To Rene
from one Hookergate
Grammar School
pupil to another

Stuart
August 84

DAYS THAT USED TO BE

STUART BELL

DAYS
THAT USED
TO BE

SAGITTARIUS PRESS

Printed in Great Britain by Ramsden Williams Publications, Ann Street, Consett, Co. Durham.

ISBN 0 903692 03 1

To Ernie Bell, who lived it.

Our civilization, pace Chesterton, is founded on coal, more completely than one realizes until one stops to think about it. The machines that keep us alive, and the machines that make machines, are all directly or indirectly dependent upon coal. In the metabolism of the Western world the coal-miner is second in importance only to the man who ploughs the soil. He is a sort of caryatid upon whose shoulders nearly everything that is not grimy is supported.

GEORGE ORWELL:
The Road to Wigan Pier.

In quiet thoughts I live again the days that used to be.

Ray Holt could hardly get to the north that day.

The Arabs had decided to ration oil to the west, the government had decided to introduce what amounted to the ten bob gallon of petrol, the oil tankers were lying empty off the straits of Bahrain and with rationing considered imminent the dealers were already cutting supplies to the garages, the garages were refusing to serve other than faithful customers, even then you could only get a gallon or two, and so Ray did not see how he would get his car out of London let alone to the now defunct coalfields of the north.

This was December 1973.

It was also the time when the government was capitulating on the price of a barrel of oil to the Arabs and telling the miners they could not have a penny more. The Arabs had to be paid at all costs, and Anthony Barber had to travel to the ski slopes of St. Moritz to do a deal with another oil producer who was not Arab, the Shah of Iran; but back home the miners had to be forced from a work-to-rule to an official strike, the country had to be placed on a three day week, it was to be the miners or the government, so the government said, and in the end it turned out to be the government.

How did it all come about?

How had the nation gotten to the state where its economy was governed by sheikhs living in tents, by Messianic moslems, by feudal kings living among sifting sands and in poker-hot sunlight. And not only were they governing the economy, but they were also being paid in hard currencies, so that the entire capitalist west found itself at their mercy, as they deposited millions — or was it billions — of dollars with one country merely to withdraw it for deposit in another for a quarter of a point interest more. What had happened to all those gifted economists who spent years on economic science, telling students how to purge the capitalist system of its sins, yet by seeing the mote in the other fellow's eye had not seen the beam in its own. Who in hell had been advising the economies of the west? Or was it all part of some great design? After all, we were told, we had coal for another two hundred years, the Arabs had oil for only another twenty, at the present rate of consumption; so let us use the oil of the Arabs and keep our coal for future use in its anthracite veins beneath our soil.

Meanwhile, the Dutch and the Germans and the Italians and the Luxembourgeois and the Swiss cut their Sunday driving, and that day, only with difficulty, Ray managed to reach the north of England.

He pulled the car off the road onto the cinder verge. He left his new wife in the car and walked forward a little. The road dipped and rose again and kept on rising through the fields and woods towards the hills that were the early slopes of the Pennines. The land fell directly from him, and where in summer there was gorse and bracken and furze, with fluffs of dandelion that swirled about the pink clover and docken and coarse nettle, now it was cold and the cold was stiff to his cheeks. From below, in the allotment gardens of the past, there was a sudden start of pigeons wheeling upward, swirling and drooping again to the little white points of their crees.

His wife left the car and came to stand beside him.

"What's that over there?" she asked.

She pointed to a building on the road halfway up the hill.

"A post office," he said.

"In the middle of nowhere?"

The clouds scudding the sun sent shadows drifting across the countryside. The shadows stained the gorse bushes and weeds and remnants of hay that lay still in the fields, the hay withered now, bedraggled, abandoned. The air was fresh to his lungs and from a corner of heaven came the slightest whisper, a sign, a zephyr that urged on the clouds and rustled the willows caressing the stream that ran in the hollow below. His wife's eyes were still on the solitary building. Her hand moved to his but the fingers were cold and when Ray turned he could see the roses the air was putting into her cheeks.

"Fancy building it there," she said.

A road from the main highway ran below them. It was overgrown now by bramble and rosehip bushes, but his eyes strayed that way because years ago he had come this way with his father who had told him there had been highwaymen in the olden time. Highwaymen indeed. But he remembered Gerald out too that day, running from hedgerow to hedgerow down to the stream where cows stood up to their knees in mud, sullenly lifting their heads as he came by. He was looking for birds' nests but when he found one the hard clay to the bottom was cracked and fragmented and there were no eggs nor young ones either.

Gerald ran back across the field to tell his father.

"Spuggied," he said.

But his father kept on walking, as they had all done, into time and history.

"I wonder if they make any money," she said.

"Who makes money?" Ray asked.

"The people who own the post office."

Ray got back with her into the car.

He thought of the green light that flowed from the harmony of the House of Commons*. He thought of the stone paving that echoed his steps like memories of the past. He thought of the dignity of the Queen's speech and the history enshrined in the slamming of the Commons door

* Ray Holt was elected Member of Parliament for the mining constituency of Runhead, County Durham, at the General Election of 18th June, 1970, the figures were:

Ray Holt	(LAB.)	23,220
Alaric Ferguson	(CON.)	14,420
Henry Jones	(LIB.)	7,241
	Overall majority	1,559

Ray Holt was made Under Secretary for Mining Affairs in Harold Wilson's Labour Government following the General Election on February 28th, 1974.

by Black Rod in the face of the Queen's messenger. Of the weary hours in the bars waiting upon the division bell, the walk in the early hours through the streets of Westminster to his apartment overlooking Green Park. The elections were over now. Devote your time to things that concerned you, events that swirled like early morning mist rising from the Thames. To your political career. But the past was as much a part of his life as the present, as the future would be.

Only the past was sure. The past he understood.

And so he came back.

Because he had been born here and lived and grown among the trees and streams and gorse bushes, the fields and copses, that were standing still, as they had always stood, even before the time they had drawn up the Doomsday book, and would be here still when all of them had gone. Only the houses had disappeared. The village. The pubs and clubs and cinemas and bingo halls, the colliery institute, the welfare ground, the pitheaps, the grocery stores and draper and butcher and sweet shops. The post office. The only building that stood still, by the side of the road, linked to the world by a single telephone wire. Naked to the breezes that sifted across the fells, the gales that blew in winter.

Standing as it did in the middle of nowhere.

Ray Holt drove up the hill past the building that had been one of the finest clubs in the district, that was called the Road End because, simply, it stood at the end of the road. Cows grazed where the pitheap had been and they were growing potatoes and kale and turnips where the colliery houses had stapled the hills leading to the Pennines. There was no traffic on the road. The welfare grounds had been turned into a pony stable and where once there had been village sports they held a gymkhana for folk who came from all over the county. At least, they had plenty of place to park. Only there was no gymkhana that day and they followed the white line down the middle of the road till they passed the post office and his wife stirred beside him.

"Where do we go now?" she asked.

It was warm in the car and she did not want to stop again.

"The cemetery," he said. "At least that's still standing."

Book One

The News

1

Alfie Bousefield, colliery clerk, stroked the fine hairs on his cheek and from his high stool in the colliery office looked down the hill to the colliery and the village.

They were burning coal tubs on the heap and in the village pulling down the houses. The flames of the tubs tinselled the soft afternoon light and carrying up the hill he could hear the tap of the demolition hammers. The skin of his forehead had dried and powdered, the tips of his cheeks were rouge where small veins had withered and of late his eyes had fallen back in his head. They were not aware of the dust in the office light, the dirt upon the windows, the reflection of the sun upon the colliery pond. They saw only the yellow tinselled flames on the heap, the sudden spiralling of dust where they were knocking down the houses.

Gerald Holt took out a new coal ticket from his drawer and came to stand at Bousefield's elbow.

He pushed the coal ticket high on the sloping top of the desk and followed Bousefield's stare out of the window.

"You can't believe it, can you?" he said.

Bousefield replaced his pen on the top of the desk and blotted what he had been writing. A nerve twitched in his upper lip but he did not reply. The skin creased around his eyes and the creases rippled back to his temples. It was true he could not believe, his mind struggled but could not accept. Always in life he preferred to recollect the past rather than visualize the future; even the contemplation of the present made him uneasy, as if he were in a room where the walls, floor and ceiling were closing in. Yet even in the past there were things he wished to forget. The lock-outs and strikes, the violence of the men picketing the office; the time they called him blackleg and knocked him from his bicycle; kicked him and punched his face till the cheeks swelled and the eyes puffed. Till they were themselves ashamed.

The time they threw a brick through his window and coated his doors with pitch because they said he was a gaffer's man.

He recalled only those memories that were as fragrant as the roses in his garden, sitting upon the lawn watching the sun sink towards the Pennines, early walks through the fields, listening to the birds in chorus from the hedgerows, the grass damp with dew, the dew soaking the polished toes of his shoes; bicycle rides so high on the fells he heard the wind whistling from the orifice of heaven. These were the moments he wished to recall, moments of sweetness and peace he knew would never come again.

Gerald wrote out the coal ticket and folding it down the middle placed it on top of the desk beside the ink stands. He patted the padding of Bousefield's shoulder.

"Better get used to it," he said.

"I suppose I'd better," Bousefield answered.

Today they were burning the coal tubs on the heap, but what would they do tomorrow?

Then he knew what they would do tomorrow. They would raze the ovens of the brickflats, dismantle the blacksmiths' sheds, the engine sheds, the joiners' shop, the machine shop, the electrical shop, the storehouse, the keeka's office, the weigh cabin, the time cabin. They would tear the wheels from the headstock and with the wheels the cage, the winding gear and the landing. They would strip the shaft of its timber, the seams of their cutters, their picks, their props, their conveyors, their girders, their haulers and their pumps. Even the fan that circulated the air. They would take the tubs and tracks from the rolleyway, they would clean out the pony stables and deputies' kist, they would leave nothing but the cold, the dark, the dust and the damp. And the rats, if the rats did not leave before they did. They would leave no memory. They would not rest till their destruction was complete, till the heapstead was stripped of its coal shutes and hopper, the power station razed to the level of the brickflats.

Till not a brick of the office where Bousefield had worked all his life was left in its place.

And the house in which he was born, where he expected to die, that in his life had given comfort, security and peace; a squat uncouth-looking house of white brick, standing in a row not one

2

hundred yards from the office; a house like so many the coal owners had built at the turn of the century. Would that come down too? Could so much be destroyed at a single stroke? Did the individual mean so little? Could comfort, security and peace be so discarded? It must be so, for as the colliery died so the village must die with it.

It mattered to no-one but Bousefield that the house had been tenanted by his father and his father before him, that he intended it for his son once his son decided to settle, as imbedded in the life of the village as he was committed to his work at the colliery. It mattered to no-one but Bousefield that by destroying the colliery where he worked and the village where he lived they would be destroying him.

"All the same," he said. "It's a bad job. A bad job for all on us."

"Not a bad job," Gerald answered. "A good job."

"Maybes for the likes o' ye. Not for the likes o' me."

"You talk like an old man," Gerald said. "As if you'd been old all your life. As if you'd never known what it was to be young. Can't you see the village is dead? It's the future you've got to look to now."

He picked from the edge of the desk the daily tonnages book and placed it on a rack above his head. The dust stirred upon the rack and rose into the air and Gerald blew a few lingering specks from his fingers. He was an arrogant young man, arrogant because he was not sure of himself, always on the attack because for him it was the only means of defence. Always he had been driven to excess to prove to other people he was not inferior, that because he lived in a condemned part of the village there was no gap between his life and their own. He realized later most people lived the same kind of life anyway, in the same kind of houses, and there were only a few in the houses the council had built behind the school who felt the way he thought all people felt. By then it was too late.

He felt others were normal, he was not. They had nothing deep down to be ashamed of.

"That's just it," Bousefield said. "Ye're a bairn compared to me. Ye can gan away the morn and get fixed up. But I cannot. Who's ganna fix me up with a job? Who's ganna fix us up with

3

a house? And who's ganna feed me wife and son whilst we're lookin'?"

"Your son's as old as I am," Gerald said, "He can take care of himself."

"And what about me wife? Who'll take care on her?"

"Why worry so much about your wife?"

"Ye'll see soon enough when ye're married yersel'," Bousefield said. "Another mouth to feed. Another tongue to tell ye what to dee. Ye'll find out then why I worry."

"Your're as dead as the village," Gerald said. "You should care."

The beginning of an evening mist tapered along the valley floor and rising up the hill softened the lines of the colliery houses. The sun shining through the haze reflected upon blue slate roofs and the honeystone brick of the older houses. From the colliery office the village was as quiet as the first day centuries ago when the first man stumbled from his cave in the hillside to gaze in the first flush of awareness upon the trees, the grass, the valley, the moisture we know as rain, the sun, the moon, the clouds, the sky. The day he sank his roots into the earth and called it his own. So that even Gerald Holt, who hated the village and all that it stood for, hated its shallowness and superficiality, felt a momentary pang, an emotion akin to regret, that the pit should die and the life with it, as a flame dies, because no-one cared to keep it alive.

"Dead, ye call it. It's been a canny friend to me all these years. It's as much alive the day as it's ever been. Ye can see it as surely as ye can see that heap o'er there. If that's not life what is it?"

"A kind of living," Gerald answered. "Not life."

"Reet alang the street doon into the village. The kids playin' and the wives shoppin' and gassin' and huggin' their bags and smackin' their bairns and tellin' them to be quiet. And the baker's van and the milk cart and the butcher and the vinegar man. And the men comin' from the pit. What's that if it's not life?"

Bousefield's hollow eyes sparkled suddenly and the lashes quivered, but the spark quickly extinguished and the lashes drooped. The shoulders of his thin frame slumped. He felt some part of him had already died. He was not intelligent enough to

4

know of an inner life that could be bruised in the manner flesh could be bruised. He did not understand there was something not the size of a kernel that had been born in him, that drew its nourishment from the senses as a flower draws its nourishment from the earth through its roots. All that he knew was that he felt different.

There was in him a deadness. He had already capitulated to change.

"I'll ask you a question," Gerald said. "If you think it's alive are you prepared to fight to keep it alive?"

Fragments of skin debris lay along Bousefield's forehead and the skin of his neck was old like the skin of an elephant. There was a pinched look about his face, the look of an inferior, a man who all his life has avoided the issues. He laid the palms of his hands upon the desk and the buttons of his sleeves scraped along the wood. He thrust forward his chin to ease the pressure of his collar upon his throat. Gerald saw that he was not old but he was sad, tired, weary of his own lassitude, wearing the same suit as on the day Gerald had first met him years ago. A man whose life had slipped away without the knowledge it had ever existed. The skin of his face had dried not from age but from weariness of a life that meant nothing.

"I'm not young like ye. I couldn't fight if I wanted tee."

"But you don't want?"

"I've seen enough fightin' in me time. The strikes and the lock-outs and the marches on Gateshead and Durham, and settin' about the food wagons, and the fist fights wi' the coppers. And where did it get everybody? Ask the men, they'll tell ye. Always they went back in worse than they come out. Their minimum cut, their hours extended. And some on them, the troublemakers, them that started it all, they never got back yet. The management wouldn't have them back."

"And you were on the side of the management?"

"I was on neebody's side. I had a job o' work to dee. And I had a canny number in the office. The management would've sacked us if I hadn't turned in."

"So you didn't fight then and you won't fight now?"

"And there was me wife and son to keep. He wasn't as big then as he is now. But he ate just as much. I couldn't miss work for the sake of a few troublemakers. I had a married man's

5

responsibilities. It wasn't mesel' I was thinkin' on, it was me family."

Bousefield's thin bloodless lips flecked white and his tongue licked nervously round the inside of his mouth. His palms remained on the desk and he continued the thrust of his chin to relieve the pressure on his throat. These were not the memories he wished to recall. He wanted to think of the roses and bees and the message that came to him on summer evenings spent in his wicker seat on the lawn. Always in the past he wished to recall the light was apricot, as if never in his life had he endured a winter, never in his life had he suffered unhappiness. He tried to forget the depression, the desperation of the men, the baton charges and hunger marches. For him they had never occurred. He thought only of the security of his house, his job, all the things that were now to be taken from him, and he wanted to be back, back in the past where he had been happy.

Gerald Holt did not want the past but the future.

For him there never had been any good days, only days of hardship and want, days when he had gone without shoes and stockings and a new pair of trousers had been an event. The only furniture he could recall in the house had been a bed, a second-hand table, a couple of chairs, a woollen carpet and several sticks of brass his mother had bought at a sale: bought because their burnished reflection gave her a feeling of riches she would never possess.

There had been pease pudding and pies at the weekend and teacakes baked in the old-fashioned stove heated by the fire. The teacakes were placed on the stone ledge outside the window and for once the odour of meal and pigs' dung from the sties on the allotments opposite was overpowered by the sweetness of baked bread. The rest of the week they managed as best they could. They lived on home-made bread, black pudding, potatoes and turnips, with never any extras. If his father were in back shift he spent the evening crouched on the street corner surveying the traffic as it passed along the road. His mother scraped her husband's boots and dusted his pit clothes by heaving them at the wall of the yard. Dadding his clothes, she called it.

It was all he recalled them doing, his father at the street-end, his mother dadding his clothes and cramping over the stove. So that even in those days, instinctively, he felt this was not life, this was only a shadow. His mother had never known what it was to live and because she had never known she had died before her time. And neither wonder when she died there had been a smile upon her face.

"So while everybody starved you were working?"

"Neebody starved. What ye talkin' about? There was always means tests and public assistance and Lloyd George. And anyway they had soup kitchens for them that couldn't afford owt. And they got extra accordin' to the number o' family."

"But you never went to a soup kitchen?"

"I never had need."

Gerald gathered up the letters he had typed that afternoon for the manager and placing them in a folder came again to stand by Bousefield.

A tremble of anger and distaste came to his hands and a little of the colour slipped from his face. He placed the folder on the sloping top of the desk and lowered his face to within a few inches of Bousefield's. The smell of dried skin was even more offensive to his nostrils than the smell of dust. Bousefield raised a hand to Gerald's shoulder and Gerald could see the short hairs around his wrist creeping back up his arm. The hand was without pressure, the fingers were pale as the face was pale, but they were not as worn as the face was worn. The skin of the knuckles was smooth, hair-covered, supple, but there pervaded the same odour of decay that came from his face, and Gerald brushed the hand aside as if he feared contamination.

"Because never in your life have you had need to fight. That's why you won't fight now. You talk like an old man, as if you'd been old all your life. Yet you're not old, just middle-aged. But what have you done with your life? What reason have you for existing? You've never even thought about it. Your life's been nothing but a slow walk from the house to the office and back again. Now something happens to change it all. Give you a chance to start again. But are you glad of the chance? Are you willing to take it? Not you. You want to go on till you reach that hole in the ground. So dying's like a yawn. But you see you're dead already. You've been dead all your life. So why don't you die now and make it official?"

Bousefield did not reply but explored with his little finger the wax in his ear.

His sandy brows came together and his green eyes peered down upon the village. He did not reply because inwardly he felt what Gerald had said was true. He felt he had been dead all these years. In life he had a wife and son, a house and job. But what else did he have? He had the memory of an imperfect past which could not always be remembered properly because there were so many things he wished to forget. He did not have a future. But then that was why he preferred to look to the past, because with all its imperfections there was always an apricot light, in the future there was only the grave. He withdrew the tip of his finger from his ear and saw on the pad dislodged particles of wax delicate as the crystals of snow. He examined the crystals as if they were his life, then slowly he flaked them from his finger where they drifted to the floor.

They mingled with the dust and were gone forever.

2

The manager's room stood at the back of the office at the end of a stone corridor and normally the manager sat with the door open, looking down the length of the corridor to the colliery buildings set a little way down the bank. His room was flanked by the surveyor's and undermanager's office, there was also the general clerking office at the front and the pay office at the back, so that when angry the manager's voice carried the length of the building. Gerald took the letters through to his room and moved to close the door. The manager swivelled back and forth on his chair, now looking out the window up the hill, now down the corridor to the fragment of colliery buildings seen through the doorway. And all the while, swivelling back and forth, he shouted into the receiver of the outside line. The afternoon light reflected on the varnished surface of his desk. He held the receiver with one hand and with the other stabbed a thumb at the corners of his eyes.

"I tell you I know these people," he shouted. "And I warn you they won't take it. There'll be trouble. They'll ask questions. They'll want to know why the pit has to close, the village come down, and they won't be satisfied with answers about surplus coal and geological conditions. And certainly not that about economic adjustment. They'll call it something worse than that, I can tell you."

The manager beckoned Gerald not to close the door but to move forward into the room. The nervous stabbing at the corners of his eyes had made them bloodshot, the rims were delicate and slightly swollen; the light that reflected on his desk reflected too upon his silver hair and coarse virile skin; he had small thick lips, the upper arching cynically, high cheekbones and a small, closely-knit brow that wrinkled back to his hair. His ears were small and had the appearance of being pinned to the back of his head. His hands too were small, plump, the skin on the fingers hardened, but the nails trimmed and free of dirt. His free hand moved from his eyes to his brow to the desk and then to the cord of the telephone. He motioned Gerald to sit and swivelling again looked beyond his head to the colliery charts on the wall.

"Why am I getting upset?" he shouted. "I'm not getting upset. I'm outlining the situation. And I tell you I know these people. They won't take it. They've suffered enough in the past. There'll be trouble, you'll see." He snapped down the receiver and pulled to him the folder of letters Gerald had placed on the desk. "Bloody fools," he said. "Can't tell them anything. Delay the announcement on the village till the men have time to digest the news about the colliery. That's all I ask. One thing at a time, I says. To smooth things over. And will they do it? Will they hell! "

"The news is already out," Gerald said.

"Not the official news. About which streets go first and which follow. They're making that announcement tonight in conjunction with the statement the Coal Board's making about the pit. Got to do it properly, they say. Might as well get it all over at once." He stabbed again at the corner of his eye. "As if it couldn't wait. As if nothing could wait."

"They'll have their reasons," Gerald said.

"Always they have their reasons. They wouldn't do anything without a reason. Not them. Because it wouldn't be judicious to the county planning department. That's the reason. As if they were of any importance."

He signed Gerald's letters rapidly, without looking at them, and passed the folder back across the desk. He brushed the cord of the telephone from the corner of the desk and with his hands free, the receiver back on its rest, his desk cleared of papers, he raised himself from his seat. The balls of his hands lay upon the varnished top and his head bent reflectively. There were many days he spent in the pit, production days he called them, going in with the undermanager or surveyor to check the lines of a new cut or the workings of a particular gallery. But this was not one of them. This was an administrative day spent in the office, garnering reports, sifting schedules, speaking on the telephone with group or area officials. Kicking his heels as he called it. He wore his sports jacket and flannels and best cherry leather shoes.

10

The shoes had crepe bottoms and the crepe creaked on the lino-leum as he crossed to the window, and stared broodingly upon the concrete shell that stood at the top of the hill.

The shell was the remains of an emplacement that had in wartime held a searchlight. The concrete was chipped and scrawled upon, but in its time it had been the village's sole physical aspect of war. Perhaps in those days they had felt the village needed protecting, but then in those days they had known who was the enemy. Did they know now, Atkin wondered. Did he know? Was it progress, was it change, or was it the indifference of an outside world, the meanness in a man's nature that persists in destruction? Perhaps it was all these things, change in the name of progress, destruction in the name of change, indifference and meanness seeking an outlet in destruction. Who was to blame? The government, for being an alien government out of touch with the people it governed, or the people of the village, perched halfway upon a hill, looking not at their future but their past, unresponsive to change and impervious to progress, unaware of the meanness and indifference of an outside world. An anach-ronism in a modern age? Atkin placed his hands behind his back and turned to Gerald. It no longer mattered to him as it no longer mattered to the village. The people who did not care were those in control, the people who cared most could achieve least.

"The voice of authority," he said. "Faceless authority. That always hits at innocent people." He stood again by the desk and as he stared at Gerald his bloodshot eyes flashed with anger and the nerve in his cheek throbbed relentlessly. "Have you ever thought how much they control our lives? Your life, my life, everyone's life. This vast faceless bureaucracy, full of maps and figures and units and digits on calculating machines? That wouldn't know a real person if it saw one? Bureaucracy! Who are the men that run it? What do they look like? And are they thinking rational men or robots? Slaves of a system that'll one day turn us all into machines?"

Gerald did not trouble to think about it. For him the point was abstract and therefore irrelevant. His weight was so comfort-able on the chair that for the first time in ten years he did not listen to what the manager was saying. Instead he asked himself how old he was, almost twenty-six; he asked what he had done with life, precisely nothing; he asked what he intended to do with

11

it, he did not know. Till that moment he had never felt certain of what it was he wanted. But now he knew what he did not want. He did not want to remain in an environment because he had been born to it. He did not want to content himself with inferiority nor coarsen himself with drink, he did not want to sink into laziness nor sour himself with worry and in ignorance call this living. That had been the existence of his people, his father, his mother, his brother, and till now of himself. Somehow he intended to change it. He intended to grasp life by the throat, grasp it with awareness, he intended to root out pettishness, shallowness, vulgarity and an obsession with smallness and seek in its place seriousness, depth, taste and a sense of proportion. It needed courage to begin again and perseverence once a beginning had been made. Gerald did not know where he wanted to go or what he wanted to do. But he saw his future as the hill outside the office, only where the hill paused at the shell the manager had seen as a symbol of the village's outlived usefulness the future strode beyond. The future had no horizon. And in the future there existed a life free from the narrowness, the pettishness, the superficiality and slow wasting that characterized the village. The living deadness he had seen in Bousefield.

"Bureaucracy's on the march," Atkin said. "Already it's begun its destruction. Already it's demanding its sacrifices. It's forgotten that this village exists. That its people exist. On this hill where they've always existed. Where they want to keep on existing. The people don't want outside interference. They don't want change. The pit closed and the men sacked, the houses pulled down and the people scattered. All they want is to go on in the same place for the rest of their lives."

"The men won't be sacked," Gerald said. "They'll only be transferred."

"It'll be like the sack to men who've spent a lifetime in the same pit. The same house. Men who've contented themselves all their lives in the same village. Where they know each other. Where they're a community. This kind of life, it's the only life they've had, the only life they want. It might not be the perfect life. But it's life all the same."

"No-one'll ever convince me it's life," Gerald said.

"It may not be life to you," Atkin said. "But it's life to them."

12

He strode up and down the room with an aggressive stride that reflected his high temperament, impatience and sharp anger. He was a small agile man, not fat but sturdily made, with strong pitmatic shoulders and thick sinewy arms. He did not come from a rich family but had worked his own way through the mine before sitting for his manager's ticket. He was therefore a self-made man and had a self-made man's reliance. He had too a stern, foreboding manner and an intolerant character that brooked no opposition. He was therefore not popular at the colliery. But nevertheless he had respect for intelligence and efficiency and for this reason admired Gerald Holt. There were not many at the colliery on speaking terms with him and he felt of the officials there was only Gerald he could trust. He swung round to face him and Gerald heard again the creak of his soles on the linoleum.

"You're young enough to seek out the meaning of life, Gerald," he said. "You still have the future before you. But for the others it's too late. They only have the past. Anyway, they wouldn't know where to start even if they knew what it was they were looking for. But you'd know. I've seen some fine qualities in you. I've trusted you and you've not let me down. There's some have, you know. Many a time."

Atkin fell again to brooding, his chin tucked into his chest. He arched his brows and without lifting his head peered beyond Gerald to the open doorway at the end of the passage. Gerald did not follow his gaze but felt the air through the open door fresh upon his neck. He uncrossed his legs and leant forward over the table for the folder. It was not till he had heard of the dismantlement of the colliery and the destruction of the village that he realized what it was in life he did not want. And it was not till that afternoon, sitting in the manager's room, that he felt his freedom. He felt the future opening like a spring bud. Soon he would walk out of the office. He would leave its dust and smouldering fire, its ancientness and decay. He would walk past the little plot of rhododendrons that bordered its front. He would even leave the village. He would forget the pig sties and pigeon crees, the hen coops and allotments seen from his window, even the house where he lived, with its chill yard and cold reflective windows. He would forget everything, even the present, in order to find the future.

"Many a time," Atkin said. "But not you. You've not let me

13

down. And when they close this colliery I'll see you get any post you like. You name the office and I'll see you're placed. The Coal Board still has need of men like you. With a bit of initiative and talent in them."

"Excuse me, sir," Gerald said. "I'm not sure I want to stay in the industry."

"Inside or outside the industry. All you have to do is think about it and let me know. There's many a business in the city that could do with the likes of you. You might do yourself a bit of good. You think it over and let me know. I'll see you get any introduction you like."

"And Bousefield, sir. What about him?"

"What about Bousefield?"

"He's spent all his life in the office. I'm sure he'd stay in the industry if he had the chance."

But at that moment Atkin was not sure he wanted to stay in the industry himself. It was a hard thing to realize that the empire he had seen each morning for the last ten years from the window of his house was now disintegrating. He had regarded it as a sturdy ox that could stand the strain forever and here it was being poleaxed by the decision of men he had never seen. A decision made with the stroke of a pen, the neatness of a map. Atkin was on the wrong side of the fence to fight, but there was nothing to stop him making a protest. The colliery had been his life, his first post on taking his ticket. In his younger days he had been goaded by an ambition to make this colliery the most efficient and productive in the area, to reach the top wherever that might have been. Ten years later his ambition was sapped, his youth vanished, he was manager of a dud colliery, a frustrated man, unmarried and in his forties, the best part of his life whittled away. Exhausted in its dedication to coal and men. No wonder, wistfully, he reflected on the advantage of change.

"All the more reason he should change now."

"That's what I told him, sir. But he doesn't agree."

"Well, that's his look-out. Not mine."

"That's why I thought, sir, if you could do something for me you could do something for him."

"Well, I can't. And that's an end to it."

He was too busy thinking of his own future to concern himself with Bousefield's. He stopped pacing the floor and raised a hand to his mouth to gnaw the backs of his fingers. It was clear he would have to start again. He would have to look forward to another job at another colliery. He would have to forget Highhill, the comfort it had given each morning to look out upon its two smoking chimneys, its smouldering fringe of heap, the lights on the heapstead. The thought that despite his celebacy, his barrenness, the cold of loneliness, the knowledge of age, this at least belonged to him. But now they would take it from him. And by taking it just as they would demolish Bousefield so they would demolish him. They might change it for something better or they might change it for something worse, but they would never exchange it for something to which he could feel so attached.

He looked again up the hill to the concrete shell. The soft golden haze that rose from the valley floor had not touched its crest and he could see the loose earth around the shell dry and dusty, the dust stirred and lifted by pockets of wind. The same shifting wind pressed back the heads of grass and scudded the frail white clouds towards the blue ridge of sky that lay above the hill. But then, Atkin reflected, listening to the sounds of the colliery that came through the open doorway, he had become more than attached, he had become involved. Involved in the lives of others, the problems of others. He had taken a mistress, he had cultivated an affair. He had lost his individuality. It had not altered his celibacy or changed his barrenness, but it had eased his loneliness, it had arrested the decline into premature age. It had made him a man. Yet he wondered now what the price would be.

"Bousefield's not the only one," Atkin said. "We'll all suffer. Each one of us in our way."

"Because the village's too small a world. That's why we'll suffer."

"How'd you mean. Too small a world?"

"The people, they won't leave you alone. Everyone knows everyone else. They know your goodness, your badness, your weakness and your strength. You're either a saint or a sinner depending on your faults. But there's nothing in between. They'll either hate you or love you, but they'll never ignore you. Or if they did it would be part of their plan to hurt you. That's why I say it's too small a world. A man has to keep moving if he wants to be free."

"You're right, Gerald. I never thought of that."

There was pain and hurt and weakness in Atkin's face as he realized now what would be the price. He would have to leave the village, he would have to abandon his empire, he would have to sacrifice his attachment to the colliery as the village would be sacrificed to the planner. He could not leave the industry as Gerald could leave because there was nothing outside a mine he could do. But he could begin again, at some other pit, in a town perhaps rather than a village, he could obliterate his involvement and remove the memory; he could become detached, disinterested, and because he was detached, disinterested, regain his individuality. He had loved these people as he had loved their life, but he would disengage himself, they would become as units to him: so many units to put the tubs, so many units to clean the conveyor, so many units to clear the face. He would forget the dust, the noise, the danger, the damp, the smell of sweat, the odour of bodies, the shine of lamp, the ache of muscles, the weariness of spirit, the waste of life. All that he had learnt at Highhill.

"I never thought of that," he repeated. "I don't know how I got involved in the first place."

"It eats into you," Gerald said. "You can't help getting involved."

"Then I'll be glad when it's down," Atkin said. "So I'll be free."

"We shall both be free," Gerald said.

3

Markie Wishart, lodge secretary, leant on the frame of the door in the clerking office and waited for Gerald to be through with the manager.

Wishart came to the office black from the pit, smelling of coal dust and damp, the fetid smell of burrowed earth and foisty air. The hobnails of his boots struck sparks as he shuffled his feet on the bare floor and kneepads attached to his belt at the hip knocked cumbrously against the door. He pushed his thin cloth cap back upon his head and the skin of his brow showed white where it had been protected by his cap. Coal dust had seeped into the pores of his skin and heads of dust were imbedded in the cheeks; dust too seeped beneath the rims of the eyes, the fissures between his teeth, the aperture of his nostrils. His lips were thick and black with dust. He licked his tongue over their dryness and the tip of his tongue showed white like that of a negro. He shuffled again his feet and fumbled his hands in his pockets. He produced a heavy pocket watch encased in celluloid and checked its time with the seven-day clock on the wall above the small red telephone exchange.

Bousefield noticed the watch and the time and locking the top of his desk put the key in his pocket. He had checked his petty cash and docketed the sick notes in the doctor's book and now he moved around the desk and replaced the covers on the typewriter and Gestetner. He paused by the window, back to Wishart, hand upon the sill, jaws clucking absently. The sandy brows remained together and in the brittle light from the window the dried skin on his forehead was white and powdery. They were still burning coal tubs on the heap but the tap of demolition hammers no longer carried up the hill. The dust from the broken houses had settled but though on the heap the flames had lost their tinsel glow the smoke had thickened and fused into the haze.

The fires might burn all night before they died of their own accord and in the morning when the men returned there would be nothing but ash and the odd scarlet ember. Bousefield brought his hand from the sill and moving back round the desk placed the telephone on the night exchange.

"Neebody cares any more," he said. "Not even Gerald. Born and bred in the village. And not even he cares."

"What makes you think I ever cared?" Gerald asked.

"Sure ye cared," Wishart said. "And probably still do. At heart."

"The village is dead. You can't fight for dead things."

Gerald placed the folder of letters on the top of the desk and stood with his back to the fire, hands open so that he could feel its heat to his palms. A small arrogant smile played around his lips but the eyes were hard. He had grey eyes that could be very cold and sullen and rarely laughed with his lips. Now they followed Bousefied with slight amusement as he took the stamp book from a drawer and began sealing the letters. He glanced at the clock on the wall and noticed it was three minutes to half-past five. In three minutes his day would be over, he would leave the office, he would inhale the freshness of the air to his nostrils, he would walk along the cinder path towards his home. And also his future. He felt the fierce heat of the fire to the backs of his legs and the palms of his hands and moved a little nearer the desk.

"Some of us might say at this stage it's more alive than dead," Wishart said. His hobnails clattered on the floor as he came to lean his elbows on the desk. "It'd be a simple world if we all accepted things as they were without wantin' to change them. Simpler still if people were left to live their own lives without others interferin'."

"He doesn't care what happens to any on us," Bousefield said.

"He's entitled to his opinion," Wishart said. And then to Gerald. "Ye think it's dead, fair enough. Ye think it's had its day, good luck to ye. Others have their doubts. Bousefield here's one o' them. I happen to be another. Yer brother Ray and yer father Tom. The whole pit from the lads at the face to the hands at bank. Ye'd not have to ask them twice. To them it's alive, it's always been alive. And if ye try to kill it by killin' the colliery somethin'll stay alive. Because it's beyond killin'."

Gerald slipped himself onto a high stool by the desk and looked into Wishart's eyes. In their hollows he saw the same stricken expression he had seen in Bousefield's when he heard the news of the colliery. It was as if he had been struck a physical blow, the pain of which did not reflect in the creases of the face but was plain enough in the eyes. The rims of the eyes were tender, not a bleary-eyed tenderness that comes from drink but strain that comes from reading. They were red too and lined with dust, their whites clouded and bloodshot. Yet there was something about Wishart that puzzled Gerald more than the eyes. Something in the lines of the face, standing out from exhaustion and anxiety, something in the way that he spoke, beyond the conviction of his views, the sincerity in his voice. Something that told Gerald he was a man supporting a world likely to topple at any moment. A man face to face with history. He laid his hands flat on the desk and manoeuvred himself on the stool.

"I'll ask you a question," Gerald said. "Just as I asked Bousefield. If you think it's alive are you prepared to fight to keep it alive?"

All of them wanted to fight, Wishart reflected, fight for the past, for the past was all they had. But because the village had lived in the past did it mean it would live now? Did it mean that because there had always been a village on this hill there would always be a village? He did not know. But there had been changes in the past, changes in the rule and order of man, in religion and dynasty, changes from the primitive to the feudal, the feudal to the industrial, changes that debased a man's dignity and coarsened his nature. But there had been no changes in the temperament of these village people. They had retained their basic character. They had lost their rusticity, the smell of the country, the freshness to their cheeks, the sun from their brows, they had changed their habits and their sports, their work and their leisure, yet they remained what they had always been. They guarded their humble aspirations. They asked nothing but to live in the place of their birth and die in the place of their content. From their lives there had developed neither charm nor gaiety nor atmosphere, but friendship, an affinity to the earth and a closeness to life, something that was beyond words, yet which existed, in the air as it were, inseparable from the village. It was this Wishart

19

wanted to preserve. It was this he wished to keep alive.

"I'll fight," he said. "But only be legal means because that's the only way we can win. We cannot win by striking against authority. By force. Even by protest meetin'. Because even protest meetin's lead to force. We can only win by puttin' our point of view and stayin' within the law."

The clock on the wall indicated a minute to halfpast five. Gerald shuffled from his stool and moved to take his raincoat from a peg beside the typewriters. A couple of ponies were driven past the window on their way from the drift to the stables, trotting placidly before their drivers, their narrow sightless eyes squinting in the sunlight, buttocks swinging with the rhythm of their stride. Their trotting hoofs stirred the dust from the shale. The ponies passed with their drivers out of sight beyond the privet hedge flanking the office, and as Gerald followed the hovering trail of blue dust the sun through the windows lighted upon his pallid cheeks as if they were wax. He laid his coat over his arm and turned to Wishart. The restlessness of his hands showed his contempt. He moved for the door, but Wishart placed a hand across his path.

"I know how ye feel," Wishart said. "I know what ye think of the life we lead. Ye want a change, ye want to make a break, ye want to seek for yerself a better life. I wish ye luck. I wish I was yer age and could try the same. But before ye gan there are things to be done. And ye're the one to do them."

"The village is dead," Gerald said. "I can't help keep it alive."

"I'm talkin' about the pit," Wishart said. "There was trouble the day. Trouble that might have been bigger than it was. That might even now develop into somethin' I cannot handle. A few troublemakers got workin' on the men. They spread rumours, they told lies. They said the men would get twenty four hours notice. They said their houses would be pulled down. They said the older ones would be kicked out without a pension, the younger ones end on the dole. And the men believed them. Don't ask me why. But the fact is they did."

"So much the worse for the men."

"They're afraid. They see their homes and jobs taken from them. And they don't know what to do. Some of them panic and before ye know it they'll believe anythin'. They believed what

20

they were told the day. They threatened a walk-out. The whole pit was stopped for an hour. And the only way I could prevent a strike was to call a meetin' the night to explain the new policies to the men."

"You'd better explain your policies. See what happens then."

"There'll be trouble the night, Gerald. The men are frightened, they don't understand. They're worried about their future, their homes and their wives and their kids. The news is too sudden. They'll want to know why the pit has to close, the village pulled down. They'll want to know what's ganna happen. If they'll have a job, a house, if they can settle among friends." The dried mud on the heels of his boots caked to the floor as he shuffled his feet. "They'll be angry when I tell them."

"What will you tell them?"

"The truth. Because that's what they'll want to hear."

"They'll not listen," Gerald said.

"They might," Wishart answered. "With ye behind me. On my own it's too big. I know it's too big. I know my limitations and I can smell trouble. I don't have to mention names. But ye know as well as I do who caused the trouble the day."

"You're frightened of my brother Ray."

"I'm frightened o' no-one," Wishart said.

"Then why do you want me?"

"Things have to be done properly. Legally. The men have to learn to keep their heads. They have to learn to be united. But it's somethin' they're not used to. Ye see, they're not organized and they don't understand. And they're frightened. All they want is to live in peace. That's the principle they'll fight for. To live in peace."

"You've got to see things as a whole," Gerald said. "The country can't stop simply to discuss a village. The country has better things to do. Besides, what is there to discuss? Certain men will be moved from one colliery to another. From one village to another. It's something that's been going on all the time. Always has done, always will do."

"That's not the way the village people look at it."

"Then the village people aren't realistic."

"All I ask is yer support," Wishart said. "Yer nominal support."

Gerald pushed aside Wishart's hand and with his coat over

his arm moved into the passageway. The light that slanted through the open door at the end of the corridor reflected white upon the brown walls and stone floor, the corridor itself was pale with dust, the afternoon air sharp with the tang of grass and bramble from the hill, pine and fir from the forest, a tang of the country, heavy to Gerald's lungs slowing his blood and making him incapable of action. The same lethargy affected his friends and deprived them of the quickness he associated with living. But if he were to leave the village he would have to learn to live without it. He flung his coat over his shoulder and turned back to Wishart.

"I couldn't come anyway," he said. "I'm not a member of your union."

"It doesn't matter the night," Wishart said. "I've called an open meetin'. Ye don't have to be a member. Anyone can come."

"You mean even Bousefield?"

"That's right. Even Bousefield."

Bousefield was bent over his shoes, brushing the dust from the toes with a duster taken from the bottom drawer of his desk. He rested a foot on the open drawer and brushing at the shoes the sleeves of his jacket were pulled up his arms and Gerald could see the white wrists thin and emaciated. He could see the pale sandy covering of hair that remained on his head, lips moving as quickly as the duster over his shoes. And again a small arrogant smile came to Gerald's lips. He looked upon Bousefield not as a man but as a habit, a man who repeated the same unthinking movements day in and day out for the whole of his life. His lips stopped as he heard his name and as he looked up from the shoes the skin of his brow crumpled in an uneasy frown.

"Divin't ye cook owt up for me," he warned.

Gerald laughed and pulled the buckle of his coat. He nodded at Wishart. "Put Bousefield on your platform," he said. "He likes to know what's going on. He can tell me about it tomorrow."

He laughed again and hurrying down the passageway bounded down the steps out of the colliery office. The toes of his shoes kicked up little spirals of dust and his hand reached to grasp a twig from the privet hedge. He began striding towards the distance, the steps of a man who knows where he is going and confident of getting there. The evening haze stalked up the hill and the sun was bright upon the village. It was bright too upon the colliery. The only clouds to be seen were ribs of cirrus high against the sky and the only sound the clatter of men's boots upon the steel bridge below as they passed towards the village. The shale was springy beneath his feet, the sun warm upon his face and neck and hair. He looked up and its permanence brought home to him the advantage of youth and the endlessness of the days that lay ahead. It comforted him to think he had a future.

There was a call from the office and he turned. Wishart stood in the doorway, balancing himself with a hand clutching the inside of the door, the other rubbing the dust from his fustian pants. His cap was pushed further back on his head and his face was fretted, his lips moistened by the anxious roll of his tongue. He looked tired and strained and on the verge of a breakdown. He blinked in the sunlight and ran a hand over his brow. Gerald was surprised to find him there, Wishart was surprised himself. He looked so out of place at the head of the steps, his hobnails licking sparks as his boots scraped the concrete, the sun catching the watch chain attached to his waistcoat pocket. He felt as if he were on a platform, in a spotlight before an audience; he did not know why he should feel so and why feeling it he should be nervous. He felt so embarrassed his lips quivered. He let his hand drop from the door.

"There'll be trouble," Wishart said. "Ye cannot avoid it because they'll not let ye. Ye're one of us, Gerald, ye're in it like the rest. Ye'll never be free, son. Ye'll see. Ye'll never be free."

But Gerald turned and kept walking.

4

Gerald Holt recalled the day his mother died.

His father had been at the pit, his brother had gone for the doctor and a neighbour had gone to the colliery to seek his father. There were other neighbours downstairs in the kitchen, stirring tea, sitting round the fire, whispering together in the stale dusty air. All of them waiting. Gerald had been alone with his mother in the room. He hair lay limp upon the pillow and her eyes, when they were not closed, moved restlessly round the grey walls. Yet if her body was feeble her mind was strong. And sitting so close on the bed, Gerald could see how life had brutalized her face, how it had gorged the remnants of her pride, her beauty, yet how there remained still in the face some force, some expression. Some message in the coarse lines if only he could read it. The hands that had played so peacefully with the edges of the blanket suddenly clutched his, the fingers were crooked and rheumatic, the knuckles swollen. She wanted to lift herself up, to speak, to run her hands through his hair, but the effort was too much and she fell back upon the pillow.

"Me poor bairn," she said. "All I wanted was to see ye up. To see ye a man. And they wi'not give us that. Not even that."

He felt her fingers cold to his but did not withdraw his hand. He wanted to speak, to comfort her, but he did not know what to say. There was nothing he could say that bore any resemblance to truth. He looked down into her face, the face of this struggling woman who was his mother, who had yielded him as a flower yields its sweetness, who had given him life, breath, strength, who had nurtured him and raised him, protected and restrained him, till now he was almost a man. He looked and knew he was looking not upon age but upon suffering. Life for her had lost its fragrance, it was over, the only moment that counted was the moment that lay ahead, and the moment that lay ahead was the

24

moment of death. But she had seen so many deaths in her life there was no vulgarity in this her own. She suffered no physical pain, only the painful memory of hardship, only the ache of weariness and an impatience to be gone. She did not care what lay ahead but she knew very well what lay behind.

"I've had a hard life, son," she croaked, for the frailness of her body affected her throat. "I'm glad I never had a daughter that lived. I'm glad she died afore her time. To think she might have lived like me. To think — but I've never lived. All my life and nothin' to show for it."

"You have Ray," Gerald said. "And you have me."

But she was not listening, her mind was elsewhere. And Gerald looking round the room realized what her life had been. She was right, it had been nothing, it would end as it had begun, on a bed in a village, with a cry of surprise and pain, and between the act of birth and the act of death there was nothing that would endure. She had known pain, she had known suffering, she had known selfishness and she had known greed. And the pain and suffering and selfishness and greed had imprinted itself upon her face and called itself life. She had known injustice too: the injustice of being poor and never having been given the opportunity to rise above her poverty. There had been times of happiness and content, short times of abundance, but they had been recognized too late when they had already dissipated, when hard times were upon her again, when there was nothing before but the same unrelenting hardship. Now her life was over, she had been born unnoticed and she would die unnoticed, and the crime of life for having neglected her was no less mitigated because there were thousands like her, all over the world who came and went, lived and died, without discovering what their existence had meant.

She clutched his hand, her face already changing.

"Never known what it was to be loved," she croaked. "Never known what it was to feel real love. To feel wanted. To feel somebody cared about me and I cared for somebody. I never married for love, son, because I've never known what love was. I'd live me life again if I thowt. If I thowt I'd know passion. If I thowt—"

"That's not love," Gerald said, smoothing the grey strands of hair on the case of the pillow. "It's love what you feel for me. What I feel for you. But the other thing, that's not love."

"To feel I was needed. To feel somebody needed us. Ye'll

25

promise me one thing, son, promise me one thing. But there, ye divin't need to promise. Ye're not like the rest o' them. Ye're sensible. Ye'll marry for love, wi'not ye, Gerald. Ye'll marry for love?"

"Yes," he said. "Only for love."

"And yer wife. Ye'll save her from my kind o' life?"

"Yes," he said. "I'll save her from this."

But at the time of his promise he had not been sure he would be able to save himself. There was the village and the colliery, other villages and other collieries; there were fields and woods and open spaces, there were no towns, no cities. No way of escape. The nearest town was fifteen miles, the nearest city twenty five. And he was not clever, he had no education, he was wild as all the village lads were wild, he had no knowledge of life and what could be done with it. He had a nature that was destructive and undisciplined, ferocious and callous, and though he harboured an awareness something was missing he had not known what it was. He knew now and because he knew he felt strong.

"I'll save her from this," he had said.

"I want ye to look after yersel'. Put yersel' first. That was my trouble. Never put mesel' first. Always I put other people afore me. Look after yersel'. Look after Ray. Ye're two of a kind, I've always seen that, contrary and awkward. And headstrong. Ye'll dee some daft things afore ye're through. Mark my words. But look after him. Ye're older and he looks up to ye. He needs ye, son, when I'm gone. He needs ye."

"I'll keep him out of trouble," Gerald said.

She turned her head to the window and he could see the old creased skin of her neck. She held still his hand but he knew she was slipping. There was already to her face a dreamy contentment, diminishing the weariness, the suffering, erasing the scars, the creases, the wrinkles, so that an emotion stirred within, an emotion greater than the love of a son for his dying mother, greater even than contrition for his own weakness, the headstrong youth that had made him an ill-tempered son. An emotion he could only describe later as a senseless pity. Pity because her life had meant nothing and because it ended so ignominiously. Because there was nothing he could have done to have made it worthwhile. Once dead the world would go its way as it had before. The sun would shine upon the good, the bad, the pure,

26

the evil, the cunning, the charitable, the selfish, the indolent. It would shine with the same force, the same lack of interest, only she would not be aware of it. She would be forgotten.

The same thought crossed her own mind.

"Me poor bairn," she muttered. "Me poor bairn."

"What is it, mother?"

He saw the eyes shiny with death.

"All I want is to be remembered. Remembered by me poor bairn."

She turned slightly on her side and her clothes heaved with her legs. A few hairs had fallen from her head upon the pillow. The marks of the pillow were upon her cheek where she had been lying and when she turned back her eyes were open wide, the whites clouded now, almost grey and bloodless. The swollen fingers of her hand slipped from his. They were so cold he let them go. His eye slipped across the old-fashioned bedstead, the old-fashioned windows never meant to open, the damp patches on the wall, the chest of drawers, the cumbersome old-fashioned wardrobe. A few old fashioned pictures were stacked in a corner against the wall, one of his mother when she was young, another of himself when he was a baby. Their cardboard backing was damp and dusty, as dusty as the pitcher that stood upon the chest of drawers, throwing its reflection back from the mirror. The mirror too had been there more years than Gerald could remember. And it seemed to him, looking round the room, that everything was so much in keeping, so out of date. The curtains were drawn across the window, but he thought of people passing in the street, on their way to the pit or into the village, yet unaware of his mother, going about their business as if nothing had happened. And yet, Gerald reflected, nothing had.

He looked down for the last time and it was then he noticed the smile.

5

Even now, seven years later, coming home of an evening, so many things in the house reminded him of his mother he felt her presence strongly. He felt she was with him still, guiding, approving, sometimes restraining, sometimes sparking anger, but never once leaving his side. The carpet on the floor, holed where stood the legs of the table, edges frayed by the wear of feet, had been knit by her before the fire in winter; the old-fashioned furniture, the leather-backed chairs, leather cheap and thin and split along the ridges of the frame; the brass fenders and stoking irons, the brass candlesticks bought at a sale, the brass ashtrays never used in her time nor after her death. They carried her influence, her personality. He thought of her lighting the gaslight with a taper taken from the mantelpiece, the light casting a lemon reflection to her features, snuffing the taper afterwards with her fingers. He thought of her taking his coat and hanging it on the pegs to the side of the fireplace, wooden pegs that often cracked of an evening, as if for some reason she was angry.

Strange now to think her place might be taken by another. That his father could bring a second woman to the house.

Yet for all his mother's presence he hated this house. It ought in fact to have been pulled down years ago. He could not remember a time when the road was not breaking up, uneven, the tar cracked, the undercoating working loose, so that littered with stones and broken glass it easily cut the knees. But it had been the houses behind that frightened him most. They had been in his childhood as they were now, cliffs of gloom, two stories of decaying stone that shed their plaster with the rain. The two at the end of the street had to be supported by stout cedar bulwarks, others were able to stand of their own accord, not proudly but sullenly, indifferent to the dust they hoarded, the damp that seeped through the walls. Their ugliness had dismayed him even as a child, he had associated it with poverty, with meanness, and the discomfort he had felt had eroded through the years into a harsh anger. That he should be born into such a house, into such conditions, that never till now had he been given the urge to rise above them.

He had gone into the colliery office at sixteen, a year after the correct leaving age because the headmaster had recommended a further year's schooling to straighten out what he termed unruly tendencies in his nature. Because he lived in a dilapidated street in the slum quarter of the village, Gerald had driven himself from outrage to outrage to prove himself an equal. Fortunately for him, when neither teachers nor headmaster could tolerate him further, he saw their breaking point before they saw it themselves. His cunning intelligence told him exactly when to stop. He listened to the headmaster's admonitions with head held low, hands touching the wall behind his back, his shoulders dejected. He indicated an eagerness to learn, a willingness to repent, and coupled these with an obedience and application that gratified the head. In the last month of the school term he had been the model pupil. So model instead of filing outside the local training centre of the National Coal Board with the rest of the school leavers he had spent a further year being groomed for a post in the colliery office.

Bousefield had been on his way down even then. He had slipped first into worry, then into laziness. Finally he had relapsed into indifference. He had been a month in hospital when Gerald entered the office for the first time. The first thing they had taught him was how to wind the seven-day clock on the wall. Then there had been the simple clerical task of entering the seam tonnages into the daily records, composing a total and phoning this total to group. There was all the work Bousefield had left and all the work that would have fallen to him had he been there. The monthly consultative meetings between union and management, the manager's letters, that he took in longhand because he had never had shorthand instruction, representatives who called from manufacturing firms, the petty cash, the formulating of group and divisional reports, enquiries at the small box window opening into the passageway. All rested upon his initiative, his ability to get through the work. The manager depended on him. And the intensity of his inferiority, the fact people brought work to him be-

29

cause they were above it themselves, forced Gerald to work with a concentration he had never known he possessed. Reports went off on time, consultative meetings were accurately reported, enquiries adequately dealt with. The routine answering of the telephone, stamping of time sheets, issuing of coal tickets, handling of pay disputes, all were jacketed into the day. So that no-one complained. And when Bousefield returned four months later, the ulcers removed, his face colourless as dust, walking unsteadily and only then with the aid of a stick, he discovered to his relief he was repeatedly by-passed.

Even in those days Atkin thought so highly of Gerald he promised him better things. But the years passed and the better things had yet to come. Gerald matured, his body developed, his frame filled out, his skin lost its early acne stains, uncertainty disappeared from the eyes, his inferiority buried deep, deeper out of sight. One day he glanced in the mirror and realized he was no longer a youth but a man. The transition surprised him. He had a pleasant face, stern, handsome in its seriousness, yet in his expression there lingered a touch of disdain, that curled his lips, arched his brows and fretted his forehead. That even found its way into his walk, the manner he held his shoulders, the stride that took him down the street, measured, purposive, a man going somewhere who knew where he was going. But these were merely signs of a fledgling manhood. Everyone congratulated him, told him he had come of age, that his life was flowering. But somehow even then he had not felt it was true.

Out of boredom he had discarded all his youthful habits but that of drink. He had drifted to pubs as the other lads had drifted, accepting it as part of working class life. He had not understood it was easier to fall into dissipation than rise above it, and though he cured himself of earlier excesses he had not been able to resist the urge of cultivating new ones. One evening he had been known to drink twelve pints of beer in three hours. Some had elevated the figure to fourteen, others placed it as low as ten. It was also said that during this performance he had never once left his seat. Which ballooned his reputation even higher. It may or may not have been true, Gerald could not remember. What he did remember, clearly, were the last ugly shapes of the pig sties before falling into a pool on the way home, the following day spent between bedroom and toilet, the ruin of his face in the mirror, with eyes subdued, the lips pale, the skin discoloured.

He began to feel distaste for the pubs and the men who gathered there. He forgot the reasons that drove them, sweating hours spent in the pit, the taste of coal dust, the burr of cutters, the heaving of the roof when the cutters ceased. He forgot their desire to escape, their longing to be free of darkness and cramp and limited space. He continued to go because it was expected of him. His moment of clarity came only a few seconds before he succumbed to the impact of beer. When four pints had been consumed and the froth of a fifth damped his lips. The sweatiness of the room was such it might have been soaking his face. His weight seemed elevated, he was raised to an eminence, he could see the faces of those around him, with all that was worst, their emptiness, their narrow humanity, their lack of intelligence. He could see clearly how they lived without an awareness to being alive. And he could see too that the emptiness, the narrowness he saw in others was all that awaited him, there was nothing he could do but submit. The fifth pint soaked his throat and awareness was lost. He heard himself singing louder than the rest.

Strangely, he never remembered during the day.

Awareness was obliterated by pressure of work, a closeness to people, occupation with colliery routine that had absorbed him over the last ten years. His life ran of its own accord as a tub might run on well oiled wheels, he had little time for personal thought or self contemplation. It was only when he met Barbara Rutland that he realized the range of his personality. He was an individual, he had a life of his own that did not have to accept a pattern woven by others, that did not have to be condemned to an environment because he was born to it. He no longer wished to see each day consumed by useless routine, an occupation that left little time to discover what life meant, what its values were and what those values meant to him. Barbara had not been born to the narrowness of the village, she was not aware of its limitations, she was not restricted by its background, and therefore she was free. He had almost forgotten the wasting he had seen in himself in those moments of awareness that so easily fled the consciousness. Barbara had brought home to him the memory of his mother, she had brought home to him the wasting of Bousefield and the wasting of his father. Till now his habit of drink, his frustration at the   office, the uselessness he observed in others

31

without the knowledge to avoid it in himself, had made him feel he was on a descent that was endless. Now with Barbara Rutland he wanted to arrest that descent. He wanted to change its direction.

But it was almost too late. He was already what his brother liked to call a leader of men. Ray tried to model his life on his excess, the pit lads swaggered and boasted as he swaggered and boasted, some of them, unconsciously, even tried to walk as he walked. The older men at the colliery looked on him with indulgence. They were happy to be considered one of his friends. They stood him drinks, they hailed him in the street, they listened to his stories, his jokes, they laughed at his swearing. They trusted him because he was not a gaffer's man. Yet they respected him too because he worked in the office and could be considered above them. Now the pit was to close and the village come down. They would be glad of his advice, grateful for his guidance. They did not know how much he had changed, how indifferent he had become. Wishart knew but Wishart had not been convinced. That was why he told him he could not escape, that was why he wanted him on his platform.

Gerald pushed open the gate and walked into the yard of the house that he hated. The ashbin in the corner by the gate was filled to overflowing and the lid sat lopsided on the rubbish. Cinder crumbs led from the door to the ashbin and coal crumbs from the door to the coalhouse. There was a rush of water down a sink, and from the latrine in the corner by the coalhouse came a faint but aggravating odour. The concrete in the yard was like that of the pavement, cracked and broken, with little grass roots pushing up through the cracks, the step to the house was worn the shape of a hammock, and the only adornment to the sill of the window was a single faded line of chalkstone. The hen coops, pig sties and pigeon crees were behind him now, the odour of earth, pigs' dung and meal had receded, leaving only the smell of the latrine, the odour of dust, the less definitive essence of decay and age that pervaded the house. His step was heavy on the concrete. His thoughts dissatisfied him. His bitterness was raw in his mind, compressed to a single point. His hands tensed in his pockets. He reached for the latch and as his fingers rose so too did his anger.

He pushed open the door and entered the kitchen.

His father sat over a plate of egg and chips, with a plate of bread at one elbow and a pint pot of tea at the other. The tea he drank from a saucer. He had come from backshift and sat now in his pit clothes, blue canvas shirt with white stitching, fustian breeches patched at the knees, the buttons of the shirt open at the neck to reveal the dirt-grey hairs on his chest, the breeches pulled tight across the thighs so that the dried mud and oil shone in the light. Holt would be sixty next birthday and was stouter than normal for so small and sprightly a man. His arms and shoulders were thick, the shoulders rounded with stooping, almost hunched, the arms thick-veined and taut; his face was vigorous, perfectly shaped and expressive, but the eyes were small, pig-like and cunning. He sipped his tea in long draughts from the saucer, and as he chapped at his food he smacked his chops; he talked with his mouth open, showing a pale tongue, spraying the table with fragments of masticated food as he spat out what he did not like upon the side of the plate. He ate with hands black from the pit for he disdained the colliery baths. He claimed too much bathing was bad for the legs. For forty-five years he had worked in the pit, and for forty-five years he had returned home to sit in pit clothes and muck, eating his dinner and smoking his pipe, before making the effort to wash and change. This was his way of doing things. He would no more dream of changing than he would of climbing a mountain.

"Aye," he said, when he saw Gerald.

"Where's old Fanny Adams?" Gerald asked, slipping his raincoat onto one of the pegs by the side of the fireplace.

"Pushed off to catch the tail-end o' the gossip. A expect."

"I shouldn't wonder," Gerald said. "And where's my tea — or didn't she bother to make it?"

"Put it in the oven, A expect. Like she usually does."

"And burnt it dry as cinders. I shouldn't wonder at that either."

"Aye," his father said.

Gerald found his tea as he expected in the oven. It consisted of two pieces of black pudding, a fried egg soaked in grease, and a dozen chips that had shrivelled and dried at the corners. They were warm but only just and as he nipped the tips the grease left an imprint on his fingers. He stood over the boiler of steaming water his father would use for his bath; the boiler was attached to the fireplace and through the steam Gerald gazed at his father, not seeing him, seeing through him to all that he detested. His bitterness had gathered like a bud and the bud was ready to burst. It was like a canker that had to be cleansed. He held the plate in his hand and looked down at the grease that lay thick and yellow upon the food. He heaved the tea into the fire and laid the plate upon the table. The grease from the egg and pudding sizzled and sparked, the egg shrivelled and disintegrated, the pudding smoked, the chips turned black and ghosted away. He felt the heat of the fire to his hands and wrists as he watched the soot-like morsels dropping through the bars to the ash.

"Aye," his father said. "That's one way o' cookin' it."

"I'm not hungry," Gerald said. "I'll have a few biscuits and a cup of tea."

"Ye'll be famished later on."

Gerald did not answer but nodded at the coal black fingers of his father.

"I suppose you'll wash your hands for your new wife?"

His father spat out upon the side of the plate. "A might," he said. "Ye never knaa. But A'm not so sure when A come to think on it. She's a canny lass, she'll not be as fussy as all that."

"I'd be fussy if I were her. She's never seen you eat at a table. She'd think twice about it if she had."

"A've had supper at her house many a time," Holt protested.

"But never with a cloth set. And never when you were black from the pit. My mother never let you eat like that when she was alive."

"She did, ye knaa, when I was hungry."

"When her back was turned, you mean. Or when she was tired of you beating her."

Holt's hand suspended across the table. The knife he held hovered over the butter dish. The skin of his forehead tightened and the trammels in the skin were black where coal dust had seeped. He did not lift his head and the lids of his eyes hooded protectively so that Gerald could see the small tired veins, the skin of the lids white against the rest of the face. There was in his expression a look of surprise, a look of curiosity and wonder, as though he had forgotten and could not recall what Gerald was talking about. But Gerald could not forget. Gerald could never forget. His father had been too active a man, too coarse and unrefined to let his energy become other than brutal. It was from his father Gerald inherited his violence, it was from his mother he inherited his feeling. His mother had been worn down not only by the circumstance of poverty but by the trial of a man who when he had saved enough frittered his money not on beer but on spirit, not on light or brown ale but on rum and whisky and brandy. He did not return home drunk, he returned home demented. You could smell his breath before he staggered into the kitchen. He smashed ornaments, hurled furniture, broke crockery, he saw ghosts, demons, sprites, and tried to exorcise them by hammering his wife's head upon the stone floor, sitting on her chest pummeling and buffeting till he was dragged off and knocked senseless by a neighbour. The screams had been so piercing Gerald felt they would shatter the windows. His mother lived on the edge of hysteria. She was grey before her time. Yet she bore it because he was her husband, she was his property, and because she knew it was expected of her. The hard times in this respect had been a blessing. Money was scarce and the occasions rare his father had enough to drink himself into a stupor. But they had been often enough for Gerald, so often the screams, the uproar, the confusion, the beat of his mother's head against stone, they lived still in his memory to inflame his rage.

"You think I've forgotten," Gerald said. "Just as you've forgotten. But I'll never forget — never."

He watched for the lids of the eyes to lift and when they did saw his uncertain glance before the hand continued forward its movement. The knife cut a sliver of butter and his father plastered it upon a slice of bread. He left the imprint of his thumb on the corner of the bread and a morsel dropped to the plate as he tore at the bread with his teeth. The white tip of his tongue licked the butter from his lips and the same monotonous champing of food continued before he decided to speak.

"A haven't forgotten," he said simply.

"I'll bet you haven't," Gerald said. "I'll bet you can't remember a single thing."

"Aye, ye're reet there, mebbes A cannot. But mebbes A remember what it was like after. And mebbes A'll never forget that."

"Yet you're going to take another wife, your're going to put her through the same misery. And you expect me to clap you on the back and say, All right, go ahead, don't mind me. D'you think I'm like that? D'you think I want to see you ruin somebody else the way you ruined my mother? D'you think I'm going to let you get away with it a second time? I've had enough of you. I'm sick of you. I'm disgusted with you. I don't care what you do, I don't care how often you get drunk. But I'm telling you I won't stand that."

"There's nee need to shout, son. A can hear ye plain enough."

"I've had you wised up a long time," Gerald said. "You've squared Ray and all you want now is to square me. You think once you can get me talked round you can marry and bring her home. Live here in my mother's house. Using the furniture my mother used. Doing the things she did. Living with her own flesh and blood. You think because you've forgotten her I've forgotten her too. Because Ray never loved her I never loved her either. That just shows how your mind works, how selfish you are. With never a thought for anyone else. But you've never been any different, have you? Always it's been yourself first and everyone else a long way behind."

"A says ye needn't shout. A can hear ye all reet."

In the silence that followed Gerald realized how heavily he was breathing. His chest constricted, the nerves in his stomach were aflame, and as he passed a hand across the table he noticed the tremble to his fingers. His father ate stolidly on, head bowed, the lids lowered again across his eyes; he drew long satisfying sips from the saucer, filling the saucer again, being careful not to let a runnel of tea fall from the pot upon the cloth. He worked at his food as he did every night, taking a slice of bread, buttering it, breaking it and rubbing the morsel along the rim of plate towards the centre. Yet Gerald had the feeling behind those eyes that did not look up, behind the tight skin of the forehead, his mind was wandering, wandering back to the past. For a moment he sat, looking at his plate but not eating. Then finally a burning coal dropping against the bars seemed to break his reflection. He looked up. He smiled at Gerald and Gerald returned the smile. It gave his father confidence.

"A've thowt the world o' ye son," he said. "Ever since ye were knee-high A've thowt the world o' ye. A'm gettin' on now, ye knaa. Not as young as A used to be. And A've had a hard life

36

and A needs a bit o' comfort, and A divin't want it spoilt warrin' wi' me sons. Not at my time o' life. Ye're young, the two o' ye, ye're both young, and A cannot expect ye to think the same as A think. But all A ask is that ye give yer owld man a bit consideration. Just so he feels he belongs, just so he feels he knaas he's wanted."

Gerald's smile was a brief parting of the lips that showed the edges of his teeth, a fleeting light that illuminated the eyes and drew out their coldness. It was as though he were enjoying himself, as though his humour had moderated. It was in fact the last nervous movement of his lips before he went out of control, the only light that came to his eyes one had to beware of. It was the only indication he gave that his patience was exhausted, his logic dissolved. Then the tempest took command. He had seen it so often in his brother, the same smile, good-humoured, gentle, before the last frail strand of anger broke. He could never see it in himself. Yet even if he had it would have made little difference. His canker had to be cleansed completely not partially. He saw his father in the chair, the black hands, the open neck of his shirt, the dirt around his neck. Then he saw his face. And he saw in it all that would be, all that his father was, cold, brutal, cunning, perhaps frustrated, with life behind and nothing before, with an awareness something was missing but without the knowledge of what it was. He saw how narrow he would be, how mechanical, repeating one habit after another, with no inner quietude, no inner peace, no secret wisdom in his heart. It made him hate his father the more, it heightened the venom of his attack.

"You'll get the same consideration you gave my mother in her time," he said.

The words were so low, so venomous his father stared confused.

"What d'ye want to say a thing like that for, son? Ye're speakin' to yer own father, yer own flesh and blood. If it wasn't for me ye'd not be here, not even born."

"I say it for the sake of my dead mother."

His father dropped his eyes. He spoke reflectively at the table.

"For the sake o' the only woman A ever loved."

"Then why did you treat her the way you did?"

The eyes did not rise. He spoke again at the table.

"Ye'll understand one day, son, when ye're owlder. When ye've seen a bit more o' life. A man's as he is and there's nowt can change him. He cannot change even if he wants. There's somethin' inside wi'not let him." His head came up and he looked Gerald in the eyes, and the eyes were pleading, and the indifference had slipped from his features, and in its place was regret. "D'ye think I've never wanted to change? D'ye think A wanted to cause all that uproar for yer mother? As if she didn't have enough to put up win without me startin' on her. As though she didn't have enough trouble. Wi' nee money and nee furniture to shout about, and all them hard times we had in the beginning when things were scarce. As though there wasn't enough to make her life a misery. D'ye think A wanted to gan out and get drunk and bash her head on the cement? D'ye think A knaa'd what I was deein'?"

"Then why did you do it?" Gerald demanded, and his fist came down on the table. "Why did you do it?"

"We had our hard times, son," his father said. "Ye knaa yersel' how hard they were. It took all A could to scrape some coppers together — even a few coppers. And then wi' workin' in the pit all day and nowt to dee at neet but hang around corner ends. A man wanted somethin' just to make him feel alive. So when A had enough A went out drinkin'. Only where others stopped at beer A went on rum. That's where A made me mistake. But A couldn't help mesel', A tell ye. A just couldn't help mesel'."

"You can say that for the first time. What about the other times, when you knew what it did to you?"

"A couldn't help mesel', A tell ye. A'd tell mesel' A wouldn't dee it again, nee more for me, A'd say. Then when the next time comes, and A had a bit o' sup in us and the lads was tipsy, A just couldn't help mesel'. Then it was o'er late. Then they were all around us, these demons, men wi' nee heads, others all in white and comin' to get us, an some all mangled up in the pit and blocked wi' stone, and liftin' away the stone and showin' us their squashed chest, and then comin' after us shoutin' it was my fault. And me shoutin' back and tryin' to get away from them, tryin' win all me might, and fightin' them one after the other. Then next thing A knaas A'm lyin' in the yard win a pail o' water o'er me head. And they says A've wrecked the house and half-killed me wife, and if A dee it again they'll lock us up."

"They should've locked you up," Gerald shouted. "They should've left you to your ghosts, the things you did to her."

His father was on his feet now beside him, nervous, pleading, distressed.

Horrified by his own memories.

"But A couldn't help it, A tell ye. There was nowt A could dee. And she loved us, yer mother, and A loved her. It wasn't the kind o' love ye young'ns talk about on street corners. There was none o' this romantic lark about it. None o' this fancy passion. But it was love all the same. It was our kind o' love. Ye never in yer life heard yer mother say a wrong word about me. Never once. And since she's dead and gone have ye ever heard me blaspheme her memory? A ask ye, son, have ye ever?"

It was when he talked of love Gerald gripped the chair in both hands. It was when he talked of passion he lifted the chair above his head. The seat fell out and rolled upon the table, a a plate fell to the floor and smashed upon the stone. His father fell back aghast, his confusion deep, pain and misery and fear in his face. Gerald stepped after him, carpet rumpling between his feet, the chair raised above his head, the chair colliding with the chain that held the gaslight, rocking it in its socket. In the pause it would have taken to bring the chair down upon his father's head, his father stepped forward. And as he stepped forward his shoulders straightened, the composure came back to his features, the pain, misery and fear dissipated, and the eyes became moist. He made one small accepted shrug of the shoulder, as if what was to come was inevitable.

"All reet, son," he said. "Hit yer father o'er the head win a chair, if ye think it'll dee any good. Bash his brains in if ye like, if ye think it'll change owt. But as sure as I'll be lyin' dead on the floor, things'll be just as they always were. Yer mother's in her grave now, son. She's out o' harm's way. Puttin' me in the same place'll not bring her back. Ye'll see son, ye'll see."

Gerald brought down the chair with all the force he had in his body.

6

Arnold Atkin was kneeling on his haunches at the bottom
of the garden examining his young transplanted leeks when he
heard the telephone ring in the hall.

He did not move but upturned his wrist to look at his watch.
He sat with shirt sleeves rolled to his elbows, showing the fine
hairs of his wrists and the delicate whiteness of his under-arm.
The sun was warm to his head and forehead and the back of his
hands as he fondled the fledgling leaves of the young leeks. It was
six o' clock. The stems of the leeks he had transplanted that
morning from the small home-built greenhouse in the corner of
the garden were no thicker than a finger; some of them appeared
so frail, the leaves or flags as they were called drooping and list-
less, that they had been set in jars to draw their white; but all of
them Atkin hoped would be prize leeks for the autumn shows.
He had personally laid the trench in his spare time, in the evening when his work was over, and now he examined each leek in
turn, studying the thickness of the stems, the texture of the leaves,
running a handful of soil thoughtfully through his fingers.

The telephone continued in the hall.

Atkin stood and looked the length of the garden to the
scullery door. He had left open the door and the harsh insistent
burr of the telephone reverberated through the house. There were
times in his youth Atkin never touched the phone but let it ring
till the caller lost patience and gave up. He felt then as he felt
now that he should not be disturbed by a call which meant more
to the person telephoning than it did to him. Then, as manager
of the colliery, in his eagerness to get on, he had taken every call,
even when the phone rang at midnight and turned out to be a
wrong number, till he tired of this and in the evenings answered
only the colliery line. Now he hesitated and looked again at his
watch. It might after all be something important.

He strode through the house and picked up the receiver. "Hello," he said. "Colliery manager."

"Hello," she said, and his heart sank.

"It's you," he answered. "What do you want?"

"Ye might show a little more enthusiasm."

"It's not that," he said. " I just happened to think it might be important."

He heard her chuckle. "What makes ye think it's not?"

"All right," he said impatiently. "What is it? What do you want?"

"Just thowt I'd ring," she answered.

"What about?"

"Lots o' things," she giggled. "We could always talk about us. And the colliery."

"What about us?"

"Ye knaa. What's ganna happen, what our plans are for the future. Now they're closin' the colliery."

"I haven't had time to think about it," he evaded. "Not yet anyway."

"I'd better come along tonight then, hadn't I? So we can have a little discussion."

"Not tonight," he said. "I can't tonight."

"I'm at the callbox in the village. I'll be straight up."

"No," he said. "Tomorrow night."

But the line was already dead.

Atkin scowled at himself in the hall mirror and wandered into the sitting room. He did not feel like returning to the garden. The light from the large windows fell across the walnut table and drinking cabinet. He strolled across to the cabinet and stooping pulled it gently open. At any other time it might have taken two short whiskies to hold down the dread of her coming. But not tonight. He held the glass in one hand and poured the wine from the bottle in the other, setting back the bottle in the cabinet before strolling to the window. Tonight it did not matter. He had decided on his sacrifice. Since she was the measure of his involvement in the village she would be the price to pay to regain his freedom. Just as the planning department intended to erase the village to tidy the map he would erase her from his life to start again.

He rolled the port around his tongue so that it flavoured the

41

whole of his mouth before reaching the back of his throat. The best part of the day began for him when everyone left the office, when the clerks closed the lids of their desks, the surveyors rolled away their maps, and the undermanager clattered home for tea. Atkin could feel the emptiness of the office. And he could feel life in the emptiness. The sun glowed through the windows upon the desks, phantom particles of dust drifted in the light, drifted as slowly as the universe, the telephone was silent, set on the night exchange, the last of the fire fell in the grate, the sparks rose and fell, angry then subdued, and the ash that disintegrated through the bars billowed across the hearth like a sudden valley mist. There was life there all right, life in the stillness, as palpable as the softest waves of air against the face. Just as there was life in the colliery at night, walking among the freshly-stacked, freshly-smelling Norwegian timber, feeling beneath the feet the solidness of the heap, listening to the throb of the winding engine and power station, the tumbling of coal into the hopper, the un-harnassing of tubs from the cage, watching the ruby incandescence from the open ovens of the brickflats.

Life that would never, could never be the same after tonight.

The office was not silent for long once the clerks and surveyors left. The undermanager toddled back after his tea, overmen and deputies called to file reports, the storekeeper and enginewright to pore over their time records, the chief electrician to discuss the latest type portable generator, the safety officer to look through the accident book, the keeka to talk with the chief of the power station, the union secretary to pass an hour or so on his way home. And each impressed upon Atkin his views. How the cutters were working in the Brockwell, why the roof supports needed replacing in the Tilley, how the bargain men were faring on number three, why the half-mile length of mineral track to the screens needed relaying, why it was time Neddy Thompson — that had the accident last March: Neddy the Dodderer they called him — should be pulled from facework to datal, that Willy Amis should be transferred to bank from the rolleyway. And listening to the various opinions and persuasions, the forthright views of the officials, the pit developed soul as well as body, it developed its own traits, its own idiosincracies, its own characteristics. It became to Atkin more than life but the life he needed.

It was hard to imagine it desolate.

But that evening he had not stayed long at the office. He knew the atmosphere would not have been the same. The officials would pass as usual, but they would pass from habit. Their gossip would not have been as lighthearted. And when he came along the passage from his own office he knew it would cease altogether. They would blame him for what was coming to pass. They knew each one of them there was little he could do, but he was manager, the colliery and men were his responsibility and with them the village. They would dissociate themselves, they would lay the blame on him. He was prepared for that. He had not been a popular manager. He had been too strong, too turbulent, and in his personality there had been a stubbornness the men had not understood. He had set himself against them by his strictness, his energy, his determination to do things in his own fashion. The prior manager had been of the village, not a stranger as they preferred to describe Atkin. They had known him as deputy and overman, safety officer and undermanager, and when he took his manager's ticket they felt the merit was partly theirs. They not only liked him but were proud of him. There was established a harmony Atkin had never been able to attain. He offended as many on the surface as he did in the pit. There had been friction from the first because they did not do things his way. They had been sullen. They had promised co-operation but the co-operation never materialized. They contented themselves with working in the same fashion. They resisted change because with their conservative natures they had not seen in it progress.

Their obstinacy almost drove him mad. He had no wife in which to confide and what was left of his family lived on the other side of the Pennines, so that he felt alone, isolated. He tried drinking with the men on Sunday before dinner, but they turned their backs, they felt awkward, as if he did not belong, and even when he caught and held their eye the most he received was a nod of respect. He even entered leek shows year after year and though he never won a prize he knew if he did the men would resent it. To them he was a stranger, he would always be a stranger. They never understood the feeling he had for the pit, never understood that despite his high-handed manner, the personality he could not help, the forcefulness that was part of him, the impatience and irascibility, he was at one with them, they had little to fear, his interests were their interests. He would never let them down. But though the men grew accustomed to him, though they admired his techniques, his forthrightness, his manner of getting done the work, they never allowed him the familiarity he sought.

So that he began drinking partly because he was lonely and partly because he was frustrated. "Ye drink o'er much," she once told him. "It's not whisky ye want to keep ye warm. It's somethin' else."

She had cured his loneliness and eased his frustration and his drinking had therefore ceased. The first years of their relationship had been the happiest in his existence, a happiness he had never conceived possible, that took the wistfulness from his features and lighted his eyes, that removed the tension from his life, the care from his thoughts. She taught him the love of body to body, thigh to thigh, stomach to stomach, chest to chest, hip to hip, the sweaty earthy heat love can generate, the isolation one feels wrapped in the clothes, cut off from the world like an embryo. Making love to her was like taking a flower and stripping it petal by petal reaching into its throat for its goodness. There was a succulence about her he found incredible. She was warm and wilful and the brashness of her voice was transfused to eagerness in her body. Lying in the gloom, flushed with sweat, head sinking drowsily, he reflected what was ambition to this. Here was contenment enough. What had he been doing all these years, depriving his body, driving his mind, neglecting himself for an empire of coal that was to betray him? Ambition was as fleeting as a snowdrop, as transient as dew on a lotus. There was no happiness but that which mattered in the crucial moment of excitement and sensuality, death and rebirth, that released the contempt in which he held himself.

"You make a bad wife," he once told her, lying on his hip, trying to distinguish her profile in the darkness.

"But a wonderful mistress," she replied.

They had met on the golf course above the village. The course stood on a plateau so high one could see the ridges of the Pennines, and it was said, in the evening, the flickering lighthouses of the coast some forty miles away. The colliery and village were tucked out of sight below the plateau. The countryside undulated as far as the eye could see, a cluster of cottages, a colliery, farmhouses, pastureland, forest, the river twisting back to its source, the strut of pylons, the frail structures of the local television transmitters, the horizon sharply defined as on a landscape painting. There was always a wind on the course, sometimes as caressive as a zephyr, other times as strong and buffeting as a gale, a wind that shaped the pines flanking the fairway, that sifted the sand of the bunkers and shook the yellow blossom from the gorse. A wind that whispered of its coming across the open fields before one felt it to the cheek. The air was pure as it was invigorating, cleansing the features of worry, adding zest to movement, enthusiasm to strokes, an air that made immediate contact with the blood so that it tingled through the veins and sharpened the stirrings within.

She was in her late thirties when passing through on the course he had seen her for the first time as a woman; a fine handsome woman, tall, erect, shoulders held back by the weight of the bag, breasts firm without flatulence; her long legs striding lithely across the turf sheathed in black slacks that exaggerated the movement of her thighs. She strode with virility, buoyed on her toes by the spring of the turf, showing the edges of her white socks, buttocks moving as fluently and coherently as her thighs. She seemed to embrace life as firmly as she gripped a club in her hand, as if she lived for the moment, plucking from each minute a full sixty seconds worth of life. She had a large face, with large jaw and cheek bones, but the bones of the cheeks were high and fragile, shell-like in quality. Her forehead too was high, receding, but unfretted with worry, and her teeth were strong when she laughed. Her laughter, rich and exuberant, was as filled with enthusiasm as her body. Her rose-red cheeks and cream, lightly tanned complexion brimmed with vitality, the wind had patterned her chestnut hair, and when she returned to the clubhouse Atkin could not resist offering her a drink.

"Better not tell your husband," he said, handing her the glass. She took it and clinked the glass against his. "There are lots o' things I don't tell me husband," she said.

She playfully touched his wrists and there flowed from the tips of her fingers a charge that aggravated the tension in his nerves and sharpened the ache in his chest, a charge that aroused the muscles of his thighs and heated a sweat to his stomach. He caught and held her fingers and spread out the hand on his own. She giggled and the hot intoxicated perfume of her breath dilated

45

his nostrils. The hand was not tanned as the face was tanned but had kept its pristine whiteness. It was warm as eggs in a bird's nest are warm, the skin of the long slender fingers soft, milk-white, the nails evenly cut and perfectly shaped, and emanating still from their tips this tactile vibration when she stroked them on the palm of his hand. He realized he needed her badly. Needed to grasp and press her hand against his body, let the long white fingers explore his veins, seek him out, and their warmth against his warmth let them take him like an over-ripe fruit and squeeze till the juice throbbed warm and thickly upon her hand.

He sipped the last of the port and laid the glass on the sill of the window. He paused to watch the subtly changing shades of evening transform the colours in his garden. The blush of the lupins subdued, the hues of the wallflowers and irises deepened, the shadow of the trimmed hawthorn hedge shaded the anemones, and only the first yellowing flowers of stonecrop in the rock garden held out against the softening light. The colliery manager's house was withdrawn from both colliery and village, bordered by an open field where pit ponies were led to graze. A drive connected the house to the road leading from the office, and looking down the drive from the window he could see the colliery chimneys and heap, the reflective lines and siding of the coal tracks out of the village. The house was of grey stone, over-large for his needs, with wide windows, long corridors, spacious bedrooms, a modernized kitchen, a dining room, a sitting room converted to a study, and a bathroom equipped with bath and shower. There was also an outhouse at the back and garage at the side. Yet for Atkin its single comfort was the garden. The rest was as sterile and bereft as was Atkin himself.

He wandered into the kitchen where the table was set for tea, a plate of boiled ham with a couple of small tomatoes on the side, a spring lettuce, a little cheese, a plate of thin bread and butter and another of biscuits. Set as usual for one. The kettle had been filled and set on the ring, with the teapot beside it, and all that was required for tea was a match to light the gas. The golfing season had not lasted forever. In winter the snow fell thickly upon the course and heaped against the clubhouse, drifts blocked the road and cut off the club from the village. Her shoulders dropped, her breasts became flaccid, her thighs grew flabby, the virility that sent her striding across the turf went from her, and with it the brashness, the enthusiasm, the zest for life. She fell back into the pattern of the village, occupying herself around the house, shopping and gossiping at the yard gate, on the corner of the street. Her body grew rigid as a frozen flower, there was little pleasure now in plucking apart the petals, rather a vague dissatisfaction, till it became harsh needful repetition. The years passed and at first he did not notice the change, she became his housekeeper and in spring and summer, with the fresh air and exercise, she regained her vitality and poise. Her shoulders became stocky, her breasts grew heavy, the fat that edged her lips and thighs in winter hardened in spring but did not diminish. The blossom to her cheeks lost its luxuriance, drew into itself, so that it was now little more than two spots of colour on the cheek bones, her underchin sagged and the line of her jaw lost its distinction. Her complexion muddied, the skin developed blotches, and the light in the eyes extinguished.

So that it came as a shock one day to Atkin to realize not that she was old but that she was ugly. She had neglected herself. She felt too sure of her man, she did not have the intelligence to realize that she had to strive to keep him, keep trim her body, harness herself in corsets, dress in respectable clothes, wear fashionable heels, coiffure her hair, touch a little perfume behind her ears. Make herself an object worthy of attainment. She preferred instead to leave it to nature. She became shabby, she let her hair grow long and tatty, wore flat-heeled shoes to reduce her height, wore the same dress, the same pinafore, the same holed and laddered stockings, the same coat, the same scarf, till Atkin's carping obliged her to change. If she saw the difference in herself she did not mind. Her enthusiasm for golf grew less, she claimed the exercise did her harm, it caused varicose veins, the air was bad for her, it gave her blood pressure. She preferred to sit with Atkin before the fire watching television. Of late she had not even come for that but slipped off to the bingo club run by the welfare, just to see what it was like she told him. He saw now the meanness, the pettiness, this preoccupation with triviality, that had so transformed and coarsened her face.

He wearied of her voice. He found her conversation shallow and repetitive, corroded by village gossip. She repeated so often to him the same trifling story he wanted to clamour out. He discovered she never read a paper let alone a book. She said she did not have to since there was nothing in either books or papers that matched the goings on in her own village. Perhaps she was right, but it irked Atkin to find her so ignorant. He wanted to make her as attractive in personality as he had found her in appearance. He tried to interest her in books and serious matters but he discovered she was not only indifferent but incapable of listening. She had no capacity for attention. He became depressed because he made no impression on her. Then he turned angry. She had involved him, she had cheated him, she had deprived him of his independence. She made him feel he owed her something, something which gave her claim to him. She bullied him a little, as if he belonged to her, as if she had a right to him. As if he were her husband. This he could not stand. He hated her now, hated the sight of her, the touch of her, yet there was nothing he could do, and because there was nothing he could do he endured.

He heard her walk along the path at the side of the house and pause at the door to the coalhouse. She had come at last. A quiver ran up the back of his thighs, the same sensation a pregnant woman feels when her baby moves for the first time. He heard her take up the shovel and bucket and open the coalhouse door. He did not feel so confident now and saw the tremble to his fingers when they touched the table. He debated whether he should have another glass of port or light the gas for tea. The light from the kitchen window carved the worry in his face, the redness of his eyes. He listened to the scraping of the shovel against the stone of the coalhouse floor as she scooped up the coal and tumbled it into the pail. The sound repeated and repeated and he could see in his mind the movement of the shovel, the coal tumbling into the pail, he could see the broad of her back, the heavy flesh of her legs. He decided to light the gas beneath the kettle and picked the matches from the top of the cooker.

He sighed, preparing himself for the ordeal ahead. He had endured enough, the period of waiting was over. Now the pit was to close, the village come down. At last he had the opportunity. He had to leave now because he could not stay. He would explain and she would understand. He smiled and lit the gas, recovering a little of his confidence. The port warmed his inside, he felt fine, he felt alive, he felt the world was not such a bad place after all. All it required was firmness. You had to be master of yourself and master of the situation. It was as simple as that. He ran his tongue round his mouth to catch the last lingering flavour of port and wondered why it was it had taken the closure of the pit to see it.

The shovel stopped scooping and the quiver came back to his thighs the way a wind springs from nowhere to clasp together the tops of the pine trees. He heard the metallic straining of the shovel against the yard when she laid it against the wall. She had filled the pail now to save her the bother later. One of her tasks as housekeeper was to light the fire each morning. This had enabled them in the beginning to spend their nights together, for she had been able to slip from her own house about eleven at night and return at eight the next morning, supposedly after having lit the fire and cooked the manager's breakfast. Now with the pail filled her evening work was done. Her hand reached for the latch and the door opened. She pushed the pail before her.

And then, not for the first time, Mrs. Bousefield crossed the thresh.

7

"So you got here," Atkin said.

"Ye divin't think I'd disappoint ye by not showin' me face, dee ye?"

She pushed the coal bucket beneath the sink where the sticks were kept.

"I told you not to come. I left a note."

"Aye, I saw that. I picked it up on me way out."

"But you never read it."

"I'll read it when I get back," she laughed. "If I can find it."

She slipped out of the arms of her coat and dragged it through the sitting room into the passageway, uncoiling as she went the scarf from her neck. The kettle began steaming on the gas and its condensation clouded the windows. She returned from the passageway and brushed close to Atkin to take the kettle from the boil. She paused by him, taller by at least a head, rubbing her knee into his thigh, taking him by the shoulders and pulling him close, so close that inclining his head it burrowed into the flaccidity of her breasts.

"Say ye're glad to see us," she smiled.

He felt the softness of her breasts against his ear and could not help the excitement rising within. A hand reached automatically for her hip. The warm intimate smell of her dress hovered in his nostrils. She wore an open neck dress and the skin of the chest was red and ugly and old, so old, older than the skin of the neck, so ugly, uglier than the heaviness of the face, that he turned and crossed abruptly to the window.

"I've told you to come only in the morning," he said. "When you should come."

"I get sick o' comin' in the mornin'. I like to lie in now and again."

She slipped out of her shoes and into the slippers she kept

50

beneath the table. He rubbed the condensation from the window to have a view of the garden and eyed the leek trench at the bottom beside the railings, the trench properly skirted with timber, so that only the young fronds of the leeks and necks of the bottles could be seen from the kitchen. The steam ran down the windows to the frame of each pane. With his back turned, he heard her take and rinse the teapot and add two spoonfuls of tea from the caddy.

"Ye see," she said. "Ye were thinkin' on us all the time."

"And how do you make that out?"

"Ye put the kettle on. Ye knaa how I like a cup o' tea when I first get in."

"It so happens I've not had my tea."

"I see that," she said. "When I set it I didn't think ye'd be eatin' much. The way ye're on I'd have thowt ye'd not be eatin' at all."

"And what makes you say that?"

"With the colliery an' all that."

"I suppose you think because the colliery's closing the manager should be deprived of his food?"

"I should've thowt ye'd be o'er worried to eat."

He gave a short laugh. "Worried," he said. "About the colliery?"

There was silence between them. He heard the slight pursing whistle she made with her lips, the sound of her feet kicking her discarded shoes under the table. The effects of the alcohol had now dissipated and he felt badly the need for another port. He thumbed nervously at his eyes, aggravating the tender rims, chewing so fiercely his lip he felt pain at the corner of his mouth. He did not like to admit he was uneasy. He rode roughshod over everything to achieve his ambition of the day; intolerant and possessive, stubborn and overbearing, it was this that had estranged him from the men. Yet with this woman he felt as weak and helpless, as shorn of hair as Samson. Why? He listened as she poured the boiling water into the pot over the tea leaves, and as she replaced the lid he reflected that each man carries in his soul the seeds of his own destruction — had he read that somewhere or was it an original thought? With some it was the weakness of gambling, with others the sin of lust. Yet with Atkin it was neither gambling nor lust but frustration and loneliness, and though he had been able to drown his frustration in drink it had taken a woman to assuage his loneliness.

"Cup o' tea?" she asked.

"I think I'll have myself a glass o' port."

"What, another?"

"What do you mean another? It's the first tonight."

"Suit yersel'," she said. "Happens I saw the glass on the window sill when I went through wi' me coat."

She took a cup from the shelf and poured herself a cup of tea. Atkin went through into the sitting room and she heard him feeling about in the cabinet. She wandered in after him.

"I knew a man like ye once," she said. "Reet guzzler he was. And always on the side so no-one knew about it. But I knew, trust me. And always he supped whisky. Nowt but the best, he used to say. That's the only drop worth havin'. Ye knaa what happened? Hardly turned sixty when he gets the shakes. Couldn't keep his hands still. That wasn't so bad. But then it was his legs. Then it was all o'er. And afore ye knew it he was gone. Just like a leet. Even afore he reached retirin' age."

"That's the fifth time you've told me," Atkin said.

"Makes nee difference though. Ye drink all the same."

"So you might as well not tell me any more."

"If that's how ye feel," she said.

She was as indifferent to his shortness as he pretended to be to her affections. She stirred the tea and watched two black fragments of leaves swirl around the surface. Strangers, she called them. She asked herself why a woman of her age, with a husband and grown up son, should be attracted to a man like Atkin. Was it boredom, dissatisfaction, a weariness of the same repetitive life, pity for the man himself, admiration for his station, or something in herself which aroused appetites others did not feel? Or was it because she loved him? A little smile tightened the corners of her mouth. She scooped the strangers from the tea and dropping them onto the saucer with her spoon crossed to the window.

"Anyway," she said. "I thowt we were ganna talk about the colliery."

"Were we now," Atkin answered. "That's the first I've heard of it."

"All the men are out in the village. Waitin' for the meetin' at the institute."

"They'll talk," Atkin said. "That's all."

"They want to knaa what's ganna happen to them when they close the pit."

"They'll be taken care of," he assured.

"And what about us? Who's ganna take care on us?"

His hand shook when he poured the port and a few red rivulets ran down the side of the glass onto his fingers. "I'm going to have to leave," he said regretfully. "I don't want to, you know. I've put the best years of my life into this colliery. And I've grown attached to the village. It'll be a wrench for me. A great sacrifice. But there's nothing I can do." He sipped the brim of his port and ran his tongue around his lips. "I have bosses too, you know."

"What'd happen if they found out. Yer bosses?"

"Found out about what?"

"About us. The way we've been carryin' on all these years."

"They'll not find out. Who's going to tell them?"

The moisture from the tea sharpened the colour of her lips. "Things get round," she said. "Dickie birds talk."

"If they find out they find out," Atkin replied uncomfortably. "I'm not a doctor or a dentist. And you're not my client. One thing they can't do is accuse me of unprofessional conduct."

"It wi'not dee yer reputation any good. For the future."

"Being boss of a dead colliery does it even less."

"I divin't care if ye have to gan away," she said. "I've got a sister at Huddersfield. I'll gan and stay wi' her. Till it all blows o'er."

Atkin took an overlong draught of the wine and felt his throat dry like a parchment. He did not absorb what she said but repeated his own words over in his mind. He was boss of a dead colliery, they would care more about that than the affairs of his private life, he was head of a dud pit, they would worry more about that than they did his future. He was finished, he knew that. This little colliery with its few hundred men, its two drifts, its three seams, its four thousand tons, this little colliery had broken him. He thought of the men demanding to know what was to happen, little realizing the manager would be asking the same question. They might send him to a drift where output was running low, a colliery already on the threatened list, they might thrust him into an office dealing with manpower, production, modernization, reorganization, so that he became a bureaucrat like the planners who destroyed the village. But they would never elevate him to a position from which he could advance. Her words had yet to penetrate the firmanent of wine. The thought he might become a bureaucrat tickled his fancy and he took a more cautious sip from the glass. How was that for efficiency? Not only did bureaucracy destroy you, it incorporated you as well.

It occurred to him what she had said.

"There's no need for you to leave," he said quickly. "At least not yet. And I'll try to see your husband in another job. So he'll have prospects. So you'll have a future."

"I couldn't stop once ye'd gone," she said. "I'd have to gan wi' ye." She sipped languidly at her tea. "No, I thowt to mesel' I'd gan and stay wi' me sister at Huddersfield till things quietened down. Then I'd join ye in yer new job. They're bound to fix ye up somewhere nice. And if it was another coalfield I'd say I was yer wife. Neebody'd knaa the difference."

"You can't do that," he gasped.

"And then when everythin' was settled like, and I'd got me divorce from Alfie we could settle down proper. Nip off and get married. Make it sort of official." The light from the window reflected on the coarseness of her skin. "Still, I wouldn't mind," she added. "As long as we weren't parted."

Atkin flushed as if the port had gone to his face and felt a great weight pressing upon him. He watched her carry her empty cup back into the kitchen and take a cigarette from the packet she kept on the window sill behind the curtain. He had the feeling she spoke as she did because she felt this was as a woman in her position ought to speak. That because they had been lovers all these years it was inevitable they should run off and marry. She could not understand it was finished. He suspected even the sensation she left behind would please and tickle her fancy. And indeed this was true, for Mrs. Bousefield had concluded she was his mistress for the sake of notoriety. For the sake of being envied and admired, whispered and discussed. Only it had not worked out the way she anticipated. The men at the golf club knew and the men at the golf club had wives, somewhere others must know and somewhere others must talk. But it had never wrapped itself round the tongues of the scandalmongers. It had never been shouted from the housetops. She lit her cigarette with a match from the box on the cooker and, holding it close to her lips, the sudden sparkling flame illuminated the disillusionment in her face.

"But you can't leave the village," he said. "It's your life."

He had laid his glass glass on the top of the walnut cabinet and followed her into the kitchen.

"Who cannot? Just try me and see if I cannot. Try me and see. There's lots that'd like to stay, ye knaa, if only they could. But it's the likes o' ye that wi'not let them."

"I didn't mean it like that," he added. "I meant this is your kind of life. This is what you've been used to."

"I'll sharp get used to somethin' different, if that's what ye worried about. Ye divin't have to be frightened about takin' me places. I knaas me manners. We might look poor and we are poor, some on us, but we've been properly browt up, divin't forget that."

"You've got to think of other people," Atkin said. "Your husband, your son. How would they get on without you?"

"Other people think only o' their bellies. How dee ye think they'd manage if I was to pop off the morn? They'd have to think somethin' up then, wouldn't they now? And anyway, divin't ye dare talk to me about Alfie. He's nowt to ye, so divin't make out he is. All these years ye've gone on as if he didn't exist. He'll find somebody to cook his meals if I'm not there to cook them for him. He looks soft and he is soft, but it's his belly he puts afore owt. Ye'll see."

"But the village people don't do that kind of thing."

"What kind o' thing? What ye on about now?"

"Don't run off with other men. Leave their husband and family."

"Divin't they now? They dee if they need the other fellow badly enough."

"Things aren't like that between us," he said. "Not any more. I think the world of you, you know that. But we're not young. The best part of our lives is over. And we're both set in our ways. We'd get on each other's nerves. The little that's left between us, I mean, it would vanish. What kind of life would it be if we despised each other? Hated each other?"

"That's not the way I figured it last neet in bed."

"But that's the way it'll be."

"Not accordin' to my book," she said, letting the smoke from her cigarette exhale through her nose. "It'd be a canny life, the wife o' the colliery manager. I'd have everybody lookin' up to us instead o' down the way they dee now. I'd make mesel' up every day. I'd lie in in the mornin' and dee me shoppin' in the afternoon. I'd have a maid, one o' them fancy Swedish lasses that come o'er in boats. They reckon they're good around the house. Clean as crickets. Not like them French bits ye hear about. Always gallivantin' and flirtin' with the husbands when the wife's back is turned." She shook her head. "I'd have nowt like that."

"For Christ sake," he said. "Speak English. You can when you want."

But she was lost in her own world. She felt till now she had been wasting her time. She had given everything for nothing in return. They had got away with it for so long because they had been discreet. Though she spent many a night with Atkin they had never been seen together in the village, they met at the golf club and drove elsewhere for their pleasure, and when they returned he dropped her a little outside the village so that she could walk the few hundred yards to her home. They had never scandalized the village's idea of morality. Her husband was the manager's clerk and she the manager's housekeeper. The village closed its eyes to the rest.

She looked at Atkin. She would see they did not close their eyes any more.

"Ye talk as if ye didn't need us," she said.

"Of course I need you," he answered.

"Then why make so many difficulties?"

"Because I'm cleverer than you. And because I see further. I see the disappointment, the pain, the feelings that come after happiness. And I want to stop it before it's too late. Before there's nothing but ruin."

"Ye're thinkin' only o' yersel'," she said. "Not o' me. If I've been good enough to cuddle and kiss all these years — and a lot more besides — I should be good enough to live win. Ruin, ye say. It'll be ruin if we gan off together. It'll be my ruin if ye gan and leave us in this hole, wi' nowt to dee but wash dishes and make meals o'er a hot stove, soak clothes and weed the garden for Alfie. So he can have himsel' a bit potter round at neet. And then pop down to the shops to have a bit o' gossip. That'll be my ruin."

"The houses are coming down. You won't be here forever."

"Aye, that's reet. They're pullin' down the village. I nearly forgot that. They'll shunt us all off and we'll have to start again. And I'll have nowt to look forward tee of a mornin' and nowt to look back on at neet. And that's how it'll be forever and ever Amen. Why, I'd rather put me head in the gas oven. Rather dee away wi' mesel' than put up wi' that."

"You'd forget in a little while."

"How long's a little while?"

"The time it takes to settle in a new house. Make new friends."

She smiled and stubbed her cigarette in the sink. "Just the time it'd take for us to slip away and settle down. All our troubles'd be well nigh o'er by then. I reckon two years'd just about fix it. Me divorce'd be comin through, we'd have the house fixed, and the people'd be gettin' to knaa us as yer wife."

The thought pleased her so much Atkin knew there was nothing he could do. He had already given up. His mind wandered to the past to take him out of the present. He thought of his arrival at the colliery ten years ago, with his manager's ticket, his ideas, his ambition, his hopes, his aspirations and his enthusiasm. He had wanted to make this the most thriving colliery in the group, run it efficiently and without accidents, increase its output and its productivity. Yet he had failed. He had applied himself with energy, devoting his life to the task, sustained by a philosophy for living, a will to succeed, that was strong, creative, nourished on a confidence in himself and his ability. What had happened to destroy him? This woman held the answer. She held it as she held him in the palm of her hand. His weakness had destroyed him as his weakness had destroyed the colliery. His weakness had been his loneliness. And this woman, lacking education, knowledge and refinement, with a mind that observed only the superficial, had instinctively discovered this, had battened upon it, manipulated it, till now she was mistress not only of his body but his soul.

He felt her hands upon his shoulders. She pulled him close and nursed his head against her bosom. The nicotine smell of her breath repelled him as did the hard domesticated hands upon his shoulders. But he did not protest or withdraw. It was as if he

57

were held by the magnetism of her body. She snuggled him so closely, so intimately, he knew she was already in the future. Her hand stroked his neck and the back of his head and he felt the long slender fingers upon his hair. At last he tried to withdraw but she held him so firmly he had to pull against the weight of her whole body. A weight that overwhelmed him, a weight he would have to carry all his life, a symbol of his failure to the men, to the colliery, and to himself.

"Ye'll take us wi' ye," she said. "When ye gan?"

"I don't know," he said. "I'm a responsible man. I have to make responsible decisions. Ye'll have to give me time to think it out. Think of the consequences. There's your husband and son. There's my reputation and future. Your future."

The grip of her arms tightened around his shoulders. Her lips pressed to his ear.

"Ye can have all the time ye want," she said. "All the time in the world."

8

Gerald Holt brought down the chair with all the force he had in his body and his father would surely have fulfilled his own prophecy of falling dead upon the carpet had Ray not taken the blow on his arms and shoulders and wrenched the chair from Gerald before he could raise it again. The seat of the chair fell from the table into the grate and stirred white ash around their feet. The chair toppled over behind Ray and thudded upon the carpet. Ray had wrenched the chair away with a shout and stood so close Gerald smelt the faint raw carbolic of the pithead baths. The fire glow was raw to Ray's face and the flames of the fire reflected to the depths of his eyes. Crumbs pitted his lips following his canteen meal and were licked away by a lizard-like nervousness of his tongue. Ray's mouth was twisted out of shape, the thick lips angry, fretful, but the anger and the fretfulness were under control.

"Take it easy, Jay-boy," he said. "We divin't want the neighbours in."

Gerald pushed at Ray and reached for the bread knife on the table. Ray stood firm, balancing on his heels, and pushed the knife out of Gerald's reach. He was as tall as his brother yet not so well developed, either in build or personality. Physically he was much thinner, less attractive, with the same colour eyes; his forehead was larger, wider, and his hair that was damp from the baths had to it a ginger cast. There were acne eruptions around his chin, a few blackheads around his mouth, and his skin had a greasy youthful pallor. He was four years younger than Gerald, highly-strung, impetuous, with as little control over his emotions as his brother. But where Gerald's anger was against the village, the life, the waste he had seen in his mother, the waste he saw in himself, for Ray it was against authority, indifference, the pressures that were for change. His body was riddled with a rest-

59

lessness that showed in the lips, in the eyes, in the hands, in the taut energetic perambulations that kept him always on the move. His grip was firm on Gerald's wrist and the pressure tightened as Gerald again tried to move for the knife.

"Easy boy," he said. "We've seen enough o' this in our time. We divin't want to see any more."

Gerald looked beyond Ray's shoulder to his father.

But his father would not turn to look at him. He crouched against the stencil of the door, the wood a comfort to his back, hands concealed behind his thighs to hide their own independent trembling. Through the pit dirt his skin was yellow and his lips powdery with dried spittle. He was not sure which frightened him most, his confrontation with Gerald or the confrontation of his sons, each with his own violent nature, an inch apart, locked by the wrists. Neither his eyes nor his tongue could rest. His tongue ran over the dried spittle just as his eyes ran over the room. He saw the upturned chair, the seat half-buried in the ash, he saw the shattered crockery, the swinging gas lamp, the rumpled carpet that had unsettled the dust, and he could not believe this was his house, that this was happening to him. Among the chaos of the table a saucer of tea remained to be drunk. It reminded him of his content walking along the heap, the shift behind him, pockets bulging with empty flask and bait tin, tread heavy from the weight of the boots. The rest was from his past, a past he wanted to forget, that he feared might one day come again, so that instinctively he began searching for his wife, seeking her beneath the table, in the corner among the books, beneath the slope of the stairs. Pinned against the wall by the lopsided chair.

He brushed a hand along his forehead and found his fingers were still quivering. He felt inside a sickness and his breath was laboured, weary. Gerald saw that he was old, very old, the vigour drained from his skin, the expressiveness lost from his face but gathered in the eyes. His shoulders, that were already rounded and stooping, had drooped so suddenly and permanently they crooked the shape of his whole body. Gerald felt he would never see them straight again. If he saw a man he did not see a father. He saw a stranger who had worked forty-five years in the pit, forty-five years of all kinds of work, pony driving, handputting, hewing, on windy picks, on cutters, in water, boring new seams, opening new faces, sinking new shafts; forty-five years of musty air, cramp in knees and thighs, muscles perpetually flexed, wasting now with damp and over-use. Gerald did not understand the impact this had on a man. He did not understand a man's knowledge is as wide as his experience, there was nothing to be learnt from books, and that if a man's experience has been nothing more than that of a mole unaccustomed to light then the man himself would be as narrow as the seam he worked, as insensate as the rock he hewed.

"Now pa," Ray said. "Divin't ye get upset."

"It's not me, son. Not me gettin' upset."

"It's o'er and done win now. We'll not have the neighbours in. Not again. They're nosey enough to start win. We divin't want them to think we're a bunch o' savages. Now then, ye just gan into the back and I'll see to the water for ye bath. Take it easy and divin't let things worry ye. Ye get the tub out and I'll fix the water. It's all o'er and done win now."

"O'er and done win for me. But is it o'er and done win for him. That's what A want to knaa, is it o'er and done win for him?"

Gerald abruptly turned and went to stand by the window. Through the small square panes he stared across the yard to the allotments and waste space between the gardens where ran the dark cinder path. The white spikes of the pigeon crees thrust themselves into the air and a few released homers flighted down and hopped contentedly from one spike to another; the coarse grass clumps, strands of bracken and shrubs of docken were ugly accretions upon the wasteland, whilst the heads of the dandelions fringing the path, standing on pale slender arms, sunned themselves in the evening light. Gerald stood with his hands behind his back. He felt no sorrow, no regret, no sympathy, no understanding. Only a slight easing of his dissatisfaction as he might with a boil when a little of the steadfast has been removed.

"A want to tell ye, son. A want to tell ye frankly. A cannot gan on like this. All this fightin' and warrin'. Just 'cause A want a bit o' peace. Just 'cause A want to settle and have a wife like everybody else. A'd rather die the morn in the pit — rather be carried out-by than gan on like this."

"We'll talk about it after yer bath," Ray soothed. "When ye've got off all that muck and ye feel better."

"All A want is a bit o' peace and quiet. Does neebody understand that? Just a bit peace and quiet for me last years. For when I retire and A've nowt better to dee than stand around corner ends.For when there's nowt to look forward tee but owld age. And this business, it's killin' us, d'ye hear. It's killin' us. A cannot gan on like this, A just cannot gan on."

"We'll talk about it after yer bath," Ray repeated. "When ye feel better."

"But A cannot gan on, A tell ye. A just cannot gan on."

"After yer bath, pa," Ray said. "After yer bath."

The soothing quality of the steaming water eradicated from Holt the panic that had closed upon him like a coldness when he stood in the kitchen and seen the chair rise above Gerald's head. He had only once in his life been so frightened. This had been in camp during the first world war when he heard for the first time the sound of shells whistling overhead. He had only been in the army for a few months before war ended, but then as now he had longed for escape, he had longed to be anywhere other than where he was. That evening in the kitchen he had longed for the misery of the pit, the heat of the pub, the cold of his bedroom, the comfort of sleep. Anywhere but in the sight of the hatred he had seen in Gerald when he raised the chair. He felt with the selfishness of a man who thought only of himself that there was nothing he had done to deserve this. Nothing. He felt he had given his son everything only to see his son turn on him in his age. But now the door to the kitchen was closed, the hatred that had turned Gerald's cheeks to stone and taken the colour from his lips could no longer reach him. And as he steeped his arms into the water he felt safe, protected by the habits of a lifetime.

"I'll wash yer back if ye like," Ray said.

"Thank ye, son. Thank ye."

"Ye're not hummin' the neet. Like ye always dee."

"A tell ye, son, A'm not in the mood. Not in the mood for owt."

Holt had brought the bathtub in from the nail on the outside wall, dragging the tub to the centre of the floor, and now with his arms steeping in water, he felt the comfort of the heat. The water discoloured quickly as the dirt rinsed from his hands. He bathed automatically, from habit, kneeling upon rags meant to protect the carpet, slapping the water over chest and head, crinkling his face against the warm rivulets that chased to his neck. The rivulets coursed black, the soap starched the hair on his chest, and the silver hair that all his life he had shaved himself was plastered to his head. He was stripped only to the waist and the broad leather belt that held his breeches was tightly drawn, making a paunch to his stomach. His boots he had taken off and laid under a chair beside the tub. He tried to bathe the dirt from his eyebrows and lashes and Ray noticed when he lifted his head that the eyes were like beads, like birds' eyes, narrow and sunk into the head.

"D'ye knaa where it'll all end, son? This carry on. 'Cause A divin't, A divin't knaa where it'll end."

He dipped the flannel into the water and a series of air bubbles floated up and the soap from the flannel sudded the surface.

"This is as far as it'll gan," Ray said. "It'll end here and now. Ye'll see if it doesn't."

"A'm not so sure. A only wish A could believe ye, A only wish it was true. But A've seen and heard things the day A'd never have thowt possible. Never in me whole life. Me son, me own son, wantin' to strike us down for nee reason, nee reason at all, just for the sake o' badness. And ye, son. D'ye knaa what A heard about ye?"

Ray picked up the flannel his father had dropped into the water and lathered onto it a little more soap. The soap left a creamy froth to his hands. He rubbed the flannel along his father's shoulders and collarbone, sweeping away the thin layer of dirt that somehow seeped through his vest and shirt during the day's work. The movement of the flannel left the skin damp and glistening and scooping into the flannel some of the rivulets that channeled down his father's back towards the broad band of his belt he lobbed the flannel back into the tub. The dark skin forming on the water rippled back to the tub's iron rim and water dripped from Ray's fingers to the rags surrounding the tub as he took up the towel to wipe the lather from his hands.

"Ye heard it was me that stopped the pit and had a meetin' o' the men in the Brockwell," he said. "Ye heard it was me that wanted to call a strike, to have the men down tools and walk out the pit then and there. Without a minute's notice." He laid the towel over the back of the chair and looked down at the red skin of his fingers where they had just been dried. "But ye divin't have to worry about things like that. Ye get yer underbody washed and I'll bring in yer shirt and pants and pullover and ye can get yersel' changed and pop out the backway. There'll be nee need for ye to come back through the kitchen. I'll settle wi' Gerald for ye."

"Whatever ye dee, son, divin't differ. For God's sake, divin't differ."

Holt raised himself from his hunkers and began loosening his belt. He slipped out of his breeches and thin woollen leggings and began loosening the laces that tied his black pit stockings. He had granite-like legs thick with muscle. Shanks that would not have shamed a pit-pony, he often said. But though they looked sturdy enough they were less steady than his sons realized. The muscles were wasting. He could walk no more than two hundred yards before a deadness set in, a numbness that forced him to pause and rest before going further. When he left the cage at banktop he got as far as the edge of the heap before the deadness forced him to stop, sometimes coming out-by he had to let the other men go on without him, and if he wanted to cross the village to visit the pub near the council houses he had either to take a bus or pause on the seat normally reserved for retired workers. His sons did not know this, nor could Ray guess it as he watched his father take and run the flannel down the inside of his thighs.

"A divin't care what ye dee about the pit, son," Holt said, not looking up, back turned to Ray. "Ye're owld enough to knaa what ye're up tee, and it's yer own look-out, whatever ye dee. But try and be sensible and cause nee trouble. Yon Wishart, he's a canny chap, we've come to nee harm under him. Leave it to him to work things out. Just think o' yer owld man and all the trouble A've seen in me time. And just remember A divin't want to see nee more."

Ray did not answer but lobbed the clothes he had sought in the kitchen upon the chair by the tub. The redness had left his hands where he had dried them with the towel and now standing by the door he felt the corns hard on the skin of the palms, he felt the two large cuts on his thumb, the thick ungainly fingers ridged and grooved with ingrained dirt. He had loved the open life as a boy and the hard skin on the palms of his hands had been caused by the climbing of trees in the wood. The hard skin had rounded into corns when he went into the pit. The hard skin and corns would not leave him now till he retired, but as he stood by the door he gazed toward the window and the light that filtered upon his father's pale naked body, so that it came back to him, that afternoon, the meeting he had held at the deputies' kist, the pale faces, the strong lights, the shuffle of bodies, the clatter of boots. The smell of men and pit dirt and pale foisty air. The tension and excitement, the emotion of men in harmony, men accepting his guidance, wanting to be led where he wanted to lead them.

He heard the news on number nine, the worst face in the pit because it was low, because it was wet, and because it had developed a fault. Bousefield, pieceworker and son of the colliery clerk, brought in the news, crawling from the mothergate. Ray had been alone on the middle of the face examining a fault, and as Bousefield pulled himself through water, using elbows and knees, shoulders knocking against props, helmet scraping the roof, Ray could not see his features for the brightness of his lamp. The lamp was attached to the socket in the helmet, but as he crawled forward dislodged splinters of bluepost fell from the roof upon his face, he dropped his head and the lamp fell from the socket into the mud and water through which he was crawling. Water seeped up his arms and the shins of his breeches, dripping uncomfortably upon his neck, running cold down his back against the cold skin. Ray habitually worked on the face and had been issued with oilskins, Bousefield worked elsewhere in a seam that was higher and cleaner, this was the first time he had ventured into the wet and the expletives he spat out in a stream lacked nothing in force because of their familiarity.

"Well," Ray asked. "What's up?"

"It's just like ye say," Bousefield said. "The word's got round, the whole pit knaas about it."

"And what do they think. Are they mad?"

"Mad! Mad's not the word. Hoppin' mad, but not mad. They're just about demented. They knaa they're ganna lose their jobs, they knaa they're ganna lose their houses. They knaa the pit'll close and the village pulled down and they'll have nee option. Mad, ye say. I tell ye it's not the word."

"All reet then. So what do they want?"

"Owt ye have a mind. Ye name it they'll dee it. If ye want them to strike they'll strike. If ye want them to burn down the offices they'll burn down the offices. They'll even wreck the pit if ye want. Wreck it as sure as I'm lyin' here."

"Ye're a good lad, Bouser," Ray approved. "I'll see ye get a medal."

Bousefield jerked his head in acknowledgment so that his helmet hit the roof and the lamp fell again from its socket. The light fell against the stone floor and its white beam reflected upon the thick black mud that separated him from Ray, not ordinary mud but coal dust made thick by water dripping from the roof. His hands were already thick with mud, and lying in the confined space between belt and face he felt it oozing up his wrists, seeping through the fustian to chill his shins. He struggled to replace the lamp in the socket, twisting his head so that water dripped upon his cheeks. The conveyor ran ceaselessly past him, there was only a yard between the belt and face, there was no space in which to turn, and to get out Bousefield would have to slither backwards the way he had come, feeling his way with the soles of his boots. He got the lamp back into the socket and again the light blinded Ray.

"There's ganna be a meetin' in the west district," Bousefield said. "All the men in the Brockwell have stopped work. They're pacin' up and down the engine plain as if they could start their wreckin' now. Featherley and Walton's gettin' the news to the others. They'll have nee bother, once they hear what they've got to say. Ye'll see, they'll be as mad as the rest."

"And what about Wishart. Will he be at the meetin'?"

Bousefield spat on his hands and laughed. He rubbed the spit on the palms and the pit dirt peeled in streaks. "They'll hang him on a girder if he is," he chortled. "But he'll not be there. He'll not dare show his face, not for his life. Anyway, he works the hauler at the drift. They'll have to send for him if they want him."

"Somebody'll send for him. Even if it's the manager."

"Let him come if he wants. They'll hang him on a girder all the same."

"But who'll speak for the men if it's not Wishart?"

"The men are for action, not for words. They knaa they've been sold and all they want now is their own back. They want to get their hands on the blokes that's let them down. They want to get their hands on the manager and the lodge secretary, they want to smash somethin' and the sharper the better. All they want is somebody to tell them what to dee, where to start. They'll see it's done after that."

"All the same who'll be their spokesman?"

"There's only one bloke in the pit — me and Walton's seen to that. And ye're the one, Ray, ye're the one they want. They knaa ye'll give them nee sop. They knaa ye'll tell them what to dee. They trust ye like they trust yer lad. All they want is ye come and talk to them, give them a lead."

"Ye've done better than I thowt," Ray said. "What'd ye tell them?"

"I says ye'd take the pants off the colliery manager afore he could reach for his braces."

Bousefield grinned, showing his teeth, teeth that were rimmed with dust. He felt now the damp seeping through him, he felt it not only to his hands, his feet and his face but to his shins, his shoulders and his chest, pervading his skin to chill his bones. He tried to relax, letting the fight go out of his body, leaving only the fight in his eyes, one leg twisted and touched a prop, boot toeing the coal face, the other prodding against the rollers of the conveyor, boot scraping through the mud of the floor. His heart beat against the stone and his hands were tense, stiffened by the cold and dirt. He had pushed back the helmet from his brow, showing a few strands of dark hair, but the water dripped from the roof upon his forehead, so that he tucked down the brim of the helmet and screwed up his face to prevent a sneeze.

"They're all behind ye, Ray, son," he said. "All the men in the pit. And ye've got me and Featherley and Walton. We'll not let ye down, ye knaa that. And there's yer lad in the colliery office — everybody knaas we can count on him. Just tell us what ye want, Ray. Ye just tell us. We'll see that it's done."

"How long will it take to gather the men for the meetin'?"

"About half an hour. By the time we get together all the men from this part o' the pit. All they want is for ye to come and tell them what to dee, they're cryin' out for a lead, cryin' out I tell ye. Ye just come and speak to them. Come and tell them what to dee."

A prop cracked sharp and ugly and a slice of bluepost fell

upon the conveyor. Neither Ray nor Bousefield moved. Bousefield let his lamp play upon the knotted timber props red with damp, Ray glanced indifferently at their flat tops splintered and cracked where they held the weight of the roof and the weight of the timber cross-supports. From further along the face, at the tailgate, he could hear the dull voices of men shouting, he could see the play of their lamps upon the damp walls, he could hear the sound of cutters being pulled back, the throb of the rubber belts as they ran on the well-oiled cylindrical rollers. Then he turned his head back again, his eyes moved from the conveyors to the props and then to Bousefield. Bousefield adjusted the beam of his lamp so that it fell directly upon Ray's features. Ray did not blink or turn away but accepted the white brilliance of the beam.

"Ye will come wi'not ye, Ray?"

"I'll come," he said shortly.

"I thowt ye would."

The cutters fell silent when news of the meeting reached the men at the tailgate, the conveyors stopped suddenly as someone switched off the current, the play of their lamps ceased against the damp walls, and the dullness of their voices deadened still further as they shuffled off the face onto the rolleyway. Bousefield began pulling back the way he had come, his lamp silver upon the roof, boot hooking behind a prop, levering himself with elbows and knees already sore with effort. In the excitement of the moment he had left his kneepads on the face where he had been working and he knew there would be little skin on his knees by the time he got back. The props cracked around him as he strained himself back, he humped himself like a rat so that the base of his spine hit the roof and forced him to slither closer to the water he was trying to avoid. The back of his head bumped continually against the roof and he had to twist his neck to ensure the soles of his feet were leading in the right direction.

"I'll spread the word," he said. "I'll see they're all there in half an hour." He twisted his neck again to see how far he had to manoeuvre. The face was some hundred yards long, Ray had been examining the fault somewhere in the middle, so Bousefield had another forty or fifty yards to go before he reached the mothergate. "At least," he said. "I hope I'll be able to tell them. If there's owt left on us by the time I get out."

"There'd better be," Ray said. "If ye want that medal o' yers."

"We should all have a medal," Bousefield said. "Every one of us. God knaas why I came down here in the first place, 'cause I divin't."

He knocked his head against the roof and his lamp dropped again from its socket. It was a battery lamp, with a battery hitched to his belt, making it all the more uncomfortable for him to manoeuvre backwards. The current was relayed along an insulated tube, and this time he let the tube and the lamp drag along after him. He hesitated when he encountered a mound of coal dust and groaned when the soles of his boots splashed into a pool that had gathered in a hollow. He scrambled through the pool as quickly as he could, his virile curses travelling along to Ray as they had when he entered the seam. Ray had switched off his lamp in order not to dazzle his friend, and now with Bousefield's lamp being pulled along the face in the dust, he sat on his own in the darkness listening to the sound of percolating water, feeling very cold and cramped, legs so long in the same position. He sat listening to the water, listening to the splash of Bousefield through the pool, and like Bousefield he wondered why he found himself where he did, why he had ever come down in the first place.

And also why it was there were those who were afraid of hell.

9

Often his father told him how in the days of coal owners a manager called on a workman with a son at school-leaving age and reminded him of his duty to send his son into the pit. In those days, not only was a man dependent on the manager for his job, the upkeep of his family, he was dependent on him for his coal, his house, his lighting and his recreation. If he was sacked at one pit there was little chance of his getting on at another. And since you were indebted to the manager for the privilege of living it would be selfish not to let your son benefit of the same privilege. Under nationalization there was no pressure upon a father to send his son into the pit, it just happened because it had always happened, because it had become the custom. And because mining folk never changed, could never change, but followed the same pattern from year to year, age to age, birth to death. Therefore a son followed his father into the pit, he expected it, his father expected it, and the only way it could be avoided was by giving his son an education.

The slide began for Ray Holt when he failed his eleven-plus. He had been relieved at the time for his brother too had failed and he wanted so much to be like his brother. He preferred to be one of the admirable failures who called grammar school boys toffee-suckers, who wet their legs in the stagnant froth of the local burn, who soaked their feet and spoilt their shoes, and threw their fine crested caps among the reeds and mud where cattle came to drink. He had felt pity for the lads as they chased among the reeds on their pin-like legs. He did not pity them now, sitting in the cold of the pit, stroking one of the papules on his cheek, listening to the drip of water, feeling damp and stiffness spreading through his body. They were the new managerial class. They used their minds rather than their muscles. When they left the grammar school they left the village, they went to college, to university, to training school, they came back with larger caps and posher blazers, not to crawl in eighteen inches or work faults in the coal but to lord it over those who had once scoffed, bullied, mocked their intelligence. They would never know what it was like to rise at two o' clock in the morning. They would never know what it was to reflect on school days as the only happy days. To think of things that might have been instead of things that were, of who they might have been instead of who they were.

But Ray's failure at eleven had been only the first stage on the way. The second had been a callow misconception on his part. He admired his brother more than he admired anyone. His father was a figure in the background, to be feared rather than loved, someone who set no example and required no emulation; his mother had died without his ever understanding what her life had meant. But Gerald had been a meteor whose course Ray could follow. He had been notorious at school, respected by friends and feared by teachers. Now he was notorious at the club. He could outdrink the most seasoned drinker, outswear the coarsest pit lad, always there were men to buy him drinks and listen to his stories. He was as free as the air and independent as the wind. He was a man before his time, so that Ray too wanted to be a man before his time. He wanted a man's respect, a man's admiration, a man's right to drink, to smoke, to swear. And to work. He wanted to follow his brother in everything, but there was one thing he could not do and therefore his emulation was not complete.

He could not follow Gerald into the colliery office. There had once been talk of making Ray a surveyor, or at best a linesman that helped the surveyors. But nothing came of the talk. Besides, he was told, with a nod and a wink and a jar at the ribs, he would be better off as one of the lads. So when schooling was over and before the end of the last school holiday off he went to the divisional training centre to be taught mining in the modern age. To be taught the intricacies of undercutting jibs, sheer jibs, turret overcutting jibs, the advantage of the latest hydraulic-type mechanical supports, the friction type that worked with the new cutting devices. Even a trepanner which had as its cutting element a rotary head with overcutting and undercutting jibs. He remembered how very proud they were of themselves at the centre. They told him in five years there would not be a pick or shovel in the pit, everything would be so mechanized that on the really good faces only a handful of men would be needed to produce several hundred tons of coal a day. That productivity per man-shift would be higher than it had ever been in the history of the industry. But the irony of this was lost on Ray since at the time he did not understand the effect this would have on men not selected to work the machines, men employed at collieries where the seams were so shallow they could not take a power loader never mind a trepanner working on an armoured face conveyor.

His first job at Highhill had been on the stapple bottom. When Ray related this to Gerald he had not known what a stapple bottom was and by the time he finished explaining his brother was not even listening. The stapple bottom was in fact a landing at the foot of a miniature shaft. Ray had to unload the full tubs from the cage that came down the shaft and couple them to the main set which hauled them to the landing at the shaft bottom. He had also to uncouple the empty tubs which came back and putting them into the cage signal for the cage to be hauled to the stapple top. He saw no-one but the men who worked the coal in the seam above his head and only then at the beginning or end-ing of their shift when they were hauled in the cage. He found the work physical and therefore tedious. He unlocked the tubs and hitched them to the set and in between spent his time casting stones at an old carbide lamp he had found one day travelling in-by. He was lonely, he felt cheated. He listened for the bell that signalled a fresh set of tubs were on their way and reflected angrily this was not the work of a man but a boy. Yet he lived with it, he accepted it. He watched the corns hardening on his hands and felt the unaccustomed coal dirt clinging to his cheeks. It reassured him, for as long as he went home black he felt he kept his status as a man.

He began counting the noises that came to him along the engine plain and the gallery above his head. The rumble of full tubs, the lighter more buoyant rolling of empty ones along the narrow tracks, the midway rollers toiling under the speed of the hauler, tubs clanging into the cage at the stapple top, the cage creaking its descent to the stapple bottom. Soon he bored of this and began taking with him magazines into the pit. He read Reveille and Weekend and Titbits. He grew tired of magazines and moved on to books. He borrowed works from the library at the institute and read in the light of the battery lamp. It was fun in the beginning because he knew he was doing something he should not be doing. But then his interest flowered into a passion, he read again at home in the evening, in the back room looking out upon the picture house. He read of the early efforts to establish a miners' union, the struggle of the union for recognition, the right to deal with the claims of its members, he read of the struggle for a stable minimum wage and settled working week, the strikes and lockouts and soup kitchens. The marches on magistrates' courts where leaders were being tried, the dispersing of the men by the violence of the police. He read of the battle that went on not for months but for years to gain only the rudiments of decency, the battle between men and employers — snakes in the grass, as his father called the coal owners. One had to fight for safer conditions, one had to fight for a public holiday, one had to fight for pay on bank holidays. One awoke in the morning not knowing whether one worked or not. But the fact which impressed Ray most of all was that in the whole history of trade disputes only the miners could say they went back worse than they came out. They never in their history won a strike.

When Ray went to work on number nine his daily book reading was eliminated. Even had he the time he would not have had the mood. At first it was impossible for him to believe this was happening to him, he could not understand this was the reality of being a man. He had filled out in his teens, he was six feet tall, and the proximity of roof and floor, with his shoulder scraping against one and his arm jammed against the other, made him certain that one day he would so lodge himself no amount of straining and heaving would get him out. Often the men talked of falls but rarely of death. They talked of the size of the rock that flattened a man to the sodden dusty floor, how they had known ten men unable to lift it, so that it had to be broken with picks before the man could be lifted out. And always as they talked Ray felt there was something the trapped man should have done to avert his calamity. He should have insured his timber was safe, that the stone beyond the conveyor was properly canched; he should have kept his senses clean, his instinct sharp, he should have been aware of the slightest noise that threatened disaster. Now he realized the nonsense of his thoughts. There was nothing one could do. One could not scramble for safety at the crack of a pit prop, for always somewhere there was a pit prop cracking. And if one day there was a fall what could one do? What could a stout man do trapped between two layers of rock, or a thin man but scamper like a mouse in the hope he was scampering out of the fall and not into it?

Ray came to know fear and panic and hate, a sullen hate he took out of the coal, a slow-burning hate that set him working with jaw tight, teeth set, muscles stiff in his cheeks. A hate that tightened the muscles in his arms and shoulders, that made them work savagely and ache afterwards. He had no longer felt so boastful, so much of an equal, so much of a man. How he hated reality! He could not let his mind wander for a moment before he was reminded of it by the ache in his limbs, the water dripping upon his face, the discomfort he felt in his muscles. He hated himself for having been deluded, he hated his father for not having enlightened him. He hated work and the men he worked with, hated them because they talked only of sex and perversion, used four letter words that were meaningless and described nothing. And worst of all he hated bait-time, when the cutter ceased and the lamps extinguished, when there was only the darkness and the sound of creaking props, the conveyor and men settling uncomfortably before speaking of their secret loves and sexual experiences.

It depressed Ray, in the depths of the earth, to listen to such outpourings. If he lifted his head it collided against the roof, if he stretched a hand it became clammy with mud. Yet he listened to the rustle of oilskins, the chewing of jaws, the swilling of tea from a flask, the tea slopping back and forth as the flask was tilted, and he wondered why it was man should be so profane, why he should work in such conditions. They were so engrossed with sex they asked each other how they would like to make love here, in the water and mud and confinement of number nine. Then suddenly it occurred to Ray that none of the stories were true. Sex was at the front of their minds because darkness and claustrophobia, regret and longing were at the back. They talked of nymphet widows and nightly flips because they wanted to forget. Because they were all wretched together. And because buried so deep they let their minds run as a sewer to give themselves importance. They had so little to boast of, you see, in daylight.

He realized they had been trapped as he had been trapped.

74

They too had learnt what it meant to be a man. They had left
school eager to be rid of childish things, to be grown up, to be
part of the world, not a bystander. But they had learnt too late.
Ray was young, just out of school with only six months in the
pit, but for these men school was so far behind it was not even
a memory, their only recollections were of coal and dust and pit
work, day in and day out, stretching far back into the past and
far ahead into the future. He began to respect the men now that
he understood them. And the more he understood the more he
began to hate authority. He hated it because he felt it was
responsible for such wickedness. To hell with economics, he told
himself. A man was born to be free, to hold his head high, to
walk with shoulders erect, work on the ground not beneath it, he
was born to feel the sun to his brow, the air to his cheeks, the
breath of life to his lungs not the chill of dust to his nostrils, not
the staleness that scurried through airways.

And not only did Ray respect the men, he became proud of
them. He wanted to protect them from authority. It had infringed
enough, he wanted to ensure it did not infringe further, it had
taken enough, he wanted to ensure it did not take more. His
reading taught him how it had oppressed in the past, keeping the
men down, neglecting their conditions, indifferent to their suffer-
ings, how it had not been content only to exploit, to exact more
in return for less, but to drive and to goad till the men could
stand no more. He knew things were not the same under nationalization. But authority remained the same, authority with its
indifference, its remoteness, its ignorance of the men and their
simple desires. Its will always to subject, to afflict, to punish. The
closing of the pit and the dismantling of the village was another
act of authority striking at the men, of not taking their wishes
into account but encroaching still further on their rights. For if
the men disliked the pit they loved the village. It was all they
had for their families, it was all they had for their children. And
to fight for the village one had to fight for the colliery. One had
to fight the authority that wished to destroy.

Ray lay in the cold and loneliness of the pit and listened to
Bousefield dragging his way back to the mothergate. He was
conscious of his body, conscious of its discomfort, and as he
switched on his lamp its beam shone on the dust and damp and
glistening conveyor. His joints were stiff now with so little

activity, but he knew with his restlessness, his aggressiveness, his anxious diarrhœtical speech, filled with passion if not good sense, he was the one man in the pit who could articulate the men's feelings. Feelings he knew they were not aware they had till they heard Ray express them for them. The light of Bousefield's lamp no longer played upon the sullen coal as finally he pulled himself onto the rolleyway. And suddenly as if making some decision in his mind Ray hurried after him. The oilskins protected his back and stomach, the battery he attached to his side, he used his kneepads to the best advantage, and the steel tips of his boots furrowed the dust behind him as he wriggled forward between face and conveyor.

Wriggled as rapidly as he could to strike his first blow at authority.

10

He stood in the back room of his father's house, back against the latch of the door, rubbing the corns on his hands, the light from the window accentuating the acne stains on his face. His damp hair flopped over his brow and he had the nervous habit of jerking his head to remove it from his eyes. The acne stains were aggravated by the fine unshaved hairs on his cheeks and chin and the small veins in his temple stood out in the light. The tip of his tongue licked uneasily over dry lips and he was conscious of the strong beat of his heart and the nervousness in his legs as he recalled his address to the men from the deputies' kist. He felt hot after his shower at the pithead baths, the steam in the room from the tub on the floor made him uncomfortable, and already he felt sweat gathering beneath his arms and behind his knees.

"It'll not be me that causes the trouble, pa," he said. "It'll be them that cares less than me."

"A knaa son. A knaa how ye feel. Ye've never given us cause yet but there's always a first time. And A divin't want ye to start now. Just listen to a word from ye owld father, that's all A ask. Divin't bring nee trouble to the house, that's all A want ye to dee."

He took the towel from the back of the chair and began drying his arms and chest. The rags around the tub were soaked from the drops that fell from his body and the imprint of his feet where he had washed them in the tub. He stood by the side of the tub, in the light from the window, back muscles flexing with the movements of his arms as he stooped to dry his loins. With his face and hair dried the yellow patches around his eyes were more prominent, he had a small perfectly shaped head with small set ears, but the skin on the face was puckered, its vitality draining, there were pouches beneath the eyes and small lines tugging the corners of his mouth. The muscles in his neck were taut as he turned and the light to his body reflected its strength and hardness.

Ray did not hate his father as Gerald hated him. The hatred he had felt in the pit had been short-lived. He felt for him now as he felt for the other men, he felt the need to protect, to safeguard his interest, and since he knew how his father had been shaped, he knew how he had been trapped as other men had been trapped, he understood. And because he understood he could accept. He watched him stoop to rub the damp from his feet. He saw him pull at a core of hard skin on the side of his toe. He saw that the movements were slow, automatic, the actions of a man tired, depressed and bewildered. With his head stooped he did not seem aware of his son by the door. But when at last he straightened, when he took the towel in both hands and began rubbing his back, he turned slowly and stared at him with his beady, bird-like eyes. His thin lips tightened and he frowned, as if brought back to reality.

"Another thing," he said. "Afore ye gan."

Ray had turned and reached for the latch of the door. His father had seen the movement, tossed aside the towel and began picking up his clothes from the chair. As he faced Ray the thick hairs shadowed his chest, the light dabbed at the shoulders where they had been dried, and as he pulled on his clothes his lips moved softly, gently, head shaking as though there was something he could not understand. But Ray understood, his face softened and his eyes grew moist, he let go the latch and as he turned the rigidity slipped from his hands.

"Ye divin't think what A'm deein' is bad, d'ye son?" Holt asked. "A knaa ye're not the same as yon bugger in the kitchen. A knaas A can talk to ye. A've never been able to talk to him. But then he doesn't understand, he doesn't understand owt. He doesn't knaa what it's like, he's never knaan. Ye knaa what A'm tryin' to say, divin't ye, son? Ye knaa."

"I thinks I knaas, pa."

"A'm owld now, and when ye're owld ye're different. Sometimes when A look back A divin't feel the same men. A feel somehow A've changed. But A'm owld as A says and in five years A'll be finished the pit and the pit'll be finished wi' me. And A want somethin' to put in its place. A divin't want to sit wi' them other pensioners on the seat and watch the traffic gan by. A had enough o' that afore the war. All A want is a bit o' comfort. Ye divin't think A'm bad wantin' that, dee ye?"

Ray stared at the dirty water in the tub, the damp rags on the carpet scattered by his father's feet. He stared at the pit clothes thrown aside, breeches lying in one place, shirt in another, belt twisted beside his boots, its dirt-encrusted buckle silver in the light. Crusts of dirt had already peeled from the soles and heels of the boots and soon the dirt would be trodden into fragments to take its place with the dust that lay along the skirting boards, saturating the cushions of the easy chair. Speckling the old-fashioned drawers with its huge mirror framed against the wall. Holt stood before the mirror to adjust his collar and his throat bobbed as he fingered the stud into the small aperture at the neck of his shirt. His cheeks screwed as he strained to attach the collar, but his eyes never left the image of himself in the glass. His cuffs flapped around his wrists but even when he paused to roll them up the eyes remained concentrated on the reflection the mirror threw back from the drawers.

"She's less than my age, pa," Ray said. "If ye marry her."

"A knaa, son. A knaas all about that. And there's some thinks A'm daft and others that she's dafter for marryin' us."

"Why is she marryin' ye, pa?"

"She's a strange lass, A cannot fathom her at times. The men say it wouldn't be so bad if A had money, but A haven't ye see. A've got nowt. And she's got nowt neither so there's a pair on us. But A'm still strong, ye knaa. A can give her a family if that's what she's after. She'll have nowt to worry about there."

"But they're shuttin' the colliery," Ray said. "Pullin' down the houses."

"They'll not pull down this house," his father said. "It's ours. It's always been ours."

Ray smiled at his simplicity. "This street'll be the first to gan," he said.

"Ye mean they'll pull it down afore they start on the others?"

"That's reet. Ye'll have to pack up, pa. Ye and yer wife and Gerald and me. Unless ye want to stop and fight."

"A divin't want to fight son," Holt said. "A divin't want to fight neebody."

"Ye'll not have to fight," Ray said. "There'll be others to

79

fight for ye. All I'm sayin' is if the worst comes to the worst, if we fight and we lose and have to pack up, she'll not mind. She'll gan wi' ye all the same."

"She'll come all reet," Holt said. "She's like that. And she fancies us, ye see, and A fancy her. Ye understand that, divin't ye, Ray, son? Ye understand that."

"Some o' the men, they say it's her owld lady shovin' ye into it. They say she wants her off her hands 'cause she has her eye on somebody else. 'Cause she wants to marry again and leave the whole tribe, but she cannot as long as she's got Dolly around."

"It's nowt like that," Holt protested. "They're talkin' out the back o' their heads, like they always talk. The owld woman, she thinks the world on her, she wouldn't let us harm a hair on her head. Only ye knaa the way they live. Ye knaa how the folk have their knife in them. That's why they gossip the way they dee. That's why they're always pullin' them to bits."

"They reckon she's got gypsy blood. Reckon even the mother doesn't knaa who the father is."

"It's bull, A tell ye. Sheer luney talk. If A ever get me hands on the bloke who says that A'll bash his head reet in — and A'll not have me family sayin' it either. D'ye think A'd marry her if A thowt that? D'ye think A'd have a lot o' gypsy kids runnin' round the floor."

"I'm just tellin' ye what they're sayin' in the pit."

"They'd better not say it when A'm around. Listen, son, A'm by mesel'. A've got neebody in the world but ye and Gerald. But ye're gettin' on, the two on ye, ye'll be marryin' yerselves afore long. Ye'll be settlin' win a house and family o' yer own. Ye'll not be thinkin' o' yer owld father. That bugger in the kitchen cares nowt about us now never mind when he's married. So there'll only be ye. And what's ganna happen when ye marry and turn yer back?"

"I'm not ganna marry," Ray said.

"That's what ye say now. A said the same mesel' when A was yer age."

"Even if I did I wouldn't turn me back."

"All the same," his father insisted. "We need a woman in the house. Ye see how it's fallin' to wreck and ruin. Ye see how owld Fanny Adams keeps it. Yer mother was never like that in her time. She was always neat and clean and tidy, nee fuss and nee bother, get it done so it was smart. That was her motto." He nodded to himself in the mirror. "Ye get used to a house like that."

Ray had the feeling his father talked not to convince Ray but to convince himself. And though Ray understood him there were times he wondered what went on in his mind, there were times he wanted to reach out and touch his father, touch not only his body but his soul. Yet as he stood before the mirror, face framed in the double edges, there was only to his features a distant inward look which told him nothing. His face was sullen with concentration, the lines in his brow and cheeks deepened and the eyes narrowed. His mouth tugged selfishly. He was like a man cornered, a man lonely, a man at bay against his loneliness, a man lonely all his life who even now refused to accept it, who fought against it and sought in its place comfort and companionship. The comfort of a home, the companionship of a wife. He ran his tie round the inside of his collar and looped the tie in front of the stud at the neck.

"I'll not turn me back on ye," Ray said. "I'll never turn me back on ye. Me and ye, we see eye to eye, we have nee fancy ideas like Gerald. If it makes ye happy ye get yersel' married. It doesn't matter what people say behind our backs. They'll never dare say it to our faces, that's for sure. If it makes ye happy it's all reet wi' me."

But Holt shook his head. He sat himself on the easy chair, unsettling the dust on the cushions, and holding his thumb against the backs began pulling on his boots, easing his foot gently into each so as not to strain the stitching. Ray saw his face flush with the effort of leaning forward, silver hair shining on the crown of his head. He seemed to be only half-listening. "If only he'd see it," he muttered. "If only there was some way A could make him see it."

Ray lifted the latch on the door.

"I'll make him see it," he said.

11

Everything was as he had left it in the kitchen. The chair remained upturned in the corner, feet to the ceiling, seat in the ash of the fireplace, the remains of a plate lay against the skirting board, splinters scattered beneath the furniture, the carpet was rumpled, out of place, revealing the dust beneath its corners; the ash had settled back in the fireplace and the fire dropped below the bars, the hard coal was crimson but there was no flame, only the pattern of the embers and the slow curling smoke of gas burning in the coal. The gaslight had ceased to swing but one of the links that held it in its socket had broken so that the lamp hung lower than normal. The kitchen was darker than the back room, for the sun had passed round to the other side of the house, but where in the back room the smell of his father's clothes on the floor, the water in the tub, yielded a smell of the pit, of dust and damp and earth, there was no such smell in the kitchen. There was only the faint aroma of eggs and chips and black pudding, the dust that lingered, the ash in the fireplace, the staleness and decay that so aggravated Gerald.

He stood by the window, head and shoulders cut out of the light, hands behind his back. There was something artificial in the thrust of his shoulders, and looking across from the door, eyes not accustomed to the change of light, Ray saw he had the same shaped head as his father, small and perfectly rounded, the ears inset, neck small and slender. He did not turn when he heard the latch drop, the door swing awkwardly open, catching the thickness of the carpet, but Ray knew just as he had known when he called for the clothes of his father that he was aware. And not only aware but on his guard. He could tell by the sudden straightening of his body, the sharp alertness that came over him, the sudden tensing of his hands as Ray stepped into the room.

"I suppose it never occurred to ye to clear up the mess?"

82

The back of his neck blushed and a hand came from behind his back to finger the curtain. He stared beyond the yard wall, beyond the allotments and waste space, to the bus garage and row of Co-operative houses stumbling back up the hill. He could see beside the corrugated ugliness of the bus garage its oil drums and stack of threadbare tyres, he could see its rubbish heap of cartons and cylinders and frayed rubber tubes. And beyond the garage he could see too the lines of the houses softened by twilight, dust coloured, the dust rinsed through with sun, houses with neither a sense of beauty nor a sense of ugliness but a sense of peace. A peace that dwelled behind the curtained windows, protected by the grey stone walls. A peace that soothed Gerald, relaxed his shoulders, his muscles, the tautness in his neck and arms, that filled him with anticipation, with tranquillity, so that the watchfulness went from him and with it the tension.

For Ray by the door, staring at the back of his brother's head, he felt the world closed in, he felt time suspended, he felt only the two of them existed in this moment, in this kitchen, the door to the back room closed behind them. With no sound from the outside world but the flush of water to a sink and inside only the ticking of the clock on the mantelpiece, the shuffle of movement from the next room, the restive escape of gas from the fire. He felt uncertain of himself, uncertain of his brother. And in the silence it occurred to him that with time suspended, with the warmth of the fire against his face, conscious of his feet on the carpet, the sweat drying beneath his arms, the discomfort of his jerkin and corduroys, it occurred to him, feeling isolated, abandoned, with only the two of them in the world, that there was nothing of value. Neither his anger with the management nor Gerald's with his father, neither his determination to protect the men nor Gerald's to leave the village, neither his desire to be involved nor Gerald's to be disinterested. Neither his wish to resist change nor Gerald's to accept progress. That everything was as meaningless as the dust in the air, as pointless as the corns he felt on his hands.

Then he looked down and saw the shattered plate, he saw pieces littering the floor, he saw the distorted carpet, the seat in the grate. He stirred and not only did he hear himself breathe he heard the beating of his heart. He swallowed and felt his throat and mouth dry. He licked his lips, his thoughts began moving again, and with his thoughts time and with time the world, and with the world himself, his feelings, his prejudices, his aspirations, his yearnings. The prejudices, aspirations and yearnings of his brother. He bent over the shattered plate and began collecting the pieces to lob them into the grate beside the half-buried seat of the chair.

"Why d'ye have to gan and dee a thing like this?" he asked.

"He'll get the same as he gave my mother," Gerald replied.

"As if ye treated her any better yersel'. As if ye never shouted and bullied her when ye had the chance."

The blush deepened along Gerald's neck and he tugged nervously at the curtain. The weight of his body rested on his left leg and with his right pushed forward, cap of the toe touching the wall, he swayed slightly as he stared out of the window. He heard his brother clearing away the confusion caused by his anger but felt no inclination to help. There was in him no repentance. The storm had blown itself out and left in its place a little tiredness, a little exhaustion, but no regret, no sadness. And the tension that had left his body came flowing back, his face flushed, his breathing became difficult, laboured, and he tried to hold it back as he held back his thoughts. The fingers of the hand behind his back opened and closed and the nails scraped fretfully at the palm.

"Maybe I didn't," Gerald said. "At least now I regret it."

"And I suppose ye think he doesn't regret it?"

"He'd think twice of taking a new wife if he did."

Ray scowled and felt the sides of the teapot. The teapot was cold but the contorted image of his face was thrown back to him from its silver lid. He removed his hands from the side of the pot and saw they were trembling, so that he became aware of a slight dissatisfaction that did not amount to anger. He picked the seat from the fireplace and dusted the ash from its cover. The ash fluttered back to the grate, leaving white the pads of his fingers, and as he ran them down the sides of his corduroys he felt the pressure of the tips against his thighs. He wondered what new thing had annoyed him. He wanted to remain composed, in control of himself. Nevertheless his pique continued till he understood what was the cause. He leant across the table and hauled the upended chair from the corner, setting it upright and slipping the seat into its proper place.

"I'll tell ye somethin', Jay-boy," he said quietly. "Somethin' ye'll never understand, never in a month o' Sundays. The owld man, he loves ye. He loves ye more than he's ever loved me. When we were kids he hammered me just like he hammered me mother. And when we gets on a bit always it was me that got the back o' his hand, it was never ye. When the teacher comes to the house and asks to see me father and asks to let ye stay another year at school to make a good'n on ye he never lets out a chirp, even though we were hard up and needed the money. And when it comes to pushin' a pen in the colliery office wi' next to nowt for yer pay, only the seat of a chair to polish, what's his crack? Did he say owt? If it suited ye it suited him, that's all he says."

"I suppose with you it was different?"

"Aye, but ye'd never see it. Ye're like the owld man. Ye care only about yersel'."

"If you mean I've not got the interests of the men at heart you're right, I haven't."

"I'll let that pass, Jay-boy, since ye think it's clever on ye. But ye see ye were the favourite, ye were always the favourite. There was nee extra year's schoolin' for me. Everybody tells us how much a villain me brother was and how I'd better mend me ways if I didn't want to turn out like him. But they never asked me to stay another year, there were nee fancy jobs for me. It was time I got mesel' a job o' work, time I paid for me keep. That was the owld man's idea."

"D'you think I care about your life story?"

"Like I say, ye only care about yersel'."

Ray gathered the crumbs from the table and threw them into the fire. He stared at the red caverns hewn out of the coal, black petals of soot quivering on the bars. Strangers on the bar, his mother called them. She looked for them daily in the belief they signified visitors to the house. He recalled her sitting over the fire, elbows on her knees, legs splayed to get the full advantage of the heat, brass knob of the poker hanging loosely between her fingers. He recalled the fire lighting her face, lighting the cracks and crevices and wrinkles, as she searched for the strangers. And with his brow on his arm, looking down at the trembling, fragile petals, he wondered what she would think of the latest stranger, the woman his father intended shortly to bring.

"Ye're the favourite," he said. "But ye divin't see why ye're the favourite."

"Even if I did I wouldn't care."

"He's makin' up for things," Ray said. "He's makin' up to me mother for treatin' her bad all them years. Ye were her favourite, so he made ye his favourite. She never treated ye bad, so he never treated ye bad either. That way he feels better. Now he says he wants to gan and marry again, bring a bit o' stuff to the house, and I says it's all reet wi' me. I says that because I knaa even if it wasn't it'd not make any difference. It's ye he thinks about, it's ye he wants to tell him it's all reet. Not me."

Ray picked up the poker and thrust it into the hard shell of the coal. The scarlet caverns were dimming now, like an evening sky when the sun has gone, but the thrust of the poker cracked through the shell and the dead coal burst alive. His dissatisfaction stirred with the flames, only he felt it stronger, fiercer, he felt the heat of the flames against his face and palms, and with it he felt the sudden glow of his anger, his dissatisfaction expanding like a bud as it had once expanded in Gerald. The shuffle had ceased in the next room, he heard his father pulling back the curtain around the door, the sound of the door opening and closing, the clatter of studded boots in the yard. He flung coal from a bucket onto the fire the way he worked at the seam in the pit, with intensity and energy, as if this would help purge his anger. The flames swept up the chimney and outward waves of heat dislodged the soot from the bars.

"Ye think the owld man's naturally bad," he said. "But he's not. He's not even what ye might call a sinner. He's just weak like the rest of us. We're all weak inside. That's why we've got to stand together, fight together, so people divin't see how frightened we are. So they divin't take advantage. The owld man, he's just like the rest of us. It's only ye that wants to be different."

Gerald discerned the bitterness in Ray's voice but did not turn from the window. He held the same stance, one hand behind his back, fingers of the other tugging the curtain; the blush had left his neck, but a muscle throbbed in his cheek as he watched the colours on the waste space changing in the softening light. The pigeons had all been gathered now, the long strands of bracken stirred with the air upon them, the dandelions by the side of the path no longer beamed and curtsied in the sun but were as dull and coarse as the grass and shrubs of docken. There was movement on the allotments as men moved out to feed their hens and pigs, do a little gardening before the meeting at the institute. Gerald saw the scattering of meal in the hen crees and heard the squeals and grunts of the pigs as they slobbered over their mush. The sun threw a crimson haze above the roof tops and a hawk flighted into the haze, paused and blackened into a shadow, before dropping like a stone into a field. Gerald watched its descent as disinterestedly as he watched the shades of evening, the men on the allotments, taking them almost as much for granted as he took his brother.

"I heard about you in the pit today," he said.

"Aye, and ye'll hear a lot more afore I'm through."

"Why d'you want to get involved. Don't you realize it doesn't do you any good?"

Ray laughed harshly and crossed to the corner beneath the stairs to gather up several bound books that lay on the floor. Gerald turned from the light of the window to the gloom of the room and watched him take each book, balance it carefully, measuring its size, testing its weight, before rubbing away the dust and laying the book on the side of the table. His jerkin was streaked with oil, there were damp sweat patches beneath his arms, his hair fell over his brow and his acne appeared less acute in the dull light. His lips moved continuously and the eyebrows came together as he studied each book before setting it on the table.

"What are you going to do with them?" Gerald asked uneasily.

"Takin' them back to the institute," Ray said. "Where they belong."

"All of them. Tonight?"

Ray grinned cheekily. "Ye can help us carry them if ye like."

Even now, Gerald reflected, there was time. But soon there would not be time. In a few moments he could go to the institute and take his stand with Ray against Wishart, he could prevent the excess to which he knew his brother was liable. Or he could climb onto the platform and support Wishart against Ray, not open his mouth, not say a word, merely by his presence quieten and restrain his brother. But this was the moment of decision. This was the moment to bring events under control. Once this moment slipped through his fingers there would no longer be time. And all that would happen to the village and its people, the colliery and its workers, the struggles, the hopes, the violence, the triumphs, they could all be traced back to Gerald. By his arrogance, his aloofness, his refusal to be involved, Gerald helped no-one, not even himself. But he was not to know this as he moved from the window to stand beneath the broken chain of the gas lamp. He was not to know this as he fingered one of the biscuits that remained on the table.

"Listen, Ray," he said. "And I'll tell you what it is you're fighting for."

"I knaas now without ye tellin' us."

"You're fighting for a house you've lived in all your life, that was condemned before you were born. That has no bath, no hot running water, no electricity, not even a toilet attached to the house. But they're proposing to move you out of this house into a better one, they're proposing to move you into a house like the ones the council built behind the school. They're going to give you hot water, electricity, a proper bath, a toilet, a fridge. There'll be a plug for the television, and maybe there'll be central heating. Even a garage for a car if you like."

"Fat lot o' good all that'll dee when I haven't got a job."

"You're fighting for a job you hate, that you all hate, each one of you, in a pit that's outdated. Where the seams are narrow, output low, where you have to crawl in on your belly, in water, with your back to the roof, just to get at the coal. You spend your lives dreading the next shift. You drink to forget. But they're closing this pit. They're going to transfer you to another where the seams are high, where you have a chance of making real money, where you walk in and out like a man not creep like a rat. A pit that's modernized and economic, with seams not too far from the shaft bottom. They're offering you a new life, Ray, a better home, a better job, a better opportunity. A chance to get out and broaden your experience, enjoy life, enjoy it like everyone else. Why won't you take it, Ray, why won't you take it?"

Ray pulled the books around the table and undid the zip of his jerkin. " 'Cause ye're wrong, son, that's why. 'Cause what's at stake is not just a house and a job, it's a way o' life. Our life.

There're people in this village never been further, never wanted to gan further. They're happy here, they've always been happy. Now they're tellin' the people to pack their bags and get out. They say it just as if the people had nee reet to live their lives in their own fashion, as if they had nee reet to decide what they did or didn't want to dee. So they'll get a new house and the house'll be like ye say, they'll get a new job and the job'll be like ye say. D'ye think they care, d'ye think that's what they want? Gan and ask them. Come wi' me to the institute, ye'll see what they want. Give them the choice between a new house and an owld'un, a new job and an owld'un, and ye knaa what they'll say just as I knaa."

Gerald swivelled on his toes and on impulse grasped Ray by the collar. The sudden movement surprised Ray, he stumbled and caught his knee against the leg of the table. His hand upset one of the books so that it fell upon the cloth. The muscles tensed in his arms and along his shoulders, his stomach curled, his chest constricted, his hands closed and his fists came up, but he was pulled so close to Gerald they were hemmed against his chest. He stood so close the pores of Gerald's skin were magnified, the face was strong, healthy, cleansed of its youthful acne eruptions, the cheeks flushed with a yearning to live, the eyes a desire to experience. Strength shone from his face, the strength of them all, of Ray and Bousefield and Wishart and his father. Yet was that strength enough? Was there no weakness, no frailty, no uncertainty? If it existed Ray did not see it. If it was there it was well hidden. There was as little weakness in the line of the jaw, the strong curved lips, as there was in the grip on his collar.

"The art of living is to live," Gerald said. "And to live you have to take life by the throat. You have to shake it like a cur till it chokes. That's what you have to do with life when you find it. And you won't find it without seeking. You won't find it in a village that's been dead so long one wonders if it ever lived. You've got to seek it out. It's as difficult to catch as the fly in your hand. But it's there if you can find it. Worth holding once you do."

Ray disengaged Gerald's hand and shrugged himself back into his jerkin. He looked at the clock on the mantelpiece and turning back to his books on the table casually closed the one which had fallen open. Gerald tried to see in him the narrowness he had seen in the colliery clerk, in his father, in his drinking companions at the club, he tried to see the shallowness he hated because he feared one day to see in himself. But if it was there he did not see it. He saw only the pallid, starch-like quality of the skin, the colour dried out of the face, blackheads offensive if one stared at them long enough. He saw a vigour and determination and hardness that surprised him because he had not seen it before. Ray placed the books in the front of his jerkin and with difficulty zipped the front as far as it would go. He steadied the books with his hands and walking to the door supported the books with a knee as he reached for the latch.

"Ye forget one thing, Jay-boy," he said as the door hinged open. "The village is life and the village people are real people livin' real lives. It's not the life ye suddenly want, but to them it's life. And that's what counts. It's all they've been used to. It's all they want. If ye destroy the village ye destroy the life, and if ye destroy the life ye destroy them." He pulled the door further ajar with the heel of his shoe and the evening light flooded over him. "Another thing," he said, adjusting the books in his jerkin to balance their weight more firmly in his hands. "If ye destroy the village and deprive the people o' the reet to live how they want, where they want, it'll not be long afore ye're deprived o' yer reets. To lead the life ye want, where ye want. That's how it turns out in life, that's how it always turns out."

"And that's why you'll fight?" Gerald asked.

"That's why I'll fight," Ray responded.

12

Markie Wishart gathered up several handwritten notes and shuffled them on the table.

He pushed the notes into his briefcase and looked down the hill from the house to the drift at the bottom of the bank; the drift had an entrance of red and white, but as coal was never brought to the surface here there were no ugly tramways and no heaps; only white carbide hills where in the old days men emptied and filled their lamps. The house was not of colliery stock but a bungalow set halfway down one of the banks leading out of the village. The land was uneven at this side of the hill, liable to sudden drops and sharp uplifts, and from the bottom instead of levelling rose like a bird's wing, so that across from the window Wishart could see the face of a sandquarry and the doll-like structure of a farmhouse sheltering beneath the horizon. A line of protective fencing lay along the top of the quarry and in the yard of the farm he could see several silvery urns of milk awaiting collection. A burn ran at the bottom of the bank, bordered by fretful willows and silver birches, and beyond the drift the colour of the gorse lay upon the land like a stained bruise.

There was peace here, Wishart reflected. The wayward dips of the land, the drop of the scarp, the sky beyond the hill, so crystal and polished, so pulsating, that one could not tell which was finite or infinite, the sky or horizon; the air rich with the freshness of the country, the scent of grass and herbs, of flowers growing wild, silver birch and willow, bracken, gorse and broom; the beauty that came and went with the sun, the splendour of dawn that tipped and shot the clouds with rose. The decay of the evening sky when the sun threw back its golden image from the windows of the farmhouse that was sunset. Beauty, peace and life. Wishart stood absently rubbing his hands before the window, the lines having relaxed from his face in this moment of tranquillity. He saw the world as it really was, as it had been in the beginning before man flexed his muscles, he saw how it was always meant to be, an outward serenity to match his inner thoughts, the one influenced by the other, related, so that he came within reaching the heart of wisdom. Life should always have this tranquil quality, he could absorb it as he could absorb sun. And he could understand it. Life was all that lay before him. This was the reality. Life did not change, change it left to people. Man could progress as he wished, in the manner of his choosing, each with a history of his own, a future of his own, composed of prejudice, meanness, selfishness and self-interest. But life asked no questions, made no distinctions. It was as it was, as it had always been, as it would always be.

He heard his wife crying in the bedroom.

He glanced at his watch and saw he had half an hour before the meeting at the institute. He had bathed away the pit dirt and changed his clothes and stood now in sandals and flannels and silk sleeveless shirt, letting the peace of the evening sink into him. He felt a tightening of the muscles in his chest the way a dying man must feel when his soul wrenches to be free. The sandmartins hovered above their nests in the face of the disused quarry and the scented air from the fields at the bottom of the bank was rich to his lungs. He had seen it all, he had breathed the inner content. This sudden insight had brought him near to the kernel of truth. But soon it would be lost as sight of a mountain top is lost to its vapours, the pressures of his own existence, the cares of his life, would sweep it away. And the sadness was it might never come again.

He turned and wandered slowly through the passageway to the bedroom. His wife lay twisted on the covers with her head to the pillow so that Wishart would not see her crying. The muscles twitched in her arms and legs and she convulsed and squirmed like an addict under the effects of a drug. Wishart did not touch her immediately but stared at the trembling shoulders. She had been knitting with her back to the frame, but the needles and wool had fallen to the floor, and the pillows supporting her back had slid down upon the mattrass. The skin on the back of the hands was pulled tight by her stiff frantic movements, the bones were stark and white leading back to the wrist, and the nails so scratched the pillows Wishart could see threads of cloth on the floor from the cases. With her face pushed into the pillow the light shone upon her neck and mouse blond hair, upon the veins in the calves of her legs. The tail of her blouse had been pulled from the skirt and the skirt itself unhooked, and as she wore no vest the light shone too upon the white sweating skin of her belly. There were red weals on the skin where her fingers had pinched and the curve of the stomach was ugly and distended.

Wishart rested upon the edge of the bed and pulled her up by the shoulders. She yielded willingly to his touch and brought her arms around his neck to burrow into his shoulder. Her face was damp with sweat and tears, hot through the silk of his shirt, and the tension in her body transmitted a febrile warmth to his hands. Her throat throbbed as she sobbed again and when he raised her face the rims were raw and swollen, the skin of the cheeks a puffed angry red. Her brow and chin were shiny with sweat. She closed her eyes against the tears, but they flowed hot and bitter from beyond the soaked blond lids, chasing down the narrow valleys between nose and cheek.

"My dear," he said. "Please. For my sake."

"I know it's selfish," she sobbed. "I know it is. When ye've got that much on yer mind."

"It's my fault," he said. "For neglectin' ye."

She made an effort to bring herself under control, but the tears flowed on and she sniffed them away as best she could before he handed her a handkerchief from his pocket. She dabbed her eyes and nose and the sobs came less frequently as the tension went from her. She was a woman of her husband's age, in her late thirties, with a short, stocky body that had once been slim, comely and attractive; she had an overlarge face that was plump now, the cheeks liberally fleshed, the line of the jaw flabby. Her hair was streaked at the front where it had caught the sun and her large snub nose, so cold in winter, glistened with sweat in summer. The eyes in their red shells were pellucid and hysterical, and when she dabbed them with the handkerchief the whites were brilliant through the mirror of tears.

"Ye were goin' to tell us about the doctor," he said.

"Yes. The doctor."

"He said ye were all right. Nowt wrong?"

"I'm all right," she laughed. "Only me nerves."

"He gave ye somethin' to take?"

93

"He gave us some pills," she said. "To help us sleep."

He patted her hand and she smiled gratefully.

"I'll see ye take them," he said gently.

He took the handkerchief and dabbed the eyes himself. His own were red and tired, slightly puffed, the pouches a light pencil blue, and though he carried with him the fragrance of the bath there remained along the lids a fine thread of coal dust the soap had not been able to remove. His hair, grey and thinning, was pushed back from the temples, but it had not properly dried and lay damp along the back and sides. He had a strong thick neck for so slim a body and the skin, coarse around the throat like that of a turkey, showed white where he had not fastened his shirt. The features were sallow, the lips pale, the only colour to the skin being the small blue scars of mining cuts on the forehead. Scars that deepened when he felt her trembling hand.

"And what did he say about the baby?" he asked.

She lifted her blouse and looked at the expanding mould of stomach where the skirt was pushed down. The flesh was firm and strong and glowed with vigour. The marks were fading where she had pinched the skin but there was one a darker hue where her nipping fingers had bruised the flesh. She rocked back and forth, knees on the bed, and stared fascinated at the womb that held the baby. It was as if she could not believe she was carrying life, as if she could not believe there was in her something which breathed and absorbed, a heart which beat as her own. Slowly she lifted her head. When she spoke her voice was high with anxiety. Hair fell around her forehead and through the tatty strands her grey eyes reflected her fear.

"I'm four and a half months pregnant," she whispered. "He gave us blood tests and urine tests, and he pressed his hands into me stomach. And the nipples o' me breast to see if I could breast feed the baby when it comes. To make sure they weren't chapped. And he asked us if I had any trouble with me back. And how many times I got up in the night to go to the toilet. And when I told him he said it was normal. Perfectly normal, he says. And then he asked — he asked."

"What did he ask?"

Her nails bit so deeply into the palms of his hands he winced and prised them loose.

"He asked if the baby had moved. And I told him not yet.

And he told us not to worry. He said it should move about now but not to worry. They take their time, he said. But he said to let him know. When it moved. So he could judge. But Mark, oh Mark, it has moved, it has. Just like a mouse running along me stomach."

He smiled. "That's all right," he said. "If the doctor said it was normal."

"But it means it's alive," she cried.

"Of course it's alive."

"Oh Markie, Markie, it can't be alive! It can't be."

"But it is."

"But I don't want it alive," she screamed. "I want it dead!"

She paused, taken aback by the words that escaped her quivering lips. The lids of the eyes drew inward and the pupils contracted. Her quivering hands extended to cover the womb and her fingers made little shadows over the hot skin, the muscles stiffened in her face and neck and there was a thickening of her throat. She gasped as if jabbed in the ribs and her hands kneaded the flesh that girdled the womb, so that Wishart felt uneasy. He felt a quickening of his heart, a little flame that licked around the walls of his stomach. He could see rising in a flood from her chest to her throat a wave of hysteria neither he nor she could stop, a pain that flushed and changed her face, darkened the eyebrows and lustred the eyes. Fear swept like a vulture from the back of her mind, fear so vivid she felt the foul bird flapping its wings in her face, its stench to her nostrils, talons clawing the flesh to the tips of her nerves. She shook her head and a feather from the pillow fell to the bridge of her nose. She screamed and twisted from Wishart to hide her face in her hands.

He had grasped her wrists to steady her, but now he let them go as helpless as the feather drifting to the floor. The feather was not the size of a petal and he stopped to pick it up, holding the fragile thing in the palm of his hand where it drifted and rode upon the hard polished skin. He looked sadly from his wife to their wedding photo on the wall above the bed. The photo had been taken against the church wall away from the gusty wind that fluttered the veils and lifted the hem of the bridesmaids' dresses. But even in the shelter of the wall little gusts ruffled the bride's veil and dishevelled the hair of the groom. It had been a white wedding, the groom not handsome but dignified, tall slender frame erect and only his hair out of place, the untried wife linking his arm flushed with the exaltation of the moment. Her cheeks that day had a colour he had not seen before or since. And there was a light to her eyes, not the curious distempered light he had noticed of late, but a glow radiating from within because she was marrying the man she loved and because he was offering all that she asked. The security of a home, the prospect of a family, the comfort of a husband. He looked down upon her quivering ugliness. He was afraid now even to touch her. The heartbroken sobs were stifled by her hands and the pillow was already damp with freshly-sown tears.

Mrs. Wishart felt the texture of the pillow against her swollen cheeks as she burrowed away from the hovering bird, burrowed from its sharp greedy talons sinking root-like to her nerves. She could feel against her neck the air from its wings and the darkness of its shadow lay across her shoulders. She quivered and squirmed and hid her face from its touch. She closed her eyes and the light was grey beyond the sealed lids. Her hand dropped from the bed but the fingers did not reach the floor, and as in her childhood dreams she felt she was falling, falling from a cliff, hurtling down but never reaching the bottom. She had been so nervous a child she slept with the light on and if it were switched off she woke in fright, steaming and sweating, hands trembling, till her mother came to switch it on again. And when she grew into her teens if she returned in the evening to an empty house she wandered through every room and switched on every light. If she had been to the cinema and lingered with friends till the crowds had gone she walked home down the middle of the road rather than trust herself to the well-lit pavement. At seventeen she suffered such persistent shingles her mother took her to see a nerve specialist in the city. The first question the specialist asked was whether she looked under the bed at night before climbing beneath the sheets. She replied no. This heartened the specialist since he knew from experience most nervous women looked under the bed at night before going to sleep. He asked why she did not look under the bed. She said because she was afraid she would find someone there.

It had amused the specialist. It had not amused her mother.

But then she had not realized her daughter's neurosis could be ascribed partly to upbringing and partly to the temperament inherited from herself. Now that she was dead Mrs. Wishart thought often of her mother and the stories she related of an evening over the fire. Some of the stories pleased Mrs. Wishart because they were humorous and jolly and dealt with times she had never known and would never come again. But there were others made her uneasy. The one which frightened her most was of the huge alsation which jumped upon her mother when carrying her first baby. The dog had been friendly enough, only a little high-spirited, but its paws upon her chest thrust her back so that she stumbled and fell. The dog scrambled over her and began licking her face. Her mother's screams brought out the street. The incident occurred during the sixth month of pregnancy and the conviction she would lose the baby so obsessed and terrified her mind she was never the same again. Even a few months before she died she could not recall the incident without plucking the skin of her neck, a pitch of nervousness slipping into her voice. After the baby was born she found her brain so weakened no thought ever occurred that could not be converted to an object of worry. She worried if the water in the tank would be hot enough for her husband coming from work, if her daughters were getting their feet wet, when the plumber was going to come to fix the leak in the cist. Even at night she tossed restlessly in bed, staring at the blue colliery lights, seeking further disaster. Until finally when she did sleep she dreamt of the boiler blowing up the kitchen, taking the house with it, and woke screaming and sweating, clutching the pillow for safety.

Her one legitimate worry was Mary, the future Mrs. Wishart, who had pneumonia a year after she was born and underwent an operation so serious she had only a fifty-fifty chance of recovery. The fluid was drained from the lung and she had to that day a scar the roundness of an apple where the operation had been. When she came out of hospital the doctor warned her mother Mary was a delicate child who ought not to be subject to strain. And since she still had the tubes in the lung to remove the remaining fluid she was not allowed to whimper let alone cry. The habit continued long after the tubes were removed and the back healed so that she grew pampered and spoiled, a child whose every want should be satisfied, every whim obliged. A child never allowed out without a coat lest she catch cold, nor long walks in the country lest she wear herself out. Mary knew she was not as other children. She knew because her mother would never let her forget. Her mother had set her apart like a princess, a frail slender tropical plant never meant for this world, with eyes soft and docile, sometimes brilliant, sometimes strange, but always disconcerting. They startled even her mother. As if they reflected a mind peopled with fears and dreads, nourished on the thought of ultimate catastrophe. And so of course it was, for Mary was so much under the influence of her mother that as she moved into her twenties the one thing she cherished above all else was security.

Her mother encouraged Mary's inclination towards Wishart because he offered all the security she was ever likely to get in a colliery village. He had a satisfactory job at the pit and as an official of the union enjoyed the respect of the management as well as the men. He was too slow of mind, too cumbersome of gait, to be regarded the best local catch, despite his tall frame and intelligent face, but he was dependable and probably had never done a rash thing in his life. Probably he was incapable of a rash thing and with a little pushing would give Mary all the security she needed. Her mother said there was nothing like a solid roof over her head. She spoke from experience, for she spent the first eight years of married life in a single room rented from an Irishwoman at a time houses were impossible to get. She had three children in this room, one after the other, and with each the rent was increased. One of the children died when very small but the rent did not come down. The colliery worked badly and jobs were scarce, her husband was out three years save for a week here and there at the brickflats, they had to accept charity, they were thrust upon the guardians. And always they lived under the threat of expulsion, always there was notice to quit if they did not pay their way. These were the hard times her mother endured, the times the whole working class endured, but they were times she wanted her daughter to avoid by having a house of her own. That was why, five years after living in a house supplied by the colliery, Mary persuaded Wishart to plunge all their savings into the bungalow halfway down the bank.

Wishart was at first uncertain. Buying a house was the biggest thing he had done in his life and he wanted to be sure. He looked over the property himself and then with the surveyor of the building society. The surveyor described it as a nice piece of land.

There was a large garden at the back and front, with a lawn and small greenhouse, and also a garage at the side with a narrow drive round the back to the road. The bungalow was neat and unostentatious, built of russet brick with a red tiled roof that jutted pagoda-like and cast a shadow upon the crazy paving. There were two bedrooms in the house, a passageway, a sitting room, toilet and bathroom combined, a kitchen with a modern sink unit, electric cooker and refrigerator, and a coalhouse set in the outside wall. The rooms were light and airy and the scent of the country sifted always up the broad undulating slopes. Wishart stooped over the soil of the garden and saw it was good. But the price was high and he hesitated. He looked to his wife.

Security was the one thing in the world Mrs. Wishart lived for. She felt if she lost that she had lost her soul. It mattered little that the deposit on the house and solicitors' fees would exhaust their savings, that the mortgage would take twenty years to pay, the interest rate wobble with the bank rate, so that if the one increased the other increased with it. That they would be paying almost as much interest a month as they were repaying the money they owed. The house would be theirs when they grew old. It would be for their children when they grew and married and needed a home. She had wanted five children. She wanted them to keep white mice and rabbits and tortoises, help her husband stoke the greenhouse boiler; the girls she wanted to pass for the grammar school at the foot of the village, the boys to play football for the local school; but above all she wanted to hear their laughter, their sobs, their feet on the pathway, their fingers lifting the latch on the door. So that she knew she would never be alone. But her mother counselled delay. She recalled how, coming so early in married life, her three children had thrust her upon charity and so destroyed in herself the little pride she had left. She did not want that to happen to Mary. She could not have a mortgaged house and five children. Better to sacrifice the one to have the other, to wait till part of the mortgage was paid, better to see how things went. As always Mary took her mother's advice. Till now it was too late, she was too old, time had passed, and she could never have the five children she yearned.

Mrs. Wishart's mother had died six months ago of cancer. It was then Wishart had seen the neurosis in his wife. Over the years he had noticed a brittleness to her voice when she laughed that was not quite normal, and sometimes looking up from his papers as he worked at the table, he found her staring with a fixity that troubled him. But the break had come when her mother died. She stayed always at the bedside, holding her mother's hand, and for days he had not seen her home. She watched the flesh ghost from her mother's frame, she saw huge clefts appear in the cheeks, hollows in the temples, the flesh of the neck shrivel and disappear, leaving only a scraggy chicken's neck. The eyes withdrew into the head, the irises perished, the pupils decayed, her sight dimmed and finally died. The skin bleached yellow when the cancer reached the liver and with her false teeth removed the mouth began to drop. She was so transformed at the end the only semblance of herself was in the three worried frets in the forehead. And there pervaded an odour of death that clung to Mary's hands long after she left the bed, so that it terrified her. No amount of washing would rid it from her hands. And as she saw her mother break up and smelled decay and death she began to break up too. The fear and dread that brooded in the eyes came to the surface. Her hands shook, she stuttered as she spoke, her cheeks stiffened and grew paler than he had seen them; the hair became tatty, an eczema developed on her hands and she began to put on weight, as she did when she worried. She began to smoke too, but the cigarettes so trembled in her mouth she gave it up and turned to drinking endless cups of tea and wandering restlessly around the house. When her mother was dead, she woke screaming and flailing her arms, claiming she had seen her mother's shadow flickering on the wall beyond the bed. As if the shadow were beckoning, as if her mother wanted her to cross over, make the perilous journey. As if she were waiting for her death.

It was then they decided on the baby.

13

Wishart picked his wife gently but firmly by the shoulders and swung her from the pillow.

He wanted to shake her, to slap her, even to beat her, yet he could not find his heart. And he remembered the baby. Instead he drew himself from the edge of the bed and pulled her with him. She screamed, wriggled and twisted, but he grasped her wrists and held on. She felt she was being plucked by the bird, the foul bird, and swept high into the air. The ground swirled and she felt sick and dizzy as its shadow fell across her face. Its talons dug deep into the veins of the wrists. She sailed higher and higher and another wave of prickly heat flushed over her. A button flipped from her blouse and the skirt slipped lower over the hips, baring her pregnant breasts and stomach. She caught her shins on the iron bedstead and panicked with pain. She beat at the sailing shadow and odour that overwhelmed her, but her nails clawed not at the feathered toughness of the bird's underwing but at the soap-scented freshly shaved skin of her husband.

She opened her eyes. He held her still by the wrists.

"Ye have to calm yerself," he said. "Calm yerself. Ye mustn't let yer nerves get the better o' ye. It's not good for ye. It's not good for the baby."

She looked over his shoulder out of the window to the edge of the greenhouse and railings. Beyond the stark tips of the railings, she could see at the top of the bank the social club at the end of the road, and beyond the club the first houses of the village, the smoke of their chimneys like a veil across the twilight. She felt as a woman just returned from a journey, their familiarity comforted her and she brought her attention back to the room. The button from her blouse had rolled against the wall and covers from the bed draped the floor. There was a small medical chest beside the bed and upon it stood a lamp and box

101

of calcium pills she had received from the doctor. A newspaper she had been reading had fallen to the carpet at the bottom of the bed and upon it were slippers kicked from her feet. The runner carpet where she had dropped her needles, wool and pattern was rumpled in a lopsided hump beneath their feet and the wardrobe at the foot of the bed stood ajar, so that her face and body reflected in the mirror. She started when she saw the image and a quiver came to her lips.

She looked at her husband. He would not let go her wrists.

"That's better," he soothed. "That's much better."

She checked her quivering lips and noticed the scratch marks she had made despite his hold upon her.

"Yer bit face," she murmured. "I've scratched yer bit face."

"It's all right," he answered. "It'll gan off. Ye didn't break the skin."

He let go a wrist and placed his arm around her shoulder.

"Come through into the other room," he said. "I want to show ye somethin'."

He helped her through the passageway into the sitting room, one hand upon her shoulder, the other feeling the throb of her pulse against his fingers. She did not protest but allowed herself to be led submissively, snuggling close, grateful for the firmness of his grasp upon her wrist. Her legs were so weak she clung to him as if she were going to fall, but her breasts heaved less and some of the tension left her face. He brought her to stand by the window and together they looked upon the landscape. The rhododendrons were flowering in the garden and the skin of the buds on the rose trellis pulsated with a dark shiny life; the first fragrance of the herbaceous border had subdued with the passing of the sun, was now less of a glory, more of a crimson flame; but the beauty, the movement, the colour, the quickening, breathed a heaviness that drowsed his lungs. The light had changed and with it the wayward dips, sharp drops and sudden uplifts of the land. The sun had passed from the farmhouse windows, the gorse had deepened, the quarry darkened, the sky paled, the horizon grown less distinct; patches of bluebells were scattered by the hedgerows, and from the willow at the bottom of the bank the willow wrens warbled and chiffchaffs pecked the silvery bark of the birch. A slight wind sprang up with the twilight and the countryside stirred at its soughing.

"There," Wishart said. "Ye see, nothin's changed. Everythin's as it was, there's nothin' to be frightened of. It's all in yer own head. It doesn't exist outside yerself." She brought her head from his shoulder and he lovingly stroked her hair. She stared out of the window. "That's right. Now don't think of anythin'. Let yer mind run down. Just look there and tell me what ye see. Nothin' much, ye think, only a few fields and trees, a bit gorse, only a farm and sand quarry. Nothin' ye've not seen before o'er the last five years."

"It's peaceful," she said quietly.

"Yes," he said. "It's peaceful. And it's ours. Always remember that. So let yer nerves wind down. Let the peace sink into ye. Let's enjoy it together. Breathe the freshness of the country. Let it fill yer lungs. Let it seep into ye, calm ye. So that ye don't feel upset. So that ye don't panic." He squeezed her wrist. "So ye feel relaxed and content."

Wishart had a voice too flat and monotonous for oratory. But he had learnt years ago to speak simply and sincerely, and it was the strength of his sincerity, the simplicity of his words, that helped his wife now. The bird that hovered over her uneasy brain wheeled away. It took with it the suffocating heat that pressed upon her like a weight. The sweat began to dry on her face and body and the air was cool against her skin; the tenseness that had aggravated her nerves subsided and anxiety shed from her face. She looked afresh at the rolling country. The twilight wind fluttered through the green unripe hay in the higher fields and shivered the catkins of the willow tree. The perfume from the flowers in the garden, the scent of herbs and grass in the country, was like a luxury to her blood. And she could feel the peace, the contentment, the tranquillity, she could feel it as surely as she could see the movement of the wind through the meadows. She smiled. She felt relieved. There was no problem that could not be faced with this inner tranquillity, there was no fear, not even of the darkest prison, if one could grasp and hold this inner kernel of content.

She rubbed her hands along the line of her husband's stomach and laid her head upon his chest to let him know how grateful she was. She was like a tame fledgling that requires only to be stroked and petted. Her hands joined around his waist and she could feel the silk of his shirt against the skin. He stroked the soft down on the back of her neck and watched the peace enter into her. He marvelled at the change. Yet he wondered how long it would last. With one hand stroking her neck, the other around her shoulder, his watch was turned from him so that he could not see the time. But he knew it would not be long before the meeting at the institute. He would have to gather up his briefcase and leave this house. He would leave it to stand upon a platform and address the men, tell them something they did not wish to hear. There would be no quietude or serenity then. Wishart stared at the softly changing shades of evening, aware of this house that was his own, this wife nestling into his chest, the world shut out so that only the two of them existed. And he wondered which was reality. This moment of cleansing, healing peace, or the moment at the institute, standing upon the platform before the men, the world clamouring to be in with all the violence of a flood unaware of its own destructiveness. He increased the pressure of his hand upon his wife's shoulder and lifted the frown from his brow.

He decided he did not wish to know the answer. If there was an answer.

"Markie," Mrs. Wishart said. "Ye promised to tell us what's goin' to happen now they're closin' the colliery."

"Nothin'll happen," he said. "We'll gan on as before."

"But the house. The mortgage has fifteen years to run."

"I know," he said. "But we'll manage."

"But if the pit's closed ye'll be out of a job."

"Not out of a job," he said. "Fixed up at another colliery."

He felt rather than heard her contented sigh. "I'm so glad," she said.

She felt free for the first time since that morning when she heard the news of the village. Wishart had conceived a child in the hope it would draw them together and take her mind from her mother's death. In the beginning, it seemed this would be so, for there came a bloom to her cheeks, a softness to her eyes, the eczema faded from her hands and with it the trembling, the stutter dropped from her speech, she ceased drinking endless cups of tea and stopped her restless wandering. She even began to sleep well at nights and did not wake dreaming of her mother. But of late she seemed to have slipped back into a world so wrapped in herself that rarely did outside events penetrate. She hardly noticed Wishart. She made his meals, ran his bath, cleaned his boots, his pit clothes, brushed his helmet, made his bait, prepared his flask, dusted his room, made his bed. But never once allowed him to enter the tightly contained inner world of herself. She hardly listened when he told her that morning of the colliery. Indeed, a little frown darkened her forehead, as if she resented being disturbed. Her mind peered out to examine the problem, but when it decided no problem existed retired back to its own inner wandering. It was only later when she called to see the doctor about the baby and heard the news of the village that she related the two and understood what it meant.

An uneasiness spread over her as she recalled the tears that had clustered her eyes.

"But Mark," she said. "Ye don't know where ye'll be workin'. At which colliery. It might be miles from here. Maybe another coalfield."

"It might," he said. "I don't know."

"And all the other men. All being transferred as well."

"We might have to move," he admitted. "Someone'll have to."

"That means we'll have to sell our house. Our beautiful house."

"It's not sure yet," he said. "Nothin's sure yet."

"But Mark. Who'd want to buy a house in a village that's dead? Miles from anywhere. With no shops and no houses? And not a town for miles. Only a dead colliery? We'd lose all our money, Mark. All that we've striven and slaved for."

She brought her head from his chest and looked into his face. The skin was even more pallid in the light from the window and a shadow underlined his jaw where he had shaved. The scars in his forehead were deep and accentuated. She withdrew her hands from around his waist and stepped back to the edge of the table. Her mind was like a snake biting back upon itself. She felt the peace slipping. She felt it had already gone. Markie watched her nervously hitch her skirt and finger the protruding tail of her blouse. He tried to smile when he saw the change in her face, but the smile did not extend beyond his lips, and she knew the peace had slipped from him too. She recognized worry in his face and sleeplessness in his eyes. And then it came to her. A revelation that leapt like a lightning flash across the uncertainty of her mind.

"Not all the houses'll be comin' down," Wishart said. "There'll be some left."

"Ye mean the council houses behind the school?"

"Probably. And a few private houses they can't get their hands on."

"But all the ones up the bank. Up there past the club. They'll all be comin' down."

"No-one knows yet," he said. "Nothin's been published."

"But it's right," she said. "And ye know it's right."

After the lightning came the thunder. She realized she had been right after all. Her tears had been justified. The colliery would die and the village with it. The houses would come down and the streets left deserted. If she stayed she would have to endure loneliness for the rest of her life, loneliness for herself, loneliness for the child that was to come. Never more would she be comforted by the sight of the houses at the top of the bank. There would be nothing but decay and rubble, the houses stripped of their walls, their timber, their windows, their roofing, with only harsh ugly chimney stacks left standing, the rats among the rubble, the rooks above the stacks. And if she left? The thought sent her reeling from Wishart till she felt the table against the back of her legs. She could not stand the thought of being cut off from the world. But neither could she conceive of a life outside the village. Were they to leave this house it would be their ruin, they would hardly get enough to cover their deposit. And she would lose security for herself, security for her child. Once she had wanted five children, now she wanted none. She would rather see the one she carried killed in the womb than born into a world that was not secure. She would rather die herself than face the insecurity she dreaded for her child.

These had been her thoughts that afternoon when she heard the news of the village. They were her thoughts now as she stood against the table facing her husband. She held her mouth tightly closed as if she were going to be sick with the tears that cluttered her throat. The one thing that saved her from disintegrating was faith in the strength of Markie. He had reassured her once that evening. He would reassure her again. She understood now why he was going to the institute and what he had to do to secure their future.

"Markie," she said relieved. "Ye'll fight, won't ye?"

106

"Fight for what?" he asked.

"Why, for the colliery. For yer job."

"The colliery's dead," he said. "To fight for the colliery is to fight for the past."

"But the men. They'll want to fight."

"For the village maybe. Not the colliery."

"But the village cannot live without the colliery."

"If it has a future it'll live," he said. "And a will of its own."

She could not believe what he had said. She did not understand the polemics of futures and pasts, fighting for the village but not the colliery, the one living the other dead. She saw only what was going to happen to her life. To their lives. She could see so vividly it was like a torture. There would be hardships as cruel as any her mother had endured. They would be thrust from pillow to post, living with strange people in a strange place, with no home of their own and no security, burdened with a family that could not be supported, far from the memory of her mother and even further from her grave. She shook her head. She understood the dilemma. She could not stay in this house, but on the other hand she could not leave. Her mother would not approve. Just as she did not approve of having a family that could not be supported. This was the meaning of the flickering shadow. This was the reason of her summoning death.

"Markie," she said.

There was something in her voice that for the first time changed his weariness to fear. He looked at his wife and realized she was a stranger to him. He did not know what went on behind those eyes that had fallen again to brooding. He blamed himself for what had come to pass. He had cared more for union affairs than he had his wife. He had sat over his papers in the back room and not considered whether she was happy or not. He attended union meetings, consultative meetings, welfare meetings, delegate conferences. Arranged cavels, compensation, rehabilitation, the men's complaints, their disgruntlements, seen to their dues, their membership, their coal allowance, their pension. And never once had he reflected his wife might be lonely. That she might prefer him as a comfort in the home to elsewhere dealing with the affairs of others. Never once had he sat down and held her hand and asked how her day had been. Never once had he taken her to the pictures. Only now when she was ill had he ceased taking her for granted. Only now when it was too late did he want to help.

"Just tell me what ye want," he said. "Just tell me."

"Is there anythin' we can do?"

"About the colliery?" he asked. "No. There's nothin'."

"Not about the colliery. About the baby."

He did not understand. "What about the baby?"

"Is there anythin' we can do?"

She saw again the pain that cleaved his brow and turned away. For as she could not bear pain in herself nor could she bear it in others. He put his arms around her and pulled her close to his chest. He rubbed his chin against her cheek and she smelt the freshness of the soap that had so lately bathed his face. But she could not enfold her arms around him nor snuggle close as she had before. Instead, she stared over his shoulder to the bedroom where the light from the window fell across the bed. The clothes, slippers and knitting on the floor, the bedside lamp, the box of pills, the pillow to prop her legs. She had the feeling they did not exist but were merely an impression on her mind. The pillow for her head was speckled with shadow where the tears had yet to dry. The room was filled with shadow, shadow that seemed to move in the light from the window, so that everything in the room seemed to move in the light. She heard Wishart murmuring, murmuring softly in her ear, but his was like a voice in a foreign language. The words had no significance. Only the shadows in the room had significance.

"My dear," Wishart said. "Never let me hear ye talk like that again. There's nothin' in this world can make things as bad as that. Do ye hear, nothin'."

He held her close, anticipating the tears, the useless sobbing jerks of her chest. But they did not come. There was only a limpness, a heaviness he did not understand. "Look," he said. "Everybody's in the same boat. In a panic because nobody's sure what's going to happen. I don't even know myself. But one thing I do know. It's not going to be as bad as everyone thinks. There'll be a way out because there's always a way out."

She came back to him from a great distance.

"I don't know," she moaned. "If only it'd be so."

"It will, I tell ye. It'll be just like I say. I'll be fixed up at another colliery. And we'll see what's to be done about the house

108

when the time comes. When we know where I'm fixed up and where we stand about the village." He held her at arm's length and tried to look into her eyes. But she held her head tucked into his chest so that he could not see. "Remember," he said softly. "It's my child as well, you know. And if I want it there's no reason why ye shouldn't."

He lifted her chin to his face but even then she tried to avert his gaze. Till at last her eyes steadied and he saw, for the first time, beyond the fear and anxiety and neurosis, the tension and hysteria, a hint of madness. A sickness that could not now be stayed. His inside ached with a prescience of what was to come. He would think often of this night and this look in her eyes. It would have told him much had he understood what it meant. But then the night was young, there were other things too he would not forget. Ahead lay the meeting at the institute, behind the peace of the evening, the manner in which his words had soothed his wife. The truthfulness that led her back to despair. He would think of this too late when it would change nothing instead of understanding it now when it could. He dropped his hand from her chin and turned to the table. The light fell upon the faded straps and tarnished buckles of his briefcase and upon the worn gold of his initials embossed upon the leather.

"I'll tell ye what," he said, taking the briefcase from the table and laying it upon a chair. "I'll make ye a cup o' tea before I gan. That'll settle ye down a bit. Take yer mind off things. What d'ye think o' that?"

"Ye mean ye're leavin' us?" she asked.

"Only for a short while," he said. "Just for the meetin' at the institute."

"But ye cannot leave us tonight," she said. "Not tonight."

"Only for an hour," he said. "I'll be straight back."

"Oh please, Markie. Please. Not tonight."

"I have to," he said. "It's my duty."

"Please don't go, Markie. There'll be trouble. I know there will."

"There'll be no trouble," he said. "At least nothin' I cannot handle. Now sit yerself down in this chair and I'll put on the kettle. And I'll empty the pot and put in the tea. So ye'll just have to pour in the water from the kettle and let it mast."

"But what will I do. When ye're not here?"

"I'll not be long. Only an hour. Ye can get yourself a wash and brush up for a start," he said. "Then give the place a dust. So that it's tidy for when I come back. Just to give yerself somethin' to do. Just to take yer mind off things."

He went into the kitchen to set the kettle on the gas. He could hardly reach the tap for dishes that filled the sink. The bench was cluttered with potato peelings, egg shells and bacon rind his wife would throw out when she washed the dishes. A few small flies hovered over the peelings and a bluebottle buzzed over the table. It had not been cleared since breakfast, the milk bottle, cornflake packet and egg plate were as he had left them, and that evening he had to clear a space for his tea. Even the oven reflected his wife's neglect, cluttered with the frying pan and chip pan, so that he had to set one of them on the floor to make room for the kettle. Layers of dust engrained the window frames, the windows too had to be cleaned, the stove smelled stale with grease, crumbs were scattered on the floor, and an odour of drains came belching up from the sink. He lit the gas under the kettle and opened the window to let in the air.

"There," he said. "The kettle's on and ye can make yerself a cup o' tea. And then get yourself washed and changed and into the kitchen. Give it a clean out. To pass the time. And before ye know it I'll be back. Ye'll not even know I've been gone."

"I wish ye wouldn't go," she said. "I wish ye'd stay with me."

"I'll be straight back," he said. "I promise."

"There'll be trouble. I know there'll be trouble."

"Not from the men," he said. "I've worked with them all my life."

"Maybe," she said. "But they'll change everythin'. I know they will."

She sat on the easy chair and he brought his head close to kiss her lips. But she turned slightly from him and stared into the dead fire. She would not let his eyes meet hers and there was a shyness about her that surprised him. As if she had reached a decision of which she wanted him to know nothing. It unsettled him. He went into the passageway for his coat and hesitated. She sat placidly enough, hands upon her lap, not smiling but not crying either, quietly surveying the dead coals. Yet he wondered whether he ought not to stay after all. He could leave it to the chairman to explain the policy and answer the questions. He had been at the consultative the evening before and knew as much as did Wishart. And he had a justifiable reason for staying away, his wife was ill, she was expecting a baby, her nerves had got the better of her, she needed him in the home. Yet he knew he had to go and slowly he took his coat from the peg. The men were looking to him for guidance. He would be letting them down if he did not go tonight. He would be letting himself down. He had to explain, even if the men would not accept his explanation, he had to be true to himself even if they did not think he was being true to them. He shuffled into his coat and wandered back into the room.

He bent again over his wife, hands on the arm of the chair.

"Now ye're sure ye'll be all right?"

He patted her shoulder and stooped for his briefcase.

"And remember," he added. "I'll be back in an hour."

She did not answer and he went out of the sitting room through the kitchen to the door. The bluebottles continued to buzz over the plates and flies hover over the peelings. He pulled the door open with difficulty, for it caught the edge of the mat and dragged it back to the wall. The evening was bright, the sun had yet to sink, and standing in the doorway hand upon the stencil, he raised his eyes, not to the village and heap but the sky-line above the open fields. He stared at the stunted rowan trees, the strip of cloud skirting the hill, the sun sitting stately upon the cloud. Suddenly he became aware of the weight of the briefcase in his hand. The handle was coarse to his fingers and the fraying bottom bumped against his knee. He recalled his self-conscious-ness on the office steps, looking down upon Gerald Holt, feet licking sparks from the concrete. He recalled he had felt in a spotlight, on a platform, and the uneasiness came back as he pulled closed the door and set off down the path.

He paused by the gate and looked back, but the windows of the house were dark in the shadow and he did not see his wife looking out to wave goodbye. He pictured her by the fire staring into the dead coal. The uneasiness that rose within was more persistent and he turned for a final look at the country. Nothing had changed but the light. Nothing would ever change but the light. It rippled across gorse and hedgerow and sand quarry like a poet's fingers across a keyboard. He watched the wind through the willow tree and heard the warbling of the wrens. A cuckoo called somewhere in the open country and he discerned in its throat a hint of mockery, a hint of pride, a hint of content. There may also have been a hint of indifference. The land was so tranquil Wishart wanted to weep. For what? He did not know. He pulled open the gate and passed through onto the stone paving. He knew what he had seen that night he would never see again, what he had felt that night he would never feel again, what he had found and held that night he had lost forever. Yet he wished to cherish the memory.

It would comfort him one day to recall that at least once in his life he had known peace.

Book Two

The Meeting

14

Markie Wishart and Ray Holt reached the institute at the same time but by different routes.

The institute was a single storey building, squat but stoutly built, with a narrow path leading to a narrow entrance, large open windows at the front, high narrow windows at the back, and a plaque above the door reading: Highhill Colliery Miners Institute, June 5, 1901. The date signified when the institute had been opened by the colliery owners. Beyond the narrow doors stood a billiard hall, a cardroom, a reading room, and a kiosk for cigarettes and lemonade. There was also a passageway with a notice board and an enclave where the caretaker could be reached. Inside the billiard hall were two tables, the trough lights swung low over the green cloth, the cue racks set along the wall with the scoreboard. Always there was someone playing brag on the bare, initial-carved tables of the cardroom, beneath the brooding canvas of Keir Hardie, whilst in the reading room bookies' runners watched the older men study racing commentaries in the newspapers before writing their bets. Outside were the welfare grounds, tennis courts and bowling green, a pavilion for darts and table tennis, a rest park surrounded by a tall clipped privet hedge, with a lawn and a rose garden, and a miniature fountain bubbling artesian-like from the grass. The welfare football and cricket fields were set apart, the one not far behind the colliery manager's house, the other at the end of the village near the council houses. Across from the institute stood the children's playing fields and opposite the colliery maintenance yard. The main road turned past the institute up the bank towards the golf course, and from the windows of the cardroom one could see the crest of the hill and the highest houses in the village.

The institute itself stood at an intersection of two shale paths. One of the paths led along by the side of the institute into a

115

coppice and from the coppice to the open fields. The other laboured from the bottom of the village, rising so steeply torrents of heavy rain had guttered the shale to its underflesh. Markie Wishart did not turn onto the main road that would eventually bring him to the institute, but preferred the short cut across the open fields. There was only one way for Ray Holt and that was up the shale bank. He strode up the bank with his books under his jerkin, thighs thrusting tight against his corduroys, holding the books steady with his hands like a woman carrying her breasts. Markie cut through the gaps in the hedgerows till he came to the Tilley drift and crossed the tracks to join the path at the coppice. He heard the swings creaking in the playing field and saw the heads of the children above the long dry grass. Their voices carried to him as he turned into the institute.

They confronted each other by the gate to the pathway, the hands of both reaching for the latch, neither certain whether to let the other pass. Ray had paused on the flagstones to steady his books and had not noticed Wishart's approach. And Wishart had been so occupied with his thoughts he had not recognized the tall figure till their hands touched on the latch of the gate. Ray lifted his thigh and pressing his knee against the railings secured a better balance for the books he adjusted. Wishart rubbed the palm of his hand against a blunt railing tip and scrutinized the white leaves peeping from Ray's jerkin. A shy smile drew apart his lips and the threads of coal dirt were dark around the rims of his eyes. He held open the gate to let Ray pass and nodded at the books.

"First I've heard ye're a readin' man, Ray," he said.

Ray hoisted the books with his open hands and noticed with distrust the flickering smile. He brought back his foot to the flagstones and straightened his back and shoulders, drawing into himself as does a snake before striking. Crumbs no longer pitted his lips but had been licked away by the movement of his tongue, his hair had dried in the light of the sun but continued to fall over his brow into his eyes, whilst the anger and fretfulness were still in the twist of his lips. His heart pattered at the walls of his chest and his legs ached to be in the hall. Impatiently he shuffled his books, tossed his head and raising his elbows as if they were bird's wings, glanced to the porch of the institute. A group of men lingered around the notice board and the echo of their steps upon the concrete carried to him as he tried to stare Wishart down.

116

"What makes ye think I'm a readin' man?" he asked.

"Ye've an awful lot o' books if ye're not."

"I'm takin' them back to the readin' room, see. For me father."

"But the readin' room's shut the night."

"So I hear," Ray said. "For the meetin'. But ye'll be openin' it, I hope, when the meetin's o'er?"

"Maybes," Wishart said. "But ye should've saved yerself the bother. Brought them another night."

"It's nee bother," Ray said. "And I could always stand on them for the meetin'. Divin't ye think? Give us a bit o' height."

"Ye could always read some o' them while ye were on," Wishart answered. "Give ye a bit o' learnin'."

A bus pulled up the bank away from the institute, gears changing for the stiffer climb that lay ahead. Ray watched the bus over the tips of the railings, looking into the back to see if there was anyone he knew. A flush moved through his body and his tongue flicked between his lips. All the way up the bank his legs had urged him to keep pace with his thoughts, so that he had found himself at the gate of the institute without being aware the bank had been climbed. Now there was an ache to his thighs and the pressure of the books lowered the zip of his jerkin. The edges of the books pressed against his chest and his breath aggravated the discomfort. He watched the bus move up the bank, its dark petrol exhaust flattening across the road. The faces that stared back at him were indistinguishable through the dusty windows and his gaze swept back to Wishart.

"Now I never thought o' that," he answered cheerfully. "And if I stick me toes in I might even get to be union secretary."

"Ye might," Wishart said. "If ye thought it worth yer while."

"That's reet," Ray answered. "If I thought it worth me while."

A murmur of men and shuffle of feet came from the billiard hall where the meeting would be held. Along by the walls of the maintenance yard other men stood or knelt, drawing on their cigarettes, running blades of grass through their teeth and chewing at the stalks. Biding their time. They knew the meeting would not begin till the secretary entered the hall and Ray felt their eyes upon him as he surveyed the bus now halfway up the bank. He turned past Wishart onto the path, but Wishart moved a hand across him so that he could not pass. His fingers brushed against the sleeves of Ray's jerkin.

"Always got somethin' to say, haven't ye," he said. "Always full o' little flashes."

"That happens to be me jerkin ye're touchin'," Ray said. "So if ye'll not waste me time."

Wishart removed his fingers from the sleeve but did not drop his arm. "I'll not waste yer time," he grunted. "I just want to tell ye what I told ye in the pit the day. Make sure ye understand. Ye're gettin' a little big for yer boots. Just a little o'er big. One o' these days somebody's ganna have to cut ye down to size. And I just hope it's not ganna be me."

"When the time comes," Ray said. "I'll make sure it's not ye."

"Clever again," Wishart said. "But I'll tell ye now what I've told ye before. Ye're o'er young to meddle in union affairs. If ye want to have yer say get yerself to the union meetin' on a Sunday mornin'. And if ye care that much get yerself elected to the committee. I'll even keep a place open for ye if ye like. But do a bit o' constructive work for a change, instead o' gettin' all our backs up with criticism."

"I'm a union member," Ray said. "I pay me dues like everyone else. I have a vote like everyone else. And it's a democratic union, so they tell ye. Ye can open yer mouth when ye like. Ye can shout when ye like. It's all part o' the great public debate. The big democracy we live in. So divin't tell me what I can and cannot dee."

"Ye're talkin' to the elected secretary. Voted in on an open ballot so I could speak for the men. So I could put their point o' view. It's me that's got all the experience and it's me that's got all the facts. And if ye don't like what I'm doin' ye'll have a chance to say so. But in the proper manner, at the proper time. At the next ballot when the lodge has to elect another secretary."

"That'd suit ye," Ray said. "At the next ballot, when there's nee colliery, nee lodge and nee officials to vote for. That'd be a feather in yer cap. Keepin' us quiet till then."

"There'll be other lodges at other collieries," Wishart answered. "Other officials to vote for. Ye can have yer say then, if ye like. Not before."

Ray took Wishart's wrist and removed the arm from his path. The wrist was warm and bony, the thin hairs golden in the light. A tremble rippled through Ray's thigh and as he set aside the wrist his stomach set to quivering. He felt tired now, tired and nervous, weary with the heaviness of the books, nervous because time was not moving quickly enough. He looked up the broken concrete to the entrance, the stone pillars that supported the porch. the gloom that lay beyond. He had hurried up the bank to bring the future close, but the future was still before him, somewhere in the institute, beyond the dullness of the billiard hall, beyond even the meeting. It was a future he wanted to reach out to touch, to grasp, just as his brother wanted to grasp life. He wanted to run, to shout, to be reckless and irresponsible, but he told himself to be patient. Yet the more he tried the more his inside set to quivering, and the more he hated Wishart his composure.

"Ye've seen this comin' for years," he said. "Yet ye did nowt about it. Ye let things slide and hoped for the best. Now they're ganna root us up like garden weeds. They're ganna send us to live somewhere else, work somewhere else. And ye'll not lift a finger even to protest."

"Ye talk as if ye were the only one that cared. With yer big mouth and fancy ideas. Ye had everythin' sewn up in the pit the day right down to the men's marchin' orders. But I put me foot on it then. And I'll put me foot on it again the night. The men'll be told the truth. And when they know what the truth is there'll be no more talk o' protest."

"Ye mean ye'll tell them yer idea o' truth. Not the real truth about what they're givin' up. It's more than a house and job, ye knaa. More than a roof o'er their heads and a seam to work. It's their contentment, their peace o' mind. Not just the comfort o' the village."

"Ye think they'll put that before their wives and kids? Ye'll see if they do. They're not as daft as ye think, ye know. There'll be a smooth transition that'll guarantee everybody's job and everybody's livelihood. As ye'd find out for yerself if ye'd listen to what I have to say."

"I heard enough in the pit the day," Ray retorted. "When ye blacklegged on the men."

The hurt went deep to Wishart's eyes. The pouches closed and a nerve ticked in his cheek. He straightened his shoulders and stepped closer to Ray on the concrete. "That's a fine way to talk to a union representative," he said. "I could have ye disciplined for that. Ye can fight for the village if ye want, but not the colliery.

119

That's finished, no matter what anybody says. Ye'll not change anythin' because ye protest."

"That's somethin' ye'll not knaa till ye try, is it?"

"Maybes not," Wishart answered. "But the men'll decide on the advice o' the union. And I'm the union. I'm the one givin' the advice. So there'll be no calls for strikes or stoppages or protest meetin's unless it's done by me after a free vote o' the men. Blackleg, ye say. After all the trouble ye caused the day I don't know how ye have the nerve."

The sun slanted upon Ray's head and the acne eruptions on his chin. His eyes and lips moved together and a little smile pulled the corners of his mouth. He felt the muscles tighten in his arms and his fists closed around his sweating palms. He thrust his face so close to Wishart's he saw the skin of his lids tighten as his eyebrows upraised. And standing so close Ray saw not the face of Wishart but the face of authority. Authority he hated and wished to destroy. He tapped the front of his jerkin and the tips of his fingers made a wooden sound against the books.

"We'll see who has the most nerve afore the neet's out, Wishart," he said. "We'll see. The men might've voted ye in. They'll not wait for a ballot to vote ye out."

He tapped again the front of his jerkin and lifted a finger warningly. He turned and moved up the path in long strides and did not even pause by the notice board as did some of the men but went on into the hall till he was lost in the gloom. Wishart by the gate watched him go. His lips were bereft of the flickering smile and as he did not breathe through his nose he held his mouth a little open. His hair was silver and a little sweat had gathered on the temples. The eyes were redder in daylight, the veined pouches puffed and accentuated, his lips were dry and scaly, and only a pale tip of colour freshened his cheeks. He did not hold back his shoulders but let them droop unconsciously and walking to the high entrance he barely lifted his feet from the concrete. Ray's words vibrated still in his mind as he crossed the porch into the passageway. Never once in his life had Ray been to a union meeting, never once in his life had he taken an interest in union affairs; for all Wishart had known he had not existed till a few hours ago in the pit; yet here he was interposing himself between union and men, management and union, in a way disastrous to all.

He was like a dormant cancer cell that suddenly awakes and

120

shoots through the body to destroy the harmony of a lifetime.

The doors of the reading room and cardroom were locked and Wishart had to push his way through the small crowd around the noticeboard. The billiard hall was already three quarters full. The trough lights had been raised and the tables pushed sideways to form a platform at the end of the hall. The playing surface of the tables had been protected with tarpaulin, planks had been laid across the tops of the tables, and several chairs and a small table set upon the planks. This had last been done ten years ago for a delegation of miners visiting the coalfield from the Donbas region of Russia and invited by the lodge to exchange banners. The chairs were for the secretary and chairman and members of the lodge committee, the table for Wishart on which to lay his notes. There was no microphone on the table and he would have to raise his voice to be heard by the overflow in the passageway.

There were more men at the institute that night than he had ever seen. Certainly more than had attended the ceremony for the opening of the pithead baths. And certainly more than for the exchange of banners with the Russians. They wore their baggy suits, their caps, their shiny boots, their sports jackets, flannels and trilbies, with home-knitted pullovers, ties and shoes to match; small men for the most, with stocky thighs and arms, rounded shoulders, sturdy backs and muscular stomachs; disfigured where coal dust had found its home under the tissues of old cuts, pale from lack of air or weathered to coarseness with their work on bank. Already the press was so great in the hall their voices reached up to the rafters. And murmuring among themselves they spoke a vernacular unique to this village, that changed with the next and kept on changing throughout the coalfield. So that a village was recognized not by the dialect common to all but by the vernacular particular to each. They stood diffidently now in threes or fours or drifted singly till they found their marrows; the younger ones gathered at the back of the hall to stand on chairs dragged from the caretaker's enclave, or tried to hoist themselves up on the racks that held the cues; whilst others shuffled unobtrusively near the fire extinguishers by the doorway, ready for an early departure when the meeting was over.

All were self-effacing men who faced danger every working day of their lives yet thought as little of it as they did the light through the windows. They were never heard of till a mining disaster illuminated this danger and shot them into the headlines. But if they lived with danger they lived too with awareness, an awareness that the country needed coal and that it had fallen to them by birth to supply it. They did not look upon it as monstrous they should be flung into the earth and once there should walk for miles along low galleries, as hump-backed as rats, to seams no more than twenty inches high, often with floors that were wet, roofs that were dangerous, choked by dust or affected by damp. Merely to do a job of work. To hew coal so that the country may be nourished. The men did not go down the pit for gain. Nor did they go because they liked it. They went because it was expected of them. Because this was the heritage left them by their fathers and this the heritage they would leave to their sons.

But as no-one was in the hall that night because he liked the pit all were there because they could not conceive of a life without the pit. Underground they could do anything. Drive a way, bore a seam, work a bargain, drill a hole, fire a shot, fill the coal from face to belt, shoot a canch, haul a set, drive a pony, seal a board-room. Above they could do nothing. Their skill lay not in their hands but in their experience. They might be fit for labouring if there were any contracting firms to hire them. They might conduct a bus if the local company had any vacancies. There were the alloy works in the valley if the alloy works were still taking men when the pit closed, the tile plant on the moors if there was transport there and back. There was the city twenty five miles away with its alien ways and skills and ideas, and there was the labour exchange, the dole, the spectre of the thirties they thought had been hanged by the neck. There were the queues and soup kitchens, the waiting on corner ends, the listlessness, the idleness, the frustration of able-bodied men out of work. And though they hated the pit they preferred it to that.

Nor could they conceive of a life without the village. For their life was traditional, flowing as a stream flows, from a source that is hidden, hidden in the past. Here was generation upon generation of miners. They came of a stock that had withstood invasion and conquest, upheaval and cataclysm, changes in religion, in dynasty, changes from the primitive to the feudal, the feudal to the industrial, changes that debased a man's dignity and coarsened his nature. Hundreds of years in the same environment had developed an instinct that could not be changed. They were dedicated to the same house, the same manner of speech, the same habit of gait, the same outlook on life. Even the same past. Education pushed back their horizons and widened their imagination, radio and television brought the world to them and the combustion engine took them to the world. Time altered their habits so that they drank not at inns but at pubs, followed football rather than cockfighting, racing rather than whippets; their wives had their bingo, their whist and their institutes, cookers and washing machines and spin-driers. But they stayed together as a community. The stream flowed on, the pattern remained the same.

There was a quietude about the village the world could not emulate. There was an affinity among its people outsiders could not understand. And since they could not understand they despised, and because they despised they wished to destroy. The middle classes in their suburbia, the bureaucrats with their plans, the government, fossilized and archaic, that looked to the horizon and thought it the future. These were the people who brought change to the mining villages. The middle classes discarded coal and turned to oil, the bureaucrats devised what they described as 're-deployment of population' schemes. And the government? They decreed that if a colliery could not pay its way it should close, the men should be transferred, they should be retired, they should be made redundant. And a village without a colliery? It should be pulled down. The people should be scattered. They should be asked to move. They should not be allowed to remain in the place of their birth, the place of their death, the place of their content.

Because you see only money mattered, maps and money, but people did not matter. They were like tools to be discarded, cattle to be organized, they were not allowed to have a mind of their own and because they could not have a mind of their own they could not have a life of their own. It was not for them to decide where they did or did not want to live. The village had not existed for the bureaucrats till they noticed it on their surveys. The government was oblivious till the colliery ran into difficulties. Now the people could be squeezed out of the only life they had, the only life they knew, and it could all be explained with a wave of the hand and a reference to figures. But tradition may not be measured on a calculating machine, a community cannot be gauged by the number of its members, and what is happiness that it may be uprooted so lightly? You may take and study a pound note, take and study a survey, but you cannot take and study the soul of an individual. You cannot halve or quarter it by surgery, you cannot photograph it like an X-ray; you cannot say this is happiness and this sadness, this maturity and this experience; this a goodness one was thankful to behold, this an evil it was a mercy to forget. But then what is the individual and what is happiness? And how can you understand either one or the other if you live in an impersonal world of steel and stone and concrete, built not upon warmth and friendship but upon cold and loneliness? How can you understand that a village perched halfway upon a hill is not God-forsaken, that its people walked close to God because they were close to the earth from which man in his origins had sprung?

But you cannot understand it, you will never understand it. Because you live in an age of eroded values. An age where the few instruct the many, tell them what to eat, what to drink, how to sing, what to dance, tell them how to feel, how to think, tell them what is good, what is better, what is best. But never what is bad, what is worse, what is mediocre. Tell them what is whitest, brightest, lightest, most hygienic, most effective. But never once how to live. To feel alive. An age of excess and superfluity, bureaucracy and ineffectuality, of frustration for those who care, easy evasion for those who do not, an age which makes a rebel an outcast, an outcast a heretic. An age of human adjustment. Where security is found in conformity and contentment in indifference. Where principle and honour, character and decency cease to exist, where only material things exist. That is the age in which you live. It is the age of the faceless man. And how can a faceless man understand that the closure of this colliery, the dismantlement of this village, was for these people like a premature death, like attending their own funeral? That there was no other way of describing it? But there is nothing — nothing — a faceless man will understand.

And so it was left to Wishart, alone on his platform, to explain to the men what was happening, why it was happening, and what could be done about it. He was of course not physically alone, for there would be the chairman and treasurer and lodge committee; the compensation secretary, the lodge delegate, the welfare secretary, the pit representative, the seam representative, bank representative; all elected to ensure the smooth running of the union and protect the men's interest before the management. Most of them were re-elected without contest in the yearly ballot so that Wishart had known and worked with them for many years. They turned up regularly for union meetings and ran the affairs of the union with little complaint from the men. That evening Wishart would be glad of their support. But as he hoisted himself upon the planks and laid his briefcase on the table the light reflected on the seats and support panels and cast thin shadows from the frames to the planks. Only one of the chairs was taken.

Sanderson, lodge chairman, leant forward to offer a hand. Wishart stroked the hairs of his wrist and nodded to the empty chairs. "Takin' their time the night, aren't they?" he said. "We'll have to get a start in a minute."

Sanderson stroked his fingers down the sides of his cheeks. "Ye'll wait a long time if ye wait for them," he grunted.

"Ye mean they're not comin'?"

He shook his head and brought his hand back to his knee. "They're here already. But not up here. Doon there wi' the men."

Wishart turned his gaze from the pale green walls above the platform to the men in the hall below. Some of them pressed so close to the jutting ends of the planks their faces were only a few inches from the table. The light from the high windows fell across their caps and trilbies and upturned faces, and ripples swayed through the ranks as latecomers tried to move past the throng in the doorway. The men at the front protested, the men at the back complained, but the movement went on till not an inch was left in the hall and the crowd began filling the passage and pathway. The faces of those on the path were waxen in the sun, and looking beyond the path through the oblong of light that was the entrance, the grass by the wall of the maintenance yard and darkened cinder path was like an imprint of colour upon a colourless photograph.

Wishart's fingers loosened the straps of his briefcase and threw back the leather cover. He took out his notes and shuffling them in his hands laid them upon the table. A frown creased his face and he scratched around the strap of his watch. He turned his eyes to Sanderson. "But here's where they should be," he said. "Not down there with the men."

"It's yer own fault, Markie. Ye should've called a union meetin' instead of an open meetin'."

"All the same," Wishart said. "I was bankin' on them. Bankin' on their support."

Sanderson looked from the strong timber rafters to the oblong light of the entrance. The wind rustled the grass by the maintenance yard and the smoke of the men's cigarettes curled away from their faces. The men stood along the railings of the pathway and when there was no more room on the path spilled upon the cinder of the bank, so that the view of grass and maintenance wall was blocked by their bodies. He watched Wishart remove his briefcase from the table and place it under the chair beneath his feet. The gold emboss of the initials on the flap was turned to him and he studied them as he spoke, so that his words were directed not at Wishart but at the tarpaulin. His voice was thin and subdued and Wishart had to strain to hear above the noise of the hall.

"I towld them that, Markie," he said. "I towld them ye'd want them up here. But they reckoned since it was an open meetin' ye'd prefer them in the hall oot the way. But I says no. I says ye'd be wantin' them up here."

"They're takin' a lot on themselves all of a sudden," Wishart grumbled. "Supposin' what I want and don't want. And what about the officials' union? The shotfirers and deputies and over- men. They were at the meetin' last night. They know it affects them as much as it affects us."

"They reckoned the same as the committee," he said. "Say ye're the one that called an open meetin'. Say they'll be havin' their own meetin' at the club on Sunday. Say they'll thrash it oot then what's to be done."

"But they'll not have stopped their members comin' the night, I'll be warned."

"That's reet. I says if ye divin't want to come on the platform ye should bar yer members from the meetin', but they say no. Say it's a free country. Say if a fellow has a mind to call an open meetin' there's nee reason why officials of another union should support him. On the other hand, there's nowt to stop members o' that union gannin' if they want. So the whips is off. They can come if they like, stay away if they like. Owt they have a mind."

Sanderson leant back in his seat and the planks sighed beneath his weight on the chair. He was a stout man, heavy in build, heavy in thought, with dark wavy hair flecked with dandruff, skin red and shiny where the razor had passed, and a heavy double chin that jowled above the tightness of his collar. His wrists were thickly-curled, hands large and clumsy, the skin on the back pulled tightly across the veins; the fingers were dyed with nicotine, there was nicotine on his upper lip, and grey ash lay like a fine dust in the folds of his suit. His teeth were strong and even, but stained too with nicotine, and when he exhaled his breath was strong with the aroma of cigarette. He suffered an excessive smoker's cough that heightened the colour in his cheeks and loosened the ducts in his eyes, so that they were permanently weak and bleary, the points overwhelmed with the fat that coiled his pouches. His voice was normally strong and gruff, his manner abrupt, but tonight he was almost timid and his voice so frail it was no greater than the sighing of the planks beneath his weight. A silk scarf was wrapped around his neck, the tasselled ends tucked under his arms.

Wishart breathed deeply and the muscles tightened in his chest. The pain was so sharp, so excruciating he let the breath go quickly from him. "Well," he said. "I reckon it's no good beatin' about the bush. We're on our own and that's all there is to it. I'll sit myself down and ye can open the meetin'. We'll not get many more in there the night."

Sanderson felt the upper support of the chair across his shoulder blades. He did not follow Wishart's gaze into the body of the hall but stared down at the flies of his waistcoat, creased and raised by the pressure of his paunch. He noticed the fine ash in the folds of his suit and flicked it off with his thumb where it drifted toward the planks and settled upon the polished caps of his shoes. The softness of the air blew over the heads of the men from the passageway and was like a hand stroking his cheeks. And when finally he lifted his eyes from his waistcoat and stared over Wishart's shoulder the panes of the high windows were blue with the sky beyond. The hall had grown quiet, the protests and complaints subdued, the frolics of the young ceased. Even the murmuring and shuffling quietened as the pasty faces set towards the platform and the men waited silently for Sanderson to open the meeting. But Sanderson did not move from his seat.

"I would if I could, Markie," he said. "But ye see I cannot. It's me throat, it's dried up on us. It must've been all that dust in the Brockwell the day. Ye knaa it's the dustiest part o' the pit. And it's clogged me throat up proper. I can hardly hear mesel' speak never mind make mesel' heard in the hall."

"The men'll not mind yer sore throat," Wishart said impatiently. "Now come on, give us a bit o' time to get myself ready."

Wishart pulled his seat forward and its feet scraped upon the planks. The planks creaked still further as he fell into the seat and began fumbling in his pockets for his glass case. He took the glasses from the case and rubbed the lens on his sleeve before holding them to the light to see if they were clean. When satisfied they were he slipped them on his eyes and stretched across the table for his notes. He would read through them quickly as Sanderson opened the meeting. He tried to let himself relax, feeling his weight on the seat and back of the chair, the weight of his feet to the planks, but he was too aware of the tension in the air to relax completely. The hostility that rose towards him from the men was more palpable even than their silence. His bowels quickened and for a moment he felt the world slipping, he felt everything was passing out of control; a panic rose within and set his hands to quivering and his feet to shaking under the rail of the chair. He noticed Sanderson still in his seat.

"Look, Jack," he said. "Ye've been chairman o' this lodge longer than I've been secretary. So ye know what the men are like. Ye know their moods. Ye know what they can get up to if they come across somethin' they don't like. Now look down there. Have ye ever seen as many men in this hall in yer life? And everyone o' them trusts ye as they trust me. As they trust the lodge committee."

"Only the lodge committee's not up here, Markie," Sanderson said. "It's doon there."

"That's why I wanted them up here. So we could show the men we were united. So they'd know where we stood. Because if they saw we were agreed they'd know it was good and there'd be nothin' to worry about. But as ye say, the committee's not up here, it's down there. And the men are goin' to notice that and wonder about it. Now ye tell me yer throat's bad and cannot speak. Ye with fifteen years standin' as lodge chairman. With the respect of every man in this hall. Now what conclusion d'ye think they'll draw about that?"

A fretful uneasiness clouded Sanderson's face. And with his face close to his Wishart saw the coarse shiny skin, the blood vessels broken down, dried and purpling with age, the dandruff thick on the wavy hair. His eyes were no longer distinguishable in their fat, the lips thin and moist, the tip of the tongue showing. And the narrow brow was creased and disturbed. His heavy hands lay still across his knee and the fingers tugged uneasily at the creases to his trousers. The stoutness of his loins pulled the material tight across his thighs. He shuffled his feet on the planks and crossed his knees but found himself incapable of raising his weight from the seat. "I just cannot, Markie," he said. "I just cannot."

Wishart sighed and let his strength go from him. The silence of the men seemed to lie heavily upon him. And in the pause it took to run his tongue around his mouth, straighten his legs, stand and glance for the last time at his notes, impressions tumbled upon him; the smell of dried earth and pigs' dung from the allotments the men had just left, the odour of carbolic that had so lately rinsed their bodies; the softness of the air, the planks that creaked as he tested them with his feet. He stepped to the table and his mind took in even the chips and stains on its surface, the scratchmarks and woodworm, the initials carved by prior union officials and with the initials the date of their artistry. From within the hall came a series of sharp nervous coughs, a final rustling as the men settled themselves, and from without the extraneous sounds of the night. A tennis ball thudded in the courts below, linnets and thrushes sang from the coppice behind, and from the pityard, travelling up the bank, came the steady drone of generators serving power to the pit. They were sounds he hardly noticed but which were sharp now upon his consciousness.

His eyes focussed on the foolscap pages he held in his hands. He had learnt long ago the men respected notes more than they did the spoken word. Why this should be so Wishart did not know, but it was a fact he had done well to remember; so his notes were ready, even though on this occasion there was little written down. What there was to say was all in his head. His nerves had steadied now and he felt composed, a quiver unsettled his legs and there was a trembling to his hands; but these were normal things, caused by the tension of the moment, the seconds before speaking. They would leave him once he began. This was how he felt when he made what he considered the most important speech of his life before the Russians from the Donbas. This was how it had been at his first major speech before the Durham miners' leader nine years ago on the opening of the pithead baths. Then again, in this very hall, before these very men, when they presented him with this very briefcase to commemorate his fifth anniversary as lodge secretary.

And this was how it was now as he gathered his phlegm, licked his lips, and declared open the meeting.

15

Tom Holt stood one foot on the thresh and the other on the step below and gazed through the open door beyond the scullery to the kitchen.

The nervous scraping of his boot chafed the thresh and his fingers brushed timidly against the green-painted panels; the fingers of the other scratched absently at his knee. His eyes squinted into the gloom and as he swayed forward his body to see more of the bedstead in the kitchen he saw the white shine of a person's leg on the bed, he saw toes prodding against the frame, the rails of the frame black in the shadow of the light from the window. Holt stared beyond the sill of the window to the overturned earth of the garden, grey and parched from lack of water, he saw the dusty shoots of the privet hedge, the sooty undulating roofs of the prefabricated houses across the yard. And bringing his attention back to the bed he heard the springs creak and saw a hand drop over the side as the person moved.

"Is yer mother in, Dolly?" he asked, still by the door, scratching again at his knee.

Dolly Walton followed her hand over the side of the bed and stared at Holt on the step. He took off his cap and as he smiled the wrinkles creased around the eyes and crumpled the yellow patches on his temples. He wore the same type corduroys as Ray, with a brown striped jacket that bulged where he had pocketed his tobacco; the white lip of his clay pipe showed above the line of his breast pocket and the knot of his tie had slipped to reveal the silver head of the stud. One of the wings of his collar had creased and slightly upturned, the toes of his boots shone with polish, and his hair seemed extraordinarily white in the light. He ran the rim of his cap around his head, still balanced in the doorway, feeling the celluloid lining of the cap with his fingers, studs of his boots chafing and fracturing splinters from the thresh.

"She's oot," Dolly said. "Seekin' coal."

"D've think A can come in and sit down. Till she comes back?"

"It's not my house. Ye can dee what ye like."

"Thank ye kindly, Doll. Thank ye."

Dolly lay on the bed in a red cotton smock buttoned at the front and curled just a little above her knees. Her clothes lay at the end of the bed and Holt knew from habit she wore nothing underneath. She worked on the local milk float, beginning at five in the morning, so that she had to be out of bed by four, out of the house by halfpast. She returned about three in the afternoon, sipped a cup of tea, stripped and changed into a smock, flopping upon the bed to doze till the rest of her mother's tribe came screaming home from school. Even then she did not get up immediately but continued to lie on the bed, resting, while the tribe returned to play and her mother gossiped in the yard till it was time to prepare tea.

"Where's yer mother seekin' coal, Doll?"

"Doon the street. She heard Mrs. Turner got in a load and she thowt she'd be hankerin' to sell half on it. Seein' there's nee room in her coal house."

"She can always have a load o' mine, ye knaa," Holt said, advancing a little, still fingering the inside of his cap. "There'll be nee need to worry on that chalk."

"Ye'll need all the coal ye can get. When they close the colliery."

"A've towld her she'll have nowt to worry about, nowt at all, once we're married."

"Once we're married," Dolly said.

Holt set himself down on the arm of the easy chair and studied the fire in the grate. The fire had been set that morning by Wally before he left for back shift. Several sticks and a few large cinders were perched upon a mound of papers so arranged to allow tapers to protrude through the bars, a match would be set to the papers and all that would be needed to get the fire going were a few choice pieces of coal to nourish the sticks and cinders. A blazer stood against the wall by the hearth to fan the flames once the fire had been lit, but across the hearth there was no fender, so that white ash had spilled over the floor and lay like trails of sand upon the oilcloth. Dolly shifted her legs slightly but did not bother to adjust the smock. The odour of her warm sweating body filled the room. She did not feel the need of a fire, but on the contrary, with no underclothing to absorb the sweat, feeling the warm current of air through the open doorway, her skin was sticky and uncomfortable.

"Anyway," Holt said. "Ye should've had yer Wally's coal last week."

"We should've had. But we never."

"How's that then, Doll?"

" 'Cause wor daft Wally sold it back to the colliery and got an extra thirty bob for his pay. Me mother argued wi' the coal man when he delivered a load next door, but he says there's nowt he could dee about it. He points to the red ink on the coal ticket and says to take it up wi' wor Wally. But me mother says what's the good o' that, ye get nowt but lip and back answers. And anyway he's supped all the money by now. So she gans on at the coal man instead."

Her head and shoulders rested on a pillow propped against the frame and her hands folded across her stomach. They were coarse hands, the nails bitten, the skin hard, fingers short and ugly and lumped with corns. Her oily hair straggled round her neck and her face was greasy because she had not washed that morning nor cared to wash since. She had thick, full-blooded lips that needed no lipstick to accentuate their opulence, eyebrows thick and dark, arched high into her brow, and brown eyes that peered from under dark handsome lashes. Eyes that were very rarely still, that seemed always deep down to be aflame. Even now, numbed as she was, feeling a little dull, feeling a little sleepy, they were startingly bright, a little wild, a little primitive, and to Holt a little frightening. It was the wildness in her eyes, the darkness of her hair, the pigment to her skin, that suggested gypsy blood. Yet notwithstanding her untidiness, her indifference to personal cleanliness, she was an attractive girl hardly turned nineteen, but not yet afflicted with the ugliness that can harden the features after years of repetitive life.

"Did she say what time she'd be back, Doll. Yer mother?"

"Back when she comes, A expect."

She stretched her shoulders against the pillow and lifted her arms so high above her head they touched the faded calendar on the wall. The movement pulled her smock tight against her body and the hem shifted to her thighs. The light shone upon her knees and as she raised her legs her breasts pressed against the tightly drawn cotton of her smock. She yawned and let her body go rigid and the mould of her stomach thrust tight against the cotton. She was not tall but sturdily made, with strong calves and thighs, square shoulders, full breasts, a body that curved strongly and firmly. Curved like a cat so that she felt the tiredness to her muscles, her knees, in the backs of her thighs. It was a tiredness which gave her pleasure and when she smiled her lips peeled back and her teeth were white in the darkening light.

"The council'll have put the leets back on now, A expect," Holt said, watching the shadow of the house lengthening across the garden to touch the privet hedge. "At least they'll be gettin' round to it."

"They'll not, ye knaa," Dolly said, shaking her head. "Not for a long time yet."

"Aye but they will," Holt insisted. "A gave yer mother the money to pay the bill. Here ye are, A says, and slaps it into her hand. Ye get yersel' down to the electric office and have it paid. Them were me very words. A divin't want ye or yer mother to think A'm mean, Dolly. A'm owt but that, ye'll see."

"Ye might've given her the money," Dolly said. "But she never paid it."

"How d'ye mean she never paid it? She must've paid it. A gave her the money A tell ye, reet slap into her hand. A says to her — ye knaa how A talks to yer mother, Dolly, A always like to let her knaa there's nee fleas on me — so A says."

"But she never paid it, A tell ye."

"Then what'd she dee win it if she never paid it? A told her to get down and pay it. Have a bit o' leet for a change. And she says All reet, she says she'll gan the morn. A hope she never spent it on the bingo. A hope she never supped it again. A've told her afore about that."

"She never supped it either," Dolly said. "She went to pay it but she never reached the office. She sees a table in the store window that she fancies, so in she pops and buys that instead. Says what's the good've fancy things like electric leet if there's nowt to eat off. What's the good o' fancy plugs and sockets when ye haven't even got a table for yer elbows."

Holt let drop his cap upon the seat of the chair and took

from his pockets his pipe and tobacco. The colour of the chair was stained and greased from beige to grey and from grey to a muddy brown. There were dark coal streaks along its arms, the cushioned seat had long ago been discarded and replaced with a pile of old newspapers one of the tribe had removed from a neighbour's bin, the back of the chair had been slashed and certain of the springs protruded. Holt unscrewed the silver cap from the bowl of his pipe and knocked the cold ash onto his hand. The new table stood in the corner by the window, a plain deal table, modest in style, simply varnished, legs already reflecting the knocks and kicks of a spirited family. Its top was a battlefield of unwashed cups and plates, cutlery, fragments of bread and pots of jam; its chaos reminded Holt of the chaos he had left in his own home, so that he stirred and felt a little uneasy. He garnered the tobacco from the pouch into the bowl of his pipe and re-screwed the silver cap.

"We had a canny table in the owld house," Dolly said. "Bigger'n that one in the corner. But it got eaten up wi' wood-worm. The council sayed to take it oot and burn it if we wanted to come here. Sayed they couldn't have their fancy cupboards eatin' away by wor kind bringin' woodworm in. Huffed me mother reet proper, but there was nowt she could dee."

"So ye destroyed it?"

"Aye, but the council never gave us another. Me mother was huffed about that'n all."

Holt searched for his matches by patting each pocket the way he did before he left for work to ensure there was nothing he had forgotten. He stared down at the strip of coco-matting that ran the length of the floor parallel to the bed and the holes in the oilcloth where a table had once stood. Beneath the bed, lying on their sides, he could see the smoked brown lips of empty beer bottles, the labels on the bottles grey with dust, the smell of the beer suddenly to his nostrils. He narrowed his eyes and watched the flame of the match lick alight the tobacco through the apertures in the cap. Through the first contented puffs of blue smoke he scrutinized the candles on the mantelpiece, wicks black from their last snuffing, the candles burnt down, runnelled where drops of wax had chased from the flame. He was aware of the wireless in the corner beside him, set upon a chipped lop-sided stand, its glass panel and station indicator missing, as were the knobs which controlled the sound, the wavelength and tonality, so that even in the days of electricity supply Holt had never known it work.

"And what did the man say about the furniture, Doll?" Holt asked. "Did he say owt about bringin' it back? Ye were on the other day about how ye were ganna gan down and see him. Ask him what he was ganna dee. Did ye gan like ye sayed, Doll?"

"A went all reet," Dolly said. "And he says he'll bring it all back as soon as me mother pays the installments. He says neebody gets owt for nowt these days. Not even me mother. And he says he cannot afford to wear oot any more shoe leather. He says the man from the shop wore oot three pairs, comin' to see me mother, comin' every day for a month and gettin' not a ha'penny oot on her. Not even a cup o' tea."

"What'd ye say when he says that?"

"A says he'd be lucky to find the fire on never mind a cup o' tea. And as for the shoe leather A says he's lucky to have three pairs o' shoes to wear oot, A says it's three pairs more than A've got. And A says it's not me mother's fault she's got nowt to give. But he says it makes nee odds to him whose fault it is. He says me mother shouldn't have signed a paper if she couldn't afford to pay. And A says me mother signed nee paper 'cause she doesn't knaa hoo to write, but he shows us the cross she put and says that's good enough for him. He says as soon as she pays the back money she owes he says we can have the furniture back — not afore."

Dolly felt the first twinge of hunger and using the palms of her hands pulled herself higher on the pillow. Above the line of the privet hedge she could see the flash of a rope as children played in the street, she could hear the slap of the rope against tarmac, the clamorous voices of the children penetrating the window. The heaviness she felt after her work and doze was leaving her, but not as yet her laziness. She would not leave the bed till her position became uncomfortable and her mother made tea, though as on other nights the tea would be cold unless her mother returned with some coal to nourish the fire. Dolly was a nightjay, that it she loved the evening and hated the day, she associated the day with work and the evening with pleasure. She might be hot, sweaty and uncouth now, but once the sun slid over the hill and the warmth went out of the air, she would be frantic with energy, washing and changing and rolling on nylons, powdering her face and brushing the tats from her hair. She watched the shadow of the house lengthening still further with an anticipation that did not include Holt, leaning against the back of the easy chair.

"A cannot figure yer mother," Holt said, sucking his pipe. "She's a mystery to me. A cannot fathom her at all."

"She's daft as a brush, we all knaa that."

"But why does she dee it, that's what A cannot figure. Why doesn't she pay, Doll, like everybody else? Ye're workin' and yer Wally's workin' and she's got her family money on the bairns and the bit o' assistance she collects at the post office. Why doesn't she pay up and have a bit o' comfort for her money? It'll dee her good, it'll dee ye all good".

" 'Cause she's daft, that's why. And 'cause everythin' ye tell her gans in one ear and comes oot the other. Ye cannot get nee sense into her head, nee matter hoo hard ye try. She says she'll pay, she says she'll gan first thing the morn, but she never does. She keeps puttin' off and puttin' off till it's o'er late and the money's gone and she has to wait till the next week comes around."

She was so uncomfortable on the bed she could feel the springs under the thin mattress. She felt the warmth going out of the air and a chill to the draught that came in through the doorway. There was a chill too to her feet and a crick in her neck from holding it so long against the pillow. And in the small of her back, at the base of her spine, there was a dissatisfied ache that caused her to lean forward so that the pillow fell slightly against the frame. The smoke from Holt's pipe rose and crumpled in the air, forming a frame around Dolly where she sat, and through the frame shone the dullness of her forehead, the darkness of her brows, the flabby line of her cheek. The flames in the eyes that brightened and burned at Holt without seeing him.

"Where's the bairns, Doll?" he asked, discomforted by the light in the eyes.

"Gone out to play. Give me mother a bit o' peace."

"And that lanky brother o' yourn?"

"Gone yer way, A hear. To meet Ray at the 'tute."

She lifted her knees and folded her hands around her cold feet. Holt blew the smoke from his vision with a wave of his hand.

"And hoo's that bugger Ray gettin' on?" she asked. "Not in any trouble at the pit?"

"What makes ye ask that?"

"Nowt special. Only A heard some o' the folks gossipin' when A come off me float. As if he'd been in a bit o' trouble, an accident, or somethin' like that."

"That's all they seem to dee in this place," Holt said. "Gossip on corner ends."

"Anyway, their tongues were gannin' sharp enough the day. They never seem to finish wi' that Gerald o' yourn. Hoo he does this and hoo he does that. Hoo he drinks o'er much and brags o'er much. And thinks o'er much o' hissel'. Hoo he cannot walk down the street for swank. They were on only the other day hoo he was ganna marry that snotty-nosed Rutland tart from down the bank."

"And is he now," Holt said. "Then they knaa more than me. 'Cause that's the first A've heard."

"It'll not be the last, A'll be warned," Dolly said. "But it was Ray they were on about the day. A couldn't make it oot when A comes past in me float, but they had their heads together all reet, and like A sayed their tongues were gannin' sharp enough."

"Ray's all reet," Holt said. "There's nowt the matter wi' him."

16

Just as he finished the shadow of Mrs. Walton fell across the doorway. Her dark hair fell around her face and shoulders and as she paused over the thresh, weary from walking up the bank from another street, her bosom and shoulders rose and fell with the wheeze in her chest, her breath caught asthmatically, and the muscles tightened in her face and neck as she struggled to breath. She held her mouth open to assist the passage of air. She swayed on the steps as if it were an effort to stand. One shoulder fell against the frame of the door and as she leant forward she supported the weight of her body by resting an elbow on her knee. The thickness of her body was concealed beneath a black sleeveless blouse and skirt, the pinafore tied at the waist, but nothing could conceal the massive heaviness of her breasts, the strength in her sloping shoulders, the stoutness to her hips. A pair of black slip-ons graced her feet, but she wore no stockings and the pallid whiteness of her legs was stained and ugly along the shins where the veins had perished.

Gerald Holt might have said of Mrs. Walton she had never lived. But if she had never lived she knew what it was to create life. She had learnt on a bed, beneath a single yellow light and festering damp ceiling. She had learnt in the loneliness of pregnancy, the pain of childbirth, a loneliness and pain that sharpens the instinct and heightens awareness. There had always been pain for Mrs. Walton, if not a pain of the body at least a pain of the mind. She had never been aware of any change in herself, any sudden flowering of her body, her life, her personality — there had been no transition from childhood to youth, youth to womanhood. All she recalled of childhood was the river which flowed past her house, the reeds and mud, the woods rising on the bank; of youth she recalled the five mile walk from the village to the bedding factory, before the first light with the birds waking in the forest, the walk back again at night, in darkness, the birds sleeping. And of womanhood she recalled the ridges of her body peeling with the delivery of each child, first a girl then a boy, then death interposing itself; sometimes wilfully, sometimes tragically. Life flowing continuously, endlessly, unchangingly, till finally she was freed of her home by the river and came to live at Highhill.

Mrs. Walton lived in the council houses behind the school in what Gerald called the posh end of the village. The day she moved in was the day the neighbours had drawn their curtains, the day they had gone into mourning. For she brought with her from the house by the river all that she had, she brought her poverty and her family. She hired a horse and cart and stacked the two together. A bedstead, a picture frame, a mattrass, pots and pans, cups and saucers, a chest of drawers and a dressing table, spared woodworm but not damp, a couple of carpets rolled and thrust along the flanks of the cart, an easy chair, one huge mirror with the mercury peeling, and a few brass jugs to match a few brass-knobbed pokers. And her seven remaining children, three that were up and three Mrs. Walton wished were up, a daughter that was bald and another that was loppy, a son who suffered from rickets and another from a cast in the eye, one who had seen the inside of a sanatorium and another the inside of an institution. And a seventh who worked on a milk float and destined to marry Holt.

He eased himself from the arm of the chair when he saw her and took his pipe from his mouth. She stared at him with soft docile eyes that were moist, like a dog's eyes; but there was pain in the forehead, in the arch of the brows, the set of her cheeks, the sullenness of her lips. A pain that might have been transient and spasmodic, a permanent pain that would always fret her face and tense her body. She ran the flat of her hand along the line of her stomach. She might never have been young let alone pretty. Her face had been narrowed with years of caring too much for others and not enough for herself. Her cheeks were blown out and florid and the skin glowed with sweat, there were two moles on her cheek, a little above the upper lip, an angry red where she had been picking at the hairs. Several teeth were missing from the front of her mouth but those that remained were little more than brown carious stubs. There was no cruelty about Mrs. Walton, only the pain, the ignorance and the yearning. A yearning to be loved that shone out like the sweat on her face.

140

"Noo then, Holtey, son," she boomed. "We stand for nee ceremony here."

"A just thowt."

"A knaa what ye thowt. Ye thowt ye'd show us all up wi' yer politeness. Noo get yer cap off that seat afore A flatten it through to the oilcloth. All A want is to sit down and get back me blow." Holt reached for the cap and held it uncertainly. Mrs. Walton pushed him impatiently towards the bed. "Oot the road," she said. "When A tell ye. And watch where ye're droppin' the ash from yer pipe. A see'd ye let it sly from yer hand on me good carpet. Noo get yersel' sat on the bed aside yer bit fancy woman so A can have a look at the pair on ye."

She flopped into the seat and let the air go out of her in a long sigh. She leant back in the seat and ran her arms along the coal-scuffed sides of the chair. They were a fish-wife's arms, fleshy but thick with muscle, pocked at the elbows with the scars of psoriasis. Her legs were aching with the walk up the bank, and with the ache in her shoulders and bosom, the tightness of the muscles in her face and neck, she felt exhausted with the wheeze in her chest. The pain slipped for a moment from the knits in her brow but when it came again she struggled a hand beneath the pinafore to unhook the safety pin that held her skirt. When the fumbling stopped and the hand reappeared the safety pin came with it. The strain left her face and she sighed again, half with pleasure, half with relief, when the pain eased.

"That's better," she said. "That's much better."

"Ye should get that pain seen tee," Holt said. "It might turn out to be somethin' serious."

"A'm all reet, Holtey, son," she said, getting back her wind. "It's ye A worry about. Ye're lookin' a bit pale round the gills. A was thinkin' of offerin' ye a drop o' rum to buck ye up. Get a bit colour into yer cheeks."

"Nee rum for me," he said, words strange and thick. "A'm off rum now — reet off it. A've never tasted a drop for years. Neither at the house nor at the pub. A glass of beer if ye like, if ye've got a bottle in the house. But not rum. Owt but rum."

"There's nowt but rum in the house," Mrs. Walton said. "Either ye take rum or ye take nowt."

Holt fell back upon the mattress and turned to Dolly. She stared back at him indifferently, hands behind her head, eyes not upon him but beyond him, beyond the garden and privet hedge, the roofs of the prefabricated houses. Projected into the night where she would be enjoying herself. Holt sought for her comfort and assurance to ease his troubled thoughts. The last smouldering fragments of tobacco in the pipe had burned themselves out and he pushed the pipe back into his pocket. The skin puckered on his forehead and his eyes receded still further into the wrinkles. His boots had pulled the coco-matting a little out of place and he looked down at the dust the matting had gathered. His hands trembled and were so unsteady he almost let drop his cap. He stretched a hand to touch Dolly's foot but when the pads of his fingers caressed the skin she pulled her feet out of reach and his hand fell against the clothes.

He turned back to Mrs. Walton. She laughed and her breasts shook and her eyes tinselled. Her upper lip quivered as if trying to suppress her amusement. "What's it to be, Holtey, son?" she whimpered. "Ye'll take rum or ye'll take nowt?"

"A'll take nowt."

"Good for ye," Mrs. Walton chuckled. "Anyway, the only rum we have comes oot the tap."

But Holt did not hear. He watched Dolly turn from him, lying sideways on the pillow, he saw her cheeks pasty in the light, eyebrows dark as charcoal. And he wondered if she knew, if she had heard what happened to him when he drank, if she knew of the coarseness and brutality of which he was capable. He did not know, he had never been close enough to ask, never been sufficiently intimate to find out. But as he contemplated her, eyes quizzical, hand fidgeting on the bed, he tried to focus his thoughts. He tried to reason why he wanted to marry, why he wanted to take for himself a second wife. And he realized it was not because he was lonely, not because he was tired of living in a house where little was done for him, not because he feared retirement and the pastime of sitting upon the bench watching the traffic along the road. Not even because he dreaded old age.

It was because he wanted a second chance. He wanted to prove he was not a brute, that it had never been his real nature to drink himself beserk, stagger home to smash ornaments, overturn furniture, beat his wife's head against the stone floor. This had been a passing phase, a residue of the hard times, times that drove a man to excess when he had a little extra. Holt wanted to

142

show the better side, the true side of his nature, his kindness, his gentleness, his consideration and his generosity. Because he had drunk in the past it did not mean he would drink in the future, because he had been cruel once it did not mean he would be cruel again. But he had to have the opportunity to prove himself. And he had to have someone young enough and unselfish enough to appreciate his kindness and generosity, his gentleness and consideration. Someone who could bear him a family that could be brought up to love him, to offer him the love of which his own sons deprived him. That was why he wanted Dolly Walton. That was why despite the whispers and gossip, the ridicule of friends, the mockery of mates, the hatred of his son, that was why he was determined to take her, to have her as his own.

"Noo then," Mrs. Walton said, serious now. "So it's all fixed up?"

Holt brought back his attention. "That's reet," he said. "All fixed up."

"It'd better be," Mrs. Walton said. "There'll be nee bother from the family?"

"Nee bother."

"Ye're sure?"

"A'm sure."

Dolly pulled herself up on the bed and shook the hair from around her cheeks. She ran a hand across her lips and found they were dry, that her whole mouth was dry, that even her tongue when she ran it round her teeth was parched. Her eyes were on Holt now and they smouldered and flamed deep down. "What about Ray?" she asked. "What does he say?"

"It's all reet wi' him. If it's all reet wi' me."

"And the other snotty-nose. What's his crack?"

Holt hesitated. "He doesn't care twopence either way. He says — "

"Oot win it," Mrs. Walton said. "What does he say?"

"He says if A want to put me head in the noose A can. If A want to hang mesel' A can."

"And if ye want to get married?"

"A can dee that'n all."

Mrs. Walton grunted and by applying the toe of one foot against the heel of the other eased her feet out of the slip-ons. The slip-ons clattered lightly to the floor. She held rigid her legs and stared at her feet. They were dark grey with dust. She frowned as she leant forward and putting one leg under her began scraping the dirt from between her toes. The frown did not leave her face and Holt could tell by the set of her lips she was studying. When she had treated the dirt lodged between the toes of her other foot she eased back into the slip-ons and plucked at the hairs on her moles. Her eyes settled again on Holt, the frown deepened, before finally she nodded, as if having settled something in her mind.

"All reet, Holtey, son," she said, extending her hand. "A'll trust ye. Noo shake on it like the man A knaa ye are. If A wasn't so sick o' men and kids A'd think o' marryin' ye mesel'. But since A've had me whack o' both A pass ye on to me daughter. But mind, A'm warnin' ye, ye'd better take care on her."

"A'll take care on her all reet. Divin't worry about that."

"Ye'd better. 'Cause if A hear on ye bashin' her about ye'll have me to contend win."

"That's o'er and done win," Holt said wearily. "A'm past that now."

"Ye'd better be. Ye knaa what ye'll get if ye're not."

"A'm past it, A tell ye. What d'ye keep harpin' on for?"

Mrs. Walton whimpered again and her breasts shook. "Keep yer shirt on, Holtey, son," she laughed. "A'm only makin' sure we've got each other straight. A'm tellin' ye noo so ye'll knaa hoo the land lies. Lay a finger on her and ye'll have me on yer back."

Dolly swung her legs from the bed and tested the cold floor with her feet. The odour of her body swung around with her. She found the floor too cold and with her big toe pulled closer the coco-matting. She was thirsty now as well as hungry. She looked enquiringly at her mother and nodded to the fire. "A managed to get a bucket oot the owld sod," Mrs. Walton replied. "And a few sticks. Ye'll find them outside on the step." Dolly stood her full height on the matting and stretched, smock pulling up with her arms, running a hand up the back of her neck to feel the strands of hair. The other hand smoothed down the length of her body from her stomach to her thighs. She stood facing the door, the heaviness of sleep and laziness leaving her now, a smile parting her lips, a smile that would have astonished Holt as it would her mother. A suggestively innocent smile, as full of anticipation as it was inscrutability.

She laughed lightly, she felt so amused. Mrs. Walton looked up.

"All reet," Dolly said. "Ye leet the fire and A'll fill the kettle."

17

"Ye all know," he said. "Why I called this open meetin' the night. Ye all heard the rumours bandied about in the pit the day. And ye all know who it was who bandied the rumours about. They told ye every man at this colliery would get twenty-four hours notice, twenty-four hours for his job, twenty-four hours for his house. So that ye'd be put in the street. Ye and yer wives and yer bairns and yer furniture. That's what the rumours were and that's what ye believed. Now don't ask me why ye believed them. The fact is ye did. Ye believed them that much ye were ganna shame the record o' this colliery, shame yerselves and shame this lodge, by walkin' out on an unofficial strike. And lose a day's pay into the bargain. That's what ye would have done if I hadn't called this open meetin' the night."

Wishart once suffered a chronic catarrh that obstructed the cavities of his nose so that now when he spoke his voice was thick, but his tones modulated, reaching well beyond the hall to the men on the pathway. Saliva issued quickly to his mouth and as he had the habit of swallowing his adam's apple bobbed and his throat was tight against his collar. But his attention was on the men and the phrases that formed in his mind. He did not have a sharp thrustful mind that leapt among thoughts as lightning among peaks, but his ideas were reasoned, his logic firm, and behind his words the weight of ten years experience as union secretary. He knew what he wanted to say and his concern was to say it well. His words were resonant and increased his authority. And as his confidence grew, the quiver left his legs and the tremble his hands; the sounds of the hall, submerged in a realization this was a meeting like any other, that these were men like any other. That he had gauged the atmosphere and measured his strength and the task was not above him.

He touched the frames of his glasses and settled his gaze on the paper.

"What I'm about to tell ye now is official. As official as all the rumours ye heard the day are false. It's not true the men o' this colliery'll get twenty-four hours notice. It's not true ye'll be put into the street with yer wives and bairns and furniture. These are the fabrications of a few troublemakers out to make the most of a difficult situation. The management committee has never once suggested to this union it was contemplatin' such drastic action. Never once has the question of a twenty-four hour notice been brought up. And I might say if it had we'd have told the management committee what to do with it. Because it would have been contrary to the spirit o' co-operation and mutual assistance that has dwelled in this industry since nationalization. Contrary to the goodwill the management bears us and the goodwill we bear the management. But as I say, this question has never been brought up. So here and now, once and for all, let me tell ye to put such rumours out o' yer head."

Bousefield, son of the colliery clerk, and Featherley his mate stood by the cue racks to the left of the hall and followed what Wishart had to say.

His words resounded through the hall and they detected in his voice a hint of scorn which made them both uneasy. Featherley stood before Bousefield and Bousefield against the wall had laid his hands upon his shoulders. Featherley did not mind the extra weight, for his own hands were pushed down to his thighs, held there by the press, but now he tried to raise them as he turned and swivelled as best he could to face Bousefield. He was of the same age, less tall in height, but thicker in build, with a cleft chin, a scar below the cleft, and skin so sallow he might have suffered a defective liver. A twitch contorted his right cheek, pulling the corners of his mouth and the lids of his eyes; he had large hollows for eyes, with pale whites and a brown speckled iris, eyebrows thick and brown one of which was divided by a scar. His hair was flecked fair at the front and divided at the left by an uncertain parting. And since he used a razor that did not cleanly shave the skin there was always a shadow to his cheeks. His nose was sallow and drooping, inclined to the left, and his teeth were broken where he had fallen at bank upon some iron sheets.

"Ye were the one spreadin' rumours," he accused. "Ye and Wally Walton by the door."

146

"For God's sake," Bousefield said. "Turn yersel' round and keep quiet."

"All the same," Featherley repeated. "Ye're the one 'cause I heard ye. Ye told two blokes on the rolleyway their pay packets'd be waitin' for them on bank. And another gannin' out-by his wife had notice to quit and they were puttin' her furniture into the street."

"I'll put ye in the street if ye divin't keep yer mouth shut."

Featherley had freed a hand from the press and waved it excitedly in Bousefield's face. The fingers were rich with the smell of manure and pigs' dung, but the nails were black, cracked and broken, one of them badly bruised where a rock had fallen. "But ye're the one he's gettin' at," he said. "Ye were the one spreadin' the rumours."

Bousefield swayed against the wall and lifted a hand to Featherley's wrist. He brought down the wrist and swivelled him back by the shoulders to face the platform. He punched him in the back above the kidney and brought his knee up into the muscle of his thigh. "I says keep yer head turned and yer mouth shut. Just think o' them pigs o' yourn and listen to what he's got to say."

Wishart sensed the men's hostility as he did the wind from his house by its soughing through the willow tree. But if they were hostile they were anxious too, eager to be told all was well, to clutch straws, to be told there was nothing to worry about, yet sullen and resistant. They had to be plied with words as his hands might ply putty. They had to be treated not as individuals but as an audience with a single head, a single heart, a single soul, a single emotion to be cultivated as one cultivates a flower. They might be violent or sympathetic, agreeable or argumentative; they might see a point or not according to their humour; but what was the mood of one was the mood of all. They would think the same, feel the same, respond in the same way if he handled them carefully. And if he did not? He changed a page of his notes and tapped his knuckles on the table. The echo of his knuckles brought the men's attention back to the platform.

"Now as I said, the announcement I'm ganna make the night is as official as all the rumours are false. The news has to be accepted and we'll have to make the most of it in the circumstances. It's not good news in the way we like to think o' the word, but as we cannot make a better on it we might as well get used to it. Ye know, there's many of us, stuck as we are on this hill, that think we're masters of our fate. That what happens here is no concern o' the world and what happens in the world is no concern of us. But ye see, we live in a country not a village. What affects the country affects us." His eyes glinted behind his glasses and a smile shaped his lips. "Now I know that seems straightforward enough to ye down there in the hall. But there's many a folk never been further in their lives, and because they've never been further think the village is the beginnin' and end o' the world. But it's not. That's why I repeat, what affects the country affects us. Now we've all heard o' the recession in the coal industry. We've all read about it in the papers and seen how it's affected miners in other parts o' the country. We've even seen how it's affected some o' the pits in this coalfield. Now it's time to see how it's affected us at Highhill."

He then read the announcement that had been agreed upon the evening before. "At a meetin' with the management committee on May 30, 1960, the management committee informed the Highhill lodge o' the National Union o' Mineworkers that owin' to geological conditions and other factors Highhill colliery has become increasingly uneconomic. The National Coal Board has therefore decided to close this colliery as of December 31, 1960."

He laid his notes on the table and gazed over their heads to the oblong light of the entrance.

"That, men, is the announcement. The pit'll close. It'll not close in a day and ye'll not get twenty-four hours notice. The village'll come down because if there's no colliery there's no work and if there's no work it's pointless for people to stay. But ye'll not be put in the street. And I guarantee ye now, to put yer fears at rest, that the closure o' this pit'll not affect yer livelihood. Ye may not be workin', in the same pit, but ye'll be workin'. Ye may not have a house in the same village, but ye'll have a house. The money'll still be comin' in. Yer kids won't go hungry. Yer wife'll still have enough through her fingers to pay the bills and the hire purchase. There'll be changes, that I grant, but changes ye should welcome. Changes that'll offer ye better workin' conditions, an opportunity to make more money for less work, an opportunity to live in a good modern house instead o' the old fashioned ones ye have here. To increase yer livin' standards, yer security, not only for yerselves and yer wives, but for yer bits o' bairns still growin' up. So that when they're our age they can have a good stable life to look back on." He brought his gaze down to stare at the men. "That's the opportunity ye're being offered the night. And in my judgement it's an offer ye should be grateful to have and even more grateful to accept."

Bousefield watched the audience as closely as Wishart to detect their reactions. The faces had lost their distinctiveness, for the light had changed, the panes in the window had deepened, and only the solid white of the entrance remained the same. The crowd swayed forward and back, pressing him to the wall. A cue handle knocked against his head and Featherley's shoulder blade jabbed into his chest. The air was so dry a cough tickled the back of his throat and automatically a hand reached to scratch beneath the line of his chin. His shirt was open at the neck, the wings of his collar over the lapels of his coat, so that his fingers explored to the hairs on his chest. The fingers were pressed against the plate-like bone as Featherley half-twisted to face him, shoulder swinging deep into his chest. And in the confined space there rose from his clothes an odour of pig scent that would have been overwhelming had not Bousefield accustomed himself to it. Now it hardly twitched his nostrils as he perched on his toes to scan the hall.

"Ye see," Featherley said. "Everythin' in the pit the day. It was bull. All bull."

Bousefield did not reply but stared over his shoulder to the heads of the men. He had a face that was cold, cold and cruel, colder and more cruel than that of Ray Holt because where Ray was galvanized by his emotions Bousefield was cool and more precise because of those he lacked. He looked from Wishart on his platform to the men in the hall and felt so unemotional he would not have known he was excited but for the strong beating of his heart. And as he leant against the wall there came over him a curious feeling, one of doubt that this could be him, another of incredulity that this moment could be real. He recalled the same feeling stooping to crawl onto the face at number nine, but then as now he had been too involved to pause and seek for an answer. Only whereas in the pit it had been the discomfort of the narrow seam so now it was the confused face of Featherley that brought him back to himself. He fell back onto his heels and stared at the bubbling lips.

"Look," he said. "If ye divin't keep yer mouth shut I'm ganna take this cue from the rack and screw it in yer ear. Dee ye hear?"

A twitch pulled the corner of Featherley's lips and closed the lids of his eyes. He looked reflectively at the polished stock of the cue but did not reply.

"That's better," Bousefield said. "Now we've got to get ourselves organized. I'm ganna push me way through to Walton at the back. Ye can get yersel' o'er in the middle beside Ray."

"But I'll never get through that! "

"Ye will if I screw that cue into yer ear. Now gan on, dee as ye're told. And when ye get there if there's owt Ray tells ye to dee just dee it, ye hear? Nee questions and nee arguin'. Just dee it."

Bousefield eased from the wall and began moving towards the entrance. He butted forward with his shoulder and tried to clear a way with his arms. His shoulders were bruised and scraped following his scrambling that day in the confinement of number nine, and pain shot up the muscles into his arms. His coat was pulled from him as he moved sideways and a button torn from the stitching. He heard it drop somewhere below his feet. Featherley turned and squinted through the mass of men to where Ray stood in the centre. Ray's hair fell over his brow and the papules on his chin were dull inoffensive blotches in the light. The men packed tightly around and his hands were held close to his chest. The press between the wall and the centre seemed thick, too thick, but when Featherley turned to explain this he saw the red nose and close cropped hair burrowing away till Bousefield was just a head among other heads three or four yards from him.

He called across the heads and Bousefield, suspended among the bodies with his feet off the ground, turned to see the edges of his broken teeth. Three frets etched deep between his brows and the cleft in his chin was a dark shadow beneath his lips. "Just tell us one thing," he called. "Afore ye gan."

"All reet," Bousefield growled. "But for Christ sake hurry on."

"Just tell us what me pigs has got to dee with all this."

Bousefield smiled and shouted his answer above the murmur.

"Ye'll see soon enough," he said. "When they close the pit."

The men allowed themselves to be pushed and butted by Bousefield as they listened intently to Wishart on the platform. "Now," Wishart said. "There'll be questions ye'll want to ask. And I don't blame ye for askin' them. Ye'll want to know why this pit should be closed. Why we should be singled out. We've done all that was asked of us, we've held output steady, we've had a low accident rate, low absenteeism, hardly any disputes and never once a strike. We've got the best first-aid team in the coalfield, that've won five divisional championships. We've got pithead baths and a canteen and a welfare, a football and cricket field and institute that couldn't be bettered anywhere in the country. But ye see these are not the things that count. Ye heard the announcement I just made about adverse geological conditions and other factors. It may seem a bit vague to ye, but that's the kind o' language the management committee like to use on these occasions. Now ye all know that this pit is old, one o' the oldest in the district; the faces are that far from the shaft bottom ye have to walk miles before ye get there and miles before ye get back. And the seams are narrow. There's not one in the whole pit above thirty inches. One o' them is even as low as eighteen inches. And ye all know how uncomfortable it is to work in that. But the setback is not so much the discomfort, not so much the travellin', but the fact that some o' the seams develop faults more than they're worth, and because the faces are that narrow they cannot be mechanized the way the management would like.

"Now ye all know the Coal Board has done its best since nationalization to make this colliery pay. It dug a new drift, that some o' ye called the golden slipper, but that was really the Tilley drift. It opened new districts in the Brockwell and Towneley. It put in new cutters and picks and beltin', to make the toil easier and the output higher. There was a new spirit o' co-operation and goodwill that the men had never known before. And yet despite all this — the new drifts, the new districts, mechanization, and the new comradeship — despite all this it's not worked out the way the management and union expected. The seams in the new drifts were too narrow for full mechanization, the new districts were soon worked out and abandoned, and since the new machinery consisted mainly of windy picks and Anderson Boyes output didn't increase the way we expected and we've not been

151

able to compete with the more modern machinery in other pits. But even then, after all the investment, after all the forecasts and projected forecasts, just when it looked as if this colliery were goin' to get on its feet and make money instead o' losin' it, the coal industry ran into difficulties that had nothin' to do with this colliery.

"But then, ye ask, how is it this pit's not economic when other pits are? We have an output o' four thousand tons a week. With a labour force that's not big. So it's not bad considerin'. How is it we cannot pay our way and other pits can? I'll tell ye. It's because the colliery loses £7 on every ton it produces. £7 a ton, mark. So on an output o' four thousand tons a week ye figure out just how much we're losin' the Coal Board! But how is it we're losin' all that money? First because as I say the seams are narrow and difficult to work and haven't paid for the cost o' the investment. And secondly because the coal we win at this colliery is the very coal the Board cannot sell because it's the very coal bein' discarded as the country turns to oil. What we produce here is household and cokin' coal. But household coal is in less demand than ever as householders install their oil burners, so that once it reaches the pithead it has to be heaped at special sights, guarded against combustion, and kept there till the Board decides how to dispose of it. And all the time billin' up charges for storage. Now in the case o' cokin' coal the Board had to close our own beehive ovens because they were uneconomic. They were uneconomic because they weren't gettin' the orders because there was a recession in the steel industry and because some o' the works began experimentin' with oil. One o' them brought an oil-heatin' plant all the way o'er from Sweden because they said it'd cost them less than burnin' coke. Never mind what was goin' to happen to the miners producin' the coal that made the coke! But I'm happy to say the experiment hasn't worked out as expected because they couldn't get the same heat with oil as they could with the coke. So the quality and temper o' the steel suffered. But by that time our own coke ovens were closed and it meant that the Board had to haul the coal to the nearest works twenty five miles away. And the cost o' the haulage had to be added to the loss in production. So ye see we might only be losin' say £2 a ton winnin' the coal and gettin' it to bank. Where we lose the other five is haulin' it thirty miles and stackin' it, sometimes for days, sometimes for months, at special sites. That's how it happens this colliery's losin' money. And that's how it is with the best will in the world the Coal Board cannot keep it open."

Wishart searched in his pocket for a handkerchief to wipe the spittle from the corners of his mouth and reflected on the anomaly of a nationalized industry being asked to pay its way in a capitalist society. It could not be done. It could never be done unless the original nationalization acts were so interpreted to reject the very aims of nationalization. For if a nationalized industry is to work at all it must work in a nationalized society. Industry in a true socialist framework is not required to make a profit but to fill the needs of the people, and the losses of one are balanced against the profits of another. In this country, for example, if all industry were nationalized the profits of the chemical industry would be employed to offset the losses in the coal industry rather than buy out competitors in a search for greater and larger corporations. And this could be done without detriment to the efficiency of that industry. Another half dozen such sectors, the car industry, the steel industry, the electrical industry, the newspaper industry, cigarette and brewing concerns, each without loss to their own efficiency, and each without detriment to their own workers, would more than offset the debts of the Coal Board in providing modern pits, improved working conditions, better wages and living standards for the men. Which after all were the very aims of a nationalized industry.

But of course if the government really wanted to help the mining industry it had only to impose a higher duty on the cheap imported oil causing the damage. This is the legitimate policy of a country wishing to protect the interests of its own particular industry. It was not done in this country because it would have blemished the doctrine of private enterprise, the principle whereby one industry throttles another and the government lifts not a finger. Nor was it done despite a statement in the House of Commons that fuel oil was being dumped from continental refineries at prices below those of the crude oil from which it was made. The fact that only a quarter of the oil used in our industry came from home refineries. That the gas industry was spending huge sums on the construction of plant to make gas from oil when there was in the Durham coalfield something like seven hundred thousand tons of the best coking and gas coal in the world. And

153

despite a warning that in time of war the country's interest may be jeopardized by over-reliance on a fuel imported rather than won from our own soil.

But Wishart was aware of the union rule that disallowed political discussion at a union meeting, even an open one like this. So he wiped his mouth with the handkerchief, replaced it in his pocket, and continued. "Now then, gettin' back to the special consultative meetin' that was held with the management committee last night. The management committee informed the union that the majority o' men will be transferred to other pits in the locality. There'll be places in the Staffordshire coalfields for them that want to gan. But if they want to stay here with their kith and kin there'll be no pressure put on them to leave. A few elderly workers'll be kept on for salvage. A few reachin' retirement age will be retired with full superannuation. And in the case o' men being made redundant these men'll get a lump sum equivalent to twenty-six weeks pay. But as I say, the management committee have confirmed to the lodge that such redundancy will be kept to an absolute minimum. So not one man in this hall has anythin' to worry about. Not one o' ye. That's why I repeat, it'd have been a tragedy to have walked out the pit the day. It'd have been a tragedy not to have waited and heard what I had to say the night."

Wishart paused for breath and almost felt the sigh of relief that moved through the hall. A mild cheer rolled round the walls and there was clapping too, sporadic not spontaneous, from men still uncertain, sensing all was well yet still reflecting. Chewing over what he had to say. They were almost convinced, yet they did not want to believe the colliery could close with nothing to be done, and they resented Wishart for not holding out the slightest hope. If they had not wanted to fight at least they wanted to protest. They had wanted to show the world that at least they cared, that though others may be indifferent there were still some who were attached to their homes and their jobs. But they had sought assurances and these Wishart had given. They had wanted comfort and this he had given too. So that now they felt ashamed and could not understand how they had allowed themselves to be misled. And because they were ashamed and because they could not understand they searched out Ray Holt to scowl their disapproval.

He had laid his books on the floor and straddled them with his legs. He felt as alone on the floor as Wishart on his platform.

Only now he did not feel so sure. He was aware of the change in the men and indeed felt a little of it in himself, a warmth, a friendship towards Wishart, an understanding that he had not sold the men but on the contrary was doing for them what they could not do for themselves. He was protecting their interests. Ray listened to the mild cheering and sporadic clapping and wondered if his action that day in the pit would have been the same had he known what he knew now. He did not know. He looked down the stained front of his jerkin where the light caught the zip and in his irritation kicked at the dark pile of books to displace their neatness. The top book tumbled upon its side but the rest were held in place by the legs of those around him. The legs swayed and a heavy boot stepped upon the displaced book. Ray stooped to pick it up and as he raised himself from his knees a shoulder thrust into him so that he lost balance. He steadied himself and turned violently upon the trespasser. A curse rose to his lips, but the curse was never uttered when he saw the trespasser was Featherley.

"I never thowt I'd make it," Featherley gasped. "But I did."

Ray smiled and brought his attention back to Wishart. He slipped the book into the front of his jerkin and fingered the brittle edges. Now was the time to act. He could stand up on his books and make his bid; he could tell the men why he had acted as he did, he could harass Wishart, embarrass him; or he could remain a drop of water in the stream, a man like any other, a member of the audience to be persuaded and comforted and reassured. If it worked as Wishart said all would be saved. And if it did not? The colliery would be closed and the village destroyed, its people scattered, and Wishart's words would be as the dust of the demolished houses, the waste of the razed heap. But as Wishart said, he had the information and the experience. And as his father had told him the men had come to no harm under Wishart. He looked into his face and saw a sincerity he admired and wished to emulate, but yet he could not get it from his mind that Wishart had changed sides, that now he was on the side of authority against the men. That too many years of working in a spirit of co-operation with the management had corroded his sense of responsibility. But he could not be sure and because he could not be sure he hesitated, and because he hesitated he knew all would be lost.

A hand tugged at his sleeve and turned to find Featherley dragging an arm from the press and shuffling back into his coat. The sweat stood upon his brow and a nerve twitched his cheek. He looked to the windows and across to the door to reassure himself that despite all he could not understand his life was as he had left it before coming to the meeting. He ran his sleeve along his forehead and the buttons of his cuff were cool to the skin. He wanted to ask Ray if he thought the meeting would last much longer, if he cared for a pint at the club when the meeting was over. But his lips changed the question his mind wanted to ask and he said, "Why didn't ye heckle him, Ray? Like ye sayed. Why didn't ye shout him down, like we agreed?"

"Let him have his say," Ray said. "He deserves it."

"All the same ye should've heckled him. He's had the field all to hissel'."

"He's handling it pretty well," Ray admitted. "He's not put a foot wrong yet."

"So it's all spoilt. Everythin's up the creek."

"If ye keep talkin' like that everybody'll get the same impression as Wishart. That at heart we divin't really care. That at heart we're just out to cause trouble."

But the atmosphere had changed for the better and Ray knew it. He could tell Wishart knew it too, for his shoulders straightened and his head raised, the muscles relaxed in his face, he ceased to pat at his pockets and the tension went out of his hands. He controlled his audience and was not controlled by them. He was moving them, moving them with his voice as a conductor moves an orchestra with his baton. His voice was clear and strong and the sincerity of his tones was conveyed to the men. He knew instinctively all they wanted was to go home and tell their wives there was nothing to worry about, that they should stop their nagging and fretting, for their lives would go on as before. They would not be separated from their mothers, they would not be separated from their friends and their neighbours and their relatives, their children would still be able to go to the village school. The wives knew the pit was a man's problem, but they knew too what affected the pit also affected the village. And the village they felt was their problem. It would be good to reassure them.

He felt the leather of his briefcase against the heel of his foot. He had his wind back now and was satisfied with the response. A thought ran through his mind confirming his belief that truth existed, that no matter how gross the deceit, how deep the confusion, it would always find its way to the light. He looked back at his notes and waited for the cheering and applause to subside.

"So now," he said. "Ye have the facts as I know them. And they're simple facts, they need little digestion. The pit'll close but the men'll not be out o' work. There'll be little or no unemployment. So the future of each one o' ye is secure. Now as I see it there are two ways open to us at this colliery. The first is to accept the facts I have just outlined. The second is not to accept them. We can all think o' the happy years together as a community, livin' the same lives, helpin' each other, fightin' each other, squabblin' with each other, sympathisin' with each other. When ye think of all the drinks we've shared, all the hard times we've had, the good times an' all. And when ye think that none of us in this hall have any fancy ideas, ambitions, hopes or aspirations, just happy to live and let live, to let time pass, to distrust change, to find comfort in days that went before. And thinkin' o' these days we can refuse to accept what is happenin'. We can refuse to accept the disruption of our lives. Refuse to accept the facts as they are before us. We can say we'll fight, we'll strike, strike for a past that belongs to us. That's what we can do if we think it'll be any comfort. If we think it'll do any good."

He raised his voice again. "Or we can say we'll accept the future. Accept all that it brings. We can say we'll go out and face it, make the most of it, let it enrich our lives, deepen our experience. Make better men of us. Let us not turn from it. For remember, memories don't feed our kids, they don't pay for the electricity bill and the insurance. They don't pay for the television in yer parlour. But the future pays for all these things and more. So let us look forward and not back. Let us see things as they are instead of as they were. Let us say that we shall accept change, accept all that it brings, not only for ourselves but for our wives. So that we can show the world we're not an old-fashioned people clingin' to an outmoded life. Show them that we live for tomorrow and all that tomorrow offers. That we are no longer the downtrodden underdogs of yesteryear, that we don't want to work in a pit that's dead, for a past that's dead, but that we live for the present and the future that is to come. Let us say that we too are of the modern age. And let the world say of us that here was a people who worked and gave of their best, who loved their village and its life, but who were not afraid to change when the times demanded it. Let the world say that we accepted change, willingly and with equanimity, that we made the most of it, the best of it. That we were not afraid to face it. And let us walk out o' this hall the night, brave and strong as the poets say, not into the night but into the future."

He turned and fell into the nearest chair. For the first time that evening he relaxed and for the first time that evening he realized how tired he was. Tired and old. Yet he was only thirty six. He recalled how when he was eighteen he had tried to project himself into the future and imagine what life would be like at twice his age. He could even recall the day he had made the projection and the reason why he had made it; he had been sitting in his mother's parlour listening to the wireless, and he had made it because those were war years, years of toil and scarcity and blackout; years he had never thought would end, with friends dead and gone and others on the way. But end they did and eighteen years later, sitting on his platform, Wishart listened to the cheering and clapping and realized this was the greatest success of his life. He had accomplished what he had set out to do, he had dissuaded the men from violence. He had swept aside their hostility to the closure of the colliery and now he would arrange an orderly resistance to save the village. He had elaborated his ideas that night on his way to the institute. For just as he had seen the colliery could not resist change so he had realized the village must change too. The old houses must be destroyed, the old quarters condemned; but what was to stop new houses rising in their place, new flats soaring from the rubble? What was to stop men living here and working elsewhere? What was to stop Highhill becoming a dormitory village which people left in the morning and returned to at night. He stretched his legs under the table and folded his arms. And listening to the cheers he decided there was no reason, no reason at all.

The cheers were full throated now and the clapping of calloused hands rippled down the back of the hall, rounded and swelled, reverberated from the walls and waved over him and then bounced back towards the back of the hall from whence it had come. The men had heard Wishart out. And they were convinced. They had been wrong that day in the pit. They ought never have allowed themselves to be misled. But just as Ray Holt with his anger and passion, his hatred of authority, had expressed one part of their feelings, so Markie Wishart with his flat oratory, his simple manner, his lack of gesticulation, had expressed another. For years the men had been kept down, for years they had been little more than dirt. But now they were respected, now they were equals, there were no coal owners to bully them, no public to frown upon them. Yet to be free carried with it the responsibility of freedom. You had to act sensibly, you had to refrain from violence; otherwise you would lose the respect people had for you, you would lose the right to such respect. This is what Wishart had expressed, this is what he had taught, and that was why after the meeting that night they would be eternally grateful.

The men surged towards the entrance.

Their cheering had even infected those not in the hall but in the passage and on the pathway. They had followed Wishart's discourse as best they could, listening to his voice rolling from the hall, standing so long on the path the muscles ached in their legs and the hardness of the concrete felt through to their soles. Now they peeled away, happy, content, satisfied, anxious to be back to their club, their pigeons, their allotments; not having any clear idea of what it was about, yet feeling the relief that came from the hall, eager to get the best out of the day before sunset; hurrying back to their television in the hope of catching a favourite programme. It was all so trivial they wondered why they had come. Those chewing stalks of grass discarded the pale squashed strands, those leaning against the railings felt a stiffness to their buttocks where they rested against the wood, and those smoking cigarettes nipped closed the gently smouldering tobacco and dusted the dead ash from their fingers. They darted down the cinder path, down the main road past the maintenance yard, scattered up the bank towards the highest houses in the village, along the side of the institute towards the coppice. Their feet kicked up dust from the cinder or pounded on the pavement. They had good news to tell and they were eager to tell it.

For them the meeting was over.

18

Bousefield and Walton stood by the stencil of the door to the entrance of the hall and looked from one to the other and then to Wishart on his platform.

The last of the men in the passage clattered down the path and the dust from their feet rose and lingered before settling again to the stone floor; the light through the doorway reflected on the green baize of the noticeboard and the white china-like handles of the doors to the reading room and cardroom. Bousefield and Walton each felt the discomfort of the stencil against their back and moved to stand across the entrance. The air from the door was cool to their necks and warm and stifling to their faces from the hall. No windows had been opened in the hall and sweat stood out on cheeks and temples as men tried to make their way out. They pressed thickly round the entrance, but neither Bousefield nor Walton moved, and swaying on their heels pushed back the crowd as it swirled against them.

The crowd was in too good a mood to protest. Besides, both Bousefield and Walton were over six feet tall, Bousefield with wide shoulders, deep chest, arms thick and hefty, Walton tall and heavy, with not an inch of surplus fat, so broad and strong he could right on his own a displaced tub. The veins stood out on his wrists and the blond hairs that curled down his forearm were thick and golden as he pushed back the bodies that pressed against him. He wore a pair of flannels and a white sleeveless shirt which showed his arms burned milk-brown by the sun. His eyes were pale blue, that caught and reflected the light, but which matched the smooth tender skin of his face; the skin was so fine and delicate he did not have to shave, and a light golden down clung to his cheeks. He had a small, perfectly formed mouth, pretty like a girl's mouth, a throat delicate and white like the throat of a flower. The line of his chin was regular and even, his nose

160

straight, the nostrils thin and finely shaped; there was not a single fret to the creamy skin of his brow, and his pale, straw-coloured hair had been so raggedly cut strands projected at the sides in fine wisps. He ran his hand quickly through his hair and the upturned palms that pushed back the crowd were less calloused and grooved than those of Bousefield.

"Just a minute," Bousefield shouted. "Cannot ye see Sanderson's got somethin' to say?"

The men stopped their heaving and turned. It was true Sanderson was on his feet. He had lifted his weight from the chair, pushed it back on the planks, and resting the palm of his hand flat upon the table, bent his head over Wishart. The nicotine stain above his lips was damp where he had licked his tongue and sweat reflected on his temples and cheekbones. Little perspiring beads ran down the line of his nose and the skin of his cheeks where the razor had passed had coarsened in the darkening light. The aroma of nicotine from his breath was hot and tangy and as he had opened his coat because of the heat the tassels of his scarf tucked beneath his arms dropped loosely upon the table. Sweat from his armpits had affected the silken tassels and his fingers were so damp they stained the pattern of the scarf as he lifted the tassels from the table. When he spoke his voice was not the frail reed it had been before the meeting but strong and powerful, gruff like the call of a corncrake.

"Ye did reet well, Markie, lad," he said. "Reet well."

Wishart had turned away to avoid the aroma of nicotine and sweat. He turned back now and his eyebrows pulled back into his forehead. He peered at him above his glasses. "As a matter o' fact," he said drily. "I might've done even better if yer voice hadn't conked five minutes before the meetin' started."

"Aye, ye might at that," Sanderson replied. "But ye did reet well all the same."

"I'm glad ye think so," he answered drily.

He looked at Sanderson with his steady eyes and Sanderson turned to look away across the hall. He brought the palm of his hand from the table and stood his full height, placing his weight on his feet where it belonged. The planks strained and protested and the stock of the billiard table beneath sighed its lamentation. He pulled the scarf from his neck, folded it in four and pushed it into a pocket already sagging with cigarettes and matches. The

161

last of the ash in the folds of his suit dropped gently to the planks, and the suit, creased and baggy where he rested a hand. His face was red and puffed and he began delving for a handkerchief to dab the perspiration on his nose. The fat had uncoiled somewhat from the eyes, leaving them weak and shiny, so that he dabbed them too before replacing his handkerchief in his pocket. He turned back to Wishart and the skin of his face glowed with the sweat upon it.

"Now then," he said. "What d'ye say I declare the meetin' closed?"

Wishart leant back in his chair with hands in his pockets, back pressed hard against the supports so that the front legs of the chair were off the platform. The question so surprised him he brought his hands from his pockets and pulled himself forward so quickly the legs jarred upon the planks. He took off his glasses and began fumbling for his case. The pouches of his eyes were pale pink, the lids heavy with fatigue, and though his movements were slow his manner remained pointed and his voice sharp. He laid the glasses in the case and snapped it shut.

"Ye're jokin' though," he said. "An hour ago ye couldn't even hear yerself speak."

The fat wrinkled again round Sanderson's eyes and the muscles expanded in his chest in an effort to contain a cough. His cream collar was neat and fresh where it had been protected by the scarf and showed like a pale rind above the lapels of his coat. He fingered the knot in his tie and lifting his chin tickled the flesh on his throat. "It's the heat, Markie," he explained. "It's loosened me larynx a bit."

"Has it now. Well, sit yerself down and let the heat shut it up again. Ye're closin' no meetin' here."

"But it's the usual procedure," he said. "It's how we always wind things up."

"Not the night it's not. It's the usual procedure to open meetin's before ye close them."

"As ye like, Markie. But ye say yersel' it's easier to dee things proper than not at all."

"Ye mean it's easier for yer conscience if ye closed the meetin'. Seein' as ye never opened it. Ye think it'll gan down better on Sunday when I have it out with the committee. Is that what ye mean?"

"It's not that, Markie. But it's me job. That's what I'm here for."

"Ye're here to open meetin's. Not to close them."

"But somebody'll have to close the meetin' for the men to get home."

"They'll get home all reet without ye interferin'."

Wishart reached across the table for his notes and then under the chair for his briefcase.

He hauled it between his knees and placing it on his lap felt the leather to his fingers, the buckles warm to the tips. He traced the gold emboss of his initials on the flap and looked to where Sanderson stood by the table, a hand still playing around his neck, the skin rippling as he gave a little cough to clear his throat. It was he who had presented the briefcase on behalf of the lodge. He was on the store committee, a member of the Labour Party, a ward representative on the local urban district council, and labour candidate at the next county council election. He had been chairman of the lodge five years longer than Wishart had been secretary, and indeed when the post had fallen open he declined to be nominated, declaring Wishart the better man. He had never failed to support Wishart in all his difficulties; the time a miner had not wanted to join the union and the lodge had demanded his dismissal; the controversy over bargain men using an excess of shot instead of the stipulated handpicks; the time Atkin insulted the lodge treasurer and refused to make an apology. Even to the threat of a strike that day in the pit. Could it be he would desert him now in the hour he needed him most? Wishart worked loose the straps of the briefcase and throwing back the flaps slipped inside the papers.

He fastened the straps and slipped the briefcase down by the side of the chair to rest against his leg. He knew the Brockwell was the dustiest part of the pit, in some places water being used to keep the dust down. He had worked there himself and suffered many a sore throat before being transferred to the hauler in the drift. "All reet," he relented. "Close the meetin' if ye like, I'll not stop ye."

A lock of dark greased hair fell across the red skin of Sanderson's forehead and when he smiled he showed the yellow nicotine on his teeth. "Thanks, Markie," he said. "I knew ye'd see it in its proper leet."

He turned to the audience and raised a hand for order. His body seemed bathed in sweat, so that his trousers and collar were tight, the cotton shirt irritating the hairs on his chest, the sweat staining the shirt between his shoulder blades. It reminded him of a time as a lad, working in a mine deep and stuffy, how taking off his shoes the sweat ran from them like water. In those days he wore only a pair of shoes and hoggers, short pants that clung with sweat to the thighs, so that they could be wrung as one wrings a shirt from the wash. The men worked in the light of a midgie lamp, that consisted of a candle in a socket, backed by a small iron shield to throw the light forward, so that its shadows were sombre and frightening upon the rock face. The air travelled listlessly through airways and as they hewed and cleaved the coal their arms were sticky with sweat, dust clinging to them like tar. Now the sleeve of his shirt was warm and damp to the skin and as he held his arm upraised the cuff links against his wrist was the only cool thing about him. He brought down his arm and turned back to Wishart.

"I'd better ask if there's any questions," he said. "Divint ye think?"

"For Christ sake," Wishart said. "What d'ye want questions for?"

"It's the normal procedure, Markie. It's what we always dee afore we wind up the meetin'."

"I'd rather ye just closed the meetin' and left the questions for another night."

"As ye like," Sanderson said. "But one question'll not dee any harm. And it'll keep the procedure reet."

Wishart closed his eyes and leant back in the chair. The sweat of Sanderson, the heat of the hall, the scent of tobacco from Sanderson's mouth, floated over him and added to his lethargy. The lids of his eyes sealed so heavily he felt they would never open again. The tiredness seeped through his body, so that he felt his lungs, his chest, his bowels collapsing, everything slipping away in this attitude of rest. He no longer felt the support of the chair against his back, the weight of his feet to the earth, only a feeling of drift, of contentment and satisfaction, the indulgence of a man who has won a famous victory and can afford to be generous. He opened his eyes and was surprised to find everything as he had left it.

"Ye and yer procedure," he said wearily. "Ye're like a bairn."

"It'll only take a minute," Sanderson said. "Just to get it o'er win."

"All right," he said. "If ye like. But mind, just one question."

The light switches were at the end of the hall near the doorway. There were four switches in all, in the same white china-like material as the handles of the door to the reading room and cardroom, the white flaking in places, showing a copper underskin; two of the switches were for the trough lights normally suspended above the billiard tables but which were now pulled close to the roof, two for the lights set in lamps along the walls above the cue racks and scoreboards. They were set in a panel near the fire extinguisher to the right of Bousefield's head. He stood hemmed with his back to the stencil. Walton's shoulder pushed into his chest, one arm held to his side, the other free above the press, so that he could extend it to the panel and with his fingers stroke the switches. The lights above the scoreboard and cue racks came on immediately, the trough lights slung to the roof shuddered and flickered and then flooded on, catching the men suspended, half towards the entrance, half towards the platform. The light reflected on the heavy beams and walls that ran with sweat, the pale windows crystal with the sky beyond, the tables and chairs on the platform, suddenly small in comparison with the bulk of the lodge chairman.

"Now then," Sanderson said, lowering his head, blinking at the lights. "Has there anyone a question to ask afore this meetin' closes?"

There was a pause and then a voice from the centre of the hall.

"Yes," the voice said. "I have a question."

"All reet," Sanderson said. "Ask yer question and get it o'er win. Ye've not got all neet."

Ray had almost turned to drift with the rest of the men. He had paused because he could not rid himself of the feeling something was not quite right. His books were no longer between his legs but scattered along the floor by the pressure of the crowd, the one taken from the pile remained still in his jerkin and his hands fingered the corners as he chewed at his lip and watched the men move towards the door. An impatience swept through him as he realized how easily they could be led. He had swayed them one way that day in the pit and now in the hall Wishart had swayed them another. There was also in him a feeling of frustration and anti-climax, frustration because the future he had striven to bring close was not to his liking, anti-climax because things had not turned out as he had planned coming up the bank from his house to the institute. He edged the books together with the toes of his shoes and pressed the one in his jerkin flat against his chest. Featherley tried to stumble past towards the entrance, glad the meeting was over, eager to be away, but Ray twisted him by the shoulder and lifting himself up stood precariously on what was left of the books.

"My question'll not take all neet to answer," he said. "But I think it should be answered afore the men gan home and tell their wives the good news." Featherley tried to twist around and Ray would have lost balance on the books but for the firm grip he had on his shoulders. His voice was strong and emotional, quivering with the excitement he felt in his chest, but ringing clearly to the rafters. "Now then," he added. "We're all happy to know there's nowt to worry about, that we'll all be fixed up at other pits. But maybe the lodge secretary'd like to expand on his statement that some o' the men at this colliery'll be sent to work in the Staffordshire coalfield?"

Wishart straightened his legs, brought his hands from his pockets, and pulled his back from the seat. He listened to the question with his hands on his knees. It was so easy to answer he did not trouble to think about it. Instead his mind went out of the hall into the future. He thought of the houses that would rise on the foundations of those to be destroyed. The water, gas and electricity mains would remain, so too would the drains, where there was no electricity it could be added, so that the houses of the new village would have all the amenities lacking in the old. They would have cookers and refrigerators and sink units, perhaps a garage for cars, hot water as well as cold, even oil burners to replace the ancient fireplace and hearth so useful in the old. But that he reflected, would be too ironic. The men would never accept it. He remembered reading of a clerk at one of the area headquarters, who on receiving a divisional memorandum urging him to save money, had promptly ordered the installation of oil heating to replace coal, because he said it was more economic.

The order had been squashed when the area manager got to know of it. He rose and leaning both hands heavily on the table blinked against the light. His thoughts travelled full circle and the silence of the men brought him back to the hall. His tired eyes searched out the man who had put the question and he tried to shuffle out of his tiredness when he realized it was Ray Holt.

"I never said some men'd be sent to the Staffordshire coalfield. I said there'd be places for them that want to gan. Because ye know the prospects in Staffordshire are better than they are here. For one thing the pits are young and less worked out, the seams are high and have the advantage o' full mechanization. Some o' the seams are even two to three yards high, worked by machines that cut and fill at the same time, so the men fall o'er themselves to beat records. And since most o' them are on bonus work ye can see what I mean when I say the prospects are brighter than they are here."

"But where would the men live if they went down there?"

"The Board has gone into the question o' the men's livin' quarters very carefully," Wishart said. "And any man willin' to leave his home in the north'd be made very welcome in Staffordshire. For example, the Board are buildin' somethin' like three thousand houses in areas where there's work and there'll be special allowances for men prepared to move. And if there's a group that wants to gan off together the Board'll see to it they'll be housed together in the new coalfield."

"Ye say the houses are bein' built," Ray said. "Which means they're not built yet?"

"That's reet. So in the beginnin' the men'll have to spend their time in lodgin's. Digs, I think they call it down there. But anyway, I know for a fact the Board are makin' every effort — and will make every effort — to provide houses near the pits where they'll be workin'. And in addition to the three thousand homes the Coal Board are buildin' they've takin' the matter up with local authorities so that these local authorities have themselves promised to provide another four thousand houses. So any man in this hall contemplatin' a move south'll have nothin' to worry about when he gets there."

"And what about the allowance? Ye say the Board are prepared to grant an allowance."

"The allowance'll be for men that decide to make a move.

For example, each man that leaves his home in the north for the Staffordshire coalfield will be given a settlement grant of fifty pounds. And the cost o' movin' his furniture'll be paid by the Board. So will the cost o' the fares for his family. The man himself'll get twenty-four and six on arrival and a weekly livin' allowance of forty-nine and six. So I can only repeat what I've just said. Any man that leaves this colliery for Staffordshire has nothin' to worry about. In fact, in my opinion, he's a man with a future."

"And if the man doesn't want to go to Staffordshire does that mean he'll lose his redundancy money?"

"Not in the least. What I said was — and I'll repeat it now so ye'll understand — that there are places in Staffordshire for them that want to gan. For them that want to stay there'll be places at other collieries in the area. So no-one'll be obliged to leave against his will."

"And these jobs at other collieries. Will a man transferred from this pit be doin' the same job there as he is now? Or will he be doin' somethin' else? And if he's doin' somethin' else does that mean his salary'll be adjusted accordingly? Or will it be the same as it is here?"

"To take the first point first. We should all be grateful we'll have work. And even more grateful the work'll be in this area. That's the first thing I'd like to say. Now for the second. Ye know as well as I do that the question o' salaries and conditions at other collieries'll have to be raised at a later date. Because it's a question that'll have to be settled between the management and union. Not between the men and their union. So if the member who asked that question — his sixth by my reckonin' — 'll only be patient everythin'll be settled for the best."

"Ye say it'll be settled between management and union?"

"That's reet. I'm glad to see that for once the night ye've got somethin' reet."

"But the management o' what colliery?"

"Why the management o' this colliery, of course."

"Then tell me what the management o' this colliery's got to do with other collieries. The collieries where ye say the men'll be fixed up. Ye know as well as I do that each colliery has its own management. Each colliery its own lodge. Now a faceworker at this colliery might not be a faceworker at the next. He might be gettin' twenty to thirty pounds a week here. What's to say he'll be gettin' that when he leaves to work somewhere else?"

A stir of anger ran through the crowd, anger not at Wishart but at Ray, that he should ask such a question. That he could break their illusions. Yet they felt uneasy. They had never considered that. If it had puzzled some of them they had preferred not to think about it but to slip it to the back of their minds. They preferred to leave it to the hands of Wishart. Now they stood beneath the lights, sweat puffing their faces, scratching the sides of their cheeks or rubbing their hands in their pockets, looking from Ray to Wishart and back again with the fascination of spectators at a tennis match. Only they were not sure what was going on, what was being said, but they knew it affected them, their livelihood, the livelihood of their families, the promises they had been given that night. So they stirred and murmured when they felt their promises threatened and despised Ray for theatening them.

They hemmed closer, but he turned fiercely upon them with a sweep of his arm. "They might give ye promises," he shouted. "But what's to say the management of other collieries'll keep them? They might give ye guarantees. But what's to say they'll be valid once ye leave? And then ye'll find it's too late. There'll be nothin' ye can do. There'll be nothin' I can do. There'll be nothin' any of us can do."

The crowd looked to Wishart and saw that he hesitated. He leant heavily on the table and bowed his head as he reflected. The light shone on the thin silvery strands and the sweat that powdered the forehead. He lifted his head again, slowly, wearily, and realized it was true. There was no guarantee. But this was one of the problems to be solved before the colliery closed. There were fears in his own mind, fears that had to be put at rest, but discussion and negotiation took time, the management had to refer back to the Coal Board and the union to the men, so that not everything could be settled in a day. Nevertheless he grappled with what Ray said and uneasiness stirred within. He saw the picture Ray was painting, he saw what might happen once the men had been disbanded, once they had been transferred to other collieries, so that he tried to seek a way out. But his mind did not work quickly enough, he could not visualize the future, he might imagine what it would be like but he could not see the reality. He could only fall back upon the truth.

"I must admit," he said. "This has not been given my consideration. But there's six months before the closure o' this colliery and the transfer o' the men. Six months to get all the guarantees necessary to protect their interests. So ye can be sure this lodge'll take up with the management all the questions raised the night. And when it has satisfactory answers to these questions it'll refer back to the men in the usual way."

"That means ye'll look into it and let us know?"

"That's reet. I'll look into it and let ye know."

Ray smiled and shook his head. "Ye don't have to let us know," he said. "I know already. Faceworkers at this colliery won't be faceworkers at the next. Deputies at this colliery won't be deputies at the next. Nor will stonemen be stonemen. Bargain men in bargains. If ye want to know the truth, ye'll be lucky if ye're not on bank. At worst, that's what'll happen. At best it'll be datal work in the pit with a chance o' facework later."

"It won't be like that," Wishart said. "Ye know it won't."

"All reet," Ray shouted. "So tell us what it will be like."

"I've already told ye, at this stage I don't know. But I promise again — for the second time the night — that before this colliery closes I'll find out and refer back to the union."

"And the men redundant, the elderly workers as ye call them. Will ye find out about them while ye're on. Or do ye know already? Like ye know about the jobs we'll be doin' at the next pit?"

Wishart blinked against the light. The heat seemed overbearing. His knuckles were white with his weight on the table, so that he stood his full height, withdrew his hands and tugged at the bottom of his coat with his fingers. There were no notes to finger now, no handkerchief to seek, his hands seemed out of place, superfluous, seeking to scratch behind his thigh, probing his breast as if there was something he had forgotten. The back of his neck was red with the heat, the skin crinkled and lined, ragged with side hairs that needed cutting. He looked down to the faces of the men a few inches above the protruding planks, eyes set curiously upon him, mouths half-open, skin stiff and yellow in the light of the bulbs. The sweat glowed on their foreheads and high cheek bones. They seemed somehow disinterested, yet attentive to his replies, and as he lifted his gaze to scan the hall he saw everywhere it was the same, the men curious and puzzled, uncertain.

"I never said the elderly men'd be made redundant. I said that some o' them'd be retired before their time. But in the event o' redundancy the men'll receive compensation to the tune o' twenty six weeks pay. The equivalent of two hundred pounds plus what they've paid in superannuation. Money they've been payin' in all these years. And during the twenty six weeks they're drawin' this money the Board'll make every effort to find them a situation."

"So they'll lose their compensation."

"Not so they'll lose their compensation. So they'll be able to reach retirin' age with contented minds. The Coal Board doesn't look at the problem the way ye think they do. They're not the kind o' men that were in power in the thirties. Ye're o'er young to know that. But the others, they know it. At least they should if they don't."

"All we know is what ye're tellin' us. And when we get down to brass tacks ye're not tellin' us very much. In fact, ye've told us nothin' at all. Only that this pit'll close and our future jeopardized. Ye're passin' to us what the Coal Board passed to ye and what the government passed to the Board. But what ye don't mention is what ye as our representative told them. How ye protected our interests. From where we're standin' it doesn't look as if ye protected them at all. It seems it wasn't so much the union but the management that did the talkin'."

"That's not true," Wishart said angrily. "And ye know it's not true."

"Ye say it's not true. But all we know is what ye've told us. And so far we've no proof that the men's interests were protected by the union. Ye leave us the impression the management committee told ye what they intended to do with the pit and then walked out to let ye discuss it among yerselves."

"The management committee put these proposals to us and gave us the assurance the men'd be fixed up at other collieries. That was the assurance the union accepted on the part o' the men. They had no alternative but to accept."

"It was an easy assurance to give. But an assurance ye ought never have accepted without first consultin' the men. For one thing we pay our dues, we have a right to consultation. We have a right to know what people are plannin' for us. How do ye know what ye planned behind our backs'd meet with our approval? Ye didn't know. Ye took a chance. And I say ye're not elected to take chances but protect our interests."

"The men's interests are protected," Wishart said. "And if ye took a bit more notice o' union affairs ye'd see they were protected."

"So tell us about the men retired afore their time."

"I said some'll be retired. Others'll be kept on for salvage."

"And what's yer definition of a man reachin' retirin' age?"

"My definition of a man reachin' retirin' age is a man gettin' on for sixty-five. That's to say, he's passed the sixty mark. He's worked fifty years in the pit, if he started like most o' them did at fourteen, and after a lifetime o' hard work he's gettin' to feel he needs a bit o' rest. So he's lookin' forward to his retirement. And to help their manpower situation the Board are goin' to set him to graze a little afore his time."

"So yer definition of a man reachin' retirin' age is a man about sixty?"

"At least he'll be that. That's reet."

"Now tell us the Board's definition of a man reachin' retirin' age. Because if it's sixty a man has a right to work till he's sixty-five. And if it's fifty it means half the men at this colliery'll be made redundant. Half the men, mark. It'll not affect my job maybes, but it'll affect every man in this hall. Because every man in this hall is either o'er fifty or has a father o'er fifty. So tell us what the Board's definition is of a man reachin' retirin' age."

"Ye've got to see reason," Wishart said. "Ye've got to keep calm and look at the problem logically. In a rational light. Ye've got to try and see things as they are and not as they might be. This lodge has worked with the management committee in a spirit of harmony for several years. We understand each other. We see eye to eye. And I tell ye they don't make promises they don't intend to keep."

"I accept that," Ray said. "I accept all that ye've said. Now tell us their definition of a man reachin' retirin' age."

Wishart searched his mind for an answer and realized there was none. No definition had been given. It would probably be given before the colliery closed but it had not been given yet. When the meeting had been held between himself and Sanderson, the chairman of the officials' union, Atkin and the area industrial relations officer, he had been too overwhelmed to put the questions he ought to have put. Atkin had not fore-warned him of what the meeting would be about, possibly because he had not known himself, and though Wishart suspected some decision might be reached on the closure of a seam or district he had not been prepared for the dismantling of the colliery and the destruction of the village. It had been too sweeping for him, too devastating. And though he had taken note of everything said by the industrial relations officer he had left the questions to Sanderson, only interrupting to receive the promise of a future meeting before reporting back to the men. But events had gone too quickly for him, he had had no opportunity to expand on the general outline, and the report back had been called before the questions could be put let alone answered. So that now he searched his mind for a definition and finding none fell again upon the truth.

"I must admit," he said. "No definition of a man reachin' retirin' age has yet been given."

A gasp of incredulity rose from the men and Wishart gnawed his lip to contain his dismay. He was upset not because he believed what Ray said but because he had failed in his duty. He had not pursued the men's interests as vigorously as he might. He was a leisurely man, with a great dislike of action, and since normally a fortnight passed between a consultative meeting with the management and a report-back with the men he had wanted time to collect his thoughts. He had not realized the news would get out. He had not realized how the men would react. He had been as surprised as the management at the threat of a strike that day in the pit. And then, realizing the temper of the men, realizing his own deficiency, he had seen that perhaps the task would be above him. That was why he had called at the office and asked Gerald Holt to appear behind him. That was why he was disappointed the committee had not seen fit to offer him their support. He hesitated now, unsure of himself, of his facts, turning to Sanderson to see if he would intervene and close the meeting. But before he could catch his eye another question rose from the centre of the hall.

"So ye don't know whether it's a man o'er sixty or a man o'er fifty?"

"At this stage, no," Wishart said. "I don't know."

"So if it's fifty half the men in this hall'll be out o' work. On the dole. And where will they find a job at their time o' life? How d'ye think they'll fill their day? Ye say they'll get twenty-six weeks pay. But that's not even a year. And in the meantime the Board'll look for another job, and they'll have to take it no matter where it is. Even if it's in Staffordshire and they don't want to go. So the whole rhythm o' their life'll be broken. Their homes shattered. Everythin' they've worked and lived for broken to pieces."

The gasp of incredulity strengthened into a roar of protest. The men stamped and clapped, whistled and hooted, heads and faces and caps oscillating in pandemonium above the floor as they turned to growl among each other. They were angry at Wishart now, not at Ray, angry because he had let them down, because he had built up their confidence, taken their trust, and let it run through his fingers as water. The heat and hours in a confined space, with little air and less room, legs aching, shoulders sagging, made them all the more irritable, so they longed to be free, longed to be into the freshness of the night. But no-one moved to go. They dared not move. They saw their lives in the balance, saw promises flaking before them, flaking to dust, the real future standing out stark like the frame of a new building. And they were frightened, as a man about to die is frightened, because he does not know what lies before him. The fires that had burned their innards that day in the pit flared again, the flames leaping upward, licking the nerves, changing them, consuming them, till they were no longer themselves but their emotions. So that they turned to the only man in the hall who could lead them, probe out for them something else they did not know.

"Will the lodge secretary say whether or not it's true there's enough coal in this pit to keep us all workin' another twenty years?"

"There's enough coal to keep twice the men workin'," Wishart said. "But for the reasons given before — the fact this colliery's losin' money, the fact seams are difficult to work — it's been decided this pit cannot be kept open. Not with the best will in the world."

"But how d'ye know these reasons are true?"

"I don't know they're true," Wishart said. "At least, I've not figured them out for myself. I'm takin' the word o' the management because I know them to be honourable men. Because I've worked and lived with them for more years than I can remember. And because I'd rather trust their word than I would yers down there in the hall."

"And what about the institute? That was built more than fifty years ago. Built to give recreation to the men o' this colliery. Is it true it'll be closin' at the end of the month? So there'll be no more billiards and no more cards. No more readin' o' papers and writin' bets. Is it true it'll be shut up so we'll be driven to the pubs?"

"Ye've got to be logical, Holt. I've told ye before and I'll tell ye again. It's only natural that if the colliery's to close the institute'll have to close with it. And with the institute all the other recreational amenities provided for by the welfare committee."

"Ye mean they'll be closin' everythin' else as well?"

"That's reet. As far as I know the bowlin' green and tennis courts, the football and cricket field, in fact all o' the amenities connected with the colliery. Even the canteen where the men have their dinners. They'll all be closed at the end o' the month."

"But why do they close before?" Ray shouted. "Why don't they close after?"

Wishart turned to Sanderson. But Sanderson's eyes were on the windows in the roof, the panes filming with the heat of the hall. Beyond the panes, in the dusk, the rhododendron blossom around the institute closed their petals against the night, the brown leaves from the laurel shrubs lay in stiff decay on the earth by the walls, and the purple irises drooped with age, the yellow innards of the petals gaping soft and moist in the thickening air. A slight wind pressed back the leaves of a copper beach, and the leaves were quick with the life that rustled through them, upturned and white with the light upon them. The path from the institute to the village was quiet, as quiet as the deserted bowling green and tennis courts, the rose garden where spouted the miniature fountain, the water sparkling to itself, the rosebuds on the trellis shaped like the onion domes of eastern churches, tinged with red, fluffed with the petals of a rose already showing forth. The sparrows flew in and out of their nests in the eaves of the pavilion, and the thrushes that fluttered in the coppice chirped to

175

themselves and the night. But their music did not penetrate the clamour of the hall.

"I don't know why the institute must close before the colliery," Wishart said. "I don't know why the bowlin' green and tennis courts should close. The football and cricket field and canteen. It's a question for the welfare committee, not for the lodge. It's a question I'll take up with them if ye like. But it's not a question I'm entitled to answer the night."

"Why didn't the union support the men when they wanted to strike?"

"Because it wasn't the wish o' the men. Only a few troublemakers."

"We voted on it. And we had a majority. The men wanted to strike. They wanted to protect their homes and their families and their futures. They wanted to do the job the union should've been doin' for them. Why didn't the union support the wishes o' the men? Why didn't they support the men against the management?"

"Because this union doesn't support strikes. And certainly not the kind that was called for this afternoon. There's enough conciliation machinery, enough arbitratin' and negotiatin' bodies to make strikes not only avoidable but unnecessary. So I repeat, there never was a need for the men to come out on strike the day. There never was nor will ever be as long as I'm lodge secretary."

Ray dug his hands into the pads of Featherley's shoulders to stop them from trembling. The sweat on his face aggravated the spots till he wanted to scratch; but instead he pushed his tongue against the walls of his mouth and tightened the muscles in his cheeks, only to make the spots ache still further. A cist was beginning to develop on his chin, in a crevice of blackheads; but it would never reach a head, only redden and sore till it withered of its own accord and dwindled from the skin. Ray felt as he had often done at school, playing football in the yard, sticky and unclean with sweat, showing the skin of a pale white neck. His corduroys held the sweat to his legs and he felt so clammy he could not bear the touch of his knee to his trouser. With his toes perched on the books he stood high above the men as if in a pulpit. Yet the muscles trembled in his thighs so that he fell repeatedly on his heels, scrambling to keep his balance on the books.

He was no longer himself. He did not know what he was. He did not know who he was. His breath was short and his voice quivered when he shouted. At times his eyebrows pulled down, his brow was fretful and angry, and there was anger too in the light of his eyes; his nerves troubled his stomach and chest, his whole body seemed to crumble; yet at other times there was on his face a smile that widened to a grin, as if he were not concerned with the fate of the men, the fate of himself. Only concerned to smile and be merry, to be as other men, to laugh like other lads. But those who knew Ray, who had seen him that day in the pit, shuddered when they saw that smile. It meant as it did with his brother that the strand of reason had broken, the hurricane was at its height, that nothing could stop him for he could not stop himself. He hated Wishart. He hated the sight of him before his eyes. He hated the words that even now issued from his mouth, the promises that crumbled before him, the half-truths and vagueness, the generalizations that meant comfort to Wishart and ruin to the men. And he remembered his love of the men, the men in this hall, who had worked and struggled all their lives, struggled in darkness to forget the destiny that was theirs, suffered nystagmus and pneumoconiosis, dermatitis and silicosis, because they had been trapped by birth to a life they could not escape.

He hated authority. He hated it because it wanted to deprive and dominate, crush not for reason but for power, crush men it had never been able to conquer, that were above conquest, but who were ill-armed and ill-prepared, not equipped to lead any life but the one to which they had been born. So they could be misguided and confused. They could be promised houses and given lodgings, they could be offered jobs and made redundant, they could be retired before their time, they could be transferred, they could be set to work on bank, on datal, jobs they had left years ago for the skilled work of the face. They could be told any lie, any evasion, any shabby half-truth, so that the bureaucrats and planners, the forecast men and relations officers, could lead their own lives in peace. And later, if there were cries, if there were protests, if reality did not correspond to imagination, facts to promises, then no-one could pin you down. For you see, you had not really promised. You had only generalized. You had not informed, only explained. In fact, you had said nothing at all. For others had said it for you. So that Ray Holt hated Wishart, hated him as the mouthpiece of authority, because he had changed sides, because he had once supported the men and now supported authority.

"We've been betrayed," he shouted. "The colliery'll be closed and the village pulled down. He said we'd all be fixed up at other collieries. And it turns out we'll be workin' in cavels fetchin' eight to ten pound a week less. He says there'll be no redundancy, only men reachin' retirin' age. And it turns out his idea of a man reachin' retirin' age is fifty. So half the men o' this colliery'll be lookin' for work. He says there's enough coal here for twenty years, but he says we cannot work it because it's not economic. And when I ask how he knows that he says he doesn't, he's only goin' by what he's heard."

"For God's sake, let's stop this talk o' betrayals," Wishart said. "Nobody's betrayed anybody. As ye'd see yerself if ye looked the facts in the face. And I'm on yer side. Because it's the only side I could possibly be on. But if it looks the night I've not done my duty it's only because there's not been time to look into things. To see how matters really stand. But here and now let's not have any more talk o' betrayals."

"So tell us about the village," Ray shouted. "What'll happen to the village?"

Wishart shook his head. He laid the flat of his hands upon the table.

"I don't know about the village," he said. "At least not yet. I don't know yet."

"Ye see, he's just admitted it. After all the promises and guarantees he says he doesn't know. He'll tell us owt to get the colliery closed and the village pulled down. The people scattered. Wives and bairns put into the street. He'll say the first thing that comes into his head. Just to deceive us. Well, I say I've had enough. I say it's time we put things into our own hands. I say we leave this hall. I say we have our own meetin'. I say that since the future affects us we have the right to decide what it's goin' to be like."

"Violence'll not do ye any good," Wishart shouted. "It never did ye any good before and it'll not do ye any good now. Can none o' ye remember what it was like in the old days? How ye went back worse than ye came out? How sometimes the management locked ye out for good? Shifted ye out o' yer houses and black-listed ye so ye couldn't get work, not only at this colliery but every colliery in the area? Can none o' ye remember that?"

"He says it'll not dee us any good. He says we shouldn't stand up and fight for our rights. As if we weren't free men livin' in a free country. He wants us to remember the old days. But that's what's comin' now. The old days are comin' back. And if we listen to men like Wishart we'll be right back where we started from. Homeless, jobless, kids without shoes. Standin' on corner ends with nothin' to dee. That's what ye get if ye listen to Wishart."

"Listen to me," Wishart pleaded. "For God's sake, listen to me."

But Ray did not let him finish. He plucked the book from his jerkin and flung it with all his strength. His aim was direct, his throw strong. The book turned through the air like a sputnik, falling open in flight, the white pages fluttering between the hard backs. It seemed an age before it struck. And in that age Wishart knew he had failed. He had not saved the future of the men, he had jeopardized it, and just as he had not saved the men nor had he saved the village. All his fears that night had been justified. And now the worst had come to pass. The book caught the corner of his eye and tore the skin along the bone. He staggered back against the chair and his arms sailed out as he tried to keep balance. His mind asked if the fault lay in him or in circumstance, if it was true what Ray had told him, that he let things drift and hoped for the best. But then his whole philosophy was one of drift. Of not planning ahead but letting events take their course. It had not occured to him others might not be content to drift, that they might plan, that they might wish to control circumstances and not be controlled by them. The blood leapt out upon his cheeks and dropped upon the lapels of his coat.

He floundered among the chairs and fell to the boards. His hand grasped at Sanderson's knee as he tried to raise himself up, but he stumbled back again, legs bending beneath the weight of his body. His face was tight with astonishment, eyes blinking against the light and film of blood that covered one of the pupils. The walls spun round his head, the rafters, the windows, the iron bars, the faces of the men, and the red baffled face of Sanderson, standing beside him peering down. He could not rise to his feet but slowly tried to pull himself up on his knees. A chair crashed behind him and he heard the scraping of his toes on the boards.

"Violence," he pleaded. "Can none o' ye remember?"

He looked down at the drops of blood on the planks.

179

Book Three

The Rutlands

19

Mrs. Rutland stood with her hands on the balustrade and looked beyond the garden to a car that appeared on the crest of the forest road.

The sun shone on the bonnet and roof of the car, but its yellow rays subsided to a gentle white as it sped towards the house; the dust from its tyres followed it like a shroud, rising white from the granite chips to obscure the grass that bordered the road. Mrs. Rutland squinted against the light and let her fingers play on the cool iron as she watched the car approach. The forest bordering the garden had been clipped by the forest commission to leave an undergrowth of bramble and dead leaves, bracken and hazel, that preceded the first young shoots in a new plantation. Rising out of the centre of the plantation stood a ventilating shaft that served the local colliery. And beyond the ventilating shaft, on the horizon, beyond the crest of trees and grass, stood the blue arid bareness of the Pennines. The car dropped out of sight in a dip in the road, and across the road Mrs. Rutland saw the firs swaying together, clasping the sky, while beneath their overhanging fronds the shadow of the interior was dark and disquieting.

The car swept out of the dip in the road and continued towards the house.

Mrs. Rutland stood on a balcony overlooking the garden. The balcony ran along her bedroom window and in a corner of the garden fringing the forest she could see the poplar trees she herself had planted, held erect with ropes and canes, the wind across the undergrowth rustling through the slim foliage. Beside the poplars were her fruit trees, apple trees with drooping branches, cherry trees that had never yielded fruit, nut trees rising like iron from the ground, the sun shining with promise on the stained, grub-eaten leaves. The light of the sun shone through the trees upon the lawn before the window, at the centre of which stood a disused well encircled by a path of crazy paving. The well had been filled with earth and in the earth pansies had been planted. An old wheel had been suspended above the well and the balustrades that attached it to its lips were wrapped in climbing roses. The roses had yet to bud, but a few shrivelled petals from the year before lay around the young plants. A cobweb clung to one of the balustrades, and the iron wheel above the well held a rusting chain once used to draw water. The lips of the well itself were green and yellow with lichen. There were three rows of tulips in a bed beyond the lawn, one row yellow, the other red, the third yellow and red together, and at each side of the bed a tree of forsythia, yellow as buttercup. A herbaceous border stood behind the tulips, pale pinks and purples, reds and violet, the wind tipping the leaves of the shrubs, the leaves dark green, pale and light green too, the fledgling buds green and brown and white in a nest of leaves.

Mrs. Rutland watched the pale white flowers of other shrubs show their stamens to the sun. Some of the herbaceous leaves had already withered, others were wilting, brown and drooping, choking buds that still struggled for life. The frail petals of discarded blossom lay upon the grass, and beneath the shrubs insects scurried on the dried scales of the dead leaves. Mrs. Rutland opened her garden twice to the public. She opened it once for the exhibition of tulips and forsythia and rhododendrons, and again for the roses she cultivated in the garden at the front of the house. The roses grew on trellises as high as bedroom windows, the blooms pink or vermilion, creamy yellow or pure orange, flowering from late June till the first heavy frost. The first of the two fetes would be held the following Saturday in aid of the local church. Refreshments would be served, and there would be coconut stalls, penny-a-book stalls, second-hand clothes stalls, lucky dips, shuggy-boats and a roundabout for children. The fete would be held in the corners of the garden opposite the fruit trees and the gardener was busy with canvas and frames, the tap of his hammer echoing like a rifle through the woods.

But Mrs. Rutland came out onto the balcony not for the fete but for the sunset. The sun slipped down over the green forest and blue horizon and bathed the hills in an aureole light. In the evening with the day behind her, she liked to place her elbows on the balcony and watch the sun. She liked to quieten her senses and open her mind, to hear the peewits calling in the forest and see the woodpigeons rising from the undergrowth, flapping heavily to the branches. She liked to feel the cool iron of the balustrade and smell the richness of the country, the dampness that came with the dusk, and with the dampness the odour of flowers and grass, of trees in the forest, hay ripening in the fields. And of course the sun, that was never the same two nights running, one night a solid brilliant white that changed slowly to a pale deepening yellow of golden dust, the other a scarlet tinge bursting to a radiance with the glow of its own warmth, the red slowly sinking, shooting across the sky to illuminate distant clouds. But tonight the sun was still high in the sky and standing on the balcony she had to shade her eyes against its glare.

She could not see the village from her house but she could feel it. She could feel its peace, its security, its humanity, stretching out to her like a hand across the fields and forest. To see it she had to walk to the little white gate at the end of the grounds, cross the road where she had seen the car, and stand at a stile leading to the fields. From there she could see the red tiled roofs of the bungalows on the lower slopes, the headstock and crusher of the colliery, the roof of the power station, the office, the concrete shell at the top of the hill, the last climbing houses of the village, the sun on their windows, the light on their roofs. But she did not have to see it to know it existed. For just as a baby in the womb is attached to its mother by a cord so Mrs. Rutland was attached to the village by her past. Her mother had run the first traps from the village to the railway station in the valley. In those days there were always men coming to Highhill, men looking for work, men on the dole, men collecting for pits on strike, some staying to work, others drifting on, and those collecting returning not with money but with bread baked by miners' wives. Her mother carried newspapers and medicine and preparations for the local chemist. She carried the post too, carried it and brought it back, and with her passenger traffic and goods service her traps did so well she was able to introduce to the village its first bus.

This was an army lorry bought at the end of the first world war. It had benches for seats, but with its tarpaulin cover and strong engine it made a dry if jolting journey, stopping rarely on the way, so that the time it took to reach the valley floor was less than it is today. Mrs. Rutland had somewhere a photograph of her mother taken years later when she bought her first properly constructed bus. The bus had about twenty seats and ran on solid tyres. In the photograph she was dressed in leggings and leather jacket, arms bent like wings at the elbows, hands in her pockets. She had a heavy, masculine face, with dark eyebrows and dark hair cut short like a man. She was of course considered eccentric by the village people, but her bus did so well she was able to extend the service from the station in the valley to the town itself. And later, when her fleet increased, she made regular trips to London, in the early days driving the bus herself. Mrs. Rutland often accompanied her mother on these trips and found them not without humour. For in order to fill the bus they collected passengers from other villages, but when they stopped at the pithead it often happened the passengers were not there, so that others had to seek them. Then the passengers arrived but not those sent after them. Seekers were sent after the seekers and it was often two to three hours before they got away.

During the year of the general strike, when miners were locked out for seven months, her mother did not hesitate to use her buses to bring flour and pigs' blood and potatoes, oatmeal and sugar, to the people of the village. She set up a committee to organize soup kitchens for mothers and their families. She organized relays of men to go into the wood and cut fuel. She organized concerts and sports meetings and football matches to keep the men's minds from violence. She offered trophies for darts and dominoes and prizes for the best-knit mats. Many a miner was kept at home by his wife on a carpet when he would have been in the street throwing stones at police escorts protecting covered wagons said to be carrying essential services. Violence was inevitable when men were locked out for seven months, with no money, no food, living under the threat of being turned into the street. But her mother did her best and for that the people were grateful.

Eventually, she married a man who had himself been a miner till he retired because of chest trouble. He received a small pension from the colliery, but earned the rest of his living from the shops left by his father. He owned a fruit shop, a fish shop, a greengrocery business and a paper shop. Apart from the paper shop, his business did badly, for the shops were a relic of a system known as tommy shops. These were shops owned by a relative of the colliery manager, or viewer as he was then known; the miner was obliged to purchase at these shops, and any credit that happened to be outstanding at the end of a fortnight was automatically deducted from his pay. And since the miner worked almost for nothing, suffering penalties for any brass or stone he might have hewed, it was possible after reductions for the tommy shop that there would be nothing to collect at the end of the fortnight. The system had been abolished and the shops bought by Mrs. Rutland's grandfather, but years passed before the miners overcame their reluctance to deal at such shops. They preferred to deal at others introduced when the village was thriving.

Mrs. Rutland's mother overcame such resistance. She found the shops ill-organized and badly run. Too much was ordered that had to be destroyed. The shopkeepers were more interested in taking out of the till than putting in. They spent most of their time in the back drinking tea than at the counter serving customers. She changed the shopkeepers and delivery services, she painted the fronts and improved the display, she introduced hygiene, she stopped credit when the village was prosperous and introduced it when it was not, relying on customers to remember her generosity when times picked up. By the time of the second world war she had added to her empire a chemist shop, a grocery store, a fresh fish business and a fleet of hackney carriages. Her bus company she merged with a larger firm running the same route, losing control but retaining a third of the shares. The company had its garage in the village and continued to ferry passengers as her mother had done before. And when war broke out she still had sufficient fortitude to demand renewal of her driving licence, so that she became the only woman driver on the road when manpower was short.

It was the war, however, that broke her mother. In the harsh winter of 1940 her husband succumbed to the chest trouble that had been ailing him for years. She had three sons all of whom went to the war, leaving only Mrs. Rutland at home. She bore the loss of her husband and in the time left after an eight-hour day on the buses continued to occupy herself with her affairs. The chemist shop and grocery store she sold to the local co-operative society. She found them too much for herself and daughter, with her sons away, and the money she invested in armaments, not because of the interest she was likely to get but because that way she felt she was helping her country. Then, in 1943, she lost her second eldest son, Alan, in the desert fighting, and hardly had she the time to digest that when she received a telegram to say her youngest son, Harry, was missing presumed dead. Of the three, he alone had joined the air force. He was rear gunner in a beaufighter and though he wrote many a cheerful letter, sending Canadian comics for Barbara, and telling of a girl he had met and intended to marry, it was evident he was afraid of flak. Her mother never got over the shock of the telegram. She sat in the sitting room and stared at the model of his plane on a stand by the mantelpiece. The plane had gone out on a mission and had not returned. Yet no-one could tell what had happened, if it had come down in the sea, if it had come down on land; and if it had come down on land might not he be prisoner in some foreign camp? It was possible, she reflected, anything was possible. But she did not know and the woman who had been able to support the death of her husband, the loss of her son, could not bear the uncertainty of knowing whether her youngest was alive or dead.

Her hair and eyebrows grew white, there was a tiredness to her face, she left her affairs to her daughter, and when her sight began to fail withdrew from the buses. Her sight grew so frail that a neighbour calling to use the phone and handing the three pennies for the call saw her place them on the palm of her hand and peering close look for them with her eyes. She owned a house in a private street opposite the school and took to sitting in the garden looking at the children playing in the yard. The sun did not shine for her now and the trees were bare. She did not notice the buses that passed on the road to the town. She could not recall it was she who had made the first journey and that now in the valley buses were so convenient hardly anyone used a train. All that was the past was forgotten. All that she had built was neglected. She took the telegram from the drawer and ran the pale yellow envelope through her hands. She listened for the phone and when it rang leapt to answer. She believed one day the war office would ring to say there had been a mistake, that her son who was lost had been found, that her son who was dead was alive.

And when the call she expected did not come she took to

188

telephoning the local exchange to ask why. She grew discontented and restless, impatient with herself and overbearing with the servants; her mind began to wander and she took to rambling through the house, looking through the rooms, banging doors, seeking 'wor Harry'. Always in her life she spoke with the broad accent of the village, and despite the riches she accumulated, the property she managed, she had never seen fit to change. Not finding her son in the house she took to crossing the road and catching a bus. 'Gannin' to see wor Harry', she told the conductor. Mrs. Rutland had to watch her as one watches a thief. But even then there were times when her mother slipped out and she had to race after the bus in her car and collect her at the next stop. Then she went out to the garage at the back to take from it his first bicycle. She would wheel it out onto the pavement in the back yard, turn it upside down till it rested on its seat and handle bars, and begin fumbling with the nuts to take the cycle to pieces. This was what she had shown him when he was very young. She could take a bicycle to pieces and put it together again without leaving a single nut or screw on the pavement. But now in old age she was interrupted by the phone and rambled back again into the house. She fell rapidly into decay. Yet despite her senility and wandering senses she listened to the news with the little perspicuity she had left. She yearned for the day war would end but died before surrender was announced, never knowing whether her son was alive or dead.

She went to her grave the uncertainty still showing on her face, the telegram that had brought her ruin pinned to her breast.

She left her fortune to her son and her business to her daughter. He never returned to the village after the war but stayed in the army to obtain a commission, and after years of distinguished service was now a retired colonel in the south. Mrs. Rutland had not left the village because it had never occurred to her to leave. She was proud of her mother, proud of her heritage, proud of what her mother had done. She wanted to carry on the tradition. She owned a fresh fish business, a fleet of hackney carriages, a fruit shop, a paper shop, a green grocery business and a fish shop. She had also retained her mother's shares in the bus company and added to her interests a small dress shop that fell vacant in the early nineteen fifties. Mrs. Rutland had not of course inherited her mother's masculine drive and enthusiasm, but she was efficient, she was shrewd, she kept a certain distance between herself and her affairs, and though she was detached she had a prudent nature and intelligent outlook. She continued her mother's standards of organization and cleanliness, she kept her shopkeepers on their toes and though she did not meddle there was very little that escaped her notice. And they in turn respected her confidence, admired her common sense, trusted her guidance and liked her personality. They felt with her they knew where they stood. There was to her a certain quality, a certain distinction which kept them in place; but she never accentuated this distinction, tried always to put them at ease, and was never short with them and never angry. In fact the only person who had seen her angry was Herbert Longley.

And that the evening before when he told her of the village.

20

"One of my friends in the Board's planning division let it drop today," he said. "He says there're twenty collieries in the coalfield earmarked for closure. Of course, not all at once. But within the next few years. And each colliery like this supporting a village of its own. He says they've done their best. But there it is."

"And this colliery. What did he say about this colliery?"

"He said it's on the short list. It'll be first to go."

"And the village. You said they'd pull down the village."

"They're going to pull down the condemned houses and refuse permission to build others in their place. So by the time they're finished, since all the older mining houses are condemned, there'll be nothing left except private and council houses."

"And me," Mrs. Rutland said. "And my shops."

She had been kneeling against the wall of the house when Longley came out into the garden. A few weeks earlier she had planted a new kind of climbing ivy and already the tentacles were hooking themselves into cracks in the stone and mortar that adhered the stone together. She knelt by the wall to the corner of the house to see how the ivy was getting on. It was now three feet tall and she bent on the border to the house, one hand across her knee, the other caressing the young leaves already showing their faces to the sun. She pressed the earth round the base of the ivy and dusted her hands on the sides of her trews. She wore tartan trews, with a black sweater and short white coat that went well with her short-cut silvery hair. The hair was divided by a parting, with a quiff that fell a little over her brow. The light caught the silvery strands and there were freckles to her brow from the sun; she wore shading to her eyes and a touch of rouge to her cheeks; there was a pale lipstick to her lips and a soft white down beneath the line of her jaw. Her only signs of age were the coarseness of

191

the skin to her chest and the brown pellucid tightness to the back of her hands. But her chest was covered by the high neck of the sweater and only the hands showed as she raised them to her eyes against the light. She looked up at Longley and with her hands against her forehead a red shadow covered her face.

He knelt by the border of the house and ran a stick through the gravel. He was a man in his early fifties, dressed in a tweed suit, a waistcoat, a cream shirt and what resembled an old school tie. The toes of his shoes were polished, but there was a slight click at the side of the turn-ups where his heel had caught the wide bottom. He had pale cheeks, the skin coarse and dry, the skin of his brow creased and puckering back to his forehead; he had brown hair, very thin on top, so that the light shone upon his baldness, but a handsome brown moustache twirled across his upper lip. He did not look at Mrs. Rutland as he spoke but continued to stroke the stick through the gravel. His hands were very large and well kept, the nails manicured, the tips without any trace of nicotine or manual work. There were thick brown hairs to his wrist and with his hand holding the stick she could see the rich cream of his cuff, the gold cufflink glittering with the movement of his arm. Only when he had finished did he set the stick aside and arching his brows lift his head to look into her eyes.

"What else did your friend say?" she asked.

"Nothing much," he replied. "Only that they'd done their best not to have this happen. You know, trying to cut down on output. Stopping recruitment and overtime and Saturday work. But things are running too fast for them. Times are changing. And it's not possible for them to do everything the way they want."

"But this colliery. What did he say about this colliery?"

"Only that it'll close about Christmas. And if they can get the men out on time the house'll come down immediately after that."

Mrs. Rutland rose from her hunkers and fumbled her hands for her pockets. Her bottom lip trembled and despite the rouge Longley saw the colour heighten to her cheeks. Even now he was not sure whether she was angry or reflecting. She looked over his shoulder to the sun catching the tips of the fruit trees and felt the muscles constrict in her chest as she tried to bring herself under control. She took it first as a woman and then as a business

192

woman. She thought of the village as it was, as it had been, not only in her mother's time, but throughout the ages. And she wanted to weep, not for the past but for the waste, the waste of human effort, human determination, human stubborness and skill that had made the village what it was. Then she turned her head away from the sun and Longley saw the muscles tighten in her neck. The trembling lip came under control but the colour deepened in her cheeks. Her hands found and slipped into her pockets. She felt as a business woman she had been out-manoeuvred. She would be destroyed because she had not been in the know. She had read of the closures up and down the country, she had read of the ominous trend to oil away from coal; but tucked in the fold of this hill, with the security of the village, she had not known that somehow it would destroy her. But even had she known how could she have seen that someone somewhere would decide that if a man cannot work in a village he could not live in a village. That because the structure of his colliery should be destroyed the structure of his life should be destroyed also?

She could never have seen it and because she could never have seen it she felt better. Her anger subsided, her feelings tightened within, and her mind began to probe the future. She turned to Longley and took his arm. "All right," she said. "You're my accountant. You tell me what I'm supposed to do."

They turned and walked along the side of the house. Against the wall were several crates of orangeade and pepsi-cola for the village fete; there was also a box of coconuts and several grey hens of ginger beer; and standing against the wall, covered by tarpaulin, the dismantled ironwork of a shuggy-boat, several folded tables and chairs, and parasols in the event that it rained. Facing the wall were Mrs. Rutland's three greenhouses. In the first she bedded tomatoes and cucumbers, in the second chrysanthemums that flowered till Christmas, carnations, begonias and petunias she transplanted in time for the summer show. And in the third the tropical plants cultivated in the spare time she had left after her affairs. These were strange plants of many kinds and colours, some with leaves like papyrus, others on hairy stems with red underskin, and still more with thick red veins and flowering heads, the petals as fragile as the petals of a geranium. But all growing sturdily in the humid temperature of the house. They walked toward this house now, Longley stopping a pace behind and resting his hands on his waistcoat as she pulled open the door.

"As I see it," he said. "There are three things you can do. The first is nothing at all. You can bury your head in the sand and go on as if nothing had happened. Of course, your trade'll be reduced, as there'll be hardly any houses and hardly any people. It means you'll have to start drawing on your bank for a change instead of relying on your profits. It means you'll have to cut down on your way of living. Cut down on your house and your grounds and your garden. But you'll get by. At any rate for a little while."

"And the second?"

"The second thing you can do is sell out. It's a bit late in the day, I admit. Six months ago you'd have had a better chance. And it's tonight the Board are explaining the position to the union. So by tomorrow it'll be all over the village. Which means probably you won't have any buyers tomorrow. But in a little while, when the panic's over, maybe you'll get a few offers. After all it's not as if the village'll be pulled down altogether. There'll still be some houses. And the people in those houses have to eat. They'll have to buy their stuff somewhere. But your selling price'll take a drop. And by the time the demolition men get to work you'll be lucky if you get half the value."

"And you think the value'll drop on my house too?"

"Probably. Who wants to live in a fine house like this in a village that's dead?"

"But what if I didn't sell out. What if I kept my shops. What if I converted them into depots and set myself on the road with travelling shops. That way I'd be better off. Because instead of concentrating on this village I'd concentrate on every village in the area. That way I'd make money rather than lose it."

"And how much d'you think it'd take to convert your shops and buy the vehicles for the road?"

"It wouldn't cost me anything. It'd be an investment that I'd deduct from my tax returns. And that way I could convert every shop I owned. All except my paper shop and my fried fish shop. And even my fresh fish shop I could convert, running the vans from there and serving fresh fish to every village in the area."

"It might pay in the short term," Longley agreed. "But not in the long term. You see, this is a dead area. There'll be no development in this part of the world at all. And just as surely as this colliery closes at Christmas others'll be closing in the years ahead. Of course, they'll not close all at once. They'll not close in six months. But little by little they'll be nibbled away, a seam here, a district there. Till by 1970 there'll hardly be a colliery left in the area. And if there's no development there's no jobs. And if there's no jobs there's no people."

"So though I might make money now I certainly wouldn't be making it in ten years?"

"Exactly."

Mrs. Rutland walked down the pathway between the rows of plants. The door closed and as the door closed so did the atmosphere around them. The air was thick and Longley felt the heat to his face and neck gradually pervading to the rest of his body. With the hot air, the humid soil, the damp vegetation, one could almost feel the jungle. The plants were set in pots on a plateau of dark cinder and under the plateau, in cement troughs, lay the water that was constantly used to nourish them. Mrs. Rutland had built the greenhouse herself, devising and submitting the plans to the local council, ordering the bricks, the mortar, the sand, laying the foundations, supervising the work, piecing together the sections and putting the glass in the frames. She ordered the boiler and the boiler pipes. She followed the work carefully and assiduously. And when the greenhouse was finished she introduced the varieties herself, saw to it they were constantly watered, and gauged the temperature of the boiler. It was the nearest she ever got to her mother's masculinity. But she liked the strange purple heart of the leaves, the small anemone-like flowers that blossomed from the stems. There was something about the primitive that appealed to her.

"And the third," she said. "You said there was a third."

"The third would solve all your problems," he said. "It'd guarantee you an income. It'd mean you could sell your shares in the bus company. It means you could sell your shops and your cars. Your house if you wanted. It'd mean you could have a stable home and a stable future. Not only for yourself but for your daughter. So that Barbara could continue the life she's been used to till she decided to marry and settle of her own accord. It means you'd be happy the rest of the days of your life."

"Sounds interesting," she said. "What is it?"

"You can marry me."

195

21

Longley saw the skin of her neck flush and her outstretched hand waver. They were now at the back of the greenhouse, among plants that reached to the panes. They had large iris-like leaves, green with white edges, the edges jagged with minute, saw-like teeth. He had to sway his head to avoid the soft green ferns of other plants suspended from the roof. He watched the tremor in Mrs. Rutland's hand as it carried forward to fondle the large velvety petals of a plant on the stand before her; the petals were open like clams and he waited in suspense for them to close around the soft white fingers. Wooden blinds were drawn across the panes of the greenhouse windows and outside he could hear the play of hoses on the lawn at the front. He stepped forward to touch her shoulder and as she turned she saw the length of the greenhouse, the gardener's wellington boots that he left in a cranny by the door, the tins of various chemical compounds on a ledge at the side, the slim red tendrils of her plants, with flowering white and yellow heads. She placed her hands on his shoulder and he in turn placed his on her wrist. Then softly, stooping forward, she kissed him on the brow.

She looked him in the eyes. She had soft hazel eyes that were damp now with surprise and tenderness. She had always known that he loved her but had thought she would never see the day he would propose. Her eyes wandered over his shoulder and she looked down to the dark cinder among the pools where lay the broken leaves and fallen petals snapped from the plants. He loved her so much he had been afraid to ask. For with him it had to be all or nothing. And he was afraid if she said no it would be nothing, and if it were nothing he would go away and never return. He preferred uncertainty to that. Her husband had been very much like Longley. He went with her several months before he held her hand. It was a year before he plucked up courage to kiss her and another year before he managed to propose. They had been married in the summer of 1938, when the tension in the air was so brittle one felt it must break. And break it did, so that when Barbara was born in the spring of 1940, her father had been conscripted, drilled, trained and shipped, and three years were to pass before he was ever to return to see the child of his loins.

Rutland had been son of the colliery undermanager. His father had promised him an opening in the pit, but he had preferred to make his own way and joined a small contracting firm in the city to train as a surveyor. The pay was nominal and he refused to take from his people; he refused to take from Mrs. Rutland too, so that in the early days of their courtship their meetings were confined to walks in the woods, lunches at their respective homes, and Saturday evenings at the local cinema. He was a very serious young man and when not with Mrs. Rutland worked all the time. He attended day school as well as night classes, took classes in English as well as mathematics; he passed his early qualifying examinations without difficulty, stumbled, when he failed his intermediate, but rallied to pass that and his final in successive years. In the interval, he changed his job several times, leaving his original firm to work for a major contractor, switching again to work for a builder in the village a couple of miles away. He claimed this way he got experience. His ambition was to settle and work for the local council. He achieved this only a few days before he was called up and indeed the day he received his official appointment was the day he received his papers.

He went through the war without a scratch. He fought in the desert campaigns, the battles to and fro in the sands of Libya, he landed with the Americans on the tip of Sicily, he took part in the battles for the mainland, he fought in the battle of Cassino. And on his off-days, in their advance up the highways of Italy, he cut the hedges along the route to make it pretty for a famous general. Later, he was transferred home to fight the battle of Normandy. He landed on the beaches, he fought his way through a country of corn and hay and derelict chateaux, a land of broken down mills, deserted farmyards and demolished houses. And so on to the Ardennes. He had been playing cards in an army jeep before the Battle of the Bulge. They were playing brag and he had picked up the only ace prile in his life when an American officer pushed his face through the window and told them to get the hell out. They had only one can of petrol to get them back to their lines before the enemy rolled over. And then when the enemy rolled back he made the historic crossing into Germany. He returned home with a pair of German binoculars for himself and a tin of boiled sweets for his daughter. He had nothing for his wife. Except, as he told her, the honour of feeling he had done enough fighting to win the war himself.

He found the village greatly changed when he got back. His wife's mother and father and two brothers were dead. His wife was in sole charge of the business and on the verge of a breakdown. She felt she could not stand for another minute the house that had brought so much tragedy. He helped her with the affairs till she was able to surmount her grief and then, when things had settled, and when he had himself taken up his work for the council, they sold their house and moved to the property in Highhill lane. The house was owned by the manager of the local colliery, anxious to get out in anticipation of the Nationalization Act. He was an ageing man who did not want to stay on under public ownership. In fact, he retired as soon as the house was sold, and being a widower went to live with his sister in Northumberland. There were four bedrooms in the house, a nursery and bathroom, a sitting room, dining room, kitchen, scullery and maid's quarter. There was also a tennis court, a drive lined with chestnut trees, a vegetable garden large enough to meet their needs, and of course two greenhouses where Mrs. Rutland kept her tomatoes and bedding plants. The only disadvantage was the price.

It took the Rutlands all the money they had in the bank and all they were able to get from the sale of their house. Even then it was not enough and Mrs. Rutland had to borrow the rest from her brother. They hesitated before they actually signed the deeds of transfer. But they reasoned it was worth it. They intended to have more than one child. Mr. Rutland intended to enter the life of the community. He intended to open the grounds for fetes, have tea parties on the lawn, cocktails in the house. Mrs. Rutland, once her affairs were organized, intended to enter local organizations, the local women's institute, the local co-operative guild, the church fellowship society. In all these the house and grounds would be useful. And if it left them broke what of it? Her husband had prospects with the council, and though her shops had not done well during the war and with rationing were not doing well now, the pits were to be nationalized, the miners themselves become owners, their wives have more through their fingers. There would be an upturn for the village and with the upturn all that they had spent would be made up.

The winter of nationalization was the most cruel anyone in the north has ever known. The snow began to fall in January and did not stop until March. For a time the roads to the village were cut off and a special snow plough had to be bought by the council to sweep aside the drifts. By the end of the second month, though the roads were clear, banks of snow were piled twenty feet at either side. All cars were advised to use chains. In the village the snow was three and four feet high on waste ground and on the pathways crushed so compactly it rose by three feet the level of the pavement. It was so bad children were not allowed home to lunch but kept at school till the evening. They developed sores on their mouths with all the icicles they sucked. And when they did get home the wind whistled round the chimney pots and the snow fell again, so that by the following morning new paths had to be made, the roads swept again, the pavements rose another inch, and again drivers checked the chains on their wheels.

Mr. Rutland never wore chains. He toured the district directing the snow plough, seeing which roads were useable and which were not. The blizzards through which he drove were worse than any sandstorms in the desert. But he liked the snow, he liked the excitement, it reminded him of the excitement of the war, so that where others were content to stay in the office by a radiator he took to the road as often as he could. He drove carefully up the winding twisting roads that made their way from the valley floor, trees climbing steeply away on the one side, falling steeply to the river on the other. Only in those first weeks, with the snow piling above the level of the car, it was easy to forget that a valley ran below. The wheels of his car skidded and swivelled through a bank of snow. He tried to check the skid by stepping on the accelerator. Instead of advancing the car twisted quickly sideways. The rear fell through the railings and the car dropped into the ravine. The blizzard continued and the snow soon covered the tracks the car had made. It was several days before they found him and when they did he was dead at the wheel.

Longley had been in the same regiment as Rutland during the war. They teamed up in the last year and returned to England on the same boat. Their experience on the crossing was almost as

199

adventurous as anything they had endured during the war. For a band of fiery highlanders, discontented with the food, attacked the galley and bound up the cooks. They barricaded themselves in and refused to move. They threatened to cut the throats of the cooks if anyone tried to enter. It meant that during the last two days of the voyage the rest of the boat had to live on the tinned meat and raw vegetables the rebels condescended to throw out, but having survived the war fighting the enemy they preferred this to hazarding their lives fighting their own. The mutineers were much chastened by the time they reached harbour, but they were still holding out when the ship unloaded, and it was not till the last bottle of beer had been drunk, the last tin thrown out of the porthole, that they eventually gave up.

Longley and Rutland went to their respective homes without ever finding out what became of the rebellious Scots. But they would often talk of it, sitting in deck chairs on the lawn of the new home, watching the wind through the trees. In those unsettled days after the war Longley came often to their new house. He liked to come. It seemed he had nowhere else to go. He had worked as an accountant in the city before being called up, but now that war was over he did not quite know what he wanted. Mrs. Rutland offered to find him a place in the village and run her shops. But after years of so much action he claimed the village would be too quiet. Finally he decided to make a break, and a few months before Rutland was killed sold his house and left to join an accounting firm in the Sudan. Later he was transferred to Cairo and there he stayed till the Suez crisis forced him out in 1957.

Much against his will, he returned to his native north and joined an accounting firm in the city. In Cairo, he had been running the business on the lines of an agency, so that on returning home he found rather irksome the restriction of working for someone else. Nor did he find the climate any better. The only inclemency one had to watch in Egypt was the sandstorm. It appeared as a shimmering purple line moving steadily closer from the horizon, so that one had time to get home, lock the door and shutter the windows, seal any cracks or skylights, retire to bed and wait till the storm passed. There was nothing so dramatic in the north, but there was damp and cold, snow and frost, there was always a wind from the moors, there was bronchitis and rheumatism and lumbago, and very little sun to compensate these in summer. Longley did not find it so bad when he left the firm to work on his own. For then if he felt like a change he could always take a plane to London. Besides, he did quite well out of his independence. He did the books of several large corporations, including one of the leading soap manufacturers, he now had an office and staff of his own, so that his own work consisted mainly of entertainment and supervision, treating the clients to a cocktail and seeing to it their work was properly handled. The only books he ever did himself were those of Mrs. Rutland.

She had felt the loss of her husband more than she felt the loss of her family. At first there was an impact of shock and bewilderment. She could not understand how a man could fight his way through a war and be found so ignominously. Then after the funeral, after the shock and bewilderment, it began to dawn on her she had never really known married life. She had known him only long enough to conceive their child. And hardly had he returned from the war when he had been taken from her for good. It was more than she could stand. She lost faith in herself and in her church. She fell into indifference. She neglected her house and her business, her grounds and her gardens. It was pointed out that receipts from her shops were lower than they had been during the war, but she could not rouse herself to understand its significance. She fell behind in her bills. Her brother had to remind her, somewhat delicately, that he was still awaiting the first instalment on the money he had loaned her for the house. And getting his letter she felt it had been a mistake. They should never have bought. She even began to feel all this had happened because of the house. That if they were still in their old house in the village he would still be driving down to the council office. That their life would be rolling on as before.

She decided to sell her house and return, but hardly had she called in the estate agent when she remembered her daughter. She had been neglected in the grief she felt for her husband. But he was dead, she was alive. Yet in many ways he was living still in her. She was his face, his walk, his mannerisms; she was the way he clapped his hands with excitement, the way he smiled, the gentleness in his eyes. The little instinctive movements that had memories for no-one but her. She recalled his intentions on buying the house. The fetes he had wanted, the parties on the lawn, cocktails in the house. She remembered that she too had planned to enter the life of the village, join local organizations, play her part in the community. What had happened to her determination? Where was her mother's strength of character? She recalled what she had read, that even the gods cannot alter the past. She felt it her duty to look after her house, develop her business, groom her garden, cultivate her grounds. She owed it to a husband living still in her daughter, she owed it to a mother who had made it possible, and she owed it to herself to lose sorrow in work that was constructive. So that she could honour the memory of her husband and secure the future of her child.

Longley was very good to Barbara. He was very good to Mrs. Rutland. He worshipped Barbara as he might his own, bringing something for her each time he came, treating her not as a teen-age nuisance but as an equal, so that they were able to exchange confidences, secrets that brought them together. She was almost a woman now, he was like a father, and it was what she needed. Mrs. Rutland saw this and it pleased her. She began to look forward to his comings and regret his goings. She was upset if his business detained him and rang if a week passed without his coming. She determined that if he proposed she would accept. She was sure her husband would approve. He did not want her to be alone all her life. He would not want her to sacrifice the future for the sake of the past. He would understand that Barbara was growing rapidly, that soon she would marry to a life of her own. Then she would have no-one. At any rate, she had decided. But the years passed, she watched his fondness turn to affection, his affection to love, and never once did he intimate that he might want to take his love a stage further. Never, that is, till tonight.

"You know," she said. "I wouldn't want you to propose out of sympathy."

"It's not sympathy," he said. "You know how I feel. How I've always felt."

"I know," she said. "And I'm grateful."

They came out of the greenhouse into the air and he felt the coolness to his face and neck. The sun was shining through the foliage of the fruit trees, tinging the leaves with red and casting a red shadow to his cheeks. He squinted and turned against the light and Mrs. Rutland could see the folds in the skin of his neck, the dark eyebrows, very thin, pencil-like, and the small curls in what was left of his hair. He looked somewhat forlorn and lost.

As if he could not disguise his loneliness. The creases were thick in his forehead and there was sorrow in his eyes. Ever since his return from Egypt he had looked so out of place. It was as if he had learnt that all the money in the world will not make a man happy, that always there is required something else. And in his case the something was Mrs. Rutland. She took his hand and together they walked along the side of the wall to the house.

"It's too much for me," she said. "This and the village."

He patted her wrist with his hand. "I know," he said. "And I understand."

"All I need is a little time. A few days to think it over."

"Not a few days," he said. "Only a few hours."

"You mean you couldn't bear the suspense?"

"Not after all this time."

"It's the village I can't understand," she said. "It's hardly possible."

"Wait until tomorrow," he said. "You'll hear for yourself."

"And you'll come tomorrow night?"

"If you want me to come."

"Yes," she said. "Come tomorrow night. Then I'll be able to tell you."

She stood on the balcony and watched the car sweep toward the cottage at the end of the forest road. The road dropped suddenly and came out at the offshoot of the village that was Highhill lane. The main road came through here and on a few hundred yards to the village. She turned and went into her bedroom and took her stockings from the bed. She pulled on her stockings and slipped into her shoes. This evening she wore a black dress with a single row of pearls and a set of pearl ear-rings. She had dabbed a little perfume behind her ears and the odour of it still clung to her fingers as she fingered the row of pearls on her throat. She heard through the open window the tip-tap of the gardener's hammer and listened for the sound of the car on the drive. It would drop down from the wood, make a narrow right hand turn and pull up to the house through the alleyway of chestnuts. She went downstairs smiling with pleasure, a hand lightly touching the balustrades. There was a screeching of tyres on the gravel, the sound of a car door opening and closing, and then feet on the steps to the house.

She knew it was Herbert Longley coming for his answer.

22

Even now she could hardly believe it was true. She had risen early that morning to scan the newspapers. She had expected to find nothing in the nationals but perhaps a paragraph or two in the provincials. Then she remembered Longley had told her the news was unofficial. Only the night before was it being passed to the union by the management. Probably it would be some days before the official announcement was made. And even then perhaps it would not be published. The world had better things to do than concern itself with the fate of the village. So she settled down to wait. She decided she would not call anyone but let others call her. If it were true what Longley had said and a special consultative meeting had been called the evening before it would not take rumours long to fly. And then there would be many anxious telephone calls for confirmation. Normally, in the morning, she allowed no calls from her shops but settled to scan the trade journals and read the mail. She always held ready the waste basket in which to drop her circulars. But that morning she brought her coffee to the settee, pulled close the phone, settled back her head and waited.

She did not have long to wait. The manager of the grocery store was first on the line. He asked if she had heard the news. She replied she had not. Whereupon he settled down to details. Only it was plain to him there would be no delay before the closure of the colliery and destruction of the houses. The pit would close in a week and families not out by then would be put on the street. He took pride in his facts. He had personally done well out of Mrs. Rutland and had built himself a bungalow on the lower slopes of the village. He would not be affected by the closure but nevertheless took pains to point out that others who were would be obliged to live like squatters. He even went so far to say that he had heard those deprived of their homes would be transferred to nissen huts used to house German prisoners during the war. She had hardly put down the phone when others telephoned to ask if it were true. The stories were getting more fantastic every minute. She therefore authorized her shopkeepers to pass to their customers the true version. But by then it was too late, imagination had taken hold, and the last call she received was to tell her that night shift men going in-by had so excited the back shift men still at work they had threatened to walk out then and there and only union intervention prevented a strike. That decided her. And before Longley entered the sitting room to settle himself on the settee her mind was made up.

"You said yesterday there were three things I could do."

"That's right," he said. "The first was to bury your head in the sand. Go on as if nothing had happened."

"And the second was to sell everything. My shops, my garage, my house. Even my shares in the bus company. All that my mother worked for and built up. All that I've struggled to consolidate. And at half price, half value. Just to have done with it all."

"And you won't do that, will you?"

"Why should I? When I know their value can't be weighed in money. When I know they're worth more to me even if I'd sold them months or even years ago. Why should I sell to make it easier for those who want to see my destruction? Allow myself forced out by the whim of some bureaucrat who wants to change something that for years has been unchangeable."

"So you won't do that either?"

"It's not what my mother would have done," she said. "Or my father either for that."

"Which brings us," he said. "To the third."

He leant forward to help himself to a glass of whisky. He did not take his whisky neat and there was beside it on the tray a bowl of ice and jug of water. He had not been to the office that day and was casually dressed in a pair of cavalry twills, a white shirt rolled to his elbows, and a small silk scarf tied round his throat like a neckerchief. The wind through the side windows of the car had deranged slightly the sparse curls to the side of his head. He hitched the crease in his trousers as he leant forward to reach for the bottle. The fire had been lit in the hearth and as it spluttered and crackled the light of its flames was reflected in the amber of the whisky. It was an old fashioned wood fire set in a large stone grate and across its hearth was suspended a spit on which Mrs. Rutland roasted her fowl. The rest of the fires in the house were coal fires, but she claimed wood gave a better heat for the roast. Longley watched the ash falling to the hearth from the embers, the wood of the logs burned the shape of honeycombs, sparks showering up as one of the logs fell. He picked up his glass and turned his gaze to Mrs. Rutland.

She stood by the window and looked toward the sunset. Her neck was yellow with the light from the window and the reflection of the panes shimmered against the wall. She held her hands before her and played absently with the wedding ring on her finger. The light caught the silvery pearls of her necklace and the silvery strands of her hair; it caught too the delicately poised throat and profile of her face. It floated over her like an underwater radiance, and the warmth and the gold, and the silent unconscious beauty of her standing there licked the flames within Longley as he sat with his whisky. There was still loneliness in his face, loneliness and sadness, like a man who had been trapped and cannot understand. Only in his case he had been trapped by life. He held the glass on his lap and stared down at the dwindling chunks of ice. He wanted her, not for herself, not for her body, not for the sake of possession, but for such moments as this. For the happiness she could bring, for the loneliness and sadness she could diminish. But he was not sure if it would be as he watched her graceful body move from the window, the breasts uplifted, the mould of her stomach strong and firm. She came and stood by the settee and straightened the curls in his hair.

"Might there not be a fourth," she said. "A fourth alternative."

"I wouldn't know," he said. "Might there?"

"What's to stop me from staying here to fight?"

"Fight for what?"

"For the village where I live. The life that I lead."

"You can't do that," he said. "That's socialist talk. And a woman in your position wants no truck with things like that."

"But the men in the pit. They're all Labour men, I suppose, so it's all right for them. All they're giving up is their homes and their jobs. Not even that. Because they'll be given other homes and other jobs. But I'm giving up everything I have in the world. And without a penny compensation. Yet I can't fight. I have to sit here and let things take their course."

She moved away from the settee across the floor toward the racks of fishing rods her husband had intended to use to fish in the river. The racks were set on the wall of the living room between the door and stairs. In the corner was her television and on the sills of the windows various tropical plants taken from her greenhouse. It was an old house and across the roof were slung strong timber beams, some of the beams eaten by woodworm, others gnarled with ancient knots. Smoke that did not escape by the chimney sifted along the beams and the wood cracked with the persistence of a tread on the landing. She looked out of the window at the sun that cupped the leaves of the laurel shubs, at the mollusc-like shells that drifted down from the chestnut blossom, and from his seat by the fire Longley could see the white soft skin of her neck, the zip which fastened her dress at the back. He placed his glass on the small table and leant forward on the settee.

"You're thinking of the past," he said. "Your mother and father."

"Maybe I am," she said. "But I know what they'd have done in my shoes."

"The world's changed since their day," he said. "They were pioneers and there's no room now for pioneers. Just for hard-headed businessmen and bankers. And you've got to feel like them, be like them, if you want to get on. That's the essence of the modern world."

"You mean I have to conform?"

"That's right. Conform. There's no room these days for the individual. They went out with the pioneers before we were born."

"I don't believe that," she said. "I'll never believe that."

"That's your trouble," she said. "You won't face reality. You won't face the world in which we live. It's a good world, yet you despise it. You shut it out. How often do I see you watching your television? And your car. How often is it out of the garage? You don't feel the need of it, you say. You prefer to walk if you have the chance. Walk through the woods, walk through the village. Dreaming of a life that's as dead as the wood on that fire."

"But if I conform, if I give up my dreams, I give up my business."

"And you go into retirement. Honourable retirement."

"But what do I do then?"

"You marry me. We'll go away together. We'll see the world.

I'll take in partners and leave the business to them. We'll play the rich couple. We'll stay at expensive hotels, eat at expensive restaurants, order expensive wines. Then, when we're sick of travelling, we'll come back and settle. Not in this grey country. Where everything lacks colour and life. We'll settle in the south. We'll have friends like ourselves. People who've lived and understand what life is. So that together we'll have a future."

"Whereas if I stay I've only a past?"

"Not even that," he said. "A handful of water."

"And if I fight what have I got?"

"Fight for what?" he asked. "And against what? Against progress? Against time? Against change? You can't fight those things. They're not people. They're not even arguments. They're events. Circumstances that destroy. As they'll destroy you if you don't take my advice."

Mrs. Rutland had in fact decided not to marry Herbert Longley. The love she had felt in those early days, after his return from Egypt, had dissipated. It had been a reaction to years of loneliness she had not noticed till his return. Had he proposed then perhaps over the last two years they would have been happily married. But in those early months he had attributed her affection to the wartime relationship he had had with her husband, the fact he had returned against his will to a part of the world he did not like. And later, when his own affection turned to love, he had not wished to abuse the memory of his late friend. He had not wished to put forward a proposal which might have embarrassed her sensitivity. And of course there was his fear of losing her. So that he had left it late, almost too late, her love for him had withered, her feelings had changed. Till there remained only a residue of fondness sufficient to make any marriage a success.

"And if we married and went away," she asked. "What'd we do with Barbara?"

"Take her with us," he said. "That is, if she wanted to go."

"And if she didn't?"

"Let her stay at home. Our home. Till she's finished her schooling."

"You have it all arranged," she laughed. "I wonder why you haven't bought the tickets."

"Because first," he smiled. "There'd be the banns."

There were other reasons too why she should marry Longley.

She had not been doing as well as she might in the fifties. The up-turn she had expected following nationalization had not come until the end of rationing, and it was not till then she had been able to pay back the money loaned by her brother on the house. Things had gone well in the middle of the decade, but since then if it had been a time of prosperity for the country it had not been a time of prosperity for her. The local co-operative society moved in with its own funeral and wedding service. She had hardly put on its feet the dress shop when the first cheap fabrics were intro-duced, and instead of buying hand-stitched dresses made to measure customers went to the local town and bought off the peg. The bus company acquired new rolling stock which had yet to be paid for, or indeed pay for itself, so there had been no dividend on her shares since 1957. Her greengrocery business began to falter when the store introduced travelling shops, so that in the age of television and hoovermatics hardly anyone crossed their doors to buy a loaf. The same was true of her fruit business. So that only her paper shop and fresh fish shop were doing well, the rest were not even holding their own.

Mrs. Rutland knew exactly what she should do to counteract this. She knew there was little she could do about her shares in the bus company or the co-operative's travelling shop; but she could convert her greengrocery store into a small supermarket, replace her hackney carriages, introduce a club to her dress shop, and sell the fried fish shop suffering in competition with television. She knew there would be no lack of buyers. And though her club scheme was a form of credit she knew it was the only thing to make her dress shop pay. The greengrocery store she would re-design in such a way it would be completely self-service, she would offer at a discount her hackney carriages, arranging flowers and providing bearers in the event of a funeral, arranging the catering and providing ushers in the event of a wedding. And into her fruit shop she would install the village's first line of frozen food. The one thing she lacked was money for investment. She had never believed in harbouring capital for the sake of capital. She required enough for the upkeep of her house and grounds, the schooling of her daughter, the standard of her life, and a small cottage in the valley for the time she retired and left everything to Barbara. It had not worried her to know she had merely enough to do these things. For what she lacked in capital she had in property. It would be sufficient to guarantee a loan on the bank to cover the investment. She had not seen what could be done to the village and her property. She had not seen that the decision of a planning officer would leave her almost bankrupt.

That was the reason why she should marry Longley. She had thought over all that he had told her the evening before and realized it was true. She could sell her shares in the bus company, sell her shops and cars, even her house if she wanted; she could settle for a home and future away from these people, the life she had known and the life she had lived; a home and a future not only for herself but for her daughter. Now that her feelings for him had diminished she realized that perhaps for her the age of love was over, that never again would she meet and love someone, really love them, as she had loved her husband. But with Longley she could lead a comfortable life. It would be a change but it would be a change for the better. There would be no more concern for the village, no more concern for her shops, no more concern for Barbara. Everything would be assured. She stood by the window and held back the lace curtain with her hand. She watched the light shake in the laurel shrubs as the wind rippled through the leaves. She knew she did not love him, but she was determined to put security before love.

And yet, she reflected, could she put security before honour? Mrs. Rutland believed in being true to herself. She believed if she was sure of herself she could be sure of everything; but a person not sure of himself could be sure of nothing. She understood there was ninety-nine reasons to justify a mistake but only one to vindicate a course that was right. That one was the truth in her heart. She did not believe in justifying herself to herself. For her it was never necessary. She lived by a goodness in her that needed no justification. Now she knew that the honourable thing was to stay and fight. She could enumerate the ninety-nine reasons why she should marry Longley, but she knew the one true reason why she should not. That one was the truth in her heart. She knew wherever she went, whatever she did, she would always know she had run away, that she had run from her village and her heritage at the very time she should have been true to both. And no matter where she went in the world she would know that at least once in her life she had not been true to herself.

Mrs. Rutland also believed in character. And she was not

sure whether Longley had the kind of character she admired. In the years since his return she had seen him get ahead not because of any strength of character but because of a capacity to work, a capacity that was not borne of ambition but of loneliness. He had no great desire to make money. He had no great capacity of decision. She had therefore come to the conclusion he was not a man of character. For no man of character would have returned to a town he did not like and lead a life of loneliness for which he was not adapted. No man would support such loneliness for three years without putting forward to the woman he loved the question which burned at his heart. He was lonely and she felt sympathy for such loneliness, but only he could resolve that. And if he could not find happiness in himself how could he find it for other people? She knew that a man could have everything in the world, yet if he lacked honour, if he lacked character he had nothing. Her mind drifted to the men that day in the pit. By Longley's standards they had nothing. Yet they had honour. And they had character. They had been prepared to fight for something in which they believed, probably not because they knew they would win but because they knew they had to be true to themselves. And if they, who had neither property nor wealth nor education, if they were prepared to fight, to be true to themselves, why should she not fight with them? It was this that had decided her. It was this that had changed her decision.

"I prefer to stay and fight," she said.

"You mean you put the village before me?"

"No," she said. "But I'm a realist. I see my life without the village is nothing. You said before that it's the past. And perhaps you're right. Perhaps I'm living in the past. Perhaps all of us in this village. But don't you see, it's my past, no-one else's. It's the only thing that belongs to me. That and the little plots in the graveyard where my mother and father and husband are buried. And if you take those from me there's nothing."

"I didn't say the village was the past," he said. "You said it for me. But it's true. The village is dead. Or if it's not dead it's dying. And if you stay — if you reject my offer — you'll die with it."

"Which means if I were to marry you I'd still have to sell. Because you wouldn't want to live here."

"We wouldn't have to live here. We'd be able to get out.

211

Follow the sun."

"So I'd still have to sell my shops. I'd have to sell at half the price. And my house too — everything at half its value."

"You wouldn't need money then," he said. "You'd have me."

"No," she said. "I wouldn't have you. I'd have your money."

"What's the difference? It's my money and I don't care. And if we married it'd be your money too."

"And what about Barbara? All her life she's been brought up to believe she'll be running the business instead of her mother. Carrying on the tradition. Even now she's studying at a business college in the city. And she likes it here. She likes the shops. She likes the business."

"She'd like it somewhere else just the same."

"But you don't see. If I were to marry you. If I were to sell. I'd be depriving her of a future. In five years my money would be gone — everything. What I have in the bank. And what I'd get on my property. The money on the house'd only be enough to buy me one somewhere else. So by the time she's twenty-five there'd be nothing for her. Absolutely nothing."

"Then marry her into money. Like everyone else."

She crossed from the window with her head uplifted, hands clasped together on her stomach.

"You're so old fashioned," she laughed. "As if anyone in our family would ever marry for money."

Longley leant forward to drink the last of the whisky. He felt cozy now, with the warmth of the whisky and the heat of the fire. Yet he felt sad too. For some reason that he did not know he was reminded of an Englishman he had met in Egypt, a painter who had wandered Europe in his youth. He once left London to spend three weeks in Sweden, but instead of three weeks he had stayed three years. He learnt the language and living in the villages sold his paintings to the country folk. Once he lived six months in Spain on an amount that would have seen him through a month in Paris. He was a painter of the impressionist school and went to Egypt because he thought the light would suit his paintings. He wanted to paint the sphinx as Monet had painted Rouen cathedral. Instead he became infatuated with an Egyptian belly dancer whom he met in one of the many sleazy clubs and when they married described it as the most divine experience in his life. Unfortunately, she was soon redundant, she turned fat in middle age, and as she

212

turned fat she turned quarrelsome. He never did finish his paintings of the sphynx. He had a wife and family to keep and came
to Longley for a job. Longley gave him an introduction to a
shipping office where he worked as a clerk dealing with shipments
of vegetable oil. He had lost his youth and his talent, his spirit of
adventure and his lust for travel, but how and why he had lost
them he could not understand. Longley felt his back against the
cushion and as he held the glass in his hand let the whisky on his
tongue roll a gentle flavour down his throat.

"So you're prepared to put the family tradition before your
own happiness?"

"The men in the colliery today were prepared to strike. They
were prepared to strike for something in which they believed.
D'you think they were doing it because of their jobs? D'you think
it was because of their homes? No. It was because of their life.
It's always been their life. And they always want it as their life.
And if they were prepared to strike to save the colliery — their
life — why shouldn't I be prepared to strike to save mine?"

"But how will you strike? What can you do?"

"Shall I tell you?" she said. "I've not the faintest idea. I
don't know how and I don't know when. But there's six months
to go yet and something'll turn up, you'll see."

Longley suddenly realized why it was he had remembered
the painter. He had remembered him because when last they had
met he had nothing to look forward to but death. Just as now
Longley had nothing to look forward to but death. Because he
had been trapped as the painter had been trapped, not by love but
by age, not by Egypt but by his own indecision. He ought never
to have come back to the north, he ought never to have delayed
so long his proposal to Mrs. Rutland. Now he saw his future as
a long glide to the grave, with his work and his rotary club, his
cocktails with clients, his lunches in hotel buffets, his trips to
London, his act as the big provincial businessman seeking security
with the people of his kind. People who sought security with him,
who were lonely as he was lonely, who drank at expensive bars
and paid expensive prices to warm their stomachs and make up
for the chill they felt in their breasts. He knew now he would
never leave the north. He knew now he would never take in
partners and hand his business to others. Even his visits to this
house and these grounds were numbered.

"I wasn't going to say this," he said. "But now I'm in the situation I have to say it."

He picked up the glass and juggled the dwindling lumps of ice against the rim.

"I'll marry you," he said. "And I'll stay here and fight."

"But you can't fight," she said. "You've nothing to fight for."

"I'll fight for all the things you want to fight for. All the things you want to save. I have money and friends and influence. And I'll make your cause my cause. Anything which you believe I'll believe." He looked up into her eyes. "If only you'll marry me."

She came and knelt at the side of the chair and took the glass from his hand. She laid the glass on the tray beside the bowl of ice and took his hand in hers. Her face was still uplifted and he could see in it all the strength that he lacked, that he so badly needed to pull him up. And she felt sorry for him then. For he would never know how close she had come to accepting. He would never know that but for the tidings he had brought, the sudden revelation of what the village meant to her and what she meant to the village, the action of the men that day in the pit, she would have married him. She would have placed him before herself and her past. Before the future of Barbara. She would have been prepared to leave if it had not been forced upon her. She would have been prepared to sacrifice if it had not been against her will. But he would never know because she would never tell him. And so she stroked the back of his head, feeling the soft dark hairs that curled round his thumb, the warm throb in his wrist, and looked into his face already lined with sadness.

"My dear Herbert," she said. "You're condemned by your own mouth. You've just said the village is dead. So how can you fight for a thing which is dead. Something in which you don't really believe?"

"I'll make it something," he said. "You'll see."

"No," she said. "You have to fight not for things which are true, but which you believe to be true. It's not a question of intellect. It's a question of heart. It's all very well now, in this moment, to say you'll fight. You'll use your money and your influence. And your friends. It'll be a different thing doing it for months or even years. And if you didn't really believe you'd be a traitor to yourself."

"I'd be a traitor," he said. "If that was what you wanted."

"But it's not," she said. "Either of you or any man."

They walked out to the car that stood at the front of the house. The water sprays were still playing on the lawn where the shadow of the house was cast, and the blossom continued to fall from the chestnut trees. It fell like a pale delicate snow and lay along the sides of the drive and around the daisies upon the lawn. A large copper beach at the end of the lawn opened its leaves like hands to catch the sun, drooping when the sun frowned behind a cloud, gathering its strength when it smiled to fill the cups of the open leaves. The rose trellis reared up at the front of the house, but the buds themselves were still in green. A sparrow flew out of the trellis as it heard their feet on the gravel and swooped to tread the husk-like blossom that bordered the lawn. They watched it nibble at the husks to while away the time. In the shadowed light of the house Mrs. Rutland saw the dried skin of Longley's face and the red tips of his cheeks where he had caught the sun. He turned, opened the car door and scratched the top of his lip with his finger nail.

"So there'll be no marriage," he said. "And no trips abroad."

"Not for me," she said. "At least not yet."

"Nor for me either, I suppose."

She did not say anything and they stood together for a moment at the side of the car.

"Tell me," he said. "Frankly. What'll you get out of it. If you fight and you lose?"

Mrs. Rutland raised a hand to her necklace and he saw again the smooth delicate skin of her throat. He saw too the soft silken strands of her hair, the freckles to her brow. And in her face the character, the honour, the honesty, saw them in the set of her lips, the firmness of her jaw, the uplift of her head as she looked over his shoulder towards the village. He saw here a woman who had lived and because she had lived had learnt the value of life; he saw a woman who had suffered too, yes she had suffered, but yet who had learnt to surmount her suffering. So that now she was able to stand erect, her shoulders straight, her back upright, as upright as her character. Reflecting on what he had said. It took a while for her to answer. But when she did she turned her head back to him and he saw a little moisture glistening the whites of her eyes.

"I can't lose," she said. "You can never lose. If you're true to yourself."

215

23

Gerald Holt met Barbara Rutland in a clump of silver birch trees near the river. To get to the clump one had to walk along the road where Mrs. Rutland had seen the car and drop down through the lines of fir trees to the group of forestry commission buildings known as Fiddlers' Green. The land dropped sharply then and the river ran below. In the blackberry season the road was so cluttered with cars driven from the city that a special car park had been sited in a clearing of the wood. The road tapered past the forestry commission buildings and dwindled to a narrow path of brown mud, gorged in winter by freshets, hard and dry now with the sun upon it. There were clumps of harsh tussocky grass on the path and at either side, fringing the young plantation, patches of gorse and broom, briars and nettles. The sun shone on the yellow heads of the gorse and the fronds of broom swayed weakly in the wind that stirred across the tops of the young firs. The sun was sinking rapidly now, its rays shooting across the heavens so that the thin fingers of cirrus that clung to the roof of the sky were red and scarlet and red again, shot through like silk. The river twisted silver and the leaves of the silver birch were powdered sage-grey in the fading light.

Gerald stood at the crest of the path on an eminence from which he could see the valley spiralling back towards the source of the river. He could feel the pallid strength of the sun upon his cheeks and forehead, the slight stirring of the wind through his hair. The land rose steeply on all sides, so that he could see at the head of the valley the water coolers of the nearest iron works, the dark cindrous heap where they poured the useless slag, the slag glowing incandescently in the night. There were the television masts at the highest point of the country that transmitted all the local and national programmes. And on the horizon, across from where he stood, a row of trees shaped like the back of a mole, and

216

further down, on the valley slopes, villages and collieries, heaps and pasture, with cattle in the fields, cattle so distant they were small irrelevant dabs of colour on the greyness. The crags to the river were steep and sharp and dangerous, but the water ran cool beneath, the current running swiftly through reeds and shoals of pebbles, past banks of sand, guiding the river through the wood to where the valley broadened below.

He dropped down to the ledge above the clump where she was waiting. The ledge was green with lichen and his tread so soft upon the moss she did not hear him coming. He had with him his raincoat slung across his shoulder, the coat tapering down his back so that the belt touched against his thighs. A horde of midgies darted above his head and somewhere in the plantation above the chiffchaffs were singing, whilst from the river below he could hear the current against the crags. She lay on her breasts and stomach in a green dress that laid bare her back but for the thin white strap of the bra that showed against the skin. Her shoulder blades rippled as her hands moved and from where he stood the skin of her back was soft and white and delicate. She had kicked off her shoes and with her legs stretched behind her, nylons twisted, she buried her toes in the soft grassy earth. She held in her hands a twig she had plucked from the ground and when she snapped the twig between her hands the crack of the wood set a wood pigeon hovering from the branches above her head.

She half-swung round when he dropped from the ledge and his restless hands had only to continue the movement to press her shoulders to the ground. Her hands and legs came round, her hips swivelled, her dress crumpled against her thighs, and dropping quickly beside her his hands fell across her thighs and stomach and breasts before they reached her shoulders. Above on the rock he had smelt the freshness of the fir trees and vegetation, below on the ground he smelt only the freshness of her body. He pressed her quickly back and gently kissed her lips. The sun burned through the trees upon his head and a dull red shadow from its glare crossed his eyes. Her hands stretched to his shoulders and his body was strong against her breasts and stomach and his face warm against hers. She had dimples for knuckles, but long tapering fingers, white and cool, that tenderly stroked the blond hairs on his neck. His raincoat billowed out upon the grass and the broken stick she had held in her hands fell back on the soft earth.

217

"I suppose you thought I wasn't coming?"

"I thought maybe by this time you'd gone to the meeting," she said. "At the institute."

"Everyone wants me to go to the institute. As if it had anything to do with me."

"You work at the colliery," she said. "And if they close the colliery they'll close the office."

"I know," he said. "But you see, I'm the only one who has nothing to worry about."

"How d'you mean?" she asked.

He rolled his weight from her chest and fell back upon his shoulders.

"I had a talk with Atkin today," he said. "And he's going to fix me up. He's going to find me a job in town. Give me the break I've been looking for."

He laughed and his laughter pealed out across the forest. His nerves were alight and as he rolled over on the grass he felt alive, so alive he wanted to shout, to sing, to laugh again, to tell the world he was alive. The scene he had had with his father that night no longer disturbed him. The talk he had had with his brother was out of his mind. He was glad to be out of the house that he hated, glad to be able to breathe the air of the country, to be able to move his limbs freely on the springy earth of the clump. And though he no longer thought of his father, though he no longer considered Ray, he knew the violence had done him good. He felt he needed a little violence to make him alive. He plucked up the stick Barbara had broken in her hands and flung it high among the leaves of the silver birch. It broke a twig from a branch and the two together fell to the earth like stoned birds. He felt his life was flowing, flowing not as a song, not as a melody, but as a landscape in nature. A landscape dark and brooding, bright and sunny, full of the sounds of thunder, the flicker of lightning. He wanted to be all men and no man. He wanted to be ten men in one and one man in ten. He rolled over and over on the turf and when he rolled back his coat was around his shoulders and his white shirt clustered with the threads of roots, the blades of grass.

"The way you're acting you'd think you were glad the colliery's coming down."

"Glad," he said. "I'm over the moon."

"And the village too, I suppose."

She turned her head from him and looked up through the trees to the sky where the cirrus was crisp and golden in the setting sun. The shape of the powdered leaves was stark against the cirrus and as the wind rustled through the twigs the sky seemed to tress and flutter like the wings of a bird. She was just twenty years old, every bit her mother's daughter, with the same complexion, the same soft skin, the same attachment to the village. Only where her mother's hair had silvered with the years Barbara's was still blond, streaked at the front where it had caught the sun. She had a large face not beautiful but pretty, the cheeks large with no accentuation of the bones, rich with natural colour, the lips large too but well formed and moist, like her eyes. Her body was large like her face, the breasts well formed but the hips large and heavy, her body rigid. She felt her weight against the earth as she looked up, head resting on her hands, heels prodding at her shoes, her legs feeling the softness of dried fir needles blown into the clump from the wood.

"I can't understand," she said. "Why it is you hate the village."

"Because it's dead," he said. "Because all the people who live in it are dead. And because I'm alive. Because when I walk down the street I see their dead faces. And I want to cry at them. Tell them how dead they are. Tell them to crawl away and really die. Get it over with."

She rested her head on her hands and brooded at the sky. She did not understand Gerald Holt. She had never understood him. He was a new force in her life, a force she had never known before, the force of discontent. She had been brought up quietly and peacefully by her mother, with her father dead, living in a house that was perhaps too large for their needs, but never wanting anything, never desiring something that was beyond her. She had never in her life asked for something which she had not got. To her life was like that, each man was born according to his station, each one was given the rudiments of his existence. And everyone was happy. She had never let anyone who wanted to grow out of his environment. Never met anyone who was angry at his birth. She turned from the sky and watched Gerald rake his fingers through the turf.

"You don't know what it's like," he said. "To feel alive — to know you're alive — and to see that life stifled. To want to shout from the rooftops. Swing yourself away into the air. Just because you feel alive."

"And yet," she said. "There's something else. Isn't there?"

Gerald's mood was as shifting as the shades of twilight. He raked his fingers through the turf, sitting with his back to her, leaning the weight of his body on an arm, looking down at the army of life his nails had uprooted from the turf. There was a softness in the air as the dusk grew near and the wood became alive with strange noises. The rustle of mice in the undergrowth, the croak of crickets by the river, the sound of firs rustling their tips, a cuckoo calling in clear tones across the clear space. He picked up the second part of the twig she had broken in her hand. He was aware of her eyes upon him as he looked down at the dried brown wood, the end rotting, the rottenness rich with insect life. He felt along the ridge of knots and peeled a little of the shrivelled bark with his hands. It dropped to the earth and immediately a small dark ant clambered upon it. He let the stick drop from his hand and turned to face her.

"I hate the village," he said. "Because I hate myself. I hate my origins. I hate the fact I was born poor. That I have to work in a job that means nothing to me. Absolutely nothing. Because I have a father who's ignorant and stupid." He stretched a hand to stroke her cheek and she felt the tips of his fingers gently stroking the skin. "And because I made a promise to a dying mother that I would only marry for love. So that I'm not sure what love is."

He laid his head on her breast and with his hand still caressing her cheek looked into her eyes. His were grey eyes, very pale but very direct and to her disquieting. They fixed upon her now and a little smile played about his lips. It was a guilty, uncertain smile, as if he had said too much. As if he had not wanted to say what he had said. But yet relieved now that it was off his chest. The weight of his head was pleasant upon her breasts and as she stroked a hand through his hair she plucked at a strand of root that had lodged behind his ear. She smiled back at him, showing her teeth, yet feeling uneasy, uncertain how the mood would take him. He was so moody often she could cry, at other times so bitter she felt his single ambition was to hurt. She lifted a hand to his wrist and felt the knuckle of the bone. She looked into his eyes, but they fell closed and she could see only the pale blood vessels in the lids.

"Do any of us know?" she said. "What love is?"

"Maybe none of us know," he said. "And maybe none of us'll ever know."

"But some people must," she said. "To get married."

"Then find out afterwards it's a mistake."

He was thinking of his mother lying on the bed and wondered what her life would have been had she not met his father. There were times he could see clearly the life of his mother, at other times he could not see it at all. She was a woman dedicated to the village and had she not married Holt she would have married someone else, a miner perhaps, or a tradesman, but certainly a man like Holt, only less coarse, more refined. A man less brutal. She had talked often of such a man, a man she thought she loved and intended to marry. He had owned the sweet shop on the corner by the cinema. They had been engaged and when he went to fight in the first world war she had promised to marry when he returned and the war was over. But he never did return. He was wounded in the arm and then in the back and finally gassed by his own company, the wind blowing back the gas over the wrong trenches. So her life took another turn and she married Holt instead.

"We still haven't answered the question," she said. "Of what love is."

"Perhaps I know it," he said. "But I'm not sure. If it's a beating of the heart. A pounding of the ears. The impulse to do crazy things. Then perhaps I know it. And if it's a warm affection, a kind of understanding, something that goes beyond feeling, beyond words, then I can recognize it, and I can say I know it. And if it's desire, strong lustful desire, then I know that too. But I distrust it. And because I distrust it it makes me uncertain.

"And which is it," she said. "You feel for me?"

He pulled his head from her breasts till his lips were close to hers, till his eyes were close to hers, till his hand could hold the tresses of her hair. His body lay at an angle to hers on the grass, his thighs and shins feeling the soft virility of the earth, his toes crinkling in his shoes. He did not know whether he loved Barbara or needed her to escape. He could not forget the promise he had made his mother. But he had not seen how such a promise would complicate his life. He had not seen how it would make him uncertain of what love was. His father claimed his mother had loved him because she accepted him. Yet his mother had told Gerald she had never loved in her life. Never really loved. And Gerald had promised that he would save his wife from the neglect, the cruelty, the coarseness that had driven her to the grave. But that did not teach him the definition of love. Till now he had shied of the village girls because he saw in them the shallowness he hated. He read their future in their faces. They had a contentment with menial things he disdained.

Barbara was not a village girl. He told himself that because she was born in the village she was not of the village. She had been educated in the city. She spoke with an accent that was refined, strange to his ear, with a nasal thickness that had nothing of the dialect of the country. And she was rich. She was cultivated in books and paintings, her outlook was broader, more intelligent, more understanding, than that of anyone he had known. And since she had money as well as leisure it seemed she could seek out the meaning of life, the meaning he was seeking himself, beyond his environment, beyond the confines of his birth. Gerald had few friends now, no-one to understand him. He had cut himself off from the pubs, the slothful drinking bouts that made him so popular. His friends thought him aloof, they thought him fanciful, they thought he was trying to cultivate airs that were above him. They thought he was hankering to marry into money. So now they discarded Gerald and followed Ray. They respected him still because he worked in the colliery office, they remembered with admiration the drinks he had swilled, the jokes he had given. But they let him go his own way, they did not bother him because he did not bother them. So that he was free to turn in the direction he wanted, seek refuge in the haven he had found, the counsels of Barbara Rutland.

But did he love her?

She was not an easy girl to love. She had never been taught the value of human warmth. She had never really discovered the exuberance of unrestrained feelings. In her childhood she had never been allowed contact with the village children. And when she began attending private school in the town there was no-one she had taken to as a friend. She found town children too distant, too wrapped in their own affairs. So that when Gerald met her, by accident at a city dance, he found her cold, unresponsive, her body too heavy, too rigid, and when he kissed it was not like kissing at all, more like flirting with a statue. She could not let herself go. She held her mouth closed when they kissed and his tongue could not penetrate her tightly set teeth. He had the feeling too that her eyes were open, that she was looking at him in a curious disinterested way, to see what he was getting out of it, waiting patiently till she could occupy herself with less embarrassing things. He felt she was not made for love. She left him frustrated. She was too cold, too withdrawn, her feelings too deeply hidden, to allow herself to be taken and crushed and born again, born and cleansed in the tenderness of love.

Often he asked himself why she went with him at all. Perhaps it was for the sake of his ideas, perhaps because at the time of their meeting she had nothing better to do. It did not occur to him she was going with him for the sake of himself. He thought perhaps as the village lad handling coal tickets in the colliery office he flattered her sense of superiority. He knew she was taking a commercial course in the city so that one day she might take over her mother's shops, but he could not rid himself of the feeling that she was being groomed for better things. She was being groomed to marry a university student or professional man, a man to be floated into society on the raft of a degree, a man already established, a solicitor, a doctor or dentist, someone devoting his life to the care of children's teeth. Someone who could offer her comfort, security and leisure. All the things she had been used to in her life. It did not matter to Gerald. He knew she would never marry him.

Yet he would not let her go. She had an intellect he admired, she was rational, she was sensible, and with her education, her learning, he felt he could talk to her. He could express himself, and by expressing himself he found he came to know himself better. His ideas crystallized, aspirations began to shape, he began explaining to her what it was he valued, though till the moment of explanation he had never quite understood himself. She was for him a stage on the way. And as he talked to her there was to her eyes a light of understanding, that he had looked for but never seen in his friends, that he had searched for but not found in the village. For that he was grateful. He felt all he needed was comprehension, the feeling he was not alone. So that he looked forward to seeing her, to talking to her, yet sometimes bitter because he knew he could not hold her, sometimes hurtful because he knew

223

she would never be his. Always as he slipped down to their meeting place among the trees there was at the back of his mind the knowledge that one day she would not come, that he would wait for her and still she would not come. He would learn then she had been sent away. And that, he knew, would be the end.

For Barbara Rutland, Gerald Holt was an experience that came once in a lifetime. She was not quite sure of Gerald and because she was not quite sure of Gerald she was not quite sure of herself. Now that she was twenty she told herself she was a woman. She must not attribute her mistakes to the errors of youth. She must act with maturity. And to act maturely one had to marry and settle and lead a stable life. This she felt became all women. But to marry one had to love. And did she know what love was? The same question troubled her as it troubled Gerald but for a different reason. She did not love her mother the way Gerald had loved his. She did not love her because Barbara considered herself a child of the village, just as her mother had been a child before her, but her mother had never allowed her to be part of the village the' way she herself had been part. This was not because Mrs. Rutland had anything against the village. It was merely because she wanted for her daughter the best education that money could give. And such an education was to be had not in the village but in the town.

The result was that Barbara had never had any contact with the village children. They were as strange to her as she was strange to them. She took the bus to school in the morning and took the bus back again at night. She wore the school uniform, tie, beret and blazer, and when she returned at night, clambering off the bus at Highhill Lane, the village children lay in wait for her by the gates to the estate. They lay in wait to pull the knot out of her tie, tear the beret from her hair, throw mud at the crest on her blazer. So that in order to escape she had to scramble over the wall into the estate rather than risk running the gauntlet to the gate. Sometimes the children even followed her across the wall, pulling off her shoes, lobbing them high among the limbs of the chestnut trees, where often they lodged till the gardener shinned up to collect them.

The children thought she was a snob. They thought she was stuck up. And she had only to open her mouth to confirm their opinions. After a while she began fighting back, kicking and scratching and pulling at ears, but often there were too many of them, so that she lost not only a little more of her dress but her pride as well. In those days her mother was too busy getting over the death of her husband to concern herself with her daughter. But even had she taken an interest Barbara would have been too ashamed to tell her. She had to think out for herself a course of action. She took to alighting from the bus at the churchyard a little further down the bank, creeping into the estate across the fields and through a break in the hedge at the back of the grounds. Later she took to going on into the village itself, cutting back across the fields to enter the gate by the wood. She never alighted at the same stop twice. Sometimes she took to excusing herself from school in order to catch an earlier bus, at other times she lingered deliberately in the town to catch a later one. So that in a while the children grew weary, their restless minds turned to other games, other pastimes, and it was not long before they began to leave her alone.

Barbara secretly blamed her mother for the attitude of the children. She reasoned if she had been sent to the village school she would not have been obliged to wear uniform, she would not have learnt to speak as if she had a plum in her mouth. She would have been no different from other children, and being no different they would have found no reason to pick on her. She did not like the town children. She found them narrow and self-centred. She preferred to remain aloof, withdrawn. Often she would be deliberately spiteful to any girl who tried to befriend her. She told herself she did not want their friendship. She felt she did not belong among them. She did not tell her mother what she felt, but often she asked why it was she should go to school in the town when others went to school in the village. Her mother replied that it was in her own interest; that she would benefit of it later, even be grateful for it. So the schooling continued, she moved from the primary to the junior, the junior to the grammar, and always she had to wear uniform, she had to wear a beret and tie and blazer, she had to take the bus in the morning and the bus at night. Only now there was no reception when she alighted at Highhill Lane.

Now she was twenty and the days of uniform were over. She attended a business college in the city where the dress was informal, where the girls were allowed lipstick and powder and nail varnish, the men casual shirts, bright ties and socks. But the reserve she had for her mother continued. Her mother would not allow her to attend a dance in the village till she was twenty-one. She claimed this had been the rule of her own mother and she did not see fit to change it for Barbara. Her daughter retaliated by asking what was the point in training her mind to take over the village shops when she was forbidden any contact with the village people. But Mrs. Rutland remained adamant. She was not so much influenced by the rigidity of her own mother as by the fact that the dance in the village had a reputation for rowdiness. She hoped the rowdiness would subside by the time her daughter was twenty-one. When she was twenty, however, she did concede to her attending an afternoon dance in the city, provided of course she went with a friend and returned in time for tea. Barbara made more friends at business college in the city than she did at school in the town, so it was not difficult to persuade at least one of them to attend the afternoon dance with her when college was closed.

Gerald rarely went to a dance in the city but had been persuaded by a friend to go one afternoon when recuperating at home after a night's drinking at the club. They had taken the bus to the city with the intention of taking in a film when the dance was over. He did not, however, find the dance interesting and wished he had gone first to the cinema instead. The band and the dancing were a little too sophisticated after the village hop. There was no foot-stamping here, no bee-bop, no little group of jive fiends dressed in wedge shoes and long-tailed coats the way you had at home. Everything was quiet, everything sedate. Even the cigarette smoke seemed to rise politely. He lost his friend and spent most of his time on the balcony sipping orangeade, looking down at the girls who converged at the left of the hall when each dance was over. One of them seemed familiar. She was a tall blond with a thick creamy neck, red cheeks and heavy face. She wore an alluring black dress with a silver string of pearls. He did not know why it was he should find and single her out, he did not know why it was she looked so familiar. Nor did he understand why he should be attracted. She was no better nor worse than any of the other girls in the hall. Indeed, looking around, there were many more beautiful then she. But attracted he was. He sipped his orangeade, waited to make sure she was with no-one in particular, then slipped down into the body of the hall to make his introduction.

Gerald Holt was different to the other boys who asked Barbara up to dance. He was five years older than she and therefore not one of the ruffians who years earlier had waited for her by the gates of the estate. She thought he was pulling her leg when he told her he came from Highhill. She thought he had been dancing with one of her friends. Yet in many ways he too was familiar. And his accent, though less rugged, with an effort at refinement, was of the colliery village. The striking thing about Gerald was that he said nothing to agree. She noticed other boys would say anything to make themselves pleasant. Gerald would say anything to make himself opposite. She told him she hated the city and loved the village. He told her he hated the village and loved the city. She told him she was being trained to run the business of her mother. He replied all training was worthless unless coupled with a philosophy for living. He was so sure of himself, of what he was and where he was going, of what could be done with life if he had the opportunity to live it, that as he swung her rapidly round the floor she almost had the feeling he was hurrying the future close. He never considered for a moment the opportunity he sought might never come. His grip upon her was so strong and forceful, and as they danced he spoke with so much feeling, so much emotion, that she was captivated. So captivated that when the dance was over she had not realized he was taking her home till he slipped off the bus at her side at Highhill Lane.

But did she love him?

It was a question she could not properly answer. In all the time she had been going to the dance in the city she had never allowed anyone to take her home. She had not even allowed anyone to kiss her. When her suitors discovered where she lived they lost all anxiety to take her to the step. And since she never accepted a date they never did get an attempt at the other. So that though she wanted to let herself be loved by Gerald she did not know how. She did not tell Gerald this was her first experience with a man. And because he did not realize this he believed her coldness came from within, her disinterestedness in him as a lover. There was no way she could make him believe otherwise. She wanted to marry and settle, settle to a stable life, a life of usefulness and effort, but since she could not let Gerald love her how could she ever know if she loved him? She lay on the grass and pondered this. He remained still with his head on her chest.

But now he had moved even closer and her lips were damp to his, his eyelashes tickled her cheeks, and the hairs on his neck were warm to the touch.

"What is it," she repeated. "You feel for me?"

"For you," he said. "I feel all of these things. A beating of the heart. A pounding of the ears. A rage because I know I can't hold you. And then I feel affection, a tenderness because I can talk to you. And because you listen and understand."

"Is that all you feel?"

"Not all," he said. "There are times — like the present — when I want to love you. Really make love to you. Suck the goodness from your body. Take the flower of your goodness and crush its goodness with my hands. But when I think like this, and I realize what I'm thinking, I'm disgusted. And I turn away from myself."

"And you think that's love?"

"I don't know," he said. "Maybe. But is it lasting love? That's what I want to know, is it lasting? Maybe my mother — maybe she felt like that for my father in the beginning. But you see it didn't last. And with me it's got to last. I couldn't go on. I couldn't live if it didn't."

He turned his head and his eyes looked out across the clump. He was thinking of the anger in his own nature, that turned so easily to violence, that could lead so easily to the irrevocable. He was thinking too of his mother, how he had loved her, really loved her, with a love that transcended sex, yet despite the strength of his love he had treated her badly. Why? What had made him so ill-tempered a son? What had made him so sharp and brutal? He did not know. He could only suppose he had inherited his father's nature, his father's instinct to hurt, his father's will to destroy the goodness he had seen in other people, a goodness he hated because he had not seen it in himself. For him, as for his father, marriage to a woman of goodness would be a disaster. So too would marriage to a woman who wanted to lead, to bridle his unruly nature. He could not tolerate guidance. He could not tolerate other people telling him what to do. So that his love might curdle, his life would be that of his father, the life of his wife that of his mother. And that he dreaded most of all. That for him would be the irrevocable. He let his eyes close and felt the skin of Barbara's chest warm to his ear, he smelt again the fragrance of her perfume.

the warmth of her body, and turned his head again to look into her eyes.

"And what kind of love is it," she said. "You feel for me now?"

He raised himself slowly from her chest and supporting the weight of his body on a hand felt the earth rich to his fingers. His open coat was creased where he had been lying and the knot in his tie was pulled down from the open collar. His free hand straightened the coat and dropped to press back the strands of her hair to the earth. The hair lay on the ground like strands of silk soft to the tips of his fingers. He smiled and his lips twisted, and lying across her body he brought down his head to kiss her ear. She felt the tip of his tongue against the sensitive inner skin and she brought her arms round his neck and pinioned his head close to hers. His face was above hers and as he looked into her eyes he saw they were helpless. His hands pressed back her shoulders to the earth, and in that moment he knew she was his, with her he could do anything, anything in the world. Yet he could do nothing. He brought up his hand till it touched the white of her throat, skin soft and golden where the sun had caught, so that he felt its delicate softness to his touch as he ran his hand to her chest.

"You know what it is," he said. "I feel for you."

24

They kissed and she closed her eyes and held her arms around his neck. The ache in her body accentuated when he ran the tip of his tongue along the lining of her ear, but now the stirrings she felt were like the pangs of a birth gathering momentum. The shadow of his face fell across the lids of her closed eyes, but as his lips peeled back her own his tongue met with the barrier of her teeth. His fingers explored between the rim of her dress and the rim of her bra and she felt the gentle pressure of their tips to the valley of her breasts. She held herself stiffly, clumsily, the touch of his fingers pleasant, exhilarating, and when she opened her eyes she saw that his own were closed, lost in the rapture of the kiss. A thought crossed her mind and she stared at him curiously. She saw how serious was his face, how strong, how handsome in its strength. The skin was pale, but the sun had brought out the freckles on his brow, it had dusted too his eyebrows, so that they were blonder than she had seen. The small hairs were blond on the tips of his cheeks, but the hair on his head was golden, carefully brushed and parted, so that he looked even younger than he was. She was still scrutinizing when he broke the kiss and opened his eyes and saw that her own were staring. He turned from her and rolled away on the grass.

"Always," he said. "The eyes open."

"I'm sorry," she said. "I was thinking."

"You're supposed to feel," he said. "Not to think."

He turned his face to the sun and its rays washed over his pale features. The rim of the sun crested the Pennines and bathed the valley in its light. The silver of the river was strengthened, the light flowed over the firs, and at the head of the valley the works were clothed in a thin haze. Even the colour of the long bone-like hills seemed sharper as the sun dipped down beyond the ridge and the light of its rays thrust across the sky in rose and yellow and gold. Gerald poised his elbows on the earth and rested his face in his hands. The rose tipped the furthest cloud, the yellow and gold rinsed through the valley, and with the sun dipping like a phoenix into its own fire, Gerald felt the air to his cheek changing perceptibly. The scents of the night seemed to rise with the setting sun, the tang of fir and thicket was quick to his nostrils, even the grass on which he lay seemed to offer its scent in immolation. The birds flew in and out of the haze and beyond the ridge a plane passed through the fire, and the fire glowed upon its fuselage.

"And what," he asked. "Were you thinking?"

She rolled over from her back till she was beside him.

"I was thinking there are lots of people in the world poorer than you. Much poorer. Only they don't feel about things the way you feel."

"That doesn't make things any better for that," he said.

"No, but everyone has to work. No-one in the world can escape that."

"That's right," he said. "Even if I was born the richest man in the world I'd still have to work. I'd still have to run myself into the ground, give myself heart attacks, just to make money. For myself and other people. But d'you think it was like that in the beginning? You'd think if God really wanted man to spend his life in an office he'd have sent him into the world properly equipped. With an umbrella and bowler. And a briefcase under his arm. But you see he didn't. He sent him with only enough to fend for himself."

"And what about environment? Don't forget, you're born where you're born, and that's all there is to it."

"That's true. But he gave him something that would help him climb out of environment. He gave him something that allowed him to endure in the hope of better things to come. Something above ambition, above shame. Above the despair you feel when you know you're poor. That enabled him to climb out of the deepest rut, the darkest hovel. So that he had the chance to make his own way."

"And what was that?"

"He gave him hate."

The plane moved out of the fire and the birds dropped down from the haze into the valley. The sun was gone now, but the strength of its glow did not weaken. The red and yellow and gold deepened, there came to the sky a tinge of green and purple, and as the sun plunged on its trajectory the colours widened the length of the horizon. The haze at the head of the valley began thickening to a mist, the light over the firs began to dim, and the silver of the river began to dwindle. Then slowly the red began to sink, began to weaken, began to fail, but the yellow continued to burn, the gold thickened in the valley, the furthest clouds held the glow of the sun's warmth and its last dwindling rays tipped the new clouds that appeared on the horizon. Only now the rays no longer touched the goldness of his hair, the blondness of his brows. Yet though the sun had gone the splendour of the sunset would not yield. And as the clouds continued to burn and flare, so the scents of the evening continued to rise, the air stayed soft to his cheek, and from the banks of the river the call of the crickets was sharper and more insistent.

"But if you hate the village so much," she said. "Why don't you leave now? Why wait till the colliery's closed?"

"Because first I've boozed all my money away. And second I have to see what Atkin turns up by way of a job."

"And if he does turn up with a job, what will you do then?"

"Depends first of all on the job," he said. "It's bound to be in the city. I wouldn't take it if it wasn't. Then when I had the job I'd move out. I'd leave the village. I'd lose my origins. Even if I have to burn down the house with my father in it — and Ray too, if he's around — just to make sure it's all dead. Then I'll go out into the world and live."

"But how can you live if you say you don't know what life is?"

"I'll find out," he said. "I'll live with awareness. I'll study everything I come across. The streets where I walk. The people I meet. I'm going to scrutinize those people. The way you scrutinize me when we kiss. I'm going to find out what life means to them. And when I find out what it means to them I'll find out what it means to me."

He brought his arms down to the earth and relaxed his chin on the back of his hands. He could see it as clearly as the sunset before him. He could feel it as palpably as the air against his cheek. He knew once he left the village there were many roads he could take. He could decide to make business his career, he could decide to travel, to see the world, or he could decide to remain a simple employee on the bottom rung of the ladder. With never an ambition to climb higher. His life would be in his own hands. It would be for him to decide whether it would be a success or a failure. It would be for him to decide whether it would be worthwhile. If there was success the success would be his, if there was failure the failure would be his too. Nothing would happen to him that he did not want to happen. His destiny belonged to him and to no-one else. He nuzzled his chin contentedly into the back of his hands. His thoughts warmed him as the sun warmed the clouds. The air was as exhilarating to his cheeks as was fancy to his mind.

"You'll not need me for that," Barbara said.

"But I will," he said. "I will."

"You'll need my advice," she said. "Not my love."

Probably it was true. He did not care to think about it. He knew there would not be many more meetings like this, her mother would find out and stop her coming, the colliery would close, the people disperse, and he would no longer be here himself. Once established in the city he would never see her again. There would be no reason. For him that stage of the way would be over. He would no longer need her to talk to, he would no longer need her to understand. He would meet with his own kind. With people who were alive, not dead as the village people were dead. He may even find then that Barbara was not alive at all. That he had only imagined she was alive. That in fact she was as dead as the rest of them. And yet there was a sadness within as he thought he might never see her again. So that he told himself one night he would wait for her outside the college. Just to give her a surprise. He would take her for a coffee, even to a dance, just for the sake of old times. To show her she was not forgotten.

"You know as well as I," he said. "Your mother would never let you marry me."

"My mother says I have free will. She says I can marry who I like."

"Even the clerk in the colliery office?"

"You'll not be clerk for long," she said. "But if I wanted, yes. Even the clerk in the colliery office."

He brought his chin from his hands and turned to stroke the skin of her back. The skin was warm with sweat, stained a little

233

with dirt where she had lain, with hairs of roots clinging to its warmth. He plucked the hairs away and let them drop from his fingers to the grass. His fingers came back to the skin and she felt them round the white strap of her bra. She had not turned her head but continued to look out of the clump through a break in the trees where the glow of the sun still shone in the sky. He could see very clearly the three knits in her forehead as she stared at the glow. They were not knits of worry but rather bemusement. As if she could not cope with the thoughts that flowed through her head. As if she still found life too much to grapple with. He placed his fingers under her chin and gently turned her face.

"That's not true," he said. "You know it's not true."

"You think because my mother happens to be a rich woman she's the kind that would want to plan my life. You think she's already got someone mapped out for me. But she's not that kind of woman. She's not got that kind of nature. She's too busy arranging her own life to worry about me."

She lifted her hand and removed Gerald's fingers from her chin.

"And your mother," Gerald said. "What will she do when they pull down the houses?"

"I don't know," Barbara said. "But I know what I'd like her to do."

"What's that?"

"I'd like her to stay here and do something about it."

"But you don't think she will?"

"No. I think she'll probably marry and go away."

Gerald turned on his back and laughed and again his laughter pealed across the forest. A few stray children answered his call and their voices carried to him like an echo. The children played by the river, the elder ones swimming in a pool cut out of the rocks below one of the crags, the younger ones skirmishing in the thicket, playing a game learned from their elders. Gerald cut his laughter short and listened to the splash of water, the breaking of saplings. The cuckoo no longer called across the open spaces but high against the sky a kestrel circled, and below the level of the fir trees the wood pigeons sped to their plunder. He watched their smoke blue tips against the sky. He laughed again and flung his feet high in the air, and his shoulders shook against the earth. The mice rustled in the undergrowth and the wood stirred uneasily under the strain of his voice.

"Marry," he said. "Your mother?"

"And why not?" Barbara asked. "She happens to be a very handsome woman."

"Maybe she is," he said. "But I never thought of her marrying."

"You don't understand my mother," Barbara said. "There's many a person wouldn't mind the chance. If she'd let them close enough."

Gerald swung himself back on his chest and his trousers were powdered with dust where he had lain on the grass. He grew suddenly very quiet. There was a clump a little beyond his extended hand, the clump not flattened by his rolling, and he reached forward to pick at the longest strand, removing the stalk neatly from its sheath, so that its end showed slim and white like his wrist. He placed the end between his teeth and sucked the juice from the stalk. There was a brittleness about him, a tension she did not understand, but which she had learnt to treat carefully. She did not know what went through his mind but she knew if she waited long enough she would find out. She stretched a hand to touch his fingers. And when still he did not respond she took the stalk from his lips and dropped it over his shoulder. He turned and looked at her.

"And does she know about me. Your mother?"

"Of course she does. She knows everything."

"You mean she knows I work in the colliery office?"

"It was the first thing I told her."

"And she knows where I live. In the slum quarter of the village."

"She doesn't care about a thing like that. Most of her customers live in the slums."

"She knows I'm a drunkard. That I drink like a fish?"

"You're not a drunkard," Barbara said quietly. "At least, not any more."

"That I'm a failure. An inferior?"

"You're not that either," she said. "Not in my eyes you're not."

"Then why don't I leave the village? Why don't I get out now? Why do I wait for the colliery to close. For someone to give me the opportunity. Why don't I make it for myself?"

235

"Because you're uncertain," she said. "Because you haven't the money. And because you've not the contacts to make the opportunity for yourself."

The softness of twilight lay across the country. The glow began to seep out of the clouds, the yellow that tipped the horizon was filtered through with crimson, the colours of purple and green that had accompanied the setting of the sun began to weaken and fade, with no longer a phoenix flame to nourish them. The sky returned to crystal, the crystal glowed with the twilight, but the light over the land was less sharp, less distinct, more sombre and grey and ugly. There was no longer a silvery thread to the river, only a muddy meandering brown, the water coolers and ironworks at the head of the valley were already lost in the thickness of the haze, and soon the haze would turn to mist. Only the Pennines to the left held their pristine sharpness. The heaps at the other side of the valley were dark shapes among the green fields, the village houses vague forms against the grotesqueness of the heaps. And the red structures of the pitheads were already lost in the greyness.

"So there's hope for me yet," he said.

"Of course there's hope," she replied.

"And you think one day I'll make the break. Leave it all behind?"

"We'll make the break together," she said. "If you want."

He pulled himself close to her on the grass and looked deeply into her eyes. They were green eyes, the green cloudy and speckled, the whites not exceptionally white but a little pigmented, a little muddy. He looked to see if she were playing with him the way he often played with her. But all he could see in the eyes was honesty and sincerity. And he realized that perhaps she loved him, that perhaps for once in his life his inferiority was wrong, that she could be his if he wanted, his origins meant more to him than they did to her. That there was nothing to stop them marrying and settling, that the experience of a father need not be repeated in the son. He rolled her over by the shoulders so that she lay on her back and looked up into his eyes. All he had to do was bend down and take her, not only for this moment but all the moments that mattered in the history of the world.

"Would you really marry me," he asked. "Really and truly?"

"I don't know," she said. "Maybe."

236

"D'you think we'd get on. If you did?"

"I'm not sure," she said. "We might."

He gave a little shake of his head and turned from her.

"You're too young," he said. "Your mother'd never let you marry me."

"I may be too young now," she said. "But in a few months I'll be twenty-one. Then she couldn't stop me if she wanted. And she wouldn't. If I really and truly wanted to marry."

He lay across her body and kissed her again. And this time he did not open his eyes to see whether her own were staring. He held her close, closer than he had ever held her, closer than he had ever dared hold her. So that he felt the heat of her body against his. He felt the touch of the body less rigid, more supple, less heavy, more lithe and co-operative. And for once she let his tongue pass the barrier of her teeth, she let herself yield, yield to show that she meant what she said. That there was hope yet. That there was nothing to stop them marrying if they wished. She placed her arms around his neck and felt again the weight of his body across her breasts. She felt the touch of his hands to her shoulders, his thigh against her thigh, her stomach bearing the strength of his. But she did not see the lids of his closed eyes. She did not see the sky through the foliage of the trees. She did not see its subtly changing crystal, the slight wind that clasped together the sage-tips of the leaves. For this time her own were closed.

"Gerald," she said. "Is it true about your father?"

25

The kiss was broken now and her lips were damp from the pressure of his.

"What d'you mean," he asked. "Is it true?"

"That he's going to marry one of the Walton girls. The one on the milk cart."

"I didn't know you knew anything about the Waltons."

"I don't," she said. "But I know enough."

"Yes," he said. "It's true."

"Just think of it," Barbara said. "A mother-in-law younger than yourself."

"I haven't even proposed to you yet," he said.

"I would be though. All the same."

With his weight no longer across her body, his head to one side staring at the clumps of grass, she could see the sky above her head no longer tressed and fretted in the light of the sun. The cirrus had drifted on, the stars were not yet out, and beyond the foliage of the trees there was only the sky, limitless, darkening now, the darkness reaching back to its own infinity. Would her own future be the same, she wondered. Her life would collapse with the village, her mother would marry and go away, there would no longer be her shops, her cars, the shares to manipulate in the bus company, there would no longer be a house too large for their needs, with grounds opened twice to the public. There would only be she and Gerald Holt, making their own way, probing the darkness, seeking for themselves a new life with neither of them involved, a life based on happiness and content, but not attachment. Was it the life she wanted? The question was so selfish she felt it did not deserve an answer. It would not be what she wanted but what her husband wanted. She was twenty now and she was a woman and a woman's place was with her husband.

"I'll put it to my mother," she said. "That we get engaged.

At Christmas. And then if we still feel the way we feel now we'll marry and go away. We'll settle down together."

"With the blessing of your mother?"

"With the blessing of my mother. But she'll want to see you. She'll expect you to come to the house and talk things over. That's her right."

"I'll come," he said. "Gladly."

So it would come out as he expected after all. All that he had envisaged in the kiss would be his. He would leave the colliery office, he would take new work in new surroundings, he would live in the city and not a village. But more than that, he would have Barbara and he would have money. He would have the culture, the width and breadth of education that money could bring. He would not always have to work, perhaps once married he would be able to seek out the life he wanted without it, he would be able to forget his father, he would no longer concern himself with his brother. It came to him, what his mother had once said, that he should look after Ray, that he should take care of him, because the two of them they would get up to some daft things before they were through. He did not know why he should remember this and why remembering it should stay in his mind. But now he would be free of his brother as he would be free of his father. He would break the chains that held him, he would rise above his class, he would pass beyond the gravity force of the village that till now had weighed him down. And once he was free, once he was weightless, he would let nothing stand in his way.

Nothing.

"And what will you do about your father?" she asked.

"What about him?"

"How will I explain him to my mother?"

"Probably she doesn't know."

"She may not know yet. But she'll find out."

A dimness closed around them and on the horizon lights began twinkling. In the crystal sky the first star began to appear above the still distinct line of the Pennines. But from the river Gerald could no longer hear the splash of water and from the thicket the break of saplings. By now the children had gone and the silence around them was the silence of the forest. Soon it would be broken by the call of night jays, the call of owls, the flap of returning pigeons, the tread of foxes. But for the moment the silence lay around them like the dark. The trunks of the silver birch trees stood out in stark relief against the crystal, but now the crystal was deepening, darkening to blue, the blue darkening to black. Already it was losing its polish. So that he could no longer make out the plantation of firs, the muddy brown of the river, even the blades of grass in the tussocks beyond the strands of her fair hair. The glow of headlamps swathed through the dusk from a car along a country road and the blue pinpoints on the horizon sharpened in the gloom.

"I'll fix him," he said. "Somehow or other. I'll fix him."

Book Four

Ray's Secret

26

In the dusk Ray Holt led the men from the institute down the cinder path to the social club that stood beyond a patch of sparse grass near a small disused heap.

He led them down the path where he had carried the books and paused beneath a narrow low-slung bridge that linked the drift with the colliery. Beyond the bridge, skirting the heap, were the houses being demolished by the council. The houses had been vacated some years earlier because of the encroachment of the heap, but it was only now they were being destroyed. The windows to the houses had long since been broken, the frames rotted, beetles and cockroaches had lived in the dust and damp, docken and dandelion allowed to grow in cracks in the floor. Occasionally mice had scampered in and out among the ruins in search of food. But now the mice had been frightened by the sound of the demolition hammers, the beetles and cockroaches choked by dust, docken and dandelion uprooted with the floors. Now the dust of the day's work had settled, walls were flattened, pavements uprooted, timber rafters and cross beams left to tumble among the broken slate and brick, fireplaces had been pulled out, stairs and ceilings destroyed.

And only the chimneys allowed to stand against the sky.

The men flushed from the hall and followed Ray down the bank. They followed without knowledge of where he was going, where he was leading. But they picked their way past boulders and channels in the cinder in the hope he was leading somewhere. They had been too long in the meeting. There had been revealed things which angered them, but more than that had made them afraid. They had asked for facts and been given promises, they had asked for promises and been told lies. Now they were glad to be out of the heat, away from the sweat, the confusion they had seen in Wishart. They wanted action and not words. Some were already so stirred they expected Ray to lay destruction to the colliery, others to set upon the house of the manager. But he did neither of these things. Instead he brought them to a halt at the bottom of the bank. Those behind pushed over the heels of those in front, they pushed and floundered, and tipping their caps and fumbling their hands in their pockets muttered, growled and threatened among themselves. Till they saw the chimney stacks against the sky.

And each one realized, without communicating with the other, that what he was looking upon was not the destruction of a handful of houses but the destruction of himself. Here was not brick and mortar being destroyed but body and soul. Each one remembered the tap of the demolition hammers he had heard that evening on his way home from the pit, each one remembered the tinsel flames he had seen from the tubs already being destroyed on the heap. And each one realized that perhaps even now it was too late, the destruction had begun, not the destruction of the village but of himself. And not only his life but the life of his wife and children. Each one looked in the same direction and each saw for himself the dust that lay in the street. Each one saw the paper that hung ghost-like from broken walls, the white shadows on the stacks where the fireplaces had been, the cornerstones broken asunder, the bulwarks that framed against the crystal sky. And each looked to Ray Holt to see what he would do.

Ray led the men across the sparse grass to the social club. It stood below the pithead baths in the lea of the disused heap. To get to it from the direction of the institute you had to cross a small footbridge which spanned a burn that suddenly came out of the ground through an iron grill and disappeared fifty yards later through another grill. The burn carried pit water down toward the river. Opposite the club on the side away from the heap were the co-operative houses Gerald had seen from his window, and at the bottom of the houses stood the corrugated bus garage, with its concrete apron, its petrol and water tanks, its heap of refuse and stack of threadbare tyres. There was no recognized road to the social club, no pavement till you reached its door, only a bouldered track that led from the footbridge, another that led through the nettles from the co-operative houses. But for all its lack of trimming, the club was a tall magnificent building, two-storied, with bars upstairs and down, several committee rooms often hired for private parties, a lounge with a television, a select, a room furnished specially for bingo, and upstairs a concert hall known as the singing end.

It was in the singing end that Ray held his meeting. The hall was larger than that of the institute, with a platform for artists, and on the platform a piano, drum and cymbals carefully covered, three chairs and of course a microphone that could be adjusted to suit the height of the speaker. The microphone was connected throughout the building so that everyone in the club would hear what Ray had to say. Chairs and tables had been left in the body of the hall and drinks would be served from the bar in an alcove to the right. There were two pumps in the bar, one for mild and one for bitter, rows upon rows of glasses, and beyond the glasses on ledges before the mirror, bottles of brandy, whisky, rum, sherry and gin. And beside them on the ledge a single bottle of eggflip. Only the eggflip would be left before the end of the evening. The men flooded into the hall and stood or sat around the tables. They stood around the bar. And when the hall could hold no more, when the seats and standing room were taken, they filled the passage and stairway or filtered to the public bar, the lounge, the select, even the room furnished for bingo. And all of them were thirsting not only for drink but for action.

Ray waited patiently for the men to settle, to slake their thirsts and ease their tired feet. They were in a vicious mood, he knew that, a mood he had to treat with care. Just as he had to treat himself with care. He had made one mistake that night, he did not want to make another. He told himself not to lose his head, he had to be governed by his intellect, not by his emotion. He had to chart the course that he had elected for himself. He had to steer the men to that course. But they were as a tiger to be ridden, they wanted action now and not tomorrow, they wanted him to strike tonight with violence and anger and hate. Just as they had in the old days. Just as their forefathers had done before them. Then when they were discontented with the management they threw the corves down the shaft, or upset the gin that hauled the coal to bank. Now when they were angry they wanted to be led upon the heapstead. They wanted to destroy the time cabin, the weigh cabin, the screens and the engine sheds. They wanted to tear up the tracks with their hands. They were seeing their own lives destroyed and in turn they wanted to destroy something else.

Ray adjusted the microphone to suit his height and flung off the jerkin that made him sweat. His throat was still open at the neck and the sleeves of his grey shirt hung round his wrists till he tidied the cuffs round his elbows. The air in the hall was cool and fresh after the institute. The lights seemed sharper, less brittle, the windows were already open to let in the air, the current that sifted through was soft to their faces, and the sounds of the evening were drowned by the voices of men and the tramp of feet on the stairs. Already the steward was filling pints at the bar. And already Bousefield and Walton were ferrying drinks among the tables. Ray licked his own dry lips and felt his hands cool to the metal of the microphone. He felt in need of a drink, badly in need, but he decided to wait, his speech might be better if his throat were dry, he had as much to say now as he had at the institute, only he had to be careful how he said it. The men's voices raised in a crescendo around him. He blew into the microphone to see if it worked and immediately he did so the crescendo ceased. And suddenly, in the silence, all he could hear was the pulling of pints, the sliding of glasses along the surface of the counter, the scraping of feet as men turned from the bar. Turned to hear what he had to say.

"So now," he said. "We knaa where we stand. We knaa exactly what the situation is. Everythin' I said in the pit the day was reet. And everythin' Wishart said was lies. Everythin' I told ye in the pit the day was based on fact. And everythin' Wishart told ye at the institute based on hearsay. Hearsay given him by the management to keep us quiet. To keep us in our places till they close the colliery and destroy the village. Wishart says there'll be other jobs for us. But jobs where our wage'll be cut by ten pounds a week. Wishart says we'll have a settled future. So we can all reach retirin' age wi' contented minds. But it turns out his idea o' retirin' age is fifty. So half on us should be retired already. And the half that's not'll soon be wishin' they were. But Wishart says we've nowt to worry about. Neither for ourselves, nor for our wives and bairns. Everythin's ganna be all reet. Accordin' to him.

"Wishart says they're ganna send us to collieries where the seams are higher. Where the work's better. Where there's not so far to walk from the shaft bottom. Where we've got a bit o' height so we divin't get cramp in our backs. But when I ask him where all this is. Where we've got to gan to find these conditions. He says

Staffordshire. And when I ask him where we'll be livin' when we get there he says in houses. And when I ask what kind o' houses, he says houses that's not yet built. That's what he says, ye heard him yersel'. So when I asks where we'll be livin' afore the houses are built he says we'll be livin' in lodgin's — digs he thinks they call them down there. And I'll warrant ye now that when ye get there ye'll find that his digs'll turn out to be huts. Huts not fit for wives and families. Not even fit for a man that's got to gan out each day to dee a hard shift's work.

"But it's all reet, ye see, because accordin' to Wishart ye divin't have to gan if ye divin't want. Because there'll be plenty of other jobs here. In the area. For them lucky enough to be fixed up. But what kind o' work and in what kind o' pits? Datal work. In pits just like the one here. Pits that are losin' money, pits that have narrow seams, pits where ye have to walk miles to get in and miles to get out. Pits turnin' out the same kind o' coal as we are. Coal that cannot be sold. That has to be heaped on bank. Pits that'll close themselves in a year. Because the economics that apply to this colliery apply to every colliery in the area. So if this colliery's got to go ye can bet yer boots there'll be others not far behind. And as surely as we'll be transferred from this pit we'll be transferred from another. As surely as there's a few men laid idle here there'll be a few more the next time. And so it'll gan on, driven from one colliery to another. Till ye get to the end o' the line. And for us ye knaa what kind o' line that means."

"That's reet," Walton shouted. "The dole."

The press was so great in the singing end he could no longer ferry drinks among the tables. The sweat was damp to his hair and stood out in white globules along the rim of his forehead. He brushed back his hair with his hand and dabbed at the sweat on his brow with his fingers. He stroked his fingers down the side of his coat to rid them of their dampness. He had hurried down the bank ahead of Ray and the rest of the men to forewarn the steward of their coming. And since the first man had entered the doors after Ray and made his way to the singing end Walton had not himself stopped for a drink. So that he longed to enclose in his fingers the handle of a pint and glanced from Ray on the platform to the men who turned from the bar. Froth still clung to their lips and to the sides of their glasses where the beer had been drunk. He did not return their glance but ran his hand again down the side of his coat and swallowed at the dryness of his throat. He felt a tug at his arm and turned to find the steward with a glass of brandy.

"Here," the steward said. "Take a sip o' this. It'll soon quench yer thirst."

"Ye mean ye're treatin' us to a brandy?"

"I'm treatin' ye to nowt," the steward said. "It's not me that's payin'. It's him up there."

"Ye mean he's payin' for all the drinks. Everythin' that's bein' supped?"

"That's reet. It's all on the house, he says. Every drop on it."

Walton took the brandy and turned back from the bar to stare at Ray. Ray spoke with a feeling and emotion that were apparent in his voice. He did not have to shout as he had at the institute, for with the microphone he had only to speak softly to make himself heard. At the institute he had let slip his dialect, he had lost the roughness from his voice, he had tried to speak as clearly and as precisely as Wishart. But now at the club there was little need for such pretence. He could speak in his own voice, his own dialect. He could use the vernacular of the village of which he was proud and would not change for anything. For contrary to his brother he was proud of his origins, proud of the fact he was born poor, proud to be part of a community he loved so well. He grasped the microphone with his right hand and stretching out his left pointed at the wall in the direction of the colliery. He gesticulated with his hands and clenched his fists to make his points. His hair continued to fall over his brow and he flung back his head to remove it from his eyes. He did not speak too quickly, too rapidly, but he made his points with force, with deliberation, so that his voice carrying through the club was everywhere understood by the men.

"That's reet," he said. "On the dole. Or at best takin' yer chance at Staffordshire where Wishart says there's work. Where Wishart says the seams are high. But what he didn't tell ye is that the higher the seams the fuller the mechanization. And the fuller the mechanization the less hands required. So that by the time ye get there, by the time ye settle in a hut with the chance of a house in the future, there'll be what they call another contraction in the industry. There'll be more men laid off. There'll be more coal produced but less men producin' it. And who d'ye think'll be the

248

first to get the sack? D'ye think they'll cavel for it the way we dee here? Not likely. It'll be last in first out. So that even if ye did get yersel' down there, even if ye did want to live in a hut, even if ye did want to separate yer wives and families from their kith and kin, it wouldn't be long afore ye're in the same boat there as ye're in here. Without a job. Without a settled weekly wage. With nowt to look forward tee and nowt to look back on. With nee future in the industry ye've worked in all these years. That yer fathers worked in afore ye. And yer grandfathers afore that.

"But what's there in Staffordshire for the likes of us? The people down there are not our kind o' people. They divin't even understand our kind o' language never mind our kind o' ways. They're not a community the way we're a community here. Here, we're all friends, we're all neighbours, we share each other's troubles, we buy each other drinks. It'll not be like that down there. Ye'll be on yer own. Yer wife'll be on her own. Ye'll not knaa yer next door neighbour from Adam. And what's more ye'll never get to knaa him. 'Cause he's not interested in ye and yer life. He's not interested in where ye come from and who ye are. He's only interested in hissel'. His own life, his own little troubles. They're all like that in the south. There'll be nee canny folks the way they're canny here. So let's not think o' shiftin' down there. 'Cause this is our home. This is where we live. So why cannot we be left in peace? Why cannot we live our own lives. Why cannot they provide jobs for us near our homes instead o' buildin' us houses near jobs. Why cannot they see our point o' view instead of always askin' us to see theirs?

"I'll tell ye why. 'Cause at the bottom o' them they divin't care. They're bureaucrats, ye see, and bureaucrats divin't care about neebody. In fact, they wouldn't knaa a real person if they saw one. For them we divin't really exist. That's why when they destroy the colliery they want to pull down the village. 'Cause they cannot understand how anyone can be attached to such a place. That for them has neither use nor ornament. That's not even part o' civilization. Ye see, for them we're people not worth respectin'. We're just country hicks stuck in the backwoods. So we can be pushed around, we can be told to live here, we can be told to work there, we can be told the first thing that comes into their heads. 'Cause for them we've not got a past, we've not even got a present. We've only got a future. Their kind o' future. A future they figured all by themselves without askin' us whether we want it or not.

"But what's their reason for pullin' down the village after they close the colliery? 'Cause ye see even bureaucrats and planners have to have a reason. It wouldn't be fun if they didn't. So what's their reason for destroyin' our little bit o' lives, the only lives we've got, the only lives we want? I'll tell ye. It's 'cause they understand that everythin' in the village revolves around the colliery. So they reckon if they close the colliery they might as well pull down the houses. 'Cause if there's nee work, if there's nee colliery, there's nee reason why people should stay. So they decide they'll shift us away. They'll shift us into the valley where there's plenty o' work. They'll see to it that we have all the advantages o' what they call the affluent society. 'Cause it's not the first time they've done this. And it'll not be the last. They even have a fancy name for it. They call it conurbanisation. Which means they're shiftin' people about against their will. They're shiftin' people to places where they divin't want to gan. They say there's nee work for us here but they'll direct us to places where there's plenty.

"Only they forget one thing. Maybe there is plenty o' work in the valley — and maybe there's not tee — but if there is it's not our kind o' work. 'Cause the pits are not in the valley, they're in the hills. And that's where the Coal Board say they'll fix us up. At collieries in the area. So though the Coal Board's movin' us to work in one direction, the planners are movin' us to live in another. So instead o' walkin' from yer front step onto the bank top ye'll have to take the bus ten to twelve miles. And in some cases maybe even further. But what'll ye dee in winter time? How will ye dee when there's three and four feet o' snow and the buses cannot get through? Will ye walk the twelve miles there and the twelve miles back? Well, good luck to them that's willin', that's all I can say. Good luck to them that's prepared to dee it for a datal wage."

The men stirred restlessly. It seemed to them there was no way they could turn. But they did not feel now as they had at the institute. The air was less stuffy, more fresh, their feet did not seem so hot or so tired, the beer had damped their throats and filled their stomachs. It had reached too their blood stream. So that they were no longer disgruntled at standing so long in a confined space. They were no longer so anxious to destroy the colliery and attack the house of the manager. They were in what so many describe their natural habitat, the social club where they spent so much of their leisure time. Clubs that had come down in history, as they themselves had come down, that were as much a part of their working life as the headstock that stood on the heap. There were three such clubs in the village. And each club was run by the members themselves. They elected a committee, appointed a chairman and secretary and steward, they had their annual darts tournament, their leek show, their vegetable show, their weekly concert and their go-as-you-please. They brought along their wives at the weekend but never during the week. For then they discussed their pigeons and their allotments, their luck with the football and the horses, they had their bingo nights, their buff nights, their domino nights, their dart nights, their snowball.

So that if the village revolved around the colliery their social life revolved around the club.

Bousefield drained his pint and pushed the empty glass across the counter to the steward. The steward had dropped his own glass into the silver trough beneath the pumps and feeling the touch of water to his knuckles began rising the pint glasses to be washed, setting them on the silver bench to drain. He took Bousefield's glass and filled it automatically from the pumps and passed it back across the counter. The red plastic on the counter was stained with the rivulets of beer, the water that dripped from the steward's hands, and the glass slid through the rivulets till it reached Bousefield's elbow. Without turning he raised the glass to his lips. He was too absorbed with what Ray had to say to notice the tug of the steward's hand on his elbow. But when the steward tugged again he laid down the glass and turned. The steward indicated the glass and nodded to Ray on the platform. "Ye'd better get that one up to him," he said. "Divin't ye think? After all, he's payin' for it. He might as well have one hissel'."

Bousefield looked at the pint. "Ye're reet," he said. "I never thowt o' that."

He began his way from the bar around the wall to Ray on the platform. He held the glass above his head as he forced his way through the press. Ray did not see him coming, for he was intent on what he had to say. There was in him a sense of power, a knowledge he could do anything with these men. There was in him still the urge to do something drastic, but he remembered

Wishart at the institute, the spots of blood upon the platform, and held himself in check. Yet as the men's tempers began to cool his own began to rise. For his words affected him no less than the men. Only where they had beer to cool their tempers he had none. His voice began to crack with the dryness of his throat, there was no more saliva to be licked upon his lips, even his tongue had dried on him. As he continued to speak his cuffs fell around his hands, he pushed them loosely aside till they flopped again, he could not keep still his body, and his feet shuffled on the platform. Yet his voice, though controlled, remained clear throughout the club.

"So what I say is this. I divin't mind if they pull down this colliery, I divin't mind if they take us off the face at number nine. With its eighteen inches o' dust and damp. I divin't mind if they leave nowt but the rats, if I divin't have to get up any more for fore shift. There's some, they reckon they work fifty years in the pit and still never get used to gettin' up at two o' clock in the mornin'. In fact, the older they get the more they come to hate it. I cannot imagine I'll hate it any more in twenty years than I dee now. I'll be resigned to it, maybe, but I'll still hate it. So divin't get the idea I want to fight because I love the pit, divin't get the idea I hate and dread the next shift any less than ye. Because I divin't. It's because there's nowt I can dee outside the pit. And if they close this colliery they jeopardise me livelihood, if they move us somewhere else they make it harder for us to make a livin'. Till the day comes when I cannot make it at all."

"But I say I divin't mind if they close the colliery. Provided they let us stay in the village, provided they let us stay in the place where me father has lived, where me grandfather lived afore him. And where all me forefathers lived afore that. This is a democracy, so they tell us. And the first reet in a democracy is that ye can live where ye like. It's a free country, so they say, and in a free country ye live where ye want to live. Not where the government tells ye. So I say this to the planners. I say I divin't mind movin' house, I divin't mind if ye deprive us o' the only life I've ever known, if ye find us another job, find us another village. Find us a house where the people are strange, find us a colliery where the work's different. Even pay us the salary ye have a mind. But on one condition. That ye planners, ye faceless men, ye come with us, that ye give up yer house, yer job, yer security, yer little bit o'

252

peace and happiness. That ye give up everythin' yer askin' us to give up, dee all the things ye're askin' us to dee. Then I'll gan. And peacefully at that."

He took the drink that Bousefield handed him and raised it to his lips. The beer washed over the dryness of his throat and he could trace its course to his stomach. He closed his eyes and felt the glass lightening in his hand. He had the men where he wanted them, he had persuaded them from immediate violence. He had soaked their anger with drink and let inaction stiffen their bones. Now he would tell them about their homes, the demolition that would deprive them of the village. He would see to it that their anger matched his own, that despite the rest they had taken, the drink they had consumed, they would be stirred again. He would tell them what he had planned. He would reveal to them what he intended. And just as he revealed to them so he would reveal to the world. That not only was their patriotism to a country but patriotism to a way of life, not only would man defend his native soil he would defend his native home. He let the beer roll over his tongue and with eyes closed saw everything as it would be. He saw it as clearly as he had envisaged it that day in the pit. But now was the time of action. He handed the glass back to Bousefield and as he swung round to give his attention to the men caught sight of Featherley in the hall.

Featherley had a place of his own at the back in the only spot where there was room for manoeuvre. For unlike Bousefield, the men were not accustomed to the smell of pigs' dung and manure that clung to his clothes. They could not abide the rich odour of pigs that rose from his hands. Those that had endured his proximity at the institute had seen to it they did not endure it again. And those placed near him at the back of the hall had quarantined him as best they could behind a table. With the result that despite the flood of beer that issued from the pumps some had yet to reach him. His look was therefore one of dejection and bemusement. He had followed Ray down the bank and listened carefully to his speech from the platform. But there were so many things beyond him, so many things he did not understand. His eyes wandered to the ceiling and in his dejection the scar across his eyebrows was more accentuated. In his bemusement the twitch in his cheek grew more convulsive. He heard someone call his name and stirred to see from whence the call came. It was not for

253

a moment he realized it came from Ray on the platform.

"Alfie Featherley," Ray shouted. "Ye're a neighbour o' mine in Ramsay's. Ye have a house in the same street. Ye keep yer pigs on the allotment opposite yer house. But what d'ye think is ganna happen when they pull down the house? What d'ye think is ganna happen to ye and yer father. And what d'ye think'll happen to yer pigs?"

"I divin't care what'll happen to me father," he said. "It's me pigs I'm worried about."

"All reet then, never mind yer father. What ye think'll happen to yer pigs?"

"I divin't knaa," he said. "I keep askin'. But neebody seems to knaa."

"I'll tell ye," Ray shouted. "Ye'll be shifted out yer house to a council house in the valley. Ye'll have runnin' water, ye'll have electricity, ye'll have a garage in case ye decide to run a car, ye'll have a garden to keep up, ye'll have a 'frigerator in the house, ye'll have cookers and stove and everythin' ye want. Ye'll even have a plug for the television."

"But me pigs divin't watch television."

"I'm not talkin' about yer pigs. I'm talkin' about ye and yer father."

"But I divin't care about me father. All I care about is me pigs."

"Ye'll have to shoot them wi' yer gas gun. Ye'll have to auction their carcasses for the best ye can get, ye'll have to raffle them in the club in the hope ye'll make more that way than if ye sold them in town. Because movin' to a new house is like movin' to heaven, ye cannot take them wi' ye when ye gan. There'd be nee place for them. And even if there was they'd not be allowed. But this is not only Featherley's problem, it's all our problem. Men with allotments, men wi' hens, men that rear pigeons. That have greenhouses full o' plants and tomatoes. They'll all be left behind. Left here wi' the past."

He flung out an arm and indicated someone in the centre. "Jackie Ling," he shouted. "Ye live at the other end o' the village. Ye've a wife and three kids — and the littlest only three. Ye're born o' the village and so's yer wife. Ye divin't want to leave and neither does she. But it's not what she wants, and it's not what ye want. 'Cause yer street'll be the first to gan. Cardiff Square,

254

Glossop Street, Long Row West, Short Row East, Towneley Terrace, Ramsay's. They'll all be down afore Christmas. And if ye're not out by then ye'll be carted away in buses, ye'll be scattered like fluff off a dandelion. And there'll be nee reet to protest.

"Tommy Gibson, ye live in a house next to the colliery. Next to the canteen. Ye're comfortable there, ye've lived there all yer life. And d'ye want to move? D'ye want to start again at yer time o' life, tramp through ten miles o' snow in winter time. For a datal wage? But ye're ganna have to dee it. 'Cause yer street's on the list like everybody else's. East Terrace, West Terrace, North Terrace, Johnson Terrace. They're all on the list. They'll all come down when the others come down. And if ye're not out when they say they'll brand ye a squatter and make ye live in the street.

"Kenny Mews, ye're a young lad just like mesel'. But married and got two kids. Ye wouldn't mind a move if ye thowt ye'd be better off. If ye thowt owt good'd come of it. But d'ye think they'll let ye gan where ye want, d'ye think ye'll be able to pick a place o' yer own? A village o' yer own? Not a chance. But ye'll be movin', that's for sure — and afore Christmas at that. 'Cause ye live in Watson Street and Watson Street's on the list like everythin' else. Just like Collingdon Road and Jessop Street. It's all got to be razed afore Christmas.

"So what'll be left? A handful o' council houses, a handful o' private houses. A couple o' schools, a few shops and a few pubs. But hardly any people. Hardly any life. A ghost town in fact, for them that stay. Wi' them that's in the council and private houses the ghosts. Lopped off from their friends, lopped off from their relatives. Wi' the whole life gone out o' the village, with only the graveyard at the end o' the line. But that'll not affect us 'cause we'll not be here. How many of us live in private houses, how many in council? We're all in the houses comin' down, we're the ones to be lopped off. And I'll tell ye now and I'll tell ye frankly. I'd rather be in the graveyard than that."

He paused sufficiently to roll his sleeves to the elbows. His throat felt better now and he was able to lick the dryness of his lips. The cist in the crevice of blackheads that had started to swell at the institute was still coming up, the sweat had taken the colour from his hair, the hair lay flat to his head, and the sweat to his face added to the discomfort of his spots. He felt the solid-

255

ness of the boards to his feet as he stepped back and forth on the platform. His pale white throat bobbed with his adam's apple and the white buttons on his grey shirt stood out in the light. The yellow walls of the hall glinted above the heads of the men and moths that passed through the window crushed themselves on the hot white bulbs near the ceiling. All around him was the smell of beer and men and foisting air, the atmosphere of the club he knew so well, that intoxicated him when he was drunk and excited him when he was sober. The gesticulation of his arms grew with his temper, but in the pause after rolling his sleeves he realized how weary were the muscles. Ye he was too much alive, too much on edge to feel tired.

His emotions were carrying him away with his tongue and his tongue carrying away the emotions of the men. But every word he said he believed. Everything he uttered he knew to be true. The men did not have to take his word for it, they could read it for themselves in tomorrow's paper. He did not want them to be excited by him, he wanted them to be excited by facts. The facts as he saw them. And he meant what he said. He would rather be in the graveyard, he would rather be dead than see it pulled down, he would rather kill it himself than have others kill it for him. His gaze dropped from the yellow walls to the men below. And as his fingers groped for the stem of the microphone he knew the men would prefer it too. They felt as he felt, the same comradeship, the same intoxication. They felt close to their origins, close to their ancestors. They had the smell of beer to their nostrils, the taste of beer to their throats, the flow of beer to their blood stream. And as the blood reached their heads it made them excited. It also made them reckless.

For they knew what Ray had said was right. None of them lived in the private houses and only a few in the council. All the rest lived in the houses to be demolished. Not only lived in them but had lived in them all their lives. Cardiff Square, Glossop Street, Long Row West, Short Row East. They were as much a part of their life as the colliery. Towneley Terrace, East Terrace, West Terrace, North Terrace. As much a part of their life as the club. As the allotments, racing pigeons, pigs and hens Ray had said would be destroyed with them. They could not envisage an existence without their house, they could not envisage a life without their allotment. They could not understand what it would be like to move away their furniture, their families, their associations. And in the heat of the moment, the comradeship of the club, they were prepared to do anything — anything — rather than face a journey into the future. A journey that for them was like a journey into death, into the unknown.

"Ye see," Ray said. "This is a democracy. This is the kind o' society in which we live. This is the kind o' trick they can play. In this land where everybody's free. Free to vote, free to think, free to speak their mind. But what's the good o' havin' a vote if the party ye vote for never gets to power? What's the good o' havin' freedom to think, to speak yer mind, when neebody takes any notice o' what ye say? What's the good o' democracy if it doesn't look after its people? Of a government that only concerns itself wi' keepin' in power? What kind o' democracy is that? And what kind o' freedom is that? And what kind o' country is it that lets these things happen? That turns a blind eye to the troubles o' the other fellow 'cause, ye see, what affects ye doesn't affect anybody else? 'Cause yer troubles aren't their troubles, so there's nowt to worry about?

"But what we're seein' here is not democracy. We're seein' the erosion o' democracy. When ye destroy a man's reet to live where he wants, work where he wants, die where he wants. When ye destroy that reet, when ye uproot people as if they were weeds, when ye transplant them like flowers, when ye herd them away from their homes like cattle. Oblige them to leave the village where they've lived all their lives. Ye can be sure the decay has set in. The decay o' democracy. And the erosion that eats away the reets of a minority the day'll soon be eatin' away the reets o' the majority tomorrow. And when that happens ye can no longer call yerselves a free country. Ye can no longer say we have somethin' here other countries haven't got. So I say to them that turn their backs on us the day, I say to them, take care. 'Cause it'll come, it has to come, a day o' reckonin'. When not only do we lose our reets, but where ye lose yers tee.

"And in the meantime what we ganna dee? How we ganna save our colliery and our village, how we ganna save ourselves? We that have the freedom to vote, to think, to speak, freedoms worth nowt because neebody takes any notice o' what ye say. How ye vote. Are we ganna let ourselves be scattered? Our houses and jobs taken from us, our families uprooted, the ground cut from

257

under our feet? Or are we ganna utilize the one freedom we have left, the one freedom we can use to make everybody sit up and take notice. United we can force them to save the colliery, we can force them to reprieve the village. Scattered there's nowt we can dee. Disunited we're helpless. They can make us redundant, they can offer us compensation, they can tide us o'er till we reach the dole. They can offer us any kind o' house, any kind o' lodgin', any kind o' hut. Just to ease their conscience. Just so they can live their own lives, tidy their maps, in peace.

"But we're free men, we hold our heads high. We know what it's like, the bitterness o' the dole. We know what it's like, the humiliation o' bein' out o' work. Able bodied men standin' around corner ends. We know what it's like to have nowt in the house. And the wife, she knows what it's like not to have a house where she wants. 'Cause we've had it all afore. It's all from our past. And the past's comin' again. But as I say, we're free men, we're ganna show the world we're free, we're proud men, we're ganna show the world we're proud. And neither Wishart nor his union nor the management'll stop us. Neither the bureaucrats nor the planners'll stand in the way. Ye want a lead, I'll give ye that lead. Ye want action, I'll give ye action. But tell us the kind o' lead ye want, tell us the kind of action ye want. And I'll see that ye get it."

He let his shoulders relax and his hands drop by his sides. He turned from the men and with his head inclined listened to their calls. They were so loud, so raucous, they seemed to echo out of the window across the village, they were so full of defiance, so full of spirit, they seemed to echo out of the county across the country. Even to the farthest corners of the world. With his eyes closed, the darkness upon his closed lids recalled to him the darkness of the pit. He recalled that day sitting upon the face at number nine, Bousefield shuffling his way through the dust and damp towards him. He recalled how he had addressed the men at the deputy's kist, how he had forced upon Wishart the meeting at the institute, how he had led the men towards one kind of violence and led them back from another. Till now he had them calling the very word he wanted to hear. The very word he had planted upon their lips. And hearing the word he turned his head and saw the men, all of them standing now, raising their glasses and shouting uproariously. Faces eager and triumphant because the talking was over and the action about to begin.

258

"We'll strike," Bousefield shouted.

"We'll strike," Walton echoed.

"We'll strike," roared the men.

"Aye," Ray said. "We'll strike. We'll challenge authority. We'll weld together our voices. We'll make them a single voice to be heard the length and breadth o' the land. We'll strike for the sake of our dead mothers. For the sake o' their livin' sons. We'll strike for our wives and families. And above all we'll strike because we're free men. Because we've been deprived of our reets as free men. And because that's the only reet that's left."

And strike they did.

27

Markie Wishart looked at the specks of blood on the boards and knew that he had failed.

He knelt upon the boards and tried to raise himself from his knees. One hand groped for the table, the other for a chair, but with the blood from his eye still affecting his vision his hands slipped, he fell upon his face and rolled on his back. The empty chairs crashed from the platform. He hit his head upon the boards and a sharp pain passed from his skull to his brain. A shutter of darkness closed upon his eyes. And in the darkness there was peace, there was content, there was no failure, no defeat, no humiliation. There was not even the warmth of the blood that throbbed upon his cheek, the sound of men leaving the hall, their boots tramping the passageway. There was only the hardness of the boards to his back, the smell of dust to his nostrils, the sound of chairs crashing from the platform. Then there was nothing.

When he came to the blood had stained the lapels of his coat and the silk of his sleeveless shirt. Already the blood was stiffening upon his throat and neck, he could feel its taste to his mouth, and as the flow continued across his eye it stiffened upon the lids. The eye would not open and another chair was knocked sideways on the platform as he tried to rise. For a moment he did not know where he was. He did not know what had happened. There was an ache to his head and a sickness to his stomach. His legs were weak and would not support him, there was dust to his face where he had fallen, and the only sound he could hear in the silence was the sound of his own breath tearing from his chest. He pulled himself round and saw the pale dusk light through the oblong of the doorway. The grass was no longer discernible by the wall opposite the cinder path. The hall was empty now and with his one good eye he looked at the cue racks against the wall, the chairs pushed to the back, the caretaker's kiosk locked for the night. He saw too the brittle lights and pale green walls, his brief-case against the leg of the table, the pile of books Ray had left on the floor at the centre. And then he remembered.

The sound of movement on the platform recalled to him how he had been deserted. How his own lodge committee had preferred to stay with the men in the hall rather than face the men from the platform, how the officials' union had refused their support but not disbarred their members from the meeting. So that Wishart had to explain to them as well as to his own. He had counted on Gerald Holt but Gerald had not seen fit to come. He tried once more to rise, keeping his hand steady on the table where he made his speech. Only Sanderson had not let him down. Only Sanderson had sufficient courage to climb upon the platform and support him. He would be grateful for that to the end of his days. He steadied upon the platform like a fighter taking the count, a knee and foot resting upon the boards, a hand across his thigh, the other leaving the table to finger the cut across his eye. The blood dropped upon his coat sleeves and flannels, there were fresh drops upon the boards, and seeing it upon his fingers he began fumbling for his handkerchief. He had used it to wipe the spittle from his mouth when he addressed the men. But now searching in his pockets he could not find it. The sound moved closer on the plat-form and a handkerchief passed to his hand.

"Ye'd better hold back yer head," a voice said. "Keep back the blood."

He took the handkerchief and wiped the blood from the lids of his eye and from his cheek. He looked down through the thin red haze that continued to film the pupil and was surprised to see the colour of the handkerchief. It was like the knapsack of a tramp, red with a few white spots where the blood had yet to soak. He stared again at the briefcase by the leg of the table and the books that littered the floor. Above his head the moisture caused by the heat of the hall, the sweat of the men, was beginning to evaporate from the windows. His cheek was beginning to stiffen, he could feel the pain of the torn skin, but no horror at the sight of the blood, only surprise that the blood was there. The blood began dripping again from his eye and flowing down his cheek. He held back his head and closed his eye and the sickness and pain came over him again. He had to grope again for the corner of the table to prevent himself from stumbling. The windows above his head began to turn and his good eye closed to shut out the spinning.

"I want ye to know, Jack," he said. "How much I appreciate yer standin' by us the night."

There was an uneasy shuffle on the platform but no reply. Wishart looked for the florid face of the lodge chairman. With head held back his eye swept down from the roof, from the windows and rafters, across the empty chairs and table on the platform. He looked for the wavy hair flecked with dandruff, the red shiny skin of his cheeks where the razor had passed, the heavy double chin that jowled above Sanderson's collar. He looked for the solidness and dependability that characterized fifteen years union effort. Effort in his own time, that was unsung, unpaid, unwept, with great inconvenience and little privilege, yet which he accepted as Wishart accepted, in the interests of the men. Men who had that night betrayed him. He saw the ash on the floor that had fallen from the folds of Sanderson's suit. He smelt the faintly lingering odour of tobacco that he carried with him. But he no longer heard the creak of the boards beneath his weight, the bark of his smoker's cough. He no longer heard the gruffness of the voice that asked for questions before the meeting closed.

Instead he saw a pair of hobnailed boots pawing at the planks. He saw the caps of the boots highly polished, the boots laced high, laces fastened tightly in a knot around the ankles. He saw a pair of faded corduroys, the bottoms frayed, a brown striped coat fastened at the front, the white lip of a clay pipe above the line of the breast pocket, the pockets pouching where he held his tobacco. He saw a pair of shoulders rounded and slumped, a back that was no longer straight, that would never be straight again. He saw hair white and shaved close to the skull that in the brittleness of the light shone like silk. A face perfectly round, expressive, the skin drooping, haggard, with wrinkled yellow stains around the eyes, the eyes very small, bird-like and cunning. And he realized it was not Sanderson at all. It was Tom Holt.

"What happened to Sanderson?" he asked.

"He went out," Holt said. "Wi' the rest o' the men."

"Ye mean he left us. Left us like this?"

"Just to see what's up, A expect. Probably be back in a minute."

Wishart steadied himself on his feet. He tried not to think. His head swirled, but the flow of blood was less now as the wound began to congeal. The flesh around the cut was beginning to swell and for the first time he felt anger in the sharp aching throb of the pain. His face had changed since he felt the blow of the book. It had changed even since he climbed from the boards. The whiteness of the skin accentuated the blue veins of his mining scars, the astonishment that had tightened his cheeks lingered still in the hollows of his eyes, the lines were deeper, sharper, more ferocious, his one good eye seemed redder and more tired, and not only had dust streaked his face where he had fallen but his chin was scraped where he had hit the boards. The boards were no longer steady beneath his feet and his legs so weak he could hardly stand without the support of the table.

He realized for the first time that the men were gone.

"But the men. We'd better gan after them. Bring them back."

"A'd stay here if A were ye. Ye've had enough for one neet."

"But they might set about the colliery. The house o' the manager."

"Even if they did," Holt said. "There's nowt ye could dee."

"I could gan after them. Persuade them."

Everything to Wishart was clear now, clear and sharp. And in the clarity there was bitterness, in the sharpness the knowledge he had failed. Thoughts that had flashed through his mind before the book tore the skin came to him again. He had not saved the future of the men nor had he saved the village. His whole philosophy had been one of drift and because it had been one of drift this had been allowed to happen. Now all that he had planned he would never see, all that had been in his mind's eye would never come true. A new village would never arise from the foundations of the old. Or if it did the credit would not go to him but to someone else. The men would fight but they would fight in vain. Or if they did not the success would not be his but the persons who had led the fight. His eye steadied again on the books at the centre of the floor. He would not believe it was true but for the pain of the cut, the blood on his face. The weakness of his legs that wanted him to sink to the boards never to rise again.

"The men can look after themselves," Holt said. "That eye o' yers cannot."

"It'll all be all right. Once I get it bathed."

"Ye'll need more than a bit water," Holt said. "Ye'll need a doctor."

"I've no time for a doctor," Wishart said. "I promised the wife I'd be back in an hour."

"She'd rather have ye a bit late than gannin' back like that."

Holt looked down at the blood that continued to ooze from beneath the handkerchief. It seemed to him it would never stop. There were dabs upon Wishart's forehead, veins that had run down by his nose and ear, that had coloured the paleness of his lips and carried on to his throat. It reminded Holt of the wounded being transported from the front during the first world war. And not only the blood but the whiteness of Wishart's face, reflecting a shock that cut deeper than any wound, that would still be there even when the wound had healed. It reminded him too of a scene in his own house, that had occurred only hours earlier, but which seemed to him more than an age but a lifetime. There had not been blood then but he knew what Wishart had seen in Ray he had seen in Gerald. The same hatred, the same determination to destroy. Only the hatred and determination were aimed at different things. And but for that, but for the vein of sympathy in Ray as well as the vein of violence, the pain and hurt he was seeing now in Wishart he would have seen in himself.

"But the men," Wishart said. "What's he ganna do with the men?"

"He's me own son, Markie. Me own flesh and blood. A knaa him like A knaa the back o' me hand. And there'll be nee more devilment the neet, A'll be warned. Ye see, he's like the other bugger A've got. He needs a bit o' commotion now and again, just to make him feel he's all there. But the neet he's passed the limit. And he'll knaa he's passed it. There'll be nowt more to worry about the neet, ye'll see."

"I cannot understand why he gets himself involved," Wishart said.

"It's nee good askin' me, Markie, son. 'Cause A divin't knaa neither. He's young and full o' spirit — full o' wind and water some might say — but there's nee call for what he did the neet. Nee call at all. A'll talk to him, if ye like. Not that it'll dee any good. A'll tell him what A think on him. Not that he'll change his opinions."

"He should keep his opinions to himself," Wishart said. "Leave things to people who know better."

"What's done's done, Markie, son," Holt said. "And nowt's

264

ganna change it now. But A'll tell ye one thing, just to put yer mind at rest. He's got nowt against ye personally. A knaa that for a fact. He thinks ye're a fine upstandin' fellow. But ye see he thinks ye've changed sides, he thinks ye divin't work for the men any more. He thinks ye work for the management. And not only he thinks it, all the men think it. 'Cause if they didn't they wouldn'tve left the hall like that. They'd still be here listenin' to ye."

"If the men don't know better they'll never know better," Wishart said.

"A'm just tellin' ye, Markie, so ye'll knaa. So ye'll understand how they feel."

Wishart did not reply but let himself be guided from the platform out of the hall into the night. He knew Holt was taking him to the doctor's but he did not care. He knew he was leaving behind his briefcase but he did not care about that either. He would call and collect it tomorrow if he remembered. Or perhaps he would never collect it. For he knew as he stepped onto the institute path he was leaving behind more than a briefcase. More than his precious blood upon the planks. He was leaving behind his authority and prestige with the men, authority and prestige built up over ten years of effort. He tried to turn and look back, for what he had lost he did not want to lose lightly. He tried to see the speckled boards of the platform, the briefcase against the leg of the table. But Holt's hand was firm upon his elbow, guiding him up the last of the cinder path to the road that led through the village.

Wishart looked up at the sky where the first stars were beginning to appear. He saw the roofs and gable ends of houses as he walked, head tilted, and smelt the timber and paint stacked in the corners of the maintenance yard. He saw chimney pots and aerials and heard the echo of his steps upon the pavement. There were no people on the street nor waiting at the stop for a bus. But lowering his head he could see the dim glow that flickered through the curtains where they watched television. And with the light through the curtains he felt the privacy of their homes, the shuttered security of their lives. He felt behind each curtain there was a separate life and with each life a separate soul. A soul that should be preserved and protected because it was the only thing man had worth keeping. Now such protection was going to be

265

destroyed with their comfort. It was going to be destroyed with the houses. And once lost it would not be so easily restored.

He knew most of the village would be destroyed by the county planners. Yet not a house would come down that was not condemned. And it was for this condemned property that people would fight. Most of the streets were named after contractors who had built them. Many were of large sombre houses, solid in appearance, built of stone from a local quarry, but with windows designed never to open and only one door leading out at the back. All had the toilet in the yard next to the coalhouse. Some did not have electricity. And one particular street was so ancient and had been condemned so long habitants born into it had since died. The houses in this particular street had no bath, only a boiler next to the fireplace, they had no proper oven, only a brick kiln heated by the fire; they had two bedrooms and two pantries, the water tap was kept in one pantry and foodstuffs in the other. There was no sink under the tap, only a pail to catch dripping water. Yet people who lived in this street wanted to fight more than anyone in the village.

The doctor led Wishart through the waiting room into his surgery and sat him under a light.

On the way from the institute the handkerchief had clotted to the cut and clung now to the skin. The doctor peeled it ruthlessly off and bent to examine the eye. He tilted back his head and Wishart felt the cool fingers upon his cheek and brow. Despite the dust on his face where he had fallen the cut of the eye was clean. The blood had ceased to flow and the pain to nag, but as the doctor prised open the cut the blood began to throb again upon his cheek and pain shot along the nerve was bloodshot the pupil and iris were undamaged.

He stood back with hands on his hips.

"If I were you," he said. "I'd call across the road and take out a summons."

"You mean call at the police's?"

"That's right. File a charge for assault and battery."

Holt stood at the back of the surgery with his cap in one hand, the fingers of the other upon the back of the chair. He had his head bent, the light shone upon his silver crown, and there was a dried spittle on his lips. When he raised his head he saw only the doctor's back. But over the doctor's shoulder he saw Wishart with his eye closed, the blood down his face and on his lips, down his neck and throat, upon the lapels of his coat, the silk of his shirt, even his sleeves and flannels. And there came to his stomach the old sickness and shame, fear that he had felt at the institute but that he had felt too years ago. Fear of the policeman to his house. He moved his weight from one foot to the other and brought his eyes from the blood of Wishart's face to the head of the doctor.

"I want no trouble," Wishart said. "Only me eye seein' to."

"Suit yourself," the doctor said. "But I know what I'd do in the circumstances."

He brought from a shelf his syringe and changing the needle took down a small bottle from the racks that lined the walls. He gave Wishart an injection to calm his nerves and filling a basin of warm water from the sink at the end of the surgery bathed his face with strips of cotton wool. Wishart sat on the chair with his head to the light, hands clasped between his legs, feeling the effect of the injection upon his nerves, the soothing balm of water to his cheeks. The doctor gave him a second local injection to freeze the wound and began threading the needle that would insert the stitches immediately but paused for the wound to stiffen. He stood with arms outstretched, hands on the mantelpiece above the old-fashioned surgery grate, not looking at the men, ignoring them. Looking instead at the eye chart on the wall above the mantelpiece.

He was a small wiry man, born and bred in the north, with a temper that sharpened as he grew older. The village people claimed he did not have a civil tongue in his head and often told him so to his face. He did not take offence, only laughed and told them not to be cheeky to the family practitioner. Yet despite his ill grace he had a thriving practice. The people seemed to enjoy the scourge of his contempt. Besides, he was the only doctor they had and a good one at that. He treated them carefully and with expertise, he never failed to answer a call, did not mind their sniffling complaints, and despite long waiting lists he was the only doctor they knew who could get them into hospital within days. And not only get them in but visit them whilst they were there. He had been their doctor for thirty years. He knew their first names and called them by such. The only thing was his temper, but they had known him so long they could even take that for granted.

Now he was fifty-five. Yet with his thin colourless face, his meagre cheeks, his bald head, his tired eyes, the withering of the skin on his throat and neck, he looked more like seventy. He was still to them as sprightly and alert as ever. He listened attentively when they visited his surgery. He answered their calls and arranged their hospital and despite pressure of work continued his visits when they were confined. Never once did he lose his familiarity. Yet there was about him a heaviness. His temper deteriorated and he stared with a detachment they had never before noticed. Often they wondered what was going on in his head. They wondered if he were happy. But how could he be otherwise when he had everything in life worth having? A thriving practice, a fine house, a new car every year and a fortnight's holiday abroad. And of course he had money.

But often the doctor reflected what was the point of having money when you did not have anything else. He had no wife, no children, only a past tied to the village. And since the village would soon be destroyed he would not even have that. He did not have happiness just as he did not have freedom. He had one day to himself a week, but for the other six he was as chained to his practice as was a convict to his prison. It was not what he had anticipated when he graduated medical school. It was not what he had expected when he came to the village. He was not old but he was weary. He stood with his hands on the mantelpiece and recalled his predecessor. He had been a heavy stout man who had retired at the age of sixty. He had been surprised to discover when the doctor retired the people of the village had not subscribed to give him the customary present. Then he was told why. A few weeks before he left he had refused to treat a man sent home from the pit after an accident. The man belonged to another village and was therefore under another doctor. It was early morning before the first buses were running and the man had to walk his way home. He had collapsed and died on the road. An autopsy showed he had a broken rib protruding his lung. He had been lucky to walk at all.

The village people were so incensed they could never forget it. And when the present doctor had been told he had been as shocked as they. But he had been more than shocked. He could not understand how such a thing could happen. Now he could understand. It was easy to make mistakes when you were tired. It was easy to allow your judgment to be tempered by your feelings. But no-one would understand that a doctor might be tired, that he might be worn down, that there might be days when he preferred not to see a surgery full of patients, nights when he preferred not to get out of bed to answer the phone, dress and drive to a call. That there were occasions when he might simply wish to stay at home over the fire. That was what he meant when he reflected he could never be free. He could never be free because he could never relax. People were always either coming into the world or going out. And in between never a day went by without their being sick. But though he was tired, though he knew he was tired, he pulled himself together sufficiently to tend his patients. He dreaded the same error of judgment that had afflicted his predecessor. He dreaded misjudging a major complaint for a minor ailment, a mistake which might he knew cost someone their life. It had not happened yet but he decided the day it did was the day he too would retire.

There was also the psychological weariness of being a doctor. A man he had known thirty years might complain of a pain in his stomach. There would be a check at the hospital and then an operation. It would be found that the man was suffering from cancer. The cancer would be removed, the doctor would receive a letter from the surgeon congratulating him on the speed with which he had caught the growth, informing him too that the operation had been a success. But — and this the surgeon underlined — if the cancer should reappear within two years the man would be beyond surgical repair. Often the two years rolled into three, periodic checks on the patient were discontinued, restrictions on his diet lifted. The man fell back into the routine of the village. Four years after the operation he returned to the surgery. The doctor noticed how the flesh had slid from the lobes of his ear, the folds of his neck, how his shirt seemed no longer to fit around the collar. The man did not need an examination, the worst was written on his face. A cancer cell had escaped to the blood stream during the operation and plotted its own sinister course. His lease of life had expired. He would be dead in six months.

The doctor saw the wonder of birth, the misery of death, and wondered what it was all for, this masquerade, this never-ending humanity, that continued to reproduce, to procreate, without reference to history, to life. That seemed to drift like the universe, without purpose, without aim, without ambition. He asked what was his own part in such drift, where did he belong in the

269

masquerade? Death and birth touched him equally. Pain was something he observed in others but did not feel in himself. And though he loved these people, though he was involved in their lives, there was always a part of him he kept to himself. He shared in their sadness and their bereavement, their joy and their elation, but he shared in it as a spectator. He sterilized the needle that would stitch Wishart's eye and felt the flesh around the wound to see that it was cold. He looked down at the face swollen and scraped, that was meek, pathetic, waiting to feel the stitch of the needle, the pulling together of the skin. And it came to him again, the foolishness, the pointlessness, the lack of purpose. And again the question nagged at his mind.

"Do you know?" he asked. "What it's all for?"

Holt stirred uncomfortably and looked at Wishart.

"Depends," Wishart said. "What ye're on about."

"This life we lead. That all of us lead. Do you know what it's for?"

"I'm sure I don't," Wishart said. "Sometimes I often wonder myself."

The doctor turned to Holt. "I'll bet you can't remember the time you came knocking at my door at three o' clock in the morning. Telling us to come and see your wife when she was laid up wi' the second one. I gave you the gas to carry down to my car and you grumbled all the way. Said it was heavy as a hundred-weight tub. I'll bet you can't remember."

"A'm sure A cannot," Holt said.

"And you, Markie. I'll bet you've forgotten the night you came wi' blood streaming down your face. Just like the night. With a hand o'er your eye to stench the flow. It must be twenty years ago. Maybe even more than that. But you'll have forgotten. Yet I can remember. As plain as if it were yesterday."

"I remember," Wishart said. "Vaguely."

"Vaguely, he says. I wish I could remember things vaguely. There was a lass came in the day. That I brought into the world myself. And she says to me, she says, I want ye to examine us, doctor. I want ye to have a good look at us. But I didn't have to examine her. I could tell by the look in her eyes. You're expecting, I says, aren't you. Ye're supposed to be tellin' me, she says. Not me tellin' ye. So I has a look at her and sure enough she's pregnant. I says I suppose now you'll want to tell your mother. That's reet,

270

she says. And the lad's that's 'sponsible. And I look at her, and I saw her not the way she is now but the way she was when she was born. And I remember the look in her mother's eye when I laid her in her arms. And I think of the night when she finds out. And wonder if her mother knew then what she knew now." He paused and stared at them. "That's why I ask you to tell us what it's all for. What in heaven's name it's all for."

He stitched the wound as Wishart sat with his head to the light. Wishart did not listen but thought of the night years ago when another wound had been cut across the lid of his eye. The cut had been caused by a stone fight on the heap between lads who lived at the top of the village and those who lived at the bottom. Some of the boys went home before the fight began, one sat upon an upended tub and watched it as a neutral, the rest fought it out with pieces of slate they picked from the heap. The fight ended when a piece of slate cut his eye and the blood began down his face. He had been taken into a house by the canteen and when the eye was bathed sent on to the doctor. Later, when he got back to school, the headmistress paraded him before every class, claimed he had ten stitches instead of only one, and pointing to the bandage that swathed his head warned everyone this was what happened to boys who fought. The scar had been conspicuous till he went into the pit. Then the insidious coal dust crept into the cut to make a small blue vein, and other blue veins were added from cuts he collected during the years.

"And your legs," the doctor asked Holt. "I see you're still standing."

"How did ye knaa they were bad?"

"One of your marrows told us. Said you had a bit of cramp behind the thighs."

"But it's not serious, doctor," Holt said. "Only when A walk."

"And about getting married. They'll see you down the aisle, I hope?"

Holt fumbled with his cap and brought his hand from the back of the chair.

"Who told ye A was gettin' married?"

The doctor laughed and for the first time that evening the fatigue lifted from his face. "There's not much you can hide from the family doctor," he said. "You might not be hankering to tell us how Markie got that gash on his eye the night. And you might be puzzled as to why I don't press you. But I'll know soon enough the morn. There'll be half a dozen rushing in to tell us before I'm even out of bed. Mind, I've not been told who's the lucky bride to be. But I'm not worried about that. As long as I get an invitation."

"It's not ganna be a big weddin'," Holt said. "Only a family affair."

"You mean it's all fixed up?"

"That's reet. For three weeks time."

"At the church?"

"At the registry office. The wife's mother, she's not got much cash, ye see. So we thowt we'd have it quiet. Nee white weddin'. Nowt like that. O' course, if ye fancy callin' by for a drink ye'll be welcome. And there'll be a do at the club later on. Ye can come then, if ye like."

"Well," the doctor said. "Now that I have an invitation we'll see. But I cannot promise."

There was no bandage this time to swathe Wishart's head, only an elastoplast to protect the stitching. He sat stoical, hands still clasped between his knees, face pale, starch-like, taking little interest in the doctor's banter. Something had crossed his mind on his way down the bank from the institute and now he wondered what it was. With the wound cleaned, the stitches inserted, he felt better, fresher, soothed by the sedative, the pain numbed from his eye. The astonishment had eased from his face but the lines on his forehead were as deep as ever. The blood had yet to come back to his lips, but the strength had returned to his legs, and when he stood he did not have to reach to the back of the chair for support. He felt almost normal but for the blood that had dried on his clothes. Yet he could not put his mind to the thought he wanted to think.

"You're sure you'll not cross the road to file a summons?" the doctor asked.

Wishart pulled his face stiffly and looked at Holt.

"I'm sure," he said.

"Suit yourself. I'll expect you back at the surgery in a few days. So I can see how it goes."

"I'm sorry I've spoilt yer night, doctor," Wishart said.

"Don't worry about that," the doctor said. "I can hardly wait till the morn to find out what it's all about."

272

They heard him close the door behind them as their steps crunched down the gravel path from the surgery to the road. Holt no longer held Wishart's arm and Wishart did not have to tilt his head to the sky. He felt a different man from the one who had tottered down the bank from the institute. There was no longer a sickness to his stomach, a dizziness to his head, a weakness to his legs. And somehow he did not feel so badly about leaving everything behind at the institute. There was only the dullness to his mind as he tried to think the thought that had occurred to him on the way down. It had been something to do with Ray and the men that day in the pit. They passed the schools and private houses, grocery shop and fish shop, and carried on towards the pub. They heard the gurgle of a burn that passed through a field near the road and the soft swaying of the chestnut trees in the grounds of the school. Their steps echoed along the deserted street and he saw ahead the blue star that attached itself to the pub. Then he remembered.

It had occurred to him that Ray Holt had never wanted a strike that day in the pit. He had merely used the threat of a strike to force upon Wishart the meeting that night at the institute. Somehow he had known that Wishart would not be ready. Instinctively he had known he would not be prepared. And instinctively he had known he would not be supported by the officials' union, nor by the committee of his own. Perhaps he had even intimidated them not to support him. Perhaps he had even intimidated Sanderson. But why? What was his motive? Why had he not been interested in a lightning strike? Why had he wanted to isolate Wishart and then destroy him? Why had he wanted to call his own meeting? What violence was he planning for the morrow? There was a pause in Wishart's thought and a pause in his step. He looked up at the blue ensign of the pub flickering above their heads.

"If ye divin't mind, Markie," Holt said. "I'd like to stop for a pint. Afore closin' time."

"I don't mind," Wishart said.

"And Markie," Holt said. "About the neet. Ye understand?"

"I understand," Wishart said. "Even more than ye think."

He continued along the street past the farm that smelt of manure, the railway bridges, post office and houses to be destroyed. In his mind he tried to imagine the bridges pulled down, the line taken up. He tried to picture the destruction wrought by the demolition of the houses. But it could not be as bad as his imagination painted. There must still be time to secure building permission from the planners. Perhaps there was even time to save the colliery. He strolled rapidly through the village, his stride trying to keep pace with his thoughts. He realized now that the men wanted action. And even against his better judgment he would see they got the action they wanted. He would protest to the manager, he would see the matter taken up in arbitration. The dullness cleared from his mind and his confidence returned. Tomorrow he would call at the men's homes before they left for work, he would persuade them against whatever Ray had decided upon that night. He had no doubt this time they would listen. With the cut across his eye, their own feelings subdued, they would be ashamed of the night before. They would listen no matter what Ray had said.

He paused at the top of the bank and looked down at his home. He felt better than he had all day. Pre-occupied with his thoughts he had not noticed the quietness of the streets. He had not realized he had walked the length of the village without seeing a soul. He breathed the air of the country and it seemed to give him strength. He felt the softness of the air to his cheek and it seemed to soothe still more the bruise around his eye. He realized he had lost that night because he had not been prepared. But having once been taken by surprise he would see it did not happen again. And tomorrow, after the call on the men's homes, he would call on the manager, he would ask for the additional information he required. Then with this in hand, he would hold another meeting, an official meeting, properly announced, with notices on the heapstead, with the committee behind him, a chairman better able to keep order. He would reveal to the men the proper position. He would demolish the arguments of Ray, just as planners would demolish the houses. Then all the things he had planned for the village, for the future, all that he had seen in his mind, would come true. He would make it come true.

The sky along the horizon was still a faint glimmering crystal, but the darkness overhead was gently reaching down. The evening mist sifting up from the river had yet to reach the village. The night was warm and the village so quiet he could hear the twittering of the night jays from the bottom of the bank. Looking down the bank, he could see vaguely the dark stains of gorse, the willow and silver birch trees that clumped the stream, the faint line of the sandquarry, and on the crystal horizon the houses of another village. The houses were stark against the sky and the lights of the farmhouse by the sandquarry reassuring. The vigour of the countryside lifted up to him, he felt it as he felt the air to his cheek, and in him there was pride and satisfaction that at least part of it belonged to him. He looked affectionately at his house halfway down the bank. It was tucked away in the gloom, the jutting pagoda-like roof vague and indistinct, with not a light to show there was anyone at home.

And then he remembered his wife, remembered her not as a name but as a person. He remembered her neurosis when she heard the news of the village, he remembered the tears that had stained the pillows, smarted her cheeks, the convulsions that had shaken her shoulders and squirmed her body. He remembered too the promise he had made to be back in an hour, how again he had placed the affairs of the men before the affairs of his wife. So that the ingratitude he had felt on leaving the institute returned, that the men should treat him as they did, that he should have devoted to them ten years of service, ten years of life, ten years he should have devoted to his wife. And he remembered the look in her eyes before he left, he recalled the fear that had twinged his heart, the reluctance he had felt at leaving. And suddenly he did not want to go home at all. He wanted to wander the village, potter the heapstead, walk the woods, he wanted to double back for a drink, stay out in the country, savour the air, savour his thoughts, his dreams, his ambitions. Even climb on a bus and leave the village. Anything rather than face reality.

He pushed open the door and peered uncertainly into the kitchen. He switched on the light. He found everything as he had left it. The bluebottle had ceased to buzz but small flies continued to hover, there was a smell of grease and unwashed dishes, the potato peelings, egg shells and bacon rind were as they had been earlier, the table as he had left it at dinner. The oven registered his wife's neglect, cluttered with frying pan and kettle, the rings thick with grease, chip pan on the floor beside the crumbs that scattered the carpet. The window frames remained engrained with dust, an aroma of dust and staleness twitched his nostrils, his pit clothes lay in a heap on the floor, boots yet to be scraped, layers of dirt encrusted on his shirt and breeches, oil stains on his cap dull in the light. He stepped over the rumpled carpet and pushed

275

his way into the sitting room.

He did not immediately switch on the light but paused to allow his eyes accustom themselves to the gloom. The curtains had not been drawn and a soft light floated in from the windows. And in the soft light he could see the objects that littered the sill of the window, he could see the china fruit bowl at the centre of the table, the silver candlesticks and electric clock on the mantelpiece. A car pulled up the bank toward the village and as its headlamps swathed the room he could see the dead coal of the fire in the grate showing the ashy white of its underskin. He could feel the cold hostility of the room, a hostility that seemed to contrast with the vigour that lifted up from the country, so that he paused one hand on the door, the other on the switch. The aroma of dust from the kitchen was still to his nostrils, but in the sitting room it was diluted with a different odour, rich, pale, exotic, an odour he had never smelt before. A shiver unsettled the muscles in the backs of his thighs and it took all the courage he had to switch on the light.

His wife lay face down in the passage halfway between bedroom and kitchen. She lay with her legs crumpled, her clothes twisted to show the bare skin of her back, arms above her head, head tilted to one side. He had the impression of a doll, a broken doll, with her tattered mouse coloured hair, her face so white, red where the tears had flowed. An empty bottle lay across the hearth, a glass lay unbroken beyond the reach of her hand and from the passage as from the sitting room there came the sickening odour of gin. The light caught the backs of her legs and large bulbous nose. He leapt forward and grasped her hands. He found they were cold, so cold.

"Oh my God," he said. "What have I done."

It was then he saw the slow curl of blood from the corner of her mouth.

28

"Ye're late," Ray said.

"What d'ye mean, A'm late? A've been here an hour."

"I've been waitin' ten minutes. Ye weren't here when I come."

"A went doon to the field. See if ye'd gone there."

"What makes ye think I'd gan there?" Ray asked.

She giggled. "If ye divin't knaa," she said. "It's nee good askin' me."

Ray stood in the side of the tall hawthorn hedge that bordered the path which led to the cricket field. He watched the mist from the river thicken around the houses and felt the softness of its vapour to his cheeks. He stood so deeply in the bush its prickles were uncomfortable to his neck and the shoots of the hawthorn damp to his cheeks. With his jerkin zipped his body felt as hot and sweaty as it had at the institute. He had run along the village from the club and his spots ached with the sweat still drying on his face. He was breathing heavily and his heart continued to beat loudly against his chest. He heard it as clearly as her steps along the path. She almost missed him, but with his hand stretching out from the hedge he pulled her close to his body. He ran his hands through her hair and stroked the soft down on her neck.

She peeled back her lips and smiled.

"A had the feelin' that somehoo the neet ye might be changed."

"What makes ye say that?" he asked.

"Just a feelin'. D'ye want to gan doon the cricket field noo or later?"

"Later," he said. "When we've had a talk."

He pulled her tightly to him and felt the tenderness of her breasts against his chest. Her thighs and stomach rubbed into his and with her arms around his neck he could feel the pulsating heat of her body. She wore a simple frock and with her low neckline

277

his hands fell against the bareness of her back. The beat of his heart quickened and a new kind of tension overwhelmed him. He closed his eyes and as they kissed the tip of her tongue explored between his teeth. The ache he had felt in his face he felt now in his chest. He was no longer aware of the hawthorn shoots and prickles to his cheeks and neck, only her thighs, breasts and stomach against his, the soft yielding succulence of her lips. And with her hands probing his neck and hair, her scent to his nostrils, the heat and sweat to his body seemed no longer tolerable.

"Why," she said. "Ye haven't changed a bit."

"Never mind about that," he said. "What did the doctor say?"

Her arms fell by her side and she stepped back a pace.

"Just what A expected," she said. "A'm two months pregnant."

"He cannot be sure. Neebody can be sure. Not till it's three months."

"He's the doctor," she said. "And if he says A'm two months pregnant A'm two months pregnant."

She looked up at him sullenly. Her opulent lips pouted and her eyebrows pulled down, but her eyes were watchful under the dark lashes. She had brown speckled eyes with flames deep down, flames that could smoulder or flare whichever the humour struck her. Now they were subdued and cunning and watched every expression on Ray's face. Even with the mist he could see the sharp profile of her cheeks, the hue of her skin, the long dark hair that hung around her neck. He paused for a moment uncertain and looked down at her cunning eyes. Then he took her by the shoulders and pulling her close reached for her face and lifted it to his. She stooped her shoulders and dropped her head. She closed her eyes against his stare and he plucked them open with the pressure of his thumbs upon her lids. The flames were almost luminous in the dark.

"Now look us in the eyes," he said. "And tell us it's true."

"It's true," she said. "And ye knaa it's true."

He dropped his hands from her face and looked across her shoulder. The mist thinned for a moment and he could see the shapes of the prefabricated houses that skirted the wood. It was almost midnight and the only sounds he could hear were those that carried across the countryside, the sound of a car along the road, the tut of an engine from another colliery. And of course

278

there was his own breathing, the throbbing of his heart against his chest. For the first time that night he seemed drained of strength. He felt he had run a great race and was ready to drop. He grew conscious of the prickles to his neck and moved slightly from the hedge. His feet rustled the grass and a twig snapped underfoot. The mist had damped the blades of grass and avoiding her gaze he looked down at the wet toes of his shoes.

"All reet," he said. "I believe."

"So what ye ganna dee about it? That's what A want to knaa."

"I'll acknowledge it. If that's what ye mean."

"And ye'll pay?"

"I'll pay," Ray said. "Owt ye have a mind."

Dolly Walton held back her head and laughed. The sound seemed to echo through the mist and night. She had lost the sleepiness that besotted her lying on a mattrass in the sitting room of her mother's home. She had lost too the dullness from her eyes. When Holt left for the meeting at the institute, she had washed and changed and after tea helped put to bed her mother's tribe. Then she had gone off to a dance in the welfare hall of another village. She loved to dance more than she loved anything. A single band toured the local halls and visiting one hall a night it was possible to attend six dances a week. This Dolly did. Music seemed to throb in her primitive blood. Her lithe body loved to test its suppleness in a rhythm. Normally, she danced with her sister, but since her sister was now in a sanatorium with tuberculosis, she stood on the edge of the hall and listened to the music. As always that night it had excited her. And as always the excitement she felt still in her veins was reflected in her voice when she laughed.

Ray took her wrist with one hand and with the other slapped her face. She fell immediately serious.

"In that case," she said. "A marry yer father."

"Ye'll not," he said. "I wi'not let ye."

"There's only one way ye can stop us," she said.

"And how's that?" he asked.

"Marry us yersel'."

"I've told ye," he said. "I divin't want to marry. At least not yet."

"Then we can gan away together. Quiet like. Get married when ye like."

"And what kind o' life would that be, d'ye think? Livin' in a strange place. Not even a village, maybes a town. Wi' nee friends. Nee proper place to live. And maybes nee work either. Only what ye can pick off a milk cart. What kind o' life d'ye think it'd be for ye. And what kind o' life would it be for me?"

"Ye'll have to leave the village anyway. When they pull it doon."

"Maybes," he said. "But I'll leave 'cause I'm forced. Not o' me own accord."

"Then it's all settled," she said. "A marry yer father."

"All reet," he said. "Marry me father. See if I care."

She leant against the railings at the other side of the path and threw back her head in defiance. Yet her eyes were still upon him, looking always for weakness, seeking indifference in what he had said. Her hands were on the railings behind her back and with her shoulders stooped they recalled to him the night she had entered the heat of a local beauty competition. The competition had been organized by a local newspaper and the purpose of the heat had been to pick the most beautiful girl in the village so that later she could enter the finals. Dolly did not win the heat. In fact she was not even placed. Not that she was less pretty than the rest of the girls, only she did not wear a bathing costume, she did not wear a finely tailored suit, she wore only the cotton frock she had on that night. Nor did she hold herself as elegantly as did the rest of the girls but stepped upon the stage with hands behind her back, her shoulders self-consciously hunched like those of a cripple. It was not a stance to show off her figure. Nor was it a stance to gain her applause. But then she did not know that just as clothes and elegance counted for a great deal audience reaction counted for more.

Ray sat at the back of the hall with the rest of the lads. For them the competition was nothing more than a hilarious outing. The heat did not begin until nine o' clock, they had therefore time enough beforehand for a drink, time enough in fact for several drinks, so that when they entered the hall at the end of a Darby and Joan their mood was even more irreverent than usual. The hall was an old cinema and they lined themselves along the wall next to the projecting room. They clapped and cheered, booed and stamped with the same enthusiasm. They whistled and catcalled to their hearts' content. They encouraged the girls in the bathing suits, admired the girls in the tailored costumes. And derided Dolly Walton till they were again dry in the throat. Even her own brother joined the clamour against her. He even began a few bars of the song, dance gypsy dance, which caused great amusement among his friends. Only Ray did not join in the clamour. But then only Ray had not been to the club for a drink.

He had stayed at home studying and met with the lads only at the bottom of the stairs leading to the hall. He was therefore able to watch with detachment how Dolly reacted to the howls of her contemporaries. She straightened her shoulders and brought her hands from behind her back, she tossed her head till the ebony hair shook around her neck, but she did not blush with shame. She did not retreat from the stage in disarray. Instead her eyebrows arched and her eyes ran along the line of detractors till they settled on Ray. She realized only he among the lads was not making fun of her. Only he had the decency to be polite. And it seemed to him, analysing the situation, his head uncluttered with alcohol, that for Dolly he was the only one that mattered. That if he were to laugh now, even to smile, her evening would collapse. She could bear the whips and scorns from others. She could not bear them from Ray. And in his detachment, sitting with his back to the wall, hands across his lap, listening to the jeers of his friends, he decided she was not a bad-looking girl. She did not have the demure prettiness of the other contestants. She did not have the lines of the girls who dressed in bathing suits. But she had a sensual beauty that was scarcely concealed in the thickness of her lips, the darkness of her brows. The flames that licked from her eyes.

He had waited for her outside the hall after the competition. He had wanted to tell her how pretty she had been, how she should not mind the sarcasm of his friends. Even the vulgarity of his brother. But if she had not minded in the hall she certainly minded now. She called them all the names imaginable. She threatened to claw out their eyes. And as for her brother, when she got hold of him. They walked along the village towards the council houses. She startled Ray with her coarseness. Yet she excited him too. Normally he shied from women. He wanted them but could not understand how they could like him with his spots. They gave him a sense of inferiority. He had no confidence in himself where they were concerned. But with Dolly it was different. He could forget about his spots, he could forget about his distrust. And how could a man feel inferior before a woman who used the language of a trooper? He recalled only the sensuality he had glimpsed that night in her face, the flames deep down in the eyes. And when her temper cooled and she had run out of expletives, he had taken her by the hand and led her round the fell.

After that they had always met in secret. He told her if ever it got round he was seeing her he would break it then and there. He could not forget the reaction of his friends the night of the competition. He could not forget the jokes bandied about the pit and he knew once the word got round it would not be long before the jokes were bandied about him. They might not mention them to his face. But they would never be forgotten behind his back. Dolly knew he meant what he said and therefore respected his request. Besides, it pleased her to have a secret she could keep to herself. She felt it was the only thing she had that really belonged to her. She did not have a girl friend in the village. They despised her as much as they despised her family. Yet at the bottom of them she knew they would do anything to have the kind of affair she was having with Ray. Only they did not have the opportunity, and they did not have the nerve. Dolly had both. And because she had both she felt her affair with Ray gave her stature, if not in the eyes of others at least in the eyes of herself. She had entered the beauty competition because she had wanted to show that if she was not the prettiest girl in the village at least she was as good as the rest. Now she felt even better. And just as before the village girls had looked down on her now she felt she could look down on them. For once in her life she was superior. The only thing she required to make that superiority complete was marriage.

But Ray did not want to marry. She had first broached the subject standing as they did now in the side of the hedge. He had reached for his face and fingered the papules on his cheek. As he did so all the distrust he felt for women returned and with it the inferiority. She had spoken of it lightly, as if she were not serious. But nevertheless as they went down to the cricket field he began to feel uncomfortable. He began looking for ways to effect a break. He knew her environment as well as anyone in the village and searching her character for motive he began to feel that for her marriage would be a release. Release from the dirt and discomfort that surrounded her mother, release from the gossip, the foolishness, the poverty, the drudgery imposed by her mother's tribe. The everlasting despair of knowing that not only was she poor but that she would always be poor. Ray understood her desire to escape, but he did not see what it had to do with him. Besides, he did not love her. He did not feel he could not live without her. And just as he had not wanted to attract the ridicule of his friends in courtship he certainly did not want it in marriage.

Then there was the question of her gypsy blood. It may or may not be true, Ray did not know. But he recalled that when Mrs. Walton had come to live in the village she had brought her legend with her. And part of that legend had been that in washing the hair of her youngest daughter with bleaching chloride the hair had fallen out and left the daughter bald. Now it was true the daughter had no hair and was obliged to wear a wig. But Ray had learned later this had nothing to do with Mrs. Walton. The child suffered a disease of the scalp that had destroyed the roots of its hair. Ray therefore believed the story about Dolly might be equally false. Certainly there was to her skin a greasy pallor. And certainly the darkness of her brows and opulence of her lips were more Romany than he cared to think. But was she really gypsy? He could not tell. Nor had he dared to ask. But if it were true, if there were gypsy blood in her veins might it not be inherited by their children? Might it not descend from one generation to the other so that not only would he have to suffer the ignominy of a half-gypsy wife but a half-gypsy family?

But when he told her he did not want to marry she turned nasty. All the venom she had turned upon his friends she now turned upon him. They slipped down the path to the cricket field, no longer hand in hand, walking separately, she stumbling over the roots and stones imbedded in the path, he listening with indifference to her abuse. It seemed just the opportunity he wanted to make a break. And instinctively it was as if she knew this, for once over the stile into the cricket field she had clawed with her nails at his face. The movement almost took him by surprise. He swayed out of reach and grabbed at her wrists. She lifted her foot to kick his shins and then her knee to butt his thigh. He sidestepped, blocking the blow to his thigh by turning inward his leg. He placed his own knee behind her and forced her to the ground. She had the strength of a cheetah and forcing free her hands she scratched the skin of his neck. He resisted the impulse to punch, but when her hands came round to claw his eyes he slapped her

283

face till she screamed. She quietened then, and with the breath knocked from her, with no longer the strength to fight his weight across her body, she had brought her arms around his neck, she had kneaded the skin where her nails had torn. She had raised her thighs to take the weight of his. And she had let him make love.

Yet it was her nature that decided him against her. His honesty told him if she was worth loving she was worth marrying. It also told him that if she was worth marrying it mattered little if she was half-gypsy or half-jap. And the ridicule of his friends should count for even less. But he could never marry a termagant. He could never marry anyone with a nature as fiery as that of his own. He wanted someone gentle and understanding, someone who would not contest his will but leave the decisions to him. Dolly would not make that kind of wife. She was too headstrong, too impulsive, too much like himself. She would push him, she would goad him, she would drive him repeatedly to see how far she could go. Then when his temper broke, when she overstepped the limit, he would put her sternly in her place. She would be gratified then, proud she had married a man and not a mouse. But sooner or later the process would begin again, the same manoeuvring, the same needling, just to see how he would react. And sooner or later he would have to react, for once she had driven him to the wall, once she had got the better of him, she would lose her pride and her respect. And he would be her slave for life.

He had not believed when she told him she was pregnant. He thought it another trap to force him into a marriage he did not want. He had taken great care to ensure she would not have a baby. To his young mind there were only two things in life that were irrevocable. One of them was death and the other making a girl pregnant you did not love. He knew he could not avoid the first but he had tried his best to avoid the second. There was only one night he had not been as careful as he might, and that had been the night of the fight. It had left him uneasy for a while, but he had pushed it out of sight in his mind. He refused to believe that a single slip could place her in the state she claimed she was in now. He had told her to forget it, not to worry, it would come all right in the end. After all, had he not heard men tell how they had tried years for their first baby? And was not the finest joke in the pit about a man ignorant in sex and shy of talking it over with his wife, who had tried years and years without success, but whose

284

wife had advised one day that they should try it 'the other way'? What on earth for, he had replied. Well you know we'll have to some day, she said. If we're to have a baby. But that was a joke. This was reality.

Dolly had met his father when her milk float ran away and she had been knocked to the floor of the cart among the crates. One crate had fallen from the cart to the ground. His father had been returning home from work when he heard the sound of breaking glass. Despite the cramp that seized his legs, he had stepped into the road and intercepted the runaway horse. He had picked Dolly from the floor of the cart as gently as he could. His intention had been to take her to the doctor's, but apart from a bruise on her knee she was only shaken. She recognized who he was and expressed her thanks. Then she invited him to the house to meet her mother. There had been at the back of her mind some vague idea of enlisting his support in her struggle to persuade Ray to marry. Holt, however, construed her intentions in a different light. And since no-one disillusioned him his visits to the house continued. The neighbours peeping from the curtains believed he was calling to see Mrs. Walton. They felt with her husband dead he was being cultivated as her fancy man. They were as astounded as the rest of the village when the truth was gossiped about.

When Dolly Walton told Ray she intended to marry his father he had laughed in her face. He realized now he ought not to have done that. For later it occurred to him that what Dolly had said had been nothing more than a threat. Possibly it had amused her as much as it amused him. But when he degraded her with his laughter she had either to go back on her word or carry it through. And being a headstrong girl, callow and unschooled, angry with Ray and determined to hurt, she had decided to carry it through. But even then she believed Ray would not put her nerve to the test. She knew he might not marry under the constraint of the baby, but she did not see how he could ignore the ridicule that would follow her marriage with his father. But Ray dismissed it as a joke just as he dismissed her pregnancy. So that her determination hardened. She accepted the proposal with the support of her mother. And before Ray knew it the story was all round the village.

Ray had not believed it was true till he noticed the reaction of his father. He had said not a word to him personally, but he could tell by the way he avoided his eye, the way he preferred to drink alone at the club, the way he tried to be out the house when Gerald came home. That night was the first time it had been raised between them. Gerald had shown what he felt by swinging the chair above his head, Ray had pointed out to his father the things that were being said behind his back. But listening to his father talking, explaining, understanding his motives, his loneliness, seeing through him to his past, to his years underground, seeing how he had been moulded by environment, by forty-five years in the pit, he could not find his heart to reveal the truth. The real reason why Dolly wanted to marry. Therefore he had washed the soap from his back, brought his clothes from the kitchen and returned to talk with Gerald while his father slipped out the back. He knew he was going to see Dolly. He knew too there was nothing he could do unless he could persuade Dolly to call it off of her own accord.

"Look," he said. "If ye're deein' it to spite me, ye're makin' a mistake. I couldn't care less."

"What makes ye think A'd dee it to spite ye?"

"There's nee other reason I can think on."

"That only shows ye cannot see farther than yer nose-end."

"I've told ye I'll pay," he said. "There'll be nee bother about that."

"Nee bother for ye," she said. "Plenty for me. Ye'd think A was a prostitute the way ye talk. Ye'd think ye'd picked us off the corner end. Ye'll pay, ye say. As if that was all that mattered. As if there was nowt more to worry about than that."

"Then tell us what it is ye want. See if I can help."

"A knaa what ye'd suggest if ye had yer way. But A'm havin' nowt like that. Neither from ye nor neebody. Ye divin't knaa what it's like to be a mother. To be carryin' a bairn by someone ye love. For ye it's only a problem o' the moment. Somethin' to get oot on the best way ye can. It's not like that for me. It's a time to be o'er the moon not doon in the dumps."

"That doesn't explain why ye're marryin' me father."

"Like A say, ye cannot see farther than yer nose-end. Ye think this kid A'm carryin'. Ye think it means nowt to ye so it means nowt to me. But ye're wrong. When it comes A'm ganna look after it. A'm ganna take care on it. See that it gets browt up proper and decent. See that it's not dragged up from the gutter the way A've been dragged. But it's got to get off to a good start. And to get off to a good start it's got to have its proper name. Its real name. Not the name of any Tom, Dick or Harry. And ye knaa what its real name is. Ye knaa the name A want."

"I've told ye I'll acknowledge it. We'll even take it to the courts if ye like. Give it its proper name."

"Another easy way oot. Just like payin'. But ye see A want more than its proper name, A want a 'spectable background. So that it gets the chance to be browt up decent. So that it has a proper father as well as a proper mother. But A want it 'spectable in such a way there's nee scandal for me mother. She's had enough in her time, what we wor Wally bein' to Borstal, and wor Annie in a sanatorium, and always people talkin' about the way we live. Talkin' behind her back as if they had nowt better to dee. So A'm ganna see they divin't get their tongues around me."

"But ye daft bitch. Divin't ye see they'll gossip anyway?"

"That's reet. 'Cause A'm marryin' a man owld enough to be me grandfather never mind me father. But ye see it'll be the reet kind o' gossip. It'll be the kind o' thing they'll expect from our family. They'll say, have ye heard about them daft Waltons? Marryin' their daughter off to a chap owld enough to be her grandpa. But then they'll say, what can ye expect? The way they've been browt up. But if they found oot A was carryin' a kid withoot a weddin' ring we'd never live it doon. And me mother — me poor mother — she'd never hold up her head again."

"Have ye told her yet? Yer mother."

"Not yet. She doesn't even knaa A've been to the doctor."

"I suppose ye'll tell her when ye get back."

"That's what the doctor sayed. Ye'll tell her when ye get in, A expect. Mebbes, A says. And mebbes not. First A've got to tell the lad that's 'sponsible. Then A'll think about tellin' me mother. But ye see A'm frightened to tell her 'cause A'm ashamed, 'cause if A did she'd howk me eyes oot. Not that A'd mind that 'cause A knaa A'd deserve it. But ye see A'd think o' all the trouble A'd be bringin' her. And A couldn't stand that."

"And ye'll tell her about me?"

"A'll tell her nowt. That way it's better for her and it's better for me. It'll be better for ye tee 'cause if she ever heard she'd sharp be along to knock yer block off. So A'm ganna marry yer father, ye see. And when we're married and settled and there's more water under the bridge, A'll tell her then. And she'll think, that was sharp. That was quick. But that's all she will think. Nowt else."

"And the folks in the village. If they get their tongues around that?"

"A'll be 'spectably married. There'll be nowt they can dee."

"Ye've got it all figured," he said. "Ye divin't need me for owt."

"That's reet. Ye've done yer work. Ye've made it all possible. Now ye can gan yer way and forget about us."

"I didn't mean it like that," he said.

"A knaa what ye meant. Ye're like the rest o' the village. Ye've nee respect for us. If ye had ye'd marry us even if ye didn't love us. Ye cannot understand that people like me — poor people, people that has nowt nor ever will have owt — that they can have a bit o' pride and self-respect. That they can worry about scandal and things people say behind their backs. There's such a thing as honour, ye knaa, even for folks like us. There's only folks like ye, folks that call themselves 'spectable, who think they're decent. Who divin't knaa what honour is."

Ray looked through the mist that was beginning to clear and reflected that perhaps she was right. Perhaps decent folk were never really decent, respectable people never really respectable. Otherwise why did they not show their decency to people like Mrs. Walton? Why did they cocoon themselves in their respectability? It was a strange world, he reflected, the people who needed respect never got it, the people who needed it so little had more than they could manage. Dolly stood still against the railings on the opposite side of the path and he brought his hand down the dark warm line of her neck and looked into her eyes. But he did not see her. Instead he saw her mother, walking through the village in her ancient brown coat, carrying her green bag, rolling along in her tired weary fashion, her brown trusting eyes fixed ahead, her mouth drooping like that of a dog, the two moles on her cheek, her black greasy hair lying flat around her neck. Always dragging with her at least one of her tribe. Yet who could imagine that such a woman might be injured by scandal, that she might yearn for respect, that at heart all she longed for was to be as decent and respectable as other people?

He saw Dolly then, not looking at him, looking into the swirls of mist, her brow fretted, her face sullen. And he realized how little he knew her. He knew her body, that was true, but he knew it as a surveyor might know a map, by its contours and watersheds, not by the quality of the country. He did not know what went on inside her head. But looking into her eyes, seeing the dark greasy hair falling around her face, he saw that she was a product of her mother. She had her mother's temperament, her mother's pride and her mother's defiance. He realized now the qualities that had made her hold her head high on the night of the competition. And he realized now why she had looked so much to him. Because she felt she had seen in him the same pride and the same defiance. But more than that she felt she had seen in him the same honour. And it was this honour that had prevented him joining the others in their clamour against her. He realized then it was true what she had said but what he had never believed. That she loved him. And that she was driven more by that than the thought to be free from her environment.

"There's another reason," he said. "Isn't there?"

"Aye," she said. "Always there's another reason."

"I think I knaa what it is," he said. "And if it's what I think I divin't want to hear it."

"Ye're ganna hear it," she said. "Whether ye like it or not. If ye divin't want to marry us that's yer look oot. But A'm ganna live wi' ye as best A can. Even if it means A have to marry yer father. Even if it means A have to share two men. Yer father'll not always be in the house. There'll be some weeks he works neets. So we'll have the house to ourselves. There'll only be me and ye and yer brother. And he'll not mind."

"But I'll mind. And I'll tell ye now, there'll be nowt like that."

"Not even when yer father's at work?"

"Not even when he's at work. And I warn ye, if ye gan through with it, then it's finished. I'll have nowt more to dee wi' ye. Not even when we're under the same roof. And as for the bairn, it'll not be mine. It'll be his. And after ye're married, if ye try to pin it on me I'll deny it. I'll deny everythin'."

"If A kept me mouth shut afore marriage A'm not likely to open it after, am A?"

They stared at each other a moment. And again he saw her looking for weakness. And this time he felt uneasy, as if she held over him something that was greater than himself. He had never before made love to a woman and he did not know the power that

289

sex could have over a man. Since she had raised the subject of marriage he had told himself their affair would soon be over. He promised himself one day he would make a date with her and not turn up. He made many such dates and settled himself at home before the fire, listening to the wind against the windows, feeling the heat of the fire against his legs, thinking what she would say when he did not arrive. She would be angry for a while, but gradually she would forget him just as he would forget her. He sat with the book upon his lap and listened to the alarm clock ticking on the mantelpiece. He decided to retire early and so be in bed before the time of the meeting arrived. Yet always at the last minute, for a reason he did not know, he would snap shut his book, pull on his coat and race through the village to be there on time. In most cases he was there before she was.

Dolly was not a clever girl but she sensed the sway she had over him. She sensed there was in him some power greater even than himself and she knew somehow she could manipulate that power to control him. She saw the uneasiness in his face and slipping from the railings reached on her toes and brought her face to his. "Then why divin't ye dee the sensible thing," she said. "Save us all the bother."

"And what d'ye call the sensible thing?"

"A've towld ye. Marry me."

"I couldn't," he said. "Even if I wanted."

"Then ye're as daft as A am. For lettin' us marry yer father."

"Ye divin't understand," he said. "Ye'll never understand."

"Understand what?"

"Why he's marryin' ye."

" 'Cause he's daft like the rest on us. And 'cause me mother pushed him into it."

"It's more than that," he said. "More than ye can imagine. It's not just 'cause he's lonely, not just 'cause he's facin' owld age and doesn't like the idea. It's not just 'cause he wants somebody to keep him company for when he's retired. It gans deeper than that. D'ye knaa how he used to treat me mother?"

"A heard about it. He'd better not try the same wi' me. A'll have his eyes oot afore he knaas he's sober."

"There'll be nowt like that," Ray said. "He's passed that now. But ye see he wants another chance. He wants to prove to himsel' that what he did wi' me mother — the bashin's he gave her when he was drunk — he wants to prove that wasn't the real him. That he's not like that. That he can be nice to a wife just like anybody else. But he's owld now, time's gettin' on, and he hasn't a wife to be nice tee. So that's why he wants to marry again. That's why he wants a second chance."

"He should look for somethin' owlder. If that's what he wants."

"It' s more than that," Ray said. "Ye see, his wife has to be young, just like ye. She has to be young enough to give him a family. Ye see, he's got Gerald and he's got me. But he knaas Gerald hates him for the way he treated me mother. And me — maybes he thinks I hate him tee. 'Cause of all the beatin's he used to give us a kid. Anyway, however he looks at it, he doesn't think he's got the respect that he's due. So not only does he want another chance wi' his wife, he wants another chance wi' his family. A family that'll grow up and respect him. That'll give him a bit o' comfort in owld age. The kind he'll never get from the likes o' me and Gerald."

"He towld ye that?"

"He didn't have to tell us. I can read it in his face, the way he looks sometimes. I can see it in the bend o' his shoulders when he walks across the heap. I can tell the way he sits o'er the fire and pokes the flames. He's me own father, I can read him like a book, the way he can read me. We've got the same nature, ye see, him, me and Gerald. So we all understand each other. Except Gerald. He doesn't understand him. But then that's 'cause he's never been down the pit."

He thought of his father leaning over the tub in the sitting room, white hair plastered by water to his scalp. He thought of him walking across the heap, his knee pads attached to his belt, helmet thrown back on his head, revealing the white line of his brow where the coal dust had to seep. And there came over him again that strong feeling he had for his father, which transcended human reason, but which he could never explain in words. Ray had to protect his father just as he had to protect the rest of the men. He had to protect them from being dragged by the scruff of the neck into the modern age. They were two of a kind, each resisting change, one because he felt he was too old, the other because he did not see why it should be imposed against his will. Only where his father hoped his fighting days were over Ray felt for him they were only about to begin.

"What ye mean is ye feel sorry for him."

"If ye like," Ray said.

"And ye'll let him marry us 'cause o' that?"

"Not 'cause o' that. I'd stop it if I could, but ye see I cannot. His mind's set on it and that's all there is to it. Ye see, at the bottom on him he thinks the world o' Gerald. Only Gerald doesn't think the world o' him. And the neet Gerald nearly bashed his head in with a chair. Just 'cause he sayed he was ganna marry ye. But still he's bent on carryin' it through. So if there's nowt Gerald can dee to change his mind there's nowt I can dee."

"So it's all fixed up. In three weeks time A marry yer father."

"I've told ye," Ray said. "I'll have nowt more to dee wi' ye if ye dee."

"That's what ye say noo," she said. "Wait till A'm married."

"All the same I've warned ye."

He felt her arms go round his neck and the dampness of her hair to his cheek. He placed his arms on the bare skin of her back and found that too damp with the mist upon it, yet the skin held its pristine warmth and standing so close, with her breasts crushed to his chest, he could smell the primitive odour of her body. She smiled and her teeth sparkled in the dimness. Her tongue sought his ear and he bent to kiss the nape of her neck.

"And in the meantime," she whispered. "What we ganna dee?"

There was only one thing he could do. He took her by the hand and led her along the path toward the cricket field. The field lay in an ampitheatre of woods and standing on the crest of the path looking down they could see the mist lying shallowly upon it. The mist was so thin now they could see the moon through its silver. She placed his hand to her lips and laid her head on his shoulder. His body no longer felt hot and sweaty, the sweat had dried on his face and his spots no longer ached, the tiredness he had felt momentarily standing by the hedge left him, he felt alive, alive in every muscle. The ache in his chest sharpened to the point of a dagger. His heart continued to beat against the walls of his chest. The earth was springy to his feet and looking down he could see in the mist the vague shape of the cricket pavilion. He felt the pressure of her fingers against his, the weight of her head to his shoulder, the odour of her body to his nostrils. He turned

292

her face to his and still holding her chin kissed her violently on the lips.

"Ye're sure ye'll have nowt to dee win us when A'm married?"

"I divin't knaa," he said. "We'll have to see."

They stumbled on down to the cricket field.

Book Five

The Fight

29

A. F. Donnolly, MP, rested against the sill of the window and with his back to the frame, hands folded across his chest, looked out from the council chamber to the rain that fell in the street. The light from the window broke across the pellucid blue scars on the strong but not handsome face, the strong white hair brushed from his brow; it fell too upon the lapels of his dark suit and the polished caps of his shoes. His temple rested against the cold glass of the pane as he looked across the street. Through the railings that surrounded the council building, Donnolly could see rain upon the roofs opposite, water sprayed from the gutter by cars along the road; he could see too starch faces peering out from the shelter in search of a bus, and even in the council chamber, through the thick plate of the windows, he could hear the hiss of wheels on the damp surface. In the flower bed below the level of the window raindrops clung like pearls to the blue skins of the irises and their yellow stamen tongues gaped in distress. A gust of wind lashed drops against the window and Donnolly withdrew his temple and began patting his pockets in search of his pipe.

He could not find it and realized he had left it in London. He had travelled up on the afternoon train the day before to be in time for what he described as his constituency surgery on the Saturday morning. His constituency comprised four urban districts and each Saturday in the month he visited one of the council offices to hear complaints from his constituents. He had been MP ten years now and never once had he tried to abandon this practice. His predecessor had been an intellectual, a minister in the Labour government between 1945 and 1950, and though he might have rendered distinguished service to his country there was little anyone could recall him doing for his constituency. That was one of the reasons why Donnolly, a local man, had been chosen to succeed him. And that was why he held his surgery every Saturday in the month.

Few people now attended the surgery. Though still advertized in the local press few realized it still existed. Nevertheless, Donnolly kept it on for the regular handful who called, some with real grievances, others with imaginary, some who were old and cantankerous, others young and innocent, all of them having complaints and all of them asking his help. They told him of their faulty water supplies, their leaking roofs, their electricity bills, their rates, their rents, sometimes their salaries, the old how difficult it was to live on their pensions, the young of the high interest rate on mortgages, the cost of agents' and solicitors' fees on a house. He listened sometimes with sadness and sometimes with amusement. Sometime there was something he could do and sometimes there was nothing. Often all he could do was offer advice. But on the whole his surgery was as dull and tedious as the debates in the Houses of Parliament. That day, however, he knew it would be different. He knew it as soon as he saw Markie Wishart striding up the path towards the council entrance.

"They say it's the early bird that catches the worm."

"I thought I'd get here sharp," Wishart said. "Seein' there's that much to talk o'er."

"So what can I dee for ye? Is it yer plumbin' or yer drainage that's wrong?"

"Neither one nor the other," Wishart answered. "And ye know as well as I do why I'm here."

Donnolly did indeed know. He knew all about the closure of the colliery and the destruction of the village. He knew of the threatened walk-out that had forced Wishart into calling an open meeting, he knew how the meeting had gone, how first his committee and then his chairman had deserted him, how that same night the men had held their own meeting in the singing end of one of the village clubs. He knew what the men had decided at that meeting. He knew why they had decided. He knew the part played by Ray and the part played by Wishart. He even knew how Wishart had cut his eye and what he had found on returning home when the meetings were over.

"They've been down three days now," Donnolly said. "They'll not stand much more o' that."

"That's what I said on the first day. And then on the second."

"Well, that's what I'm tellin' ye on the third."

Wishart shrugged out of his coat and shook the drops of rain from the shoulders. He took the seat Donnolly offered and folding his coat laid the damp side across his knee. His thin silver hair was plastered to his head and driblets of rain ran down his temples and cheeks to his neck and collar. When the drops reached into his shirt he took a handkerchief from his pocket and wiped away the damp. His face was paler in the light with the moisture upon it, the pouches tired under the eyes, the lids red-rimmed and angry, the elastoplast still across the stitches by the corner of the eye. He wore the same shirt and coat as on the night of the meeting, there was dried blood upon the sleeves and lapels and dark stains upon the shirt. It was not, however, the blood Donnolly noticed but the tremor in his hand, the tremble in his voice as he spoke.

"The latest I've heard," Wishart said. "Is that when the food's run out it'll be a hunger strike."

"And how long d'ye think a hunger strike'll last. In them conditions?"

"I don't know. They've stood it three days with food. Maybe they can stand it longer without."

Donnolly leant forward and rested his elbows upon the table. He did not look at Wishart but at the dull white light that broke across the worn tops of the desks. Against a window at the opposite end of the chamber stood a chestnut tree, its blossom forlorn in the rain, the serrated sides of the spear-shaped leaves pressing against the panes, the bark furrowed and ridged, dark and sleek with the rain upon it. Donnolly had spent many an hour in committee staring through that window. In winter when the tree was bare he had seen the water coolers of the power station built on a bend of the river, the tops of the houses slipping down the bank to the water's edge. In autumn he had seen the pregnant expansion of the green prickly cases that held the young chestnuts. Now he looked upon the blossom and the green shiny leaves and pulling his hands across the desk leant back in his seat.

"Ye knaa as well as I dee, Markie, the significance of a stay-down strike. It's a special kind o' protest, made by an individual with a grudge against the manager. Normally it lasts twenty-four hours. Sometimes it might last a week. But most cases it ends after three days, when they carry the man makin' the protest back to the surface. Sufferin' from cold and exhaustion. Now this time there's a hundred men down. And as I say it's the third day. Now it cannot last more than that. Otherwise ambulance men'll be down to bring the men up."

"I'm not so sure," Wishart said. "They say they'll stay down till they get satisfaction. And there's nobody offered satisfaction yet."

"Nor will anybody offer satisfaction. Not till they call the strike off and get back to normal."

"But they'll not do that. So it's stalemate."

"Stalemate between the men and the management," Donnolly said. "Not stalemate for ye."

"And what d'ye mean by that?"

"Ye knaa what I mean, Markie. It's up to ye to get the men back. It's up to ye to get the men out so that negotiations can begin."

Wishart became aware of the damp coat across his thighs and lifting it from his knees placed it over the back of the chair. There was a troubled look to his eyes as he turned. He thought of all the things he had intended walking home from the doctor's surgery, the call on the men's homes, the additional information sought from the manager, the official meeting he proposed to hold, with notices on the heapstead, with a committee behind him and a chairman capable of order. He had intended to demolish Ray as the planners would demolish the houses. Yet three days had passed and this was the first he remembered. He leant forward in his seat and folded his arms across his knees.

"That's why I've come to see ye, Albert. Because I'm not in a position to do that."

"Ye're the lodge secretary, Markie. If ye cannot neebody can."

"But ye were lodge secretary before me. And I thought with yer prestige, yer reputation, ye might be able to talk them o'er."

"Ye mean ye want me to gan down the pit and call the strike off?"

"It'd be a load off my mind if ye could."

"It'd be a load off everybody's mind. The only thing is what am I supposed to tell them?"

"Tell them they've made their protest and no matter how unofficial it's been noted by the lodge. Tell them the lodge'll make an official protest to the management and if the management doesn't take it up within five days it'll gan further. Tell them we'll get a man down from Durham and he'll take it up at area. Tell them everythin'll be done to safeguard their interests. Tell them everythin' they've been told by Ray Holt is rubbish. That they'll all be fixed up at other collieries, that there'll be no redundancies and no reductions in pay when they transfer."

"Ye mean they'll all be fixed up wi' jobs at other pits?"

"That's reet. And gettin' the same money they're gettin' here."

"So there'll be no redundancy after all?"

"None that I can think on."

"In that case why divin't ye gan down and tell them yersel'?"

"Because they'll not believe it if they hear it from the lodge secretary."

"Whereas they will if they hear it from me?"

"That's what I'm hopin'," Wishart said.

Donnolly leant back in his seat and looked at his hands. They were large worn hands, heavily lined and padded, yet the callouses had long since disappeared from the pads, the coal dust seeped from the lines. It was ten years since he had last been down a shaft. There were many MPs invited by the Coal Board to inspect faces where the latest type hydraulic props and trepanners had been installed; they were taken down specially by a manager or undermanager, wearing white overalls and helmet and photographed on their way back stepping from the cage. Yet these MPs were not the most vociferous in the House. Those who had most to say on coal and its industry were those who would not know a pit prop from a lamp post. Donnolly was a rare speaker in the House. Nevertheless he continued to study fuel and power and was therefore able to sit back and reflect objectively on the fate of Highhill. He knew all about the recession in the coal industry, he knew why there was a recession. He even knew where the recession had begun.

"If I heard reet, Markie, what ye mean to say is that ye've spoken to the management."

"I've not spoken to them yet," Wishart said. "But I will."

"So to be honest, it's not what the management say. It's what ye say."

"But I'm sure the Coal Board'll guarantee it if it means gettin' the men back to normal."

"Ye think they'll guarantee there'll be no redundancy and no reduction in rates when the men transfer?"

"I'm sure of it."

"Divin't ye understand, Markie, that everythin's come about
the way it has because ye made promises ye couldn't keep. And
because it was shown ye couldn't keep them? Now ye want me
to gan down the pit and repeat the promises. Ye're bankin' on my
reputation and my prestige to do yer dirty work for ye. Ye want
me to gan down the pit and make a liar and a hypocrite o' mesel'
just so that the strike's broken and the men get back to normal."

"I'm askin' it in the men's interest," Wishart said. "I cannot
sleep at night thinkin' o' them down there in the cold and damp.
With hardly any air and no light. I think o' the way they're
jeopardizin' their future, the national agreements made with the
Coal Board. I keep thinkin' o' their wives on bank, some o' them
standin' round the yard, worryin' about their husbands and their
sons. Lost because there's no baits to make up and bottles to prepare and boots to scrape and clothes to dad. I want to see things
back to normal. That's all I want. Everythin' back to normal."

"Then ye shouldn've let things get out o' hand in the first
place. Ye shouldn'tve listened to all that twaddle spat at ye the
other night by the industrial relations officer. Things are the way
they are, Markie, because ye never handled the men proper. Ye
knaa and I knaa this colliery's finished. And in their heart o'
hearts maybes the men knaa it tee. But they'll not admit it. So
they were lookin' to ye for guidance. They were lookin' to ye to
tell them what to do. How to fight. And the top and bottom of it
is, Markie, ye never told them."

"Ye cannot fight for things which ye don't believe."

"It's not what ye believe. It's what's in the best interests o'
the men. And even if ye divin't believe ye still have to be diplo-
matic. Ye should have filed yer protest then and there, at the consultative meetin'. Then ye could have reported back to the men
with a clear conscience. Ye could have told them ye'd filed yer
protest and they'd have been happy. And then after a few months
and a bit o' negotiation, when tempers had cooled, when the men
were gettin' used to the idea, ye could have reported back and
said there was nothin' to be done. But all the same their interests
were safeguarded. That way everybody would have been satisfied."

Donnolly folded the papers he had deliberately scattered on
his desk and tucked them away in his briefcase. He avoided

Wishart's eyes. There was a gulf between them now, the friendship of a lifetime had been severed because for Wishart events had passed beyond his control. He was an unexceptional man dealing with exceptional circumstances. He would have been better handling the organization of an accepted decision. He would have been at home explaining to the men how the transfers and redundancies would be organized, how cavels would be drawn, how first out would be those last in, or those with a persistent record of absenteeism. But this was not an accepted decision, things had not been handled as they should have been, and the circumstances remained exceptional. Donnolly replaced his briefcase against the leg of the desk and gazed over Wishart's shoulder to the portraits of distinguished councillors that graced the chamber walls.

"So there's nothin' ye can do?" Wishart asked.

"Sure there's somethin' I could dee. Always there's somethin'. I could gan down the pit if ye want, I could talk to the men, I could tell them everythin' ye say. But there's nee certainty I'd be comin' up again, once I heard their point o' view. There's nee certainty at all that I wouldn't stay down with them and join their strike. Because it seems to me there's not much security in what they've been told up to now. Transferrin' them to doomed pits, offerin' them jobs in Staffordshire, tellin' them to move into houses that's not built. That's not my idea o' security. Never was and never will be."

Wishart rose from his seat and turned to go. He plucked his coat from the back of the chair and pulled it over his shoulders. Water had dropped from the lapels upon the floor and there were bars of dampness across his thighs where first he had lain it. He pulled himself into the coat, stiffly, jerkily, feeling its dampness round his shoulder blades, clumsily fastening the buttons and turning up the lapels round his open neck. Water ran slightly from his hair to his face and he wiped it away with his hand. He had been out of work three days now and already the hands were losing their coarseness, were softer and whiter, the nails less broken and black. But the hurt Gerald Holt had once noticed in his face was deeper and more permanent. His movements had always been slow but now they were slower and Donnolly was not sure if the pause he made was deliberate as they turned towards the door.

"There's another thing I wanted to ask," he said. "Before I

gan."

"That's why I'm here, Markie. So I can answer questions."

"Who d'ye think's at the bottom of all this?"

"I should've thowt by now everybody knaas who's at the bottom on it."

"Everybody thinks it's Ray Holt. But it's not. It's somebody else."

He pulled up the back of his collar and thrust his hands into his pockets. He continued towards the door as a new gust of wind and rain lashed the windows. The light through the window flooded upon the linoleum and the tops of the desks in the council chamber. On the desks he could see the initials scratched through dull committee or council meetings, the ink stains of a hundred responsible councillors. The radiators in the chamber were not working and standing by the door he became aware of the cold dampness, a chill that made him shiver. Outside the window, in the border that surrounded the offices, the blue irises were torn and drooping where they had been bludgeoned by the rain, and the earth of the border was darker and richer with the rain upon it. He could see the sky above the glistening blue of the slate roofs, grey and overcast, the clouds scudding heavily by from the west. He brought his hands from his pockets and his fingers reached for the handle of the door.

"How d'ye make that out?" Donnolly asked.

"The night o' the meetin'. He knew more about the colliery than I knew mesel'."

"He's just well informed. That's all there is to it."

"It's more than that," Wishart said. "He knew everythin' about the village too. He knew which streets were comin' down first and which were to follow. He knew when they were comin' down and why they were comin' down. And he knew it all before it ever reached the pages o' the papers."

"Maybes he made enquiries and found out."

"That's what I thought in the beginnin'. Now I know it's not true."

"And how d'ye knaa that?"

"The meetin' he held in the singin' end o' the club. After the meetin' at the institute. I would say there was o'er a hundred men at the meetin'. All with throats as dry as blottin' paper. And d'ye know what? All the drink was free. Every glass and bottle in the

304

place. So there wasn't a drop left by the time the meetin' was finished. I had a talk with the steward the next day. He told us it cost at least a hundred and fifty quid."

Wishart opened the door and together they walked along the corridor towards the council exit. Donnolly was not alone in holding a surgery on Saturday morning and the office was full of people waiting patiently outside the doors of the various council departments, waiting to see the clerk to the council, the housing manager, the public health inspector, the sanitary inspector. They sat in hard-backed chairs along the wall and the corridor was filled with the odour of dampness coming from their clothes and hats and umbrellas. Clerks shuffled in and out of the various departmental offices and from the direction of the typing pool there came the rattle of a tea trolley. There was a draught to their faces as Wishart opened the door and the draught grew stronger and colder as they moved along the corridor towards the exit.

"So who d'ye think it is if it's not Ray Holt?"

"To my way o' thinkin', it could be any one o' three people. The first I reckon it might be is Atkin, the colliery manager. Everybody knows how much effort he's put into this colliery, how bitter he is because it's bein' closed. He'd be in a position to give information if he wanted. I'm not sayin' he did mind, but he could've done. And there's no reason why he shouldn't if he thought he'd get away with it."

"And yer idea o' the second?"

"There's his brother Gerald. He works in the colliery office, he'd have access to all the information he wanted. Only I don't think it's him. It could be, but I doubt it. He couldn't care less if the colliery shut or not. He's stuck-up at the best o' times, thinks he's goin' places, thinks he's above us. He'd not stoop to give information to anybody. Least of all his brother."

"Which only leaves the third."

"The third I thought on was the local MP. He's born and bred in the village, he was lodge secretary for nigh on twenty years before me, he drinks at the club every Sunday dinner time. And he knows everyone in the village by their christian names. If anyone could lay hands on the right information he could. And there'd be ample opportunity if he wanted to pass it on."

The large heavy doors to the council building were open and pulled back to the wall and Donnolly leant against the frame to

305

look into the street. He had known from 1944 that one day he would be candidate for Parliament and therefore he had looked carefully and meticulously for someone to fill his place. He had wanted someone for the council, the county council, and secretary of the lodge. Sanderson had more interest in local politics but Wishart more interest in the men. It was true he was a moderate, he did not have in his belly the fire of his predecessors, but with nationalization the industry had need of moderates, they had need of men who would see to it that union rules would be adhered to, agreements kept, that there was a proper relationship between management and men. Donnolly had never expected great things of Wishart, but he had trained and cultivated him as best he could, and over ten years he had watched with satisfaction his handling of many difficult situations. Now for the first time he felt something other than satisfaction, not anger, not hurt. Only disappointment.

"Ye honestly think I'd dee a thing like that?"

"I didn't say ye did. But ye could on."

"The first thing I'd like to say, Markie, is that ye're not the fellow I used to knaa. A man of honour and character, a man who always seemed to knaa what was best. Ye've changed a lot o'er the last few days and I understand why ye've changed. It's not easy when things get out o' control. It's harder to bring them back than it is to let them gan. All the same, the first thing ye learn in politics is to be careful what ye say."

"I didn't want to cause offence, Albert. If that's what ye mean."

"Ye're an old friend o' mine, a friend o' long-standin'. So I'll not take it amiss what ye said. But others might. Gerald Holt, for example. And the colliery manager. They're not daft, ye knaa, either o' them. They'd have ye in court afore ye could turn yer garden. So if ye're bent on makin' enquiries I'd be careful how ye gan about it. Otherwise ye'll see the day when ye regret it."

"So what it boils down to is, it wasn't ye?"

"The first I heard o' the strike was what I was told by me agent o'er the phone in London. O' course, everybody knaas it's an old colliery and anybody with any sense must've known it'd have to close sometime. Just as all the pits in the area'll have to close. And the houses were condemned afore I was elected to Parliament. Even afore the start o' the war. They should've been down years ago. I've said it afore and I'll say it again. But I never thowt it'd turn out like this."

"Then there's only the manager."

Wishart braced his body to face the rain, but as he moved to step onto the pathway Donnolly eased from the frame of the door and lifted a hand to his arm. Wishart paused and for the first time their eyes met. In the light from the open doorway Wishart's grey eyes were white and shiny, red veins ran riot in the whites, the rims remained red but were no longer darkened by coal dust, the soft pouches were the colour of small bruises, and the lines had deepened round the corners. There was grey stubble to his cheeks and strong haggard lines ran from his nose to the corners of his mouth. His face seemed whiter and more finely drawn. There was no blood to his lips but a vein throbbed nervously in his temple and there was a dark edge of dirt around the elastoplast. He tugged against the pressure of Donnolly's hand but the fingers were firm on the gaberdine.

"Where ye off tee now, Markie?"

"Ganna see the manager. Put to him the same question I put to ye."

"Then mark what I say. Watch how ye gan."

The gaberdine slipped from Donnolly's fingers and as Wishart walked down the pathway a gust of wind blew a damp scrap of paper limpidly across the pavement, the blossom of the chestnut trees lay sodden in the gutter, and the rain danced a butterfly dance off the road. The rain whipped at Wishart's face and hair and clawed at the white elastoplast. He winced as he walked the length of the pathway to the pavement. He walked slowly and deliberately, his tread heavy, and when he reached the end he turned to face the full brunt of the rain. His head bent slightly and the wrinkles gathered round the eyes. His brow crumpled, his mouth slightly opened, and the rain ran down his cheeks like tears. Yet he did not seem to notice.

He just kept walking, walking into the rain.

307

30

Ray Holt led the men down the pit as he had led them down the bank from the institute.

He led them with full bait tins and bottles, bulging pockets and chests, carrying as usual their lamps and tokens but also dart boards and dominoes, cards, dice and monopoly. They waited for him in the pityard so that he would be first to step into the cage. He walked past the colliery offices and looking down into the yard saw the sun upon the polished crowns of their helmets, their scarred faces pale in the light; they cheered as he walked past the office, holding his hands to his chest, this time not to withstand the pressure of books but to contain the sandwiches and biscuits he had stuffed into as many spare tins he could carry. He kicked up spurts of dust as he dropped down the cinder path, his helmet pushed back on his head, his spots showing less in the light, hair gold with the sun upon it. The men parted to let him through, still cheering and clappping, but the cheering and clapping ceased as he stepped onto the iron sheets before the mouth of the cage.

The studs of his boots scraped the sheets as he turned, slightly out of breath, holding with one hand his chest and lifting the other to rest on the iron frame of the cage. The cage was used not only to haul men but to haul tubs and there were small tracks in the cage to facilitate loading at the shaft bottom and top. The tubs were hauled along the engine plain from coal reservoirs fed by belts, loaded into the cage in pairs, and once at the surface rolled off again and hauled to the screens. The rails in the cage were shiny with use and caught Ray's eye, glinting in the light. He looked from the rails to the wheels of the colliery stock, strong and proud against the sky, silent and motionless too, the winder man out of sight, waiting, ready to control the flight of the cage to the unknown. To the bowels of the harmless earth. The greased cables of the hauler glittered and the paintwork of the stock was dull and red, showing patches of rust where the paint had flaked.

Ray felt the pressure of the tins against his chest and looked around as if for the last time. His gaze swept beyond the heads of the men to the sparse grass of the embankment, the street of officials' houses overlooking the colliery. He saw the sky a pale fragile blue, the clouds low and white, skimming from over the hill. He listened for the sounds of the colliery he heard each morning tramping across the yard, the hiss of steam from the engine sheds, the clatter of coal down chutes, tools from machine shops, he looked for the shower of sparks from the blacksmith sheds, the smoke that puffed from the chimneys, he waited to hear the rattle of tubs, the sound of unloading from the storehouse. But this morning there was nothing. There was only the sight of the sun upon the colliery pipes, the shuffle of men awaiting his sign, the ceaseless drone of the power station serving not only the colliery but the village. The last white wisp of smoke where the day before they had been burning coal tubs on the heap.

And as he looked around he smelt to his nostrils the air of the country, fresh and unpolluted, not heavy with dust, not damp or fetid, stale and unhealthy, but clean and invigorating, not limpid or dead with passing through galleries and air doors. He smelt the air and felt the cold iron to his hands and thought of the cold below, so that there came again the old hatred, the old disgust, that men should work underground, that they should walk along galleries as hump-backed as rats, as blind as moles but for the light that shone from their helmets. That they should have to risk their lives in seams eighteen inches high, the weight of the world held from their shoulders by small slim props. With only water seeping through drop by drop, upon neck and face, hands and wrists, forming puddles and pools, giving dermatitis and rheumatism, wasting muscles, cramping tissues. Bringing them all to an earlier grave. But that they had to fight for these things because this was all they had, this and the village, and if they lost the one then surely they would lose the other.

He brought his hand from the iron and despite the weight of the tins straightened his shoulders. He looked up to the colliery office. He saw the pebbledash walls, the open doorway, the blue slate that shone on the roof. He saw the windows cast in shadow, and beyond the shadow, out of sight and out of reach, he felt he saw the figure of authority, that wanted to destroy not only the men but also their families, not only their past but also their future. And he looked to the men. He saw them not as they had been the night before, in fustian breeches, shabby coats, canvas-thick shirts, carrying from habit their kneepads and mackintoshes, lamps already fitted to the sockets of their helmets, the batteries attached to their belts at the waist. He saw their faces starched white, with no colour to the cheeks, lips dry and flecked with spittle, and in their eyes he saw the same understanding, the same comprehension. As if they understood what the battle was for and why it had to be fought. So that there rose in him again the same urge to protect and defend, to safeguard their interests.

But once in the pit the first impulse of the men had been to destroy. They had wanted to set about the cutters, sabotage the belts, damage the pumps, pull the props from the faces, even tamper with the fan that circulated the air. Their tempers had cooled overnight, but in the morning, on the delivery of the papers, they had skimmed through the pages to see if what Ray had said was true. And sure enough, in the provincial paper published in the city, there was an article given a second lead on a middle page, proclaiming the destruction of the village and the dispersal of its inhabitants. The paper of course did not take the same view as the people of the village. They followed the line given them by the county planning department. They highlighted the kind of houses into which the people would be moved and listed the amenities that would be provided. They indicated the advantage of commuting a shorter distance into the town and in order to fill out the story gave a list of the village streets that would be affected.

That was enough for the men. Any doubts they had were swept away, they did as Ray told them, they slipped into as many woollens they could lay their hands on, they took out gloves, swathed themselves with mufflers, and had their wives fill as many bait tins and flasks they could. They cut the article from the paper and had the cuttings pinned in all the galleries of the pit, along the engine plain, in the various districts and seams, even on the cutters they had wanted to destroy. Their idea had been to dismantle one of the cutters and send it to the surface as a gift to the manager, with copies of the articles pinned to the pieces. But Ray warned against such violence. He said he wanted the support of the public not its hostility, he wanted its sympathy, not its

310

animosity. And just to make sure his counsel was followed he had pickets placed on the main faces, he had the men separated into districts, giving one district to Bousefield and another to Walton, but each well away from the other so there would be no antagonism. He had Featherley act as his special liaison, wandering from district to district, gauging the mood of the men, carrying messages, listening to any complaints, and relaying these complaints back to Ray. Ray also placed pickets at the mouths to the drifts that were linked to the main workings, he also had them on the bank top so that now what he described as unauthorized persons would be able to use the cage.

The unauthorized persons were of course Wishart and the manager. Reporters could come down if they wished, but permission was refused by the management, though television cameras were allowed to take pictures of the pithead. Wishart worked the hauler in the drift but had not shown up for work the day the strike began, and later when he did show up he had been refused to set foot in the cage. He had telephoned the pit from the colliery office but each time he called no-one appeared to know where Ray was. Atkin made no effort to go down the pit and talk with the men. He claimed that since the stoppage was unofficial it was in the hands of the union. The Coal Board agreed with this. Which was just as well for the manager, since the men threatened to hang him from a girder if he so much as showed his face. On the day the strike began Ray had called upon other collieries in the area to come out in support, and once the story hit the paper, though the strike had no official backing, other collieries came out in protest. There were many stoppages and loss of output before finally the men were persuaded to go back.

The only colliery where the men did not go back was of course Highhill.

It was only natural, however, that the men should want to be violent. They were not clever men, they had no higher education, they saw only the obvious and that when it was put to them. They had come from the land to the mine to be exploited by speculators eager to make the most of the land they had bought. Through the centuries they had been bullied by owners, badgered by overseers, taunted for barbarity and want of intelligence, made to work in pits whose only ventilation had been a fire at the bottom of the shaft to keep moving the air. But when there were explosions, when fire ignited pockets of coal damp, when men were killed and nothing was done, when conditions after the accident were the same as those before, the men acted in their own interests. They set about property, they set about life, they inflicted damage where they could. Then they went back to work, sheepishly, foolishly, paying for their damage to property out of their wages, their injury to life in the courts. It was true those days were history, the miner of today was not the miner of yesterday, only faced with the same injustice his instinct did not change. Faced with an obvious wrong the instinct rose to set it right.

So that now they had to fight again. They had to fight for their colliery and their village. In the past they had fought for a higher minimum wage, shorter hours, better working conditions, they had fought for the right to a holiday, the right of compensation after an accident. Now they fought for the right to survive. And in order to fight they had to face the elements they hated most, the dark, the damp, the cold and the loneliness. They had to stage a stay-down strike in order that their voices could be heard, their claims met. But a stay-down strike is not the best of strikes, even when staged by a hundred men. Fears are like shadows that enlarge themselves in the reflection of a light, the mind begins to wander, to take on eerie thoughts, a chill attacks the feet and despite the welter of garments moves up through the body like ice in the blood stream. Darkness and damp are everywhere and so too is loneliness, the loneliness a man feels when he is not with his wife, when he is not in the heat and sweat of a club, when he misses the warmth of a bath, the comfort of a bed to ease his aching muscles.

Now, after three days, the mood of the men was beginning to change. They were beginning to falter. They were missing their wives and their homes. They were tiring of each other's company. The exuberance of doing something daring was beginning to wear off. They were cold, they were stiff, they were hungry. And they were disgruntled. They were beginning to ask themselves why it was their colliery should be singled out, why they had to fight and not their union, they were beginning to wonder what they were doing there, why it had happened to them and not to someone else. For three days Ray had let them do what they liked. He had restrained them from violence, but he had let them play their cards and their darts and their dominoes because instinctively he had known reaction would set in, the glamour and adventure wear off, the humour of the men begin to change. So that when the change came he was ready. He was not surprised. First he cheered their spirits by distributing copies of the district newspaper that ran a story on the strike, together with the names of the men taking part. Then he summoned together the men and held his first meeting at the deputy's kist along the rolleyway.

The kist was a white-washed cabin where deputies met to write their reports. The cabin was set in one of the walls of a gallery wider than most where tubs were filled from the coal reservoir and coupled to the set to be hauled out-by. In the kist there was a desk similar to the ones in the colliery office. The desk was polished with the passing and repassing of documents and on its top stood a telephone linked to the bank. On the wall above the telephone there was a calendar revealing the shaped back and curved buttocks of a nude woman, and to the left by the notice board a green-painted medical box bearing a red cross in a white circle. The box contained a phial of morphia used by deputies and overmen in the event of emergency. The emergency was a serious accident, but the morphia had not been used for several years, not since a joiner travelling in-by had thrown his bag of tools on the incoming set. The strap of the haversack had remained round his arm and dragged him under the wheels.

The set had now been pushed from the loading point and in the cleared space the men sat on their haunches the way they sat around the corner ends. They sat patiently, stoically, hands folded across their chests or embracing their knees, looking up to Ray on an eminence above them. He had taken off his helmet and gloves and thrown them into the kist. He sat on an upturned tub as the men sat on the tracks. His hair was pressed flat to his skull by the constant wearing of the helmet, the hair was streaked with dust, and little heads of dust had embedded themselves in the roots. Though he had done no work, his hands and face were black, streaked where he had rubbed his gloves, his face seemed thinner, leaner, the bones more prominent. But his hands and lips still moved in harmony, moved restlessly and impatiently as he spoke.

"First of all I'd like to say how grateful I am we're still all here. A hundred on us began this strike and a hundred on us are carryin' it on. There's neebody changed their mind yet and there's neebody tried to sneak out the back way to the surface. I knaa

313

how many of us must have thowt on it, I thowt on it mesel'. But here I am and here I stay. Till we get satisfaction on the points we've put to the management. Till we receive assurances this pit'll not close, that there'll be no redundancies and no transfers, that they'll not pull down the houses — our houses — and move us about like cattle. That we'll be able to live where we want to live. Die where we want to die. That's all the guarantees we want, nowt more and nowt less. But here we are and here we stay till we get them."

He gathered on his tongue a gobble of dried dust and turning his head spat it upon the tracks. He wiped his sleeve across his mouth.

"But what do the management say to our proposals? Do they say they'll take them into consideration. Do they say we're reet to demand a bit o' security for our wives and families? Or do they say we have to gan back to work, back to normal? But even then they still divin't say things'll be any better, they still divin't give any promises. Any guarantees. They say they'll negotiate, they'll take it up wi' the union. But the union's already sold us once and who's to say they'll not sell us again? So what's the point o' negotiatin'? What's the point o' sittin' round a table? Either they're prepared to grant concessions or not. And if they're prepared to grant concessions why divin't they grant them now while we're on strike? Why do they want to sit us round a table? I'll tell ye why. 'Cause they've no intention o' grantin' concessions. 'Cause once they start negotiatin' they'll do the talkin' and the union'll do the acceptin'. That's how it was afore and that's how it'll be again."

He leant his elbows on his knees and looked down upon the wheels dismantled from the upended tub. He did not feel the tension he had felt before his confrontation with Wishart, nor did he feel the excitement that had roused him as he related the facts about the village. The rims of his eyes ached with tiredness and the ache between his shoulders was sharp as he hunched uncomfortably. He did not look at the men but at the lights above their heads strung trinket-like along the rolleyway. He knew they would not like the proposals, for he knew their thoughts before they knew them themselves. But he knew too they would accept because there was nothing else they could do. They could not return to the surface and tell their wives they had failed. They could not say there was no hope for the colliery or the village, that

314

they would have to accept defeat because they had accepted it themselves. To do this was to accept not only defeat but surrender, to lose not only their homes and their jobs but their self-respect. And that, he knew they would never do.

"So what we ganna dee in the meantime? I'll tell ye what we're ganna dee. We're ganna continue this strike. We're ganna stay down till we get satisfaction. If it takes a week, if it takes a month, if it takes a year. So that they'll understand we mean business. So that they'll understand we have reets and we want to see them reets respected. And if it means we'll have to suffer then we'll suffer. If it means we'll have to dee without then we'll dee without. If it means a few more days of aches and pains, then we'll accept the aches and the pains. And we'll accept them not only for ourselves but for our wives and families. So that there'll be work and wages, a roof o'er our heads, so that we'll have the security o' the colliery and the security o' the village. So that we'll have a future. But we're ganna have to suffer, suffer long and suffer hard, suffer cold and suffer cramp. And suffer gladly at that."

The men listened quietly, uneasily, some sitting now on the cold rock between the rails, some on the rails themselves, rubbing together their hands, others drawing fingers in the dust, stubbing the caps of their toes against the chocks. They wanted to be told good news, they wanted to be told their strike had been a success, that they had gained their reward. But instinctively they had known what Ray had to tell and because they had known when they heard their resentment was sharpened. Even the younger ones were less enthusiastic. For three days they had rode the miniature cage coupled to the stapple bottom and top, they had walked the pit with a yardstick, they had organized rat hunts, they had explored old workings, seams narrow and dangerous, boardrooms long since sealed, but neither beer nor cigarettes had crossed their lips. For Ray had banned both and all had been stopped and searched at the shaft bottom the day the strike began. They had slept on girders, they had slept on timber, they had told dirty jokes and stories to lull them to sleep. And when sleep came they had grown oblivious to the smell of dust, the discomfort, the draught, the austerity of their beds. The red eyes of the rats that peered from the gloom.

Now they were stunned at what Ray had said. For it was

Saturday and Saturday was a big day in the village. Saturday was what they had looked forward to all week. On Saturday there was drink to be had, racing on television, there were wives to be taken out, wives and fancy wives, there was the local hop for the village lads, Dixon of Dock Green for the stay at homes. There were papers to read and brag to play. There were allotments to tend, pigeons to train, leeks to supervise, tomatoes to cultivate, pigs to feed, seed to plant. In short a whole village rising from a week of slumber. For strange though it may seem in the second half of the twentieth century, there are still people who live their own lives, follow their own hobbies, who take pleasure from simple things, things done by their fathers and their fathers before them. Who entertain themselves and are not always entertained by others. So that, sitting in the cold, thinking of the week behind, thinking of the week ahead, a grumble of protest rose around Ray.

"But hoo we ganna live?" someone shouted.

"That's reet. Hoo we ganna keep ourselves alive?"

"I'll tell ye how we'll live," Ray said. "And I'll tell ye how we'll keep alive. Ye've all had a bit of a holiday up to now. Ye've run around and done pretty well what ye like. And I've let ye dee what ye liked 'cause like ye I thowt a few days strike would suffice. 'Cause I thowt the management'd see our point o' view. But it's not turned out the way we thowt. 'Cause they divin't care, really care, like they say. Otherwise they'd have promised somethin' just so that we could get back to bank. Get back to our homes and our beds. But they're not really interested if we get back to these things. They're not really interested if we're alive or dead. So the strike continues. So we'll have to get organized. And the first thing we're ganna have to dee is move out o' here up into the owld workin's. Where we can keep warmer and drier. And we're ganna utilize the straw o' the pony stables, and make ourselves palliasses. So that we can stick it out for as long as it takes the management to see reason."

"But hoo will we keep warm? What'll we dee about that?"

"We're ganna work," Ray shouted. "That's reet, work. Face-workers are ganna get back to their faces and clean them up, stone-men are ganna dee a bit o' canchin, datal workers are ganna busy themselves in the main galleries, layin' stone-dust, white-washin' kists, maintenance men are ganna repair belts. And a few others, instead o' lazin' about down here complainin' o' the cold, they're

316

ganna get themselves up to the owld workin's where we'll sleep, they're ganna clear them out o' rats and dung and wipe away all the fungus that's hangin' from the roofs. And each day we're ganna find somethin' fresh to dee. Each day we're ganna work a few hours, not to produce coal, not to help the manager, but to help ourselves. To keep our minds and bodies occupied, just enough to get the blood circulatin'. Just enough to take the cramp and ache from our limbs."

"But hoo we ganna take the cramp from our bellies. What we ganna eat?"

"We'll not eat," Ray said. " 'Cause of now it'll be a hunger strike. And it'll stay a hunger strike till the management relent and send food down or till the management accept our demand for steady employment and security o' future. And don't ask how long that'll be 'cause I divin't knaa. But I dee knaa that no matter how long it is ye'll still find me down here to the last. Till there're guarantees of a house and job not only for me but for everyone in this pit. And remember this, we're not alone down here. Ye heard about the token strikes at other pits — strikes 'cause the men there knaa that what they're seein' here they'll one day see themselves. Ye heard about what was on the television, and ye've read yerselves what the papers say about us. And ye knaa I've got a brother in the colliery office. A brother that's on our side, always has been, always will be. So we'll get by, divin't worry about that. We'll stick it out till our aims are met, ye'll see. Till we have the management on their knees, offerin' any concession we like, owt we have a mind. If only we'll call the strike off."

Even as they sat the men felt the ache in their bellies. Their bait tins and flasks had long since emptied, the little food packed by their wives exhausted, for a day now they had not known what it was for food or drink to cross their lips, and more than ever they missed the taste of nicotine to their throats, beer to their tongues. But they had contented themselves by pretending the strike would soon be ended, they had amused themselves by thinking what they would eat, what they would drink once they reached the surface. Now they looked around the loading point. They saw the black belts that carried the coal from the face, they saw the dark iron of the reservoir, they saw the light reflecting on the girders, the shiny dusty walls. And they saw Ray Holt, standing now on the tub, but bent with his hands on his knees; they saw

the light behind catching the fairness of his hair, they saw the
white of his teeth, the paleness of his lips and tongue. And they
saw his eyes. They had never been distinguished eyes, always a
little grey, always a little blodshot, but now they shone out of
his blackened face, shone with strength and determination and
courage. Courage that could damp but not quell the protest.

"But them that's gettin' on in years. Hoo will they stick it
oot?"

"They'll not," Ray said. " 'Cause I'm sendin' them back to
the surface. 'Cause they've had enough o' the pit without havin'
this. And 'cause it's time we younger ones fought their battles for
them. For as ye knaa it'll be the owlder ones that'll be hit by the
closure o' the colliery. They'll be the ones retired afore their time
— at the age o' fifty accordin' to Wishart — they'll be the ones
made redundant. And they'll be the ones that'll not get a job.
'Cause there's nowt they can dee outside a pit. But as I say it's
time we fought their battles for them. So from the day any man
o'er fifty'll be sent back to bank. And with him'll gan any man
who doesn't feel he can continue the strike. Who couldn't care
less whether this colliery closes or not. I divin't want this kind o'
defeatism round me. Any man who thinks this strike'll be a failure
can gan back. Any man who puts the interest o' himself afore that
of his wife and bairns can pick up his helmet and pads, bait tin
and battle, and leave now."

But no-one moved. Their hearts and their bellies and their
minds told them to do as Ray said, to gather their helmets and
pads, their bait tins and flasks, to take their aching limbs away
from the cold, their minds from the dark, but their legs did not
obey the order. They felt the cold to their buttocks as they might
feel damp. Their hands too were stiff, so stiff no amount of rubbing
would bring back the circulation, so that they tucked them under
their arms or began patting their pockets in search of gloves. But
still no-one moved, not even the older ones Ray had said should
return to the surface. For what Ray had known was right. They
could not return, they could not accept defeat, they could not lose
their self-respect. They were bitter at the thought of what lay
ahead, they did not relish the prospect outlined by Ray, but they
would not return to the surface to admit surrender. Instead their
eyes turned to the news cuttings pinned to the walls, the paper
already grey with dust, yet the print still legible, outlining what

would happen to their village, to their lives, so that they felt again the same anger, the same stubborness. The same will to defy.

And Ray was glad they did not move. For a moment he had seen the collapse of the strike, he had seen the men returning, leaving only he and his friends to carry on to failure and victimization. He was like a man walking a tight rope, not really sure of himself, uncertain like the rest, but trusting his instinct, trusting sense of right and wrong, gauging the thoughts and feelings of the men and trimming his speech to these feelings. Standing there, hands on his knees, head uplifted, he wondered how it would end. Yet with the men not moving there was only one way it could end. The strike would be a success, there would be no redundancies, no transfers and no closure of the colliery. Even the houses of the village would be saved. There was still some distance to go, he knew that, the men would suffer more than they bargained, the strike last longer than expected, but they had either to put their faith in Ray or put their faith in the devil. And since they worked each day with the devil on their shoulder, since they faced the hell of the pit all their working lives, they placed their faith with Ray.

"So it's all settled and above board. The owlder ones gan back and tell the world we're deein' fine, that we've stuck it out till now and we'll stick it out for longer. That none of us'll gan back till we get the guarantees we ask. Guarantees not only for ourselves but for them returnin' to the surface. That's the message they'll take back, not that we're wiltin' but that we're only just startin'. That we've just begun. That from now on, not only will it be a strike it'll be a hunger strike. And it'll stay a hunger strike till they dee somethin' about it. And for the men that stop let me tell them this. It's a fight to the finish, make no bones about that. And once ye make the decision to stay ye stay till we get satisfaction. Whether it's for a day or a week or even a month. There'll be nee slinkin' back to the surface. There'll be nee allowance for sickness and rheumatism. Not even for death. So make sure while ye have the chance this is what ye want.

"But if ye dee stop, just think on this. This is the only means we have to put our case, this is the only means we have to be heard. But not only are we fightin' for ourselves, for our families, we're fightin' for somethin' bigger. We're fightin' not only for the reet to live where we want, work where we want, we're fightin' for a principle. That a man means more than a machine, that money can never mean more than a man. Ye see, there're people that's forgotten that. They've forgotten there're still human bein's in the world. For mark my words, what's happenin' here'll soon be happenin' all o'er the country. All o'er the world. The bureaucrats that are deein' this to us'll soon be deein' it somewhere else. Not only in the pits but on the railways, in the shipyards, everywhere machines can dee the jobs o' men. Everywhere money counts more than machines.

"So not only are we fightin' for ourselves, we're fightin' for all those people in the future. All those that'll suffer the way we're bein' made to suffer. And ye knaa, if we fight hard enough and long enough maybes we'll change this emphasis from money. We'll put the emphasis back where it belongs. We'll put it back on dignity and decency and respect. We'll put it back on the individual. Where it should be, where it should always have been, and which it should never have left. So remember this. 'Cause if we fail it's a failure for humanity. And if we win it's a victory against mammon. Against the gods that worship money. And remember, ye should be proud to be part o' such a strike, a strike that took the first step to create a world where man had restored to him his proper reets, his proper place in society. And not only remember it now, remember it all the days o' yer life."

Tom Holt stood with the small of his back against the inside wall of a refuge hole, hands behind his back, feeling even through his gloves the cold steel of a girder. His face was blanched, the skin pinched at the cheeks, and despite streaks of dried dust the yellow stains were prominent around his eyes; his eyes were almost closed, closed with weariness and fatigue, the veined lids drooping listlessly. His helmet he had placed with his pads on the knuckle of a yardstick in the hole, his hair shone in the light, and the deep lines in his forehead were filled with dust where the rim of his helmet had been. He was lower in the gallery some thirty yards from Ray. This was the main road out of the pit, dipping before its haul to the shaft bottom, and with the rain on the surface the hole was already inches deep in water. The water seeped through the tongue of his boots, over the rim of his ankles, and Holt felt a chill to his feet as he felt to his soul. But hemmed as he was by men suffering the same he had no inclination to move. So he left his aching back against the support of the girder and looked over the heads of the kneeling men to the kist where Ray was still speaking.

Ray stood upright now, shoulders rounded and hunched, but hands and voice controlled, his words authoritative, yet sincere and touching, moving Holt as they moved the rest of the men. Holt recalled what the doctor had said, how he had carried the gas the day he was born. And he remembered the anecdote of the girl who had seen the doctor for confirmation of pregnancy, so that she could tell her boy friend and perhaps her mother. And how the doctor had reflected on the day the daughter was born, if her mother had known then what she was to learn that night. Well, had Holt known the day Ray was born that one day he would be leading such a strike, had he known that his protest would stir not only a village but a world? But Holt had never taken an interest in his children, neither at birth nor in upbringing. They were merely noises to him, noises to be chased into the street and strapped if they woke his afternoon sleep. Probably later he would have taken more interest had they been good footballers or cricketers, but the only thing in which they excelled was drink. And though a great drinker himself he had somehow resented it in his sons. He had accepted it in Gerald, for he was eldest and could look after himself, but he had never been able to accept it in Ray. The first time he had seen Ray in the club he had cut him dead and not spoken for months. Yet here he was now, taking on his shoulders not only the responsibility of the men but their families, not only of the colliery but the village.

Holt would always be grateful to his son for releasing all those over fifty. He had never known how the pit could take a man, take his thoughts and twist them into delirium and obsession. He had never known how much he would miss the tub of steaming water that awaited him after each shift, the cold chilly bed in the cold chilly room, in a house that had for him no warmth or comfort. Even the meals of Fanny Adams, that were always overcooked, the egg congealed, the bacon overcrisp, chips limpid with fat. And brandy, that he had not sipped for years, not since the death of his wife. He felt it would take at least half a bottle to thaw his inside, to bring the glow back to his stomach. He brought his back from the wall and stretched a hand to take his helmet from the yardstick. The water stirred and squelched beneath his feet and he found it an effort to raise his boots. He thought again of Ray and what he was doing. He placed the helmet

on his head and reached a hand for his pads and stick. He began
out of the hole upon the tracks. He stepped over the tail-rope that
drew the set to the shaft bottom. And as he stepped onto the tracks
he saw Ray standing before him.

"Not ye, pa. Not this time."

"What d'ye mean not me? Ye said all them o'er fifty."

"I knaa I did. But ye're stayin' wi' me."

"But ye said A wouldn't have to fight. Ye said it yersel'."

"Nor will ye. There'll be others to fight for ye."

"Then why d'ye want us to stay down here. In this hole?"

" 'Cause it's the only thing I can think on."

"But A cannot stay down here. A've had enough. Enough, A
tell ye."

"It's only for a little while, pa. Not very long."

"But A cannot stand it. Another day and it'll finish us."

"I'll look after ye," Ray said. "I'll see ye come to nee harm."

Already the older men were making their way to the shaft
bottom. Holt watched them over Ray's shoulder. Suddenly he
thrust him aside with the yardstick and made to move after them.
He stumbled over a midway roller and fell to his face on the tracks.
The cramp that afflicted his legs gripped so tightly the muscles he
could not move. The cramp had started years earlier, beginning as
pins and needles, forcing him to rest every mile or so he walked.
They were the product of bad conditions, working in low and
working in wet, so that not only were the muscles cramped they
were wasting. In the early days when first affected he had rested
in refuge holes and let the men go on ahead. He told them he had
a little stitch, a little wind, that he would catch up later. But he
never did catch up and now they were so bad he could walk no
more than two hundred yards without resting. And standing so
long in the hole they had seized up altogether. He scraped his
wrists as he fell and jolted a knee against the track. Ray hauled
him to his feet and stooped to gather his stick and pads, the helmet
that had rolled from his head.

"Ye're just like the rest," Holt said. "Ye divin't want us to
get married, that's what it is. Ye knaa A've set me heart on it, ye
knaa it's all fixed up for three weeks. But ye divin't care. Ye think
if ye can keep us down here long enough, she'll forget about us.
She'll find hersel' somebody else. So there'll be nee talk. And nee
scandal. But A'll not put up win it. A'm takin' nee notice, see. A'm

ganna gan back and get mesel' married and neebody's ganna stop us."

"It's not her I'm thinkin' on, it's ye. It's not yer weddin' I'm worried about, it's Gerald. Ye knaa what he nearly did the other neet. Ye knaa what'dve happened if I hadn't come in and took the chair from him. He'd have caved in yer head and thowt nowt about it. And ye knaa what he thinks o' ye gettin' married. Ye knaa he's just waitin' his chance to get at ye. So who's ganna save ye when I'm not there? Who's ganna look after ye then?"

"A'm not worried about Gerald. If that's what ye think."

"No, but I'm worried. 'Cause what I see in him I see in mesel'. Ye saw what I did to Wishart wi' the book. I didn't mean to throw it at him, I didn't even knaa it was in me hand, till I saw the blood spatter his coat and shirt. Till I saw him fall to the boards. And it'll be the same wi' Gerald. He might not want to harm ye. But once he sees ye, once he starts to thinkin', then there'll be another row, worse than the last. And I'd rather have ye down here wi' me than six feet under somewhere else."

"Ye think it's as bad as that?"

"Worse. Ye knaa he doesn't like the idea o' somebody takin' me mother's place. But more than that, ye knaa he's hankerin' to marry that Rutland tart from down the bank. But d'ye think she'll marry him when she finds she's ganna have a mother-in-law younger than hersel'? And d'ye think her mother'll let them marry? She'll not and Gerald knaas she'll not. That's why he'll put a spoke in yer wheel. So take my advice, stop down here. Ye'll come to nowt but harm up there."

"But me weddin'. What'll A dee about that?"

"She'll wait for ye, pa. Even if it does take more than three weeks."

"Are ye sure, son. Ye're sure she'll still be there when I get back?"

Ray stared into the small bird-like eyes of his father and realized how much it meant. He saw in the fleck of the irises the pain of being unwanted, the ache of loneliness, the desire to give meaning to a life that was meaningless. And he remembered a mist through the trees, a moon through the mist, he recalled the dew on the grass, the cobwebs of damp against his face, the taste of hair to his mouth. He recalled a succulent body and gently moving buttocks, arms around his neck, the ecstasy that swelled through his body like sea against rocks. The great climax of heat and energy which made him wonder what it was all for. What in heaven's name it was all for. But there was no answer. There would never be an answer. There was only the swirl of water round his feet, the sound of men as they made their way out-by. He handed pads, stick and helmet back to his father and wiped the dirt from his face where he had fallen.

"I'm sure," Ray said. "Neebody can be more sure than me."

31

Arnold Atkin watched Markie Wishart mount the steps to the office. The telephone rang on his desk.

"Hello," he said. "It's you again. I was wondering when I'd be hearing from you. Yes," he added. "I've got news for you, but I cannot say it's good news. Half the men on strike are on their way back to the surface. That's right. But the rest staying down are making it a hunger strike. That's what I said. And they say it'll stay a hunger strike till they get satisfaction. Whenever that'll be."

He swivelled his chair from Wishart and gazed up the hill to the shell of concrete at its peak. The rain sat like silver pearls upon the windows, but through the pearls he could see the concrete dark grey with the rain upon it, the dust around its base washed to mud by the storm. Rainheads came low and ragged over the summit and rain lashed pitilessly the cattle that grazed on the coarse tussocky grass. Streams ran turbid brown down the hill and Atkin saw the channels they carved in the paths. He did not look at Wishart but stabbed at his eyes with the ball of his thumb. The eyes were so bloodshot it was as if a vessel had burst in the conjunctiva, the rims too were red, the skin dry and peeled; the skin of his face was leathery, the lips wrinkled and keened, pulled tightly across his teeth. They parted slightly and Wishart saw the white tip of his tongue as he swivelled back and talked again into the phone.

"Well, since you're losing seven pounds for every ton you're drawing if the strike lasts a month you'll be saving thousands. I know, I know, it's not the line you take. It's bad for public relations. But what you really mean it's making a precedent bad for the future. For when you start laying the axe to other collieries. You're frightened they'll all do the same there. You never said that? I know you never said that. You haven't the courage. That's why I'm saying it for you."

Atkin of course sat with the door open and Wishart entered without formality. Water dripped from his coat the length of the passageway, it dripped too from the end of his nose, the point of his chin; his hair, face and ears were soaked and despite the elastoplast the stitches ached where the rain had lashed at the cut. The rain was on the caps of his toes and in the turn-ups of his trousers. He took off his coat at the end of the passageway and shook a shower of drops upon the floor, then hanging his coat on a peg he entered the office. He wiped face and hands with the same handkerchief he had used at the council. There was a large fire in the grate and he picked up the poker to stab at the coal. The fire hissed and sparked, ash fell through the bars to the tiles of the hearth, and as the flames licked hungrily up the chimney, their reflection burned brightly upon his cheeks. He placed the poker back on its stand, and turning to feel the warmth of the fire upon the back of his legs saw the flushed face of Atkin as he shouted into the phone.

"Listen," he shouted. "Don't take that attitude with me. I told you what'd happen the night it all began. I told you to delay the announcement about the village till they had time to digest the news about the colliery. But not you. You had to have it announced the same day. Simultaneously. To meet everybody's convenience. So the men went out on strike and half the pits in the county came out in support. And it's not finished yet, not by a long chalk. But you'll never learn, never in a hundred years."

He placed the phone back on its rest and looked across at Wishart.

"One of these days," he said. "I'll get to meet that fellow."

He raised himself from the chair, resting the balls of his hands upon the varnished top of the desk.

"So it's true after all," Wishart said. "About the hunger strike."

"You heard what I said on the phone."

"So what we ganna do now?"

"It's not what I'm going to do," Atkin said. "It's what you're going to do."

The draught blew cold through the door and he came round the desk to stand by the fire. He glanced at Wishart but did not hold his stare. He had the same reluctance to look him in the eyes as had Donnolly before him. It was not from guilt, not from shame, merely from a sense of embarrassment.

326

"That's why I've come to see ye," Wishart said. "See if ye can help."

"I'll listen to what you have to say," Atkin said. "But I cannot make any promises."

"It's not a question o' promises. It's a question o' guarantees."

"Guarantees have the ring of concessions," Atkin replied. "And it depends on the concessions you want."

"All I want is for ye to tell me now, in this office, that there'll be no redundancies, security o' work at the next colliery and no reduction in pay when the men transfer. And in turn I guarantee that the strike'll be o'er by five o' clock the night. That the pit'll be producin' by Monday."

Atkin rested his hands on the mantelpiece and with arms outstretched looked up at the geological chart on the wall. The light reflected on the glass frame and he could hardly make out the strata that lay between the colliery surface and the first seams of coal. There were layers of shale and sand, chalk and clay, limestone and granite, bluepost, hardpost and of course troughs of water. It was the discovery of large underground water deposits near the upper workings that had led to the closing of the first seam. This, Atkin reflected, looking back, had heralded the closure of the pit, for though the difficulties in working the seam had been great they had not been insurmountable, and it was only because the industry was beginning to place the emphasis on money rather than coal that it had closed at all. Now the rest of the pit was to follow, not because it was old, not because it was low, not because there were faults in the main seams, but because it was uneconomic. He dropped his hands from the mantelpiece and for the first time, turning to Wishart, caught and held his stare.

"An easy promise to give," he remarked. "Seeing the pickets'll not let you past the bank top."

"They will if I have them guarantees behind us."

"But who's to say I could give them even if I wanted? You forget I'm only the colliery manager. There's the agent at group, there's the area general manager, the divisional chairman. There's the Coal Board in London. And above the Coal Board there's the government. So I might give you the guarantees. But there's nothing to say others'll back them up."

Wishart saw the look in Atkin's eye as he turned. He had seen it before, at the consultative when the area industrial relations officer was explaining the mechanics of the closure, when Atkin had sat silent, brooding, and Wishart like a stricken sheep, leaving the questions to the lodge chairman and representatives of other unions. That look in Atkins eye had awakened him from his bewiderment. It was as if like Wishart he saw in the death of the colliery the death of himself, not the passing of a life but the passing of his own life. There had always been understanding between Atkin and Wishart. Only once had there been a dispute. This had been years earlier, when a datal worker had not wished to be a member of the union; Atkin had supported the datal worker, and Wishart had been obliged to call in a union official from Durham. Apart from that, however, Wishart appreciated what Atkin had done for the colliery, and though aware he was disliked, was probably the most detested man at the pit, he knew he had done more than anyone to make it pay. Now like Wishart he was face to face with failure. And failure was in each of their eyes as they stared.

"So everythin Ray Holt told the men was right. And everythin' I told them wrong."

"Depends on your intepretation of the facts," Atkin said. "How you look at the problem."

"He said stonemen wouldn't be stonemen at the next colliery. He said faceworkers wouldn't be faceworkers, deputies deputies. In fact he said they'd be lucky if they weren't on bank. At worst, that's what'd happen, at best it'd be datal work now with a chance of facework later. Now ye're tellin' me what he said was true. 'Cause if ye'll not offer these guarantees it means they're not for the askin'."

"I couldn't offer them in the first place because the men are still on strike. Because we've made it plain there can be no negotiations till everything's back to normal. And in the second because as manager of this colliery I'm responsible for the men whilst they're here. But once they leave, once they work somewhere else, they're out of my jurisdiction altogether."

"Which means the men'll not know what they'll be doin' till they're transferred?"

"Exactly. But of course you've got to look facts in the face. If the men want to work in the area, in pits similar to this, you can't expect them to walk into the best jobs straight away. Otherwise there'd be a stink with the regulars at that colliery. They'd

328

have to bide their time. So in part what Ray Holt said was right. In the beginning it'd be datal work now with a chance of facework later."

"Meaning a drop o' wages from eight to ten pounds a week."

"Granted. But remember this. The alternative's the dole. Because around here there's precious little outside the pits. So if you're not fixed up there you're fixed up nowhere. You'll have to sign on. You'll have to hang round corner ends. Take walks in the country. But you'll never draw a living wage. Of course it'd be different if the men were to go to Staffordshire."

"To live in huts. In houses not yet built."

"That's not true, Markie. And you know it's not true. You're just repeating what Ray Holt told the men. And what the Coal Board have since denied. There's a chance of good money in the Midlands — probably that's where I'll end myself — and if the men are prepared to leave there'll be accommodation. And not only for them, for their wives and families."

"The Board went to a lot o' bother denying conditions in Staffs. But I notice they never mentioned redundancy."

"You heard what the industrial relations officer said. He said it'd be kept to a minimum."

"The only trouble is he never specified what the minimum was."

"Look, Markie, son, there's not many jobs in the area. So it's only natural there'll be a bit."

"But how much is a bit?"

"About a third of the labour force. Now don't lose your head. I know it sounds a lot. But it's only a question of a hundred. And most of them'll be the older hands reaching retiring age. And they'll get their superannuation. They'll get two hundred and three pounds to send them off. And in the case of younger men being displaced they'll get twenty-six weeks pay, and in the meantime the Board'll keep looking for jobs in the area."

"And if there aren't any I suppose they'll be offered places in Staffordshire?"

"That's right. And as I said there's many a worse thing they can do than move there."

"But if they don't want to gan. Does that mean they'll lose their redundancy pay?"

"Figure it out for yourself, Markie. They'll be offered jobs.

Isn't that enough?"

"It's not enough. And ye know it's not."

"Listen, Markie. The Coal Board's job is to run the coalfields. And its statutory obligation is to make the industry pay. Now it's not for the Board to take into consideration the social structure of these mining villages. It's not for the Board to take into consideration whether there's other employment in the area. You might think the Board has a certain responsibility to the men. For what happened under private enterprise. But for the most part they have discharged that responsibility. And they're still discharging it, if you look a moment at the facts."

"The facts are they're deprivin' the men o' work. They're doin' them out of a job."

"Only some of them, Markie. Not all. And it's not their fault, it's not even the fault of the government, it's the fault of the times in which we live. You see, everywhere men are taking an interest in figures. They're looking to see if they can cut costs, increase productivity, reduce overheads, increase efficiency. They're looking to see where they can make economies. Just as they're doing in the coal industry. Do you know, there are studies going on of every pit in the country. Studies to see how economic they are, how profitable, whether output can be increased with less manpower. And with this pit losing seven pounds a ton it's lucky to be given the grace it has. It's lucky to be closing in six months and not tomorrow."

A gust of wind clashed shut the door at the end of the passageway. The door banged against the thresh, but the heavy rusting hinges soon swung it outward, and looking down the passage, through the widening aperture of light, Atkin saw the scurry of dust along the stone floor, he saw the light upon the brown-painted walls. The hedgerows were black in the rain, the colliery lines rusted from disuse. The white hand-points stood forlorn in water, water stood in pools outside the office, and the swollen ugly pipes that pumped from the pit throbbed their contents into the colliery pond. The surface of the pond was like the surface of a mirror shattered to fragments where rain lashed and cut the ripples. The rain had damped the fires on the heap, and in the rain, in the cold chill light, with the sky grey and heavy, bearing low upon rows of idle tubs, the heap was even more ugly than it seemed before. The door banged again, flames stirred in the grate, and the draught along the passageway scuffed the cuttings on Atkin's desk.

"I've a good mind to resign," Wishart said. "Here and now."

"Resign if you want. They'll only elect Ray Holt in your place."

"But why wasn't I told all this the other night," Wishart asked. "When I could have done somethin' about it?"

"You were told, Markie. Only you weren't quick enough to read between the lines."

"And the men reachin' retirin' age. What's the position on that?"

"They'll be the older ones. Over sixty at least."

"All o' them. They'll all be o'er sixty?"

"Maybes not all. But most of them."

"Ye're sure ye don't mean o'er fifty?"

"Some may just be over fifty. We'll not know how many till we allocate the jobs."

"I've a good mind to resign," he repeated. "Even if they do elect Ray Holt."

The caps of his toes and turn-ups of his trousers had dried in the heat of the fire, and his face was puffed and shiny where it had been lashed by the rain. His hair was still damp, flattened to his skull, but his hands had dried, the skin tight from the heat of the fire, so that he brought them from the range of the flames. He lifted them to his face and felt the skin tender round his eye where the stitches had been inserted. Pain throbbed again as he patted the wound with the tips of his fingers. He looked down and realized for the first time since the meeting he was still wearing the same shirt and coat spattered with blood. He had been so distracted finding his wife unconscious on the floor that he had not thought again of the meeting, and once realizing his wife was safe, that she was not going to die after all, he had bent all his energies to breaking the strike and getting the men back to normal. It had been a hopeless task, he knew from the beginning it would be hopeless, but the responsibility was his, he could not shirk it, and try as he may he could not shrug it upon the shoulders of others.

Yet neither wonder he had failed when all that he had told the men had been untrue. Neither wonder they believed he had sold their interests. He turned from Atkin to the mantelpiece and placed his face in his hands. If he could cry he would. If he could release the misery that choked his throat he would let it flood forth

331

in sobs and tears. Even then moisture came to his eyes and his lips trembled. And he wanted to cry, cry as a woman might cry, cry as his wife had cried when she heard of the village, cry not because the colliery was being destroyed and he had lifted not a finger to help, but because he had failed in his duty. He had deserved the destruction of his reputation. He had deserved to be stricken by the book. He had deserved the insults of men not privileged to be part of the strike. And Donnolly was right. Everything had come about as it had because he had abrogated his responsibility. Because he had not filed his protest at the consultative, because he had been too bewildered to collect himself, too upright to question the word of men unused to detail, accustomed only to vague generalization.

And Atkin beside Wishart did not look on with contempt. He looked on with compassion. For he too had almost wept when he realized his empire would be taken from him, that he would have to begin again, at another colliery, in another village, with one failure behind and another before. With the knowledge that though they may offer him another post they would never offer him one from which he could advance. But he had not minded that, he had not even minded he would have to start again, provided he could start afresh. But it was not to be. Wherever he went he would have to take Mrs. Bousefield with him. She had decided and because she had decided there was nothing he could do. She had learnt to manipulate him, to control him, just as he had manipulated and controlled the colliery. So that like Wishart he had wanted to cry, to cleanse himself of the bitterness of frustration and defeat. But like Wishart it was not to be. The defeat and frustration were to stay with him coiled as a lump in his throat forever.

He touched Wishart's shoulder.

"I know how you feel," he said. "I've felt the same myself. What I've just told you — those are my official views. Views I'm obliged to hold as manager of this colliery. But they're not what I really believe. I know this colliery is finished. I know there's nothing to be done to save it. But if there was — whatever it was — believe me I'd do it."

"So ye're the one behind it?"

"How do you mean. Behind what?"

"Behind the strike. Behind Ray Holt."

"What gives you that impression?"

"Ye said it yerself. If there's anythin' ye could do ye'd do it."

Atkin listened to the door banging at the end of the passageway. The door to his own office was held by a coal paperweight that normally stood on the desk. The coal had upon it the impression of leaves and had been dug out of the colliery during the first week of his management. As a souvenir he had had it mounted on a stand and inscribed with the date on which it was hewed. It was kept regularly dusted and cleaned, so that the impression could be clearly seen, and the coal shone almost as brightly as the zinc on which it was mounted. Atkin removed the paperweight from the floor and replaced it upon the desk. He closed the door and stood for a moment with his back to the frame. Wishart heard the closing of the door and turned towards him. In the light from the window the keens to his lips were more accentuated, the eyes redder, angry, the virile skin pulled tight across the high cheekbones, furrows deep in the puckered brow, the light throwing dabs of silver on the high forehead.

"So you've the same impression as me," Atkin said. "You think there's more behind this than Ray Holt."

"A lot more," Wishart said. "And I'm ganna make it my business to find out."

"You can if you want. It'll not make much difference to the issue."

"It might. If I could find out and expose him to the men."

"The men'll not take any notice. Even if you did expose him."

"Depends doesn't it. Who it is that's behind him."

Atkin felt through the cracks in the door a draught to his shoulders. He pushed himself from the door and crossing again to the desk picked up the paperweight. It had stood so long on his desk beside the trays, telephones and pens that to the staff it had become just another fossil. But to Atkin, looking at it each day, it had given as much pleasure as the view of the colliery seen from the bedroom window, the smoke and noise that drifted up the hill from the pityard. It had been for him a symbol of his dedication to coal, to the colliery and the men. But symbols become meaningless, dedication reaches the point of exhaustion, so that now it gave no pleasure to run his hand over the fossilized leaves. How many centuries had it lain in the earth? How many milleniums before it transformed itself to coal? And how many more before coal was discovered by men? Once in his hand it

333

had seemed light, beautiful and alive. Now it was dull, heavy and ugly. He replaced it again on the desk.

"I always thought there was someone behind Ray Holt," he said. "Ever since he brought the pit to a stop after the consultative."

"Apart from the fact he knew more about what was goin' on than I knew myself."

"And the fact he made such a good job of destroying the reputation of the lodge secretary. Why do you think he did that, do you wonder? Because he didn't like you? Because he let his temper get the better of him? Or because all along he was planning a stay-down strike? A strike that'd last? But in order to have such a strike he had to destroy the reputation of the lodge secretary. Because he knew more than anyone that in the event of an un-official strike it'd be up to the lodge secretary to get the men back. And with the lodge secretary out the way, the union and manage-ment sticking to national agreements, the strike'd last for as long as the men could stick it out."

"Well, he's burned his boats now," Wishart said. "With half the men back on the surface it'll not be long before the others wilt."

"Wrong again, Markie. The strike's not finished, it's only just begun. All them back to the surface are the older ones. Men who cannot stand the strain of a long strike. Ray's getting rid of them now so that in a few days they'll not break the ranks. Now the only ones in the pit are the diehards. Men who'll not mind a bit of starvation, a bit of discomfort. Who'll back Ray to the hilt, stick it out to the last. Till as he says they get satisfaction."

"Ye seem to have it all figured," Wishart said. "The only thing ye haven't said is who ye think's behind it?"

Atkin looked at the chart above the mantelpiece.

"If you want my opinion," he said. "I'd ask the MP."

"What makes ye say that?"

"Nothing particular. Only a feeling."

"As a matter of fact," Wishart said. "I did ask him."

"And what did he say?"

"He said to ask ye."

"Well, you have asked me. And I know nothing about it."

The pain in Wishart's eye had ceased to throb, the muscles no longer ached in his face, but he felt discomfort where his shins and feet had been damped and where his hair had yet to dry. The office was so warm with the door closed he felt no envy to leave. He had no desire to return home. His lips had ceased to tremble but his eyes remained moist, and the thickness was still in his throat as he spoke. He watched the rain against the windows and wondered where he should go, what he should do. He knew he should call by the surgery so that the doctor could look at the stitches, he knew that as lodge secretary he should perhaps go to meet the older workers as they returned to the surface, but he knew the pickets would not let him past the bank top, he knew despite the rain there would be others to do the meeting for him, and even if the pickets did let him through, even if he did enter the yard, he would only risk further humiliation. Then he remembered the third possibility. He remembered the last person who might have supplied information to provoke the strike.

"That only leaves Gerald Holt," he said.

"Gerald Holt? It's nothing to do with him."

"I'm not so sure," Wishart said. "I thought the same myself till a few minutes ago. Till I got to figurin' the leak must come from the office. And if ye say it wasn't ye then it must be Gerald."

"You're barking up the wrong tree, Markie. The only information that was brought to the colliery office was for the consultative the night before. Even then it was all in the head of the industrial relations officer. There was never anything on paper. And the only person who could have told Gerald Holt was me. But I never told him anything, because I know he's not interested. There's nothing I can imagine him doing to keep the colliery alive."

"All the same I'm going to ask him."

"You'll get short shrift when you do."

As Wishart went to seek his coat Atkin tidied the cuttings on his desk, and hearing him clatter down the steps into the rain he replaced the paperweight at the base of his door and moved through to the general office at the front of the building.

The office had been washed that morning by the cleaner, the linoleum was still damp on the floor, there came from the desks the odour of wax, and pervading the office was the sharp manure tang of the pony stables: the stableman had passed that morning to gossip with the cleaner as she scrubbed the floors. There was no fire in the hearth, though one had been built of paper, sticks and coal, as unaware of the storm as the storm was unaware of them. Yet were there any phantom particles of dust in the air, the light was grey across the dull tops of the desks, the coal drawing book, the house repair and doctor's book were all in place, the caps on the inkwells, the covers on the typewriters and gestetnor. The filing had been done, the spikes containing the multifarious doctor's notes and housing complaints ranged neatly on the sill of the window, the stamp book and pens all removed into the locked desks. So that there was nothing on which Atkin could occupy his hands. The office was as neat and tidy as a corpse.

Yet it was a corpse. Its life had gone with the decision to close the colliery. Not so long ago, before the clerks decided to add half an hour to their day and cut the Saturday morning, Atkin remembered the office vibrating with life and activity, with pay claims at the window, deputies checking sick notes in the doctor's book, with clerks compiling figures, overmen and surface officials preparing time sheets at the back, manager and undermanager discussing at the front. And even when the clerks ceased to come officials still passed. They passed to collect the mail in their respective boxes, they passed to feel the warmth of the fire to their thighs, to talk shop, to bring the colliery to life by their words. But now the colliery was dead. And from now till its closure officials would not pass. They would have to be coaxed, they would have to be summoned. And as for their company he would have to seek that at the officials' club next to the office. He would have to seek it hesitantly, uncertainly, because he knew they might not associate with him even there.

He rested a foot on a chair and one hand on his knee, the other on the cover of the typewriter, looked out upon the village. All was shrouded and veiled in rain. It shone on the honeystone walls, the slate roofs, the privet hedges, it ran down windows, down gutters, it dulled the lines of the houses, darkened the black of the telegraph wires, it danced off the road and pavement, it obscured the pitheaps and pasture at the other side of the valley. It cleared the streets of people. It forced those in the pityard to seek shelter in the time cabin and storehouse, engine sheds and machine shop, even under the hoppers. And it kept coming, coming over the crest of the hill, sullen grey clouds, low with the burden of water, low with the sorrow of oceans, yet indifferent to the sorrow of people, the people of the village, indifferent to the men below, as unware of the storm as the storm was unaware of them. Yet like the men impressing itself upon the world by its strength, its violence and its determination.

The telephone rang again in his office. He had that morning put the line through direct from the switchboard and now he looked to the board to see which of the colliery lines was ringing. He dropped his foot from the chair, hand from his knee, and turned to take the call in the general office. One hand moved to depress the small controlling switch and the other reached to pick up the receiver. As they moved they wavered, there came again to his thighs the nervous twitch of the muscles, he became suddenly aware of the dryness of his lips, the aridity of his tongue. The tightening of the muscles in his stomach. The telephone continued to ring. He knew it might be important. He knew it might be area, it might be journalists seeking new developments, it might be the county council offering new angles on the village. But he knew too it was none of these things. He knew who it was even before he depressed the switch and the phone stopped ringing.

It was Mrs. Bousefield.

32

Mrs. Walton knew Gerald Holt was coming long before he arrived.

She knew because she had seen that morning a stranger on the bar, a flake of soot blown down the chimney by the storm; the flake clung to the bar, quivering in the draught like a sensitive gold leaf in a physics laboratory. Other soot had been blown down the chimney and lay like dark snow on the white ash of the dead fire. The coal Mrs. Walton borrowed from a neighbour had all been consumed, the last flame sputtered out in the night, but since her son was in the pit, and since it was his job to clean out the grate, no new fire had been prepared with the usual paper, sticks and ash. Soot from the chimney had billowed out beyond the hearth to the floor, it lay under the bed and table, under the easy chair, the stand on which stood the radio, the children had dragged their feet in it that morning and their shoes carried its imprint through the house. Mrs. Walton had not since bothered to clear it up. She would wait to see what further soot would be blown down by the storm, what other mischief her family could wreak, before deciding to move.

Her strangers on the bar had never let her down yet, though often she made a mistake as to who the stranger might be. Once she thought it was the doctor come to see about the pain in her stomach when it turned out to be a removal van come to dispose of her unpaid furniture; another time she thought it was the public assistance when it turned out to be the electricity board to cut off the current. But this time she knew it would be Gerald Holt. She had therefore left open the door so that he could walk in from the rain. Normally the door was locked and bolted, the curtains drawn across the windows, for the only visitors her strangers regularly anticipated were the rent collector and housing manager, the one seeking his arrears, the other on a tour of inspection. There were also agents who passed from time to time to collect their hire purchase, but these had long since given up in despair. The rent collector and housing manager too came rarely now. For with the door always locked and bolted, the curtains drawn, with Mrs. Walton sitting upstairs deaf to their supplication, their only course had been to make a dignified retreat.

Gerald Holt did not have to make such a retreat. He stood in the doorway and let down his umbrella. He shook the umbrella on the step and watched the drops shower upon the linoleum that petered out by the thresh. The rain had dusted the shoulders of his coat and toes of his shoes, the wind ruffled his hair, but protected by the umbrella there was no rain to his face and hands, no rivulets down his neck to his collar. He wore his best brown suit, recently tailored in the city, with narrow turnup-less bottoms, the lapels hand-stitched, with no flaps to the pockets, the creases razor sharp in the trousers. He wore a red tie and cream shirt, with gold cufflinks showing at the wrists; the lacquer on his new shoes shone despite the rain on the caps, and with hair soft and golden following its wash, chin recently shaved, he felt as he had meant to feel, more than a little superior as he stood in the doorway and rapped his knuckles on the panels.

"Ye're warse than yer father for ceremony," Mrs. Walton said. "A've towld him and noo A'll tell ye. We stand for none o' that lark here. Either ye come in or ye stay oot, it makes nee odds to me."

"I've not come to see you," Gerald said. "I've come to see Dolly."

"A thowt there'd be a catch somewheres. A couldn't imagine ye makin' a social visit."

"Just tell me if she's in or out. That's all I want to know."

"She's oot, see. And a good job tee, for ye."

"That's what you think," Gerald said. "I'll wait till she comes back."

"Ye'll wait an awful lang time tee, if ye ask me. She's away doon to the 'lectricity office to pay for the quarter. And when she gets back she'll be callin' for the bairns at a party doon the road. So if ye have owt to say ye'd better say it to me. It makes nee difference in this family. All for one and one for all. That's our motto."

As Gerald hesitated by the door the last drops from the umbrella fell upon his shoes and the wind through the door flapped his coat around his loins. He moved out of the draught into the scullery. He felt beneath his feet the hardness of the coco-matting and looked up at the copper boiler above the stove. There was none of the warmth, the comfort of a house regularly lived in. There was only the smell of dust, a pale ugly smell that reminded him so much of his own home, that flared his nostrils and deadened his tread even as he walked into the yard, not merely the smell of dust but the smell of poverty, a smell he felt could never be washed from the pores of the skin. It was idle to see from whence it came. It was everywhere, pervading every corner, every room, on each article of clothing, each item of furniture. Not even fumigation would rid its essence from the air. So that instinctively Gerald looked back at the light from the open doorway. He looked down at the razor creases in his trousers and smelt the newness that sifted from his suit.

"A suppose ye've come to see about yer father?"

"That's right. And since I can't lay my hands on Dolly I'll have it out with you instead."

"That's nice o' ye, A must say. But if ye waited ye could have it oot wi' yer father. He'll be up about noo wi' the rest o' the men."

"I thought that myself," Gerald said. "So I went to the pithead to collar him when he came up."

"And what'd he say. When ye saw him?"

"He didn't say anything because he never came up. That brother of mine kept him down out the way."

"Which means somebody in the family's got a bit o' sense."

"That's what you say now," Gerald said. "You'll be changing your tune if the strike lasts another three weeks and you have to call the wedding off."

"The registry office can wait," she said. "Not like the church."

"But in three weeks maybes he'll change his mind."

"Ye mean ye and yer brother atween ye. Ye'll change it for him."

She had seen Gerald many times in the street but this was the first time they had ever spoken, she had seen him hurrying through the cut towards Highhill Lane but this was the first time he had deigned to cross the step. She saw at a glance there was in him a great deal of his father. It was true he had his mother's features, the pale eyes, the pallid skin, the slightly over-large nose, but there was in the tilt of his head, the curl of his lip his father's arrogance, his wilfulness, his urge to destroy. A hard-ness that may or may not have concealed a sensitive nature. Yet there was too in his youthfulness, reflecting from his strength, a desire and a will to get the most out of life, something she had once cherished for herself and since abandoned, but yet which she now nurtured for her daughter. She finished wiping her hands and re-nurtured for her daughter. She lumbered toward Gerald clenching her fists, a nerve twitching in her cheek.

"Ye'd like a spoke in the wheel, wouldn't ye?" she said. "Ye'd like somethin' to happen that'd put it all off."

"You're not trying to tell me it's a love match. A marriage that has to take place or the world'll stop?"

"Maybes not," she answered. "But it's what they want. So why cannot ye let them be?"

"Because it's not what they want. And it's not what my father wants."

"He's the one that asked her. He's the one that popped the question."

"But who's the one behind it. Who's the one that did the shoving?"

"A did see, if ye want to knaa, but A never had to shove very hard, A can tell ye. Yer father was shovin' me harder than A was shovin' him."

"Then you made a mistake. Because you shoved the wrong man. He's not got money, if that's what you think. Either in the bank or under the bed. All she'll get out of him is cuts and bruises. Her head bashed against the pavement. Years and years of drudgery, that's what she'll get just as my mother got before her, because that's all he's capable of. Not love, not affection, nothing that she'll be proud of. There'll be no happy life, if that's what she's after."

"He says he's changed. Say's he's not the same fellow."

"Changed, that's a laugh if ever there was one. How can he change, how can any of us change? You heard what Ray did to the lodge secretary the other night. You know how my father used to treat my mother. And my father probably told you of the night I almost bashed his head in with the chair. Change! He can no more change his nature than I can mine or Ray his."

341

"Just let him try and lay a finger on wor Doll. Ye'll see what'll happen. Just let him try."

"There'll be no-one to help the way there was to help my mother."

"Let him try it once, that's all A say. Just once. A knaa wor Doll. Her big brother, he used to aggravate her all day lang till one time she crept up ahind and bashed him o'er the head win a stone dish. The dish was never any good after that. Cracked reet doon the middle — and his skull tee, A should think. Had headaches for months. A always reckoned he was never the same again. Always reckoned he'd never've been sent to that 'tution if wor Doll hadn't hit him o'er the head wi' the dish."

"It'll take more than a dish to crack my father's thick skull," he said.

"Wor Doll'll crack it. If he lays a finger on her."

She lumbered back towards the dishes and took down from the pipes a tea towel. She tossed the towel into Gerald's face.

"Better make yersel' useful," she said. "While ye're here."

The towel dropped from his face to his hands and since the pipes were cold he felt the dampness to his palms from its last use. It was not really a tea towel but a strip torn from an old dress, its texture rough to the skin, the pattern faded, the colour stained, the edges frayed, so that threads of cotton draped his hands. He gripped it in his fists ready to throw it back. Yet he did not throw it back. He remembered he was here to lord it over Mrs. Walton. He was here to look down upon her, to treat her with contempt, not to lose his temper because she was affronting his vanity. The natural and dignified thing to do to show his superiority was to dry the dishes. The alternative was to pass into the sitting room and wait for Dolly. Slowly he unhooked the umbrella from his arm and slipped out of his coat. He slipped out of it carefully, patiently, so that the full effects of his suit would not be lost on Mrs. Walton. Then, placing it on the hook behind the door so that the gaberdine did not touch the pit clothes, he turned his attention to the dishes.

"I suppose when they marry they'll be coming to live at our house?"

"Ye divin't suppose we'd have them here, d'ye. Win all my kids on the floor?"

"But it's my mother's house. The things in the house are her

342

things."

"Yer mother's been dead and gone seven years. She'll not mind where she is."

"But I'll mind. And they're still her things all the same."

Mrs. Walton did not reply but filled the kettle and took it through to the sitting room. It was only when she placed it on the ash that she recalled the fire was dead. She was at heart a lonely woman, despite the work made by her family, the work she had around the house, and though there were many things she could have done to occupy her time she preferred to pass the days wandering between kitchen and sitting room, looking out of the window to see what was happening in the street. Also she preferred to think of days that were gone rather than days that were here. When she was young she had had the chance of marrying rich but instead had chosen to marry poor. She could not understand how this had come about and often wondered how things would have turned out had she decided otherwise. Her own mother had only been sixteen when she was born, she had lived her early life in the village, and later they had moved to a house that stood on the valley floor by the river. Her mother had died of bleeding piles, a little unbalanced at the last, claiming they were bombing London years before the first bomb was ever dropped. Mrs. Walton had been only twelve years old at the time and from then on had to struggle as best she could.

Mrs. Walton took the kettle from the dead fire and laid it among the ash on the hearth. She lifted herself up from her haunches and listed back into the scullery. She forgot the soot that littered the hearth and as she trailed back into the other room she left a further imprint among the dust on the stone floor, there was soot to her knees like black psoriasis, and lumbering past Gerald she smudged the soot from her hands into the folds of her pinafore. She opened the two small doors to a fire designed to heat the boiler adjoining the stove and took out the few sticks her son had chopped before going on strike at the pit. She would try and light the fire with the sticks and old coal and a few tapers of paper. If she were lucky she might perhaps get sufficient flame to heat the water in the kettle so that she would not again have to drink cold tea. She laid the sticks on top of the boiler and as she did so a spelk lodged itself in her finger. She plucked out the spelk and pursing together her lips gave a long sigh.

"Listen," Gerald said. "Haven't you any sense of shame. Don't you know the scandal you'll cause?"

"We've had enough o' that in our time," she answered. "A bit more'll not dee any harm."

"But just think of their ages. Look at the difference. My father's sixty year old, he'll be retired in five years at the most — sooner if they close the colliery. And how will they live after that, on his superannuation, the pension he'll get from the post office? And just think, by the time he's seventy, by the time he's really an old man, your Dolly, she'll not even be thirty."

"That's ten years away yet," Mrs. Walton said. "And ten years is a lang time — even in this life."

"But she'll still be young, she'll still have her life before her."

"The way ye're on," Mrs. Walton said. "Ye'd think it was really her ye cared about."

"You don't think I'm talking for my father's sake, do you?"

"No, but ye might be talkin' for yer own."

Mrs. Walton did not laugh but showed her brown carious teeth and her shoulders shook as though like a dog she whimpered.

"I couldn't care less," Gerald said. "In a few months I'll be left the village. After that I don't care what happens."

"And the Rutland tart doon the road. The one ye're hankerin' to marry?"

"What about her? I didn't know you knew anything about her."

"A didn't, as a matter o' fact. Till A went to pass the order for the car and had a row wi' the hand in the garage 'cause he wanted us to leave a deposit. A sorted him oot all reet and then he gets nice as ninepence and tells us he'd seen ye and her in the wood."

"Well, what's that got to do with it?"

"Nowt, A suppose. Only A was wonderin' what her mother'll say when she finds oot yer father's marryin' wor Doll."

"You forget," Gerald said. "I'm marrying the daughter not the mother."

"So ye say. Still, the mother might have an opinion. Seein' they're that rotten wi' money ye can smell the stench every time they pass. And seein' the daughter's not twenty-one."

"She may not be twenty-one yet," Gerald said. "But she'll be twenty-one by the time we marry."

"Anyway," Mrs. Walton said. "A just wanted ye to knaa ye're nee better than me."

"Nobody said I was. But I wouldn't do a thing as daft as the one you're doing."

She lumbered past Gerald again and carried the sticks back into the sitting room. He had by now dried half the dishes and placed them among the debris that still scattered the kitchen table. The cloth was as damp to his hands as a sponge and throwing it into the crook below the copper boiler, leaving the others to dry on the tray, he turned and followed her into the sitting room. The family had carved their initials on the door, the bed was unmade, the plant pot stood empty on the sill of the window, the plant being in the yard with the coco-matting. The candles were sunk low in the brass sticks, the beer bottle still protruded from under the bed, he noticed the dabs of soot like paint stapling the walls, and on the floor the imprint of soot like the paws of a dog. He saw the varicose veins in the back of Mrs. Walton's legs as she lowered to her hands and knees over the fire, ash sticks and paper ranged to one side, and for the first time he noticed how black and greasy was her hair. He advanced into the room slowly, uncertainly, as if distrusting the floor to his feet, unsure that it might not at any minute swing from under him.

"A knaa ye think A'm daft," Mrs. Walton said. "A knaa everybody in the village thinks the same. Some say they divin't knaa who's the daftest, wor Dolly for marryin' yer father or me for lettin' her marry. But if it suits her book it suits mine and A divin't see what it's got to dee win anybody else."

"But you still haven't told me why you're shoving her. What you hope to get out of it."

"Nowt for mesel'. A lot for wor Dolly." Her hand went again to the side of her head, she shook the hair around her neck and glanced up at Gerald. "Just look at us," she said. "Just tell us hoo owld ye think A am. And tell the truth. Ye divin't have to worry about hurtin' me feelin's."

"I wouldn't know," Gerald said. "Around sixty, I should think."

"That's reet, sixty ye say. And some days A look seventy. And some days A feel seventy. But d'ye want to knaa hoo owld A really am. Forty-five. Not a day more and not a day less."

"Maybes I over-reached myself," Gerald said. "Maybe I

should have said nearer fifty."

"Sixty ye sayed and sixty it is. And that's hoo owld wor Dolly'll look when she's my age, if she marries the kind o' fellow A married. If she has the number o' kids A've had to bring up. It's nee fun for me, ye knaa, havin' to knock at people's doors for coal, burnin' candles instead o' 'lectricity, havin' to keep a bed doon here 'cause there's nee room up loft. Bashin' the bairns in the street just to show the snotty-nosed neighbours it's not yer fault the way they've been browt up."

"Neighbours are the same the world over," Gerald said.

"Except that none o' them let on to ye around here. None o' them even bother to nod their heads. They think A'm dirty, they say A'm scruffy. And ye see for yersel' hoo things are. But hoo d'ye expect them to be? Some days, some days A says to mesel', A says A'll get a good start, get up sharp and put things reet. So A works me fingers to the bone, A cleans oot the house, A shakes the mats, meppoes the brass, blackleads the stove. But the next day everythin's as bad as the day afore. And the day after it's warse than when A started. So A says to mesel' what's the good, what's the good o' owt."

"But Dolly. You won't save her from this by marrying her to my father."

"A will, ye knaa. Ye'll see if A divin't. Sometimes A sit here and look back. A gan o'er things that happened years and years ago, such a lang time back it's a wonder ye can ever remember. A think o' the time when the fellow wi' rinken boots slapped all them gold coins on the table, the time me mother wi' her piles used to walk out the house at six in the mornin' to find a fence to sit on, just to get a bit relief. She never had hopes for us, never knew what hope was, but all the same she'd turn in her grave if she saw hoo things turned oot. And if she was to come back and see the house as it is noo she'd ask the same question A keep askin', where did A gan wrang. Where did A make the mistake. And o'er the years it's come to us little by little, if only A'd not had all them kids, if only A'd not had one after the other."

"And you think if you marry Dolly to my father she'll have none at all."

"She might have one or two. She'll not have more than that."

"Some men can give kids right up till they're eighty."

"But not yer father. He'll be lucky if he's capable after sixty-five."

Mrs. Walton, having cleaned out the grate, packed together the paper and began to build on it the ash and sticks. She dislodged the particle of soot that she had described as a stranger on the bar and though she had raked the poker through the bars she had not bothered to clean out the flues, the fire would draw badly if it drew at all, but since she was only interested in a cup of tea she would leave such other chores for another day. There was a box of matches on the mantelpiece, next to the spots of tallow that had run from the candle, and as she reached up Gerald handed the box to her. The brass candlesticks reminded him of his own home, he recalled the dissatisfying odour that quivered his nostrils as he walked up the yard, the gloom that met him as he opened the door. Still, his own house could never have been as bad as this, it could even have been better than it was, for it was he who resisted change. Many a time, since the death of his mother, his father and Ray had wanted new carpets, new furniture, a new radio, even a television, but always it was Gerald who refused. He refused because he feared it would dull the memory of his mother. He threatened to smash up anything new they might buy. Still, a new wife in the house would change all that. Dolly might have had nothing at home herself, but with someone else's money, some-one else's house, with credit here and there, it would not be long before there was change.

Anger stirred within, but it was only a glimmer of what he had felt the night he had spoken to his father. He asked himself why he should care when he was going to leave. Why should he worry about things which would no longer concern him. But hardly had the thought bubbled up in his mind when another followed it to the surface. It said he should always care, he had always to care about anything which concerned his mother. But then the real reason why his anger could not rise was because of the similarities between his mother and Mrs. Walton. Both had been born poor and both had been worn down by their poverty: his mother by an overbearing dogmatic husband who used his fists as the only support of an argument, Mrs. Walton by an indifferent ignorant husband who knew nothing about childbirth, who made love to his wife immediately she was on her feet from her last pregnancy, and who did not understand that the most dangerous period for conception was immediately after a birth. Who even had he known

347

would doubtless not have cared.

So that both women reached the age where they too cared no more. His own mother had taken refuge in death and Mrs. Walton, judging from the pain that reflected in her face, the deadness in the soft brown eyes, would not be long in following her. The world would then go its own way after her death as it had after the death of his mother. The similarities between the two women were greater even than Gerald realized or could possibly have known, for years ago they had both been members of the same spiritual church, had sat in the same congregation, attended the same meetings, and could if asked have recalled the same memories. The time an Indian guide appeared through one of the mediums, how they had smelt the tang of his grease, seen and heard the crack of his whip, the time one of the mediums had almost choked because someone at the seance would not answer a call from the beyond. But Gerald did not know of such things. He only felt for a moment that he saw his mother bending over the fire, a feeling that rid him of his sense of superiority and placed in its stead a sense of understanding.

"All me life and nowt to look back on. Everythin' past and done win noo, only a pain in the belly for me troubles, sick o' the sight o' the whole damn lot, but nowt to dee, nowt to dee, just keep on. Wor Alfie, he was lucky. Picks up a bail o' hay and drops doon dead. Knaas nowt about it. A wish A could find it as easy as that. But as A say all me life and nowt to look back on. Forty-five year owld and never once had a holiday. Never once seen the sight o' the sea."

She took the matches Gerald handed her and lit the tapers she had twisted through the bars from the paper. She leant back on her knees and wiped the dust and ash from her hands upon her pinafore. As the fire ate up the paper and its flames curled around the dry sticks, Gerald saw its reflection upon her face, he saw the moisture of her lips, the limpidity of her eyes, bright and yellow upon the backs of her hands. And in the brightness of the flames her face seemed to change. The blankness was lifted from her brows, the weight of indifference from her cheeks, the lids hooded down a little over her eyes, he saw the lashes dark against the yellow flickering light, and for once he saw her lips peel back, he saw a smile break across her face. For a moment she seemed to forget the fire, the kettle, her thirst for a cup of tea, even the weight of the thoughts she had tried to unburden upon Gerald. She lifted herself to her feet and her smile was so wide he could see the brown carious stubs of her teeth.

"But there, A have got somethin' to show for it, at least one thing. At least one memory that makes ye think it was worthwhile. A've knaan what it was to love. A've knaan what it was to feel for a man what ye're supposed to feel. A've never towld neebody this, not even me own family, A divin't even knaa why A'm tellin' ye, only A hope ye'll keep it to yersel'. He was a gypo, ye see, used to park his caravan on the football field opposite the houses. But he was a real gypo, swarthy skin, win a silk scarf round his head, a pair o' gold ear-rings the size o' hoops pierced in his ears. And he had white teeth, like A've never seen afore in me life, and eyes that had a way o' flashin' strokes o' lightnin' when they looked. A was married at the time wi' three kids on the floor, but then A says to mesel' what odds. Another'll not make nee difference. And it didn't. And A was reet, it was worth it. Worth every minute."

"So it is true. What they say about Dolly."

"Aye, it's true. But it's none o' yer business, nor anybody else's. Only divin't let on ye knaa, never let on. She'll only scratch yer eyes oot if she found oot. And it was worth it, A tell ye. Just to have had somethin' to look back on."

"And what happened in the end?"

"Wi' the gypo? He went away and never come back. A towld him A was carryin' his bairn, but he wouldn't believe it. Said A was tryin' to trick him. Said A was tryin' to get him like the other lasses. A says he was daft, towld him it didn't matter to me if A was carryin' another one or not. So he changed his tune. Gives us a rabbit he'd caught and says not to worry. Says it wasn't like other lasses, says A had a husband to look after me. Then he says maybes if A wanted we could gan away together. Says he knaas another gypo that'd exchange his caravan for another, a bigger one where we could live together. Said he'd be back sharp and not to worry about owt."

"And you never saw him again?"

"But it was worth it, A tell ye. Worth every minute."

She bent again low over the fire and picking up the kettle tried to crush it down upon the flames. The smile was no longer to her face, the blankness and weight had fallen again, she looked

349

anxiously at the fire burning round the kettle, and rubbing her hand along the line of her stomach, seemed to forget Gerald altogether. He had been standing at the side of the fireplace, one hand resting upon the frame of the bed, the other in his pocket, but now he turned and walked back into the kitchen. He was himself far away. He was remembering another such room, another such bed, at another time in his life, smoothing the hairs of his mother's head upon the pillow. He was remembering the last confession she ever made, the one that meant something to her most, that meant too she was dying with a regret, and taking his gaberdine from the hook behind the door he pulled it over his shoulders. He no longer noticed the corrosive odour of dust, the washing in the corner opposite the door, the partly dried dishes among the crumbs of the table. He did not even notice the coco-matting and plant drenched through with rain as he walked out of the yard towards the gate.

He was thinking of his mother and Mrs. Walton. And he was thinking of himself. He knew he was leaving the house more in sorrow than in anger. He knew too he had almost forgotten the reason for his visit. But again he could not help wondering if he would ever be able to lift himself above his origins, the environment to which he was born, or whether all his life he was doomed to suffer as his mother had suffered, as Mrs. Walton had suffered, poor because they had always been poor, wretched because that was the only condition they had known. He did not notice the rain upon his head and shoulders, as he walked towards the cut. He thought only of the poor throughout the ages, all over the world, born to ignorance and poverty, childbearing and misery, without a philosophy, a meaning to life, living without knowledge, without awareness, yet clinging by their fingertips because they preferred this to death. So that for a moment, but only for a moment, he began to realize why it was his brother was fighting. He began to understand what it was he was doing in the pit.

He strode through the cut towards the cinder path that led to the main road. He could not understand why the rain lashed at his head and shoulders in a manner it had not done before. The path was already a reservoir of rain, one vast lake along the wall of the school; a ridge of ash protruded the surface of the lake, but the only path was through the sodden grass that fringed the cinder. The lacquer on Gerald's shoes were already tarnished with rain and rain ran down his face and neck from his head. It was then he remembered the umbrella. He had left it hooked to the table at Mrs. Walton's. When he returned he found her staring down at the dead fire, outstretched hands touching the mantelpiece. She did not seem to notice he had left. The flames had consumed the paper, charred the sticks, but failed to grip the ash. The kettle was not boiled, the water hardly warm, and the fire already dead. Gerald picked up his umbrella and paused before the doorway. Then, without realizing he had anything to say, without even realizing the words were on his lips, he spoke.

"I wanted you to know," he said. "That one of these days — I don't know when — I don't even know how — but one of these days I'll see you get that holiday."

He turned again and this time, unfolding his umbrella, properly equipped, went out again into the rain.

33

"Hello," Atkin said. "It's you again. What d'you want this time?"

"Same as I wanted last time," Mrs. Bousefield said. "Want to knaa if ye've made yer mind up yet."

"Look, can't you understand we're in the middle of a strike. The biggest thing that's ever hit the pit?"

"Makes nee odds to me," Mrs. Bousefield said. "Only means wor Alfie's nowt to dee and the lad's down the pit."

"It also happens to mean I'm a very busy man. I've no time for private problems."

"Well, ye'd better make time for this one."

"Listen, the pit's my responsibility. I'm working night and day to make sure everything's all right with the men."

"The men can look after themselves. It's me ye've got to think on."

"I am thinking of you," Atkin said. "But I've told you. At the moment I've other things on my mind."

In his impatience, receiver still in hand, he turned to look at the rain against the windows. Through the rain he saw a car coming along the road towards the office, a car he had never seen before in his life. This might once have filled him with curiosity, but now he watched its progress with indifference. So many cars stopped these days at the office, so many carried on towards the pityard that another could not arouse his interest. As her voice droned on and on he leant his elbow on the small high desk on which stood the switchboard and reflected the car would probably carry on beyond the office and storehouse to the pityard. Perhaps it was a relative come to collect one of the older workers returning to the surface. Or perhaps it was an official come to spend another hour in conversation, not discussing how to bring the strike to an end, merely repeating the Board's stated position. He reflected if as much was said about bringing the strike to an end as there was why the Board could not intervene the strike would not have lasted beyond the first day. But her voice brought his thoughts back to the telephone, he heard the same words repeating over and over again, till he was forced to reply.

"Of course I'm listening," he said. "What d'you think I'm doing?"

"Then why divin't ye answer. When I ask ye."

"Because there's nothing to say. I haven't decided yet."

"But when will ye decide? That's what I want to knaa."

"I don't know yet. Probably by the next time I see you."

"That's what ye said the last time and the time afore that."

"Well, this time it's true. This time I mean it."

"Ye'd better. 'Cause if ye divin't ye knaa what ye'll get."

"I wish you wouldn't talk so stupidly," he said. "It doesn't make it any easier for me."

But this time it was his words that were lost on her. She had already put down the phone.

He heard the slamming of a car door. The distortion that confused his vision cleared, he saw the car before the steps to the office, the windscreen wipers idle now, raindrops gleaming on the silver handle like little crystal beads, the crystal shattered, the beads broken, as the handle of the door turned and a woman stepped out. A beautiful woman, graceful, elegant, upright, hair carefully combed, cheeks carefully rouged, a well-kept woman whose refinement and grace reflected in her face. And whose face reflected her character, and not only her character but her soul. Her nose and eyes crinkled against the rain and as she stood uncertain upon the steps the wind blew through her hair, its gusts buffeting strands round her face. She wore a yellow plastic mack and carried in her hand a yellow plastic helmet. She looked up at the office and saw Atkin by the window. Yet Atkin not only saw her he saw all that she stood for. And he saw the village had not betrayed him, it was he who had betrayed the village. He had not occupied himself with beauty and grace. The woman hurried up the steps and he heard the tap-tap of her heels in the passageway.

"I've come to see you about the colliery," Mrs. Rutland said.

"Everyone come to see me about the colliery," Atkin said. "No-one comes to see me for myself."

"I hear the strike's breaking. That some of the men are already back to the surface."

"Only the older ones. The younger ones'll be down a while yet."

"And those staying down. I hear they're making it a hunger strike."

"You have a good source of information," Atkin said. "I only knew myself an hour ago."

The tap-tap of her heels reminded him of Mrs. Bousefield. He had by now forgotten the strong lissome figure that had strode across the golf course, thighs pressing against the black sheath of her slacks. He had forgotten the taut breasts made firmer and rounder by the weight of the bag pressing back her shoulders. The soft chestnut hair and virile creamy skin tanned by wind and sun and air. He remembered only the slovenliness, the sloppiness, the slap-slap of her oversize slippers as she wandered through the house; he smelled the light fragrance of perfume and was reminded of the sweaty carbolic odour that soured every room she entered. Mrs. Rutland loosened the buttons of her mack so delicately, with so little effort and so much grace, that Atkin felt ashamed, ashamed of the woman he had once loved as a wife. And preoccupied as he was by his thoughts, dismayed by the memory, it was not till she was slipping out the arms he realized he should be helping her with her coat.

"Oh yes," Mrs. Rutland said. "You know they say I own half the village — two fish businesses, a fleet of hackney carriages, a paper shop, fruit shop and grocery store — yet from what I've heard since I'm the only one who never saw what was coming. The only one who didn't have the foresight and initiative to make enquiries."

"I presume from that you knew nothing about the colliery till it was too late."

"The first I heard," she said. "Was on the night of your special consultative."

"D'you think it'd have made any difference. If you had known?"

"It might. Certainly I'd have been better organized. And it wouldn't have come as such a surprise."

"But that's just the point. If everyone had known in advance there wouldn't have been any shock. The men'd have time to think it out for themselves. They'd have seen then they weren't getting such a raw deal. Of course they might have asked their lodge secretary to protest, they might have stalled a bit, but once the transfers were arranged, once their wives settle to the idea of a new house, there wouldn't have been half the fuss there is now."

"All the same," Mrs. Rutland said. "I'd rather have been in the know than in the dark."

He pulled the arms of the coat from around her wrists and placed the coat on the hooks the clerks used next to the small box window. The window opened into the passageway and as he placed the coat on the hooks he felt a draught through the cracks. He was not surprised the fate of the colliery and village had come as a surprise, it had come as a surprise even to him. But then in that respect he and Mrs. Rutland were very much alike. They did not meet the right people, encourage the right contacts. In all his years at the colliery Atkin had tried to associate himself with the men, he had ignored the officials, he had never gone snivelling to group to pick up gossip, pry into the affairs of other collieries. One of the reasons he had welcomed the National Coal Board was because under private enterprise a manager spent too much time looking over his shoulder, he spent too much time pandering, too much time justifying himself at the expense of the men. Under public ownership this he felt was not necessary. He felt that though the organization might be unwieldy, though it might be bureaucratic, each had his part to play, his job to do. And for Atkin that job was to manage this colliery. He had therefore isolated himself from the world and got on with his work.

Mrs. Rutland too had isolated herself. It had taken some years to emerge from the mourning she had imposed upon herself following the death of her husband; it had taken some time before she began to take an interest in the affairs left by her mother, before she began opening her grounds to the public and entering the life of the village. Now she was president of the co-operative guild, a member of the women's institute and treasurer of the darby and joan, she ran whist drives and domino handicaps, organized coffee mornings and as secretary of the youth fellowship arranged its trips to the coast. Yet she was as isolated in all this as was Atkin in his work. The only person with whom she had any contact in the outside world was Longley. She knew none of the influential businessmen, the bureaucrats that counted. So that when the outside world decided to shake off its indifference, when it decided to intrude upon the compact isolated world of the village, she had been as taken aback as had Atkin himself.

But though their two worlds were of the village they followed a different orbit. Their paths had rarely crossed. Evidently, Atkin was not interested in co-operative guilds and women's institutes, and Mrs. Rutland's contact was with their wives rather than with the men. Atkin often saw her walking along the side of the road through the wood, but since always he was in his car with Mrs. Bousefield he preferred to put his foot on the accelerator than slow down to say hello. Only once or twice had she ever called by the office. The first time had been when she wanted to enlist his support for a mile-of-pennies campaign she had organized to repair the church steeple. Atkin had never been to church since his christening and had been embarrassed by the request. Nevertheless he had given and given gladly and Mrs. Rutland had been so delighted she had offered him a personal invitation to the garden party she was holding the forthcoming Saturday. Atkin had accepted, believing something might come of it, for even then he had thought her a very attractive woman. Unfortunately for him, however, Mrs. Bousefield heard he was going, dragged along her husband, and the day had been spent with the clerk and his wife admiring the roses that trellised the front of the house.

The second time she called had been on a more serious matter. A relative of her husband had been killed not getting out the way of the set. He had been a frail middle-aged man whose strength had been weakened by successive stomach operations, the first exploratory, the second major; there had been other complications and after the operations a breakdown in health. He had lost weight, his recovery had been slow, and for some months the only work for which he was capable was delivering messages on bank and carrying various inter-office mail between collieries. Later he determined of his own accord to return to the pit and it was on his first day back the accident occurred. The empty set ran over his foot and broke his ankle. The accident itself was not enough to cause a fatal, but his health was such he died on the way to hospital. Mrs. Rutland had called at the office not because he had known the man personally — he had been only a cousin of her husband — but because she had learnt his wife could not read or write. She had signed all the papers relative to the accident with a cross and Mrs. Rutland had called to ensure this was in order.

Atkin told her it was and that the claim for compensation would in no way be affected.

She had not been to the office since and now she moved around the desk to the window.

"I'm glad they're going to continue," she said. "I'm glad they've decided not to throw it all up."

"They'll decide that soon enough," Atkin said. "Once they feel the hunger to their bellies."

"I'm not so sure," she said. "Of course, I know nothing about pitwork. I know nothing of conditions down there in the dark. But it seems to me they'll get plenty of encouragement tomorrow. One of the mass circulation Sundays is running an article supporting their cause. They've gone carefully into all the facts and decided the men are right. They're not getting a fair deal."

"I don't see how they can get a fairer one. All the compensation they'll be getting if they're laid off, the time they've been given before the pit closes, all the effort that's being made to fix them up — and not all over the country but here where they've lived all their lives. Where they're born and bred. You know, it's all very well being sentimental. But the only thing that counts in this world is realism. And in their own interests they should realize the sooner the pit closes the better."

"That's not the line the Sunday paper'll take tomorrow."

"But it's the true line. It's the only line that counts."

"You're living in the wrong century," Mrs. Rutland said. "You can't treat men as tools that you pick up or lay down, that you displace or abandon. You can't just neglect them the way you did a hundred years ago. Or even fifty for that. The world's changed since then, you know. The individual has rights today. He knows he has rights. And he's not particularly impressed by all those statements you're making about reductions in labour and movements of population. He doesn't understand language like that."

"Then the Sunday paper better get its facts right. They'll be denied if they're not."

"You'll have a hard job denying it's a hunger strike. And the fact it's a hunger strike'll give it the headlines. I have a friend in the city who knows the news editor. And he says if the men stick it out till tonight, and if they really do make it a hunger strike, the paper'll give it a front page lead. At least in the northern edition."

"You'll not be disappointed," Atkin said. "It's a hunger strike all right."

"Of course, after the article's published it'll go badly for the colliery manager."

"Will it now? And what makes you say that."

"The article will be realistic. It'll describe to the last detail the conditions the men are enduring. It'll ask how they can suffer all that if they're wrong, if their cause is not right. And now it's a hunger strike, now the men are prepared to add hunger to the rest of their troubles, the country'll agree with them. They'll say they can't be wrong. That's why I said it'll go badly for the manager."

"But I am only the manager, don't forget that. I take my instructions like everybody else."

"I know you do. Only my friend knows pretty well what's going on at division. He's made it his business to find out. And at division they're saying you're the one that refused to let down food. Not the Coal Board. They say the Board's given you a free hand to enact any measure you think fit, within the framework of the national agreements, to bring this strike to an end. So it's you not the Board that's refused food."

"If my hands were as free as you seem to think I wish they'd stop calling me on the phone. I wish they'd stop telling me what to do."

"According to my friend you're not popular with area as it is. He says every time they ring you give the impression you're supporting the men. And they say the only reason why you won't let food down is because you want to show whose side you're really on. Because that way you think you'll keep in favour."

"You have it all figured," Atkin said. "I don't understand why you never had it figured before."

"Because as I said no-one bothered to tell me. I'm making sure they tell me now."

358

34

She had not looked at Atkin as she spoke but now as she turned he saw a tremor to her lips. He had not winced at her words, indeed he had looked upon them with indifference. He regarded himself as a politician or statesman who all his life had been careful what he said, but who had now discovered that it did not matter at all. He could say what the hell he liked. Besides, so far she had told him nothing he did not know. He knew he was not in favour at area, but then he never expected to be, he knew what they thought of his reflections on the phone, but he was not a hypocrite and he would not have made them if he thought later he would regret. And it was true, in some measure he had withheld food to give the impression that as manager of the colliery he would do everything to curtail the strike. But it was not entirely true. He had decided to withhold food as much in the interests of the men as in the interests of the colliery. He saw again the tremor on Mrs. Rutland's lip but read it this time not as a shiver of emotion but as a shiver of cold. He thrust a hand in his pocket for a box of matches to light the fire.

"Which would you rather have," Atkin said. "The men driven back to the surface now for lack of food, or staying down day after day, week after week, with just enough to keep going, suffering more than you or I can imagine, even more than they imagine themselves. For a cause that was lost before this strike began?"

"It doesn't really matter," Mrs. Rutland said. "The way I see it you'll be obliged to let down food after tomorrow."

"And how do you make that out?"

"Because there'll be such a hue and cry up and down the country you'll have no alternative."

"It's not what the country says. It's what I say."

"Not this time it isn't. The order'll come from head office."

"You've just said yourself I have a free hand. So if I choose

359

to disobey their instructions?"

"Why should you disobey. When in your heart of hearts you'd like nothing better than to see this strike succeed?"

Atkin bent over the fire and cupped the live match in his hand to protect it from the draught of the door. The tap of her heels followed him round to the hearth and by the desk she saw the lemon glow of the flame upon the faded callous of his palms. She saw too that as he had struck the match he hesitated. Then he lit the paper and watched it shrivel brown under the advance of the flame. He extinguished the match with finger and thumb and tossed it upon the large chunks of coal that would nourish the fire. Standing back he heard the crackle of wood as it spurted alight, sparks swirling up the chimney with the thin brown smoke. Soon the fire was spurting and crackling, throwing its heat across the hearth, its red and yellow flames reflecting sheet-like on linoleum still damp from its wash. Mrs. Rutland stood with her back to the desk, hands fingering the stool behind her, the glow of the fire on her nylons, the rouge on her cheeks, the red to her lips, the shading to her brows darker in the flush of light. Atkin lifted his head to see the colour and animation, but he saw too a smile, not of mockery but authority, the smile of a woman who has planned her campaign to a final detail.

"But supposing things turn out as you say," he said. "Supposing I am authorized to send down food."

"There'll be no supposing," Mrs. Rutland said. "You wait till Monday."

"All right. So I wait till Monday. Then what happens."

"Hardly will you get authorization when I'll be on the phone asking permission to supply the men. As I said, you know I own half the shops in the village. And you know too I have the concession to prepare and supply school dinners to the schools in the village. I run the kitchens and arrange the transport. So it'll not be difficult for me to increase the kitchen staff, bring into service a few spare vehicles, and supply the men in the same way I supply the schools."

"It seems on a grand scale," Atkin said. "I'd much prefer they had only sandwiches and tea."

"I've told you, you'll have no option by Monday. The order'll come from London to division and from division to area. The area general manager'll ring giving you permission and he'll hardly have put down the phone when you'll be back on the line telling him what you've planned. He'll only be too happy to get back to division and division to London. They'll issue a statement saying they've authorized the supply of food, news'll be in the mid-day papers, and by the time it's realized the kind of supply there'll be nothing they can do."

"You honestly believe the article will have that big an effect?"

"The paper has a circulation of over four million. It'll be headlines in the north and prominently placed in every other edition."

"But if you supply the men the way I think you're going to supply them the strike can go on forever."

"Not forever," Mrs. Rutland said. "Only till, as they say, they get satisfaction."

Her smile tinkled to a laugh as she moved from the heat of the fire. She laughed not because she wanted to mock Atkin, not because she failed to understand his dilemma, but because now it all seemed so easy. She had paced her study thinking what she could do to help, she had cut herself off from her shops, her affairs, she had thought and rejected one scheme after another because they were over-simple or over-complicated. Then that morning she heard from Longley for the first time since the strike began. He too it seemed had been thinking. He had also been busy with his contacts. He had garnered the information relevant to Atkin and persuaded the news editor to write the story. The editor had been doubtful at first because he said what he really needed was a head-line. But Mrs. Rutland had provided the headline when Longley rang and heard it was a hunger strike. Now there was nothing to prevent its publication on the front page. There was only Atkin to prevent the supply of food Monday.

"I'm not sure I could accept that," Atkin said. "Not as manager of the colliery."

"You'll see Monday. You'll have no alternative."

"But if I decided to supply the men today. Of my own accord. Before the hunger strike gets rolling?"

"You've not done it so far", Mrs. Rutland said. "Why should you do it now. Besides, I'm sure you're still thinking of that little goodwill you have left at head office. I'm sure you'd prefer the decision to come from them rather than from you."

"And if you propose to supply the men and they refuse?"

361

"By Monday the hunger strike'll be in its third day. I don't think they'll refuse, do you?"

Atkin paused by the green ledge of the window on which stood the telephone linked to the pit. He leant his elbow on the ledge, fingers coiling round the cord of the phone, feeling the dust on the cord to his nostrils, eyes on the slender stub-like props of the telegraph posts on the heap, the thin wires stitched across the hurrying grey sky. The light struck across his face and Mrs. Rutland could see the extreme redness of the eyes, the silver of his hair; the skin of his cheeks was red and chaffed, as if badly shaved, and there were deep lines in the skin of his neck. She followed his gaze out the window and saw below the heap the structure of the power station, bricks stained and ugly, she saw the soot-streaked fingers of the chimneys, not smoking now, swaying against the sky with the movement of the clouds. And in the pityard she saw the cars and people, still waiting, even though by now all the older men had returned to the surface. She moved across to the ledge to stand by Atkin.

"I know perhaps I shouldn't have made those enquiries at division," she said. "But believe me I also made them in the village. And I know more about you than you can imagine. I know what you've done for the colliery over the last ten years. I know what you've done for the men. Your efforts to associate yourself — the leek shows and flower shows, the Sunday drinks at the club."

"Efforts that had little success, I can tell you."

"Efforts you made all the same. And which at least prove your heart's in the right place."

"I doubt the men would agree. I must be the most unpopular man at the colliery."

"But unjustly so."

"Not unjustly. Rightly so. I'm manager of this colliery. And as manager I'm responsible for all that happens."

"I suppose that's why you left on the pumps. And the electricity. I suppose that's why, knowing there was a strike coming, knowing what kind of strike it'd be, you did nothing about it. You left the pityard open, you let the men go down even though you knew they wouldn't be coming up. And that's why, as you said yourself, you refused to let down food, because you didn't want the men to suffer more than was necessary."

362

"The men don't appreciate that. They don't appreciate anything."

"It's not the point whether they appreciate it or not. The point is whether you appreciate it. Whether you feel that what you've done you've done for the best, that you know in your heart of hearts you're doing all you can, so that there's nothing for which to reproach yourself. That you've stood by the men, that you've helped them. And that you'll help them again to the best of your ability."

"I don't see how I can. As manager of the colliery."

"You can help them by being true to yourself," Mrs. Rutland said. "By doing what all the time you want to do."

As she stood at his elbow the tang of dust from the cord of the telephone was overwhelmed by the fragrance of her perfume. He could see from the corner of his eye the tweed of her costume, arms still folded across her chest; he could see the shine of light upon her nylons, the tan of her shoes, the laces damp and bedraggled. But playing with the strands of the cord his attention remained on the colliery. He recalled the defiance that had stirred within when he watched Ray Holt lead the first of the men into the cage. He recalled how for three days he had eaten out his heart to do something and now, given the opportunity, he hesitated. Why? Why did he not take Mrs. Rutland's advice and do what he wanted? Because all his life he had been a responsible man, because he had subordinated his instincts to duty, and not only his instincts but those of his undermanager and overmen and deputies. So that the pit did not succumb to negligence, so that accidents were not bred of laziness.

"One question I have to ask," Atkin said. "Why should you be doing all this?"

"For the same reason as you, when you put your mind to it. For the honour of being true to myself."

"I suppose financial considerations don't enter into it?"

"You mean having all those shops in the village?"

"And the fact that pulling down the village won't do trade any good."

"It won't do it harm either," Mrs. Rutland said. "People will always come back to the village, if only out of habit."

"They'll have a hard job coming all the way back from Staffordshire."

363

"But they won't all be going to Staffordshire. According to the management they'll only be going to collieries round about. And anyway you're forgetting the roots I have in the village, roots that go deep. My mother and father were born here. And my grandfather too. Always there's been a Rutland associated with the colliery. As far back as 1842. When there was all that trouble in the county it was a Rutland who led the Highhill delegation at the meetings."

"So it's all for the sake of sentiment?"

"Not for sentiment. For the sake of honour."

"And you want me to do the same?"

"I want you to be true to yourself."

Atkin did not see that he had any alternative. There was nothing he was likely to do to stop the hunger strike, therefore there was nothing that would prevent the publication of the article tomorrow. He would receive a call Monday for the authorization of food and either he could await the call of Mrs. Rutland and pass the authorization to her or on his own initiative give instructions for sandwiches and tea to be sent down by the wives who waited in the pityard. Probably the men would scorn this scant replenishment of their bait tins but not the soup containers Mrs. Rutland would no doubt send down in their stead. And it was not necessarily so that Atkin would suffer because he helped nourish the men, it would not be necessarily true that he would be criticized for handing over the organization to Mrs. Rutland. After all the Coal Board were not ogres, they were not the landowning tyrants of a century ago, it was not all that likely they would frown upon his activities.

"You say you'll take care of the men. You'll supply them and nourish them and see they come to no harm."

"That's right," Mrs. Rutland said. "With of course your permission."

"But who's going to take care of the dependents on the surface? You've got to remember this is an unofficial strike, there'll be no wage packets coming in, there'll be no support from the union. And probably nothing from public assistance. So who's going to nourish them? Who's going to see they come to no harm?"

"After tomorrow's article the local provincial evening paper in the city'll take it up. They've already lined up a series on the whole future of the Durham coalfield. The number of pits that'll close over the next ten years, the number of men displaced. The impossibility of finding them all jobs in the area. The certainty that some are bound to have to leave."

"I hope it'll not forget everything the Board's doing to alleviate hardship."

"That'll be taken into consideration. But the fact is they'll recognize a man's right to live where he wants to live, work where he wants to work. Because that they say is the basis of a free society. They'll give the strike and all its developments front page leads and by Wednesday or Thursday, if the men are still down, they'll announce the opening of a relief fund. They'll donate five hundred pounds themselves and ask others for contributions."

"The men won't need relief if they're down the pit."

"But their wives and families will. I'll be announced treasurer of the fund. Of course I'll donate three hundred pounds myself and all other contributions will be passed to me. I'll work out some system whereby the money'll be evenly spread and of course I'll see that it's used only for essentials — food and the rest. The publicity'll encourage the men, they'll see their wives properly treated and cared for. So all they'll have to worry about is sticking it out till they're given the concessions they want."

"But what happens if the management refuses to grant the concessions?"

"How can they refuse. With all that pressure upon them?"

Atkin ceased playing with the cord and brought his elbows from the ledge. The steel of the headstock was black not red in the light, the wheels dark against the restless sky. The wheels had tumbled and spun to bring the men back to the surface, the winding engine had revved and roared to work the cage, but now the light filtered grey upon the girders, the winder itself was silent, the cage stranded, and only the headstock seemed conscious, conscious of the men it protected below. Conscious why they needed protecting. Atkin had all this time seen their endeavour as one final fling before disaster, he had admired their action, longed to participate, but seen no hope of victory. Now he realized what Mrs. Rutland had said was true. All the figures the industrial relations officer had used to persuade him of the inevitable could be discarded, all the instructions from men he had never seen, frail voices over the phone, could be set aside. The tide of bureaucracy would be rolled back. The efforts of automation and modernization, patterns that changed a way of life, could be halted.

They could be halted by people overcoming their apathy, by voices crying in the wilderness, and by organization. The organization of those who did what they wanted to do, who believed in the right of the individual over the machine. And by aligning himself with Mrs. Rutland, by subscribing to that organization, perhaps after all something would be changed. Perhaps as he had reflected no governments would fall, there would be no international reverberations, no angry constituents to face, but perhaps too if they were successful a drift would be stopped, a drift whereby faceless authority hit at innocent people, imposed itself upon individuals. Perhaps by their actions they would break the stranglehold of bureaucracy. They would retard the date it would make them all slaves of a system run by robots. That indeed would be something worth fighting for, something worth achieving!

Atkin felt like some revolutionary about to attack the last edifice of a civilization he hated, a civilization foundering on its own greed and acquisitiveness, helped by the indifference of those who did not suffer from its extortion. He felt as Ray Holt must have felt when he knew he had the men with him, when he knew he had an instrument with which to force his will on society. He no longer felt the quiver to his thighs or the twitch to his stomach, he felt only an elation that warmed his innards like a glass of port, the warmth of victory, the knowledge that by his simple decision he would open the way to saving the colliery, perpetuating the life of the village. But there were dangers too, dangers that could not be shuffled off, that had to be faced because his responsibility would not allow him otherwise. It may not be true that by helping the men he would be ejected from the industry he loved, work to which he had devoted his life. But he had to accept the possibility. He had to accept all the obstacles and pressures that would follow his being true to himself.

Whichever way he looked at it he knew it was a break from the past. He knew from this day he could never look back. From this day he had to accept the possibility of severance from coal. He was reminded of the paperweight that stood on his desk. He excused himself a moment and passed through the office to seek it. It was dull and heavy to his hand. It was such a lifeless thing again he could not understand how it had ever given him pleasure. The coal was hard and brittle, edges sharp where it had been cleaved from the rock; it was a dead pitch in the light, but the draught through the open door stirred the last garnet embers of the fire to flicker rose upon the leaves. He reflected that if he were to throw it among the dying husks the fire would fall in the grate and slowly from the embers yellow flames curl around the base and eat into the impression. He thought of a better idea and walked back through to the general office. He presented the paperweight to Mrs. Rutland.

"It's for you," he said. "I want you to keep it."

"I assume then that you agree?"

"I'll do anything I can," he said. "Anything to make the strike a success."

Mrs. Rutland took the paperweight and felt the coldness of the base to her fingers. She rubbed a finger along the surface of the coal to see if it were real, she turned it over in her hand and noticed the clear impress of the leaves. She also saw the date engraved upon the base. She knew nothing about the leaves, she knew nothing about the coal, but in some way, taking it from Atkin, she saw it not only as acceptance of his collaboration but also his rejection of the past. His decision to have done with it all and look now to the future. He was prepared for anything that might come. He was committed, as committed as Ray Holt, as committed as herself. She realized what he had decided was no light thing. She realized too he might live to regret it. But she accepted the gesture. Only she did not know how to show her appreciation.

Then lightly she leant forward and kissed his cheek.

35

When she returned home she placed the paperweight on the mantelpiece above the fireplace in the sitting room, and over the next few days, as events unfolded, often she had occasion to study the weight and be grateful to Atkin.

The Sunday national ran its story as planned and the following day, Monday, the local post office was inundated with telegrams for the colliery manager, describing his refusal to send down food as barbaric, inhuman, unfeeling, reminiscent of Buchenwald, and other worse epithets. The area and divisional offices also received calls, the BBC referred to the strike in its news bulletins, the television cameras that over the first three days had taken pictures for local transmission, returned this time for film to be relayed nationally. Reporters began again calling the office and for the first hour of the morning closed' the switchboard, so that the first Atkin heard he was wanted by area was when he received a call on an independent line that linked the different collieries.

As had been forecast, Atkin hardly put down the phone when Mrs. Rutland rang. He granted her the permission given by the area general manager and from there the operation had worked with the precision of a military campaign. Vans trundled past the office towards the pityard, huge silvery containers laden with soup were taken from the vans and loaded into the cage, the winder revved again, the wheels began to turn, slower and more steadily this time; the men who had heard the news of the supply, impoverished now, famished, were waiting at the shaft bottom, waiting with empty' bait tins at the ready. Probably on that first day, in their eagerness, more soup was wasted than swallowed, but with a little warmth to their bellies, the dizziness went from their heads, the shakiness from their limbs, they no longer seemed to mind the claustrophobia and cramp, the limited space. Even their quarrelousness dissipated and as they moved back to the higher galleries, they moved lithely and with suppleness, arms around each other's shoulders, slapping each other's backs. The soup came again later in the day, and after two days mashed potatoes and vegetables began to fill the steaming hot containers.

The days slipped by, the provincial evening in the city began its onslaught, the miners of Highhill hit the front page, there were pictures of the containers being manoeuvred into the cage, pictures of cutlery being sent down, even pictures of Atkin on the steps of the colliery office, briefcase in hand, like a cabinet minister leaving for a meeting at Downing Street. After three days the provincial paper announced its relief fund, contributed five hundred pounds itself, announced the three hundred pound gift of Mrs. Rutland and two hundred pounds from another source. The other source was Longley. Mrs. Rutland was announced treasurer, she immediately appealed for contributions, these began pouring into the newspaper office, and by the weekend the amount had jumped to two thousand. It seemed a great deal to the people of the village, and of course Mrs. Rutland was delighted, but she knew there were not only the dependents of men in the pit, there were all those striking on the surface.

She began immediately to devise how best the money might be distributed. She had thought of various schemes, but the one which seemed to offer the best opportunity of guaranteeing a fair distribution, minimizing the possibility of fraud, was the one she worked out with Arnold Atkin. Atkin proposed blank pay notes be issued to the men on the Thursday in the same manner as if they were working. These pay notes indicated their salaries and how they had been calculated. The men could therefore read over the calculations and if there were errors these could either be adjusted the following week or corrected on the day they received their pay. Friday was payday in the mining industry and against each note the men received a wage packet. Atkin proposed that instead of giving them wages, since they were not working, they be issued with credit slips. The credit would be three pounds a week per family, with four pounds for those with three or more children. Bousefield who had been in the village all his life and who knew by sight not only the men but their wives too would see to it the right people received the notes and that the right amount allocated to each family.

The credit slips could be used in the village only for the

purchase of food. Each shopkeeper would mark on the slip the amount supplied, so that the customer could not call at another shop and use the credit slip again for the same amount. Families were advised to do all their trading at one shop or store and then when the full amount of credit had been absorbed that particular shop or store would retain the slip and forward it to Mrs. Rutland for payment. Mrs. Rutland's shops were of course fully covered by the scheme, but in order that she might not be accused of profiteering she had it extended to every shop in the village, including the co-operative store. Even then there were disadvantages. For example one could not buy one's meat from the same store as one bought one's groceries, nor could one buy bread from the store selling fresh fruit and vegetables. Mrs. Rutland had therefore to waive her advice to shop at a single store and each shop had to mark not only the amount of provisions but also its name. The shopkeeper supplying the food bringing the credit to three or four pounds would then retain the slip and at the end of the week forward it to Mrs. Rutland.

She had too to stipulate the cards be marked in ink, so that no-one could cheat by rubbing out; she had memories of the erasing that went on with ration cards during the war before the invention of ball-points. Also, she warned shopkeepers that anyone who overstepped the three or four pounds limit would themselves be responsible for the collection of the extra. This however was a threat she did not carry out. Yet the very fact she made it kept shopkeepers in line and prevented widespread exploitation of the scheme. Some of the shops introduced their own credit over and above the amount allowed, others less adventurous complained they were being left out. These were the sweet and cigarette shops. They wanted credit extended to their own particular trades. Mrs. Rutland refused and advised them to introduce a credit scheme of their own, as her mother had done before the war, and as the social clubs were now doing for their members.

Also loud in their protest were the travelling shops not included in the scheme, but since few of these traded from the village Mrs. Rutland did not heed their complaints. There were also more people who said the amounts were too low, that three or four pounds a week did not compare with the cost of living, the price of foodstuffs, that anyway the amounts did not take into account hire purchase instalments — tick as it was called in the village — and worst of all, how could one be expected to go to bingo when all your money had to go on food! Most of the people, however, took it in sport, understood that they too had to make sacrifices, that they had to support those underground, that they had to accept the little they were given if they wanted to stay in the village. They were excited too by the publicity, flattered by the number of reporters who asked their opinions, promised to get their names into print, their photos in the paper. It was something they had never known before, an experience they knew came once in a lifetime.

Mrs. Rutland required that the credit slips be returned no later than four o' clock Saturday, so that the cheques could be made out by the beginning of the next week. The scheme had only been introduced Friday and there had been great confusion at the office as men and wives scrambled round the doors. At first they had not understood what was happening, believed it was first come first served, that those last in the queue would receive nothing at all. In subsequent weeks the pay notes would be issued Thursday and the slips Friday, enabling a double check by Bousefield, but that first Friday the clerks had been badly organized, pay notes had been issued at one window, credit slips at another; the slips were fresh from the printers, some were blurred, the print unreadable, and those receiving such slips queued for another. It was not till eight o'clock that all slips were issued and the system explained. Not till eight o' clock before the excitement and confusion died.

Since on that first Saturday there was nothing for Mrs. Rutland to do, she relaxed before the fire reading through the morning papers, her daughter idled by the fishing rods in the stand attached to the wall near the door. The wind had blown itself out towards the end of the week, the rain had ceased but the weather yet to clear, a mist had risen from the river, its whiteness filtering through the trees to drape the grounds. The rain had ruined the garden fete held the previous Saturday, only the stall attendants had turned up, together with a few of the faithful from the church on whose behalf the fete was being held. Even they had not been able to withstand the piercing, slanting rain, and after braving it out under dripping canvas had finally taken refuge in Mrs. Rutland's sitting room. The fete had then been turned into an indoor barbecue, there had been sherry as well as tea, canapés as well as cakes, so that the faithful were well rewarded for their labour. Barbara had acted as hostess in the absence of her mother, only she lacked her mother's familiarity, the guests were not of her age group, they talked of things which to her had no significance or importance. She found them dry, arid, without personality, and she had been glad when they took advantage of a break in the rain and left.

The stalls had been covered overnight in the hope the weather might clear and enable the fete to be held Sunday. The rain however had been more ferocious then than on the day before, the stalls had therefore been dismantled, the trestle tables and parasols folded, the chairs and refreshments removed. A few grey hens had been pushed under canvas at the end of the lawn but for the most part the garden had been left to bear the brunt of the storm alone. The pansies were torn in the bed set in the disused well, the petals of the tulips floated blood-stained in the pools around each flower, the forsythia had seen its honeysuckle shaken to the earth, the wind had torn its greedy hands through the young poplars, the ropes supporting the poplars had shaken loose, the colours of the herbaceous border were ruffled and feathery, thinned, some of the shrubs broken, stripped of their leaves. Only the rosebuds climbing the balustrade of the well seemed to have withstood, only the scarlet-tipped calyces still protected their blossom.

The mist wreathed around the fruit trees so that their trunks loomed stark in the garden, there were dull pools where the rain had saturated the lawn, the mist was damp to the crazy paving, damp to the panes of the windows, and moving a hand across the glass Barbara could see moisture dark to the flesh of the tulips protected by the side of the house. She did not like the mist. She liked it even less than she liked the rain. It made her feel cold, unclean, it set a chill to her bones, her soul, it dulled the excitement she had felt over the last few days. She did not like the journey into the city when the mist was so thick, she did not like walking in the woods, she did not like sitting at home listening to the crackle of the wood fire. But there would be nothing for her to see in the pityard, she could not persuade her mother to take her for a drive into the village, she could only idle around the stand of fishing rods thinking of some distraction. She could only flick through the Radio Times to see what there was on television, open another batch of letters deluging the house, delivered by the postman three times a day. Even look to the telephone in the hope it would ring.

"I'll get it," she said. "Probably it's for me."

The telephone stood on the sill of the window and she crossed quickly to pick the receiver from the hook.

"Hello," she said. "I thought it'd be you."

"Sorry about last night," Gerald said. "I couldn't get away because of all those damn slips your mother insists we dish out."

"Didn't they tell you? I rang the office about eight and heard you were still there. So I never went myself."

She saw her mother unfold her knees, the cuttings drop to the floor.

"So what's new," she asked. "Apart from that?"

"I went to see the old cow. Tried to get her to change her mind."

"But you didn't have any luck?"

"She has it all figured, right down the line. I told her I wasn't very keen, but she says she doesn't care about that. Says she has her own reasons for wanting them to marry and as far as she's concerned that's an end to it. She's not changing her mind for anybody."

"So when will it be. The wedding?"

"Just as soon as the old man gets out the pit. As soon as the strike's over."

36

Barbara traced a finger through the moisture of the window and watched her mother pick up the cuttings that had fallen to the floor. She let Gerald talk on but as she listened her mind was only half on what he said. He was complaining because he could not take her out Saturday night. Though in a few months she would be twenty-one the furthest her mother let her go was the youth fellowship dance held in the church hall. Even then it was only every fortnight. Once she had arranged to meet Gerald there, but this was in the early days of their courtship, his reputation as a drinker preceded him, and the churchwarden was there personally to refuse entrance. Barbara had not yet arrived and could not stand by him. Gerald had been greatly amused by this rejection on the grounds of dissipated youth, but nevertheless described it as a fine welcome for a sinner back to the fold. Barbara was so humiliated she refused ever to go again. Gerald could not often get away Wednesday to take her dancing in the city, the picture hall had been half-converted to bingo, both of them hated television, there was nowhere to watch it had it been otherwise, and therefore they had had to settle for walks in the woods.

"An intimate conversation," Mrs. Rutland said. "Anyone I know?"

Barbara put down the phone and leafed through a horticultural magazine on the sill of the window.

"Only Gerald Holt," Barbara said. "The boy who works in the colliery office."

"It's not serious, I hope. The men aren't on their way back to the surface?"

"You heard what he said. It didn't sound like it, did it."

"Holt, you say. I suppose he's no relation to Ray in the pit."

"No relation at all," Barbara said. "Only his brother."

Her mother picked up the scissors from the arm of the chair

on which she was sitting and began cutting out another article. She had opened a scrapbook the day the strike began and already it was halfway to being full. As she sat by the fire, frill of her slip showing white like a hem to her dress, knees shining in the glow of the flames, there were papers all around the chair, most of them national, only two or three local. She had pulled a coffee table close to the chair and on it stood a tall glass of pineapple. She wore an oatmeal dress buttoned down the front and pinned to the breast of the dress was a large aquamarine brooch, with a similar aquamarine ring on her finger. Mrs. Rutland had hardly in her life worn jewellery, she believed it a little too sophisticated, a little too showy. She had lost the habit altogether on the death of her husband, and seen no reason to cultivate it again, perambulating as she did the social circle of the village. Now with so many strange people coming to see her, journalists for interviews, modest men with contributions, she had opened her box again, much to the curiosity of Barbara.

Barbara was always irritated by her mother's aplomb. Often she said things that were cutting to see if she could snap her out of it, sometimes she ignored her altogether, did not speak for weeks; but once she shed her moroseness, when at last she broke her silence, her mother talked as naturally and easily as if it had never been otherwise. This irritated Barbara even more. The fact was her mother did notice, and not only noticed was upset by it, but she had never quite known how to deal with Barbara, she had lost years of experience pining for her husband, so that when she did come back to reality she found her daughter growing independently of her. There had been a barrier between them, though she had never been able to define what that barrier was. Of course in those years of puberty there had been no hostility between them, no open warfare, only a lack of intimacy, a lack of filial love. Even then Mrs. Rutland had not taken it amiss, for she recalled the same qualities in her husband. She did not doubt he had always loved her, but she could not help remembering he had taken her out a year without venturing upon a kiss.

The difficulties in their relationship had really developed over the last year, as Barbara emerged to womanhood. There had been those scenes about attending dances in the village, her dislike of travelling each day into the city for her commercial course at business school. Then of course her refusal ever again to attend a dance her mother organized on behalf of the church fellowship. She never divined the reason for that. But then her daughter seemed to be going through such a difficult period she had not thought fit to ask. She thought she had been granting concessions enough when she allowed her to the dance in the city Wednesday. Often on her return, over tea, over what she liked to consider the intimacy of the meal, she probed her about the dance, asked if anyone had taken her out, offered to bring her home. She probed not because she was curious, not because she lacked confidence — the thought frankly did not enter her head — but because this way she thought they might draw together.

Often she felt what Barbara lacked was masculine authority. And over the years she felt she had tried to make up for this by too excessive a discipline. But then she too had been on her own, there had been no-one to whom she could turn, no friend, no confidante, no-one that is except Herbert Longley. Longley, however, was not a father, he was not even an uncle, and therefore knew less about children than did Mrs. Rutland. Besides, though he liked Barbara, he had been indifferent to her upbringing, he had not noticed the change as she grew older, he had not witnessed the scenes, the tantrums, the buffetings Mrs. Rutland suffered, the misconstruction upon her questions about the dance. And each time he came Barbara went to him, she talked easily and without restraint, she held his hand, strolled him in the garden, tossing her head as if to show her mother it was not *she* who was lacking in human warmth. But Mrs. Rutland tried not to notice. She liked to think these things would pass, they were outward displays of adolescence that would leave her, like acne, once she reached twenty-one.

She did not understand most of her trouble was caused by a misreading of her daughter's character. She liked to attribute her stiffness and lack of warmth to her father, she liked to think that because she had his walk, his mannerisms, she had too his character. Yet in fact Barbara did not have the character of her father, she had the character of her grandmother. She did not have her masculine drive, her love of gadgets, but she did have her attachment to the village, her love of the country. And it was in this Barbara felt she did not resemble her mother. She did not believe her mother loved the village. If she had she would not have sent her daughter into the town, she would not have deprived her of contact with people who would later become her friends. She knew of her mother's involvement in the village, she knew the guilds she ran, the clubs she organized, but she could not rid from her mind the idea it was done impersonally not for love but for gain. Not for the sake of the village but for the sake of the shops.

That was why, contrary to what she had told Gerald, she had not mentioned him to her mother. She knew what she had told Gerald was true, her mother would never seek to enforce upon her a partner she did not want, she would never try to drive her to a business or professional man because she thought such a marriage befitted a daughter of her standing. But with her mother's indifference to the village she feared that though she might not openly disapprove she might go about things in such a way it would fall through. She would use her artfulness to see Barbara no longer liked Gerald the way she felt she liked him now. Barbara had a great mistrust of her mother's cleverness. She did not want to admit she ran her affairs well, according to Barbara she ran them badly, but she knew the results must be good, for she lived in a big house, she had a fine car, and she was popular in the village. And in business what could be more important than that?

"I didn't know Ray Holt had a brother," Mrs. Rutland said. "Still less he worked in the colliery office."

"That's because you don't get out enough. If you went to the village a bit more you'd know things like that. You wouldn't have to rely on me telling you. Anyway, I know what you're thinking, but you don't have to worry. He'll not use his influence to bring the strike to an end. He couldn't care less."

"All the same it's an important connection. I'm surprised Atkin hasn't realized it."

"Of course he's realized it. The undermanager was at him only the other day — telling him to send down Gerald and bring the men back to the surface. He said they'd take as much notice of Gerald as they take of Ray. Atkin put him off by saying he'd refer it back to area. Of course he never did, but I'll bet he gets a sweat thinking what'll happen if they find out."

"But how can Gerald have that much influence over his brother?"

"Just because your brother's never had any influence over you it doesn't mean Gerald can't have any over his. As a matter of fact, his brother's always looked up to him, thought him something of a god. It's only natural, really, since he's younger than Gerald. And of course since Gerald works in the colliery office and he in the pit. It sort of made a distinction between them."

"Then maybe it's Gerald behind the strike."

"I've just told you, he couldn't care less."

"All the same he might have passed information. If only out of mischief. I was told yesterday when I was up somebody leaked all the Board's secrets. Told Ray the whole story before it even got to the lodge secretary. That's how he incited the men, got them to settle for a stay-down strike."

"And a good job too. Only it has nothing to do with Gerald. But the undermanager thought him being so popular with the men, being a big drinker and such a favourite with his brother, he might get them back to the surface. Atkin pointed out he might not too, but the undermanager argued it was worthwhile. He doesn't like Atkin, so he put the pressure on. The only way Atkin got out of it was by making the promise to refer it back."

Barbara pulled at the hem of her lemon cardigan and crossing to the table took from her bag a powder compact. She had that week changed her style of hair, sweeping back the tawny streak from around her face, leaving her brow exposed, uneven; the hair at the back had been tied in a small bobbing pony's tail, and at the front the unevenness had been corrected by combing down a fringe. She opened the compact and looked at herself in the small mirror. The style she felt made her look much older, more mature, more like a woman than a fledgling out of her teens. It seemed to give shape to her face, take the heaviness from her cheeks, the width from her brow; it accentuated the fineness of her nose, her mouth, the speckles to her eyes, so that she looked prettier, more beautiful, more like a flower coming to bloom. She took the puff from the compact and began lightly to powder her cheeks. She tried to adjust the mirror and look beyond her shoulder to where her mother sat over the fire.

"There's another Holt I heard mentioned the other day," Mrs. Rutland said. "One getting married soon."

"It happens to be their father," Barbara said. "He's getting married to that Walton girl. The one who delivers the milk. The one who had a row with the gardener and pulled out the iris bulbs for spite. She always manages to break a bottle at the gate and scatter the glass over the drive."

"But she's young enough to be his grand-daughter."

"I know. I should have thought some of the shopkeepers, with their nose for gossip, would have told you before now. Everyone's been talking about it since the word got round. But of course, I forgot, you don't have that kind of interest in the village."

"I did hear something," Mrs. Rutland said. "But I dismissed it as gossip."

"It's even better than gossip. It's true. That's why Gerald rang on the phone. He's been to see her mother — tried to get her to call it off. Only he's not had much luck. You'd understand why if you knew her mother. She's the one who left six weeks debt at the newsagent. Said she only bought the papers to light the fire with. And since she'd never had a fire in weeks she offered to send them all back."

"I remember. She ordered the cars at the garage."

"That's where you heard. The wedding'll be on as soon as his father gets out the pit."

"I didn't even know he was in the pit."

"You thought all the older men came out a week ago. And so they did. All except Ray's father. They're saying in the village Ray deliberately kept him down so he wouldn't marry. And they say if he keeps him down much longer he'll not be in a state to marry even if he wants."

Mrs. Rutland continued the cut of scissors through paper and there was an uneasy movement of springs as she adjusted her poise in the chair. A little wood on the fire had been exposed to the rain, the smoke had risen thick and blue, the tang of its odour lingered still to the beams, a tang to which they were both now accustomed. She picked the glass from the table and gently sipped the pineapple. She thought of the relationship between Gerald Holt on the surface and Ray Holt in the pit. She could not understand how she had not heard of it before now, but then she realized probably she had, only she had not made the connection. She realized too how grateful she must be to Atkin, how much could not be accomplished without his assistance. She placed the glass on the table and thought of the second connection, between Gerald and Barbara, she began to consider why it should be important to them, why they did not want his father to marry, why they should even want to stop him doing something he so obviously

379

wanted to do. And she realized she had to go carefully, diplomatically, she had not to expose her sensitivity to yet another rebuff.

"This Gerald Holt and you. Is it serious?"

"He wants to get engaged at Christmas."

"And you. Do you want to get engaged?"

"If I did it's no good you trying to stop me."

"My darling, no-one wants to stop you doing anything."

"That's what you say now. But you've all kinds of ways to get round me. Not letting me out Saturday night, not letting me loose in the village. I know you say I have free will, you say I can do what I like, marry who I like, yet I can hardly go for a walk without you asking where I'm going. I can hardly cross the doors without being told when to be back."

"Soon you'll be twenty-one," Mrs. Rutland said. "Then you can please yourself."

"So you've told me. But I'm the only girl in the village who never gets out Saturday night. The only girl at school with no tales to tell Monday. All the time you've tried to isolate me from the village. You've tried to cut me off from its life, its people. Here I am, as you say, nearly twenty-one, and the only friend I have is Gerald Holt. And the only reason I have him is by accident."

"You'll have time enough to know people once you leave school."

"If there's any people to know. Or any village. Oh I know all the efforts you're making, the trouble you're going to, but d'you know what they're saying in the village? They say you're only doing it because it's in your interest. Because if they pull down the village you'll be ruined — and you know you'll be ruined."

"You seem to know an awful lot. For someone cut off as you say."

"Only because I overhear conversations. Not because I'm told anything."

"And you believe what you hear. What they say?"

"I don't know what to believe," Barbara said. "That's what I wanted to ask."

"If you knew me as well as you think," Mrs. Rutland said. "You should know the answer."

"You were counting on uncle Herbert to solve your problems by proposing. That's why you're making such an effort now that he hasn't."

"As a matter of fact he did propose. And as a matter of fact I was on the verge of accepting."

"Then why didn't you. If you like him so much?"

"Because he told me about the village. He told me what was going to happen. How they were going to pull down the houses. Move the people away. How I would have to leave too because there was no reason to stay. And when he told me that, when he told me the best thing I could do was marry him, I just couldn't accept."

"You mean you put the village before yourself?"

"Not exactly. I put my past before my future."

Barbara had moved her bag away from the table and now she studied a plaque of winter moths the gardener had collected during the cold months. There were people in the village who were saying about her mother worse than she had related. They were saying all those grandiose schemes for credit had been invented to ensure she had an income when the men were on strike, that she had wanted the whole scheme for herself and that the only reason she had extended it to others was because shop-keepers complained. But Barbara knew her mother had subscribed three hundred pounds to the fund at the outset, she knew too supplying the men with food was costing more than she could ever recuperate on credit. She had rejected these intimations when they had been brought to her notice by Gerald. Nevertheless somewhere inside she had believed. That was why she had wanted to hear from her mother it was not true, that was why she wanted to be reassured, comforted. She laid the plaque on the sill and came reluctantly towards the fire.

"And Gerald," Mrs. Rutland said. "Does he feel the same about the pit as his brother?"

"I've told you, he couldn't care less."

"But if they pull down the colliery it'll not be long before they pull down the office."

"He's going away anyway. He hates the pit and can't stand the village. He says it's dead — been dead for years. He says it's time they made it official. He'll not be happy till it's pulled down brick for brick, house for house. Till there's nothing left but rubble."

"But where will he go. Once it's pulled down?"

"He wants to live in the city. He doesn't really know where — anywhere as long as it's miles from here. He wants to go out into the world, see a bit life. He wants to find out what he's here for, what he's doing on this earth. Find out what life means to him. Then when he finds out what it means to him he's going out to live it."

"He thinks he'll find all that in a city?"

"He says people are alive in cities, they've got something to live for. And he wants to go and find out what it is. He wants a break, he's restless, unsure of himself. I suppose he really doesn't know what he wants. He's lunging about in the dark. But some day he'll find himself. He'll know what he's looking for. And I'd like to be around when he does."

"But about the village, that it's dead, that it's never been alive. You believe this too?"

"No, I don't. I don't see why it should be pulled down and the people sent away."

"But if he wants to leave you'll have to leave with him."

"If I love him it'll be my duty. It's what I'll have to do."

"You don't sound very sure. About loving him."

"I'm not sure, really sure. But sure enough. You see, you don't know him, you've never met him. But he's a force. He has so much strength and power — and so much confidence. He's determined to live life to the full, he says he'll take it by the scruff of the neck, he'll shake it till its teeth rattle. And he will, once he's found it. That's why I'm so attracted. Because I've never met anyone like him before."

"All the same you'd have to be sure — really sure — before you married."

"But I'll marry him if I want. No-one'll stop me."

Standing by the coffee table, watching her mother sip the pineapple, she felt the same hostility. She felt the same need to attack and thus defend. Only this time her antagonism was weakened by uncertainty, the doubts that had risen about her mother. She knew the views related by Gerald were not held by the majority of the village, she knew too her mother would never stoop so low as to put her own self interest before those of men on strike. But in her resentment she had wanted to think the worst,

382

and even now, knowing she was wrong, she still felt reluctant to admit to herself the truth. She tried to find other reasons why her mother should not marry Longley. She knew he had money, property, income, that he would see her mother settled, and herself too when the time came. She could not believe her mother would throw all this up merely for the sake of the village. Somewhere she felt there must be another reason.

"Mother," she said. "I hope you didn't turn down uncle Herbert for me."

"What makes you say that?"

"Nothing. Though it'd solve all our problems. We'd not have to worry any more about the shops in the village, about keeping up this big house. We'd be able to go away, the three of us, we could have a good time, travel around, he could take us to Paris the way he says. The way he's always on."

"But once we left the village we'd never come back."

"Probably if I marry Gerald I'll never come back anyway."

"And you really want that. That I marry Herbert Longley?"

"If you wanted to I wouldn't stand in the way."

"You mean not like Gerald Holt? But you see I don't want. Because you see I don't want to be driven from my home. I don't want to sacrifice my principles and my life, betray myself, take the easiest course, just to give pleasure to others. I like Longley — I think the world of him, and perhaps some day we'll marry, when all this is over — but not yet. Not before I've fought for the colliery. And certainly not before I've saved the village."

Barbara tidied the papers around her mother's chair and sat herself on the rug. She picked up the scrapbook her mother had set aside and looked again through the cuttings. Despite the mist the same sense of excitement rose in her again, only this time it was warmer, deeper, making her want to tremble. Not because she was doing anything for the village but because her mother was doing it. And not because of the selfish reason of profit but merely because she wanted to. Because she loved the village. She had never felt she would see the day when she would be proud of her mother. But then she had never felt she would see her mother sharing the love she had for their lives, a life that was dear to her and did not want to change. A life pleasant because it was sheltered, because she had been born to it, and because it comprised of things basic to her nature — peace and happiness and content tied to the country, their origins.

"You think it's worth it, mother. The strike?"

"Of course it's worth it."

"I didn't mean that. I meant you think we'll win?"

"Of course we'll win. How can it be otherwise?"

"I just thought — well maybe the men'll crack."

"They'll not crack," Mrs. Rutland said. "Not for a while yet."

"Well suppose there's intervention. By the union?"

"You mean that in the paper today. About the big man coming down from Durham?"

"That's right. The area secretary."

She laid down the scissors and drained the last of the pineapple.

"I don't know," she said. "I'm a bit frightened myself. He's very popular in the county and he's got a lot of standing with the men. They might take notice of what he says. Of course he'll tell them to get back to the surface, he'll urge them all to go back to work, he'll say just how bad these unofficial strikes are. And he's quite a speaker. I've heard him on a few times myself. The men might heed what he says."

She noticed Barbara's hand creep up to hers and fondle the aquamarine ring on her finger. She could not understand this sudden change, this relaxing of the cold war. She felt embarrassed, shy, and wanted to recoil from the touch. Yet feeling the warmth of her daughter's hand fusing into hers she began to divine that the change was permanent. Like the first breath of spring that told you winter was over and summer about to begin. And the sudden relief she felt, the tension she shed, made her realize how much she yearned for this love, this tenderness, how much she needed it to replace the love she had felt for her husband. She needed to be rid of the loneliness that returned for no reason at all when she heard a step on the drive, a car at night on the forest road. She needed Barbara close to her, so close she could give to her life something it lacked, the knowledge that she was needed, needed by her own.

But she began to realize that perhaps it had come too late. She and Barbara would draw together only to be separated when she married and left the village. When she settled elsewhere with Gerald Holt. She did not want to stop Barbara from marrying, have her close, always close, she wanted her courtship to end, her love to fade, though she was determined there was nothing she would do to stop it. Things would have to take their own course. She would not risk her daughter's love by interference. Yet the same thought crossed Barbara's mind. She saw she was drawing close to her mother and she saw her mother might interfere. She saw she might try to influence her against Gerald.

"And Gerald," she said. "I can bring him to see you. I can tell him it's all right?"

"Of course you can, darling. You know you can."

"You really wouldn't mind? If we got engaged at Christmas."

"If that's what you wanted I wouldn't mind at all."

"But his father. Getting married to that Walton girl."

"Some of the scandal might rub off," Mrs. Rutland said. "If you marry."

"But I'm not marrying yet. Only getting engaged."

"I'll think it over," Mrs. Rutland said. "See if it's all right."

"Anyway, I can bring him to the house. I can tell him to come."

"Of course you can. Bring him any time you like."

In her anxiety Barbara had tightened the pressure on her mother's fingers. Now the pressure relaxed, she lifted a hand to her face and felt the soft silkiness of the skin against her cheek, the cold of the ring against the bone. She could forget now the resentment, the hostility, the antagonism, she could forget her mother's refusal to attend school in the village, the dance in the store hall. She was happy because now her courtship with Gerald could be brought into the open. She could bring him home Saturday night, they could walk through the village like other courting couples, they could go dancing in the town or city. And all with her mother's blessing, her mother's consent. Now she had found her mother, found this contact, this warmth, she too did not want to lose it. She was proud she was fighting, so proud she wanted this closeness to go on forever. Then she thought of union intervention. She thought of the possibilities of the men returning to the surface.

"Mother," she said. "I hope the union don't intervene. I hope the men stay on strike."

"I hope so too," Mrs. Rutland said. "I hope so too."

37

But as it happened they need not have feared union intervention as they did.

Over the first three days the union confined itself to instructing Wishart to get the men back to work; this was in accordance with standard reconciliation procedure which declared there must a return to work before negotiations could begin. The procedure had worked at other collieries where men had come out in support, it had worked in Scotland the year before, when three thousand miners came out on strike over the closure of the Devon pit, near Alloa. There was no reason why it should not have worked at Highhill. Besides, at Highhill the men were on stay-down strike, and stay-down strikes rarely lasted more than two or three shifts never mind two or three days. But the conciliation machinery at other collieries relied on the prestige and authority of the local union, the ability of the lodge secretary to impose his will on the men. At Highhill the machinery broke down because the lodge committee supported the men, the lodge chairman was down the pit.

And because the lodge secretary could not impose his will on those at bank never mind those underground.

Therefore the strike was a runaway before the union realized. At the weekend the Sunday national had run its banner headline, Monday food began to be supplied to the men, Thursday saw the launching of the relief fund in the city, Friday the distribution of credit slips that took care of their wives and families on the surface. The men knew they had the public behind them, they saw it in gifts of blankets and warm clothing, they saw it in the amounts that quickly amassed in the fund. They were therefore in no mood to accept the union's request for a return to work. Besides, the articles in the provincial confirmed again everything they had been told by Ray, that by 1970 every pit in the area would be affected, that a labour force of 120,000 in the country had already been reduced to 83,000 and would be reduced to 55,000 by 1970. And since no new industry would be introduced to absorb the surplus labour they understood they had to fight now if they had to fight at all. They had to win now if there was to be victory. In vain did the union explain that though the labour force would be reduced, though it would be reduced in the proportion given, this did not mean a redundancy of tens of thousands, merely that recruitment would cease and retirement not be extended.

That a man leaving the industry would not be replaced.

The union of course regretted the closure of the pit on what they considered merely financial grounds. They referred to the hardship created by the government's insistence that the industry pay its way, regardless of the cost in redundancies and transfers, the upheaval that changed the tenor of their ways. They acknowledged that though there may be geological difficulties in working the coal some of it remained the best coking coal in the world, that despite the fact modern machinery could not be introduced means were at their disposal to produce sufficient to help keep working all the gas plants in the area. They regretted too the manner in which the lodge had presented the news to the men, not at a special report-back as stipulated in union rules, but at an open meeting before the facts of the closure had been properly assimilated. Nevertheless, as soon as the pit was producing again, negotiations could be held between union and management, not at colliery but area level, negotiations that would be based on keeping the colliery open, that would look into costs seam by seam, district by district.

So that the men could be assured the colliery would not close till the matter had been thoroughly thrashed out.

But Ray Holt said that if they deplored the emphasis on money rather than men why not declare their official support for the men instead of letting the strike drag on unofficially. He said they all knew there was enough coal in the pit to last twenty years but the pit had to close because the Board had authorized the closure of any seam not producing more than a hundred tons a day. He asked why the union did not intervene with the Board to rescind such arbitrary decisions instead of intervening with the men who had to endure the hardship such decisions imposed. He also rejected any attempt to renegotiate the future of the pit at area rather than colliery level. He said they had had enough of other people deciding their future. All the trouble had come about because decisions had been taken above their heads, arbitrarily and without consultation; this he said was a negation of all that a nationalized industry stood for, it was a negation of the authority of the union, an infringement on the rights of the men.

As for the assurance the colliery would not close till the matter was thrashed out, he dismissed this as meaningless, since the colliery was not intended to close till Christmas, the men could return to work, the matter thrashed out, and still the deadline be maintained.

Towards the seventeenth day of the strike it became clear only the personal intervention of the area secretary was likely to bring the men back to the surface. The secretary himself had wanted to intervene earlier but had been advised not to do so because of the militancy of the men. He had been warned that with their tales so high, supplied as they were with food, the support they were getting from the public, he was likely to suffer a rebuff that would leave the situation worse than it was now. The fact union stature was not high owing to the resentment felt against Markie Wishart, the fact Ray had weeded out the older and more vulnerable workers before the strike got under way, was also taken into account. It was considered those who remained had stamina for a while yet. Besides, given their example and the publicity that appeared in the papers the area secretary had his hands full damping down protests and threats of strike at every colliery where even the rumour of a seam closing was hinted. But towards the seventeenth day the publicity began to settle, tempers to cool, and it was then the area secretary made his voyage to Highhill.

Ray Holt, with an insight developing like a sixth sense, had seen intervention coming and decided to treat it as a matter of no importance. He jibed at the union and scoffed the secretary as a man they saw only at opening and closing time, the opening of the pithead baths and the closing of the pit. He wanted to know why they had not seen him earlier, why the union had not joined the Board and approached the government to keep the colliery open. But the secretary had more prestige with the men than Ray calculated and therefore he was obliged to change his technique. He let it be known that the area secretary was coming to declare the strike official, that in his pocket there would be plans to ensure new seams replaced those the Board wanted to close. That not only would the pit close now it would never close. Even then Ray felt uneasy, he felt the prestige of the secretary might outweigh his own, that for once the men might listen to the voice of reason rather than the voice of protest. So that he began looking round for some other distraction, some other event that would minimize the effect of the visit. He thought it would never come at all, that control was passing from his hands.

Till he heard over the colliery line Markie Wishart had resigned as secretary of the lodge.

The news came only an hour before the area secretary was to make his appearance at bank top. Ray immediately held an improvised ballot in the pit, had himself elected secretary, declared the strike official and called on the area secretary to give his support. The secretary had hardly stepped from his car when he saw himself deflected from the purpose of his visit. He was obliged to declare the strike could not be official without the support of the area union, that the union could not give its affirmation, not because the men's cause was unjust, but because there had never been an official strike in the industry since vesting day and the moment was not opportune to have one now. Besides, there was nothing in this dispute that could not be settled around a conference table. He therefore asked the men to disregard the advice of those whose views corresponded to the nineteenth rather than the twentieth century, declared that any single revolt against the trend of civilization was doomed in advance, refused to accept Ray Holt as lodge secretary, and declared the ballot invalid because it had not been held on official union ballot paper. And because as he said in the event a lodge secretary resigned during his year in office it was for the lodge committee and not the men to elect a replacement.

The men were disappointed at this attitude of the union leader. They had believed he was coming to Highhill with real concessions, they believed he would tell them of new seams to be opened, more money to be invested, the maintenance of a tradition whereby a son followed his father into the pit. They could not understand his rejection of Ray Holt as secretary. They could not understand his criticism of a man to whom they knew they owed everything. It was Ray Holt who had elicited for them the real consequences of the closure, it was Ray Holt who had indicated what transfer meant to another colliery, it was he who had organized the stay-down strike — and not only organized it, seen to it after three days of hunger they were fed and kept warm, that the attention of the world was drawn to their fight. That their wives and children should not starve while they remained un- supported and unfinanced. Therefore they did not respond to the secretary's urge they return to the surface, they did not respond when he asked for a vote to return to work. They did not even let him down the pit but stranded him on the surface, and before he returned to area headquarters approved unanimously a message from Ray informing him of their determination to continue the strike.

Wishart had resigned because for him there had been no alternative. For seventeen days he had gyrated between Donnolly the MP, Atkin the colliery manager, and Gerald the colliery clerk in an effort to persuade them use their influence to bring the strike to an end. He had tried on several occasions to get past the pickets on the bank top, or even past the pickets who patrolled the mouths of the drifts. He had put to Gerald Holt the same question he had put to Atkin and Donnolly and received the same response. He still felt bitter and disillusioned, bitter because he had not con- strued the facts as they had been put to him, disillusioned because he had placed his trust in words and because words had let him down. Yet the feelings of tears and misery had left him, had distilled into his soul, he realized now that even had he thoroughly understood the position would not be changed. The colliery would still be losing seven pounds per ton, the seams would still be narrow and unworkable, the coal still gather unwanted at the surface, the Coal Board could not do other than modernize pits or make them redundant, the colliery could not continue to exist merely because it had always existed.

The people could not always live in the past, they had some time to turn their gaze to the future.

Therefore he had resigned. He had shed the load of ten years responsibility. He had decided to fade into the background. Already, over the last few days, his appearance had changed, the stitches had been removed from his eye, the plaster stripped away, leaving a white peeling skin, the scar itself was a fresh red line, that would soon fade and blue once he returned to the pit, there was more freshness to his cheeks, he looked healthier and more relaxed, he could straighten his shoulders, his back, as if the burden he had carried all these years had been a physical burden. He was not even worrying about his wife. Three weeks in hospital had put the colour back to her cheeks, it had reduced the strangeness from her eyes, her hair was neat and well kept, brushed back from the forehead, the scrape marks where she had fallen healed from the cheeks. The baby had been saved and once out the hospital he was determined to devote as much time to her as he had once devoted to the affairs of the union. He sat on a small tubular chair near the bed in the hospital and gently patted her hand.

"How d'ye feel the day?" he asked.

"Fine, just fine," she said. "Only I wish I was out, I wish I was home."

"It'll not be long now," he said. "Only a day or two."

"That's what the doctor said. When he called round the day. Ye know, the one who looks at all the patients. The one who sometimes comes round at meal times and asks how things are, if ye like the food, if ye have any complaints. He called the day and we had a good long chat and he said just the same as ye. Not long now, he said. Just like ye. Only he wants to see ye before I leave. Wants ye to call by his office the night on yer way home."

"Probably just to tell me when ye're comin' home," he said. "So I can get things ready."

Her bed was next to the garden and out of the window she could see the tall torch-like lupins, violet and pink, that graced the path, she could see the lawn that had only recently been cut so that the damp stalks and daisy heads lay like a thin carpet on the green, she could see the hanging rustling tails of the laburnum in a grove beyond the lawn, some of the blossom tarnished now, the nectar sucked out of the honeycomb petals. And at the centre of the lawn in narrow beds of dark earth she could see the first of the summer roses, damp still nestling in the cups of the leaves, the blossom already bursting from their buds, little minute flies picking at the red that appeared among the green. Yet the fragrance that had for Wishart the freshness of opium came not from the roses in the garden but the roses that stood in vases at the side of the bed. They were double flowering roses, rouge and vermilion, with little pearls of damp sitting upon the pearls, the petals closing to press the damp to the heart of the blossom. They were early blooms at the height of flower and as he leant to finger the stems the pearls dropped to his hand and he smelt the freshness to his fingers.

"Where did ye get these?" he asked.

"The patients in the ward," she said. "They were on about the strike and I told them I lived at Highhill, and I said my husband was lodge secretary and they asked us if ye were down the pit with the rest o' the men. And I said ye were. And I said ye had to get special permission to come up and see us, and if ye came up they wouldn't let ye back. So they clubbed up and bought us these flowers."

"And ye told the doctor. I was down the pit?"

"Yes," she said. "And he said he was very sorry, and he hoped ye were all right and ye wouldn't get too cold and damp and the rest. And I said no. No because they're properly organized. And I said it's me husband organizin' it. So he can save the colliery and the village, so they're not destroyed. And I said they'll not be destroyed because he's me husband. And because — so they clubbed up and bought these flowers. Even the doctor, he clubbed up too."

"I wish ye wouldn't tell the doctor I was down the pit," Wishart said. "Or that I'm organizin' the strike."

"But ye were in the pit, Markie. Ye were. All yer life ye've been in the pit."

"Only it's in all the papers the union aren't supportin' the strike. And though I'm lodge secretary, though I'm head o' the union I've not been down since the strike started. Not once in all this time."

"But that's why they bought us these flowers. Because ye were down the pit, because I told them ye were down, and because that's how ye got yer bad eye. I said ye fell over a tub when ye were down, I said ye couldn't see where ye were goin' because it was that dark, and ye were hungry and weak and tired, and the next thing ye knaas ye're lyin' on yer belly and there's blood streamin' from the cut. And they had to send ye back to the surface and have stitches put in. And with me in hospital and the stitches in yer eye that's why they wouldn't let ye back."

Wishart held her hand in his and she felt the pads of the hand less coarse, the skin less brittle, the large cicatrices on the fingers already contracting. Three weeks out of the pit had changed his hands as they had changed his face, she noticed the dabs of colour to the points of his cheeks, she noticed the eyes less grey and shiny, the whites less bloodshot, the rims no longer so red where he had been reading. The face marred only by the fresh red line, thin and ugly, that ran from the brow of his eye to the network of wrinkles forming round the pouches. He still wore the sports clothes and flannels, for over the years not only had he neglected his wife he had neglected himself, this was all he had presentable, though now the sports coat and flannels had been cleaned, the bloodstains no longer apparent to the lapels, stains down the side of his coat round the pockets. The eyes too were less tired, less stricken, and they smiled with his lips as he pulled himself a little closer to the bed.

"Listen, pet," he said. "Listen carefully. I've resigned from the union, I'm no longer lodge secretary. I've given it all up 'cause I want to be with ye. I want to dedicate myself to ye the way I once dedicated myself to the men. What happened the other week, the night I went to the institute, it was my fault 'cause I should never have gone. And havin' gone I should've come back like I said. But all that's behind us now 'cause we're ganna start again. Just ye and me and the bairn. That's all, just the three of us."

"But the men in the pit, Markie. The fight for the village."

"The men are fightin' for the colliery," Wishart said. "Not the village. But once out of here we'll not have to fight 'cause we'll have each other. We'll live for each other just the way we did when we were married. Just the way it was in the beginnin'. And no matter what happens to the colliery, no matter what happens to the village, this is our home and this is where we'll stay. And once this baby's born, once he's sittin' on yer knee, we're ganna have others just as ye wanted. Everythin's ganna be just as ye've wanted."

"But if there's no village, Markie, what's the good of all those children?"

" 'Cause this house is ours and 'cause what's ganna happen to the village'll not affect us. But if ye think ye cannot live without the village at the top o' the bank, if ye think ye want the companionship o' the houses and the people as ye've had in the past, then I'll fight for the village, I'll fight the way ye wanted us to fight for the colliery. And ye know me, if I fight the way I say, if I put me mind to it, we'll come through, ye know we'll come through. So ye'll be happy. So ye'll never be lonely again."

393

"That'd be nice," she said. "Never to be lonely again."

As he talked of the village he had seen the fret come again to her face, he had seen the tightening of breath in her throat, like an asthmatic fearing an attack, he had seen the quiver that came to the lashes of the eyes, the tremble to her lips. The eyes glazed white and the tongue began nervously to prod an incipient mole on her cheek. She had searched his face as he spoke, looking for the confidence he had once inspired, she had thought of their years of married life, how he had been a comfort to her, a comfort to know her life was in his hands, that she could leave decisions to him. That he would never let her down. Yet he had let her down. He had let her down the night he had gone to the institute, the night she had looked into his face for strength and seen only weakness, when she had looked for assurance and seen only uncertainty. It was then her nerve had cracked, it was then she had dissolved into panic. Now feeling his grip tighten upon her hand, fingers exploring the pulse to her wrist, she searched his face again, uncertain this time what she would find, the same weakness, the same doubt, or the strength and confidence she had always known.

And she saw this time he believed what he said, he was not merely consoling her, he was not uttering the first words that came to his head merely to keep up her spirits. She relaxed and allowed herself to fall back upon the pillow. She smiled, showing her teeth; they were dull ugly teeth, stained with nicotine from the time she had smoked, the teeth at the front blue with decay. She had let them go just as she had let herself go. Yet for Wishart to see the smile, to see the ugly carious teeth, was to be taken back over the years to the day of their wedding, so that they were standing in the shelter of the wall, the wind through his hair, fluttering the veils of the bridesmaids, shivering the hems of their dresses. To the day she had really been happy. He knew now they could not put back the clock, they could not retreat to that single day of happiness so many years ago. But perhaps just as the wind had lifted the veils of the bridesmaids' headdress, so he would lift from her thoughts the veil of mania and psychosis, the shadow of derangement that so obsessed her mind. They could not turn back the clock but perhaps they could start again. Perhaps it was not too late for her to have the family she wanted. Perhaps it was not too late to have the children she yearned.

It had never occurred to Wishart how much he had loved

his wife till now. He had taken her so much for granted he had allowed his love to slumber. And it had been enough to know that she loved him, it had been enough to know she was there to see to his meals and his clothes, tend to his wants, while he got on with his true vocation, his work at the pit and his work for the men. He remembered how she had set him to the gate in those early days, walking down the gravel with her arm in his, feeling so embarrassed he looked to the road to ensure he was not being seen. She had tried too to take an interest in his work, and he had explained to her the hauler, how the set ran from the main to the surface, how as the full set sped out the empty set was hauled in, the oiled cables speeding over the midway rollers. He explained how once to the surface the coal was hauled to the screens and once screened shunted into trucks and trundled to the cokeworks in the valley. He went on to explain what happened once it reached the cokeworks.

But by this time she was not listening. She was too busy manoeuvring the dirt from the rims of his eyes.

And he wanted so much those moments back, he wanted her home now, this day, tomorrow, home to the peace and quiet of the country, the soft sensualness of the air as it rolled up the slopes from the burn, perfumed by the fragrance of silver birch and willow, the gorse and bracken, he wanted her as she had been before, thinning the lilac tree at the gate, pruning the rhododendrons that bordered the path. And he wanted it so much he went to see the doctor now, striding down the polished floor of the corridor with a pace and purpose Mrs. Wishart had never seen, tread echoing through the ward till he came to the doctor's office. The doctor was a small stunted man, hardly forty, yet with hair grey at the temples, wearing heavy framed glasses that deprived him of the little personality he had. He did not stand as Wishart entered, merely pulled at his ear and ushered him onto a seat with a flourish of his hand. He leant forward on the desk, arms folded, the backs of his hands forested with hairs, yet the fingers thick and capable, the wrists strong, nails neatly rounded and trimmed. The glasses to his eyes were thick-lensed and his eyes seemed to swim around and peer from out of the glass.

38

"I want my wife home, doctor," Wishart said. "As soon as possible."

"With the shortage of hospital beds," the doctor said. "I suppose you're wondering why we've kept her in so long. The baby's all right, you know, as I think I told you. Only a little out of place in the womb. That's not important, however, either it'll right itself or we'll right it ourselves when the time comes."

"Ye said there might be complications, doctor. About her general state o' health."

"That's right. Physically she's all right. The contusions on her arms and chest and legs have cleared up. And so too's the cut on the lip. We've given her a thorough examination as far as we can, with radio and the rest, and as I said physically, there's very little the matter. There's no reason why she shouldn't have a normal healthy baby. Follow it up with as many as she likes in the years she has left."

"Ye said physically, doctor. What d'ye mean by physically?"

The doctor pushed back the arms of the chair and moved from the desk to the window. The light heightened the wisps along his temple and the silver flecks to his hair, it reflected too upon the pale sallow skin, the line of the jaw stubbly with shadow. His office looked out upon the garden at the back of the hospital, with a lawn and a fading rhododendron at it centre, the last brave colours of the rhododendron straining to catch the sun, the grass of the lawn dulled and tarnished with dust and soot that drifted from the embankment. The embankment ran past the hospital grounds, the grounds themselves were contained by high creosoted railings, so that the only view from the window was of the signal box and points, the snake-like blackberry strands that tangled the embankment. And among the blackberry thorns, clinging to the dark cinder soil, shaded from the fading light, the doctor could see little flutters of yellow from heads of gorse, the drooping campanula of bluebells flourishing as best they could in the arid undergrowth.

"Physically," the doctor said. "She's all right. Mentally I should say she's a little disturbed, a little psychotic. That's why we've been keeping her in, that's why it's been a little longer than you expected. We've been holding her under observation." He returned to his desk and sat down. He opened a file before him. "The fact is for a while we weren't even sure why your wife took the gin, whether she merely wanted to destroy the baby or whether she wanted to destroy herself."

"But I thought I explained that, doctor. I thought we cleared it all up."

"We did. But we had to make sure your theory was correct. You said she wanted to kill the baby because she couldn't tolerate the idea of it being born into a world without security. That because the village was being destroyed she felt her security was being destroyed with it. And not only the security of herself the security of her child."

"That's reet, doctor. That's what she believed."

"So that in fact with the colliery closing and the village being destroyed, there's no reason why she shouldn't try again."

"But she won't, doctor. I know she won't't."

"How d'you know?"

" 'Cause things are ganna be different, I know they are. I'm ganna make them different. Everythin's come about 'cause she's been neglected, 'cause I never had time to take care on her the way I should've done. But that's all finished now. I've resigned from the union and once this strike's over, once everythin's back to normal, I'm ganna see she has all the peace and security she wants. And I'll see she has it even if it means I stop work. Even if I never work again."

"I believe you," the doctor said. "And I'm not doubting your word. Only I want to let you know how the position is medically. So you understand how she may feel. Medically, she's suffered an experience that may only be described as traumatic. She's always been highly strung, you told me so yourself, and I know she had a great deal of worry about her mother and the way she died. Worry that probably disturbed her judgment, so that she couldn't think straight. She couldn't reason."

"But it's only a little thing, doctor. I'm sure she'll get over it."

"Maybe," the doctor said. "But maybe not. Security means a lot to a woman — and especially to a woman like your wife. I know she doesn't look so bad in the hospital, but once she gets out, once she begins to feel lonely again, she may start to worry. She could develop paranoid delusions, she may feel she's being persecuted, that people are getting at her. That they're closing the colliery and dismantling the village just to get even."

"But why should she think that, doctor?"

"It's surprising what people think when they're suffering paranoid delusions. One woman I know thought she was being burgled, and when the welfare officer arranged for her to be collected she showed them all the elaborate obstacles she had to stop the burglers getting in. Another believed her neighbour was trying to hammer a hole through the wall from the fireplace. And another stood at the back door and gave away all that she had in the house. Said her husband had won the pools and didn't need things any more."

"And ye think me wife'll turn a bit like that?"

"She might, unless she receives treatment. Of course you haven't to think there's anything wrong with your wife, basically wrong that is. You've merely to look upon mental illness as you might look upon physical illness, a handicap you cannot help. Something which afflicts you like a cold. Something that probably you'll be rid of through time. And these days the mental hospitals are very good. Not at all like the asylums of old."

"A mental hospital! But doctor surely."

"Now it's all right, don't get alarmed. She may enrol as a voluntary patient for a limited number of days. And they'll give her a little psychotherapy, and perhaps a little occupational therapy, just to keep her mind off things, just so she sees her problems in a better light. Sees that they're not half as big as she expected. And as I said they're not like the institutions of old. They have a better understanding, a better knowledge. And with modern methods of treatment I'm sure they'd clear her up in no time."

"But she looks that well and cheerful," Wishart said. "So much like herself."

"Because as I said the change of company, the change of scenery, it's making her feel better. It's lifted the darkness from her mind — the bird she thinks is always hovering over her shoulders. But who knows what'll happen once she gets back to her old surroundings, once she sees the village she so obviously loves. Once she realizes perhaps after all she'll have to leave. Or that the village'll leave her. What then?"

"But I've told ye, doctor. I'm ganna spend more time at home. I'm ganna look after her. See that it doesn't happen again."

"Then you can send her into hospital at weekends. As a voluntary patient."

"But weekends'll be our best time together. The time I'll be with her most. The time I'll be able to brighten her up, take her for walks, take her to the pictures, so that she'll be all reet. So she'll be pulled together. And if she is all reet and pulls herself together she'll have nothin' to worry about. And if she has nothin' to worry about there'll not be need o' treatment."

"You're the husband, of course," the doctor said. "It's up to you."

"But she's all reet, I tell ye. Anyone lookin' at her can see she's all reet."

Wishart saw the muscles in his wrists and forearms tight with the pressure of his clasped hands. She was all right, he knew she was all right. And no-one who had not seen her the night of the meeting at the institute, no-one who had not seen the distemper to her eyes, the nervous sweat to her face, who had not seen the way she clawed the pillow, the bruised skin of her stomach where she carried the baby — no-one who had not seen these things could say otherwise. The woman who relaxed on the bed in the hospital ward and the woman who once had clawed at his face were not the same. No-one could say they were the same. And he meant what he said, never again would he let her fall into neglect, never again would he let things out of control. All this time he had known she had been slipping, he had known she was not herself, but he had known through his intellect and not through his emotions. But now his emotions too had stirred, had been awakened by the depths of his failure, the sight of her lying across the doorway, and he knew how great his climb would have to be, how near they had come to destruction. But he was prepared to make that climb. He was prepared to see the past did not raise its ugly head again.

"Listen, doctor. All she wants is to come home. All she wants is that we be together, that we start again. Just me, her and the baby. 'Cause she's ganna have this baby and I'm ganna see she has it. And not only this one as many as she likes in the time that's left. So that she'll never be lonely again. So that even if I'm not here, and even if we leave, leave the village, leave the colliery, she'll never know what loneliness is. Never again in her life."

The doctor closed the file and laid it on the blotting paper. He followed closely what Wishart had said, he followed too the look on his face as he said it. He noticed the moisture that came to his eyes, the expressiveness to his hands, the determination in his voice as he spoke. And the sincerity that in the past had often swayed the men now swayed the doctor. He felt he could trust Wishart and in his mind made the decision not to press it. After all, if Wishart kept his promise, if he consoled and comforted his wife in the manner suggested, then perhaps all that he had said was true, she would no longer seek refuge in hallucination and fantasy, she would lose her obsession, her drift to delusion. She would again take her place in society, she would accept responsibility, responsibility towards herself, her husband and her child. A woman like so many other women, only a woman not afflicted by loneliness, a woman cured of mania. The doctor came round the side of his desk and patted Wishart on the shoulder as he rose from the chair. He walked with him to the door.

"And you're sure you'll not enrol her as a voluntary patient?"

"I don't think it's necessary, doctor. Not if I look after her myself."

"But you will look after her. Just as you say?"

"I've told ye, doctor. I'll even stop off work. Miss a shift if it's necessary."

"Very well," the doctor said. "Tell your wife she can go home tomorrow. Tell her I'll have her out first thing tomorrow morning."

39

On the twenty-fourth day of the strike Ray Holt wandered down among the old workings till he reached and pushed open the door to a small gallery not the size of a kist and felt to his face the full strength of a fan as it whirred before him.

He let the force of the air clash shut the door and swaying on his heels, feeling the rush of air to his chest, he took the helmet from his head and set it down with the yardstick and safety lamp he used to tour the galleries. He had not thought of Wishart since the time he resigned as secretary of the lodge, in fact he had hardly crossed his mind since the day the strike began, when the remorse he had about throwing the book finally drained from his brain. Besides apart from the indifference in which he held Wishart he had more important things to think about. The last time he had been uneasy about the direction of the strike was at the time of union intervention a week ago; he had felt then possibly control was passing from his hands. Now for no apparent reason his forebodings returned, his instinct told him of tension and disaster he had never known before.

He felt a storm was gathering and the storm was about to break.

He settled himself upon the hard sharp rocks and with fingers stiff and cold began loosening the buttons of his overalls. He pulled stiffly at the scarf around his neck and let it drop to the floor beside the yardstick and lamp loosening the buttons of his shirt and vest to bare a little of his chest. The air seemed cool and fresh following the staleness that scurried through airways, and accustomed to the sound of the fan he was content to let the air slap against his chest and pinion his shoulders against the closed door. His shoulders ached with stooping, there was an ache to every bone and muscle in his body, and in a perverse way it gave him pleasure to rest the hurtful muscles against the hard panels. Even the strong soles of his boots were worn with the sharp uneven nature of the galleries; his feet ached as well as his shoulders, and his face remained stiff and sore not with cold but with the dirt that clung to the cheeks. And the rims of the eyes, the lining of the nose, the skin of the lips were all thickly lined with dust, so that it was a pain to blink, a pain to speak, a pain even to cough, to spit the phlegm from his mouth.

But these pains, these aches, these little local difficulties, were nothing to the sharp ugly pain Ray felt to his stomach: a pain like the gnawing of a rat because after twenty-four days of strike the men were still underground, because in all this time no definite concessions had been offered to bring them back to the surface.

Everything was as it had been on the first day of the strike. Only there were fifty men down the pit instead of a hundred, there was hot food served twice a day, at ten o' clock in the morning and ten o' clock at night, stews and soups and hot-pots, there was tea sent down in canisters the size of samovars, and between the hot meals, between soups laced with brandy and stews stiffened with rum there were sandwiches cut by relatives still waiting at bank top. And in the pit itself there were comfortable palliases of straw and choppy, there were blankets to keep them warm of a night and instead of restless sleepless hours in old boardrooms, on belts and landings, above loading points, the men bedded down in a disused pony stable in the old workings. The stable was near a downcast shaft where the air was fresh, their sleep was deep and invigorating, and if it was true they could not rid either themselves or the pony stables of the wretched sweaty tang of manure, if it was true their pillows were a little hard, their palliases bumpy, uneven, they were happy.

Happy still to be the centre of attraction, to be in the public eye.

It was twenty-one days since Ray had issued his proclamation that they should work, not for a living, not to hew coal, but to keep their minds and bodies occupied. It was twenty-one days since he had ordered them to begin cleaning faces, stone dusting ways, whitewashing walls, repairing belts, clearing out old boardrooms where once he had thought to live, so that in anticipation of their pit being reprieved and work allowed to start theirs would be the cleanest and best kept pit in the area. They had even enamoured themselves to the public by sending to surface for more whitewash and stone dust, so that this too was reported in the papers and this too reflected to their credit in the eyes of the public. It was also true by now some of the men had forgotten what they were doing there. Since all of them were younger men, with only a few over thirty, they looked upon it as a prank, a lark, a return to the freedom of schooldays when they were happy and undisciplined and did what they liked, so that they clambered on faces, they hewed with picks, they manipulated the hopper, swooshing down dust and coal to frighten anyone who happened to walk beneath. But never once did they get out of hand. A yardstick in the ribs from Walton or Bousefield saw to that. And there were always the older ones, those with wives and families, who tried to keep a sense of proportion, tried to see the strike in the context of their homes and future.

Ray lay upon the rocks with legs outstretched, his back to the door, the fan pummelling air to his face so that it stung through the dirt, fingers holding back the wings of his collar to bare more of his chest. He had switched off the light still socketed to the helmet, and head against the panels, dust-covered lids half drooping across his eyes, he stared at the small blue cone of flame in the safety lamp, the flame hardly flickering protected as it was by the glass. He sucked the air with great breaths, his chest jerked with the rapid expansion and contraction of his lungs, the air seemed to cleanse his mind as it cleansed his blood, he could think clearly, more sharply, but the sharpness of his thoughts, the clarity of his vision could not take away the sickness he felt with the anger in his stomach. He had been depressed for a long time now. It was as if he were in love with a girl and did not wish to admit it. He knew all the men in the pit were missing daylight, he knew all suffered the same aches and pains, the same stiffness to neck and back, that beneath the stiff coating of clay that stretched the skin to their faces, the skin was pallid, ghost-like. Just as his own skin was pallid and ghost-like. But few he felt missed the village as much as he.

He missed his evening walks when his reading was over, he missed the dew on the grass, the sight of rabbits in the fields coming from their burrows fringing the hillside, he missed the silvery vapours of the river, the wood through the silver, he missed the tang of burning refuse as men cleared their gardens, the blue powder coloured smoke rising from the chimneys of the village houses. He missed the song of the birds as he walked alone on the

403

fells, his step down the road reverberating back from the iron bridge across the lines. And above all he missed not the peace, not the tranquility, but a sense of the past, the primitive past, the village of his father and forefathers, the village that had always been there, that had always been loved. That he had never wanted to leave. And which now people would never leave unless it was forced upon them. So that often, sitting in the dark, he felt he could weep, he could let the tears roll in flood, he could let himself go, let his life go, because it was useless to hang on, it was better to lose his grip.

Drift like everyone else.

He thought often of his brother and the conversation they had had about life, how Gerald had mocked and rejected the life of the village, how he wanted to seek it elsewhere in a town. But all his life, Ray knew, his brother might seek out his meaning and never find it. To live Gerald had said, you had to take life by the throat, you had to shake it till its teeth rattled; that was what you had to do with life when you found it. But to Gerald these were words, good words, strong words, but words all the same. And though these words had been rejected by Ray, though now he had an aversion for his brother and all that he said, yet here he was carrying out the philosophy, here he was involved, grasping life with both hands. By the scruff of the neck as his brother might say. Yet because he was involved, because he was grasping life, he was unhappy. He was miserable, he was depressed. He felt he had reached out to grapple the cur by the throat, only to discover it was not a cur at all but a bear, and far from he shaking the bear the bear was shaking him.

But all this time slowly he was discovering what his brother had yet to understand, that not all of life could be explained, not everything could be reasoned logically. There were feelings and emotions beyond expression, there were things you did that sometimes you did not understand yourself. Why was it, for example, if they hated the pit, if they hated the work, they were fighting to keep it alive? Why was it that after twenty-four days of strike, without a single concession, the men were continuing their protest? He did not know, there was never an answer to the question, in fact he reflected, if you thought of it long enough, there was not even a question. All things were as they were and that was an end to it. You had to be happy now if you were ever to be happy.

404

Only this moment counted and it was in this moment one had to find one's peace. But perhaps this was the fly in the hand Gerald wanted to catch, perhaps he too had realized the significance of this moment. And perhaps just as once Ray had thought nothing was important perhaps he was right. Perhaps nothing mattered after all. Neither for his brother nor for himself, neither for the colliery nor for the men.

But though this was what he felt now, in this moment, in this gallery, feeling the backs of his thighs cold to the rock, feeling even the force of the air to the soles of his boots, hands still holding the wings of his collar, he knew it was not what he would always feel. It was a kind of thinking that came when he was alone, when his mind emptied of care and worry, when he could forget the anger and hurt that ached his stomach, let the tiredness slip from him, so that he could open his senses and be aware of all the things around him. He could disregard the roar of the fan, the discomfort of the floor, he could concentrate his attention on the cone of flame in the safety lamp, the cone of flame in his soul. He could study it and nourish it and by study and nourishment he could expand it so that it made radiant his being. But it would not always be so, the world would not always let him have this peace, this seclusion, his thoughts could not always be withdrawn, detached. There would come a time when the world would rush upon him with all the force of a door pushing open behind, the force of air seeking an outlet along the wrong passageway.

And who knows perhaps once it was lost, once the flame was extinguished, it would never be rekindled again.

40

"Well, now what's the matter?" Ray said.

"Nowt special," Featherley answered. "Only I've come to tell ye about the men. Like I always dee."

"Only ye're supposed to come through the other way. Not this door here."

"I knaa. But ye see I had to dee me necessaries. So I thowt it'd be quicker if I just cut down this way."

"And break me back into the bargain."

"I'm sorry, Ray, son, but I never thowt I'd find ye sittin' wi' yer back to the door. I thowt mebbes ye'd be examinin' the fan or hoppin' it down the other way back to the shaft bottom. Holdin' that lamp o' your'n up and down like ye always dee. Like somebody on the railway stoppin' a train. I never thowt ye'd be blockin' the door wi' yer backside."

Ray picked up his yardstick and helmet and kneeling on his hunkers retied the scarf around his neck and fastened the buttons of his shirt and vest. He buckled the belt to his waist and as he did so noticed the tremor that came to his hands. He felt too the rapid beat of his heart and there rose in him again the old irrational fear that Featherley was bringing with him bad news, he felt he was coming to tell him the men had decided to return to the surface, that they had already done so, that it was all decided and that there was nothing for him but to accept. The white tip of his tongue flicked from the blackness of his lips and he felt a curl to the nerves of his stomach. He switched on his lamp and seeing Featherley against the rock, helpless in his stupidity, coarse in his shallowness, he felt like taking the stick and beating him, beating and killing him like the Egyptians of old, not because he was the bearer of good news but because he was the bearer of bad.

He tucked the ends of his scarf beneath his arms and brought the yardstick down on Bousefield's helmet.

"So ye're here to tell us what's new wi' the men," he said.

"And it better not be somethin' I divin't like. 'Cause if it is I'll feed ye through that fan and send ye to the surface as bait for the time keeper."

"Nowt can be that bad now can it, Ray?"

"Depends what ye've got to tell us. But if there's anybody tryin' to sneak by the pickets to the surface, or any talk o' defectin' I'll mince ye through it all reet. Ye'll see if I divin't."

"Course not. Who's ganna try and dee things like that? Or even talk like that. The men divin't care if the strike lasts till Christmas. As long as they keep gettin' them hot stews laced wi' brandy, as long as they can put their heads down at night and kip, snug and cozy like in the pony stables. They divin't mind a bit. And they divin't feel the cold half so much since they took yer advice to keep on the move."

"And the concessions, the guarantees. Has there been owt said about that?"

"Nowt said. Only they cannot understand why the management divin't give in. They cannot understand why they're lettin' it drag on so long. 'Specially when they knaa they cannot win. When they knaa we cannot get beat. They reckon it's Atkin that's makin' it difficult. They reckon he's the fly in the ointment. They say he's trying to hold out and break us just to show everybody how clever he is. So he can get hissel' another job when the pit closes."

"And that's all they say. Nowt else."

"There has been another thing gannin' the rounds. Meanin' nee harm like."

"Out win it. Who's it about — me?"

"Not about ye, Ray. About yer father."

"What about me father?"

"They cannot understand why ye're keepin' him down so long. They cannot think why ye want him to suffer like the rest on us. At first they thowt ye were just deein' it to show there was nee favouritism, that yer owld father had to suffer like the rest on us, just to show how tough ye were. Just to show how determined ye were to carry everythin' through to the last. Even if it meant killin' off yer owld man wi' the rest on us."

"And after that what did they think?"

"After that they got to thinkin' ye were keepin' him down 'cause ye didn't want him to marry. And they understood that, 'cause everybody knaas just how daft she is, how they say she's

407

half gypsy, and that she's only marryin' 'cause that daft mother o' hers thinks yer owld man has money. But after a bit they got to thinkin' it mightn't be such a bad thing after all. They figure yer father's not gettin' any younger and if he fancies a bit o' batter at his time o' life they reckon he might as well have it."

"And that stuck-up brother o' mine. I suppose neebody thinks he has an opinion."

"They figure from what yer owld man says he's not so keen. And they understand mebbe ye divin't want to put in a word, seein' all the help he's givin' ye in the office. They knaa somebody's behind ye and they have a pretty good idea it's Gerald. But they figure yer father bein' the way he is, ye should use yer influence a bit. Make him change his mind."

"Ye seem to forget I've done me best for him as it is without gannin' cap in hand to Gerald. Ye knaa I picketed him at the drift mouth so he gets the air. Ye knaa I see he gets the best grub, at least as far as it's possible to see he gets it. And how I fixed him up in the overman's cabin, makin' a bed out o' the ambulance stretcher, with a proper pillow so he gets a good night's sleep. Better'n anybody in the pit by a long chalk."

"Only it's not his cup o' tea," Featherley said. "It's not the kind o' thing he should be deein' — least not at his age. O' course we knaa it's fresher at the drift mouth than it is in the pit, only it's a long hike for the grub, and it gets longer when ye walk it two and three times a day. Specially if ye have legs as bad as yer father's."

"Well, him and his legs'll just have to stick it. There's nothin' I can dee."

"I thowt that's what ye'd say. And o' course ye're reet. Only I tell ye, Ray, yer father cannot stand much more. He's gannin' round the pit tellin' everybody it wasn't his fault that fellow got caught in the picks. It wasn't his fault he's dead and gone and left a wife and two bairns. And he doesn't see why they should all set on him, why they should cast off their stones and white sheets and chase after him. He says he's told them it's not his fault. Only he says they keep comin', they'll not give him a minute's peace."

They had walked from the gallery towards the shaft bottom, feeling the pressure of the fan diminishing to their backs, the pressure ceasing altogether as they paused in an air-lock, the muscles in Ray's back and shoulders aching where they had stiffened following his rest against the door. They moved forward out of the air-lock along a narrow way between a belt and rock wall. The air was cold here, fresh and cold and damp, and Ray could feel the damp to his shoulders accentuating the ache. Featherley had raised his voice to be heard above the whirr of the fan, but with the door to the air-lock closed, the fan behind him, he still did not lower it, and the harsh jerky sentences seemed to hurry ahead to be at the shaft bottom before them. Ray let his yardstick trail through the odd handfuls of coal and stone that littered the belt, coal that was little more than powdered fragments where men had been cleaning the face since the strike began, the only slabs of real coal choking the funnel of the hopper at the end of the way. Ray pulled away the stick and paused by the top of the hopper.

Featherley did not notice the pause and collided into his back.

"And that's all the men have to talk about. Me own private affairs?"

"There is one other thing I'd like to bring up wi' ye. If ye have a minute like."

"It's not about them pigs o' yers. I couldn't stand talkin' about them the day."

"Not exactly about me pigs," Featherley said. "About the village."

"All reet. What is it ye want to knaa about the village?"

"Well ye see, Ray, it's like this. Ye say they're ganna knock down the houses and move away the people."

"That's reet. Cart them away like cattle."

"And ye say that when we gan we'll have to leave everythin' behind. Our pigeon huts and hen crees and greenhouses and allotments, and o' course in my case me pigs."

"That reet. Nee pigs neither."

"But is it reet what ye say? I mean have ye checked it. I knaa it's reet they're ganna pull down the houses, I knaa it's reet we'll have to live somewhere else. But is it reet that when we gan we'll not be able to take owt win us. Is it reet the council'll not take our hobbies into consideration. And that they'll not let us keep me pigs after all?"

"If ye think the council'll let ye keep yer pigs in the bath ye've got another think comin'."

"I divin't want to keep them in the bath — nor in the bed-

409

room either. But supposin' we write to the council for permission to keep them on some sort o' allotment near the house where I'll live. Supposin' I offered to buy a bit o' land, just a square, just enough to support a sty. I'm sure they wouldn't mind makin' a little money sellin' us it. I'm sure they wouldn't mind fixin' us up."

They stood for a moment at the hopper top and then clattered down the iron stairs to the engine plane. The voices of the men carried to him along the plane, voices with which he was now familiar. One of the men stood by the telephone in the deputy's kist, ready to take any message from the surface, others sat around the loading point, listlessly and without energy, aware of the absence of Ray Holt, filling in the time till he roused them from their lethargy. The ten o' clock meal was behind them now, so that they were all looking forward to the afternoon, when the cage would carry away the scoured canisters and return with sandwiches cut by relatives. The men had tired of their darts and dominoes, cards and monopoly, they had grown a little tired too of the work, not because they were lazy but because the same repetitive tasks had killed their interest. Ray was aware of this and as he walked from the loading point to the deputy's kist ideas passed through his mind to liven their interest.

"Ye really care about them pigs, divin't ye," Ray said. "They mean more to ye than owt in the world."

"I can understand me pigs, Ray. I cannot understand owt else. I'll never understand people the way ye understand them. And divin't say ye divin't understand them either 'cause I knaa otherwise. I'm a daft bugger, I knaas I'm daft 'cause everybody tells us. But I've not got eyes in me head for nowt. There are some things I notice."

"All the same it's people that count in the world. It's not pigs. And ye've got to live with people. Ye've got to understand them. 'Cause ye're involved in life, ye're involved from the day ye're born, and it's nee good tryin' to get out of it by lockin' yersel' away. But shuttin' yersel' up wi' pigs. The world'll soon hammer a way through to ye, divin't worry about that. And once it does ye'll have to watch it, ye'll see."

"I knaa what ye mean, Ray, I've thowt about it mesel'. But when I was young I was never any good at football or cricket, I was never even any good at makin' friends. And me father was

410

always a one for the pigs. And it used to be a comfort to us, just to spend hours and hours hangin' about the sty. Gettin' the stink to me boots and me corduroys — so everybody used to say I had the plague. So everybody used to leave us to mesel'. But ye see that way I was happy. That way it was as if me life had some meanin'."

"So even now ye divin't mind movin' house. Ye divin't mind movin' village — as long as yer pigs come wi' ye."

"If I could take me pigs with us it wouldn't matter where I lived."

"But ye cannot. And that's an end to it."

"But I might if ye wrote a letter to the council. If ye asked them on movin' house if I could take me pigs win us, not to keep them in the bath nor nowt like that, just to buy a bit o' land. Not far from the house. Just so I could look after them the way I've looked after them here. And I'm sure the council aren't as bad as that, Ray. I'm sure they'd understand if ye put it to them proper like."

Ray studied the men through the windows of the kist. He studied the manner they lolled about, he studied the pallor to their faces, and he looked for weakness, he looked for defeat. He looked for the first signs that would tell him their cause was lost. But he saw none of those things. He saw only listlessness and boredom. A boredom he knew he would have to do something about. The men had exhausted even their inexhaustable supply of stories and jokes, they had had out all their old quarrels, their old arguments, they had read all the papers that had been sent down to them, they had backed on slips of paper all the winners they were ever likely to back, thereby losing a fortune for the bookmakers and saving for themselves a few precious shillings. They had listened for the telephone to ring and when it did their interest stirred and their eyes grew animated, but when the receiver was replaced, when things went on as they had before, they settled back, the lustre from their eyes, their gaze turned to the shaft and the time when they could next expect a supply of food.

They were men in a state of siege. They were well supplied with food and drink, they slept of a night, they exercised themselves in the castle yard, they did a little work to keep supple their muscles and their minds, but they could not venture beyond the castle walls. Their freedom was restricted and because it was

restricted Ray felt uneasy. He felt some of the men must be restless, captive, eager to break the monotony, the routine, but which
of the men and what were they planning? And might it not be
planned at all, might it not be some gesture as defiant as it was
spontaneous? Ray did not know. He did not even know whether
it was merely his own imagination, that his nerve and will were
weakening, that he was not the man he thought he was, that after
all he could snap under pressure. Might it not be that he was losing his grip, that unlike the men he could not stay the distance.
He stood by the window rubbing his hands. He repeated to himself that he did not know, there was very little he did know these
days. But as his restless mind cast over these possibilities there
was something he remembered. And as he remembered the sickness
returned to his stomach.

"Do us a favour, will ye," he said. "Get yersel' to the drift
mouth and see how Bousefield and Walton are gettin' on. There's
a fresh stock o' blankets comin' in and I sent them up to take
charge. I was bankin' on ye bein' wi' them so that they didn't get
up to nee bother. But now ye're here I think ye'd better get yersel'
away sharp as ye can."

"They wi'not like us spyin' on them, Ray. They were on about
it afore."

"Never mind what they were on about. It's me that counts
around here, not them. And ye knaa how they are, the two o' them,
ye knaa how they're always dyin' to be at each other's throats. Ye
better gan and see what they're up to. See that it's nee mischief."

"But what'll I say to them when I get there?"

"Just tell them ye've come to see about me father. See he's
all reet."

"And me pigs. Ye'll write a letter to the council the way I
ask?"

"I'll write it now," Ray said. "On me best notepaper. And
I'll send it to bank when they send down the sandwiches. So they
can pop it in the post and it'll be there by the morrow. Mebbes
ye'll even have a reply afore the strike's o'er."

"And ye think it'll be all reet. Ye think they'll let us keep
me pigs after all."

"Ye were supposed to be talkin' about the village," Ray said.
"Not yer pigs. But I'll let ye knaa as soon as I get an answer."

Featherley nodded and Ray watched him hurry along under

412

the lights past the men towards the mouth of the drift. And as he watched him go Ray felt sad, though why he should feel sad he did not know. It came to him it was all for nothing, that it was all so unreal, so unnecessary, that in a year's time he would wonder if this could possibly have occurred to him, that it was like trying to move a mountain with the weight of one's mind and that one could not possibly succeed. In that moment he lacked courage, he lacked faith, he hoped that day there would not be any trouble because he knew if there was he would be unable to cope; he was at a low point, he knew that, the lowest he had been in the pit, the lowest he had been in his life. And the strange thing was he did not know why he should be so low. There was not any single reason on which he could lay his finger. But then maybe that was how it was in life, maybe the superficial reasons were never of account, it was the deeper, subtler psychological reasons that mattered. Maybe it was because he felt the strike would be a failure, that he himself was a failure. Or perhaps it was merely because he was thinking of his father and the pass to which he was bringing him.

Ray had the habit of not listening carefully to any conversation, but picking over it in his mind it always amazed him how much of the essential he retained. He had only half-listened to Featherley as he spoke of his father, not because he was un-interested, but because the impulse of memory thrust him back into the past to the scene with Gerald. And the scene with Gerald recalled to him the scene with his father in the pit. He had kept him down because he feared what might happen once he found himself alone with Gerald. At the time he had suspected the strike would be longer than most people thought, though he had not realized it would be as long as it had turned out. But once having made the decision he did not feel he could retract, he had sworn not to allow any break in the ranks and he feared to set a precedent by releasing his father. Yet following Featherley's conversation he reflected that surely if the strike lasted another month, and there was no reason why it should not, it might well finish Holt. And the irony was it would not be the fault of his brother it would be the fault of himself.

He turned from the window and leaning back upon the desk removed again his helmet. In the brittle light his hair was grey with dust and flattened to the skull, his face was leaner and there was a tightness to the cheeks, a stiffness to the lips that could only be caused by pain, a secret inner pain one wished to hide. His mind and body were tired, his thoughts were no longer clear, he lifted the boot and as he began unloosening the laces tried to reason the consequences of his father's death. He reflected it would be a good way out, clean, simple, an unfortunate consequence of the strike. It would prevent his father marrying and it would prevent a scandal to his name. It would thwart too the schemes of Dolly. Her baby — their baby — would be born a bastard, but she would have to bear that, and even if she did try to reveal the truth, even if she did try to pin the baby on him, no-one would believe since she had already been engaged to his father. He removed his boots and let them drop to the floor. He pulled himself upon the desk and let his feet dangle over the side.

He had thought very little of Dolly since the strike began. This had pleased him because he had feared in the depths of the earth, alone with so many men, cut off from women, he might have found himself thinking of her, he might have found himself overpowered by her absence, the lack of physical contact. So that he feared his resolve would weaken, he feared he would be only too glad to see her when he returned to bank. But it was not so. He had forgotten her so entirely it was as if she had never existed. And even the times when he did think of her, it was never of their lovemaking, the primitive odour of her body, the sweatiness, the closeness, it was of the times when he sat over the fire reading his books, how he had decided not to see her but had rushed out of the house to be there on time. Now, involved as he was in the strike, involved as he was with the pit, he could not understand how this had been so. He could not understand how he could have been so coarse and immature. In fact, the temptation removed, with no reason to look for excuse, he felt he could smile at his weakness, be indulgent with his faults.

But as these thoughts circled his mind he began to rise out of his tiredness, he began to see things with his habitual clarity, and he began to realize one thing he could not be was responsible for his father's death. And rather than avoid a single scandal the fact Holt died would create two others, the scandal of Ray letting him die, and the scandal of an illegitimate child being born after his death. And again the feeling of understanding and affection he had for his father returned, Featherley's conversation floated through his mind, he began to understand how his father was suffering because he began to understand how he was suffering himself. He began to realize probably the strain too was telling on him and that was why he was so depressed. But he had to rise from his lethargy, climb out of his dejection. He could no longer allow things to drift, he could no longer allow his father to die merely because he did not want to set a precedent.

And with an impulsiveness typical of his nature he decided he would go now, he would release his father, he would send him out by the mouth of the drift, out to the sunshine and daylight he so sorely missed. He realized too that perhaps in the weeks that had passed Gerald's temper had cooled, perhaps he had come to accept the idea; but in the event he had not, in the event he still felt as strongly as ever, Holt could live with the Waltons till the strike was over, till the time of the wedding. So that he would be safe from the terror of the pit. Ray dropped from the desk to the floor and stooped for his boots. An ache shot up his back and the pains were sharp against his shoulders. He reached for his yard-stick and helmet and hurried out of the kist. The decision being made he felt in a sudden panic to carry it through. He felt it must be done now, at this moment, that there was not a second to lose.

And though he did not know why, he was right there was not.

41

For the disaster he feared most occurred as Featherley hurried through the old workings to the mouth of the drift where idled Tom Holt.

Three weeks in the pit with little better to do than explore old galleries had made Featherley an expert in all these short-cuts between seams and districts; nevertheless he still retained a basic fear that one day he would so lose himself he would never find his way back, he would miss a cut or gallery and die of suffocation and neglect. Or worse his retreat would be cut off by water, water that began around the ankles, that seeped up to the knees, to the thighs, then to the stomach and chest, slimy water that ran cold to the neck, the lips, so that he could feel it to his throat, tasting of dirt and stagnation, clogging the orifice of eyes and nose till it reached the level of his hair. The very thought made the breath heavy to his nostrils and quickened his stride through the desolate galleries till he reached a sharp incline that linked two seams of coal.

The incline was known as a drift, but the drift had fallen into disuse, water poured through the roof, the lights were few and dim, the light of his lamp glistened upon the walls, upon the silvery mud that was the incline, and upon the heavy bulwark at the bottom of the drift designed to halt the course of any runaway set. Halfway up the incline, by the heavy bar, a space the width of a yard had been hollowed where older men could pause and regain their breath; but since this part of the pit was disused, since water poured through the roof, the hollow had gradually filled with dark slimy water through which Featherley would have to splash to reach the top of the drift. He disliked this particular short-cut, for the chill to the air seemed more intense, the damp more discomforting, and hardly once had he manoeuvred the incline without falling on his face. Now he tried to walk it quickly to get it over with, digging the point of the yardstick deep into the soft clay, feeling the slither of his hobnails as they failed to grip.

But as he reached the hollow where lay the pool, his feet were knocked from under him, he felt a downward force upon his shoulders, the yardstick went from his hand, his knees scraped the mud and he fell with a splash into the pool. The fall knocked the wind from his lungs, the helmet fell from his head, and the pressure he felt to his shoulders he felt now to his neck, his head dropped under the water, the dark slime ran up his nose and his ears, it rushed into his mouth so that he felt its cold slimy taste like ice to his throat, he felt it choking, suffocating, and in a panic he tried to lift his head, he tried to force his face from the water, but the pressure on his neck kept it down, the pressure scraped his nose and his cheeks in the soft flinty clay, the pain increased the panic and the panic increased the pain, and mingling with the pain and panic was the realization that this was it, this was death, that there was nothing he could do but submit. That there was no time to think, no time for reflection, no time even for last visual memories. And with the water to his chest and lungs, the water to his throat, he felt there was hardly time to die.

But he did not die.

The pressure on his neck reversed and instead of pressing him into the water hauled him out, instead of rubbing his face in the clay it brought him back to air; but hardly had he the time to open his mouth, the water to run from his ears, when the pressure applied again, his head plunged, his nose crushed into the clay, the water rushed again to the orifice of his mouth, it rushed again to his chest and lungs, and again death pressed heavily upon him. And again it claimed him for its own. And water was all around him, not only filling his head and his lungs but freezing a bitterness to his thighs and stomach; water had already drowned his head, it was only his body keeping him back, it was only his body that would not let go. Only his body for which death was waiting. Then the pressure relaxed again, and again his head soared out of itself, soared like a bird for heaven, soared away from his body till it was brought to earth by the brilliant gestapo-like light that blinded his eyes.

"Spyin' again," Bousefield said. "Up to yer old tricks."

He moved to dip Featherley's head again into the pool but Featherley floundered to be free.

"For Christ sake, Bouser. For Christ sake."

"I told you what ye'd get if I caught ye spyin'. Didn't I?"

"But I wasn't spyin'. I wasn't."

"Then what ye deein' in this part o' the pit. On yer way to the drift mouth?"

"Just gannin' to see Ray's father," he spluttered. "See how he's gettin' on."

"And ye didn't knaa we was at the drift mouth. Seein' about blankets?"

"Gannin' to see his father, I tell ye. Neebody even told us ye were here."

"Ray sent ye all the way to the drift mouth and never even said ye might see me and Walton on the way?"

Featherley tried to turn from the light but Bousefield held his head with both hands. Water and slime ran from the long hair of the scalp, the skin of Featherley's lips was broken and black and flecked red with blood, there was blood too among the dirt of his cheeks, water ran black from his brows, his lips trembled and his teeth chattered, and each time he blinked the whites of his eyes showed his fear. The nervous twitch he had to his cheeks contorted all the more his face and his mouth opened wide to show his blackened teeth as he tried to vomit back the filth that congested his lungs.

"I says Ray sent ye all the way to the drift mouth and never said ye might come across us on the way?"

"He says — he says I might bump into ye. By chance like. But he sayed it didn't matter if I did."

"So ye were spyin' after all?"

" I wasn't spyin' on neebody, I tell ye. On neebody."

"I told ye what'd happen if I caught ye spyin' on us again. I told ye I'd finish ye. I told ye I'd string ye up the way ye string up yer pigs. The way ye slit their throats and hang them upside down. Till the blood drips out o' them. So there's nowt but flesh — dead flesh."

"Divin't keep on at us, Bouser. Divin't keep on."

"I'm not keepin' on. I'm only tellin' ye what I promised in the first place."

"But I wasn't spyin', I tell ye. Win't ye believe us? He says just gan to the drift mouth, see how me father's gettin' on. And call in on yer way back on Bousefield. See they're up to nee mischief. That's all he says. But he didn't mean nee harm — it was nowt nasty like."

"Checkin' up like he's always checkin' up. Seein' I divin't kill nee rats, seein' I divin't break neebody's arm, seein' I divin't break this piece o' machinery or that. Dyin' to see if he can find fault. Dyin' to see if he can grind us down a bit more, a bit farther. See if he can make us break afore he does."

"It's nowt like that, I tell ye. And it's not his fault he's a bit nervous — win everythin' under his care."

"Only from the day there'll be one less he'll have to worry about." He pulled Featherley's head closer to his and lowered his helmet to an inch from Featherley's eyes. The light shone yellow and hurtful through the closed lids. "I meant what I said, ye knaa, divin't think I didn't. I'm ganna finish ye good and proper. I'm ganna see ye divin't spy on me nee more."

The bitter chill Featherley felt to his thighs and stomach crept up to touch his heart. The discomfort of the cold, his hands and knees in the ooze, the water to his arms, the cold to his head, the ache to his face — these were nothing compared to the cold killing intent in Bousefield's voice. Tears began to flow from the scaled lids and he began to bubble like a child, his body jerked like that of an animal, but no matter how hard he tried, how much he flounderd, he could not rid Bousefield's grip from his neck. The words were so low, the manner in which they were spoken so terrifying, he felt urine running down the inside of his leg. And making one final exertion, with a strength he had not known he possessed, he heaved himself over, he fell upon his helmet, he felt the water to his back, his neck, and for a moment felt he had rolled free of the grip. Then it tightened again on his collar, the strong beam of light darted from the stone wall and blinded again his eyes.

"Now just tell us the way ye want it to be," Bousefield said. "Ye can have yer choice — neebody'll say I wasn't generous in that. Ye've not got much time to figure it out, but ye can have yer choice all the same. Ye can drown yersel' like a dog. Ye can have a yardstick up yer throat to puncture the windpipe. Or food poisonin'. Just tell us what ye fancy — that's all I ask."

"Now, Bouser. Just listen."

"So it's food poisonin' ye want. It's a bit of a meal ye fancy afore ye gan."

"I divin't fancy owt, I tell ye. I — "

But before he could finish, his eyes were diverted from the strength of the light, he felt Bousefield's grip weak upon his throat, he saw the free hand sliding through the water a stick, he saw a thong tied to the end of the stick, and on the thong a rat, a meagre, thin-framed rat, its tawny coat ruffled and damp where it had been dragged through water, its whiskers quivering with fear and weakness and anger, its eyes reflecting that fear, turning away from Featherley to scurry through the water, floundering as Featherley floundered, almost drowning before Bousefield scooped it up with a handful of water, letting the water drain from his fingers, yet holding the neck of the rat between finger and thumb. He had caught it among the packs of the old boardrooms, tied its tail to the thong in such a manner it could not be free, and steadily watched it starve and weaken, now half drowning it, now half blinding it, now setting the flame of a match to its ears, now prodding the hot point of the match up its behind, so that the rat wanted only to die.

And was weak and angry because it could not.

"That's reet," Bousefield said. "Ye're ganna eat it. Head first. Ye're ganna rive off the head and chew it till I tell ye to stop. Ye're ganna spit out the bones like I tell ye, and then ye're ganna let the precious juicy blood run down the back o' yer throat, so that it quenches yer thirst. So ye'll never be thirsty again. So ye feel like a new man. Then ye're ganna swallow what's left, swallow it all in one big gulp, so it doesn't stick in yer throat. So it doesn't deprive yer belly o' its pleasure."

The weak frail rat bared its lips and showed its sharp stained teeth. Bousefield still held it with one hand, and with the other gripped the back of Featherley's neck. Only his grip was loose now and by a sudden rapid movement, by sliding sharply backwards down the incline, Featherley could be free. But he did not move. He could not move. He was like a rabbit frightened by the scent of a stoat. He felt weak and crumpled and defeated. Sobs constricted his chest, the twitch to his cheek affected his whole face, the tears mingled with the water where Bousefield had ducked his head, and the green-edged teeth chattered with such ferocity they almost came out of his head. He wanted to speak, he wanted to explain, but he could only grunt and moan and babble, so that Bousefield laughed at his incoherence, rejoiced in his power. He released Featherley's neck and holding the rat between finger and thumb pushed it under Featherley's nose, so close he could smell the ugly unhealthy odour of the rodent.

"Now gan on," he said. "Divin't let me put ye off. Eat."

And Featherley, in his terror, in his defeat, the rat staring him in the face, knew there was nothing to be done, death had laid its hand upon his shoulder and he had to answer its call. He had never thought of death, in fact he had dreaded even to think of it, yet deep in his sub-conscious there lay a picture of how he felt it would be, how he would look it in the face and spit in its eye, how he would sneer and laugh, how it would come to him when he lay in bed, content itself facing him in the corner, how in its leisure it would move to the foot of the bed; how he would shoo at it and tell it to go away, but how grinning it would move closer, grinning it would sit upon his legs and then upon his chest, so that he felt its suffocating weight; but still he would smile and jeer, still his nerve would not break; and not till it moved to smother his face, not till it moved to quench the thirst for air to his lips, would he try to spit at it. Would he show his contempt.

But lying in the water, death already at his throat, it was nothing like he expected. Except for the terror, except for the powerlessness of his muscles, the uselessness of his limbs, the inability to cease the chatter of his teeth, the sob to his chest, the impossibility of staring other than at the white blinding beam of the lamp — he almost thought that except for these things it was no different from any other moment. But as Bousefield moved his head the lamp swung from him, Featherley found himself blinded by darkness, the darkness of eternity, the darkness of the grave, he found there was nothing he could see, not the water dripping from the roof, not the mud of the incline; there was only the dampness to the air, the rustle of the rat on Bousefield's palm. And the knowledge he was dead, that his mind had died, and that his body was about to follow. The light came round again and the rat once more pushed under his nose.

He opened his mouth to bite.

42

"All reet," Walton said. "Ye've had yer bit fun. Ye can pack it in now."

He hauled Bousefield away and pushed him roughly down the incline till he fell against the iron bulwark. The stick dropped from his hand and slithered to the disused rolleyway. The thong detached from the stick and the poor crippled rat dragged itself away, trying to summon the energy and will to run. Bousefield would have gone after it but for the pain in his back where he had struck the bulwark, his helmet would have fallen from his head but for the thong that held it like a sombreror. He stared with surprise and incredulity up the slope to Walton. Walton had been sitting at the top of the incline smoking a cigarette watching all that passed with affected indifference. He had smoked the cigarette to the last shred of tobacco and snuffed the last dying embers between his fingers before lumbering heavily down the slope towards them.

"Ye divin't mean to say ye're ganna try to stop us?" Bousefield asked.

"Ye're like a daft bairn," Walton said. "Wi yer tricks."

"But it's not a trick. I'm ganna finish him."

"Ye're ganna finish neebody," Walton said. "Unless it's that cigarette I gave ye afore."

Walton dusted the ash from his fingers and not wearing a helmet ran a blackened hand through his hair. The hands were coarse and ugly now, just as the hands of the other men were coarse and ugly, he had tried over the first few days to keep the nails clean and trimmed, scrubbing the pads with a small brush he had brought with him into the pit. But after a fortnight the brush had worn, the bristles dropped out, nothing it seemed could stay the march of dirt and callous that grafted his hands, and therefore he had let them go as he let himself go. His face too had changed, the skin he never shaved had coarsened, soft downy hair covered the cheeks like a tawny fur, the hair that was straw-coloured had like that of Ray Holt flattened to his scalp and the smooth creamy skin had hardened and lined, rough around the corners of his mouth with prolonged exposure to coal dust.

So that it seemed just as he entered the pit a youth so he would leave it a man.

"Ye mean to tell me," Bousefield said. "Walton o' the doss-house is gangin' up wi' Featherley o' the piggery."

"Ye can cut the jokes about the dosshouse, Bouser, son. I've had enough o' them o'er the past three weeks."

"Dosshouse I says and dosshouse it is. Ye live in a dosshouse, and there's nee two ways about. And ye knaa yersel' it's a doss-house, 'cause that's what ye're deein' down here on strike. 'Cause it's the only chance ye'll ever get o' luxury. 'Cause ye knaa it's the last ye'll see of it once ye get back to bank."

"Listen, Bousefield, I've told ye to cut it out. And I'll not tell ye again. For three weeks now ye've never stopped about me and me mother and family. And for three weeks I've let ye have yer say 'cause it makes nee odds to me what ye think. But I'm gettin' sick of it now, d'ye hear. Sick and tired. So watch what ye say. Or ye'll feel the lash o' my tongue as I feel the lash o' your'n."

"The only thing is everybody talks about yer family 'cause there's that much to say. But neebody talks about mine 'cause there's nowt they can get their tongue round. We're a good, clean honest-livin' family ours. All the time we've been in the village, there's never been owt anybody could say about us."

"And I suppose ye think everybody's forgotten yer old man bein' a blackleg durin' all them troubles and strikes. I suppose ye think 'cause ye live in one o' them fancy official houses, just 'cause ye're on the face and I'm just an electrician on the rolleyway, ye think ye can boast to us. But it doesn't mean there's nee skeletons in yer cupboard. Not by a long chalk."

"But we divin't live in a dosshouse, that's for sure. And our family's clean — neebody can say they're not that."

"And ye think me mother's dirty, is that what ye think?"

"I wouldn't exactly say that," Bousefield said slyly. "Only everybody knaas every time yer mother walks along the village store everybody she meets has to be fumigated on the way back. Now ye couldn't say that about my mother, could ye."

Three weeks in the pit had not only changed Walton's features, they had changed too his temper. He stood in the hollow of the incline, feet in the water, not looking at Bousefield, not even looking at Featherley, his face white in the light of Bousefield's lamp. He had decided he had taken enough from Bousefield. He had decided he was not going to take any more. For like the rest of the men he too was feeling the effect of a long strike, he too had seen the edge of violence sharpened in him, so that he was no longer afraid of his strength. Indeed, in his anger, in his weariness, he welcomed this confrontation. He felt even reckless. And he had kept up his strength while in the pit, he had kept firm the muscles, he had kept strong his shoulders and chest, so that now, standing in the pool, he felt ready for anything. He turned to Featherley lying still in the pool.

"We'd like to see them on, wouldn't we?" he said. "We'd like to see them on."

"I divin't knaa what ye mean," Featherley stuttered. "I divin't knaa..."

"Sure ye dee. Bousefield's mouther and the manager. We'd like to see them on."

"Now listen, Walley."

"Him bein' that little, her that big. It'd be like a rabbit buckin' a dog."

Bousefield clambered up the incline to swing Walton round by the shoulder. Walton threw him from him and he stumbled and slithered to the bottom of the drift. Walton slithered after him as far as the bulwark. "For years everybody's knaan yer mother's been kippin' wi' the colliery manager. For years everybody's knaan that's why she's done his housekeepin' — supposed to nip along early in the mornin' to make his breakfast when in fact she's been there all neet. For years everybody's knaan and for years everybody's kept their mouths shut. Only divin't come here and call my mother dirty. 'Cause I knaa and ye knaa she's not half as dirty as your'n."

Bousefield's helmet finally dislodged, his lamp splashed into the mud, and rolling over to his knee, mud and slime running down his back, all he could see was the dimness of lights at the top of the incline, the heavy silhouette of Walton in the light, tense and half-crouched, the light casting fair upon the straw-like strands of hair. And kneeling there, one knee in the mud, he felt the same coldness settle upon him before he threw a brick at the store window, before he looked for trouble at the dance; the same coldness of cruelty that made him burn rats by the tail, drive and to goad by insult his fellow men. He searched for his lamp and a flicker of joy warmed his inside. His upper lip quivered like that of the rat and even from the incline Walton could see the lips pulled back, the snarling teeth. Happy because for once Walton had stepped over the mark, because for once he had allowed himself the luxury of an insult. He paused crouching on the balls of his feet. He replaced his helmet and adjusted the lamp and as he stepped forward in the mud his boot kicked against something solid, something heavy. The handle of a pick. He scooped it up and advanced towards Walton.

"I knew one day ye'd step o'er the mark," he said. "And I knew when ye did I'd be ready."

Walton saw the pick in Bousefield's hand and stooped to grasp Featherley's yardstick from the pool. Even then he realized he was ill equipped, and holding the yardstick with both hands began backing up the slope, feet slithering beneath him, bending his knees to keep balance. Bousefield came steadily towards him, eyes and teeth shining out of his black face, the skin pallid despite the glare of the lamp, moving steadily up the slope like a mountaineer stubbornly advancing towards the summit. Featherley saw him coming and tried to drag himself from the water before he got there. But paralysed as he was even by the sight of Bousefield, he buried his hands in the mud, cringed against the wall, and when he saw the pick in his hand screamed and urged again his muscles to movement. Still they would not move, Bousefield cut short his retreat by standing on his fingers, Featherley felt the hobnails across his knuckles, felt them crushing the bones to the floor, and let out a painful shriek. Bousefield looked down upon him with the same coldness, the same detachment, his face reflecting the same brutality and cruelty, his mind trying to decide whether to finish Featherley with one quick blow to the neck.

But Walton flung himself upon him and together they rolled to the bottom of the incline. At the bottom of the incline Walton threw Bousefield from him, but Bousefield rebounded from the wall to tower over him. He swung the pick viciously at his head, but Walton ducked under it; the pick hewed at the rock with such force it took a second for Bousefield to wrench it free. Walton picked up the yardstick and swung it over Bousefield's head and crushed his neck to his chest. A minute of that and Bousefield would have been dead, but he kicked viciously with the heel of his boot, Walton loosened his grip an instant and Bousefield wrenched himself free. The yardstick somehow became entangled with the pick and was torn from his grasp. Bousefield rammed the blunt head of the pick into Walton's stomach, he gasped and crumpled, and his hands went automatically to his belly as he sank to his knees. Bousefield was on him with the pick before he could rise.

Walton twisted his ankle as he fell and even had he wanted could not move from his path. Bousefield lifted his head with a hand and jabbed a knee into his throat under the jaw. He raised the pick for one short sharp stroke. And it did not seem to matter to him that the man he was about to kill was unarmed, defence-less; just as it had never mattered to him that Featherley had been unarmed, defenceless. Only he had to find expression for his violent nature, he had to manifest his hatred and animosity even toward the person who had been his friend, he had to release the bitter energies that had built up over the weeks of confinement in the pit. The consequence of murder did not trouble his mind; it did not matter to him that he might be hanged, he might be gaoled, he might be removed from society and never seen again; that he would cut himself off from his family, his village, that all his life he would be an outcast among men. He raised the pick and brought it down. Walton lifted his arm in protection. The point of the pick broke the bone beneath his elbow and with a startled grunt and sudden whitening Walton watched his arm drop uselessly to his side.

Bousefield raised the pick again and brought it down towards his head.

43

But Ray Holt wrenched the pick from him as once he had
wrenched a chair from his brother. He swung Bousefield round
and even before he let go of the shaft kneed him in the testicles
and as he crumpled, foam appearing at the corners of his mouth,
thrashed him with the flat of the pick across the neck. Bousefield
sank to his knees and rolled over to his chest. His face was contorted with pain, but Ray looking down at him in the light of the
lamp, saw beyond the pain, beyond the coarseness, the stifled look
of hatred and bitterness he had never seen, the look of a twisted
personality, a flower without nourishment, a spoilt child that had
never grown up. And he felt sorry, sorry because this was his
friend, because there was nothing he could do, because all his life
Bousefield would express himself in cruelty and hate merely to
justify his personality, his existence. But the feelings Ray had
turned when he thought of the effects his action might have on
the strike. He kicked him in the side and bent over Walton as he
lay against the rock.

Walton was neither conscious nor unconscious but lay shivering and in pain with eyes half closed, sweat cold to his forehead,
the skin showing white through the streaks of dirt. Ray did not
try to touch him. He did not even try to examine his arm. He had
seen the impact of the pick and heard the crack of the bone, besides he could tell by the manner in which it hung by his side, so
peculiarly and uselessly, that it was well and truly broken. The
only problem for Ray was to decide what to do and to do it quickly.
He rubbed at the coarse barb that had accumulated to his features
and kneeling on his hunkers heard the splash of water behind him.
He turned to see Featherley stumbling down the slope. His legs
gave way several times and he tried to drag himself along on his
knees. He tried lifting himself up on the ancient timber supports
and the props cracked in protest. Even then his efforts were feeble,
emasculated, and swiftly Ray crossed to drag him to his feet.

"What in Christ name's the matter wi' ye?" he asked.

"He tried — he tried to."

"All reet, never mind what he tried. Are ye fit enough to walk, that's what I want to knaa."

"If there's owt ye have to dee, Ray, I'll try."

"Never mind tryin', ye have to be sure."

"In that case I'm sure."

"Ye'd better be. Or ye'll get the back o' me hand across yer mouth."

"Now divin't ye start, Ray. Divin't —"

"All reet, I'm only pullin' yer leg. But listen to what I say and listen carefully. I want ye to nip back along to the deputy's kist — telephone to bank and say there's been an accident. A fall along the rolleyway. No, divin't say that, say a fellow fell on a pick in the dark and broke his arm. And tell them to get an ambulance to the mouth o' the drift — the mouth o' the drift, mind. Not bank top. And then get one o' the deputies to open the safety chest in the deputy's kist and get out the morphia. And get some o' the other men along here wi' the ambulance stretcher, so we can set him up proper. And if there's any first-aid men get them along tee. But nee panic and nee commotion, d'ye hear?"

"What about Bouser? He looks dead to the world."

"He is dead to the world. But I'll worry about him, not ye. Now ye've got all that, 'cause once ye've telephoned the surface and got the morphia and stretcher fixed up I want ye to nip back to the drift mouth, tell them what's happened, and tell them to expect an ambuluance at any minute. Probably it'll be there afore ye. Anyway, nee matter. When ye get to the drift mouth ye explain the position to me father."

"Ye mean about the accident?"

"Tell him I want him to accompany Walton to the surface. See he's all reet. See his mother's told, see that everybody knaas it was an accident and nowt else. See me father gets a good night's sleep in his own bed, and tell him — tell him — if there's any trouble wi' that brother o' mine just to kip at Walton's till he's married. Only tell him to wait till the strike's o'er, so things are settled like."

"So ye're sendin' him back after all?"

"Neebody'll get back if ye stand and gape like that. Now get them legs o' your'n movin' and dee as I say. Or I'll never post that

428

letter about yer pigs. And then ye'll never have that acre o' land ye're after. Now gan on, get on."

Featherley staggered off as best he could and Ray turned his attention not to Walton but to Bousefield. Ray felt cool now, he felt collected, the miseries and doubts that had afflicted him were dissipated, he had galvanized himself under the pressure of violence; and just as Bousefield had cleansed himself with his violence upon Walton so Ray had cleansed himself with his attack on Bousefield. He felt like a field commander who has given the orders of battle and has nothing better to do than sit back and see his plans bear fruition. He wiped the spittle from the corners of Bousefield's mouth and returning up the slope to the pool where Featherley had almost drowned took his scarf and dipped the frayed tasselled ends in the water. He returned and bathed Bousefield's lined pained face, holding his head gently, Bousefield moaning as he stirred, clenching his teeth against the pain of his testicles.

Ray wiped the dirt and sweat from his face and saw the fretted white skin underneath.

"Now what'd ye gan and dee a thing like that for?" he asked, still bathing his face. "After all the trust I've placed in ye. All the responsibility. What'd ye have to gan and spoil it all for like this?"

"Better ask him in the corner," Bousefield grunted. "He shouldn't have started on about me mother."

"What about yer mother?"

"Said she'd been sleepin' wi' the manager. Lies like that."

"I suppose ye never said nowt about his mother like. Ye'd never dream o' provokin' him."

"All the same, what I said about his mother was true."

"Whereas ye think what he said about yers was false?"

Bousefield's eyes opened and he stirred uneasily.

"Ye're not tryin' to say the same as him, are ye?"

"Listen, Bouser, son, I've got enough on me mind without worryin' about other people's problems."

"So it is true. After all."

"Neebody said it was true. Only listen for a minute while I tell ye. Ye knaa me owld man's gettin' married to the daughter — Walton's sister I mean. And ye knaa neebody's keen on the idea. Least of all wor lad. But ye knaa I accept it 'cause it's what he wants. Only ye divin't think I'm leapin' for joy. Ye divin't think I'm jumpin' o'er the moon."

429

"All the same that's yer father. Ye can understand a thing like that. Only to say things about me mother. Me own mother."

"Only ye'll have said worse about his, I'll be warned."

Ray glanced to Walton against the rock. A feeling of annoyance and frustration came over him, that he had let these two together, that all along his judgment had been correct, that they were not to be trusted, that they alone were a source of danger. Yet now that his anger was controlled he narrowed his vision to see the consequences of the disaster, and he saw the consequences were not great. He would lose Walton to the surface with a broken arm, but that in itself would provide another headline for the papers; he would still have Featherley and he would still have Bousefield, he would no longer have the source of friction between the two; and he could use the incident to send his father back to the surface. He could turn tragedy into triumph. The only thing was he would have to keep the true story dark, he would have to see those who were against the strike could not spread it abroad the ranks were breaking. The resolve of the men beginning to weaken. He let his mind run on and dropped the damp tassels of the scarf to the floor.

"I wouldn't care so much if it were true. But to knaa it's all lies."

"What difference does it make if it's true or not? The damage is done now."

"It makes a lot of difference to me," Bousefield said.

Slowly, painfully, he pulled himself to his feet. The lines sagged his cheeks and he continued to clench his teeth against the pain; but if there was animosity in his eyes it was not towards Ray, nor even towards Walton, but to some distant figure on which his eyes had yet to focus. He ignored Walton and began looking with slow stiff dignity for his helmet. He stood with hands clawing his knees, feeling short of wind and physically sick, white still fleck-ing his lips, blowing out long sighs as if this might rid the pain he felt between his legs. Then, spying the helmet among the mud, oblivious of the mud to his head, he bent to attach the sombrero-like cord around his neck, and one hand reaching for the wall began making his way up the incline towards the drift mouth. His feet slipped repeatedly in the mud, the wall was damp to his hand, but he had almost reached the top before Ray realized he was gone.

"Where'd ye think ye're off tee now?" he asked.

"Gannin' back to bank. See if it's true."

"For Christ sake. See if what's true?"

"What Walton said about me mother."

"But I've told ye. What difference does it make?"

"None to ye. A lot to me."

Ray had scrambled up the slope and now held out an arm as he tried to pass.

"I need ye down here, Bouser. Wi' me."

"Ye'll not need me. Wi' Featherley to keep ye company."

"Ye knaa I need ye more than I need Featherley."

"Ye wouldn't have thowt it. The way ye sent him spyin' all the time."

"I had good reet. Seein' what's happened the day."

"All the same I'm gannin' back. I have to gan back."

The lamp in Bousefield's helmet had rolled from its socket and snapped itself off when the helmet had fallen from his head, and standing in the dim lights at the drift top, by a set of rusting disused tubs, he had not seen fit to relight it. Ray stood so close to his friend he could feel his breath against his cheek, he could smell the earth and pit, the cold damp smell of dust and water that was overpowering to his nostrils. The contortions were less to Bousefield's face but there was pain still in the cleave of his brows, the fleck of his lips, the white powdery colour of his face that shone through the dirt. With Ray standing over him he tried to raise himself to his full height, but as he did so the muscles ached in his neck where he had been struck by the stick, pain reflected again to his face, and the brows lifting up showed the malevolence in his eyes as he recalled the source of the blow.

"Listen, Bouser," Ray said. "While I tell ye somethin' that'll make the wax pop in yer ears. Ye knaa me father's marryin' that Walton bit, ye knaa soon I'll have that scruff at the bottom o' the slope as a relative. But I've never told ye why she's marryin', why she wants to be one o' the family."

"I divin't care," Bousefield said. "It's nowt to dee wi' me."

"But it has if ye listen. She wants to be one o' the family, 'cause it's me she wants to live with. It's me she wants to marry."

"I divin't believe it," Bousefield said. "You're makin' it up."

"Makin' it up nowt," Ray said. "Ye'll see if I'm makin' it up, wait another six months till she drops her kid, ye'll see. Only

431

it'll not be me father's kid it'll be mine. And when she marries it'll not be me father she's sleepin' win. It'll be me."

"I still think ye're makin' it up."

"Suit yersel'," Ray said. "Happens to be true all the same. Only ye divin't see why I'm tellin' ye, ye divin't see why it makes nee difference to me. 'Cause everybody thinks I'm a tough guy, see, just the way they think ye're a tough guy. So if a thing like that makes nee difference to me why should a bit o' rumour about yer mother make any difference to ye?"

"All the same I'm ganna find out."

From the bottom of the incline, along the rolleyway, Ray heard the voices of men bringing morphia and a stretcher. Their voices grew more animated as the men reached the bottom, the rumble of the stretcher tub was lost to the discordant sounds, the arc of their lamps slanted off the silver walls and illumined still further the water from the roof. From the top of the incline, looking down, all seemed noise and confusion, but even before Ray half-started down the slope, other voices rose, voices of control and command, voices of men versed in this kind of situation, ambulance men trained to handle all manner of pit accidents, trained to such a degree it would not take long to examine Walton, splinter his arm, and wheel him on the stretcher to the drift mouth.

"All reet," Ray said. "Gan back to the surface. Find out for yersel'. But I'm tellin' ye now, if there's owt ye dee to jeopardize this strike, owt at all that'll make a bad impression, I'll be after ye. And not with a pick, with a gun."

"It'll be a long time afore I forget what ye did the day," Bousefield said. "Be careful it's not me that comes after ye."

"It's not Featherley ye're talkin' tee now, ye knaa. Better watch what ye say or I'll drop ye here and now. And mark what I say, cause a disturbance and ye'll knaa what ye get. And I'll find out, divin't think I'll not 'cause I will."

Ray saw the clear coldness of Bousefield's eyes as he raised his head and Bousefield the strong determination that was reflected in Ray's. But it was obvious if they understood the look they did not understand each other. Bousefield was going to do what he had to do regardless of Ray Holt, and Ray was going to return down the incline to the men he had now to manage alone. Yet as they held each other's stare neither moved. For it seemed to both once they set to walking their different ways neither would see the other again. And somehow this saddened Ray. It disappointed him. He realized not only was he losing Walton and his father, he was losing his friend, his best friend, without whom the strike could never have been possible and certainly sustained. He recalled how Bousefield had slithered to him along the face of number nine, bringing news of the unofficial stoppage, he remembered his devotion and dedication the night of the meetings at institute and club, how possibly without him, as he faltered at the institute, the strike might never have got away.

And as he remembered these things foreboding came close on their heels. The kind of forebodings that had sent Featherley chasing through the disused workings towards the drift mouth. He felt somehow he should stop his departure, he should not allow his return to the surface, that to let him go now was to commit one of the mistakes in his life, one of the costly mistakes. What had he told himself only the other day? You should not make a mistake knowing it to be a mistake before you made it; nor should you make the same mistake twice. But yet he realized too there was nothing to be done and because there was nothing to be done technically he was not making a mistake. If Bousefield wished to return to the surface no one could stop him. His will was too stubborn and his character too independent to be swayed by anyone other than himself. Yet as Bousefield moved toward the drift mouth Ray went after him. He gave him one last warning, one last message.

"Take notice o' what I say, Bouser," he said. "I'll kill ye if ye jeopardise me, I'll kill ye."

44

"And I'd kill mysel' tee. If ye left us in this hole."

"Ye've said that before," Atkin said. "But in a little while ye'll forget."

"And in that little while we could settle down cozy like."

Atkin lay with Mrs. Bousefield, head relaxed on the pillow, watching the changing patterns of light that came with the sun through the window, listening to the noises of the village that carried across the football field and lines, sounds that were as familiar as the sounds of the colliery. The yellow curtains were half-drawn across the windows, but the sun flowed through the gap, through the rayon, casting liquid tanks of light upon the wall. The light dimpled too the warm moist shoulders of Mrs. Bousefield as she lay beside him. Her face and neck were brown where she had caught the sun, the summer had brought again the youth to her face, but where the tan faded the warm unvirgin skin of her breasts and shoulders melted to gold, and even the white strap of her slip, the slight sighing of the chest stirred Atkin as he lay beside her. Mrs. Bousefield lay one hand behind her head, the other playing with a dry curl behind her ear. She did not look at Atkin as she spoke but kept her gaze to the ceiling.

"Tell us what ye're thinkin'," she said. "Ye used to tell us once. Lie there and tell us all the thoughts gannin' through yer mind."

"And you used to listen because in those days all the thoughts were about you."

"But it doesn't matter if they're not about me now. Just let's talk about the future — our future."

"I don't want to talk about the future. Or even the past."

"Then talk about anythin'. Just tell us what's gannin' through yer mind."

A little smile tugged her lips but she did not take her eyes from the ceiling. She gained as little pleasure from loving Atkin as Atkin gained from loving her. For him it was a mechanical duty, laborious, pathetic, the motion of which he repeated for reasons he did not know; for her it was an opportunity to count the flies on the ceiling. It was also an opportunity to flaunt her power. She felt for Atkin as she felt for her husband, a maternal instinct that had long since dulled, she felt too a little disgust that he could be so weak and bending. But that was why she had to continue exercising her power, to prove not only was she mistress of his body but of his mind as well. She had to prove he still belonged to her. And each time she proved it she gained her little satisfaction, her little triumph, as if she were dominating him not he dominating her. She turned on her side and placed a hand on his hip.

"As a matter of fact," he said. "I was thinking of the colliery."

"Always," she said. "The colliery."

"To think those men can stick it out thirty-one days."

" 'Cause they're gluttons for punishment, that's why. And gluttons for publicity. 'Cause they get plenty o' grub to their bellies and tea to their throats. And 'cause though they divin't knaa it they're being managed from the surface."

"Only they don't believe it's me doing the managing."

"That's where ye're soft. That's how I cannot understand why ye spend so much time thinkin' o' them. Ye risk yer neck, ye risk yer job. Ye get them food, ye get them blankets, ye get them recharges for their lamps. When there was that accident ye not only fixes up the ambulance ye even gan to see the fellow in hospital. Ye call by the house to see his mother — and a shock ye got there an all."

"And all for nothing. Because no-one ever gives me credit."

"That's reet. 'Cause it all gans to Gerald Holt."

"And Gerald never lifts a finger."

"Only neebody believes that. Everybody believes he's the brains behind the whole thing. But that was Wishart's daft fault for gannin' round tellin' everybody. But ye sittin' in yer office, worryin' what to dee next, ye get nee credit, only complaints if things gan wrong."

"All the same," Atkin said. "Ye're missing the point. I'm not the brains behind it all — someone else is. But the men have spent thirty-one days in the pit and not a sign yet the strike's breaking. Not a sign yet they'll come back to the surface. It just

435

shows how aware they are of the principles at stake. How everyone of them understands what it is he's fighting for."

"I suppose you want to gan and join them."

"No," he said. "Only I can't help thinking."

"What cannot ye help thinkin'?"

"All those men fighting for their principles. And on the surface
people like Mrs. Rutland fighting too for what they believe. So
why shouldn't I fight? Fight the way they're fighting. Take off the
gloves and get into the ring. Get in and do something really worthwhile?"

Her hand moved from hip to thigh and with a gentle rocking
motion she turned him towards her, so that her breasts were against
his, her thighs against his, her stomach felt the warmth of his
stomach, and with arms encircling his neck, pressing him close,
hair brushing against his cheek, his mouth, she really seemed to
dwarf him. He did not respond to her touch because he liked to
think response was dead in him. Yet as he looked into her eyes,
her brown eyes, he saw the lustre he had once known as she strode
across the course. The lustre of life that was now the lustre of
triumph. Her triumph over him. She was aware of this triumph
and pressing his face to hers she peeled back his lips with her own
and pressed her tongue between his teeth. And he accepted the
lips, the tongue, because for him there was no way out. He closed
his eyes and felt a hot flush stimulate his body as the kiss
prolonged.

"Ye are deein' somethin' worthwhile," she said. "Ye're
comin' away wi' me."

"That's right," Atkin said. "I'm coming away with you."

"Ye're comin' away and we're ganna live together."

"Live together," he repeated. "As man and wife."

"Till I gets me divorce. Till we can really be man and wife."

"Yes," he said. "After the divorce."

"And it's all fixed up," she said. "There's nee gannin' back?"

"No," he said. "No going back."

Atkin for once nearly slipped into dialect as he repeated what
now seemed to him the chant of some sanskrit ritual. For
the first few weeks he had held out against Mrs. Bousefield, he
had held out so completely he felt he would evade her altogether.
He had been helped in this by Mrs. Rutland and his efforts on
behalf of the men. He had also been helped by himself. When he

436

had met Mrs. Rutland he realized how much he had let himself go, how much he had succumbed to self-pity. And he had decided then and there he would have nothing more to do with Mrs. Bousefield. He would do his best never to set eyes on her again, he would cease his reckless stupid drinking, he would put his mind to the strike, to the men, he would so tire himself he would sleep of a night without the stimulants he habitually took. He had felt at the time the handing of the coal souvenir to Mrs. Rutland was not only a break with the past, it was a break with himself, the little impious self that lived within. And he had felt if only he could liberate himself from this small insignificant little self, the bondage in which he had cast himself, he would be free.

But though it had worked in the beginning it had not worked for long. He saw little of Mrs. Rutland because she concerned herself with keeping supplied the wives and families of men on strike; nevertheless she did as he said and worked night and day at the office, he dropped his disparaging conversations with officials, he sought of his own accord various compromises suitable both to men and management. And even tried to devise ways of making more comfortable the lot of the men in the pit. It was he who suggested the soups be laced with brandy and hot-pots stiffened with rum, though this he knew to be in direct contravention to the Coal Mines Act. But the passive resistance set up against him in the village did not dissolve overnight. The minds of the people fathomed back to the times of hatred and bitterness, when the management were considered mortal enemies, the war a civil war to be fought to the last, so that they looked upon Gerald Holt and not Atkin as the saviour. They continued not to speak in the street and even those who once had nodded turned away if given the opportunity. This disheartened Atkin. But more than that it defeated him. He had sunk so low in self pity he had not felt he could sink lower, he had decided to end the slide, not to carry it further. Yet here he was lacking encouragement, already defeated, and far from arresting the decline he had accentuated it, his drinking began again and with it the stimulants, so that in the end he lost even the will to avoid Mrs. Bousefield.

Yet he so hated her he dreaded to think what their life would be like together. He had ceded to her demands because in his misery he had seen no alternative. He had sold his birthright and would receive in return not even a mess of potage. Why? He did not know himself. He had heard of men, some of them acquaintances, who had ruined their lives for the sake of a woman they loved, who had shattered both homes and happiness, left wives and children, yet who had been treated ignominously, lived the life of a dog. But who accepted this life because they were in love with the woman concerned. Yet for Atkin to sacrifice the little he had merely to assuage his self-pity, that puzzled him. It puzzled him so much he felt there must be in him a force greater than himself, perhaps the force of self-destruction. He reflected how once he had thought life was in own hands, that he made the decisions concerning his life. But it was not so. It had never been so. He could no more plot his destiny than a star could chart its course through the universe.

"I hope Mrs. Rutland hasn't been puttin' ideas in yer mind," she said.

"What kind of ideas?"

"Nasty ideas about settlin' here to fight."

"She doesn't have to put them into my head," he said. "They're there already."

"Well, ye'd better get rid o' them. 'Cause I for one'll not stand them."

"I've said I'll marry you," he said. "I've said you can put in for your divorce, though heaven knows what you'll get it on. You've nothing on Bousefield and even if he has something on you, even if he can get you on desertion or adultery there's nothing to say he will. That he'll put himself to the expense."

"He'll gan to the expense all reet," she said. "I'll make him gan to it."

"You'll have a hard job. Since you're running away with me."

"But that's why he'll have to do it. 'Cause there'll be that much gossip and scandal in the village he'll have nee option. 'Cause if I knaa the folks around here they'll never let up till he's started proceeding's. So divin't worry about the divorce. I'll take care o' that."

"All the same I'm thinking of leaving the colliery, the industry. I'm thinking of resigning. Of applying all my principles as the rest of the village are applying theirs. Because I want to stay here and fight. Fight for the village as everyone else is fighting for the colliery. Of course it doesn't mean things'll be any different. Just that we'll go along as we've always gone along till the fighting's over."

"Ye divin't have to worry about nee fight startin' never mind finishin'. Yer first duty's to me and I say I want to leave. Leave the village now not next year — nor in ten years either. And I'm not interested in keeping on the way we've been. I'm only interested in gettin' away. Away from the whole damn crew o' them."

With one agile movement Atkin pulled back the covers and leapt from the bed. His clothes were scattered on the floor where he had hurriedly undressed and stooping he gathered them up and flung them onto the chair next to the fireplace. Mrs. Bousefield watched him cross to the fireplace and in the mirror on the wall above saw his weak tired face. The skin of his face and neck were of a different hue, the skin of the body a moist warm, muscles rippling the shoulders and armour-plated chest, legs sheathed with hairs. He had a perfectly-shaped body, small and thick-set, like that of the first primitive man, and as he passed through the yellow golden rays of sunlight, strutting as he always strutted, on the balls of his toes, she felt there was strength to his stride, strength to his movements. Only there was no strength to his face. There was only weakness and submission. He pulled a shirt over his head and leant across the chair for his trousers.

"I've agreed to everything," he said. "Only it's a question of time."

"Always wi' ye a question of time."

"I don't even know myself what I want," he said. "It's all in a state of flux. I've neither decided to stay nor decided to leave. But I'm going to have a talk tonight with the MP. See what are the chances of saving the village. See if it's worth putting up a fight. And if it is then we'll see. And I'll let you know."

"Ye divin't have to let us know. I'm tellin' ye the way I want it to be."

She pulled back the clothes and herself stepped out of the bed.

"Ye want nothing less than hundred per cent surrender," he said. "Don't you?"

"That's reet," she said. "Hundred per cent."

439

45

She placed her feet to the carpet and shook the hair around her ears. She carried with her from the bed an odour of sex and sweat and as she picked up her stockings and rolled them to her legs she reflected how difficult it was to believe that once she had loved Atkin. She had worshipped the ground on which he walked. She had been unable to think of anyone but him, she had made meals, washed dishes, dusted furniture, and never once had he left her thoughts. Often she had wished she could go back to the moment prior to their meeting when he had offered her a drink at the club, she wished she had slipped away then before his own round of golf had finished. It was true of course she had had affairs before Atkin, little flirtatious affairs that heightened her ego and flattered her pride, but this was the first time she had fallen in love. This was the first time she had realized how she was trapped, burdened. Till then she had been content with her life, her husband, the triviality of their ways, but now she found them unbearable, she felt she could support them no longer.

But that was years ago, this was now. What had happened to deaden her love, what had killed the little bud in her heart? She realized probably she had killed it herself. Once she had told him what she really needed was a caveman, someone of strong personality who could govern her, force his will upon her; and at the time this had pleased Atkin because he felt he was such a man. Yet when he tried to dominate she retaliated. She rebelled. Her will could not bow to that of another. She had worn him down, she had decayed his resistance, she had eroded his will, his character, so that towards her at least very little of it existed. And because very little existed, because she had broken him, she despised him. She disliked him. She was indifferent to him. She wanted to keep on dominating, continue governing, and the more she despised, the more she disliked, the more she felt the urge to bully. To exact hundred per cent surrender.

She heard a noise in the garden.

"What's that?" she asked.

"What's what?"

"I heard a noise," she said. "From the garden."

"Probably a joker from across the colliery houses. Happens to like my lettuce so across he comes every summer and helps himself to an armful. I caught him once in the act and d'you know what he said? Said he loves lettuce and mine are the best in the district. So when a thief flatters you like that what can you do to stop him?"

"Catch me lettin' people away with a thing like that."

"Anyway, come away from the window," Atkin said. "You've got nothing on."

He slipped downstairs and found on the carpet a letter pushed through the box by the clerk on his way home. Probably the letter had come with the afternoon mail, but Atkin had left the office at three o' clock to brood alone. He had told them he would be on the phone if needed. He opened the letter and read it. It was a Coal Board letter marked private and confidential. He guessed what it would be. It was from area office telling him what his next position would be "if in the light of accounting investigations the area is making into the profitability of each seam at your colliery, and subject to suitable arrangements being made with the local lodge of the NUM, the Board should decide to uphold its decision to close Highhill colliery at the end of the year." He folded the letter and placed it in his pocket. It was just as he had expected. He could not have hoped for anything else the way he had talked on the phone, he could not have expected anything else given the fact he was manager of a dud colliery.

He crossed to the cabinet and poured himself a glass of brandy. He raised the glass to himself in the mirror before he drank. Feelings of self pity welled within but he held them back. He tried to put his mind to other things. He tried to see in the letter a justification of the decision he wanted to make, that he should leave the colliery, the industry, he should plant his roots in the earth and make a last stand: the stand of the individual against bureaucracy. The only difficulty was Mrs. Bousefield. But this was not a difficulty, this was an impossibility. He let the brandy roll from his tongue to his throat. Normally he drank it slowly, carefully, but this time he felt the need of a shock, a stimulant and so he drank it quickly and in one gulp. He felt its fire to his nerves. He felt its heat to the back of his throat. He felt grim and bitter and miserable. But he placed the glass on the walnut cabinet, nodding to himself in the mirror, and took out the letter to read it again.

"I hope there's nowt passin' between ye and Mrs. Rutland," she said.

"What d'you mean — passing between us?"

"Ye knaa. Letters and the like."

"Why should we write letters when we can reach each other on the phone?"

"It's surprising," Mrs. Bousefield said. "What people dee when they're in love."

"And what makes you think I love Mrs. Rutland?"

"Ye must love somebody. Seein' as ye divin't love me."

Her green dress was creased where she had flung it to the floor, she had not bothered yet to attach her nylons, their folds hung loosely around her knees, and though she had slipped her feet into slippers she had not done so properly; she walked on the back of her heels, and as she crossed to Atkin the slippers made a peculiar flapping noise. She turned to let him fasten the hasps on the back of her dress. He looked up and saw the warm dimpled skin, the soft down on her neck, before it gave way to chestnut hair, that somehow seemed scented and fragrant as she stood so close, so that a flicker stirred within. But once he fastened the hasps, once he tasted the chestnut hair brushing his lips, she slipped from him, the flicker subdued, extinguished once and for all as she moved into the kitchen to light the gas. She called through to him when she had put the kettle on the stove.

"I heard about her callin' by the office the other week. And on Saturday too when neebody was about."

"She called about the colliery," Atkin said. "See if there was anything she could do."

"Everybody's breakin' their neck about the colliery," she said. "Except me and wor Alf."

"And even your Alf's chucking in his weight. If you consider how he controls those credit cards."

"Makes nee difference," she said. "It's all the same to me."

She lighted a cigarette and stood by the window, holding back the curtain. She could see no-one in the garden. Only the sweet peas pushing up on their trellis, the line upon line of potato heads, some of them flowering now, white flower heads suckling to the sun, the leeks at the bottom of the garden strong and sturdy, developing for the autumn shows. She pulled the tars of the cigarette from between her teeth, the tip of her tongue, and turning up the gas beneath the kettle passed back into the sitting room. Atkin stood by the window and the light caught the profile of his face, but it was a profile in decline, the cheeks grown flabby, the chin sagging, the pouches beneath the eyes swollen, expanded. And the lips that once had curled with disdain now drooped at the corners.

The face of a man with a past, not the face of a man with a future.

"Arnold," she said. "What kind o' house will they give ye wi' the job?"

"What job?" he asked, vague, distracted.

"The job after this one. The next colliery."

"Probably a colliery house," he said. "Like this one."

"Only bigger," she said. "And better surroundings."

"I shouldn't think it'll be bigger," he said. "Probably smaller."

"No," she said. "There aren't any small houses in the midlands."

"What makes ye think I'll be sent to the midlands?"

"Ye said yersel'. It was the first thing ye says."

"I'll not be sent to the midlands," he said. "I'll not even leave the area."

She smiled her tight smile and returned to the kitchen to make a pot of tea.

"Joke as much as ye like," she said. "But I knaa where we'll be gannin'. I talked it o'er wi' wor Alfie — o' course I never said nowt about runnin' away — but I said like how ye hoped to gan to the midlands. And he said there's many a worse thing ye could dee. He said they're all big collieries down there, deep but mechanical. He said if ye're given one o' them ye'll be all reet."

"If they give me one of them."

"They'll give ye one all reet," she said.

Mrs. Bousefield had thought of it so long she could not conceive her ideas as other than reality. She noticed the nylons had slipped to around her ankles, but instead of stooping to roll them up, she laid the half-smoked cigarette upon an ashtray on the mantelpiece and sipped the tea so that it damped her lips. Yes, she would have a fine house in the country, like those she had seen on television, like the one owned by Mrs. Rutland on the fringe of the village. She liked to think that, like Mrs. Rutland, she was a civilized woman, cultured, only that her culture had been stifled by so many years in the same environment; but now that she was leaving that environment, casting off her origins, she could allow her intellect and culture rein. She could do the things that secretly she had wanted to do all her life. She sipped the tea and the sound she made caused Atkin to turn from the window.

"You may have to settle in the area," he said. "If that's where my job is."

"I've told ye. Ye're gannin' to the midlands."

"But I'm not," he said. "They've transferred me to a job in the area."

"So ye say," Mrs. Bousefield smiled.

He took the letter from his pocket and threw it on to the table. It slid along the polished surface and her closed face looked at it blankly, not understanding. Then the brows came together and she stared at Atkin, scrutinizing, distrustful. He saw the light to her throat, the muscles tighten in her neck. And for the first time in their long relationship he felt she was at a disadvantage. He felt he had her on the hip. She picked up the letter and fumbled open the envelope. "If it's the same kind o' letter that ye left about me notice it'll meet the same kind o' fate," she said. But as she read the letter he saw her face change, darken, the knits deepening to her brow.

"You see," he said. "The control of a drift. Not two miles from here."

"Ye've had it typed in the office," she said. "To frighten us."

"It's postmarked area," he said. "And signed by the area general manager."

She held the letter a moment, reflecting. The frets lifted from her brow and she smiled."

"There's only one thing to do," she said.

"And what's that?" he asked.

"Change it."

"But how d'you expect me to change it? Me — manager of a dud colliery, a colliery that has to be closed because it can't pay its way? My reputation and career ruined. And you think all I

444

have to do is ring the area general manager and tell him it's not good enough. That I want a job in the midlands or no job at all?"

"Ye'd better if ye expect me to come away wi' ye."

"But even before I ring I know what he'll say. He'll say take it or leave it — work there or work nowhere."

Mrs. Bousefield had never before seen Atkin laugh. And even as she stood by the table holding the letter she was not sure if he were laughing now. But the lips were peeled back and she could see his teeth, there was laughter to his eyes and in the shake of his shoulders; there was relief to his face, but more than relief freedom. He was like a man released from prison, a man relieved of responsibility. His face had changed in an instant. The flabbiness, the sagging, the swollen expanded pouches, they were lifted from his face, the heavy saturnine scowl, the drop to the disdainful lips, belonged no longer to Atkin but to some man emerging from a dream. So that Mrs. Bousefield found her power fading, she found it diminishing, and the enfuriating thing was there was nothing she could do. It aggravated her temper. It drove her to desperation.

"I'm ganna tell ye frankly," she said. "I've had just about enough. First ye say ye cannot take us win ye, then ye say ye'll think it o'er and let us know; then ye avoid us for more weeks than I can think on, and then eventually when ye dee decide ye'll take us ye fix it so we divin't have to gan at all."

"I didn't fix it. It was fixed for me."

"Either way, makes nee odds to me. But ye'd better get it fixed different — and sharp at that. 'Cause if ye divin't I'll finish wi' ye. But more than that I'll see everybody else finishes wi' ye an' all. I'll write to the area general manager for a start. See that he knaas what's been gannin' on all these years. So ye'll hardly be likely to get a drift never mind owt else."

"But I've told you," Atkin said. "What does he care?"

"And I'll write to Mrs. Rutland. Ye'll worry more about her, I'll bet. A nice little poison pen letter tellin' her the kind o' man ye are. Weak and vaccilatin'. The kind that deprives a woman of her virtue. Ye'll not get far win her after she reads that. I'll put a spoke in yer fine wheel, me lad, ye'll see if I divin't."

But even as she threatened Atkin knew that he was free. He realized too just how supreme was the irony. The whole situation had come about because of the closure of the colliery. He had been shocked at the time because he had felt they were taking from

445

him his life; yet the solace he had was that by casting off the colliery he would cast off his past; and by casting off his past he would be rid of Mrs. Bousefield. He could forget her just as he could forget his dedication to coal. But Mrs. Bousefield had decided to come with him. So that the decision to close the colliery had placed her on his shoulders not for a few weeks but for a lifetime. And Atkin had accepted that situation, he had accepted it so perfectly he had never seen any release. But just as the closing of the colliery had placed her burden to his shoulders so the decision to offer him a drift had removed that burden. Had offered the release for which he sought.

"I wish you wouldn't talk nonsense," he said. "It makes no difference to anybody what we've been up to all these years. And even if it does what do I care? And what difference does it make to my future in the industry? Either they send me to a drift or they send me nowhere. And they're my bosses. Either I do as I'm told or I resign."

"Then ye'll have to resign. 'Cause I'm not gannin' two miles."

"But if I resign I'll fight for the village."

"And that'll not dee me any good either."

"So it's the finish," Atkin said. "Between us."

"It'll have to be if ye divin't fix them bosses. Ye think ye can live without me, but ye'll see ye cannot. It'll not be long afore ye come cringin' back. It'll not be long afore ye're on yer knees wantin' us to sleep wi' ye again. Only I'll not be there. I'll not be available. So ye'd better make up yer mind. Either ye decide to leave and take us wi' ye or I walk out this house and ye'll never see us again."

"Then I'll never see you again," Atkin said.

46

Bousefield junior stood with back and head against the wall and through the open kitchen window followed the conversation between Atkin and his mother. He heard his mother's rising voice, the words ringing clear, harshly, the harshness surprising Bousefield because he had never before noticed it. He heard the last fatal words, the final threat and rejection, and held his breath in the pause that followed. He dared not inch forward to peer through the windows. His hands scraped the wall and he felt the quarried stone against his spine. He could not tell what was passing in the silence, but he heard a door opening and closing, the sound of shoes thrown to the floor, the tap of heels moving from carpet to oilcloth, and instinctively he knew his mother was about to leave. He leapt back from the wall and throwing himself into the potato plot flung himself to the earth.

The rain had long since ceased and the earth dried, but in the furrows protected by the potato heads, the ground remained a little damp, uncomfortable to his chest and the hands outstretched before him. He had entered the garden from the line, climbing the embankment and leaping the small hawthorn hedge, crushing underfoot the fruit of the strawberry patch where he had landed. He had been walking up the path when he had seen his mother appear naked at the window. He jumped into the shadow of the outhouse and with her gaze turned towards the bottom of the garden he had seen her profile as clearly as you could see the profile on a coin. He had seen the white hand holding back the curtain, pressing against the pane, he had seen the warm golden throat, the splayed drooping breasts and wrinkled nipples, the chestnut hair that seemed to shake wantonly around the ears. The glimpse was only for a moment, in that moment he felt a sickness to his stomach, the image engraved itself upon his memory, and he turned away from the window just as she let her hand drop from the curtain.

He lay in the furrow and felt his heart beating back at him from the clay. He parted the potato fronds sufficiently to see his mother leave the house, face flushed, lips trembling, yet head held back in defiance. Though she had slipped into her coat and shoes she had forgotten her stockings, they continued to drape her ankles and she paused by the outhouse to roll them up. Bousefield saw the white flash of her legs and the dark shadows beyond the hem of her dress and slip. He saw too the lips move as if she were talking and from the pocket of her coat a handkerchief appeared, and she blew her nose. His feet stirred in the furrow and she looked across to where he lay; he had parted the stalks in such a way that only his eyes appeared, but it seemed to him, looking through the trellis of sweat peas, that their eyes met, that they queried what he was doing there. Yet though her eyes were fixed on his there was nothing she could see. For he realized she was crying. She pushed the handkerchief back into the pocket and heard the tap of her heels as she hurried round the back.

He looked along the avenue of potato heads and saw the fronds powdered a dusty green where the light filtered through, he saw little bundles of alysum beneath the path, heads of grass from the broken concrete, and as he looked he realized it was true. Everything Walton had said in the pit. All that had been gossiped behind his back. He heard the front door bang and lifting his head guessed that was Atkin leaving the house to walk to his car parked at the front gate. And not only was it true now, he reflected, it had been true for years. For years everyone had been gossiping about her and his father, for years they had been the laughing stock of the village. He heard the car door open and shut, the throb of the engine as it purred to life. He lay a long time after the car had left before finally he made a move. The damp clay had stained both knees and sleeves where he had lain, and carefully he flicked at both before he moved up the path to the back door.

He gently tried the door and found it open. He moved into the house and looked around the furniture. He knew the house well since years ago when still at school his mother brought him regularly during the holidays. He had helped tidy the house and once he had even helped with the spring cleaning. Since he had been small and nimble they had given him the task of climbing a pair of stepladders and pushing open a small trap door into the attic. There had been a little light in the attic, only that which passed through a small window, and he had been so anxious to get out he had not properly arranged the pictures and frames they had handed to him, so that for all he knew they remained as he left them, scattered over the floor. But despite the fact she gave him the worst chores somehow he had enjoyed those jaunts with his mother. She had liked to come to the house and clean it for the manager and some of the pleasure it gave her was transfused to her son.

Another memory stirred his brain and he passed out of the sitting room to the outhouse. They were still there, two large circular tins of paraffin which Atkin kept for a small paraffin heater he had bought to heat the kitchen. The tins were new and had not yet been opened. Atkin had bought them at the end of winter, before the weather changed, and neither he nor Mrs. Bousefield had yet had occasion to use them. They stood in a corner of the outhouse next to the oil heater; there were various other bric-a-brac in the outhouse, a lawn mower, two ceylon tea chests, an old bicycle, probably a relic that had been in the Atkin family for years, and of course propped against the wall stepladders he had once used to climb the attic. He hauled the stepladders out of the outhouse and returned for the tins of paraffin. He pushed open the door to the sitting room and staggered with all three to the passageway and stairs.

He steadied the steps at the top of the landing and climbing slowly carefully pushed open the attic door. The smell of dust inhaled to his nostrils and as he pushed his head through the door the smell strengthened. He shuffled on the top of the steps to ascertain the steadiness of the ladder, but instead of climbing into the attic he slipped down a few steps and stooped for one of the tins of paraffin. He carried the paraffin into the attic and saw the light through the attic window, the blue sky fretted and edged by drifting cloud. The light rippled over books and papers, picture frames and paintings, dust covering the paintings and frames, the light strengthened in the confined space, deepening the shadows in the corner. He unscrewed the top of the tin and the whiff of paraffin razed his nostrils. A few drops stained his hands and shoes as he impregnated the floor, the papers, the picture frames, the rafters; his feet left prints in the dust, the attic floor creaked beneath his feet, and coughing he inhaled fumes as once he had inhaled dust.

He slipped from the attic and carried the second tin into the bedroom where he had seen his mother at the window. She had not bothered to remake the bed, the clothes were thrown back, he could see the stained sheets where they had lain, the creases to the pillows where they had rested their heads, the three strands of chestnut hair his mother had left on the pillow. He unscrewed the top and poured the paraffin over the bed, soaking the sheets and blankets, the bedstead, gaining a bitter galling satisfaction from the knowledge this was the last time they would ever sleep in that bed. And that he was the reason why they should never sleep in it again. He laid the tin upon the tiles of the fireplace and breathed deeply the crude harsh fumes. He passed downstairs to help himself to a glass of brandy. He helped himself to two brandies. He looked above the walnut cabinet and saw his face in the mirror. He smiled and in spite of himself a tremble came to his lips. He nodded as if he were nodding to Atkin. "This one," he said. "Is on me."

He turned and began searching the kitchen for a match.

47

Gerald, who did not smoke, clumsily lit the match and cupping the flame in his hands leant towards Mrs. Rutland so that she could light a rare cigarette.

They sat in the garden, in the twilight, on little white chairs around a little white table, with a parasol to keep the sun from their heads. The maid served coffee in little white cups standing on little white saucers, she left a little white pot upon the little white table, and when she retired Gerald proceeded to bed down the coffee on the best meal he had ever had. He slumped back in the chair and watched the wind filter the leaves of the young poplars, he sat facing the wood and ridge of hills and despite the parasol, with the sun cresting down, he felt its benevolence to his face. He was filled with a contentment he had never known before. He felt this was life and these people were leading it, he felt close to the meaning he was seeking, the peace he should hold and nurture like a flame to his soul. And suddenly, for the first time, he felt by marrying the daughter, by marrying into money, he felt he could hold that peace, he too could lead the life they were leading.

Mrs. Rutland smoked placidly her cigarette, taking long husky draws, leaning casually in her chair as Gerald imagined all women of her class might lean. He had worn his best suit as he had worn it to impress Mrs. Walton; but he was conscious the parallel was not the same and he felt less convincing than when striding into the uncarpeted, oderiferous scullery of his father's wife-to-be. Throughout dinner, bewildered by the choice of wine and panorama of cutlery, uncertain which knife and fork to choose next, trying not to leave fragments of food upon the rim of the glass, there had passed through his mind a picture of his own home, the yard broken and cracked, the dust and odour of decay, the gaslamp still lopsided from its conflict with the chair. And like a child who feels the pangs of homesickness he asked himself what he was doing here, what right had he to so much luxury, so much elegance, when for so long it had been denied his mother.

Gerald had seen Mrs. Rutland often in the village but rarely had he taken notice. The image of her he recalled best was that of a woman with twin red-setter dogs, holding the leash in her hand, wearing a tweed costume and tyrolean hat with a feather plunging from the felt. This was years ago when still a boy, but the image lingered, and with it the picture of a gentle but eccentric matriarch always relied upon to open the church bazaar. He was therefore surprised to find her younger than he expected, younger and more vivacious, laughing a great deal, and not only with her lips but with her eyes. Indeed, she was so young and attractive it even occurred to Gerald in his arrogance that he could love the mother more than the daughter. The thought at first delighted then amused him and looking carefully at the red wreath of her lipstick on the cigarette, the gentle hollow of her bronzed cheeks, hair grown more silver and sun-caught in the evening light, he was stirred from his serenity.

Mrs. Rutland had by now allied herself one hundred per cent with the village; and that meant for her with the tight-lipped, tight-faced women who queued for credit cards, the men who for thirty-one days had endured the discomfort of a strike hundreds of feet beneath the surface. The things which normally occupied her time — her gardens, her hot-houses, her telephone calls from one shop to another, the garden fetes and church bazaars which had made her so typical to Gerald — those were things of the past; they had merely been a grooming for the events that now so absorbed her. She felt this, the struggle to save the village, the fight to save the colliery, was her true vocation. She therefore spared herself no effort, no energy, no finance, to further the cause of both the men and the village, to lengthen the strike and thus publicize still more the fate of its people.

She had been delayed that evening because affairs in the village had held her longer than she anticipated, and therefore there had been no familiar introduction, no hand-shaking, no superficial pleased-to-meet you. This relieved Gerald because over dinner as he waited there had built up in him a feeling he was not going to like Mrs. Rutland; he felt towards her a resentment that was difficult to explain. It was as if by thinking she was deliberatley keeping him waiting, that she had put on this show

452

to humble him, she was treating him shabbily. And because she was treating him shabbily he could therefore justify to himself the reason why he should not like her. And he did not want to like her because he feared she would not like him. Yet she treated him with respect, as an equal, not as clerk in a colliery office, and she did so subtly and without condescension, so that he appreciated it the more.

She did most of the talking while he and Barbara listened, sitting side by side, hands clasped beneath the table. Barbara sat with her head uplifted, free hand shading her eyes against the sun, not listening to her mother, not having to listen since the stories were so familiar, but watching Gerald, noticing his reactions, uncertain of him still and the temper she feared. Her mother explained how her husband had endured the war only to be killed in a road accident; how her mother had built up the several village businesses only to disintegrate on hearing of the death of her son; how in rapid years Mrs. Rutland had lost not only her mother and brothers but also her father and husband, yet how she had survived the natural calamities of her life because she felt it was in her nature to survive them. And how she felt she must survive them for the sake of her daughter. At this Barbara frowned then blushed, her fingers tightened around Gerald's under the table, and when she closed her eyes against the glare of the sun, she smelt the petalled fragrance of her mother's perfume, the blue tang of the smoke that she exhaled.

"It often puzzled me," Mrs. Rutland said, when she had related how her husband's father had been under-manager of the colliery and had once urged the same career upon his son. "About your own father. Why he ever volunteered to stick it out so long — down there with the rest of the men. Why he didn't take his chance and come back with the others when the strike had hardly started."

"I've not had time to ask him yet," Gerald said. "Atkin insisted on sending him to hospital for observation and since he came back he's not been in the house. He's been staying with Mrs. Walton."

"But won't that be bad for your father?" Barbara said. "I mean people gossiping in the village."

"They'll gossip anyway," Geerald said. "Once he's married."

"I've heard that was why he came out of the pit," Barbara

said. "So they could get married straight away."

"He prefers to wait till the strike's over."

Gerald tightened his grasp on Barbara's hand and stared her in the eyes. He noticed a flush to her face, the flush of blood rather than the flush of sun; she continued to wear her hair fretted across her forehead, with a neat blonde pony's tale at the back; the style heightened the prominence of her cheeks and widened the edge of her brow. It also made her look more like a woman. And because she was conscious of the change the style had brought about she tried to act like a woman. She tried to carry her maturity as a mother might carry her first baby. She was no longer the young girl that Gerald once had known. Personally he preferred it that way, she seemed to him more attractive, more desirable, for of late he had got into the habit merely of loving her image, now he felt he wanted to love her body. He looked at the golden dent to her throat, the sun-tarnished strands of blonde hair round the side of her head, the gold that deepened her cheeks as the blush subsided and the sun moved out of the line of poplars. And with the blood flushing warm to his own veins, he wanted her now, wanted her in conquest.

The toes crinkled in his shoes as the conversation came back to Mrs. Rutland.

"There won't be any scandal," she said. "It's not as if they were living together."

"All the same," Barbara said.

"And probably it's more convenient. So they can get to know each other better. But getting back to the strike — and talking of village scandal and gossip — everyone has it you're the one behind the strike. You're the brains behind your brother."

"That doesn't give credit to my brother, does it?"

"But someone's supposed to be behind him. Supplying him with money, getting Wishart to resign, having himself elected in his place, and just as the area secretary got here. That was a masterstroke if ever there was one."

"I've not lifted a finger," Gerald said. "Not since the strike started."

"You see," Barbara said. "Gerald doesn't believe in the strike. He doesn't believe in the village."

454

48

The maid brought from the house an ashtray and Mrs. Rutland smiled and stubbed her cigarette. She had never quite been able to settle once she understood that Ray and Gerald Holt were brothers, still less when she learnt how always Ray had looked up to Gerald, how he had followed his habits at school, how he had followed them in the pub; so that she had feared Gerald in the colliery office might utilize this influence to bring the strike to an end. That events might be taken from her hands and placed into his. And that she knew would mean an immediate end to the strike. She had of course all along believed in the strike, but for a month she had seen men persevering in the pit, supported by the local newspapers and national press, yet not supported by either Union or Board. Not supported by the forces that counted. She had never doubted the strike would be a success, indeed she worked herself so hard she did not have time to doubt, but now there were things she could not understand. She was beginning to feel the indifference of authority, the indifference of an outside world, an official world that did not care about the village or the colliery, that washed its hands of ethics and justice and looked at the dispute only in the light of a face-saving formula.

"I don't believe," Gerald said. "Because I knew in advance it couldn't be a success."

"It'll be a success," Mrs. Rutland said. "If only because it draws attention to the plight of the village."

"And what plight's that?" Gerald asked.

"The plight whereby innocent folk are herded from their homes the way they are in communist countries. Against their wishes, against their will. Sent to live in strange places with strange people, where they're not known — not even a community. That's the plight I'm referring to."

"You forget the houses are all condemned property."

"And have been for years. Only in those years why weren't

455

modern houses built in their stead. And why weren't alternative industries brought in when it was seen what was going to happen. Why has the village and its people been neglected for so long, a village that for centuries sustained life."

"Because it never did sustain life," Gerald said. "It was never capable of sustaining life."

"For hundreds of years," Mrs. Rutland said. "People were content to live here. And you say it wasn't life. That they've never lived. And even now — because they're alive, because they know they're alive — they fight to keep it. And still you don't believe the village is worth it. Still you want to see it pulled down and ruined by people to whom it means nothing."

Gerald did not have to turn his head to see the large house, the spacious gardens, the sun tangling the leaves of the poplars. He saw the sun flecking red the apple and cherry trees, the nut trees, he saw it flame upon the rhododendrons, and upon the roses that climbed around the wheel of the old well. Beyond the poplars he could see the trimmed acres of the forestry commision, the solitary air shaft stubbing the ground, the dark olive of the fir trees, tips straining towards the sky, uneasy, appealing. And he did not wish to quarrel. He did not even wish to discuss. His weight was settled comfortably on the seat and with great and sudden clarity he saw how the wind pressed back the leaves, garnered the light, how the slim supple trunks swayed gracefully. He saw the view which greeted Mrs. Rutland as she flung open the bedroom shutters and understood the peace she must feel, the inner peace, that nourished her soul as delicacies nourished her body. So that he could understand why she wanted to fight, why it was she did not want to surrender.

But he could not understand why anyone else should want to fight, why like him they did not all wish to yield to the future. He could not understand — and he felt he would never under-stand — why people should want to continue living in houses that should have been destroyed years ago, houses like his own, decayed, damp, uninhabitable, houses without modern conveniences, not even a toilet attached to the house; and he realized how righteous it was for people like Barbara and her mother who would not know what the inside of such a house looked like to talk of saving the village, safeguarding the past. How they could play upon the narrowness of the people themselves, play upon the qualities

Gerald hated most, so that they too wanted to fight, they too wanted to protest. And he thought of the squalor and misery such conditions had brought to his mother, to himself, so that for years he had felt inferior, his personality soiled, perverted, and in spite of himself a quiver came to his nostrils, the nerves lit in his chest.

"If you'd lived in one of the houses," he said. "You'd understand what poverty and poor living conditions could do to you, how they could demean you, change your face, your personality, your very soul. How angry it can make you, how it can affect your pride, your character. So that no matter how long you live you can never be free of it — never."

"You mean we're idealists looking at the beauty of a painting that has no beauty?"

"Looking to a past that not only was not as picturesque as you like to think, but could never have been as picturesque. It's all right for you, you know, talking of saving the village, of fighting to propagate a life you see as the only life. Because you don't see the meanness it breeds, the pettishness, the selfishness. And even if you did you'd not understand. Because you're not involved, you're detached."

"But if the people of the village thought like you," Barbara said. "There wouldn't be a fight."

"If all the people in the village were as intelligent as me there'd not be a fight anyway."

Barbara disengaged her hand from Gerald's. She felt she had been rebuked, she felt Gerald's sarcasm had reduced her to size, and since she could find no answer she stayed silent. She looked to her mother for support but did not get it. Her mother's thoughts were following a track of their own, her mind was still on the strike and village, the antagonism of Gerald, the lightning flashes she had seen which she thought must also be reflected in his brother. The lightning she admired because she felt it showed character. It showed strength. The strength she had looked for but never found in Longley, that she had glimpsed in Atkin, and which she was sure was possessed by Ray. And by all the men on strike with him in the pit. It gratified her to know the same strength was reflected in the man her daughter had chosen to marry.

But she thought too of their new-found love, the love that would soon be dissipated once her daughter married and left. She thought of the years of antagonism between them, years for her

457

of inner coldness, suddenly dissipated by her daughter's change
of heart, the mutual love of the village that had brought them together. And which Gerald with his differing outlook and differing
views would shortly sever. It saddened her to see the waste of
youth in her daughter, she felt she was too young to marry, she
felt that since she herself had never known married life, her
daughter would be deprived of its fruits just as they had been
deprived her. Yet she had in her life so disciplined herself to the
inevitable, of accepting the personal disasters that befell her, that
she had decided to accept this, she would sacrifice her own
happiness to that of her daughter. Yet the maternal instinct told
her she had to be sure, really sure, that by sacrificing her own
happiness she was not sacrificing too the happiness of her daughter.

"You say I'm an idealist," Mrs. Rutland said. "And of course
you're right. I am an idealist. I see the village in a different light
because as you say I'm detached. I'm not involved. I see its
history, I see its spiritual quality. I see all the things you can't
see because you're in the pool swimming whilst I'm on the edge
watching. You're too busy living to catch the value of life."

"If you'd lived the way I've lived," Gerald said. "You'd take
the view I took."

"Not necessarily," she said. "People live in the same spot
for century upon century. And there develops in them an instinct
that attaches them to that spot. So that regardless whether living
conditions are good or not something instinctive tells them this
is their home and this is where they should stay."

"We're living in the age of the mechanical tree lifter," Gerald
said. "That lifts a tree out of the ground roots and all and plants
that tree somewhere else. And what a mechanical device can do
to trees change and bureaucracy'll do to the human race."

"But you say I'm an idealist because I love certain qualities
in the village that you don't see. Yet you too are an idealist — as
much an idealist as I am. You want to leave the village because
by leaving the village you'll find the meaning to life. But how do
you suppose you'll do that?"

"By living," Gerald said. "Simply by living."

"And you think by moving from your environment you'll be
free from it. Because you've just said yourself you'll never be free.
You'll find people in cities are too cloistered; they live too much
in a jungle of stone to be other than stone themselves. And when

458

you move you'll never understand their ways; just as they'll never understand yours. Then you'll feel the draw of your environment — like a magnet pulling you back."

"I don't think so," Gerald said. "Once I leave I leave for good."

"But what will you do. Where will you work?"

"I've been offered a post by Atkin, the colliery manager. He says I can have any job I like. I name it and he'll see that I get it."

"Then it better be a good post. And with prospects. Because as you say we live in a modern age. And a mother has the right to expect the best for her daughter. She has the right to hope that her husband will provide her not only with a family but with a house and car. All the amenities of the age in which we live. So you'd have to be prepared to work hard."

"I'm not frightened of hard work if that's what you think."

"But you agree by marrying Barbara you'd be going up in the world and my daughter would be coming down?"

"What you mean really is that though you love the village, you idealize the people, the houses in which we live, you're not keen on marrying your daughter to someone who lives in them. You'll fight to keep them from being pulled down; you'll spend your energies to keep them standing; but you shudder at the thought of your daughter living in one of them."

"But you're not staying in the village. You're going to live in the town."

"Which from your point of view is just as bad. Since I'm taking her away anyway."

"You forget it's always been understood my daughter would take over the business interests once I had retired. Ours is a family business in case you didn't know; it was built up by my father and mother; I kept it going through the long years of war; I'm fighting for it now, just as I'm fighting for the village. And you can't expect me after all this time to be happy at seeing the sole heir taken from me. And not only taken from me but deprived of a life of security just to go with a man who doesn't really know what he's looking for."

Gerald was accustomed to those he attacked shrinking from him not returning the fire. He looked across at Barbara. She sat without speaking, cold in her seat, looking down at the white coffee cups and pot before her on the table. She had herself ruth-lessly attacked her mother, but it was only when she heard the bitter ruthless words of another that she understood the effect her own must have had. She toyed nervously with the gold-chained cross around her neck, feeling the warm flush of blood and sun to her cheeks, not daring either to catch the eye of Gerald or her mother lest by their gaze they ask her to take sides. And she did not want to take sides. For she did not know whose side she should choose. She was determined to marry Gerald for she felt she saw with him a life without monotony or routine, not an ordered life nor a contented one either, but turbulent and enriched with excite-ment. Yet she wanted too this closeness with her mother, this intimacy, she wanted this new-found security, this new found content. So that she was glad when the telephone rang and she was able to leap up and enter the house to answer it, leaving the shell-fire to continue overhead.

"Then marry her into money," Gerald said. "As I've always expected you to do. Because at the bottom of your heart that's what you want. Because probably that's how you got your money in the first place. Because you're so old-fashioned you haven't got the instinct for survival. If you'd had you'd have changed your ways long ago."

"We'll survive," Mrs. Rutland said. "By maintaining the traditions of the past."

"Which shows how old-fashioned you are. Just how dead you are. As dead as the village, as dead as its people. Yet you won't lie down, that's your trouble. But you'll have to lie down eventually. Because change and progress'll make you lie down. This part of the world's modernizing itself quickly; it's hurrying pell-mell into the future. It won't wait for corpses like you who hanker for the past."

"You think we're all dead?"

"As dead as the village," Gerald repeated. "As dead as the dodo."

"And Barbara too?"

"Barbara! She's like the rest of your class. Useless, utterly useless. With no backbone, no spine. No guts to go on. That's why you want to marry her into money. That's why you want security. Because she's incapable of looking after herself, because she wouldn't know what an idea was never mind a thought. Marry

460

her! She wouldn't be any good to me even if I did. She'd be a milestone round my neck. Something that'd drag me down rather than buoy me up."

Barbara called from the doorway to say the telephone was for her mother. Mrs. Rutland looked at Gerald, paused to reply and thought better of it. There was crimson to her cheeks, a quiver to her lips, and a suggestion of tears to her eyes; she was taken aback not only by the harshness and cruelty of Gerald's words but by the bashfullness of her own; but there was to her jaw a line of determination and finality which suddenly made Gerald regret what he had said. She left to take the call, stumbling self-consciously on the grass, and Gerald looked around the garden for what he knew to be the last time. He had ruined everything. His temper had defeated him. The temper he tried so hard to control but like the wind was uncontrolable. The words they had used he knew meant nothing. It was the clash of temperament that meant all. The sun had sunk still further till now it edged gold the restless tips of the fir trees, the light seemed whiter in the leaves of the poplars, he saw the same spirit rippling through the foliage, and despite his anger, his flamed nerve-ends, he regretted the peace he had found and lost, the peace that might have been his for all time. He realized now that probably he might have inherited this house and this property, this quietude and content, so that he might never have had to leave the village, he might never have had to face the indifference of the town.

But his words had changed the course of his life, his anger had thrust him back to the class to which he knew he belonged. He had tried to rise above that class and had been beaten back, he had tried to bridge the gap between his world and theirs, but he had found the chasm too wide, the abyss too deep. He thought of his past, his origins, his inferiority, and was amazed at the audacity which had even brought him through the gates never mind into the house. He recalled his earlier thoughts, that he would never marry Barbara and he realized now how true they were. But then he reflected what did he care? Regardless of Barbara, regardless of her mother, he still had the future, he still had the promise of a job from Atkin. He could still go away and start again. That would always, he reflected, be his comfort, that no matter what happened he would still have the future, he would resolutely close his face to the past, a past which he felt belonged to others not to

461

him. He rose from his chair and moved towards the house. He had left his coat on the chair and probably but for that would not have bothered even to say goodbye. He would have walked through the garden and left by the little white gate leading to the road.

"Going so soon?" Mrs. Rutland asked.

She stood by the window with the phone, hand over the mouth-piece so that the caller would not hear what she had said.

"There's no reason why I should stay," Gerald said.

"On the contrary. I have something to tell you."

He took his coat from the chair over which he had informally placed it and slipping it on his shoulders straightened his tie. If he had to leave then leave he would; but he was determined to do it, if not in a blaze of glory, at least in a manner of grace and polite-ness; he wanted to show them that though he had been born poor he did not intend to stay poor the rest of his life. He might even shake her hand and so withdraw in a formal manner. He might even bow stiffly. Barbara was not in the sitting room when he sought his coat but probably out front examining the roses to the trellis; or perhaps now that she was a woman she had taken refuge in a woman's tears, weeping upstairs in her room. He tried to listen for her tread on the floorboards, he half-hoped she would make one last appearance before he left; but when she did not he told himself that it did not matter, that nothing mattered except the future. He waited by the door and watched Mrs. Rutland put down the phone and come smiling towards him.

"I've decided it'll be all right. You can get engaged tomorrow if you like."

Gerald opened his mouth to say how much of a hypocrite he thought she really was.

"Never mind the apologies. I understand. You have the temperament of your brother and the courage of your father. And it's good to see a young man who can still have cause to be angry. Probably you'll be just what Barbara needs. Someone with a little force and strength of character."

"But I don't think I could possibly get engaged tomorrow."

"Then keep to your original plan. Get engaged at Christmas."

They came out again to the garden and he felt the fresh warmth of the sun to his face, he saw the spirit of life through the poplars and realized that after all this spirit might be his. They walked across the lawn and under the shadow of the chestnut trees, up the dusty sun-speckled path threaded with roots till they reached the little white gate at the end of the grounds. The grass was firm beneath his feet, he kicked aside a twig with the toe of his shoe; she had engaged his arm as they walked up the path, he had smelt to his nostrils the fragrance of her perfume, and felt himself roused as he had whilst sitting opposite sipping coffee. He felt courage to put his arm round her shoulder and press her breast to his. But standing by the gate, looking down towards the house, seeing Barbara coming out into the garden, he felt a little embarrassed, a little ashamed, and tried as best he could to disengage his arm.

"We're past the age, of course, when a mother lays down the conditions for her daughter's marriage. But if there's a favour you could do me I'd be very much obliged."

"And what's that?" Gerald asked.

"You don't agree with the strike, I know; you think it's foolish to support it. But there are people in the village who have a different view. A view they sincerely hold."

"And I respect them for it," Gerald said.

"Of course you do. Still, you're the brother of the man leading the strike. And you do work in the colliery office."

"What's that got to do with it?"

"There's many an official who might see the connection, who might whisper it back to area office."

"So my promise is?"

"That no matter what happens you'll do nothing to jeopardise this strike. That you'll not use the influence you have on your brother to bring the men back to the surface."

Gerald heard the anxiety in her voice and saw the anxiety in her eyes. He smiled and wanted to laugh. He felt the rapid beat of his heart and recalled the anger of a moment ago; but as with all unstable characters his emotions could quickly change and his temper cool. He had believed, as his quick mind raced ahead, that one of the conditions of his future marriage would be that he stay and fight for the village, that his love for Barbara would conflict with his desire to be free, his hatred of the village with his yearning for a life he believed was to be lived beyond its confines. Yet what she asked was so simple, so easy to give, there was little else to do but laugh. Barbara moved towards them through the trees and the relief on her face was the relief that he felt to his own inside. And he realized that despite all he had told himself, all that

463

he would have himself believe, he really did care for her, he really did love her. And probably under the influence of that love he would have made any promise, any compromise, to keep her. But the one that he had to make was so absurd that he laughed again.

"That's the least of your worries," he said. "I'd not go down and settle the strike for a pension."

49

"I know someone who'll end the strike for me," Atkin said. "And he won't require a pension to do it either."

"And who might that be?" Donnolly asked.

"I'll tell you in a moment. Only I'd like to hear your views about the strike."

Atkin stood with hands in his pockets in the living room of Donnolly's home. It was a bungalow set on a hill overlooking the river and valley; the estate on which it was built had been the estate of a long line of peers who had made their fortunes from coal; they could trace their pedigree to the first days of the young industry when men and women were lured from the land, the land that they loved, and sent to work and die in the first village pit. That was centuries ago, but through the ages the family had garnered for itself a reputation of resistance to change which made it liked and respected by every coal-owning family in the country. When there was a demand for a general advance in wages the gentry locked the men out; if the men threatened to strike over objectionable bonds of service the gentry let them; if there was a slump in the coal trade and money could only be made by selling coal cheaper than your neighbour the men were forced not only to accept the ten per cent reduction the company asked but also an extended working week. And when better ventilation was advised by engineers who studied the causes of an explosion that killed seventy people the gentry waited fifty years before the safety measures were carried out.

The class war continued right into the twentieth century, when the tide of Bolshevik revolution lapped our very shore, as one of the lords put it, the local gentry were foremost in advocating a struggle to the death, of locking the men out, turning their families from colliery houses, enlisting special baton-swinging constables to keep the peace which only the constables themselves were breaking. Hauling miners before the courts for throwing stones, break-

465

ing windows, stealing coal from private property — the property being the local pit-heap — fining and imprisoning them, the gibet being no longer fashionable, as bandits who repeatedly broke the peace. Mercifully for the gentry, sterility and death duties had all but wiped them out before the dread New Year's Day of 1947 when the wrongs of centuries were redressed, when the gentry and the rest of their kind were consigned to oblivion, thus being spared the hideous sight of miners with cars, returning home from pit-head baths clean like other men.

The principles by which fortunes had been made nullified by a simple act of Parliament.

No-one knew his history better than Donnolly and when the estates were sold it pleased him to think the local Labour party could purchase a plot and on it build a house for the local MP, and that he the son of a common miner, born of a generation of common miners, should bring his bones to rest on the land of his father's oppressors. It pleased him to think that the view they enjoyed, the peace and serenity of the countryside, could now be vested in him. He had been doing a little spadework in the garden when Atkin had arrived, a sweat shone to his brow, and the brown eyes shining from the brown skin seemed deeper and more penetrating. He had taken a handkerchief from his pocket and rubbed the dust and sweat from his hands. The spade flashed once more into the earth and he ushered Atkin into the sitting room. The room was cooler following the warmth of the evening but the sun through the glass of the long angular window rinsed yellow Atkin's cheeks as he paused to look out.

"The strike's finished," Donnolly said. "It never had a chance since the time it started."

"You may think it's finished," Atkin said. "But you're not down there with the men."

"And it's lucky for ye that I'm not," Donnolly said. "Ye'd not have seen me stand for the tripe that's been pushed into them o'er the last month, I can tell ye."

"You've seen more just strikes than you've seen pints of beer," Atkin said. "And you stand there and say you believe this one's tripe."

" 'Cause ye knaa and I knaa the men have as much chance now as they had in 1926. They were forced to strike then 'cause the vested interests wanted them to strike. Now the men are fightin'

466

for the same reason — 'cause it's the vested interest in the village that wants them to fight. And fight that hard and long people'd have to sit up and take notice."

"Ye mean the strike wouldn't have lasted a week if Mrs. Rutland hadn't stepped in?"

"And if ye hadn't helped her by slyin' in food afore the Coal Board got to knaa what kind o' food it was."

"The men stayed down in protest against the closure of their colliery," Atkin said. "And because the same day they were told of the destruction of their village."

"Granted. But they went down wi' the intention o' stickin' it out for as long as they could — as long as it would take them to get a few concessions — but their idea o' duration was three days and not thirty one. And even then they might have got their concessions if the vested interest hadn't stepped in with its propaganda and its stews and hot pots."

"You talk as though it had all been planned beforehand. As though it never happened spontaneously."

Donnolly grunted the way he did in the House of Commons when he heard a man who had never been down a pit discussing the nationalized industries.

"Ye'll be sayin' next it all came about through love o' the village."

"It all blew up on the spur of the moment," Atkin protested. "When the men heard the news."

"Listen," Donnolly said. "And I'll tell ye somethin' that ye on yer side o' the industry knaa nowt about. The most famous stay-down strike in history took place at Fife in Scotland. It's a long time ago now, but it doesn't make it the less significant for that; but when the first district union was formed, the men decided to hold a stay-down strike to enforce on the management an eight-hour day. The management weren't accustomed to all the men actin' together and so there was nowt they could dee but agree. And that was how it came about we had the first eight-hour day in the country. But the stay-down strike didn't last thirty days. It hardly lasted thirteen."

"Just because the strike here's longer doesn't make it any the less just."

"Aye, ye're reet there. But the fact is Lenin was reet when he said the British ruling classes were the cleverest in the world;

467

ye can see it any day o' the week on a national scale. But for the last month I've been seeing it reet under me nose in me own constituency. Ye talk of principle, ye talk o' spontaneity. But ye knaa as well as I dee that the motivatin' force of all this palava comes from the surface. From the people whose interest is as economic as the Coal Board's."

The yellow rinse of sunlight to Atkin's face deepened as the sun slipped lower. Just as in the early morning a haze rose up from the river, clinging to the sides of valley, so in the evening the same haze rose again, obscuring the trees, the water, but not concealing them altogether. He could see the silver of the sun upon the water, the little brown rat's teeth where the water nourished upon rocks, the green plumes of oak and chestnut, the little speckles of light and shade cast upon the dried earth. The tranquillity of the country was all around him, a tranquillity that seemed to mock the violence, the privation of forty-seven men who could endure every form of hardship for the sake of principle; that seemed to say that in order to live sunlight was enough. But some instinct in Atkin told him sunlight was not enough, could never be enough, and for the first time that evening Atkin felt a strange stirring, a vague uneasiness he attributed to the uncertainties of the future and not to any impending disaster. He tried to take his mind from this by concentrating hard on what Donnolly had said.

"You surprise me," Atkin said. "You're supposed to be the party that has the interests of the men at heart."

"So we have. But we've also got to bear in mind the interests o' the country as a whole. We're against restrictive practices in our party, just as we're against unofficial strikes. But ye knaa, what we're discussin' here isn't the rise and fall o' Highhill — romantic as that might seem to ye — we're discussin' the rise and fall o' King Cole. The way people talk ye'd think it was sentimentality that brought coal to be the country's major fuel. It was never nowt o' the sort. It was 'cause about six hundred years back the price o' wood trebled o'er and above the rise in the cost o' livin'."

"And what's that got to do with our present situation?"

"Wood priced itself out of the market. And coal achieved its prominence not 'cause o' any attachment to the owld coal fire. So just as price and abundance were responsible for bringin' coal to the fore o'er the centuries so price and abundance'll be responsible for its decline — the price and abundance o' oil. Neebody'll buy coal when they can get onto a good thing cheaper."

"And the human situation. That's what we have to consider."

"Let's keep on our historical perspective for the minute. Ye knaa Newcastle was always the centre o' the world's coal trade, but most o' the coal was mined in Durham not Northumberland. And reet through till the end o' the nineteenth century there was more coal mined in Durham than in all the other English coalfields put together. But now the county's having to pay for that eminence — 'cause now the county's worked out. Now the coalfield's dead."

"And your idea is that if the coalfield's dead the people had better get out or die with it?"

"That's the idea o' bureaucracy. It's not my idea."

"All the same," Atkin said. "You seem to agree with it."

Atkin watched Donnolly roll up the sleeves of his old gardening shirt and smiled at the forceful belligerent way in which he expressed his views. Parliament had by now gone into its summer recess, Donnolly had returned to his house and his constituency, he had as he usually did in summer ceased his Saturday surgery, and now most of his time was spent reading the newspapers, catching up on the latest political literature, and spending what was left of his day working in his garden. Like Winston Churchill laying his bricks the time in the garden was well spent, since Donnolly was able to consider not only the problems of his constituency but what he considered the most pressing problem of all, the strike of the miners at Highhill. He had not at first wished to intervene, since being a former miner himself he had considered the strike of the men to be a just strike against the uncertainties of the future. But after the first three or four days, as with the management and union, he had found affairs taken from his hands so that he could not intervene even had he wished. In fact, the more he looked at the strike the more he saw it in the terms of the class struggle, and the more he resented the arbitrary interference of the local ruling classes, Mrs. Rutland and Arnold Atkin.

Nevertheless, after thirty-one days, he realized that the strike could not be broken without the consent of either of these people. The men could never return to the surface unless they were urged to do so by the people who for a month had kept them down. The people who for a month had manipulated the men in their own self-interest. Donnolly knew of course that he had no right to criticise the self-interest of others, because he himself had till now

469

been motivated by the self-interest of the local Labour party. His party on a national basis had to support the Coal Board because the Board was intent on making the industry pay, of streamlining and modernizing till it became a sound economic unit. The local party could not nevertheless miss the opportunity of pummelling its opponents for its lack of humanity and the slow inexorable desuetude of human rights which it saw in the high-handed manner the news had been given to the men. But intervention? The party was always reluctant to intervene in any unofficial strike because of the odium it knew was attached to such strikes; but since the manner in which the men continued to sit it out had attracted the sympathy of the country, Donnolly had been advised to intervene at the most propitious moment so that some of this sympathy could be drawn to the Labour party when eventually the men came up.

But how was Donnolly to decide what his party considered a propitious moment? He knew that outside the village it was considered that the strike was running out of steam, that the men were finding it harder and harder to justify the duration of their protest to the outside world, newsmen were running out of original copy and therefore the public were running out of interest. Donnolly understood that the men had never meant to stay down as long as they had; they had counted on a short sharp strike with at least some of their demands met after only a few days; but once the press had moved in and food began to be provided on a large scale then the men could not return to the surface any more than the Coal Board could offer the concessions demanded. Now everything revolved around the question of face. The men could not return to the surface and admit defeat nor could the Board allow them to return victorious. A compromise had therefore to be found and Donnolly felt that of all the interested parties he alone was capable of finding it.

He did not like Atkin because he considered him to be the force behind the strike. He believed that had it not been for Atkin there would not have been a strike at all; by that he did not mean it was Atkin's negligence that had brought about the closure of the colliery; but that since following the meetings at the institute and club Atkin must have known the kind of strike impending and should have seen to it that it did not occur. He should have locked the men out rather than let them into the pit. In this opinion he was governed by his dislike and not by his logic. For to lock the men out would have made Atkin no better than the coal owners, he would never have been able to justify himself to area, and above all it would still not have prevented the strike because the men would have stayed out on the surface. But though Atkin was manager in a nationalized industry Donnolly could not get from his head the fact he was a member of the ruling classes and as such had an instinct for the plotting Donnolly associated with these classes. He did not see there was no advantage to Atkin from the strike, indeed from his open support of the men, the hostile attitude to the management, he had condemned his own future, and rather than gaining from the strike he had lost.

Now he was galled by the fact that he had to rely on Atkin if ever he was to get the men back to the surface.

"Anyway, ye were tellin' us about the person who might be able to end the strike."

"I said I knew someone who would go down and end it. And he wouldn't require a pension to do it either."

"Well, spit it out, don't keep us in suspense. Who is it and what can he do that we cannot?"

"You still haven't told me why you think the strike's finished?"

"D'ye never read the papers? They've not yet had a Gallup poll but ye can see for yersel' public opinion is beginning to weaken. I knaa for a fact that when the evening paper publishes its next list o' contributions towards the strike they'll be down by half o' what they were last time. And certain o' the right wing press — the capitalist press — which never gave the strike their support anyway, they're sayin' now the men should be sacked by the Board and expelled from the union."

"And who d'you think'll ever take notice of them?" Atkin asked.

"Once public sympathy starts to weaken," Donnolly said. "Ye'll see, it'll not take authority long to put the finger on."

Atkin with his attachment to the strike did not like to admit to himself that what Donnolly had said was true; but as manager of the colliery he was aware that even at area office opinion was beginning to harden; there was talk of considering the men as tresspassers not honoured guests, of waging upon them what one official described as a war of attrition; and there was even talk of sending down a mines inspector to see how many regulations were being broken. Ray had refused to allow down either cigarettes or alcohol, but since this was not a gassy pit, and since no great security measures had been enforced by the pickets, cigarettes had no doubt filtered through the drift mouth, the soups had for long now been laced with brandy, paid for from the newspaper fund, and even then, despite these infringements, had the Board really wanted to be tough all they had to do was verify that men were sleeping in the pit. Once this was proved then all those on a stay-down strike could be dismissed since this was an offence against the regulations. The Board had no wish to do this, but as in all giant organizations differing personalities held differing opinions, and now it was those who believed in more forthright measures that were beginning to hold sway.

Atkin was still convinced the possibility remained that the men would if necessary stay-down till Christmas, but now he was less convinced of its probability. Probably their physique and stamina could withstand such a long siege, but it could only withstand it if food continued to be provided in the same quantities, attended by the same publicity, which satisfied not only their morale but also their egoes. But as Donnolly had said publicity was waning, the strike had gone on so long it was no longer understood by families on the surface, of rationing, of a drabness they never wanted to see again; but since this drabness, this rationing was not extended throughout the country it was all the harder to bear. So that as the novelty wore off wives began asking the same question that had queried the minds of the men before they conditioned themselves to the cold and the damp. They began asking why they should be singled out, why their colliery should be destroyed and not the colliery of some other village.

But to Atkin as to Donnolly it was clear that if a break was to come it had to come from the surface. It was clear that the men would stay down the pit till they were told from bank to come up. What then to do? He was aware of the interest which Donnolly was taking in the strike, aware too that he had been in contact with area officials; he guessed that probably he had received instructions to intervene, but that probably too his influence would not be sufficient to bring the strike to an end. Atkin himself could do nothing in his official capacity because he had neither the confidence of the men nor the confidence of the Board, the Board itself would be reluctant to offer any new concessions, Mrs. Rutland

472

would do nothing, absolutely nothing, and therefore the stalemate would be prolonged. It would be prolonged till the men fell into a state of disorganization or till there was a total capitulation. And with pressure from their wives, with the supply of food likely to be rationed, since this too was now paid from the newspaper fund, it seemed this was the time for Atkin to utilize his secret weapon, to produce the ace that all this time he had held up his sleeve.

"I wouldn't agree with you that the strike never had a chance," Atkin said. "But I would agree with you that now it's finished."

"O' course it's finished," Donnolly said. "I'm glad at least somebody shows a bit o' sense. A modicum as I might put it in the House."

"But what about the struggle for the village?"

"What d'ye mean — struggle for the village?"

50

"Just what I say," Atkin said. "The fight for the colliery might be over, but what about the fight for the village?"

Donnolly paused over a writing table set in an alcove next to the fireplace; on the table were various hansards and mining publications which reflected his two major interests. There were also several pads of canary yellow foolscap paper which Donnolly bought specially from legal stationers in London. He liked each day to read a few speeches that he himself had heard in the House, he had watched carefully their delivery, and if he considered them really good he made a note to copy them during the summer recess. This he believed improved his own style. He was aware his manner in the House of Commons was sketchy and, in the case of Burke several members slipped quietly out when he rose to his feet. There were rarely more than five or six members in the House, he spoke always on constituency matters, and therefore he spoke to be read and not to be heard. His speeches were never given a line in the London papers but nevertheless made ample copy in the Northeast. And with a little sub-editorial advice here and there he had ceased making references to "astronomical phenomena" and "hyperbolic hypotheses".

He did not even make them now in conversation.

"Now that's a different matter," Donnolly said. "If it had been a question o' that from the start I might have subscribed to it. 'Cause there I see a chance o' success — and a very good chance at that. I could even use the bit influence I've got, get onto the minister of Housing and Local Government. Get onto the local authorities. Aye, with a bit o' effort I think we'd be able to keep the village on the map."

"The question is how," Atkin said. "How?"

"I suppose ye divin't dee any gardenin' or fishin'. It's remarkable how it clears the mind o' nonsense and makes ye get down to the essentials o' life. Ever since the recess started — apart from

474

that bad spell o' weather we had — I've been in the garden every day. And every day things have come to us about the colliery and village. And everyday it's crept up in me mind that somebody sometime is ganna put the question ye've just put."

Atkin's impatience affected his concentration and he had difficulty in carefully following what Donnolly said. Yet he was aware too of Donnolly's hostility, his antagonism, and realized he had better curb his impatience if he wanted to make him an ally. He watched Donnolly take his pipe and pouch of tobacco and fumbling for a match stand in that pensive mood which reflects deep thought but which Atkin had learnt from experience only disguised unsureness and lack of certainty how to proceed. But in fact Donnolly did know how to proceed. Only he wanted to advance in his best House of Commons manner. He lit the pipe and inhaled the dry tangy smoke, closing his eyes in brooding fashion, lobbing the dead match upon the unlit fire and clenching his teeth round the stem of the pipe before proceeding.

"It's like the lines o' Tores Vedras," he said. "We have three lines o' defence. The first line is that once ye've arranged to call off the strike I'll get onto the local council and they'll hold an enquiry into the exact state o' the houses to see if they really must come down. O' course I'm not in any doubt about the result — it's bound to be negative anyway — but apart from the fact that it'll give us a bit o' time it'll show the village people that we mean business and that we aim to get things done."

"How will it show them that if the result's negative?"

"The result has nowt to dee with it," Donnolly said. "But action's like justice — not only must it be done — it must be seen to be done. That was the whole trouble wi' Wishart. He sat on his backside and did nowt, and wondered why it was men took things into their own hands. If he'd had a bit o' sense in his head he'd have realized he'd have achieved more from quiet diplomacy than the men'll ever achieve in a month long strike."

"All right," Atkin said. "That's one line of defence. What's the second?"

"The second is that I'll persuade the local authority to rephase their plannin' — that instead o' knockin' down all the houses at once they knock down only the worst. That'll help save the village for a few years 'cause it means the council'll have to allocate to other families the houses they're rebuildin' in the valley for the people o' Highhill. And by the time they get round to buildin' other houses — what wi' the restrictions this government puts on them — years'll pass, and by then we'll have thowt o' somethin' else, and that way the village'll never die."

"But once they close the colliery the village'll never be the same anyway."

"Ye mean all the families that'll opt to move to the midlands?"

"And the fact there'll be no work in the village for the people who stay."

"That'll not be a problem in this modern age," Donnolly said. "The English language doesn't change much o'er the years, but it's changin' an awful lot quicker now wi' the introduction o' all these American words. And one that's come out lately is commuter. It means ye work in one place and ye live in another. And that's what people in the village'll be deein' — they'll live in the village and commute to other areas."

"They'll soon get sick of that."

"Wait till I tell ye what our third line o' defence is."

"And what's that?"

"The buildin' up of a new village on the foundations o' the old. Sounds easy, ye knaa, but it's not. This area's not one scheduled for redevelopment. I'd have to belabour the government in the House and attack their regional policies — or rather their lack o' regional policies. And what with all the publicity the strike's caused maybe I could even get one o' the front bench to put up a speech — naturally we'd have to keep the pot boilin', but wi' ye and Mrs. Rutland that shouldn't be difficult, should it?"

Donnolly was aware of Atkin's fondness for drink and therefore crossed to his cabinet and poured for him a brandy. Atkin watched the warm gentle liquid pour from the bottle and for some reason recalled the brandy he had had before leaving; he recalled his glance in the mirror, the nervous uncertain face that twitched back at him, and again he felt uneasy, again he felt something was wrong. Donnolly did not pour for himself a drink but handed the glass to Atkin. Atkin felt the coolness of the glass to his fingers and immediately felt reassured. He recalled that now he was a new man, now he was rid of Mrs. Bousefield, soon he would be rid of the colliery, and therefore his life would begin again. He sipped gently the brandy and felt that it cleared his head. It allowed him to see things in perspective. It allowed him to visualize what could and could not be done, to see clearly the possibilities Donnolly outlined and to understand better their defects. The brandy burnt at his tongue and slipped towards his throat.

"The one thing that strikes me," Atkin said. "Is that it's all so negative."

"Whereas ye're all for positive action?"

"The kind the men have made to save the colliery."

"But our aim's to save the village not destroy it. The colliery wasn't quite dead, ye knaa, when the Coal Board announced its demise, but it died soon enough once the men sat down in the pit. That's where positive action gets ye. Again, ye've got to live by reality. We can sit here and dream up all the plans in the universe, but if none o' them work we might as well throw them out the window."

"But surely there's something we can do. Something more aggressive?"

"Only after we've safeguarded the future of the village."

"But what about Mrs. Rutland?" Atkin said. "What shall we do about her?"

"What about her?" Donnolly asked.

"In anything that concerns the village we'll need Mrs. Rutland. And if I know her she'll not want to fight for the village till the last drop of sweat's been wrung on the fight to save the colliery."

"Then ye'll have to get the men back to the surface in such a way that it'll look as if it's on their own steam they're comin' back. Or better still throw the responsibility on the shoulders o' that contact o' your'n. So that if there's any blame to be apportioned it falls on him."

The only person who could go down the pit and urge a return to the surface was of course Gerald Holt. This was the secret weapon, the ace that Atkin held up his sleeve. And it was possible events could be so arranged it would appear that Gerald had gone down the pit of his own accord and on his own initiative. He was indifferent to the fate of the colliery and was therefore unlikely to mind. And when Mrs. Rutland chided Atkin, as chide him she would, he would declare word had got back to area office through no fault of his own of the relationship between the two Holts, and that area by offering Gerald a handsome post at some other colliery had enticed him to persuade the men return to the surface. Gerald probably would not mind that either. Atkin knew that the presence of Gerald alone would not be sufficient to bring the men back; concessions, even if only face-saving concessions would have to be offered; Ray would have to be convinced that his strike could not possibly succeed, and probably as part of the persuasion drawn into the campaign to save the village.

Atkin placed the brandy glass on top of the cabinet and picked with a finger at his brow. He saw it all perfectly in his mind. He would have to get the concessions from the Board; he would not tell them of his intention to leave, merely explain that by making one huge effort he might be able to bring the men back to the surface without the ruthless tactics that at the moment were being bandied about. It might take several days persuading the Board to offer the kind of face-saving concessions that would be required, but by explaining if such concessions could be offered, not only would they be acceptable to the men in the pit they would also be acceptable to Mrs. Rutland on the surface. The Board might then see this as a serious effort at compromise and not merely a propaganda move to provide copy for the press. The Board would also have to be convinced of Atkin's sincerity, but in this he would not utilize the support of Donnolly; then when the strike was over, when the men were back to the surface, when the Board were beginning to revise their opinion of Atkin, and even perhaps the foolishness of assigning him to an insignificant drift, Atkin would show his independence, he would make his final flamboyant gesture and resign.

Yet the clarity of the brandy told him it was all too neat, too pat; it reminded him of his plans ten years ago for the colliery, how little by little these plans had shredded and disintegrated; so that he was afraid the plans he had now, the visions, they too would disintegrate. He did not know what would happen once the fighting was over, once the shouting and the tumult died, the princes and the kings returned; all that he knew was that of now he was committed, his decision had been made, he would let himself go, let his nature go, his personality. He thought of Mrs. Rutland. He recalled what Mrs. Bousefield had said of her. What she had suggested. That he felt for her more than he was prepared to admit. And to him it seemed more important than ever that it should look as if he had no hand in the return of the men to the surface. That it should all rest on the shoulders of Gerald Holt. He turned to Donnolly and saw how carefully he was being scrutinized, how anxiously Donnolly awaited his decision. How he too was eager for the battle they wanted to see soon commenced.

"And ye'll fix it wi' the lad that'll not need a pension?" Donnolly asked.

"I'll fix it," Atkin said. "And in such a way it'll look as if he'd done it on his own initiative."

51

"There's no doubt about it," the inspector said. "It's arson all right."

"The fire's hardly out," Atkin said. "How can you prove that?"

The inspector jerked his head back to the house. A beam was dropped from the upstairs to the lawn and a new mist of damp smoke rose from the grass. "The fire started in the loft. Then it blew off the roof and sent it tumbling into the passageway. That's how it spread so quickly through the house."

"It doesn't prove it's arson because it started in the loft."

"We found a pair of stepladders at the bottom of the stairs. Scorched to pieces, of course. And a couple of tins of paraffin — empty. They'd have exploded had they been full. Appears the paraffin was sprinkled around the upstairs floor and also the loft. And a liberal sprinkling at that, I should say."

The inspector stood with his hands behind his back, now and again inclining his head and raising one of his hands to pull at his ear.

"I can't understand," Atkin said. "It's all so pointless."

"Not so pointless as that," the inspector said. "Obviously it's the work of someone who's organized. And the only people organized are those on strike. So, the first thing we'll do is get their leader to the surface. We've a valid excuse now, more than a valid excuse. And once he's here we'll give him a proper grilling."

"And what do you prove if you do that?"

"He'll not be in such good shape after his month down there. It shouldn't be too difficult to find out who's at the bottom of it. And of course once he's back to the surface it'll not be long before the others are following."

"But because it happens to be arson doesn't say it originated in the pit."

"It originated somewhere," the inspector said. "And that's

as good a hotbed as any."

"I can't believe it's true," Atkin said. "They're as much against violence as anybody."

"And what about the one that came out the pit the other day," the inspector said. "With the broken arm. Broken in two places. Said he had fallen on a rock. Only the doctor reckoned it was caused by an instrument. Probably a pick. Of course we tried to take a statement, but nothing came of it. Only don't tell me they're against violence because I don't believe it."

The firemen worked around them, plodging through pools of their own making, flecks of water glinting on their helmets; water swirled too around the feet of Atkin and Gerald and the inspector as they stood on the path, dabbing at the tops of their shoes, the turn-ups of their trousers. And around them too was the heavy soused smell of the fire that would permeate for many a day not only the village but also their clothes. Atkin scratched at his eyebrow as he did when preoccupied and over the inspector's heavy shoulder saw the flashing blue cone that topped his police car, the heavy snout-noses of the two remaining fire engines. He saw too the face of Gerald Holt. Gerald had lingered longer than the others, long after the evening cold had replaced the heat of the fire, the chill striking at his chest as he stood shivering on the path. But why Gerald lingered he himself did not know. Perhaps because for the second time in his recent life he felt sympathy for another person, because Atkin had loved the colliery yet it had been taken from him, because he had loved this house, yet they had burnt it as a torch.

And because again Atkin had been rejected by the people of the village. He was aware they had not telephoned the fire brigade, he was aware they had not formed a human chain, not even to extinguish the embers that fell from the roof to the lawn. Gerald did not believe there had been a conspiracy against this, merely that as a single mind all the village people had acted in the same fashion. Because they could not believe in Atkin as colliery manager. Because they could not believe in him as a man. Therefore, as others filtered away Gerald had stayed. He had stayed because he had wanted to show that at least someone had faith, someone had confidence, and at least someone would stand by and help. He watched the steam rise from the drenched embers, he saw through the burnt out husk the last blue plummets of smoke drifting over the railway lines towards the football field.

And he saw the visage of Atkin, blanched, showing the strain of decision and tension.

"It doesn't make sense to me," Atkin said. "All the same you can try. You're at perfect liberty to make any investigations you like. I'll even give you permission to go down the pit and interview Ray Holt. Only if I know Ray he'll want to be interviewed in the worst seam of all, eighteen inches high."

"And probably some fifty yards along it," Gerald said. "So you'll have to crawl in and crawl out."

"And even then I doubt whether you'll be able to make it stick. They're at least forty-seven men in the pit to vouch that he didn't do it. That never once has he left the pit. Probably you're right and probably they're all committing perjury. But you'll have a hard job proving it. Besides," Atkin added. "I've something to tell you."

Atkin took the arm of the divisional inspector and led him round the scorched crumbling walls to the back of the house. The leeks in his garden were still in their trench, only the trench was filled with water, ash had flaked upon the leaves, grey soggy ash that matched the colour of the whites, whites pale and liverished now like a diseased iris. The outhouse from where Bousefield had taken the stepladders and paraffin had not been exposed to the fire, but part of the solid outside structure had cracked from the house and tumbled upon its roof, so that the asphalt was charred with smouldering debris and broken granite. Granite and debris had flattened too the potato heads, the glass panes that protected a few frail raspberry shrubs were broken, the strawberry patch had been trampled underfoot by the lumbering brigade. So that with the glass, the water, the mud, the debris, the granite, the ash, Atkin looked again to the leeks, he thought how earnestly he had cultivated them, yet how with their destruction the pastime was so insignificant, so worthless and useless.

How it had all been for nothing.

Gerald on the path stared up at the blackened chimney gaunt against the sky, rising into the clear starlit evening, beyond the roof destroyed by fire or pulled down by firemen. Steam continued to rise from the smouldering furnishings cast out upon the mud of the lawn and through the gaping walls, through the hovering blue and white smoke, he could see kitchen lights twinkling from

482

houses beyond the football field, he could see doors still open and despite the cold men in shirt sleeves and women in pinafores framed in the doorway. He could also see Atkin discussing with the police inspector. Their faces reflected the earnestness of their conversation, they evidently reached some sort of agreement, for the inspector nodded, Atkin relaxed and placed his hands in his pockets, they paused together by the outhouse, Atkin brushing the flaking ash from his cuffs, the inspector a few drifting sparks from his shoulders. Together they walked around to the front of the house, past Gerald and towards the car of the inspector.

The inspector was driven off and Gerald was himself halfway down the drive when a second pair of headlamps settled upon him. He turned to stare into the lamps and immediately they were dipped. Atkin's car trundled down the drive and pulled alongside. Atkin leant across and opened the car door and Gerald slipped in beside him. He realized that since Atkin had nowhere that night to sleep probably he was on his way to find for himself an hotel and would drop Gerald off on the way. The smoke had smarted his eyes as he skirted the house with the inspector and now the rims were raw and the lids damp as he drove onto the road that led through the village. He did not speak to Gerald nor did he invite conversation. But instead of continuing along the road that would eventually lead to Gerald's part of the village, he turned left and drove on towards the summit of the hill. The street lighting reflected amber upon the tarmac and the tune of the engine changed as Atkin dropped gear to climb the hill. He stopped at the summit and opened the car door to step out.

"Thought maybe you'd like a breath of air to clear your lungs."

Gerald had no alternative but to step from the car and follow him into the field along the path that led to the concrete shell. He walked ahead of Gerald and Gerald could see the vapour of his breath rising ahead as he strode through grass already heavy with dew.

"The only way I could put the inspector off," Atkin said. "Was to tell him the strike was finished."

"How did that put him off?"

"Said the strike wouldn't last longer than a few more days. So any interviews he wanted to carry out could wait till the men got back. I said he could continue his investigations on the surface and if there was evidence that led to Ray to nab him as soon as he stepped out of the cage."

"That means my brother'll end up in gaol!"

"I doubt it," Atkin said. "The inspector'll not unearth the evidence."

"All the same, someone's responsible," Gerald said. "Someone's got to hold the can."

Atkin could feel the air fresh against his face, he could feel it fresh, untainted to his lungs, he could feel its coldness to his hands and wrists, his chest, so that for the first time he shivered, for the first time he realized how nippy it was. He paused at the shell and laid his hand upon the concrete. It was wet and cold to his palm. The valley lay before him and he could see the thin mist that garnished the valley floor, the lights at the other side of the valley, vague, indistinct, the rattle of tubs released from the cage of a colliery so distant, the sounds brought close with the stillness of the night. And despite the cold, despite the dew, there rose from the grass the same freshness, the same fragrance, the same sweet smell of the country, of herbs and flowers and dung, that cleansed his nostrils and thickened his blood, seeping into his movements, slowing down his thoughts to make him less capable of action.

"Oh, I know who's responsible all right," Atkin said. "I knew as soon as the inspector told me it was arson. There's only one person could have known about the paraffin in the outhouse and the bric-a-brac in the loft. Who'd have the nerve to sprinkle the whole show then leave the steps and tins for everyone to see."

"You mean Mrs. Bousefield?"

"Not Mrs. Bousefield."

"Surely not wor Alfie from the colliery office?"

"Not him either," Atkin said.

"That only leaves the son."

Atkin nodded. "The same one who broke Walton's arm in the pit. Cleaved at it with the head of a pick. Only because Walton pointed out to him the truth. The truth about me and his mother. That everyone's known for years, that probably he's known himself only never wanted to admit."

"So that's why he came back to the surface."

"To prove to himself it was true," Atkin said.

"But how d'you know it was him. That he really did break Walton's arm in the pit?"

"Because your father was delirious when they took him to hospital. They gave him a sedative to quieten down but before it had time to take effect he blurted it out before one of the nurses. Unknowingly, of course. She passed it on to me when I called by to see him."

"So you knew Bousefield was back to the surface," Gerald said. "You knew what was going to happen."

"I knew something was going to happen. I didn't know what."

"Anyway, since you know who did it, why don't you turn him over to the police."

"What makes you think I want to prosecute?" Atkin asked.

"But he burnt down your house. Your possessions."

"He burnt down the house of the Coal Board — I was only the tenant. And as for the possessions — they belong to the past. Let them die with the past. Besides, why should I want to prosecute? Tell the world why he did it, why he wanted to burn down the house. Because I was sleeping with his mother. Because he did it in righteous anger. And if he demands a jury the jury might condemn me and not him."

"But unless you do they'll pin it on my brother."

"They'll pin it on no-one till they have the evidence," Atkin said. "And there'll be forty-seven men in the pit to say Ray never left it. That he had no hand in it. They could of course go ahead and charge Ray and try the other forty-seven for perjury. But somehow I doubt it. I doubt it very much."

Gerald felt the cold more sharply and more cutting.

"You told the inspector the strike was finished," he said. "What d'you think he'll do when he finds out it's not?"

"He won't find out," Atkin said. "Because what I told him was true. The strike is finished. By this time next week the men'll be back to the surface."

"You mean they've declared their intention to come up?"

"No. I've declared my intention to send you down."

52

"What d'you want me to go down for?"

"To persuade them it's in their own interest to come up."

"But how d'you think I can do that? They've already said they'll come up for no-one."

"They've said they'll not come up for Wishart or the area secretary," Atkin corrected. "They've not said they'll not come up for you."

"They'll not come up for me either," Gerald said. "Unless I have concessions to offer. And how am I going to get them d'you think?"

"I'll arrange the concessions," Atkin said. "If that's all you're worried about."

"They'd have to be real concessions. Not just a face-saving formula."

"Don't worry your head about that. They'll be real concessions all right."

"But if you can get the concessions, why d'you need me. Why don't you go down and take the credit yourself?"

"Because they'll not trust me," Atkin said. "They'll not believe anything I say."

"What makes you think they'll believe me?"

"Because they respect and admire you. They think you're the one behind the strike anyway. Responsible for the tip-off in the first place, the food in the second. They reckon you're the one supplying the information. So that anything that comes from your mouth they'll believe. If it comes from mine they'll dismiss it as propaganda."

"Surely there's someone else who'll go down. Other than me?"

"There's only you," Atkin said. "Besides, the men respect you because you're a drinker. Because even though you work in the colliery office you're not above joining their company. And then there's the influence you're supposed to have with that brother of yours. How he followed you through school. How he followed you into **pubs.**"

"He might have looked up to me in the past," Gerald said. "He certainly doesn't look up to me now."

"It's no good wriggling," Atkin said. "You're the one to go down. I've already decided in my mind."

"But I can't go down," Gerald said. "Even if I wanted to."

Atkin raised his palm from the concrete and dabbed at the moist imprint with his fingers.

"And why is that?" he asked.

"Because I promised Mrs. Rutland I wouldn't go down. That I wouldn't lift a finger to bring this strike to an end."

"Why did you promise that?"

"Because I love her daughter. And because soon we're going to be married."

"And you mean she made that a condition."

"There aren't any conditions. Only she requested it of me and since I've never been committed to the strike, since I've not cared either way, it seemed an easy promise to give."

"But it's not the mother you're marrying," Atkin said. "It's the daughter."

"Only the daughter thinks the same as the mother. And as committed to the strike. So if I affront the one I affront the other."

Atkin had looked sharply at Gerald as he spoke, the lines heavy about his face, his eyes uplifted so that there was about him the impression of an owl. But now reflecting he stared down the hill towards the valley, he traced the road he had taken that evening from the house of the MP, he tried discerning the road that clung to the valley side, the road on which years previously Mrs. Rutland's husband had met his death. He had been happy driving up from the valley because he had made a decision, he had restored to his life a sense of purpose, he had disengaged himself from Mrs. Bousefield, he had worked out a plan that would end the strike and bring the men back to the surface, he had secured an ally in his desire to save the village, and together they had elaborated ideas that would achieve this aim. So that with this sense of purpose, with this goal ahead, he felt he would have restored to him his vigour and confidence. The chill of loneliness that for so long had frozen his inside dissipated. He had even felt cheerful till he had reached the outskirts of the village and seen the aura of fire to the sky.

"So you can't help me," Atkin said.

"I'd like to. But I can't."

"It's a pity," Atkin said. "Because there was something else I wanted to tell you tonight."

"What was that?" Gerald asked, puzzled.

"I've fixed you up with a job in the city. A pretty good job at that. Assistant to one of the executives in the soap business down there. He's an old friend of mine — his father was a friend of my father's. He got in touch with me when all this business blew up about the colliery. And of course when I mentioned your name he was very pleased to help."

"I'm very grateful," Gerald said.

"He said he was looking for some talented young man he could push along. Someone with a bit of vigour and go in him. The idea is he'll be able to keep you under wing and you can step into his shoes when he goes up the ladder. I explained your characteristics and he said you'd be just the man for the job."

"I appreciate it very much," Gerald repeated. "Only I can't understand why you say it's a pity."

"Because life's rather like government," Atkin said. "If you accept a cabinet post you have to give up all outside interests. You have to give up all shares and directorships. Any influence you may have. So that you don't use that influence when you're in government. Because government is really a serious business. Just like life. It demands sacrifices."

"What you mean is that unless I go down the pit and call the strike off I don't get the job?"

"The strike's bigger than all of us," Atkin said. "And it's more important. It demands its sacrifices. The men have sacrificed thirty days of light, thirty days of warmth and comfort, for something in which they believe. And what have we sacrificed, you and I? Why we'll not even have lost a moment of sleep."

"But I don't believe in the strike as they believe."

"But I do, Atkin said. "I believe in the strike and I believe in the village. I know I have no right to ask you give up your happiness, your future, just because of your devotion to me. I have no right to intrude upon your life and to ask you to choose. But you see the strike's more important than me, the forty-seven men in the pit are more important than the two of us put together."

488

"So you're asking all the same."

Atkin did not reply and Gerald realized the choice was clear. Either he went down the pit and intervened in the strike or Atkin would revoke his offer of a job in the city. It was a choice not easy to make, in fact it was a choice he should have rejected out of hand. He did not even see it was worth considering. On the one hand he had the possibility of marrying Barbara and settling into money, on the other the choice of working in the city, in a sound position, but in a situation where he earned money instead of having it earned for him. Had he a selfless nature the choice would never have been necessary; he would have been prepared to make his own money rather than marry into it. But things did not work like that. And then there was his love for Barbara and Barbara's love for him. He had no right to jeopardize that. And Atkin had no right to ask him. Gerald had never been involved in the strike, he had not even wished to be involved, yet here he was being asked to give up more than all the men in the pit put together.

But though it was true he had never been involved in the colliery if he married Barbara he would be involved in the village. Barbara and her mother were involved to the hilt, they were part of the village's vested interest, and by wedding himself to such an interest — by joining the village establishment — he would be as much involved as his brother. As much involved as Atkin. Was that what he really wanted? For that was what would happen if he refused to accept Atkin's offer. He understood he would never leave of his own accord, that had he the will to do so he would have left before now, he would not have allowed lack of money to deter him, nor lack of opportunity, he would have made the money and he would have made the opportunity. No. If he stayed in the village he accepted his mediocrity, he accepted the restrictions which the village imposed, he accepted that always he would be like a cock with one leg tied to a stake, that never would he have the freedom he sought.

The freedom to start again.

He realized then that all along he had been involved, involved in the village, involved in its life, but that if he married Barbara he would be involved still deeper. For with his sharp perception he realized the struggle to save the colliery would be followed by the fight to save the village, that Mrs. Rutland and her daughter were bound to be involved in such a fight and that consequently

Gerald would be involved too. He realized with a sudden intuition, a flash that could be either of anger or despair, that he would never, could never, marry Barbara; that he had surmounted the antipathy of her mother, the desire she had to marry into money, he had surmounted his own poor origins, the uncertainty Barbara showed towards his temperament, the clash his temperament had caused that evening, but somehow he could not surmount this final force. The gravity pull of his environment.

Atkin understood the predicament in which he had placed Gerald and was sympathetic to this predicament. He realized he had no right to ask of him sacrifice. Yet had he too not sacrificed? It was true as he had told Gerald he had not lost any sleep. But he had lost more than that. He had lost his colliery, his house, his career and his mistress. And why should he sacrifice if others did not? He felt the old self-defence mechanism working within. He felt the old need to justify himself to himself. And he realized too, looking down upon the valley, feeling the silence behind him, that his sacrifices were not over yet. That though he might force Gerald to go down the pit he would never persuade him to proclaim to the world he was doing so of his own accord, that his own part in the affair would be discovered and that the designs he might have had on Mrs. Rutland, however, subconscious, would be dissipated, never again would he have access to her inner councils, and never would he enlist her aid in saving the village. Therefore, he had more to lose even than Gerald.

Yet still he determined to lose it, still he determined upon this final sacrifice. He turned to face Gerald and saw the uncertainty in his face, the uncertainty he had so often discerned in his own as he gazed in the mirror. His eyes were not on Atkin but beyond his shoulder towards the house, the damp wreath-like plumes of smoke, the massive gaunt-stricken walls, the naked chimney, the light that somehow was sombre through the holes in the broken walls. He could hear the final clumsy clatter of firemen as they continued their ruthless stripping, the echoing hustle of tubs from the opposite side of the valley. The two together a death rattle to his aspirations. So that he felt tired and sick, his emotions were spent, all he wanted was to return home and go to bed. The cold bit deeper into him and there was nothing now to stop the shiver to his lips. He realized Atkin's eyes were upon him, he realized too he was waiting, waiting for a decision. He thrust his hands deeper in his pockets. He nodded. He had decided. His sacrifice, like that of Atkin's, was complete.

"I'll do as you say," Gerald said. "I'll bring the men back to the surface."

53

"Aye," his father said, when he saw the case. "Gannin' for a holiday, I suppose?"

"A holiday," Bousefield junior admitted. "And a long one at that."

"I suppose ye'll not have time for a cup o' tea afore ye gan."

"If that's a hint for me to put the kettle on I've not got time."

"Aye," Bousefield said.

Despite the fact it was July, Bousefield considered it sufficiently cold for his winter overcoat and cap, the coat heavily belted, the cap ugly with a peak that advanced across his brow like a vizor. Bousefield neither drank nor smoked, he did not bother himself with a garden or allotment, he played neither cards nor snooker, he rarely visited the institute, he no longer played golf, therefore his only pastime, since he did not gamble was to scan through the paper then settle in front of the little black box that was called television. He watched it from the first news bulletin to the last; on nights he was bored with it, he turned down the sound thinking he might enjoy it better; and if there was a programme he evidently did not like he waited till it was finished before he pronounced his verdict. Bousefield junior disliked his father almost as much as he disliked television; therefore the evening before he had got his own back on both by removing a valve from the set without his father's knowledge. The set had consequently not worked and that evening his father had donned his heavy coat and cap and gone to see the local television expert.

"Bit late of a neet to decide on a holiday," Bousefield said. "Divin't ye think?"

"It's the best time to decide," Bousefield junior said. "When yer mind's clear."

"But if ye leave it any later ye'll not even catch the last bus. Ye'll have to gan the morn instead."

"I'd rather walk," Bousefield junior said. "It's quicker than waitin' till the morn."

"Walk? All that way to the town?"

"All reet then. So I'll call a taxi."

"Nor call a taxi either," Bousefield said.

"Ye've just said yersel' it's better than walkin'."

"Not after the fire at the boss's house it's not."

"What's the fire at the boss's house got to do win it?" Bousefield junior asked.

"Nowt much," his father replied. "Except when they get round to figurin' who did it and start makin' enquiries it'll not be long afore yer taxi driver friend lets on about the fly-by-night that called up and asked to be driven to the town after the last bus. And it'll not be long afore the local village cop finds out who that fly-by-night was."

"Ye're not tryin' to say by that ye think I started the fire?"

"Happens I knaa ye started it," Bousefield said. "I was just passin' by the pit manager's house — gannin' to see about the television, when I sees ye poppin' out sharp by the back door. Rushed out and jumped the dyke like a stag with a hunter on his tale. I noticed ye never looked back either — least not till ye were o'er the fields and into the wood. Then I glances up and sees why ye never looked back. And in yer shoes I wouldn't have looked back neither."

Bousefield slipped his shoes down the side of the case and tried to see if it would shut. It would not and he leant heavily upon it; still it would not shut and so he raised the top and stared at the disorganized packing. He had stood with his back to his father as he spoke and even now, as the significance of his words bit deeply to his mind, he did not turn; he did not even feel the need to turn. It amazed him how indifferent he was. It surprised him to discover he really did not care. And why he did not care dawned on him so suddenly and swifty that for a moment his lips shaped to smile, his forehead relaxed, and a little white gleam reduced the coldness of his eyes. He did not care because he knew he would never be caught. It was as simple as that. They might discover it was he, but they could never prove it, and by the time they did perhaps he would be thousands of miles away, away not only from the police but the cold deliberateness he had seen in Ray Holt that last day in the pit. He took his shoes from the case and rearranging them in a different fashion tried again to close it.

"I suppose that means now ye'll be turnin' us in," he said.

"Not me own son," Bousefield answered. "I could never dee a thing like that."

"Ye would. If ye thowt ye had owt to gain by it."

"It's not my business what ye've done," Bousefield said. "Any more than it's my business the reason why ye did it. But if ye want to knaa happens I might even be proud o' ye. And happens if I'd had a bit o' gumption mesel' maybes I'd have done the same thing years ago."

"Only ye didn't," his son said. "So I had to dee it for ye."

"Aye, ye're reet there. Nee gumption and nee go, that's me. All me life I've never changed. Never changed a bit. Ye knaa, there are times ye get to thinkin', and there are times others get ye thinkin'. Like that pal o' yours in the colliery office — Gerald Holt."

"He's nee friend o' mine," Bousefield junior said. "Nor Ray either."

"All the same, ye knaa who I mean. And d'ye knaa what he said to me once? Said I'd never lived. Said all me life and nowt to show for it. I've thowt a lot about it since — what he said, I mean — in fact, I've not been able to get it out me mind. And he's reet, ye knaa, whichever way ye look at it. Me life's worth nowt. Never has been. I might as well die the morn than keep on."

Now that he was warmed through he unloosened the buckle of his belt and pulled the heavy coat from his shoulders. He took off his cap and together with the coat hung it on one of the pegs by the side of the fire. He unravelled the scarf and showed his bare collarless neck, the dried arid skin of his throat, the small stunted adam's apple that bobbed against the silver stud. He stood before the fire in the manner that he stood in the colliery office, with his back to the fire, hands behind his back, the glow of the fire crimson to his thin bony wrists. His lips, white and parch-like, moved slowly but incessantly, but there was to his eyes the same inept look that lacked understanding, the look of a man who had never understood. And who felt too old now even to try. He watched his son try, this time successfully, to close the case and haul it from the table to the floor.

"Ye're the only son I've got," Bousefield said, though why he said it he did not know. "Yet like yer mother, ye divin't care about us. Ye've never cared."

494

Bousefield glanced at his watch. With his case packed his only preoccupation was that of time. He was thinking that after all it was as his father had said. If he did not hurry he would miss the last bus and if he missed the last bus he would have to take a taxi; and though he did not care whether they discovered it was he or not he did not see the point in attracting attention. He did not listen carefully to what his father had said; he had learnt years ago that never once did he say anything of consequence, even what he did say could be rapidly contradicted, and therefore one need not open one's mind in the hope of garnering pearls of wisdom. Yet percolating to his sub-conscious, permeating his own thoughts, was something his father had said, something which registered. Something that demanded more than the monosyllabic reply. Something that made him pause and look at his father more closely and searchingly than he had ever done before. He pulled the sleeve of his pullover over the strap of his watch but continued to finger the winder.

"I'll ask ye a question," he said. "And when ye've answered I'll tell ye why I divin't like ye."

"It'll be my fault, I suppose. Always it's my fault."

"Ye've worked all yer life in the office," Bousefield junior said. "But how many times have ye been down the pit?"

"I've often wanted to gan down. In fact, I've always meant to gan down — sometime."

"But ye've never been down?"

"I divin't knaa why," his father admitted. "All I had to dee was sign the indemnity book."

"Yet ye never even signed that. Never once have ye been down."

"I'll make a point o' arrangin' it," Bousefield said. "Afore the pit closes."

"Never once have ye been down — never once in yer life. Yet ye sent me down. And not just for a visit — to work."

"There were good prospects when ye went down," Bousefield said. "Ye knaa yersel' how good they were."

"Thirty quid a week," his son said. "Workin' on them new fangled cutters."

"And they were just openin' the new drift. The golden slipper. That was supposed to supply coal for seventy-five years. Ensure the life o' the colliery. That had two hundred thousand pounds worth o' equipment invested in it. The most modern drift in the country — that was how it was billed. The best workin' conditions ye could get."

"Only I never worked in the drift. Never once in all the time I was in the pit."

"All the same the prospects were there. Ye cannot deny that."

"Prospects! " his son said. "Ye read about them fancy cutters in Coal magazine. Only ye never stopped to think the seams at Highhill were that low ye'd never get them in. Ye read of all these modern units, wi' pit props that walked — all kinds o' gimmicks like that — only ye never bothered to gan down and see the conditions at Highhill. The water and the dust and the low roofs. And ye never thowt what'd be like for me, gannin' down there, day after day, week after week, drinkin' me head off of a Sunday. Just so that I'd forget what was waitin' for us the morn. So I'd not have to lie awake all neet dreadin' the first shift."

"But all that's finished," Bousefield said. "Now they're closin' the pit."

"Closin' the pit! It should have been closed ten years back, Twenty, if ye ask me."

"Then why'd ye stop down on strike?" Bousefield asked. "Why'd ye stick it out as long as ye did?"

"To get me own back, that's why I stopped down. A little bit here, a litttle bit there, taking the guts out the pit as the pit's taken the guts out o' me. Pullin' out a prop here, pullin' out a prop there, not endangerin' the men, but fixin' things up scientific like, so the whole thing'll cave in afore the men get back to work. Takin' it out o' the rats by slittin' their throats and lettin' the blood drip drop by drop upon the lines."

"Ye did that?"

"I'd have done more if I hadn't heard about me mother and the colliery manager. The whole o' number nine, the worst face in the pit, I've drilled holes all along it, I've taken out the canched stone, I've removed pit props here and there. I've dropped a little bit o' shot in all the holes. And ye knaa what I was ganna dee the day the strike ended and the last man had got back to the surface? I'd have blown the whole face up. All hundred yards of it. So ye'd never get neebody crawlin' along nee eighteen inches again."

"I cannot understand it," Bousefield said. "I cannot understand why ye dee things like that."

" 'Cause I hate the pit, that's why. 'Cause I've always hated it, every minute of it, 'cause I'll always hate it, as long as there's breath in me lungs. The hump ye get to yer shoulders stooping to miss the girders in the roof. The jagged bits o' rock that'd cut yer head off at the neck if it wasn't for yer helmet. The damp that seeps to yer bones and the damp to yer lungs. That ye'll never understand, can never understand, unless ye've been down yersel'."

"But what's that got to dee wi' me," Bousefield asked. "I'm a clerk in the colliery office — not a stoneman on the face."

" 'Cause ye wanted to knaa why I didn't like ye. Ye wanted to knaa why it wouldn't matter to me if ye were dead. 'Cause there's nee reason on earth — nee reason at all — why I shouldn't have been clerk in the colliery office, why I should have been a stoneman on the face. Why ye shouldn't have fixed me up with a cushy job the way ye fixed yersel'."

"How could I have fixed ye up in the colliery office," Bouse-field protested. "Ye knaa there's only one vacancy every ten years. Ye knaa that as well as anybody."

"So why didn't ye fix us up in the machine shops or the electrical shops. The way ye got Walton fixed up when he came to ye. How was it ye were able to dee it for one o' me mates but ye weren't able to dee it for me?"

" 'Cause that was what ye wanted," Bousefield said. "Ye wanted to be one o' the lads. Ye wanted to smoke and drink like everybody else. And ye wanted to earn money the way other lads were earnin' it. It was yer own decision, it was what ye wanted, so divin't come to me now ten years later and say it was my fault. Ye've got neebody to blame but yersel'."

" 'Cause at that time I was young and daft. 'Cause I didn't knaa owt else. But ye knew — or ye should've done. At least ye'd have knaan if ye'd cared. Only ye never cared then and ye divin't care now. And that's why neebody ever cares about ye. That's why they'll never care."

Bousefield junior had left his case on the floor and moved to stand only a few inches from his father. His face was pale, dried of its colour with so many weeks exposed to the sullen air of the pit; his eyes were clear but the rims were red, underlaid with dust, and the redness and the dust seemed to accentuate the white of the irises. The eyes slid from his father's to a poker standing on

497

the brass stand in the fireplace. His father's eyes followed their shift in direction and when they lighted on the poker he stepped back a pace so that his heels treaded the brass of the fender. The stud burst at his collar to reveal a few pale hairs on his chest. And standing so close Bousefield could just see the dried worls of skin, the minute red tips to his cheeks where the veins had withered, the little edges of fleck to his lips. The eyes large and luminous with fear. And shocked by the bitterness of his son, the hatred that had brought the fear to his eyes, his mind was lifted to a new level of awareness, he looked at his son and saw him as if for the first time, the red nose, the cold pellucid eyes, the cruel lips, the absolute fearlessness and ruthlessness he saw in his expression.

A son he had never really known.

54

"Divin't ye speak to yer father like that," Mrs. Bousefield said, pulling back the curtain from across the doorway so that the curtain rails scraped on the brass rod. "He happens to be yer father, whatever else ye may think on him. And 'cause he's yer father he deserves yer respect."

"I've asked him a question," her son said. "And I'm still waitin' for an answer."

"I heard yer question," Mrs. Bousefield said. "And the way ye put it I reckon half the street heard it tee."

"I want to knaa how it comes about that a fellow who worked all his life in the colliery office — who never once had the nerve to gan down the pit. I want to knaa how it is he sent his son down."

Mrs. Bousefield let drop the curtain behind her and threw a letter she had been writing on the table. She noticed the case on the floor, standing on its side, the drawers her son had left open, the expression on her son's face, that perhaps could not be read by his father but certainly could be read by her, she recalled the fire-lit sky, the sparks, the flames, and could not have understood more perfectly had it been written before her eyes in black and white. There had been a chill to the bedroom and she came forward to warm her hands. Both son and husband made way, more from habit than from respect. She was already dressed for bed in a cotton white nightdress hidden by a faded woolen dressing gown worn at the sleeves. She was beginning to show her age not only in her face but also in her hands, hands that were stained at the back, stained not with marks of the grave but large white blotches that showed a lack of pigment. Her hair was in curlers, she had given her face a creamy pack that evening, but nothing could hide the decay of her beauty, and worse nothing could disguise the knowledge of that decay to her eyes.

"If ye must knaa, I'll tell ye why he did it," Mrs. Bousefield said. "Since it's that long probably he's forgotten hissel'."

499

"I've not forgotten," Bousefield answered. "Why should I forget?"

" 'Cause shame should make ye forget, that's why," Mrs. Bousefield said, looking at her son. "He sent ye down the pit 'cause that was his way o' gettin' a bat at me. He knew I loved ye, ye see, he knew I treasured ye as the only one I had, so he thought by hurtin' ye he'd be hurtin' me. By sendin' ye down the pit he'd make ye suffer for what he reckoned I was deein' to him."

"Ye mean he knew then," Bousefield junior asked. "Yet he did nowt about it?"

"Only send ye down the pit. Condemn ye to a life o' drudgery to get even wi' me."

"I cannot believe he'd dee a thing like that," Bousefield junior said. "He'd not have that much sense."

"It's true all reet," his mother said. "Whether ye believe it or not. I begged him to put ye into the store, to have a word wi' the headmaster o' the school 'cause he was on the store committee. There was a vacancy in the drapery at the time, but not yer father, he wouldn't hear o' it. Reckoned there was o'er much fiddlin' gannin' on in the drapery so he preferred ye in the pits."

"He wanted to gan down the pits," Bousefield persisted. "Always reckoned that was where he wanted to end up."

"That's reet," Mrs. Bousefield agreed. "Ye were nee help yersel', as far as that was concerned. Only ye'd have gone into the drapery all reet, if yer father had put in a word. If he'd put himsel' to the bother. But he didn't. And I knaa why he didn't, and he knaas hissel'. It was the reason I've just given."

Only one thing stopped Bousefield from taking the poker and breaking the balding skin across his father's skull. It was not that he had had enough of violence that night, it was not that he had scruples about doing an injury to his father; it was merely that he felt sick to his inside. The sickness of disgust. He looked down at his father, turned from him now, a nerve throbbing in his cheek as he gazed towards the fire, he saw the dried sandy skin of his head, the shrivelled crinkled ears, the nervous throb of his adam's apple. And he realized something else. He realized from who he had inherited his coldness. The indifference of his personality. The malice that made him the man he was. Bousefield never once had a conscience about the things he did, in fact he did not know what conscience was. But he was aware there were in him talents that did not exist in anyone else, talents which often puzzled him but which he knew he could do nothing about. He turned from his father and moved to take his case from the leg of the table.

"Just a minute son," his father said. "Afore ye gan."

"Ye said yersel' I'd miss the last bus," his son answered. "So I'm takin' yer advice and gettin' out now."

"What I've got to say'll not take more than a minute," his father insisted.

"Say yer piece then," his son said. "And get it o'er win."

"Mebbes what yer mother said is reet, I divin't knaa. She always says like the elephant she never forgets. And mebbe without knaa'in it mesel', mebbes that's why I did set ye to work in the pit. To suffer things I'd never suffered mesel'. But anyway, it's o'er and done win' now, we none of us can make a better on it, so it's nee good tryin'. Only remember this, all these years I've known about yer mother. And all these years I've kept me mouth shut."

"Only 'cause ye were that scared I'd run away and leave ye if ye didn't," Mrs. Bousefield interrupted. "Scared ye'd get neebody else to fill yer belly for ye. To make yer meals and clean yer boots. That's why ye did it and for nee other reason."

"It had nowt to dee wi' that," Bousefield protested. "Fact, I'd have done what the Holts did when their mother died — I could have got mesel' a housekeeper. Like the colliery manager, in fact. Just like the colliery manager. Only I wouldn't have kept it so hush-hush. I'd not have made a song and dance about it. I'd have been open, like."

"Ye'd not even have the gumption to get yersel' a housekeeper never mind keep it in the dark."

"I'd have had the gumption all reet, ye'd see if I hadn't. Only I'm tryin' to tell ye why I never did it. Why I never brought things into the open. It wasn't even 'cause of a sense of shame, but 'cause of a sense of honour. Family honour, if ye knaa what that means. It was 'cause I didn't want everybody to knaa I'd picked a wrong un."

"Ye," Mrs. Bousefield said. "Ye stand there and tell me ye picked a wrong un."

"Or mebbes ye went wrong after I picked ye. It makes nee difference now. And I suppose if that's the way it was I cannot blame ye. I'm not much cop as a husband, but then I'm not much cop as a man. All me life and nowt to show for it. Not even an allotment like some o' the men. Not even a garden properly kept." He shook his head sadly. "I often think, ye knaa, that once I'm dead there'll be nee trace of us, just an entry in a record book. Nee goodwill, nee little bit o' land that ye could say, this was mine."

"Self-pity'll get ye neewhere," Bousefield said.

"Like the fellow who had the golf-course," Bousefield mused. "He was a fine figure of a man. Kept the storehouse o' the colliery and comes along to the office regular as ninepence for his pay sheets and schedules. Used to bone us when I was younger 'cause I stamped them upside down. But when he dies everybody remembers him, everybody says there's a fine upstandin' fellow. Only I wonder what they'll say when I pop off. Or if they'll say owt at all."

Bousefield's eyes were fixed on the embers of the fire; he bent for the poker and absently stoked the hard crust of coal. There was in the room a silence, but it was a silence Bousefield did not notice. He did not realize he was under the scrutiny of both wife and son, and with his face reflected in the flames, he did not realize how both of them noticed in his expression not so much the wrinkles, not so much the age, but the sad frankness of a man who says this is me, take me as I am. I am naked, I am weak, but I am a man. And my weakness comes not from drink, not from sensuality, not from excess, merely from the weakness of self-knowledge, the knowledge that I am as I am, that I cannot be made better or worse, aware that its meaning lies only in himself, in what he is or is not prepared to make of it. And that he has made nothing of it. And that therefore is why he is weak. That is why his life is void of achievement.

"Anyway," Mrs. Bousefield said, turning to her son. "True or not, it's time ye were off. Or ye'll be missin' the last bus. And like yer father says some taxi-driver might remember ye as a fly-by-night. And that wouldn't dee at all. Not even for the family honour. Would it now?" she added, turning to Bousefield.

"He's not even said where he's gannin," Bousefield said.

"That's reet," his mother said. "And where are ye gannin'?"

"Join the merchant navy," Bousefield said. "If that settles yer curiosity."

"And when d'ye think ye'll be back," Bousefield asked.

Bousefield junior looked at his mother and she understood.

"Ye knaa ye're supposed to give a week's notice at the colliery," she said. "They'd be able to get ye on that, if they wanted."

"Only they'll not will they?" her son said. "Ye bein' that friendly wi' the manager."

"All that's o'er now," Mrs. Bousefield said, looking at her husband. "O'er and done win. We'll all be makin' a fresh start as of the neet. All the same, if ye like, I'll see the manager. I'll fix it up so yer notice is backdated."

Bousefield laid the poker back in the grate and turned and looked to his wife.

"No," he said. "If there's any fixin' to dee I'll dee it. I'll see him first thing the morn when I call by the office. He'll smell a rat, o' course, probably he'll have smelt one already. But now the shoe's on the other foot. Now it's time for him to keep his mouth shut. To keep things to hissel'."

The younger Bousefield picked up his case and pulled back the curtain from across the doorway. He thought his actions that night had severed finally the slim and ever shrinking contact his mother had had with Atkin, and for that he was glad, he was happy because at one single stroke, one simple light of a match, the smear of years had been washed from their name. Yet he was perturbed too by the understanding he had seen in his mother's eyes. The understanding they would never meet again. That once he had stepped across the thresh he would never return. And after all, this woman was his mother. She had brought him into the world, she had watched him grow, and if it was true she had shown neglect, if she had thought more of her lover than she had of husband and son, yet still there was between them a bond, a bond that demanded respect. She was after all a human being. She had pursued her own selfish course, she had neglected everyone else, yet because he was leaving he seemed to understand the tensions and conflicts that reigned within her soul as well as within his own. And he belonged to her, as a speck of dust belongs to the universe, but like that speck of dust they would drift apart, and he would keep on drifting through an eternity.

"Better take yer coat," she said. "Afore ye gan."

"I'll pick it up in the passageway," he said. "On the way out."

"And shake hands wi' yer father," she said. "While ye're on."

He shook his father's hand that despite the warmth of the

room was cold and without strength.

"And give yer mother a kiss. I'll be owld and grey by the next time ye're back."

He kissed his mother on the cheek, the first time he had kissed her in his life, and as he slid from her she handed him the letter she had retrieved from the table.

"One last favour afore ye gan," she said. "Post this for us as ye pass the box."

The letter was addressed not to Arnold Atkin as Bousefield expected but to Mrs. Rutland.

55

"All right," Atkin said. "You're clear."

He handed Gerald a page of foolscap which Gerald carefully folded and placed in the pocket of his boiler suit.

"You don't have to bother reading it," Atkin added. "It's all as we thrashed out last night."

"And if I want to ring you'll be on the phone?"

"The line from the deputy's kist'll be open from the time you leave the office."

"And the line to the divisional chairman?"

"That'll be kept open too," Atkin said.

"What about Mrs. Rutland?" Gerald asked. "Has anyone told her yet?"

"Once you're safely ensconced in the pit I'll give her a tinkle on the phone. I'll tell her it's the only thing possible in the circumstances. I'll explain the motives behind it and the steps we intend to take to save the village. And if we're lucky perhaps she'll tag along."

"If we're lucky," Gerald said.

He moved out of the office along the passageway into the sunlight. He had anticipated walking the distance he could so clearly remember his brother having walked the day the strike began, dust spurting from his feet, he had wanted to make his first ever descent in a cage, first being searched by the banksman, the clinging to the iron bars across the roof, suddenly being dropped into the darkness by the unseen winderman manipulating his switches. But it was not to be. He had changed at the colliery office into the old boots and boiler suit of his brother, the helmet and kneepads of the colliery manager, and instead of striding along the cinder towards the colliery yard he was hustled by the safety officer into a car and driven not to the pithead but to the drift mouth some miles away. This was because the manager did not wish to rouse the attention of the lineage men — reporters not accredited to newspapers — who lingered on behalf of the press. And because the mouth of the drift was said to have easier access to where the men were quartered.

Gerald and the safety officer called at the time cabin to deposit their tokens and Gerald feeling the unaccustomed weight of the boots, the heaviness of the battery attached to the waist, strode over the silent midway rollers and oiled cable to the dark orifice that was the mouth of the drift. There were no lights on the gradient down from the mouth, he had as yet to attach his lamp to the socket in his helmet, the ground was uneven, he did not direct its beam to the roof and therefore despite the pleas of the safety officer repeatedly he rapped his head against the timber beams and knocked his helmet to the ground. He would be dizzy by the time he returned to the surface. He would even be dizzy by the time he reached the bottom of the incline. For his attention distracted by the sight of lights ahead, the eerie sound of voices lifting to him from the bottom, he straightened for a second his shoulders, collided with a low-slung beam and was knocked completely off his feet.

Floundering among the rails and sleepers he came into his first contact with the mud. His hands groped for his helmet, he saw the trinket lights reflect from dark scummy pools, the cruel glint of girders, the air was cold to his face and already there was a chill to his feet. There was also to the air an odour he had never known before, an ashen odour compounded of dust and dank and coldness. The incline widened to a loading point, lights were everywhere now, and with the lights the neatness and tidiness of white-washed walls and stone dusted ways, of hoppers that glistened with new paint, there were piles of neatly stacked timber, pails of tar-like grease used to lubricate the axles of tubs, nylo-fasteners to staple together sheets of rubber belting. The trans-formers and compressors were carefully fenced, tubs were set for the first run to bank once the pit began producing, though of course the belts were still, the men idle, and even at the deputy's kist where loitered what Gerald presumed to be a group of strike leaders, there were only signs of a lethargic activity.

The safety officer led Gerald as far as the kist and there he left him, Gerald could not understand why. Those in the kist, with a nod that matched the stiffness of their bones, also began to disappear, to drift away to join those men sitting around the trans-formers and compressors, lounging against empty tubs, men with faces that seemed little more than blackened shrunken skulls, blackened and shrunken following their forty days of travail in the wilderness of the pit. Gerald stood uncertain what to do next, still holding the lamp in his hand, already a stiffness congealing his fingers, a dryness cracking his lips. He stepped over the tail-rope and stood before the open door to the kist. Only one man by this time remained in the kist and he did not look up as Gerald entered. Indeed, he did not even indicate he knew who Gerald was. Nor did Gerald recognize him till, slowly and sardonically, he took off his helmet and scratched the back of his head. He flattened the hair to his head with the palm of his hand and spoke in a voice that sounded thick with dust.

"Ready?" Ray asked.

"Ready for what?" Gerald said.

"Your tour o' inspection, o' course. That what ye came for, wasn't it?"

Ray did not wait for an answer and Gerald had no alternative but to follow him out of the kist beyond the tubs along a short path to a narrow stairway that led to the top of the hopper. The passage between the rock wall and belts supplying the hopper was narrow, stripped of its light to save electricity, the way underfoot was bad, and first Gerald's hand rested against the clammy wall then against the cold belt as he stumbled from side to side. The lamp he held slipped from his fingers and tumbled among his legs, the cord between his feet, and Ray had to pause and return the lamp to his brother, unwinding the cord, attaching the lamp to the socket in the helmet, so that they could go on again. The whiteness of Gerald's face was illuminated in the beam of Ray's lamp, his hands were cold as they brushed against his face, the pads hard, calloused. But standing so close Gerald sensed about his brother an animal virility he had never known before, a ferocity that for once made Gerald unsure of himself. Then the beam of the lamp was turned from him and in the light of his own he saw his brother striding along before him, the tip of his stick trailing along the coal and dust on the belt.

Ray did not speak as he arranged the lamp, nor did he speak afterwards as they wended their way along the narrow passageways, water deepening beneath their feet, sometimes mud rising beyond the level of their boots, the air around them growing limp and stale. They moved up the small sharp incline drifted to connect two seams, where Walton and Bousefield had finally clashed, they continued along where there was no light at all, where the air was positively dank, silver globules of water percolating the roof. The going grew worse, the mud in some places reached to their knees, shreds of fungus hung from the roof, Gerald had not the slightest idea where he was going, where his brother was leading, or even what his purpose was. But for the first time in their lives he felt the initiative rested with Ray. He was the superior of the two. He was the one who at that moment had the greater strength. Their progress was slow, for Gerald stumbled frequently, lost his helmet, cut his shin, felt the mud oozing over his head, so that Ray had to stop and haul him to his feet. Encourage him to keep going.

Finally, the beam of their lamps played upon the dampness of a wall that suddenly bared their path. It was as if they had been walking along an alleyway looking for an exit only to find the alley was in fact a cul-de-sac. Gerald looked enquiringly at Ray. Ray however was not perturbed. There was even a peculiar twist to his lips as he said, "here we are". And laughed. His gaze dropped in the direction of his boots and Gerald followed his eyes. He noticed an aperture perhaps eighteen inches high cut into the left of the wall. Ray removed the helmet again from his head and scratched his skull. His face seemed that of a barbarian, with the grizzly stubble of red beard, the acne stains along the forehead vivid and angry, the face made even more grotesque by the twist of amusement Gerald noticed to the lips.

"You're not trying to tell me you work in there?"

"That's the three quarter seam," Ray answered. "Or number nine as ye might prefer to call it. And divin't say ye divin't recognize it, after all the seam tonnages ye've filled in regularly for the last ten years. Ye should knaa it as well as ye knaa the back o' yer hand."

Gerald did not reply but stared down at the seam.

"Here, drop yer head," Ray said. "And I'll show ye."

Ray stooped and on all fours like an animal paused and looked significantly at Gerald. Gerald again had no alternative but to accept the challenge and crawled through the opening into the seam. It was as high as he had imagined, only eighteen inches, and he had hardly room to breathe never mind move. But it seemed his brother was haring along, despite the mud, despite the roof, despite the stiffness he must surely feel in his bones, despite the Anderson boyes cutting machine that suddenly reared before him. Ray had already manouevred the machine, crawling between props and upon the belt, Gerald's lamp caught the flash of the studs in his boots and followed like a lizard his course through the mud. But lacking practice, lacking method, his foot hooked itself behind a prop and not realizing how dangerous the obstacle was he pulled and heaved and sweated till the prop came loose. There was a crack and a sigh and a groan and the prop dropped a further two inches. He called to Ray, but Ray only laughed and told him not to mind the conversation of the roof. A few chips of post fell into his face, he heard the splintering crack of another prop and scrambled on with his fists tightly clenched.

He scrambled into a hollow that had filled with water because with the men not working the pumps were operated inefficiently. His head went under, his helmet came off, his lamp extinguished, he felt the cold fungus-like taste of water to his mouth, its ice cold shrieking at the gums, he felt its bitterness to his lips, his eyes, his cheeks, his brow, he floundered in a panic, he thought that he was dead, that he was drowning, and the final thoughts that passed through his mind was that this should happen to him, that he should find himself in this predicament, that the young man who had so elaborately crossed the threshold into the world of Mrs. Rutland should be so crudely drowned in the pit. Which reminded him in the clarity of his thoughts that he had not even signed the indemnity book. He splashed and spluttered and when he raised his head called for Ray. And even above his death thoughts, he heard the voice of Ray, the laughter of Ray, so that he was surprised, astonished, reproachful that his brother should engineer his death. That there was nothing he would do to help. Yet even when he heard the laugh, even as those thoughts crossed his mind, his head lifted from the water, he felt the strong muscular jerk to his neck and felt himself dragged to the safety and comfort of the mud.

Then again Ray was off, not waiting for Gerald, urging him to hurry, to follow his soles, to watch the props, the pools, the belts, not to be put off by the cracks and groans that now seemed all around him, the chill of the water, the bluestone that chipped from the roof, telling him there was not much ground to manouevre now, only another fifty yards, that if he could survive that he

509

could survive anything, not to let his back come into contact with the roof because scabs might develop on the base of his spine. But Gerald could not listen. His head was full of water. And even had he understood it would have made no difference. His head again came into contact with the roof, again he was thrown full length into the slime, he did bump his back against the post of the roof, he was concerned by the chips that fell into his face, the creaks and groans that were so loud and menacing they even penetrated the drumming water to his ears. So that he did not want to stop even when the only thing his lamp could perceive were Ray's heels only a few inches before his face.

Ray manouevred himself in the narrow space so that he was lying facing his brother, head close to his, his lamp switched off so that it would not blind Gerald's eyes. And suddenly reaching to Gerald's helmet he switched off his lamp too, so that the darkness around them was complete. And with the darkness the silence. Yet so close to the earth, to danger, to death, Gerald felt his senses alert, his mind clear, aware of the stone and water, cold and foist, and also the smell of his brother, of unwashed primitive man, whose clothes were threadbare, holed, whose very skin seemed so thick with dirt and unshaven hairs it would never be clean again. Only the eyes shone out, grey and piercing and angry. And to Gerald they seemed to accentuate the discomfort of the seam, the soreness to his shins and back, so that all he wanted was to be away, safe again in the colliery office, warming his back against the fire, looking out from the security of a desk upon the shallow mist that lay along the floor of the valley. Anywhere but in the darkness, anywhere where the smell was not offensive to his nostrils.

"How d'ye like to make love here, Jay-boy?" Ray asked. "How d'ye like to have a bit laid aside ye, on that belt, in that damp, a bit stripped naked and ready to take ye? A nice married bit that knaas what it's for and doesn't mess about sayin' she doesn't want it when all the time she does? How'd ye like her now, wi' the water drippin' to yer back and the mud to yer loins. Appetisin', divin't ye think?"

"I don't think so," Gerald said.

"Ye would if ye'd been down here wi' the rest o' the lads. If ye had to work down here day in and day out all yer life, lettin' yer mind run like a sewer just so that ye can forget. Just as on the surface ye drink to forget. Ye curse and blaspheme and whore to forget. So ye'll not be reminded that this is yer destiny. This is what faces ye for the rest o' yer life."

"But don't you see how daft you are. How pointless it is to keep this alive?"

"I might have expected as much from ye," Ray said. " 'Cause ye divin't understand the basic principles o' life, never mind owt else."

"Then tell me why you fight?" Gerald said. "Tell me why it's worth saving?"

" 'Cause it's all we've got. And better this than nowt at all. 'Cause if we give up this job we give up this village. And if we give up our village we give up our life. But more than that — 'cause always in the past we were first to suffer. 'Cause when coal didn't sell wages were dropped, hours were extended, men were locked out, blacklegs brought in, wives and families turfed out of colliery houses, men gibetted if ever they committed violence."

"But that's the past," Gerald said. "And the past's dead and gone."

"Cannot ye see it comin' again?" Ray answered stubbornly. "Divin't ye ever read the papers. Even the fancy adverts the Coal Board sent out tellin' ye there'll not be a pick nor shovel in the whole industry in five years time. And in fifteen there'll hardly be a man — never mind a pick nor shovel."

"But it's a good thing," Gerald said. "Taking the toil out of the work."

"Lengthenin' the dole queues, ye mean. O' course, ye divin't care about that 'cause ye'll not be in the queue. And 'cause ye cannot see the disaster it'll be for us. 'Cause the only job we can dee is in the pit. And if ye take this job from us ye take everythin' we've got."

Ray breathed heavily, finding it an effort to speak, yet sufficiently close to Gerald to make himself felt, so that as with their last meeting beneath the broken gas lamp, Gerald felt the revolutionary fervour, the anger, the kind of anger and fervour that in the past had changed the world. And the more he spoke the more excited he became. Thoughts held for so long within seemed to bubble and froth in his mind, he wanted to burden up-on Gerald all the anger he felt, not because he had spent thirty-seven days in the pit, but because throughout the centuries authority had not changed, because still it attacked the men, smothered them with its indifference. Its superiority. And because there was nothing, absolutely nothing, they could do. The rights of the individual were discarded as they were in war. But perhaps those rights did not exist, perhaps they had never existed, only at election time, when even they did not exist because the capitalist press so distorted and confused the issues that the freedom of one's choice was prejudiced anyway.

No, there was no freedom. And the men had stayed on strike thirty-seven days to prove there was no freedom. All this time they had public opinion on their side, all this time they had the support of their wives and families, the men striking on the surface, the village elite that helped supply food, the press in the city that had opened for them a fund. Yet despite this enthusiasm, this belief in the justness of their cause, they were still down in the pit, accustomed to the cold, the damp, the chill, the discomfort, men of stone not men of emotion, men biding their time as soldiers do on the front towards the end of a war. Waiting. And hoping. Till the result of their wait came as an emissary from the surface. And the fact the emissary was his brother made Ray more grim and bitter than ever. It recalled to him his thoughts in a moment of depression, it recalled Gerald's search of a meaning to life, the meaning he believed Gerald sought in vain, but which he himself felt to be at his fingertips.

"Ye seek the meanin' o' life," he said. "Ye come down here and tell us this is not for us. But d'ye think ye're the only one that wants to know what life's about. Sometimes — sometimes mesel' I've been that full o' life, I've wanted gan out into the yard and shout from the rooftops — stand on the lavatory top and call to the world — tell them all to come round, hear what I've got to say. Tell them I'm alive, that to live is enough."

"Yet it's not enough," Gerald said sadly. "Is it?"

"It might be if it wasn't for bureaucrats like ye. But as ye say it's not 'cause neebody'll ever let ye live in peace. It's like being a tortoise, ye stick out yer head and somebody comes along and chops it off. And for what? For nee reason at all. But I'm alive, thirty-seven days in the pit'll not change me idea o' that. There's only ye, Jay-lad, and that bastard gang o' yers, the Rutland set, the Atkin set, there's only them that's not alive."

512

The men too were alive, Ray wanted to say, though he did not get round to saying it. They were as much alive as he or anyone else. And they too sought their origins, the meaning to their lives, because they had no choice but to return to the earth from which they had sprung, because their roots sank deep into the earth and unknowingly they dug to seek them. Dug to seek themselves in the depths of the pit just as any collar and tie worker seeks himself in the occupation of an office where he earns his livelihood. Seeking his destiny, his meaning, his soul. But his mind was moving again, weariness had sapped his concentration, he switched on the lamp and saw Gerald's peaked face. It was obvious he was lost and did not understand, so obvious that despite his tiredness, his discomfort, it made Ray laugh. Laugh because everyone in the pit, aware someone was behind him, believed it to be Gerald.

"What's the joke now?" Gerald asked.

"Everyone believes ye're the one behind the strike," Ray said. "Ye're the one feedin' us information."

"Someone was feeding you," Gerald said. "I'd like to know who it was."

"Ye'll find out soon enough," Ray said. "Only when I want to tell ye — not before."

His white tongue wiped his lips and he moved his shoulders. He lifted a hand and switched off his lamp so that again the darkness was complete.

"Now then," he said. "The message I got on the phone was that ye were comin' down wi' definite concessions that would be satisfactory to me and the men and bring this strike to an end. I was a bit doubtful at first, 'cause if anyone was offerin' genuine concessions they'd come themselves. They'd have nee need o' me brother."

"They're the best concessions you'll get," Gerald answered. "You have to believe me when I say that."

"They'd better be. 'Cause I only let ye come on the condition they were genuine concessions and not just a load o' bull that amounted to a face-savin' formula. So ye'd better make it good, Jay-boy. 'Cause if ye divin't I'll not vouch for yer safe return to the surface."

Gerald felt as if he were lying on a bed of quicksand that was gently sucking him down. He was disconcerted by the darkness,

513

but even more disconcerted by the mud, mud that was now so cold he felt it touching his bare skin. His hands groped forward through the slime and dust to touch Ray's shoulder. It was not the conditions in which he had expected to conduct a negotiated settlement, he had expected the nearest he could get to VIP treatment, a seat in a warm cabin, near a telephone so that he could be in touch with his superiors. But he was sufficiently tough not to ask for mercy, even to let his brother know that he minded. He pulled the helmet a little further down on his head and hunched his shoulders in a uselessly protective manner to avoid the drops from the ceiling. He swallowed what seemed to be a large blob of dust and was surprised himself at the dryness of his tongue as he spoke.

"You'll believe me," he said. "When I tell you they're the best you can get."

"Spit it out," Ray said. "I'm prepared for the worst."

"You made a fuss because the welfare facilities were to close before the colliery. You remember you swung Wishart as high as the chandelier the night of the meeting at the institute on this very point."

"Ye'd better not have come all this way to tell us the Board've been sufficiently magnanimous to rescind that. 'Cause if ye have ye'd better hurry back sharp afore some o' the lads get hold o' ye and ye regret it."

"Listen to what I say before you pass judgment. The Coal Board are prepared to promise an extension of the life of the welfare till after the colliery's closed. And a long time after, if need be."

"They're still thinkin' o' closin' it anyway."

"You didn't honestly believe they'd do anything else, did you now? Anyway, I'm not finished yet. They're promising to extend the life of the Brockwell seam till well after Christmas. You'll remember they offered to hold a very thorough costing investigation into the whole pit, and even though you didn't agree they went ahead and held it just the same. And one of the things they came out with was that the Brockwell seam was the only one breaking even."

"Yet they'll only keep it open till after Christmas."

"I said it was breaking even, I didn't say it was making a profit. Anyway, for God's sake don't miss the point. If they keep this seam open till after Christmas it means there won't be any redundancy. That not a single soul will get the sack."

"Mebbe not at Christmas," Ray said. "There'll be plenty when it closes later on."

"Not necessarily," Gerald answered. "If a lot of the men elected to live in Staffordshire there'll be more vacant places in the county. And it'll be easier to fix those men working at the Brockwell into these places."

Ray listened intently in the darkness; he did not agree but did not interrupt.

"Gan on," he said. "I'm still wi' ye."

"So what I've just said constitutes a guarantee there'll be no redundancy when the pit closes. The only guarantee you'll get. And the men that'll be retired before their time'll be sixty or over — not as you once said — fifty or over. And when they retire they'll be compensated to the tune of £203."

"And the transfers? I suppose we'll still have to accept them?"

"We'll fix as many as we can in the area. But still some'll be encouraged to move to Staffordshire and Bath, places like that. They'll be given special allowances to pay for the moving of their furniture. And to offset that jibe of yours about living in houses not yet built they'll be provided with luxury caravans at God knows what expense."

"Owt else?"

Gerald breathed deeply; the mud to his chest felt now like cold steel.

"I've been instructed to make a special point of this," he said. "There'll be absolutely no victimization. Those men on strike in the pit'll be treated exactlly like everyone else. Even you and Featherley and Walton, ringleaders so to speak — and Bousefield too if he'd been around — you'll all get the same treatment."

"Disbanded," Ray said. "And sent to all parts o' the globe."

"The Board'll bear in mind people have lived here as a community," Gerald answered patiently. "They'll try to see they stay a community once they leave."

Gerald lifted a hand to his helmet and fumbling with the switch snapped on his lamp. He had expected to see confusion and uncertainty in his brother's face, but all that he saw was sadness, a sadness that moved him because it was that of a defeated man.

515

"And suppose I refuse these concessions?" Ray said. "Suppose I decide to continue the strike?"

"You'll never get better terms than these," Gerald said.

"Mebbes not," Ray said. "Mebbes on the other hand I will."

"Listen, Ray," Gerald said, feeling a dull cramp to his legs. "The only real concession we're offering you is to continue working the Brockwell; but at least it's a concession, you have to admit that. And if you think it'll sweeten the pill any I'll see to it that the Board doesn't say over much about when it'll be closed. So that the decision will have an air of permanence."

"Very kind of you, I must say. Only ye still haven't told us what'll happen if I refuse."

"You've got to accept things as they are, Ray. Not as they might be. You've got to look to the future and not to the past; or even to the immediate future. And if you agree to these conditions Atkin says he'll quit the colliery and throw in his weight to save the village."

"I'll believe that," Ray said. "When I see it."

"It's true enough," Gerald answered. "He's even talked to Donnolly the MP. And Donnolly's agreed to help. He's even prepared to raise the subject in the House when it reassembles."

"And what about Wishart? Maybe he'll raise him in the House tee."

Ray gently manouevred himself out of the seam at the tailgate and out upon the way, and Gerald did not hesitate to hurry after him. He pulled at his cuff so that he turned.

"Didn't ye hear the news?" Gerald asked. "About Wishart."

"Divin't tell us he's standin' for Parliament. I will be surprised."

"About his wife."

"They lived halfway down the hill," Ray said. "I saw her now and again on the bank."

Gerald's back had soaked where water had fallen from the roof, the dark ooze of the churned coal dust had blackened the dungarees in such a way they would never be clean again, his face too was black, blacker than Ray's who had spent so long in the pit, but already the mud was drying, he could feel its cold stiffness streaking his face, the inside of his mouth, and only his teeth and eyes seemed exceptionally bright as he reached to his full height.

"She slashed both wrists with the carving knife," Gerald said.

"She wasn't quite dead when they got her to hospital. She kept raving about you in the pit and the marvellous job you were doing to save the colliery and the village and how it would all turn out right in the end and they'd give you a medal. Only she thought you were Wishart and Wishart was you." Gerald paused. "They buried her yesterday."

The ache of the cramp had sharpened to Gerald's legs and lying so long on the seam he was surprised by the stiffness to his muscles, the agonised pains that ran up his back as he stood upright. His lips were tight with pain and with the dust in his throat, his teeth clenched, his voice did not sound his own as he spoke.

"That still hasn't answered me question," Ray said. "About what'll happen if I refuse the terms."

"You'll agree, Ray. Because you have to agree."

"But what if I don't?"

"Then probably most of you will be sacked for breaking the Coal Mines Act. And more than sacked, prosecuted. You've been breaking the law left right and centre, Ray, ever since you decided to stay down. Sleeping in the pit, smoking in the pit, brandy in the soups. There's very little we don't know of you, you know, in the colliery office. And though I won't split and Atkin won't split there's plenty who will in the hope of promotion."

"I don't care," Ray said. "Let them prosecute if they like."

"Only you'll be expelled from the union too," Gerald added. "There's been a reluctance to do that up to now, but I tell you, Ray, opinion is hardening, the public's interest is falling off, and as it's falling off there are those in the union want to take advantage of it. They think you've shown them up enough with your antics. They want to get even. And that they think is the way to do it."

"There'd be a riot if they expelled us," Ray exclaimed. "Half the coalfield'd come out on strike."

"Only that wont do you and the men much good. Since you'll be sacked and on the dole."

"We don't care about that. As long as we're still supported from the surface."

"You'll not be supported for long," Gerald answered. "I've told you, public interest is falling off. Money to the fund is falling off. There'll be enough to cover this week, but it'll be half rations next. And not only for you in the pit but for the families at the surface. And how long d'you think they'll support you on empty stomachs? Seeing as they've already stuck it out for over a month."

"The men'll like it," Ray snarled. "Even if their families don't."

"They won't, Ray. You know they won't. Already this last week you've had defections to the surface. Granted they sneaked out by the drift and at night so nobody'd know. But I know and you know, even if it hasn't yet reached the papers. Besides, why should you stick it out? It's not as if we're making you return to the surface beaten to your knees. You can come back looking as though you've triumphed. That way not only will you not have lost face, but you'll be able to return a hero."

"But you know and I know that I'm not a hero. That the end'll be exactly the same as if I'd never struck at all."

"But by that time maybe a year'll have passed. And by that time probably you'll have saved the village. So no-one'll mind anyway."

Both moved tiredly down what appeared to be a disused way, the stone dust sludge beneath their feet, the fungus hanging white from the roof, the smell of dung dry to the air so that its staleness caught at the throat. The going seemed suddenly harder to the feet, Gerald began to forget the lowness of the roof, and again the helmet was knocked from his head, and again his head ached with the force of the blow. The air became staler and staler and Gerald did not know they were making their way along a downcast shaft past old boardrooms towards the fan that circulated the air. He heard the sound of the fan but did not discern what it was. Then he saw before them what appeared to be a door, Ray hauled it back and the force of the air swept over them. Ray let the door clash behind and stood staring at the fan as if it were some god, some idol, that demanded obeissance.

Gerald could not understand this, but then he did not know this was always where Ray came to think out his problems. He watched his face and saw how sullen and disappointed it was. And he realized then that Ray's enemies were wrong, he was not merely a name-seeker, a troublemaker out to make the worst of a difficult solution, as someone had put it. He really did care about the men and what happened to them. He really did care about the village and its fate. And he had read sufficient history to know that the miners had never won, could never win, that he was in the position of the strike leaders of old, men who had failed like him, who had been fobbed off with a face-saving formula, but who had refused such formulae, who had stuck it out to the bitter end, and who had paid the penalty. Their own lives broken, the concessions offered withdrawn and surrender terms imposed. Was this now going to happen to him? Would he too make the same mistake. His face reflected his uncertainty. He turned and looked at Gerald.

Something else occurred to his mind.

"Ye asked us who it was behind the strike."

"I know who's behind it," Gerald said.

Ray shook his head. "Ye think ye knaas," he said. "That makes a difference."

"It wasn't Arnold Atkin," Gerald said. "Nor the MP."

"And certainly it wasn't ye."

"That's right," Gerald said. "It was Mrs. Rutland."

Ray held back his head and laughed. It was as if all the tension that had bound him for so long was released.

"Nor Mrs. Rutland either."

"Then who was it if it wasn't her?"

"It was me."

"I don't believe it," Gerald said.

"The night afore the meetin' at the institute," he said. "I went to see Mrs. Rutland. I thowt if anybody'd knaa she'd knaa. She'd only just heard the news from her accountant in the city. It fitted in with everythin' I'd heard by way o' gossip. I asked her what she was ganna dee about it — she said nowt at all. I told her if she'd let us have all the information she had, even get a bit more to fill in the blanks, I'd outline to her a plan o' action that couldn't fail. She listened to the plan and agreed."

"You mean the idea for the fund and the supply of food — they weren't her ideas at all?"

"I've just told ye, they were my ideas. But I must say we'd not have got very far without her — what ye might call — active co-operation."

Ray laughed again and together they began along the upcast shaft where the air was fresher till they saw before them the lights of the loading point and the blackened faces of the men. Ray was still laughing when he arrived and the men looked at him sullenly not understanding. Yet the tension of weeks had edged too their faces, and seeing the laughter of Ray they too began to laugh, uncoiling themselves, ridding from their bowels the tension. They had been waiting curiously for the return of the brothers, they had not quite known where they had gone, and they had not expected them to return via the downcast shaft. They had at first been discussing the proposals Gerald would be likely to put forward, they had argued among themselves whether or not Ray should accept such proposals, what they would do in his shoes. But now all pretence was over, whatever Ray decided they would abide by, he was their leader, their chief. So that if he laughed, they laughed. If he thought they had a right to be merry then be merry they would.

And they were merry now because they knew just as Ray knew that the strike was over.

56

Ray's eyes squinted in the brightness of the lamps that illuminated the loading point.

He had fought for the principle that men meant more than machines, that money could never mean more than men. A principle that people had forgotten because they had forgotten they were still human beings. He had tried to reverse that principle, he had tried to assert the right of the individual over the machine, but he had failed, not because the machine was too big but because it was too indifferent. Because really it did not care. Because at heart people did not care either. Only he cared, he and a few like him. You could overcome most things in life, he reflected, but the most difficult of all was inertia, lack of enthusiasm, indifference. Left to their own the men would never have had a strike, they would have accepted all the proposals put forward, and they would have suffered the cost of their indifference. After a few months, however, they would not care where they worked or what had happened. As long as they could be left alone with their closed minds and thoughts.

But even on this occasion when he had raised the men from their indifference, when he had managed to shake the village and the world, he had not been able to shake the machine. He had not been able to wake up a single bureaucrat. To have done that would be to have caused a revolution. And the British people had passed the time of revolutions years ago. He should have been alive in 1926, he reflected, then he would have made the people jump; he would have made the government jump too, he would have rid this country of its established order, he would have seen to it that bureaucracy and indifference did not usurpe the rights of the individual, bring the men to their knees, not only during the strike but for years afterwards. But then he was born thirty years too late and as with the leaders of 1926 he had accomplished nothing. Nothing. Only this time Ray had remembered not to drag out the strike too long, he had not refused concessions that later would be withdrawn, only to be replaced by others harder than the originals and which had to be accepted once the men were beaten. At least he had spared the men that.

But yet had it really been for nothing? He recalled what he had read of the strike in the South Wales coalfield in 1911, how they had held out for months to enforce a minimum wage only in the end to be defeated, yet gradually because of their strike how a demand for a national minimum had spread throughout Britain, so that though years were to pass eventually it was to be achieved. Eventually it became law. Perhaps the strike at Highhill, County Durham, had not been in vain. Perhaps some time, somehow, somewhere, its effects would be seen. Perhaps after all it would not be a failure. It might change the destiny of man only by the breadth of a snail but change it it would. Then he recalled the village. He recalled those Gerald had promised would fight. And he understood in that second that all was not lost, that perhaps after all they might win.

He felt better then. He felt after all his life had a purpose. He jumped clumsily from the tub and moved towards the kist. He picked up the yardstick and helmet he had let drop behind him and looked around the kist that had been his home for six weeks. The faded picture of the nude model on the wall was smeared and dark with coal dust. The papers that straddled the top of the desk were unrecognizable. The ancient telephone remained off the hook, as it had since Gerald had entered the pit, and for all he knew the manager was still on the other end of the line, having taken in all that Ray had said. Abruptly he replaced the receiver. He peered out of the small panes of the kist. The men were already on their way to the surface, the clatter of their boots, the laughter in their voices, echoed around him like those of men decamping.

Ray, like the captain of a ship decided he would be last to leave. But as finally he moved from the kist he saw a figure before him.

"It's all over now?" Featherley asked. "I can gan back and feed me pigs."

"Ye can gan back and feed yer pigs," Ray said.

"And all the fightin's o'er. Finished and done win?"

Featherley leant against the stencil of the door, blacker than any man in the pit, holding his helmet in his hand like a wages clerk asking a rise, and smelling of the pit as foully as he had ever smelt of pigs. Hot water had been sent down twice a week, in canisters normally used for tea; the water was of course transferred to pails and used to wash away the dirt and grime and shave away their beards. The men availed themselves of it joyfully, though very soon they were just as black again. Not so Featherley who either arrived too late or was not sufficiently forward enough to see that he got his shave like everyone else. With the result he was ten times blacker and smelled as foully as if he had been dipped in a sewer. Only his teeth and his eyes shone out, the pink underside to his lips as he spoke. Yet as always Ray could not but sympathize with him, lost as he was, for he was so much like the other men, ordinary souls who asked for little. And little was what they got.

Together they left the kist and walked across the rails to follow the footsteps of the men. Had it really been forty days and nights? Had they really spent so long in the pit? Now that it was past it was difficult to believe, yet the ache to his body, his feet, his mind, was such that it must be so. Gradually they walked up the tunnel that was to Ray unfamiliar terrain, they left behind the compressors, the pumps, the tubs and the hopper. But more than that they left a part of their lives, a part of their souls. He was not to know of the crowd that awaited him on the surface, silent and attentive, he was not to know once he emerged from the orifice of the drift he would be acclaimed by press and public alike, that the tumult of their voices would make as a squeak of a mouse the cries of pleasure uttered by the men. That the words he now spoke to Featherley would be repeated to newsmen as he reached the surface. And not only to newsmen, uttered on television, reprinted on newsreels and sent around the world.

"The fight for the colliery might be over," Ray said. "The fight for the village has just begun."